THE ABODE OF FANCY

For B.M.P.
In loving memory

THE ABODE OF FANCY

Sam Coll

THE LILLIPUT PRESS
DUBLIN

First published in 2016 by

THE LILLIPUT PRESS
62–63 Sitric Road, Arbour Hill,
Dublin 7, Ireland
www.lilliputpress.ie

ISBN 978 1 84351 663 7

Characters in this novel are fictitious and any resemblance to real persons living or dead is entirely coincidental.

A CIP record for this title is available from The British Library.

1 3 5 7 9 10 8 6 4 2

Set by Marsha Swan in 11 pt on 15.5 pt Caslon
Printed in Spain by Castuera

PROLOGUE

It had been over seven years since last he had seen Arsene the weatherman.

This discovery occurred to Mr Martin Graves just as his plane touched ground in Dublin, sliding on the runway through dint of the drizzle's wet. Glum, the singer Graves descended from the craft, and collected his baggage on the terminal's treadmill, and morosely wound through the shoals of commuters toward the exit where the buses were stacked. As he made for a vessel, he brushed past the shoulder of Boris Nigel Gillespie, arm in arm with his wife Hilda O'Mara, with whom he had just been bickering, en-route to catch a flight to Palestine, which they would board to accompany several other prominent theologians, in the services of another ineffectual peacemaking mission.

On the city-bound bus, Mr Graves peered gloomily out the window and reflected on their long estrangement, as his view was washed by sheets of the ghastly downpour, a mocking display of the drab weather he had not missed while sunbathing on the beaches during his lengthy Mediterranean exile. He had gone to Greece to clear his head, having packed in the musty actuarial duties to which for decades he was joylessly enslaved, preferring the adventure of seeking fulfilment elsewhere. For he had a fine pair of lungs, and a dulcet voice that traversed the ranges both baritone and tenor, and in his heart of hearts he had always wanted to be a singer full and proper, a skill he had seldom been granted the chance to display at home, before in his wisdom he fled to foreign lands, where his grave countenance made him a natural for crooning tearful elegies at the funerals of spinsters. His desire to sing emerged early, springing from his brightest youthful days, his first memories being of the chirp of hidden crickets, whose warble his boyhood heard but dimly, squatting amid the ashes by his mother's fireside, the warmest hearth of their midland cottage, and Mrs Graves smiled as she knitted in her armchair, and watched her youngest son crouch by the embers, peering up the sooty chimney and straining his ears to catch the angelic insect noises petering down in ghostly echo, words of heaven's code.

Arsene O'Colla the elder weatherman had also shared his passion. They bonded over their mutual love of operas and symphonies, and all other works of the greatest composers, of which canon both could boast an encyclopedic knowledge, so they found when they met by chance outside a chess tournament in the seventies, in which sport the older man had excelled. And in later life, when Arsene frequently sought free shelter whenever he came up to Dublin from his Wexford home, it was at the Rathmines lodgings of Mr Graves he most often found refuge, in a crooked domain hailed by some an architectural disaster, but nonetheless comfortable and well situated close to the canal. And Mr Graves fed and nurtured the older man of whom he took such care, and kept him company even in their lengthy silences, for as he aged the elder grew ever more taciturn, not that Graves much minded, for, like a long married couple, their hallowed wordlessness was golden, seated on their sofa nodding to the strains of Bach or Mozart, of Wagner and Verdi, or maybe Mahler or even Schubert, the favourite of Mr Graves.

And any buried resentment that Mr Graves might feel at the abuse of his services (for the weatherman so seldom said thanks for the many kindnesses shown him by the tenor, being often grouchy and surly instead), was slyly channelled into a sequence of subtle digs and little slurs with which he would pepper his sullen guest, exploiting the bitchy wit and sardonic turn of phrase and barb that his waspish upbringing had bequeathed him. And Mr O'Colla seldom sensed that he was being mocked or insulted, deceived by the warmth of the quiet tone the tenor employed to sneer at the old gnome's follies, encaged in himself, his senses dulled from the sequence of crackups he had suffered, hunched insensate like the lumbering elephant who only discerns by degrees that his back is copiously bleeding from the little bird's unceasing biting.

Though sometimes he went too far. Upon one occasion, maudlin O'Colla had begun to recount an amorous escapade of his young manhood, and was just getting into the lusty swing of it, growing fond again as his glorious conquest swam upon his rosy memories, before the tide of revelation was clammed as a consequence of the tenor's dig:

'… see, I knew this girl, yeah … and she was very pretty, yeah … and I wrote some poems for her, see, because I was a literary lad, like … and we had a date by the beach one night, like, and we sat in the car, and kissed a bit … and jaysus, I was fairly going for it. I was mad for it I was, y'know? And it was so hot, my old man was going mad, and –'

'Your old man? So was your father with you on the date, then?'

And never a word more did indignant Arsene ever say on that score.

And yet they remained the best of friends, forever travelling together to the opera festivals in company of Eugene Collins and his son. Which made this present silence of seven years all the more galling, about which Mr Graves wondered why, as the airport bus sidled into the rainy night-time city. He wondered had he done him some inadvertent wrong, or whether Arsene brooded on some other imagined hurt or slight, a grudge whose origin eluded him; and sometimes, based on numerous unanswered messages he had sent him, the sorrowful tenor more darkly wondered whether the old man had died.

The bus halted on O'Connell Street, and Mr Graves sallied out bearing his bags, and began to stroll southward through the puddles, hoisting his tattered umbrella that the wind persisted to rip, his tall wrinkled brow getting drenched through gaps in his brolly's canvas, as he trod with mellow plod through the deserted streets, slipping on the cobbles. Since his Rathmines residence was currently being rented out to a pair of trendy lesbians who kept some cats (due to which the place was now awash with the pungency of feline urine), tonight he would stay at the redbrick house of Eugene Collins (who had also gone abroad), number nine on a road called Lombardy, some twenty minutes' walk. Over the phone he had yesterday spoken to the son Simeon Jerome, the residence's wayward guardian, who had agreed, since he was himself away also, to leave the key hidden in the garden's grass for the guest's convenience, in whose thickets he should seek upon arrival.

Arriving sometime before midnight, Mr Martin Graves, much dampened and depressed by the journey, duly hunted in the grass on hands and knees, in search of the slippery key which he only barely found, well hid beneath the wetted earth, and let himself inside the dark house, his shoes squelching on the floor of the hall. He tossed the keys by the base of the great Buddha's head settled on the hall's table, a relic of the Orient, a tubby joker whose lowered lids had not yet been pulled off to sprout as green tea leaves. And in the dimness the tenor strolled around Eugene's empty household, timidly peering into room upon room, turning on and turning off the lights, many of whose bulbs were blown, sneezing at the dust that had been allowed to gather in the home's every cranny, under whose boards softly could be heard the titter of mice and rats. And then, having surveyed the lower level, Mr Graves next ascended upstairs to where the main room was set on the topmost second floor, as the wind blew and the rain teemed, casting his eyes all around the vacant ballroom, long ago a warren of bedrooms that had been smashed together as one, to let in the sunlight that fell in shafts from the skylights, since when the family had lived upstairs in accordance with the Georgian principle, lounging among the two beige couches, the two green armchairs, the television in a distant northern corner, beneath a wall of shelves upon shelves of books and photos and newspaper clippings, DVDs and CDs, a sequence of shelves spanning the length of the room, broken only twice by the intrusion of blank wall space, filled by paintings and fireplaces and flowerpots. And lastly, on the long dining table by the southern bay windows, lay a vast collection of assembled objects that caught his eye as he flicked on the light to illuminate the darkness, over to which the tenor tiptoed to survey, submitting the array to an exhaustive forensic scrutiny. He saw:

—A comic book of 994 pages, with twenty pages of acknowledgements, *LIFE OF WATT*, as written and drawn by Alfred Gary Allen, co-authored by The Mad Monk, chronicling the adventures of the titular Archibald Theodore Watt;

—A packet of condoms belonging to lapsed scholar Edwin Galbraith;

—A postcard to Eugene, depicting sunny bullrings, as sent by Mr Harry Carson, who could not send it to his Granny Marge since she did so hate bullfighting;

—A fragment, contained in a jar, of the surviving bones of Peadar Lamb's Bull;

—A postcard for a Connemara golf-course, with two hares in the foreground;

—A volume of verses in the Gaelic tongue, written by the poet Tadgh O'Mara, illustrated by his former lady love, the painter Hermione Gauguin;

—A cartoon of Watt and Sherman sailing the seas, bearing The Mad Monk's coffin in their boat, as depicted by none but the hand of Arsene;

—A chessboard belonging to Elijah the coffee-room prophet;

—A few stray hairs clipped from the White Dog's shaggy mane;

—A biography of Laurence Sterne, written by I— C— C—, with generous editorial assistance provided by Isolde Lovelace and even Sam Sly;

—A letter from Mr Harry Carson, recounting his marriage to Ivana Egorova;

—A crude cartoon of fluffy Johnny Fritzl, naked in Kyrie Elysium's arms, who smiles impishly and brandishes a knife to shave her teddy, as done by Simeon;

—A battered yet precious edition of *A Midsummer Night's Dream*, as signed by Robin Goodfellow the Puck himself, with annotations by the fat cat Moloch;

—A DVD of Bresson's *Au Hasard Balthazar*, starring the eponymous donkey;

—A photograph of Eugene's parents, the late Megan Devlin (also known as Granny Nutmeg or Maggie) arm in arm, in their Galway garden, with her husband Francis Alphonsus Xavier Collins, her solely only fearless Fran;

—A peacock feather plucked by Simeon from one of the birds who were wont to roam the grounds of his late Granny Mary's abandoned Roscommon farm;

—A sculpture of a cow whose udder The Mad Monk once suckled like a calf;

—A scurrilous cartoon, done by their uncaring son, of Mrs Esmerelda Merkel and her henpecked husband Pipefitter Pat, pussy-whipped in Phibsboro;

—The memoirs of Arsene O'Colla, a scrappy pile of pages bound in ribbon;

—A monochrome photo of Eugene Collins and his father in the Phoenix Park;

—A pilfered beermat, on the back of which was an advertisement for Mr Merriman's Mount August Inn, situated on the avenue of that same name;

—A cigarette lighter, once owned by the Pooka Fergus MacPhellimey;

—A prescription for some anti-inflammatory tablets, given to a confused youth by a nurse called Adrian in St James's, to quell the swelling of a foreskin;

—A couple of surviving poems, as writ by The Mad Monk for the Banshee;

—A bag of green tea leaves, bought for Simeon by Agatha Honeypenny;

—A cartoon drawn by Marco Grimaldi, depicting a caricature of Albert Potter transformed into a bloated testicle, with a speech bubble saying: 'MERKEL';

—A discarded scarlet dildo once owned by former tenants Gallagher and Freaney;

—An issue of *ICARUS*, as edited by Boris Nigel Gillespie, with a poem by S.J.C., under which, scrawled in ketchup, a certain Saruko had writ her name;

—A small portrait in oils and acrylics, very accomplished, as undertaken by Ms Jezebel Temple, the formidable subject being Mr Albert Potter;

—An unsent love letter from Simeon to the sublime Saruko, a fast fading printed email;

—A moleskin notebook, Simeon's birthday present from Konrad Merkel and Johnny Fritzl, with inscriptions, and a virile fingerprint from Lukas the Shag;

—A copy of *The Book of Tea* by Kazuko Okakura, with the resonant phrase 'Abode of Fancy' underlined in Konrad Merkel's green biro;

—*The De Valera Code*, a bestselling conspiracy novel by Ulick O'Muadaigh of Sligo, with a touching dedication to his departed brother Aloysius;

—A photograph of the old man Arsene O'Colla and Simeon Jerome Collins, together alone again at the breakfast table in the elder's Wexford house;

—A copy of *The Patrician*, the annual magazine of St Patrick's Cathedral Grammar School, edited by Mr Jim Bateman and introduced by Mr Bevis, the tasteful photos provided by Mr Bernard Moran, with a loving tribute to the retired physics teacher George Corbett, as written by Mr Bateman;

—A manuscript of *IKAROS*, an aborted stillborn novel by Simeon Jerome;

—A dashing self-portrait of the younger Mr Albert Potter seated by a window;

—A few scrolls of parchment, roughly torn into three parts, a tripartite division that was seemingly random, on which was written *The Mad Monk's Doggerel Epic History,* as first told to his latest lady love, Banshee Maggie Devlin.

This survey awoke strange feelings in Mr Martin Graves. He felt like a librarian confronted with a jumbled chaos it was his role to order and set in a semblance of sequence. And perhaps, if he pried further and harder, following the paper trail from document that lead on to document, and artefact to artefact, he might at last find an answer to the worries that haunted him, or chance upon a key to the labyrinth into which he had inadvertently wandered as an innocent. And maybe he would learn on the way exactly why he had not heard from the weatherman for seven years, and from there propose a solution to the absence of his old friend Arsene. And it was to the last of these items that Mr Graves first gave his fullest attention. For with all the time in the world at his disposal, as yet untiring with no desire still to sleep, the tenor decided to peruse the Doggerel-Epic for his amusement, lest any hints to the mysteries be embedded in those bathetic lines. He could do with the distraction. And so he sat on a chair at the table's top, and wrinkled his brow as he began to read, while the wind howled and the rain fell, the rain teemed and the wind blew, the wind and the rain, the wind and the rain, as the singer read on, in the quiet of the dark, alone in the black of night, with not a fire to warm him.

CHAPTER ONE

FOUND OBJECT:
The Mad Monk's Doggerel Epic History, as related to the Banshee Megan Devlin (Part One of Three)

In the black of night we sit by our fire
While without our donkey strolls by the mire.
Though bright, our furnace gives but a chill flame
That can cool a kettle, and who's to blame?
Methinks I glimpse in your looks accusing
Guilt's burden laid at my door, accruing
Thus some cause on my part for this grim cold,
Of which there's none, I assure thee in **BOLD**.
Rather I entreat thee, let's fill this void
With jocund babble, since earlier I toyed
With telling thee my tale, of which thus far
You know none, and so, by light of yon star
That grants eloquence to a mere dumb mule,
Hitherto firing thy voice to heat gruel,
Just as you spun your sob story along,
So too shall I unravel my oblong
Chronicle. But where to begin? At birth?
I was a drowsy child, of ample girth,
Indolent and much given to moaning –
I quite wore out my parents with groaning.
I cannot recall their faces at all,

Save that mother kept hers hid by a shawl,
Having once been bit by a great White Dog,
Who came chasing her out from the world's fog,
Snapping her lashes and slashing vast gashes
Out from her cheeks. Her looks were as ashes
Are to embers, after his brute assault.
Later he was my pet, kept in a vault
Deep down in Earth's core, from whence nevermore
Could he flee, save when I bade him. Before
All that, I daily bore me ma's nagging,
A poor crone, her beauty robbed, with sagging
Dugs I sometimes sucked, though my brother got
More milk – he was her dote, and I was not.
We lived in some citadel by the sea,
Whose frothy waves comprised our nursery,
Lapped by the foam and elbowing the brine,
The gurgling molluscs I would claim for mine,
And hang around my neck on a lace,
Which Father found fey, so he'd smack my face,
Bidding me shut up, silent little louse.
There were many rooms in my father's house,
Like the attic in which we did research,
Conducting strange experiments on perch,
Or the lime ballroom through which we would run,
Ripping out our budding hairs just for fun,
Or the dank cellar where first we drank beer,
Brewing our own brand when full moon was near,
Or the secret chamber of Mum n' Dad,
Where they wrought love I witnessed, and was glad,
Or the dusty pantry smeared in pastry,
From whence fled we to the tall apple tree
In the garden, atop of which we regard
The tumbling expanse of Father's vineyard,
Among which twining maze of grapes and vines,
I lost myself in gulping finest wines.
And the best fungi too were to be found,
Sought by arduous combing of the ground,
Magic mushrooms nestling deep in the grass,
Whose heads I nibbled, so my fit would pass,
And then a sweet and blissful trance would fall,
And I enraptured on my back would sprawl,

Knowing peace I was hitherto denied,
Pestered since childhood by some buzzing snide
That crushed my ears and kept me from my rest,
But now a giddy longing filled my breast
As I lay and stared toward the heavens,
Smiling at the stars, both odds and evens,
On which cosmic map I traced my own shape,
When my brain's monarch caught me twixt his cape,
And this was that same Faerie King of yore,
Waggish Oberon, an arrogant bore,
Who nonetheless endowed me with powers
On which I can't put a price, mid bowers
Of his lush and leafy Faerie kingdom,
Where mad revelry and gay abandon
Doth reign. I became his tallest kinsman,
A giant among the elves, and a plan
Was hatched to have me mate with one among
His womenfolk. And I was quickly flung
Along the greedy ranks of the hopeful,
Until I met a girl more beautiful
Than the rest, and she was the one I wooed,
And strove to charm with many verses rude
That I wrote with what scanty wit was mine,
And then at last, yes, she did draw the line,
Agreeing blushing to be my first love,
Sparking off fireworks in the sky above.
You had your Frankie, Maggie – I had her.
Well do I remember how she would purr,
And crawl catlike across the marble floor,
Bubbling for kisses, always wanting more.
Zounds! She was as tall as she was wide,
Squat and perhaps dumpy, but what a ride!
At our wedding were the Puck and Pooka,
Whom I befriended while smoking ganja,
When a chariot conjured to bear us by,
Borne by angels, came dropping from the sky,
Into which we stepped and stood by the helm,
Straddling the oars, carved from Chesterfield elm,
As through night's starry ocean we did rush,
Dipping into milky ways with their mush,
And glimpsed dour Orion wielding his axe,

And spry Mercury collecting his tax,
And Janus-faced Gemini twins at play,
Bouncing dull planets by the dark moon's bay,
By Saturn's bright shores where we did alight,
Among whose dizzy rings we took our flight
From the pedantic charioteer band
Employed to keep randy rabbits in hand,
Such as our chuckling pair who cut the strings,
Shimmering glimmering whimpering rings
Where we lost ourselves, embedded in sands,
Lovers whose contours were those of the land's,
Embracing mid joyous dust so we rolled,
Sucking galactic grit and Martian mould,
And the dirty deity was our priest,
Whose nonstop wedlock prating never ceased,
His radiant drone shone upon our match,
Glinting off our limbs as I licked her snatch,
An exalted profanity given
Blessing by the serene sun, like driven
Snow can turn to slush, so too did we melt
Like slimy slaves dunked in the marble belt
Of hurtling asteroids. But then I awoke,
And my dream dissolved in a haze of smoke.
The period of enchantment had passed,
For the spell of the mushrooms could not last …

END OF PART ONE

CHAPTER TWO

The Poet Tadgh O'Mara was of Louisiana extraction, Irish-American born and bred of Galwegian parents. He grew up among broken toys and burgers, smoke from the butts of his father's rifles and the aroma of maple syrup with which his mommy lathered their pancakes. Wheeling tricycles by the wet savannah where he dreamt of buffalo and moose and Bogart. In kindergarten, his horn-rimmed teacher remarked on how pronounced was his intelligence even then, so young, already an obscure original.

Tadgh could not fit in here. His classmates could not even pronounce his name. And come the time for enlisting cadets, in the swinging sixties when explosions rocked the oriental abroad, Tadgh chose to be a conscientious objector, pleading power to the flower, for which insolence his officer father never forgave him. An intense dislike of his father went hand in hand with a hatred of his homeland, which he believed was a haven for hypocrisy and a country whitewashed by lies, a bullying nation throwing its flabby hamburger weight around the older world like a toddler throwing a tantrum, upsetting its unstable cradle and tossing its rocketing rattle to bomb the anthills to smithereens, before applying the magnifying glass to sizzle the scuttling critters to frying toasted death.

For such beliefs, Tadgh was outcast among the bulky majority of his gung-ho contemporaries. Nor did they much care for his increasingly arcane interests, in poetry and gardening, in baroque music and nonsensical folkloric nuggets, snippets of fairy lore preferably culled from the corny history of the little island across the sea from whence his folks had fled, which land his romantic fancy built up into an idyll of promise, a dreamy refuge where he too could flee in turn. And with mounting longing Tadgh looked across the ocean in despairing hope to faraway Hibernia, dreaming of embarking in glorious exile from Capitol Hill and candyfloss, free from the cyclones and hurricanes and tornadoes that ravaged quivering Louisiana, in one of which his favourite brother lost his life when a towering cedar fell and squashed him on the head. That was the last straw.

And so one day following a fight with his father and a teary hug from his mother, he packed all his belongings into a small little suitcase, a gasping bag that burst at the seams and spilt his books, and waved down an ocean liner onto which he stowed in the hold like a beardy rat, and thus set sail across the Atlantic in secrecy and happy wonder. Life as a stowaway was thrilling in those days. He riffled peanuts and mustard seeds from the plates of affluent diners above board, and packets of grain from the leaking holdings, munching and sleeping and composing in the liner's bowels, and thereafter strolled the decks for the sake of digestion, with scarf and suit to avoid suspicion, affecting a telling limp like Captain Ahab or Byron before him, which strategy had worked wonders for that poet, and surely would reap similar fruit for this young upstart. His mysterious limp set him apart in ladies' eyes and was an easy talking point to prompt a suggestive chat. And insatiable Tadgh then bedded down the willing broads in his damp and seasick cabin deep down beneath the deck, in the murky guts of the wading ship, making moaning love mid the crates and sacks, as the vessel was bounced and heaved astride the waves, rocked by gales that swirled her sails, while fogging the peephole window with their feverish lovers' breaths, sated having copulated, falling back on beanbags whistling their joy.

Tadgh O'Mara was proudly polygamous in those days, juggling sailor girls one upon the other, sampling the oceanic babes of many colours and creeds, soon finding that he favoured best the French-flavoured gamines, to whom he could coo arty profundities post coitum, with limp gesticulating wrists and polo sweaters and crooked berets. Though he did so soon deplore their despicable habit of smoking tapering cigarillos, scent of whose ash curled the reddening wings of his nose and tainted his dainty lungs.

Inland and onshore when the ship met well by starlight the rotting Celtic dock, he travelled as a prodigal wanderer awhile with bag on back, learning slowly the ways and means of the isle wherein his ancestral roots were sowed and seeded. Ireland was not quite what he had imagined. Oft he was forced to hold his nose, put off by the native odours. There was less magic in the air than he had expected, but a lot of bile and needles on the littered streets, many clumps of horseshit to chase about the dirty alleys of Dublin, and many huddled wretches left out with the stray linen to freeze, lying supine among the shards of broken bottles, relics of oafish debauch.

Disappointed by what he saw around him, sometimes he even forgot to limp, or forgot which of his legs was meant to be the lame one that dragged behind – an easy mistake to make, and a ready way to fall out of favour in the imperious eyes of the visiting Gallic girls, who saw right through his phoniness and spat him swiftly out. Unimpressed by the Gaelic ambience, he swung to the Gauls for comfort. He learnt their language, and fell in love with all things French. Soon there was a schizoid chasm in his already splintered soul, as the Frenchman in Tadgh vied for supremacy with the Irishman, and began to win out over the humble Gael. The depressed Catholic Ireland of then was no place for an aspiring artist. Where in drab Dublin could he come upon the delicacy and heady ambience of brilliance that abounded in Montmartre or Pigalle or the Bois de Bologne, a cultured civility decried by the vulgar as snobbish frothy pretension? Sooner rather than later he yearned to flee again, and so then zipped by ferry to the Continent and roamed the green Auvergne, sniffing the burnished red backs of quizzical cows, whose meat he nevermore would eat. One of his more attractive qualities was that he abhorred any kind of violence, and so renounced the consumption of flesh – he would not even stamp upon an ant or crush the buzzing fly with a fist – dour Tadgh in some ways was vaguely drippy trippy hippie, like a young man of his time, for once.

But then, very soon, and out of the blue like a bolt, he was a married man was this queer old Tadgh O'Mara, wed to a kindly sunny bonny young filly from Fulcaragh. Hippy Wendy just happened to be an au pair on a school-term break, tanning herself on the slope of Sacré-Cœur where all the lovers were stationed come every Parisian sunset, mollycoddling and messing their hair as they hugged with limbs entwined. As she lay on the grass, she saw him ambling by with a glint in his eye, the strange dark poet who stopped to speak and flirt, and she loved him for his limp and lisp, for his lanky masculinity that did not debar a gaunt virility, for his floating voice that fluctuated between Louisiana drawl and Celtic growl, finally settling for flowery French yakking, jammy purring and buttery humming. He seemed to Wendy the most brilliant man that she had ever met, forever talking the dictionary whose leaves he pored without remit, in search of odder sounds with which he could pepper the pages of his verse, which was increasingly bilingual and stilted, rejecting all flowing idioms and renouncing the muck of mundane everyday in favour of clouds and fogs of senseless metaphors.

And very soon Wendy was welcomed to his bed, and he to hers, and they fucked a lot, and happily so. And when she was with child, as was only inevitable, she clamoured and wheedled that they soon be wed, a breathless proposal greeted by the timid Bohemian with a reluctance only matched by her dogged persistence, pointing lovingly to her swelling belly. You've made your mess, now lie in it, buster. It was not that he disliked her (though her bossy, unimaginative and aggressively businesslike approach to life rather warred with his Elysian longings) – only he nursed qualms on the grounds of his sexual appetite that veered toward the varied, juggling dates and peaches like plums as he hopped like an antic flea. A conventional marriage seemed anathema to him, a straitjacket for the libido. But in the end, after daughter Hilda was born, he eventually agreed, figuring that there would be other ways and means of getting his goodies.

So a wedding was had, in a tumbledown chapel in scenic Montluçon, with streamers and fizzle, full of fuss and ostentation at which ascetic Tadgh did bristle and bridle inside, feeling a fool as he led her down the steps with a hand around her waist, and before their cheering chums they dutifully embraced. Worse was to come. In Holland they set up camp and rundown lodging, for she was an attaché at the Irish embassy there. And so Wendy worked, and Tadgh talked, and opined, and wrote when he could, and looked after the bawling Hilda whose stinking nappies he changed, at whom he screamed when she refused to recite the alphabet letters he tried to teach the little bitch, beginning quickly soon to feel itchy and restless for novelty.

To which end, he drew up a barmy contract to which he bid wife Wendy append her baffled signature, a contract whose content she only vaguely discerned, something fluffy about an Open Marriage permitting both partners a considerable measure of freedom to indulge themselves, and rack up scratchy notches on the amorous bedpost. Puzzled Wendy, wooed by his words that sounded straightforward, signed on the line toward which gangly Tadgh eagerly pointed and panted, little knowing what next was in store for her. Such things never happened in Fulcaragh, she thought, scratching her head as she gave bosomy suck to her mewling girl. She figured that there was something fishy in the Dutch air that had addled the deluded head of her husband. She hoped naught would come of it; perhaps it was only a game, a poetic conceit of his. Alas no.

For unloving O'Mara gleefully chose then to fulfil his contractual obligation, with a deranged fervour that tried Wendy's nerves to shreds, quite outside her sphere of thought – she was hardworking and pious, having been drilled in the doctrine of faithfulness, conditioned to fear and despise the rabbit's bounding her ostensible husband now daily delighted in. He obtained a maid to mind Hilda in his absence – and the frowsy maid was the first of the other lovers he fucked within Wendy's hearing. Poor woman!

Think of the routine: coming back from the sweaty office on umpteen occasions only to find the unattended child asleep and sedated, with traces of his bedded guests strewn about every telltale corner of the seedy flat, wading through the emptied vats of wine and champagne, the mucky piles of ash stubbed in the trays, the haze of gauzy smoke that clouded their chambers, and the greasy prophylactics found nestling in the wastepaper baskets beside their broken desk, whose wood was cracked in the throes of conceited seduction. And lipstick smears embedded in the wallpaper, bottles of nail polish wedged in the skirting boards, soiled knickers from the night before joining the contents of the baskets for their weekday wash, the hints of wayward negligees and torn brassieres, tossed aside heedlessly with a flash of teeth that bit their straps, to land on the bashful teapot full of emerald fossils, sediments of sweet absinthe whose tang was sin.

None of this was fair to poor Wendy, who sat dumbly in her harried state of fretting blinkered love, rocking dozing Hilda's cradle as she worried, never thinking herself to abuse the terms of the daft contract in which she had unwittingly partaken, never dreaming herself of making eyes at a hunk from the embassy, like the beefcake bronze chauffeur who was Latinate and oiled, who always bared his grinning teeth when she passed him by with a swish of her skirt, whose olive hands she might hold and conduct to her breast, and thence conduct the rest of him back to her bed. But such an illicit act was outside of her imagination, and thus left her helpless on the shelf, pouting and crying in frustration and indignation, sulking on the settee watching lonely sitcoms that woke the yapping brat, awaiting his return. And when he did, it was always arm in arm with some other blowsy sluttish tart who liked his limp and fell for his Byronic blather, the type he met in café bars, bonding by quoting Rimbaud and Baudelaire in unison, chanting between the smoking rings that her purple lips blew toward the gangling bard who was neither exactly Gallic, nor quite Yankee Puritan, nor even wholly Hibernian. And Wendy would hear the doggish scrapings at the door as he drunkenly fumbled with the lock, then staggered reeling in with the giggly colleen hanging on the stripes of his vest, and then the muttered bluster with which he would greet and excuse his wife and child, followed by the clumsy fumble and stumble to the spare bedroom into which they would tumble, where within a riot of orgiastic sucking groans would subsequently issue, to the disgust and despair of blindly faithful stricken Wendy who would bury head in hands and weep.

It could not last. Soon they split up come a certain summer in the seventies, to their mutual relief – Wendy kept hold of Hilda, which deprivation the poet shrugged off unconcerned – he'd see her sometime later whenever anyway. The poverty of all human relations, he thought. Thus kicked out of their abode in Amsterdam, prodigal Tadgh O'Mara traipsed back across the channel to his originals, for all that there was much in Ireland that offended and disappointed him. Once upon a golden time one could sit in Grafton Street Bewley's and nurse a free glass of hot water for all the whole idling day long while one plied one's papers warm and undisturbed; nowadays such thrift was discouraged by radish waitresses who bid one either pay for a coffee or get up and get lost.

So since the eastern coast and the midlands no longer held any possible appeal for him, he looked to the utmost western part of the land in hope of finding what he was seeking. On a rickety bicycle he wheeled across the country's breadth, down brambly lanes and tarmac highways, by the crags and bottoms of a dozen chalky pins that were mountains with cloudy caps, like bewigged and gloomy judges in the sky's courtroom. Soon he came to the Mayo seashore where he boarded the puffing ferry bound for Inishbofin.

And they must have thought him to have been a bizarre sort of geezer, those shifty Bofin folk, idling squinting on the pier to watch the ship sail in, raising bushy eyebrows in mumbled wonderment as the new piece of work sallied forth from the ferry, bearing his honking bicycle and bags. He was wiry and thin with not a peck of fat on him, with flat soft cap and bottle-top glasses, big boots and creamy polo shirt, and skinny jeans and tawdry sweater knitted from artificial native wool, with a medley of mannerisms distilled from the melting pot of Gallic meets Gaelic, with limp wrists and loping stride, wiggling hips in a way that seemed fey, with a brush of frizzy beard that recalled Lytton Strachey's, among whose frazzled tangles slivers of early silver gleamed, like rustling pearls among the bush of thickets. Was he a Yank? Was he a Frog? But he was a Poet!

A peculiar, not to say suspicious, occupation to be having. For all his best efforts in the years that ensued, he could never belong here. Perhaps he tried too hard. For fifteen years he learned the language, raking those dying embers the colonial had quashed, whose own accursed tongue he now abhorred and spurned and all but rejected. Soon Tadgh O'Mara spoke only Irish and French, condescending upon a blue moon to dredge up just a bit of English, but only with extreme reluctance and intense pain, wincing at the ungainly words that were so ugly on his lips. His mistake was to attempt to be more Irish than the natives themselves, which was never guaranteed to endear him to the locals. What was worse, the Irish he learnt and spoke was gleaned from the pages of his beloved dictionaries that cherished the archaic and outmoded. He learnt words from books, not by speaking with his neighbours. And they would be regularly taken aback when he addressed them in a stuffy fashion, hailing them with queer locutions smacking of dusty study, utilising 400-year-old expressions that sang of scholarly pedantry, arid and dead since divorced from his surroundings, for he denied himself the pleasure of bonding in the bars and trading in the local gossip, shirking the pubs where the best Inishbofin Irish was spoken, following up the rigid impulse of his recent teetotalism and newly adopted abhorrence of all alcoholic beverages.

A sample of his typical speech, as rendered in English, might be thus:

'Hola, sirrah! By my troth, the air doth shrewdly bite! An ill wind blows o'er yonder chalky harbour ours. Whither wouldst thou wander for matins this Michaelmas?'

In response to which misty query, the badgered islander might noncommittally stutter, then bid the weirdo swift farewell, then snigger behind his back as he cycled away down twisting paths, deftly dodging queer stone walls that stayed upright by a miracle.

He lived in a draughty cottage with reedy roof of thatch he rented, a dwelling which for years he endeavoured in vain to purchase for his own, to no avail – the obstinate homebred breed were welcoming, but would never relinquish their lands wholly to the hands of the intruding outsiders who blew through. And he must somehow have felt lonely in his quiet state of polite alienation, though he grew to cherish his aloofness by keeping busy. For days on end he might not speak to a soul, planting spuds and cabbages in his overgrown garden, digging up turnips and windy beans to cook in slops of soup, trawling the howling shores to collect drippy strands of seaweed from which he squeezed his salt. And in the cold silence of the mornings he would always be found composing, hunched at the desk in his dark living room where the fire weakly crackled, lurking by the cobwebbed window clutching spiralling quill that traced his spidery script, browsing the lexicon with inky chipped fingertips, giggling mirthlessly as he chanced upon another antique phrase that was as webbed as was the pane of his marbled spyglass.

Those who live so long alone inevitably become set in their ways. He too became more and more of a control freak over these years of seclusion, hating any spontaneity and fearing tricks of the moment, turning aside from any displays of Dionysian exuberance, and coldly revelling in icy Apollonian order and stringent discipline. His walls were papered with sticky memos upon which he scribbled his reminders for the day's chores, every minute's activity planned and choreographed to the last detail, from buying the eggs to peeling the spuds, from pissing in the thistles to shitting in the bushes whenever the frozen boghole bowl got blocked by winter's ice.

What few guests he admitted were expected also to conform to his strictly demarcated ways, as Eugene Collins soon discovered when he came to chat

– and was aghast when he found his eloquent friend unwilling anymore to argue or communicate in the English tongue that was their shared vehicle of expression way back in the day, forced instead to stammer through the treacherous voids of his homemade speech he had not studied since school. Most often they would talk at complete cross-purposes – Eugene would misconstrue some clause of Tadgh's to refer to the mating rituals of shrews and starlings, when really the poet was talking metaphorically about how much he loved women's bodies. And soon they had nothing left to talk about at all. Eventually, in exasperation and angry English, Eugene argued that this was a dreadful imposition upon which Tadgh was insisting, however well-meant his motive, and he would not tolerate these conditions one minute further. Tadgh was put out; he had thought that Eugene would be delighted to speak Irish on the island. How about they spoke English whenever they met on the mainland? Not bloody likely, snapped the other. Just how often are you going to be coming to the mainland? Not bloody likely. And so they parted.

The poverty of all human relations, thought Tadgh. To clear his head, long walks he might make to the island's quieter patches, lying down in empty fields to stare at the darkening sky and open his gob to drink the teeming drops of sprinkling rain. There was a little big lake not far from his house, over whose algae-laden surface the swans would glide and paddle, silent ghosts threading the liquid vista by mossy edges where crumbling boats were moored, once manned by grinning skeletons of fishermen. Rare flowers grew in the hedges, sporting riotous petals in the summertime, on the voluptuous buds where scarlet black beetles copulated, six-spotted burnets pressing together their inky sexes, of which abandon the poet took note with a magnifying glass.

Yes, he loved the place, and his poetry blossomed there (though some critics chided him for the 'anthropological magpie' approach he took to the language – it was like reading a dictionary of the most obscure Irishness that had been spliced all out of order). And he swam daily in the bitter sea, for nearby was the silvery beach, in whose pampas dunes the jaded natives squatted and sucked their pipes, and coolly regarded the bony Yankee strip to his briefs to show off his haggard trimness, and tie up the tangles of his hair in a plastic bun, and lastly snap on goggles and snorkels before diving into the icy churn of cruel waves, so cold that none of the locals dared themselves to dip in a shrivelling toe.

And sometimes, as he floated on his back with belly to the sky, gurgling scraps of old songs and childhood tunes as he flapped his flippers like an angel, the scudded fluffs of clouds, hovering in the blue above, seemed to evoke in him images, pictures of comely womanly contours, of breasts and hips and buttocks, such as so long of which he had been starved, for which, under cover of darkness, he longed and lusted all the more.

So, cautiously, he began again to flirt with certain younger among the island's women, learning to love their darkly sultry windswept beauty, going so far as even to enter the bar, if only to ogle the pretty new barmaid, waggling her bust as she scooped off the foam of his Carling. Emboldened, he next conducted a dangerous affair with a housewife who lived up the hill. Their union was mostly platonic, and their hand-holding interviews were often curtailed by the intrusion of her bacon-faced husband with tubby gut who wanted his dinner, or the gaggling spree of her neglected daughter chicks, who roamed the roads barefoot (they had to sell the shoes to fund the TV licence), their spongy soles pricked by glass, smelling of piss and sadness – for their mother was mad, as Tadgh discovered, calling off their coupling when he saw her belt one of her girls with a frying pan. He dreamt of rescuing the girls from the domestic debacle in which they were trapped, and taking them home to care for them as if for his own, but then he got distracted when the summertime tourists came in by boat and logged in at the harbour.

Oft would he sit on the stony stoop by wall of the pier, and keep a hungry eye cocked lest any French damsels drop in. And once above all he was lucky, when he spotted a bird with Medusa's curls and a barmy glint in her kindly eyes, boasting a canvas in her satchel, paints and palettes in her purse, and coarse brushes in her blouse. Hermione Gauguin had not a word of Irish and only a smattering of English. She planned only to pass through for not more than a week, intending to paint the isle's foggy vales and foaming surfs where seals and dolphins reared their blinking heads, frolicking on the basking current by sunset. But it was not long before the poet approached the painter on padding panther's feet, purring sugary words in her own honeyed tongue, inviting her back to his place for supper and sex, to which proposal she chuckling acquiesced.

And so up the sandy hill toward his abode he led the lady by the hand, loving the prick of her painted nails on his palm, the jagged fangs of her kooky grin, as over his garden gate they hopped as one, and into his frosty sanctum he beckoned her in to sit and dine. Log by log he heaped on his sputtering fire, while steam from the kitchen's kettle plumed and spat, and the charcoal pot bubbled and stewed, and rosy candles on the flimsy table she lit with her lighter, glinting off their sooty knives and spoons, as stony home-baked bread they buttered, dipping chunky slices in cosy bowls of seaweed soup.

Over wine they chatted on art, and found in each other their unlikely equal, Hermione and Tadgh, a likely pair. And in the later dark of his sparkling bed they clawed like furies, the polecat and the tigress, dynamos zipping by in the night and exploding, exalted and scorched by the offbeat brilliance of their respective selves. And smiling Tadgh O'Mara stroked her sleeping breast and marvelled while she snored, believing at last that he had found the one woman worthy, the love of his life and the foremost muse.

So Hermione Gauguin moved in with him, and for a time both knew bliss. His poetry grew ravished, enraptured, every line, hitherto so wordily arid, now illumined by purple light of love; and her painting also flourished in the cool of island air. Canvas upon canvas she tossed off then hung on every one of his walls, each piece one further step toward the hazy ideal for which she yearned, chip by misty chip scratched and daubed with pellets of paint, sometimes as if hacking off distracting lacquer or unravelling a mummy's bandages, others as if piling on clods of clay to a whirling spool, stippling canvases with nib of her brushes, and blobs of pigments smeared with fingertips of the Titian type, hoisting and raising the buried city squeeze by squeeze, like dragging up the dregs of Atlantis from the inky pits of submersion, gasping anew for fresh breath.

Her works were blurry but also crisp, with the form of the hilltop castle overlapped with the dewy bauble on a cow's head and horns, colours dissolving to a final elemental grey, straggling shades fading into wispy shreds, like vermillion rags of clouded sheep, dyed violet in the turnstile with their master's branded marks. And as she slapped on the colours and cheerily whistled through her crooked teeth, her lover sat aside in his crackling armchair, with his notebook in hand, with feet upon the poof and head in the clouds, and watched her as she painted, and warmly smiled and scribbled dimples. Eventually they were moved to collaborate, and so brought out a book together, for which the words were his and the pictures hers. It was he who spoke and stuttered at the ceremonial launch over in the island's newly erected eggshell arty centre, while she gazed upon her gangling man shaking upon the pedestal as the punters bought their book, and she smiled and sipped from the wine that was free. Tadgh drank water.

But the idyll could not last. Artistic temperaments are prickly at best, and when underneath one roof, tensions between two will quickly arise in cramped confines. For Hermione, bred on the best bohemia, did so love to roll tobacco like a true puffing trooper – while anal Tadgh despised this disgusting habit, and soon would forcibly bid her step outside to smoke, even on the soggier days when the drops extinguished her lonely flame on the damp doorstep. And Hermione also loved to drink and booze and party, whereas Tadgh (himself plastered after only a birdie sip of stout) loathed the bars with their vulgar merriment – so she was resigned to crawl the isle's three pubs all on her own, befriending the locals through spirited pantomime and innately warm good nature, for all that she had not a word of their tongue worth the name. On darker and gloomier nights, she would liken the three taverns, all owned by the local mini-magnate Ruadhri, to circles of purgatory or hell, blasted by wind and waves on the seafront, shivering in the darkness when the island's electricity got cut in the frequent storms, rolling fags with blue and freezing fingers, only for all the shavings of Golden Virginia to be stolen by an unheeding breeze, plucking papers from her gaping grasp.

And the ordained diet was a further bone of contention, which Tadgh dictated must be strictly vegetarian. But Hermione soon got sick of seaweed and popping peas from their pods, no matter how frugal or healthy such foodstuffs doubtless were. For she was French and fanged – they shoot horses, don't they? Sometimes she might nip out to the shops to dine on slices of ham, guzzling piggy slivers in the sandy roadside, only for her lover to whine about the flesh on her breath, when he boned her in their narrow bed.

And often, when off wandering on hungering painting expeditions to scenic and lonely outcrops, seated sketching some heather and gorse with easel and all, her roving eye might stray from her composition, to drift and consider the form of a plump and tasty seagull sitting nearby fluffing his feathers, with a dash of blood upon his beak, and she would wonder just how easy it might be to fashion a bow and arrow and take her archer's aim, or to pick up a sharp rock and fling it at her flighty supper's ghostly head, and finally her mouth would water and drool, her very saliva mingling with her running paints, as she imagined building a fire in a cave, and charring the creature to a tangy crisp, and munching upon his succulent meat, and licking her chops clean of blood and brains, and then feeling full for the first time in bloody months.

All these and other niggling irritants combined to prey upon their pairing and mar their love. She was a free spirit who hated his control freakishness, and she found contemptible the insane degree to which his airless days were ordered, their every little trivial ritual rehearsed, and above all she hated how his reactionary manly word was always the final one on any subject. At softer moments she conceded that he was still a good man at his root, but a good man fatally misguided, tending toward monomania, however admirable was his single-minded battle against globalization and the cultural imperialism practiced by his homeland – he tried so very hard to forget that he was American, poor devil. And soon their little differences gathered force and erupted into blazing rows, in all of which he adopted the arch and condescending attitude of a disappointed parent, and she a rebellious teenager stamping her petulant foot, hissing and tearing out twigs from the manic curls of her thatch of broomstick hair. Neither would change, neither would cave – how sad, that two comets, as these individuals doubtless were, could be so much in love, and yet still be so insurmountably incompatible.

Finally, tearfully, but decisively, Hermione Gauguin threw in the towel, and packed up her bags, and bade lavish farewell to Tadgh, and stormed out of his cottage to catch the day's last wretched boat. And thus, with infinite regret and sadness and relief, the poet and painter parted company. (She later met a bus conductor in Pigalle, with whom she fell in love again, and lived happily ever after.)

The poverty of all human relations, thought Tadgh, having lost for good the most likely love of his life. Depressed, he retreated again to his monastic seclusion, mindlessly enacting his meaningless chores, reaping stale corn from the harvest of his heartbreak, inking aching lines that sung of sorrow, yet rang somehow still false.

And one midsummer eve, his quota of words set down on the scroll in pedantic array for today, he went downhill to the beach for a dip. It was deserted at that hour, save for one solitary man seated afar in the waving dunes, caressing the mane of his dog.

Tadgh squinted as he undressed by the rocks – the fellow seemed to be beardy as was he, clad in a dirty nightgown like an asylum inmate, scratching the muzzle of his little wee white corgi. Nobody I know, thought Tadgh, snapping on goggles lastly, and prancing frantically forward to meet the pulsing waves. He dove in the feathery shallows, sucked in breath and did a handstand, gurgling manically then splashing to topple. He swam and did the doggy paddle, and the angelic butterfly crawl, as the waning sunlight dwindled and gave its leave to dusk. And the poet swam until his fingers wrinkled to raisins, and soon felt a chill in his bones. Shivering, he arose from the waters reborn a new man, sorrow subsumed by seawater salt, and waded back to the rocks to grab his garments and vigorously towel. And the first stars appeared in the sky, and a greyly yellow moon gravely arose, casting the pebbly beach in silver glaze. The man in the nightgown, winded like a billowing shroud, had left the hillocks of distant dunes, and was walking the dog by the lapping shallows, some yards away from the wet poet who soon was drier. Dressed again, in jersey and jeans, he turned on a, to patchily illumine his unwitting way homeward, and began to amble upward and uphill.

But just then in the curtained darkness, as his boots crunched on the pebbles and cockleshells, he heard a growl and bark behind him, followed by a stifled shout. Turning, he saw that the dog had fled from his owner and now was mounting fast upon him, the poet his prey, keen to chase and hunt for sport. At first he thought nothing of it – only a little puppy after all. But then he saw, for whatever why, that the dog grew larger with every foot he gained, every swift approaching pad of paw, stamping and loping on the sand that bore his prints, barking and growling and howling like hell with blazing rolling eyes and drool. Feeling fear, Tadgh hastened his pace, then quickened to a run as he felt the rabid beast's breath upon his heels, chasing him higher and higher up slope of the shore, keen to pick flesh from his bones, and suck up his marrow to grease its mandibles.

Terrified, the lanky beanpole poet windily ran along, dropping his bags in sand in his fluster, darting frantic glances behind his shoulder at the blurry snowy shape of the White Dog, whose size increased and swelled until he was monstrously huge, of unearthly outsized proportions, a growling giant hunting down his quaking supper that could not scamper fast enough nor outrun him, running screaming through the night and crying in the darkness, sightlessly flinging stones behind to deter the demon's advance, blindly stubbing toes on the rocks, slipping on the dampened pampas, getting sand blown in his eyes, stumbling and tripping and crawling bolting upright with breathless stagger, fleeing the barking distraught, hearing the farther owner's voice on the shaking wind, bidding his beast desist and be good, an appeal that went ignored.

And at last panting Tadgh got to his garden's gate, and hopped over the squeaky turnstile, blundering through blackness to greet his door where he fumbled with his latchkey, and heard the hound smash down his fence, scamper roaring through his garden, and he felt its hot breath on his neck as it bit him, clamping its jaws on his elbow chomping and tearing off a smidgen flesh, the sharp scalding pain stung and the hot blood bled, but then with screech he got his key and turned the lock and scampered bleeding inside, and slammed the door against the furry fiend who thunderously pounded the boards with its thumping paws, and barked and scratched and howled and howled.

Slumped and crumpled on his landing with his battered shoulder to the door, the wounded poet clutched his bleeding elbow, and winced as streaming blood pooled darkly in the dimness. And he cocked his straining ears as the outside howls dwindled to growls, and the dissatisfied monster snuffled, and scraped about, and woofed and hissed, and then came a sound and smell of trickling pissing as a leg was lifted, and the poet's flowerbeds were burnt by the scalding canine urine. Then there was a new sound in the air outside, the sound of a giant's footsteps thudding up the desecrated path, at which the chastened dog was heard to whimper, cowed before its owner who had at last caught up. Tadgh heard a stormy kick being administered to the creature's belly, at which the guilty mutt groaned and whined, accepting submissively its rightful punishment, as all wrongdoing doggies do. And then the owner's voice rang out in the night:

'Christ, Snowy! Can't I take you anywhere?'

Silence then, and Tadgh's teeth chattered. His bloodshot eyes arched over to the window on the wall above where he crouched, through which pane hung and shone the pale and mocking moon, neither crescent nor oval, seeming to smile. Then a looming face appeared at the window and took the place of the moon, luminously shining. The face of a tall old man, with shaggy beard and hooked nose, with a sharp and pointy skull from sides of which sprung two tufts of hair, like as unto horns. Initially graven in expression as he squinted at the dim behind the glass, he began then to smile, baring jagged teeth in a yellow grin at the cowering poet who lay within, gazing fearfully upward.

'Hi there! I really must apologize for my pet's behaviour. Must have given you quite a start, eh? He's not usually so ferocious, I assure you. Last time he got that angry he tore off my mother's face, ha. Sometimes he just seems to, er, to see something sort of, eh, sort of objectionable in some people. Seems to get a whiff off of them that he doesn't like. Drives him crazy. I reckon he's not fit to be taken out in public anymore. For a long time, you know, I've had it in mind to lock him up. Preferably buried underground on the mainland. Any suggestions? You are the victim after all, it is only right you have a say.'

Tadgh thought of a postcard he owned, depicting the grave of Yeats.

'Drumcliff,' he hoarsely croaked.

The stranger considered and sucked upon a pipe.

'Where's that? ... Sligo, innit? Ah yeah, at the foot of the big man mountain's toes. Of course. Good one. Ah but I knew you were a poet only to look at you. Thank you for your time and sorry for your trouble. I do hope our paths will cross again some awful faraway day.'

And then, as if an afterthought:

'... uh, I have ... or had ... a daughter myself too, you know.'

And then The Mad Monk disappeared.

And as the night melted and darkness withdrew, when pearly dawn appeared over the starry horizon of the sea, and the black house grew grey then white with the light that flooded in through the glass and peeked through chinks in the masonry, Tadgh O'Mara lay slumped by his door and wondered over and over on what the stranger had said. And he raised his wrinkled hands, which seemed all the older and ashen, cracking their brittle fingers with pain, and rose from his swoon with groans, for his bones were crackling and aged, and looked through the fog of his mildewed mirror, and admired the frostiness of his hair and beard, which the day before had been brown, and overnight had turned white. And he considered again, and dressed the wound in his chapped elbow, and understood that there was no point in turning back. He would find his child, wherever she might be.

That day he vanished. His empty house was soon demolished, and a children's playground was erected on the dusty smoking ruins left behind.

CHAPTER THREE

The tale of Peadar Lamb's Bull is recounted often in the annals of old Athleague by the Suck Valley Way. It gave the folk much fodder to talk of.

Peadar was well known and well stood in the land. A gentleman farmer, with leprechaun looks, he was liked and loved by all who knew him, by young and old alike adored. He was a generous giver of bronzes when at the mass the collecting bowl came round, ever ready with a coin for a kid and a bit for a baby. He was revered for his stories, enlivening for his listeners bygone strange scenes that only he had the worth of wit to describe, to tell to all the tales of his tribe. And he was a family man, happily married to a lovely lady for long a year, to whom he was a good husband, and so too was he a fine father to his set of sons. Many were the tracts of fields that were his, many were his cows and pigs and sheep, and large and spacious his house and keep. And he was as amiable with animals as he was with his fellows. He was well versed in country matters.

Peadar had a lot of cows, but only one Bull, a handsome virile creature of whom the farmer was very fond. He had several names for the Bull, and though it was seldom that any stuck, the most enduring were Bosco, Alphonsus and Albert Van Zyl. He liked to talk to the Bull whenever he got the chance or had time to kill, leaning over the paddock's stony wall to pass a remark about the weather, or inquire as to the condition and merit of the grass being eaten. The Bull's replies to these queries were for the most part brusque and bullish. Sometimes, worse still, he would not even bother repay Peadar with the dignity of a reply, but instead turn his big back on the good man his owner, and with superb disdain ignore him. And it disheartened Peadar that the Bull did not love him as much as he did the

Bull, for all he ever wanted was to be friends. So their relationship, warm on Peadar's part, and frosty on the Bull's, was conducted at arm's length.

(The first danger signs were noted when Peadar's wife awoke one night to hear her husband lying by her in the bed, seeming sleeping but perfectly coherent in all he said, panting and pining for his life's lack of love, lack that the Bull refused alas alleviate.)

On one fine April day Peadar was quietly having supper with his family, when of all a sudden their peace was ruptured when they heard from without a roar, the Bull's bellow. And Peadar panicked, dropped his spoon and knife, to the concern of his wife, and got up from the table and ran out as fast as he was able, tearing through the fields scurrying within sight and sound of the Bull's roar (Albert Van Zyl he was being called this weather), and came upon the creature to see aghast that he was belly deep in the bog, stuck in a murk of mire, sinking fast, a plaintive look in his eyes that was never before seen there, as one by one the grains of his life ran thinner and thinner in the merciless hourglass.

Peadar paused. Here before him was a life to save from the grave, the life of one he loved, his best and only bull who with his concubine cows had such power of pull. But it would be an effort to save him, rope was required, to tie tight around the brute's belly, and tug and pull till he came unstuck. He could not do this alone. And all the while he paused the Bull still further sunk and bellowed, and gave the man Peadar many a look. And those looks were appealing looks, and those pleading looks gratified Peadar in a strange sadistic sort of way, who felt himself almost happy to have gained the brute's attention. And from such attention may spring affection, such as he craved.

So snapping out of his reverie he called for help from many varying quarters of his household and farm, got some boys from the barn and nearby neighbours come clamouring to aid him. And they all came a-tumbling down from their corners along the undulant dips of the field, and got some rope and made quick to tie it taut about the shoulders of the sinking giant who snorted and roared all the while, sinking ever lower all the time. And Peadar on the sidelines stood alone the better to brood, and shouted and gave orders, and ordered his lady to make a cup of tea for all the company. And having tied they tugged and heaved and strained and swore, and little children coming home from school gathered in a ring to look upon them. And the sinking Bull in agony blared.

And the springtime sun sunk in the sky as the dying day wore on, and the moon rose, and stars twinkled, and the people pulled and still they could not shift the croaking Bull from the bog. And the Bull was weakening, and Peadar was worrying, and the children were crying, and the men who were pulling were weary, and wanted rest, which at his behest with a sigh Peadar deemed fit to give them. And so the men retired, and the children were taken home to bed, and Mrs Lamb shrugged her shoulders and shuffled away. And left behind alone in the darkness Peadar with a lantern looked at the Bull, shoulder deep in the miry bog, so sad and doleful, his pride all gone, looking back into the eyes of the man who owned him and loved him. And Peadar too felt sad to see, knowing in his heavy heart that the beast whose affection he so sought only now felt for him that same feeling when on the brink of extinction.

And then knowing a sudden savagery Peadar untied and cut the rope and threw the trail away, and sat down on a mound, and with the flame of his lantern lit himself a pipe, and sat and watched the Bull sink and further sink, waiting for the ground to swallow him up and waiting for him to die. And the night grew into day, and the meadow lightened as the sun arose to find the farmer still sat on the mound, and lower sunk the sinking Bull, bellowing the less, croaking the more, his light going out as the earth crushed his sides and sapped his strength and he starved and died. And Peadar looked on with iron eyes, as dwindling life lapped. And the Bull starved and his cries grew fainter.

And it was for several days and nights that the two wore on this way in the same stance, until at long last the Bull finally died. He was so sunk by that stage that only his head and horns were still visible barely bobbing above the bog, so he was when he drew a final breath and died. And Peadar Lamb, when he was quite sure that the beast was dead, took a spade and heaped on the horns and head some shovelfuls of boggy clay, heaping until there was no more to be seen of the dead animal save for a fresh clump or mound on the ground similar to that that he had sat on. And this done, he spat a little, sniffled a little, and turned away and walked back to his home, where he was received with reserve and looks imploring, silent faces begging know why, but he would not answer.

Some months later, bereft Peadar got lucky on a horse. The horse was called Wolf the White Rider, and it was a tidy sum Peadar collected, the first such sum for many a sun he had won, and it rather turned his grieving head. In a rare instance of irresponsibility, he blew it all on a binge of boozing, and thus toured the town's three bars with lopsided traipse.

Willie Flynn (who in later life would work in the meat factory until the drink addled his brains and wound up driving a truck into the sleepy Suck – sad fate) was a youngster at the time, in the process of courting Desdemona O'Connell. Young Willie was passing by Waldron's on the evening in question (en route to a dalliance at a dance with the damsel) and was witness to Peadar getting ejected by barman Barney. Horrified Willie saw Peadar, an upright pillar of the community, now properly potted, bowler askew and lank locks wet with the sweat of a souse, giving cheek and being brash, getting flung out the door and landing on the road with quite a crash. There he lay, staring supine at the stars with a terrible smile, the remainder of his winnings spilling from his pockets.

And Willie Flynn crossed the road over to where the elder man lay, and stood over him, unsure of what to say, then decided help him up. Peadar was heavy and not easy to shift, and his truculent humour did not help. He was perfectly happy where he was and wanted only to be left alone. But soon the old shite again was upright, and by the younger got dusted down his front, his jacket lapels smoothed, his bowler set aright on his head, but as for his prodigal pennies that had wandered, there was too little light for Willie to see them, and he said sorry to Peadar that he would be winding up the less richer.

'Arragh, what is wealth that wants worth?' spat Peadar bitterly.

'Now, now, Mr Lamb, don't be talking that way now,' said Willie keen to placate, 'just get your bearings and be on your way home now.'

'My home hath no heart no longer,' Peadar dolefully said.

'Ah go away with that now, Mr Lamb, sure haven't you a fine house to call yer own, and a lovely wife and sound sons to look after you?'

'A fat bitch and a lot of loafers with empty heads and stagnant souls, she the woman fooled me a sagging nag now with droopy paps and a tongue to spit venom, and me boys, those dullards, none among them a quarter the man their father was and is.'

Willie thought further to remonstrate, but he had not the requisite know how of the world's wiles to deal with the darkness he was met with now. So after some further dustings of lapels, the younger gave the elder a shove to the north. And teetering Peadar staggered away, and Willie watched him go until the darkness swallowed him up like a ghost. And Willie Flynn was on the point of carrying on to the dance, when an idea struck. All the coins lost from Peadar's pockets rolling still the ground bestrew. Money such as was good for getting what one wanted. It smacked of sin, such as from which he normally flinched, but he felt this instance an exception. And though it was too dark to see those coins, he could yet fetch a light from some source. And Willie Flynn, whistling with devilry, went on to the dance, where he hoped Desdemona O'Connell and a candle or lantern to find, to aid him in his scheme, to acquire gains ill-gotten, to further evil ends.

Meanwhile Peadar meandered down the road, turning off down a dark path hedged by tall trees into the quiet of country. He tripped up several times on his crooked way, brought down by erect mushrooms and toadstools. Soon the sound of water was in his ears, and he made tracks in the darkness in search of that sound, hunting for the trickle and rush, sounds he knew well, the sound of the Suck.

And when he got to the Suck, the thought of suicide entered his head.

Standing there by the moonlit Suck, watching the silvery dappled river rush by, radiant as gossamer with the moon, he thought how nice it would be to jump into that river and soar along caught up by that surge, and thereafter sink. That such a jump and subsequent sink constituted suicide he only discovered by degrees, and he found himself not at all alarmed to be considering it. And it was not long before he convinced himself of the worth of the notion, smacking his palms and removing his boots and socks, and steadying himself in readiness for the decisive jump into the watery element.

And so he jumped. And he had not far to fall from the shallow bank before he landed splashing into the Suck, and then was tumbling along with the surge through the darkness. And he howled as he was carried on the back of the stallion Suck, feeling the cold of the water, wet limbs cracking against riverbed rocks. And in such a manner would he have flowed along until he inevitably drowned, had not a hand from the sky (or so it seemed) dipped down to grab him by the hair of his head to hoist him up and out. And so he was lifted free and dripping, and carried through the air, and deposited with a dump back on the bank. And on being dumped, beneath the bark of a wizened tree, his head hit the ground hard, and then, overcome by the horror of the evening, for a while passed out.

Meanwhile, Willie Flynn had managed to get Desdemona to come out from the dance with him, bearing a candle and a pack of matches, to the spot on the street where Peadar's winnings had rolled. The candle lit, and held by the querulous maiden, Willie scrabbled about on hands and knees to pick up from the paving all the stray coins, aglow and winking in the flickering candlelight. In time he had scooped them all up (fewer than he had hoped, the old shite had drunk up the bulk), and clasping them in his palm, he took his leave of the disgruntled damsel (who grumbled), giving a final peck to her chubby cheek before turning to scurry away to his digs, up nearer the river. And then the rasping wind blew out the candlelight, and she was left all on her lonesome to go home alone lonely.

After that, when Willie arrived back to his darkened digs, he was met with a sharp thump on the head from a hoof, and he saw stars as he sunk into a coma.

Back by the bank beneath the bark, Peadar awoke from witless slumber to find lying beside him in the murk a body he knew to be that of Willie Flynn, his eyes vacant and tongue lolling. And as Peadar blinked and looked around him, he saw that a ring of candles surrounded them, and their flame was as that of the stars in the heavens. The last candle was being lit by a hunched figure, dapperly dressed in pinstriped tweeds, lighting the last candle by means of a match in the shape of a crescent moon. The final candle lit, the tidy figure turned to look at Peadar, who saw with an obscure horror it was a man with the head of a goat, with looming horns, a long beard curling to a fine taper, and eyes of brightest yellow, eyes that gave Peadar a lurid quizzical look, the head cocked to one side.

Then, having assured himself that the specimen was the one wanted, the Pooka nodded and grunted, produced from a pocket a pipe, which with his lunar lighter he lit. Smoking, he sat down beside Peadar beneath the tree, crossed his legs and looked up at the stars peeking between the boughs and foliage. Silence reigned until the Pooka broke it.

'I saved your life, you know.'

Peadar shivered, remembering the hand that held him by the hair.

'You are not, I take it, a happy man, Mr Lamb?'

Peadar, heart in throat, mumbled something to the effect that he wasn't.

'Nay. But then again, what is happiness? Did you ever know it?'

Lulled by the lilt of the voice, Peadar growing calmer in his reply grew bolder. He said he thought he had been happy once, having had everything a happy man in that habitation was expected enjoy, which in that place amounted to field and family.

'But it was never enough, Mr Lamb, was it? What was that that you lacked?'

Peadar considered, then admitted at last it was love he lacked.

'How so? Surely your lady loved you? Getting spoilt for choice, Mr Lamb?'

Peadar shook his head in vehemence. There was one life above all from whom he had wanted love, love the swine stubbornly refused give, and now that that life was ended, never would. The allure of the unrequited beguiled.

'It becomes all the balder. When reciprocated, we never notice, it's always those who ignore us over whom we worry and tear our hair in woe. The Bull, eh? Old what's-his-name: Bosco? Alphonsus? Albert Van Zyl?'

Peadar's eyes grew damper, as numbly he nodded, sniffing.

'And yet you let him die, Mr Lamb. And wherefore on Earth why?'

Peadar had no answer. He buried his face in his hands and cried.

The Pooka, mature beyond his years, gave a sigh to see a grown man cry. He stood up, stretched, pared his long nails, and explained his scheme. His associate, one Goodfellow, was at the moment engaged in the chore of digging up the buried deadened Bull, whose cadaver he would shortly tow over to where they were. For a small sum, they would strike up a bargain with the farmer, wherein they would bring back the Bull, through aid of the Faerie King's Fire they had stolen, purloining its Promethean properties. And maybe then the Bull might love him; the Puck could play Cupid with his quiver of aphrodisiac arrows. All they requested in return was the remainder of the money Peadar had won on Wolf the White Rider, gold they might put into their pot. And just as Peadar was on the point of protesting that he had no means of paying them, for all his winnings were drunk up or lost, the Pooka pointed a talon to the moribund Willie:

'That oaf stole it from you, good Mr Lamb. Rummage through his pockets, you will see it is so. You see now how I, a stranger, may be trusted to save your life and lend you the love you lack, while one among your village's number reveals himself to be a shallow untrustworthy brute who will take duplicitous advantage of your incapacity.'

Peadar found the money, and pondered the point the Pooka made, aggrieved to think it all too true, feeling new horror to see the greed that festered in the hearts of men, and feeling moved that the Pooka, painted by lore a demon, should be so kind and good.

And then lo, hither came to them in the night the elfin Puck, giggling and snickering with a demon's glee, wheeling through the darkness the creaking barrow, wherein lay a bundle of bones, those of the Bull, a skeleton that was slightly askew, to whose ribs clung some tatters of flesh and meat not yet rotted, and in the sockets of the skull, lay the jellied bloodshot eyeballs, quivering as the barrow ground to a squeaky halt.

'He's yours for the having!' quoth the Puck, doffing his floppy cap.

Through foggy eyes, Peadar seemed to see the Pooka dip into a pocket, and pull out a bundle of fire he held in his palm, liquid fire that glowed with the effervescent flare of phosphoresce or ectoplasm, some gas that was not of the Earth, which ball of brightness he seemed then to rub upon the bones, back and forth as though administering a massage, to daub them and baste them with oily fire that would make them move, which indeed they duly did, tingling and shaking as snaking breath began to creep back through the empty frame. Hinges jangling, snorting, the Bull of bones arose from the barrow, and all stood back to watch it hit the turf, and paw the ground again, skeletal with furious eyes of red. It looked about, and hit upon Peadar. Who knows what memories it nursed of life? Who knows whether his image aroused buried knowledge? Who knows with what emotions the monster glared upon the man who had loved him in life, but now who cowered to see him arisen, sensing a vile thing done that was neither right nor good, nor after the natural way of the world. Who knows from whence sprang that instinct to rage – perhaps a memory had been kindled of a man who had cut the rope, and sat back to watch him sink and die. The farmer trembled, and croaked:

'No. This is not my Bull. This is a travesty. Kill it again for me.'

But his words fell on deaf ears; the Pooka and the Puck had vanished with his cash, having neglected to apply the aphrodisiac arrows. (Bastards.)

So he was left alone to deal with the beast, whose attitude quickly proved to be of a wrathful sort, quickly angered. Sensing its hostility, Peadar attempted to escape by climbing up the tree, but he was feeble, and the Bull of bones was quick. It charged headlong as he clung dangling from a branch, and knocked him down, shattering one of his ribs, and cracking both his hips, and trampled all over him as he lay groaning in the mucky riverbank, beaten and trodden as weeping he sprawled. He pleaded forgiveness as he was stamped upon, an impotent appeal that met with no relent in the assault. Willie Flynn awoke from his stupor in the midst of the fray, took fright and tried to run away, but the Bull would not let him go unpunished. It pricked his arse with the sting of its horns, which made him yowl and spring, and topple stumbling into the deeps of the Suck, in which depths he was as like as to have drowned, had not he had the wit to grab onto a jutting log that bore out from the bank, onto which he clung for his life for all the rest of a very long wet night.

And the Bull of bones stormed away from that pair of miserable men, and bound from the bog down the village's central street, and by some was seen as they exited the pub, sight of which skeleton, hurtling along and hellishly snorting, made them devoutly question their alcohol intake. Then it was gone, and never seen from that day to this.

Peadar crawled home, lamed and bloodied and maimed, where his wife attended to his wounds, soothing the sores of her husband, broken in spirit and purse. Willie Flynn was later rescued from the river by some shepherds, to whom he told his sketchy tale, none of which they believed. And Peadar too, once his grief and pain had palled, began to take cheer in the mere telling, maker of a queer fable whose moral was unsure, and whose veracity was vague, that yet made for thrilling hearing, as he propped up the bar and decade upon decade explained to the crowd how it was he twice lost his best bull, and how the fairies took all the money he had won on a horse.

And then, years later, around nowadays, he cut off his leg with a saw.

CHAPTER FOUR

The Mad Monk awoke on the seashore some years later. Coughing, hacking, he spat out sea salt as he waked. His garments stuck to his skin as he slowly began to crawl up the slope of the shore to squat on the sand. Seated, he permitted himself a smile.

It was morning, and there were no clouds in the sky, at which The Mad Monk spat a kiss, and smoothed out his shaggy beard, alive now with carp and kemp and barnacle that over the long course of his sea's sojourn had found a new home in the tangles.

He was very happy to be back.

Hearing caws, he looked up and saw two gulls wheeling about in the blue. Mindful that their bowels may want emptying, he headed with a prance further inland. As he ambled, he kept anxious eyes on the blue above, annoyed to see that the impertinent birds were following him. They cawed as closer they came lower, and he growled. Then he stooped to pick up two purple pebbles, wetly glistenening from wash of the wave. Bright eyes glinting, he laid them on his palm. He mourned that beauty be bloodied.

His eyes no longer on their target, he noted not how low by now had come the wheeling gulls, nor heard their cheeky caws and cries. The bolder of the two dipped in its flight, made a move at The Mad Monk to sit on his shoulder, and bit the sharp tip of his skull, bit enough the bald patch of scalp to bloody.

But The Mad Monk moved not, stood still as stone on the sand, eyes for nothing but the pebbles in his palm, about his face a white cloud of calm.

The gull, perplexed to be ignored, bit again. The other, less than bold, alighted on the sand at the feet of the mountain of man, and walked in circumspection about him in a circle. Curious creature. Its fellow bit again, pleased to see the spool of blood that darkly now dripped from the widening wound, from top of scalp slipping slow in a sliver down his brow, passing by the brook of nose, staining the teeth of the mouth that always seemed to smile, coming to nestle amid shags of the beard, the blood among the bristle now. And so he bled, and the bird bit. And the sun shone. And the water's waves lapped the shore. And over all seemed a lull.

But then The Mad Monk snapped from his roguish ruse, and with a roar shot up an arm, and made a grab at the biting gull, and caught it by the neck, and the squawking creature croaked as its neck was broken by the clawing fingers tightening, and The Mad Monk laughed and laughed, and his mouth opened wider to admit the bird, and he ate, and chewed, growling as he guzzled, his champing jaws dripping blood chewing in relish the feathery bones so easily broke, a miracle he didn't choke, and he spat forth some feathers that galled his gizzard, and the pulpy mush in his mouth he rolled round with his tongue, and he swallowed in sections, with consideration.

At his feet, transfixed, the other shyer seagull nestled, looking up gawking with nervous eyes at the looming ogre who had made meat of his mate. The power of flight having dissipated, all he could do was watch, and hope in vain meekly not to be noticed.

But there was no escaping notice. The Mad Monk saw all. He looked down at the little bird squatting on the sand far below him, looking up in its small sad fearful way. And The Mad Monk's cruelty melted. His gnawing hunger of before sated, the thirst brought by salt of sea abated by bird's blood, he grew kinder, and milder. And he decided it would be nice to do the gull a favour, and leave him better off the wiser. And such a feat would be no small one, and would augur well for all to come that was to be done.

He bent, sat down on the sand, crossed his legs like the lotus, and regarded the little gull (its paperweight heart aflutter with its fright, thinking yet the madman may kill me, he might!). But as the minutes passed, the gull grew calmer in the giant's shadow, growing to admire his large look, encrusted by the weed of the sea, his great ragged robe speckled by barnacles, in one palm playing with the purple pebbles, whose prior purpose had played out and whose chance was gone, yet still might be made useful, so the wise old wicked man was thinking as upon the gull he gazed, that gull who grew to love the look that glinted or blazed in alternate measure in the eyes of him who was neither Monk nor merely Mad. And the sound of the sea was soothing, the lap was lulling as soft on the sand the stirring surf bubbled gently, ebbing and eddying, casting a balm of calm on the seagull's soul. And he shut his little eyes, and began to slumber in the sun on the sand.

And The Mad Monk smiled to see the seagull sleeping, and so he then spoke, and the slumbering seagull somehow heard all that he said:

'Little bird. Thou art the first witness to my arrival. A friend of mine once told me a theory of the origins of eyes, wherein first they were formed through the process of pebbles being rubbed, mayhap for millennia, against the breasts of sea snails. These pair in my palm, pretty their purple hue, seem likely. And so for you, gully my only, I shall give thee a new pair of eyes, a new pair, a purple pair, formed of pebble and pap of crustacean. Through aid of my fine chalk all I need do is daub in a pupil or two, and slot 'em in your sockets. And those that you have I'll pop 'em out if I may – for I don't suppose you'd mind much if I ate them, would you, popping them into me mouth to chew them with the gusto I would give a grape, for Lordy knows my belly's a big one – whizz – pop – yum – tasty! There you go, anyway, all done and dusted, and you didn't feel a thing, did you? Rise up from your slumber and awake, and all will be new through veil of violet hue. Go on, give it a go, gully my goodly, go on, wake up!'

And the seagull woke up from its deep sleep.

And everything had changed.

Newly born he saw the seaside glitter before his enraptured eyes, and his waking soul beat the warmer in his breast, feeling bliss amid such splendour he had hitherto never known. And his eyes, quick as before but all the sharper now, newly purple their pupils a chalky white, saw too that he sat no longer in shadow – the man had gone. And the giddy seagull saw then too, lightly lain in the spot he had sat upon, a trim envelope, a crimson rectangle. And somehow the seagull knew too that the onus was on him to ensure the envelope saw fulfillment of its deliverance to whomsoever parties it was addressed. And the gull was happy to play a part in a plot bigger than he, in service to the saint who had wrought such a miracle, a man he would have followed to the end of the Earth, and further yet than that.

And so, approaching the envelope on tap-dancing feet, the gull inclined his head to read the writing, in a firm hand that had room for blemishes, and searing moments of spidery ejaculatory splash, tokens of the man of passion possessed of the fiery mind that moved the hand that held the quill that wrote the terse words of addressees and address:

To Messrs Goodfellow And MacPhellimey;
Stationed At The Tomb Of Archibald Theodore;
Atop The Largest Sand Dune In The World;
Somewhere In The Depths Of The Desert;
Somewhere In The Unwieldy Width Of The World (you'll get there!).

The seagull took this in with a smile, barely noticing that this marked but another milestone in his little life, one so far lead without ever having had the wish, will or tendency, to say nothing of ability, to read written words, hitherto alien to his understanding. He scooped up the message with a careless clasp of wing – his feathers finding fingers – and, strutting in a circle, pondered the import of his task. Then he turned his bold face to the sun, and spoke a parting declaration of his feelings:

'Cor blimey, I've boarded the gravy train like Boy George or Kevin Spacey!'

And with cackle and cheery chuckle, the gull took off and took wing, and left the land, and soon was sailing in the sky of blue, out into the ocean, staring down the sun, a speck in the horizon, soon but a blot in the blue, that faded, and was gone away far.

CHAPTER FIVE

Arsene O'Colla lived not far from the sea, near Bannow Bay on a southeastern shore. His house was an oblong bungalow, hedged by high shrubbery, enclosing a spacious courtyard of a grand garden. In previous years, the grass stood tall, overrun by weeds, and a legion of dandelions, and buttercups, and daisies, home to the hare, the pheasant, collared doves, and sometime springtime frogs, hopping and croaking, huddling down near the roots. All over grew fingers of the spreading grass, taking over the paving of the path that lead from his gate to his door, invading to conquer the dilapidated garage, its roof fallen in and crumpled, the cause a flash of lightning that struck, far back sometime in the seventies. But today the grass stands tall no more. On the advice of an uncaring cousin – having a mind to inherit the place only to sell it once the old man passed on – Arsene had it cut, laid to waste by lawnmower. Birds no longer sing there.

Sunlight came in through crack of the filthy curtain, a slender ray alighting on the old man's eyes. He had slept a full sleep, though not a good one, deep and dreamless as death, drug-induced. Following the gospel of Dr Lennox, he had gobbled his staple fill of pills the night before, thought to be of aid in banning from his troubled slumber the diabolic visions that in the past had put him in peril.

A groggy zombie, he lifted his head from his pillow and sat up in bed slowly, smacking his chapped lips. He looked about the bedroom's murk, the floorboards uncovered by carpet; the mirror afar begrimed by streaks of mildew; the bulb above in the sagging ceiling that had ceased to work; his dentures in a glass by his bedside, a glass once filled by water, long by now evaporated in the damp stale air. Yawning, he slowly got out of his musty old man's bed, freeing himself of the heavy smelly threadbare blanket, a fetid scent arising, the fragile bedsprings creaking. Their creak called to his mind the chirp of the rodent chorus that daily scurried hither and thither up above in his attic, or down below his feet beneath the floorboards, coming up for air to steal his food. He took his dentures from the glass and fitted them into his mouth – an imperfect fit, for those dentures were as profuse with gaps as were his real teeth.

Then he swung feet to the floor and stood up swaying, in string vest from which his pot of belly poked, and beige underpants, displaying a history of stains, tokens of the blue-moon nocturnal secretions to which he was prone. He padded out from his room into the hall, a hall lined by stacks of old volumes, cluttering the cramped passage, sprinklings of turds made by mice nestling deep in the hairy carpet. The walls were adorned by rare engravings and old prints – reproductions of military group portraits by his favourite Franz Hals – and some antiquated fin-de-siècle cartoons, satirical in nature, featuring Earl Spenser, culled from contemporary periodicals, that appealed to the blatant patriot in him. Arsene with bleary eyes gave a glance to none of this as he made his way down the alcove to the toilet, second door on the left. Fresh light of morning falling through the cobwebbed window bathed a radiant balm on the rusty bath, the drain clotted by hair, on the dampish tiled floor, on the toilet bowl, over which the old man now took his aim, holding in one hand his shriveled manhood in poise for a piss.

The flow was slow to come; and erratic when it did, splashing on the cistern, piddling down in stray droplets at uneven intervals. Having done, and forgotten to flush, Arsene, as he stuffed himself back in, all at once began to shiver. He coughed; and saw emitted in the air a fogburst of cloudy breath. Only then did he become aware of just how cold was his house. On account of the expense incurred, which seemed to him scarifying ('too fecking expensive!' he would splutter), he was loath to ever turn his heating on, even in the very depths of frosty winter, for all the chiding of his few true well-meaning friends. But the old man would never listen, for there was a deep stubbornness in his soul.

Mousetraps were strategically installed in every corner of his kitchen, and the first thing he saw upon entering, with momentary qualm, was the corpse of a mouse, crushed by sprung metal. But he disdained to do anything about it, and let it lie dead. He filled the kettle with tap water, and set it to boil, and brought forth a greasy bowl from the sink's clutter, to which he added cornflakes from a box hid up on a high shelf, topping off with a dollop of lukewarm milk from a carton left atop, not in, the fridge. This carton had spent most of the previous week sitting in the sun, as a consequence less than cool. But since the fridge door was prone to swaying open and staying open, and nothing kept cool or fresh, perhaps after all it made no difference where in the kitchen the carton was kept.

The kitchen gave way onto the suntrap of his sitting room, two of its four walls being almost all of glass, wide windows through which he could see his garden and high hedges, and the decaying box of disused garage. He carried his breakfast bowl over to a low armchair, set it down gingerly on an arm, and took from a nearby chair a blue dressing gown that hung there, into which he slipped himself. Books and dusty newspapers crammed that sitting room, crowding the table and sitting on all bar two of the chairs. There was a television over by the curtain, which he switched on, with intent to catch the morning service. But only snowy waves showed up onscreen, which put Arsene at a loss. Puzzled, he scratched his head, gazing blankly at a monochrome version of Bruegel's *Children's Games*, hanging by thumbtack on the wall by the spotty monitor.

Since visuals went nowhere, he elected on sweet music to provide his entertainment. His sound system, kindly lent him by his tenor friend Martin Graves, lay below the table, the speakers blocked by old catalogues, which he shoved aside as he got down heavily on hands and knees, to delve amid what discs and cassettes and stacks of vinyl lay hidden under there. The selection had its share of 'difficult' and 'challenging' pieces – Late Quartets of Beethoven, some snippets of *The Ring* – though Arsene in his older age found himself increasingly more inclined to slighter frivolities, which were easier to take on an empty stomach, and less upsetting for a mind prone to distraction.

After flirting with the *Pastorale*, he chose *The Blue Danube*. Its undulating strains soon filled the sunny room, knocking dust from the stacks and plaster from the chipped wallpaper. Still vague Arsene hunched under the table crouching by the music box, wondering why the tune no longer made him happier, as before it had unfailingly done.

Then he heard the rumble and click of the kettle in the kitchen as it boiled. He started back up abruptly with a grunt, banging his head on the table's underside, which threw him dizzily backwards. Alarmed, one hand flailed out, made a grab at the arm of the low armchair behind him, brushing past and knocking over the bowl of cornflakes he had forgotten he had set down there. The bowl fell from its perch not far to the floor, where its contents were spilled, and it smashed, and it broke. Arsene heard the noise and froze, and sat on dumbly, there on the floor beneath the table for a time.

Outside, a stray grey cat was roaming through the garden, creeping amid the grass on legs more wobbly than once they were. She was old, her ragged hide long lost its gloss, with only one of her golden eyes still in working order – the other but an empty socket. She was lured by the many mice she knew resided by the place, and drawn by the prospect of a saucer of milk that the aged resident upon occasion set down on the doorstep for her pleasure. Today she found none. Miffed, her ears pricked up to hear faint strains of Strauss stealing from within. Feline she flitted eagerly to the sitting-room window, upon whose ledge she hopped up sleekly, nose to glass to peer upon the interior. To see one-eyed the old man emerging from under the table slowly, one quivery hand planted on the tabletop to steady, as he stood upright again, shaking. The cat regarded coolly the old face that came into view, seen at a distance through the fog of glass, saw the jowls, mouth agape, a few tufts of ratty whitish hair atop the potato skull and eggy scalp, saw the hazy eyes dipped, inspecting the damage that lay in ceramic shards and a milky puddle of wet mush on the floor. Then he stepped over the pool, headed to the kitchen, and emerged after a minute's lapse cradling a cup of steaming tea.

The one-eyed cat saw the old man sit back down in his armchair, pot-bellied old gnome in dressing gown of blue, and sip his tea, expression inscrutable. Then he reached out one hand to the table to pick up a nondescript catalogue that was lying there. Through this he skimmed and riffled for some minutes, from his sipping lips some tea dribbling down to stain the paper he perused. Hungry for attention, the cat mewled and scratched the glass, pining. The old man heard her scratching mid music, and looked up. But there was no understanding there in the blank gaze that faced her, the mind afar. Dimly sensing that for his company she clamoured, he managed a vague nod that she barely could see, then looked back down at Mealy's catalogue, the more pressing of his priorities.

For Mealy's auction was being held in Dublin in the Tara Towers tomorrow, and Arsene intended today to travel down to the town to attend the event at which he was an annual fixture. For he was a man whose hobbies and interests gave him constant preoccupation and means of distraction from the void without and the hollow within. And since his recent retirement from the Met Service (where he had worked some thirty years in a position of scant importance that gave him ample time to browse the papers and stare at the sky, learning off by rote the cumuli and the nimbi), his hobbies had become his life, as they had to be – it was when he had nothing to do that danger loomed the darker, and he scarcely knew what madness he was capable of. So he sought refuge in his pastimes, for all that the very dearest of them – chess, in which he had been the country's champion before his first crackup – was the very one he had to abandon and give up, on the advice of old man Lennox, it being thought too risky, given his supposed heart condition, since being too thrilling. So more sedate and tranquil pursuits were encouraged, such as stamp collecting, reading, and accumulating rare Irish books at auctions such as Mealy's. Such books he bought for wildly extravagant sums, belying his miserliness in all other areas of his life's expenditure, for all that his allowance was healthy, for some of such books he bought he also sold on, for comparably tidy sums, constituting his principal means of income, in addition to his considerable pension. And he structured his day-to-day existence around the successful accomplishment of such small missions, that gave him a deep sense of satisfaction and pride, the only way, indeed, that the old man could keep going. And the impending trek to Dublin for the auction, perhaps combined with but one more consultation with his mentor and all but father figure Lennox, was just but another such mission, the accomplishment of which ought to be sufficient to occupy the remainder of today and much of tomorrow, as it had to, as it must, for sanity's sake.

Beep-beep, beep-beep

Faintly the cat heard the peculiar noise through glass, akin it seemed to her to the crickets chirping in the grass, if much less melodious, at which noise the old man started up from his armchair, spilling his tea in his consternation. Curiously, she watched as he began to blunder around the room, in search of source of the sound that was not Strauss, looking for what he kept on losing, planting a foot in the spilt milky mush of cornflake on the floor, wincing at the wetness. Finally he found it, lodged on the mantelpiece squeezed between two gaudy antique vases (bought at the height of madness, when he knew not what he did, nor why he did it), a lump of grey metal, speckled by pokeable dials, so it seemed to her single feline eye, that the old man now took up with trembling hands.

Arsene had still not gotten the hang of his newly acquired mobile phone, one he had begrudgingly bought with great reluctance at the pestering of his friends, whose badgering had worn him down to this partial concession to the times (but getting a computer and wireless broadband was still a point-blank 'NO', no matter what they said, for all that it would suit him down to the ground, a numerically minded sort who liked to keep an eye on the progress of stocks, to say nothing of the convenience it would lend him, and the dividends he might gain, through the online buying of books). He had gotten as far as being able to make calls on it, and to open what text messages he received, though replying to these texts was as of yet still beyond him. Trembling, breathing heavily from the start the beeping had given him (two shocks in short succession already thus far this day, it was too much, set him off on the wrong beat altogether), he fingered the requisite keys, pressing to open to read what was received, which read:

> Simeon will meet you at 4 pm in Kilkenny Design Centre Café on Nassau Street to give you the keys to the house—Eugene

This constituted another alteration of Arsene's regular routine for such Dublin-bound trips and voyages, wherein he was used to seeking sanctum and night's asylum in the houses of his friends Mr Martin Graves or Eugene Collins. They would cook him dinner, look after him and keep him company, and all for free, and he did not even have to bother to be charming nor especially friendly or grateful for their kindness, for they usually put up with anything, bar the occasional outburst of sulk. But now Mr Collins, trophy husband of the diplomat Desdemona, had upped stumps to move to Athens, leaving his house behind in care and custody of his son Simeon. And any such alteration in Arsene's routine was galvanic, and took time to take on board. He had forgotten the hassle their move abroad would entail him, the snags that would ensue with regard to his future visits to the town to seek refuge at their place, number nine on a road called Lombardy, which was now, so he heard, being rented out in part to some youths, Simeon's college friends. And it seemed, to judge from this text, that time on the young man's part was wanting, given that he would not be at the house until late, kept out by carousing masquerading as studying, and would be unable to admit Arsene at an hour that might best suit him, hence the need to deliver the keys in such a way as the text dictated, to allow the old man ease of access to the house at any hour of day or night that pleased him. But there would be no free dinner waiting for him there this evening, Desdemona being gone, a thought that made him melancholy.

But still and all, he felt a faint, yet keen, anticipation, almost excitement, at the prospect of meeting the boy again. For it had been a long and goodly while since last he'd seen the young man Simeon, and he wondered whether college had changed him, wondered how much in the interval he had grown, beset by wondering for that lad he'd known all his life of eighteen years, ever since the boy's birth – Arsene it had been who met his father in the bar on the fateful day his life began, and Arsene who roused the company to propose a toast to the health of his friend's newborn. And Arsene had welcomed Eugene's son as a new member of The Thursday Club, the casual social gathering of gentlemen of which Arsene was honourary Chairman, and Mr Graves and Mr Collins the most loyal members. And Mr Collins had heeded his Chairman's words, and taken them literally, as a consequence of which his son grew up among these older men, among whom he came to feel more at home that ever he was when among his contemporaries, among whom he felt always ill at ease, from whom he kept largely aloof. But among the old men he felt at home, accompanying his father every week to the bar to see them and hear them blather, to soak up their stories and listen to their corny jokes, and the old man Arsene coming gradually to seem, throughout his childhood, like an uncle, or something of a second father. And often, whenever bored of their blathering, sitting in the corner with pen and paper his father had given him, he would resort to caricaturing them, in the cartoonish style of which from an early age he was adept, and through practice grew still better, becoming satirical chronicler of the club's trivial travails, depicting their feast days, their bickering and their squabbling, their outings to the opera or to the zoo, making up little narratives all about baldy father Eugene and the singer Mr Martin Graves of the wrinkly brow and biting bitch's wit, and finding above all in Chairman Uncle Arsenic's face a wealth of eccentric attributes to milk and make fun of, to the elder man's delight, though outwardly he affected to disdain. And one of Arsene's most treasured possessions was one such caricature the lad had done him as a present, a depiction of the elder balder Collins and the tenor Mr Martin Graves and the Chairman O'Colla, sat around this same sitting-room table, a terrible trio of drooling grotesques, a drawing done some ten years ago, which hung, from the day it was done till today, on the sitting room's western wall, to which Arsene, having digested the gist of the text, now turned eager eyes to have just one more look among innumerable looks.

But over the years it had withered, and the incessant stream of sunlight pouring into the room had long faded the lines of biro's ink, and the detail of the drawing diminished to such a degree that there was now almost nothing left of the ghostly trio on that crinkling sheet, its curling edges frayed and browning, soon to be crumbling, which looked from a distance like a rectangle of paper entirely blank, hung up on the wall below Bruegel, hung up only God knows why. And Arsene was disappointed to see nothing there, having forgotten what it had looked like, remembering it had been an amusing memento of a happier time that was no longer. And as he stared he heaved a sigh.

The cat made mew, scratching again at the window. Thus hailed, Arsene saw. And knowing at last what the creature wanted, on a passing moment's impulsive kindness, he moved from the mantelpiece to open the window, to admit the ragged one-eyed cat, who hopped with a stumble into the within, straightaway scurrying to the mushy puddle of cornflake on the floor, milk she lapped up with her pert pink tongue, purring in pleasure. And Arsene shut the window and left as she lapped, left her behind alone in the room to lick up his mess, divesting his blue dressing gown that he dropped to the floor, in a pool of sunlight near where she lay, on her belly greyly licking, as the old man left the brightness for the hall's darkness, shuffling away on his bare feet, their veins varicose, from his string vest his pot of belly poking, a bulge to hide his paltry pride below.

Then the licking one-eyed cat obtained a slight scratch from one of the sharper shards of broken bowl. A scratch on her tongue that stung, a nasty nick, and she withdrew away from the pool in pain with a hiss, dripping blood in scarlet circles dotting the milk. And the *Danube* grumbled to a close, and the waltz wound up with a crash of chords, as the spinster cat rolled in her agony on her back, rolled under the table by the speakers that fell silent, cowering in the shadow cast by drape of tablecloth and table's spindly leg, her arthritic paws to her wounded tongue, whining piteously.

Then her ears pricked up to hear noises from afar from another room.

For having given his bone-dry face a token splash of water in the sink, and dressed himself with solemnity, donned his dark trousers, put on his smelly shirt and striped waistcoat and shabby jacket, and looped about his flabby neck a spotted crimson tie, and packed his hairy suitcase with the few requisite odds and ends for the night that was in it, keeping room to allow for stowing the many books he would buy, Arsene now thought to ring up his mates in the village to let them know where he was going. They were the old sods, the counter crew, local gossips who kept him abreast of the current, with whom he fancied himself one of the lads, by whom he was laughed at behind his back, being thought a weirdo, of which discourtesy he was ignorant. And so he made in succession three calls from the phone in the hall, by the front door beneath the purple yellow Wexford flag, that awoke a spur of pride in him to see, and a few of Hals hanging. The first call was to genial Joe Hegarty, a doddery lush with whom he had made several annual enjoyable excursions across the channel in a luxury liner to Cherbourg:

'Howya, Joe … how's the body … yeah … yeah … I'm going to Dublin, Joe … yeah … yeah … for the night, yeah … no … yeah … no … bye now, Joe.'

The next call was to Bart Hartigan, the obese Gulf War vet:

'Howya, Bart … it's Arsene O'Colla here … why're ye not dressed in green, ha ha ha … yeah … no, 'cause I'll be going to Dublin today, see

… yeah, for the night only, yeah … ha ha … yeah … no … yeah … bye now, Bart.'

And the last was to Michael Nicholson, the dour schoolmaster:

'Howya, Mike … yeah, it's Arsene again … yeah … oh, never better, yeah … no … no … yeah, going up to Dublin today … yeah … did I tell you yesterday already did I, yeah … oh right, so … yeah … bye now, Mike.'

And having made these calls, and touched by the bit of bright banter that warmed the innermost humanity of his heart's cockles, and made him feel a little less lonely and alone in the world, Arsene stood, and put on, as final touch, a bobble black hat on his head, to guard from the wind his frosty pate so quickly pale to cool, a hat with quite a tip and point to it, reminiscent of a garden gnome's conical cap. And thus attired in his armour to do battle, the old man Arsene sallied forth from his dusty nook into clear air, a man with a mission and a job or three to do, eager soul astir with longing for the prospect of seeing through the potential doings of his day, quiet excitement kindling in his groggy zombie's veins, as he set out with bag in hand on his day's journey to the city. He opened his door, stepped outside, and closed and locked his door, and wandered away down his garden path passing by the ghosts of weeds that were once, and was gone out his rusting garden gate, as the snap of a brittle twig the sound of its squeak as it swung shut again slowly, and so then did he walk away down the country laneway that lead to the highway, keeping close for safety in the shallow ditch's side, walking merry in the morn's strong sunshine, hearing with a dampened joy the singing of hidden birds in the shrubbery, birds that no longer came to his own garden, not since he had his grass so cruelly cut.

And so the old man Arsene was gone away from his habitation, and his house stood empty. Empty but for the one-eyed cat he had forgotten he had admitted, the cat he had unwittingly locked in. Cowering in the shadow of sitting room's table, her tongue yet a bit bleeding and dribbling blobs of blood, she heard all the calls made in the hall, and thereafter the sound of his shuffling footfall to the door that opened, and shut, and the click of the turning key in the lock, and the dying away of dwindling footfall as he walked away, leaving her behind alone, locked in. And she went berserk, stuck and stranded in this arid prison, and snarled and shrieked, and made dents in his rug, and knocked over his clocks, and ripped up his curtains, and scratched his towels, and hissed and pissed on his papers, and all but tore out her own golden eyeball in her lonely frenzy.

But then she remembered that she was far from alone, for she remembered the chorus of rodents who were there with her too, of whom there were many of that gang of mice she might hunt and catch, with whom she may play before murdering, upon whom she may feed. And so the crazy one-eyed cat set out to wage war on the little mice locked up with her in the private prison of the house of the old man Arsene. And so it was that blood was liberally spilled at all hours of the few days he was gone, splashings of blood spilt at midday and midnight and on the coming morrow's morn, a dozen little lives extinguished and snuffed, pools of their blood coagulating to harden as the dripping tallow and wax of a smoking candle similarly snuffed – and, deep in the heart of its boiler's bowels, the old house gave a shudder, for it had never foreseen, not even in its darkest dreams, that it might one day be the scene of such abominable slaughter.

CHAPTER SIX

From the beach, The Mad Monk passed as a shadow over many miles of dunes, the pampas blades bowing backwards to admit him through. And in the sky dark clouds began to rally – and in the wings of his nose came the scent of storm. So he abandoned the plains of dunes in favour of a seashore cave, a humble shelter for his noble head. And in this cave he resided for some short duration of days, as the rain came down to drench the land, and the wet of the weather to welcome him. And in that cave he built from some logs and branches a fire for himself, one that he lit from spark of some stones he scraped, and the warmth it lent, and light at night it gave, were pleasing to his senses. And for food he fed on some crabs that ambled naively into that cave, lured by firelight. He cooked their flesh in the flame, and ate heartily, relishing the crunch of their crabby shells under his iron canines. And for dessert he dined on an earthworm, seasoned with sea salt, made juicier through liberal sprinkling of the silvery slime of snail (it was his custom to collect such slime). And when he was not eating or sleeping or surveying the storm's progress, he would doodle on the walls of the cave, anointing his fingertips with pigments of his own produce, and making bold strokes on the flatter sections of stone. He drew dragons and demons, visions of the Otherworld and of Paradise, sometimes even attempting the beloved face of Watt once known. And sometimes he took stabs at sketching his own self, though through lack of a mirror, the results were mediocre. Still and all, he found it a pleasant pastime, and he reckoned he would improve, through dint of sheer persistence.

And one day there came into the cave a darting Hare, whom The Mad Monk caught easily, and would have killed and cooked and eaten, had not the Hare, who possessed great powers of persuasion, made a moving appeal for his life to be spared. He was young, and his whole life lay before him. What is more, he knew The Mad Monk of old, so he claimed, for when a baby he remembered having been introduced to that same 'worthy gentleman' by his father, one of the pillars of the haring community, who had often dealt with fairies and druids and shamans and suchlike singular folk, of whom The Mad Monk was one of the more colourful. His father had hailed The Mad Monk a hero such as might redeem the world from the ruin with which it flirted, and he made it plain to his impressionable son that such was the sort of chap he would have him try in his own little life live up to, and strive to emulate, for all he never could nor would. And as long as he lived the young Hare would never forget the words of his father apropos that paragon of all earthly creatures, that glory of the world and god in man.

So thus did the loquacious Hare plead his case and charm The Mad Monk through flattery and flowery words and cloying compliments, and though outwardly The Mad Monk affected to disdain the praise, within he was secretly delighted. And when the pageant of praise was winding down, The Mad Monk bade the Hare be quiet, and to run along like a good fellow and leave him alone – 'for my appetite that once yearned your flesh is dissipated and quenched, so well wrought your roguish ruse of waffle'.

But the Hare, getting cocky, would not leave. He had come to the cave with a specific purpose, to seek advice from a man known far and wide to be wise.

'Hang on now, my hopping hare of bandy bow legs! Leaving aside whether or not I do be wise, how is that you came to know that advice such as you seek would be readily found from one such as me in this particular godforsaken cave of all caves on the coast?'

The Hare smiled, knowing something he didn't, and elaborated. The Mad Monk's coming was no secret among the learned. For months prior to his landing, the advent of his return had been much spoken of. It all began when a ghost was seen wandering the hills, caressing the goats, murmuring sweet nothings in their ears and babbling unto them prophetic gobbledygook to make their hairs stand on end. This ghost took the shape of a bald old man with a very long beard and glowing eyes, who spoke in lofty language, foretelling his brother's impending re-arrival to redeem the wretched.

The Mad Monk started at the employment of the word 'brother' with reference to this prophet – and felt a chill to his heart. For he recognized in the description the person of his own dead brother Elijah, who knew all, and of what he knew told only a little, and that little whenever and to whomsoever few he chose. And he felt quiet horror then.

The Hare continued. The appearance of this spectral soothsayer was surely a portent, and the goats had not been slow to spread what he said. They told other goats, goats overheard by donkeys, who told other donkeys, who told the asses, who told the horses, who told the cattle, who told the pigs, who told the sheep, who told the dogs, who told the cats, who told the rats, who told the mice, who told the geese, who told the chickens, who told the ducks, who told the swans, who told the herons, who told the cormorants, who told the otters, who told the jackdaws, who told the …

'Enough,' said The Mad Monk with some firmness. And then he felt a great weariness that gave way to doubt, and to the threshold of terror. For the weight of expectancy was doomed to dog him now, in a way it would not have done had his coming to the country been made in secret. But contrary to his wishes, the multitude both high and low had long known, and thanks to the gossiping of his brother's ghost, the numbers of those in the know had day by day the greater grown. And they expected much of him, more than any mere mortal man, more than even his own immortal self, the very god in man, could ever live up to. And now his strong shoulders began sadly to sag, under strain from all the daunting weight of promise they sweating bore.

Sitting there brooding darkly, scratching his beard, digesting all he heard with a liberal dose of doubt, The Mad Monk forgot about the cocky Hare seated there before him on the floor of the cave, by light of the flickering fire, eagerly eyeing him, awaiting the moment when the old man would ask of him at last the precise advice his youthful ignorance had sought. And then The Mad Monk shook himself, remembering of a sudden something the youth had said, with regard to the reason for his coming to the cave.

'Sorry about that, lad,' he said more amiably, 'me mind's a muddle, I'm afraid. Thanks for the telling. But I seem to recall that you had need of advice to ask me? I beg you, pray, spit it out, and we'll see what needs or can be done, if anything at all.'

The Hare grew shyer, a faint blush stealing to his furry cheeks.

'Dear Sir,' he said, hopping gingerly in his shyness from one hare's foot to the other, 'It is long past the last March's mating season. My fellows and brethren males, as is common and can only be expected, went mad with mating, impregnating females all over the shop with proper impunity. And being as I was at the time newly come of age, it was my expected duty to do ditto. And I tried. But somehow, for whatever why, I could not bring myself so to do as they did. My heart was not in it. I failed in my function.'

'You are impotent, I take it?' said The Mad Monk dryly, stifling a yawn, with a sneer to his voice, already feeling a bit bored.

The Hare blushed redder and blanched.

'Oh no, no, not at all – or at least, not always – only sometimes – intermittently impotent it is I am, you might well say. But I – .'

'I see,' The Mad Monk cut across him, doing his best to be indulgent, 'Well now, Lordy knows this is a vexing matter, but not so new that I have not met it scores of times before. Your affliction is as old as the hills, as old as tyrant time, that traitor time in many men the primary cause. Cannot say I have ever known it personally, this sapping of the vital spirits, no, not I, who was always from birth a virile bounder enviably laden with a lucky loot of the bindu, but I've always done my best to help the poor bastards who are less lucky. A quiver of aphrodisiac arrows it was once my pleasure to keep, which arrows I administered with glee to the wretches, that they may know again the joy of fecundity. Is that why you have come? Because I must have you know, those arrows are stowed away in my desert hideaway in care of the Puck, who will be coming later, who may or may not bring them. I make no promises. I give thee no false hopes. In the meantime, I can cook up a potion of potency that may alleviate thy malady, if only temporarily, until the cure more lasting may come. Or not. Nothing is certain. Will that do? Is that all?'

Throughout this disinterested expostulation, the Hare wrung his paws and ground teeth in dismay, kicking himself for having gotten the emphasis and the wording wrong.

'No, Sir, that is not all,' he said finally, raising his nervous head to face down the godly yellow eyes of eagle, set in the fine face crackled by light of fire's flame, 'My concerns go beyond the mechanical squirt of seed. For I, uncommonly among my kind, have higher aims in mind, not so easily brought off, when you are an animal as I am.'

'Higher aims,' The Mad Monk drawled, tasting the sounds, 'That sounds funny. Can't say I've met many hares as yourself who ever bother aim higher, who care do more than their allotment of life permits, and their cast of mind allows, they who do no more than feed, and fuck, and try not to get killed. You begin to intrigue me, boy. In what way, then, is it that you aim higher and do so differ from your flat-headed peers?'

'It will sound ridiculous for me to say it,' the humble Hare said shyly, 'but say it I must. Unlike my contemporaries, I did not care to bound from bed to bed and from woman to woman, leaving in my leaky trail a wake of children. For you see, there's ever only been one for me. Bare but one. Only one especial lady for whom I ever had any attention or deep affection, any real care at all, ever since birth. It is more than physical – it is spiritual, if you'll allow me say so. Only for she would I squander my goods, do deeds of service and run errant errands. Only for she would I lend my life in sacrifice if the barrel of the hunter's cruel gun at her were pointed, if it meant I would die so long as she would remain and live and last. For her alone do I feel the noblest of sentiments, the greatest gift and the most galling curse, making of all my life a melancholic agony, and making me mad, mad, mad, madness that knows not the calendar's dictation nor the schedule of the seasons, madness beyond mere March, a lasting passion that never leaves me.'

His little voice broke, and he hesitated. And The Mad Monk felt a quickening excitement to hear the Hare so speak, whose eager eyes bulged as his fervour grew, tall the shadow he threw on the cave's craggy walls, dark shadow forged by the firelight that flickered (night by now had fallen thickly), as he spoke with feeling of his nameless passion, erect ears aquiver as they tautened and pricked – and, in the quiet of hesitation, the patter of rain and sound of storm filled the gap and howled, as The Mad Monk knelt forward closer to the Hare, to whom he now whispered hoarsely, his curiosity to satisfy:

'And what is the name of that feeling of which you speak?'

The Hare shivered; swallowed; then said:

'Love, Sir.'

And The Mad Monk sighed; and shut his eyes; and spoke slowly:

'Ah … yes. Love. Sweetest of dreams, our life's bitterest mystery, our foremost misery. I know the feeling well, old as I am, and have felt so frequently in my time its prick and sting, its brief and intermittent bliss that will so swiftly turn to rancour, that yet will come again to be a craving for sating, wringing our anguished hearts until we can take no more – though forever always we eternally do come back for more. Only ask the ages, and you shall see it is so. It is the oldest of ailments, the most delicious, the most destructive, affecting all manner of men from all walks of life high and low from top to toe. Still and all, for such as yourself, I mean a Hare, to speak of it so finely, is decidedly rare. Please elaborate, my boy – impart unto me the circumstances – the state – the condition of this love – the nature and character of this lady on whom you would shower it – and tell me how real – how true – how lasting this love – do but tell me all this, and ask my advice, and we shall see for sure how I might help, if help I can, as I hope I can.'

With quiet tears, the Hare expanded, and The Mad Monk with shut eyes nodded and sighed in sympathy, swaying from side to side as he listened to the Hare speak impassioned of his lady love, the one and only, a darling damsel with luscious legs and floppy ears, so sweet, so kind, so gently tender her nature, possessed of a pair of eyes, and a speaking voice, that were the most beautiful and divine he had ever been blessed to behold, or ever had the happiness to hear. She was as young as was he, lived not far nearby, and he had known her from their infancy, they were childhood friends who bonded as babies, who grew up together amid the tall grass of hill and dale and vale, among whose blades and thickets they tumbled and played their carefree childish games, knowing not a care in the world – until, slowly but surely, over the years there was begot in his aching heart a bubble of love for none but this fairest lady, love that grew and grew, giving him now, in the throes of his young manhood, nothing but the vilest spleen. And the core and crux of his angst was his deep uncertainty as to the pitch and degree of her feelings for him, his awful doubts as to whether what he felt were fully reciprocated.

And The Mad Monk sadly smiled to hear this, recognizing the seed of the oldest story – the potential unrequited that ever beguiled, ever destroyed.

The Hare, by his own admission, had not the requisite cockiness to make his move to stake his claim, to pluck his pick and take his choice and bewitching woman woo – so greatly in cowardice did he fear her rebuttal. And she had recently begun to disgust him by her seeming fickleness, having, during the month of last March when high on her first heat, gone about gadding with the other braver boys, hopping around and pulling hairs, earning a reputation as a ready ride. Already pregnant, she was expecting now a batch of babes – begat in delirious frenzy, their fathers gone away elsewhere, to fresher pastures for plowing, such as knew no love. And relations nowadays between himself and herself were strained – he wondered had she done it all just to make him jealous, to spur him on to claim her as she knew (she must know) he dearly wanted do – or whether indeed he were wasting his time and ought to swallow pride and strive to quash his doomed and futile impotent love – and wondering whether indeed she were only just another fickle hare-brained female fool, happily ignorant of any higher feeling such as that selfsame love he felt, that made him so miserable.

And then the Hare fell quiet and waited for the advice to be dispensed. But it did not come. Still The Mad Monk sat on silent with eyes closed, seeming to be sleeping – and the Hare wondered had he bored him overmuch. But he was mistaken to wonder thus. For The Mad Monk had heard all intently and interestedly, and now was in the midst of formulating a scheme, cogs and wheels grinding and clacking as he thought things through. For he was of the opinion that it was not mere advice the young Hare needed, verbal advice that could get lost, or be misunderstood, or ignored, or forgotten – rather, practical and active assistance, such as at which he excelled. For he was since time immemorial one of the most devoted servants of true love in all its forms, and the very best friend and encourager of young love in particular. For he liked this young Hare who had given him valuable information, and the picture painted of his passion's plight had touched the old man keenly, and he was determined do well by him. And in his strong heart warm sentiment stirred – and he decided that, once more again, as so oft before he'd been, it was meet that he, The Mad Monk, should be matchmaker one more time.

'Come, boy,' he said, opening his eyes, 'no more dallying. Let us make tracks. Take me to the place where this lady lives. By the mass, I must glimpse this girl with mine own eyes afore I do more. And then – then – I shall well make it worth thy while'.

And these words puzzled the Hare – yet also excited him – and kindled in his starving soul a smidgen hope. And so they got up to their feet, and stretched and sighed, and The Mad Monk fashioned a crude umbrella to shield them from the waning storm, its spokes of stick and its tattered canvas dried seaweed, and blew out in a breath the fire no longer needed, and bade fond farewell to his doodles and daubs on the craggy walls, and picked up the little lithe Hare not half so cocky, who fitted snugly in his large palm where he would not get so wet, and in thus such manner arrayed, did The Mad Monk and the Hare quit the cave and go out into the world, in search of the lady that the latter loved, the woman who, through machinations of the former, he might somehow still win.

CHAPTER SEVEN

From the seashore cave, they travelled through the wet night over dunes and dales that gave way to man made lanes lined by rickety walls of stones, some of which The Mad Monk knocked over for the lark, having no respect of boundary lines, taking a whack with a plunge of his makeshift umbrella to make the stones come tumbling down, which damage was later supposed by the locals to have been wrought by the culprit gale, that howled through the chinks and down the byways. Skipping the lanes, they bounded over fields of pasture dotted like grids all over the land, saluting the sheep huddling together in their tight flock, shivering in the dwindling drizzle, stopping awhile to converse with a company of cattle, to ask for directions to where they were going (for the Hare, giddy at the prospect of his impotent love at last requited, had quite forgotten the way).

And one particular Cow, a handsome heifer with a dung brown hide that looked lovely in the grey light of impending dawn, proved especially knowledgeable of the terrain's topography, though she lacked the requisite eloquence ('... is over there where you is going ... like, not that there, but the other there, there is where is where ...') to express coherently in words the direction they might best take. So The Mad Monk said:

'Madam, allow me to interject if I may. Since you cannot tell so well, perhaps you can show better. To which end, might you be good enough to take us there? And furthermore, would you be good enough – Lordy knows we are weary travellers full shagged with our strain – to let us ride you?'

And the Cow was very agreeable to be ridden by two such gallants as The Mad Monk and the lovesick Hare. So The Mad Monk, with the Hare on his shoulder, gave a leer, and hopped atop her back and mounted her, and the Cow, sagging a little under the weight of the ogre for all that she was plump, began to waddle along majestically, away from the little field where she spent her days in grazing, passing by her sole calf who drank from their water trough, the little calf who lifted up his goggling baby's long-lashed eyes to gawk upon his mother as she left him behind alone, his mother being rode by a rare specimen of extravagant manhood, a bigger bull than ever whoever his father was.

'Don't worry, son!' The Mad Monk yelled at the doleful calf, 'I'll look after her! Shan't be too long before ye get a chance to suckle again that glorious udder you love!'

And the Cow, a respectable lady, blushed brown to hear such coarse gallantry and boor's bonhomie, but refrained from comment, lumbering on.

This queer trio, of riders and ridden, left the field by means of a gate that the farmer, a son of Peadar Lamb, had just opened, and neglected to shut, having gone off to a wetted ditch to take a dump in the soft morning light. Thus defecating, squatting low to the ground and riffling through yesterday's paper, close to nature and near to his roots, he was too preoccupied to notice his favourite Cow depart from her habitation, and sidle away down the lane, lined by nettles and blackberries, some of which were picked and eaten by The Mad Monk astride her, his appetite insatiable, some of which blackberries he shared with the melancholy Hare on his shoulder, to alleviate his pining.

Having eaten, The Mad Monk made kindly conversation with the Cow whom he rode, asking her about her son, who, it transpired, had been born a fortnight ago. The Mad Monk was fond of children, and plied her with questions about the boy's upbringing not long in the offing, asking her how varied was his diet, how crystalline was the water in the trough that he drunk, what were his interests, what were his hobbies, to all of which such questions she responded warmly, the theme rousing her mother's pride to heights of eloquence of which she had never before thought herself capable.

Then The Mad Monk, prying deeper, made bold to ask about the boy's father, a matter about which she was cagey until with skill he drew it out of her, as it slowly emerged that there was doubt as to the sire's identity. Doubt, for the Cow could not pinpoint with any precision when the boy had been begat, nor for sure could she identify with whom she coupled and by whom she was ploughed, when the act of begetting took place. The most likely candidate among the local brood of bulls was a doddery and wilting old fogey, to whom the chiseller bore a superficial resemblance. But the Cow was unconvinced, for there was something fishy in the air, as she outlined:

'... you see, Sah, it will strange seem to say maybe, but you know better than me lots not known nor can be. See, I remember rape. Only dream could be, true, just is not sure. It is night, dark very deep, I is alone by myself in my field, like. And this bull then come to me. But he no bull like any bull I ever seen, Sah, not this bull I seen then. Or I have, I mean, such a bull like him seen, but never such a bull as was moving, like, like as was living, like me, or you, or him on your shoulder. What I mean is he was as is a dead bull, Sah, I seen lots of dead bulls lying on the ground, but this bull, no, he seemed alive, like, but looked dead. But how? Has no flesh, like, no fat nor nothing – this bull's all bones, Sah. So how's he do what he do then? Like one of them bulls of bone those peoples don't even like to eat, him's got no meat, so how does he do it, he took me then, got up on me, felt like, maybe was only what you call bad dreaming, maybe only, nightmare like, that I was raped by this bull of bones like dead bull's ghost, I dunno ...'

The Mad Monk needed no more to hear. 'He's getting round quite a bit,' he muttered, 'throwing his skeletal weight all over the shop.' And he thought with a pang of poor Peadar who had cut off his leg, whose remaining days could not be many.

Turning aside from the troubling question of paternity, the business of birthing was a torment, and The Mad Monk tutting sighed in sympathy to hear the Cow expand upon her period of pregnancy and labour, bemoaning her woman's plight and pain, describing graphically how she had swelled with the seed planted by whomsoever, and the fatal day her waters broke with the flooding tide, and the strain and suffering, the pushing and heaving, the gore and blood of birth, that galled and raked the fires of her anguish, until her son popped finally free. And the Hare, listening intently on The Mad Monk's shoulder, marvelled to hear of all that was new to him, a naïf unschooled in the world's ways, a novice who never before now gave pause to ponder on the woes of womanhood and the fatigue of the feminine of which he was blissfully ignorant, his eyes widening to discover the laws that moved the world, how every one that walked was begat through throes of the eternal maternal agony, and he was moved to new sympathy for his lady love, for all that she was fickle, who lay now pregnant and heavy with babes begat by brutes, the birthing of whom might rent and crush her, poor thing!

And The Mad Monk made further seedy inquiries: 'Is your boy a good boy? Does he like his mama's milk? Does he bite too hard as he sucks her treats of teats?'

The Cow blushed again, and for answer made only a noncommittal mumble, which was not enough for The Mad Monk. Barking, he slapped her back to halt their progress by side of the winding lane. Thereupon, he got off her back, took the Hare from his shoulder, and set him on the dirt path, and bade him attend to every detail of what he would do, for this was part of the Hare's lesson in life, and love too, or love of a kind, to a degree. The Hare, puzzled, stood and saw. And the Cow, sensing trouble, trembled.

And then The Mad Monk got down on his hands and knees and crawled under, the tip of his sharp skull and tufts of his devil's hair tickling her belly gently, crawled beneath the Cow's underside to inspect her udder, large and undulant and fleshy pink, pertly jelly dangling, through her legs a shaft of sunlight illumining the sloping side, and The Mad Monk smiled to see the primal pumps to sing of mamas everywhere, and he took the thick teats in his hairy palms, and stroked them with his fingers, fingering and massaging until they came to be moist and began to leak their load, heavy with mother's kindling milk they swelling bore, and the Cow felt his horny fingers, and gave a start and made to move, but he hushed her with a whistle, and told her to be still, and when she was calmer and her full teats rousing to dripping, The Mad Monk bent forward his shaggy lion's head, and carefully wrapped his lips around her udder's teats, and began slowly to suckle, and the Cow heaved a sigh to feel her load begin to leave her draining, her woman's eyes widening to unveil the whites, the balls of her pupils in their bliss rolling round, as The Mad Monk softly gently suckled of her milk, sucked and drunk as her calf, on the leak of her load, and the Cow shut her eyes as she was drained, and her heavy head dipped and swayed, and up above the sun shone down on the suckling scene, a calf on his knees by his mama's undulant udder, as The Mad Monk sucked up his milky drink in the morning, as the mother Cow mooed and lowed and moaned in her pleasure.

The Hare, standing to the side, beheld the preceding, stupefied.

And when The Mad Monk had swallowed his swill and fill of morning's milk, he detached his stuck lips from her bounteous bovine teats, and sat back down on the dirt with a sigh, giving a parting stroke of affection to her udder, a light pat of his careless palm. And the ravished Cow turned around her huge head to look upon him who had sucked her, and saw him on the ground by her side, squatting on his haunches in his mucky robe, licking clean his wet lips, a moustache of her milk in a ring around his mouth, sprinkling droplets nestling in the shining thickets of his beard. And his yellow eyes met her ebony orbs, and he winked like the rogue he was, and gave her a smile to show off his shark's teeth (that had not bit at her teats), and she shyly responded in kind.

And thus did god and cow commune, and come to an understanding

The Hare stood there aghast, very small and young, looking on appalled, shivering faintly in his fear though the day was warm, having a mind to flee and hop away to safety far from the strange sights to which he was witless witness. But The Mad Monk turned, and he was caught again in the glowing jaundiced gaze that held him down.

And the old man said, very quietly: 'That's how you do it, me boy.'

Thereupon, he picked back up the paralyzed Hare and cradled him warmly, sat again on the mount's back, and then their journey resumed, the delighted Cow's wet nose glistening as nostrils sucked up the damp sunny air, mooing gently in a dulcet drone.

So then did they come to their destination, a Connemara golf course, home to a thriving haring community, who nestled in roomy burrows dug in the lees of the dipping hillocks, who scampered in gay abandon under the leafy bowers, planted to give golfing men some eye candy to ogle, hares daily hit at by prodigal golfballs, that they stole and bore underground, setting them up on earthen altars to worship as pockmarked gods. The Mad Monk and his companions made entry through the carpark, where heaving automobiles were stacked in sardine rows, out of one of which was getting:

I— C— C— and Isolde Lovelace, distinguished academics in the capital's college, up for a mid-term round of golf, unloading their clubs from the boot of their swish Lexus. And I— C— C— breathed the air, and thought about Sterne.

The Mad Monk and company avoided these worthies, hopping over the picket grounds onto the course where they ambled, but broke into a run when a dry official spotted them, hailing them with a cry to get out, at which they narrowly dodged away into thicker undergrowth. Once safe, The Mad Monk stationed his adoring Cow under a tree by a pond, told her tenderly that he would not be long, and then set off with his Hare in his hand to seek and find the love interest long sought. They found her bathing her feet on the other side of the little pond. She was fat for sure, with her brown belly bulging with the babies she was carrying, their birthing soon impending. Her girth was being mocked by a cluster of cheeky ducks who swum by her feet, quacking in derisive chorus. In her eyes was a vacant look, made dopily stupid through a surfeit of vigorous and violent intercourse, and The Mad Monk, seeing her for the first time, thought her nothing very much to write home about.

'That's your lady love? Bejaysus, son, you might have done better.'

The Hare heard him not, hopping from his hand to scurry over to salute her, all agog, heart fit to burst, feeling courage on the threshold of consummation. But when she turned her vacuous eyes upon him, he faltered impotently, and halted, and stood before her dumbly, grinning weakly, newly nervous, beset by the same shyness, seeing no love there in her empty stare, feeling again his former despair. He turned back appealingly to The Mad Monk, who had sat down on the pond's bank to bathe his crusty soles.

'You see how it is, Sir!' the Hare whined, 'Do I delude myself? Where in this wretch is the beatific being methought I saw? Is love such a delirium as this, an illusory bubble so brutally pricked? Wherefore does she seem to me now as so much nothing?'

The Mad Monk, for answer, kicked splashing water at the young fool.

I— C— C— and Isolde Lovelace arrived with clubs by the pond to take potshots, discussing what Toby and Trim would have done were they then them. While nearby the damp Hare dithered. So The Mad Monk wearily dispensed his cryptic advice:

'Do but tickle her in the proper place.'

But the Hare knew not what place. And The Mad Monk sighed, and so condescended to do the job on his behalf, stretching out a long finger across the pond's narrow radius to tickle the pregnant lady in the proper place. And to be thus tickled, in such a place, in such a way, she snapped of a sudden from her stupor, gasping and panting, hot for it anew, and fell then upon the nearest male by her side, upon the addled Hare who loved her best, and threw out her chest and straddled him, her flopping weight upon him, the babies jostling around her insides, as The Mad Monk tenderly withdrew his finger and sat across to behold. And the Hare barely knew what hit him as he was mounted, panting for dear breath as her belly crushed him, and she rolled and scratched and pawed him, unquenchable appetite awoken by The Mad Monk's deft tickling.

And then the lady hare fell from straddling, landing heavily in the pond, kicking the air and howling, thrashing in the wet, startling the retreating ducks, her labour begun.

And The Mad Monk said, 'Get down there and help her deliver, boy.'

Gingerly, still shaking, the Hare slid from the grass into the pond water with a shudder, and stood over the quailing mass she was become, unsure of what to do, then bent to administer deliverance as best he could, paws on her belly exerting gentle pressure, vaguely sensing her need to push. Push she did, and heave also, as she howled, blood shedding to stain the clear water darkly, bubbling blood from her aperture. The Mad Monk sat sedately and watched, a mild smile brightening through his beard.

And the Hare grew more confident in his task, instinct kicking in to take over from his crippling intellect, made at last subordinate, finding the ropes as he went along, and she too soon ceased to shriek, coming to be calmer, beginning to feel safe in his hands as the pond water became warmer, bloodied by birthing, in the heat of the noonday sun. And, in good time, in short order, they came, a quartet of them, four babes of four fathers, and though none of them were his own, he treated each of them as if they were, as they came one by one slowly popping finally free, and he took the mewling mass of each as they came, a bloodied newborn bundle, and bathed them in the pond's warm waters, to wash off the blood in which they came encased, and set them floating on the pond, bobbing parcels of new life, having passed down the channel from one liquid element to another, to water warm as was the womb, and so they floated, mewling, the four of them. And soon they were all ejected, and the sated mother, emptied, could relax, and feed upon the afterbirth he thought to offer her, and so she sat, nipple-deep in pond water, chewing in content, languidly eyeing her bobbing babies, loving the lot of them, as any mother would. And her deliverer sat in the soup by her side, scarcely believing he ever had it in him to do as he had done, teeth chattering in his giddy elation of disbelief. Then she turned to look upon him at last, a long look upon him she cast, she who had known him all her life; he who had come back to help her at her most agonized ebb, more than ever had any of the brutes and bounders done, hunks of hares nearby in the neighbourhood, who rode her and ditched her thereafter, and would not stick around to see their seed flower. But here was he – the weedy one, yet the kindest one – and he would be her husband – for this was nothing if not a marriage. And he felt her gaze, and looked again upon her – and saw then, with a surging joy in his lovesick soul, that she finally at long last loved him as he did her. And The Mad Monk sighed to see the couple cuddling in the warm water, their bobbing batch of babes floating in a little ring around them, mewling softly.

I— C— C— dropped his clubs, and Isolde Lovelace mocked his waning virility, rolling her eyes as the hapless professor fumbled with the balls, gruffly mumbling.

The Mad Monk looked up from the happy hares in the pond to the squabbling couple with their clubs nearby, and his smile faded. And The Mad Monk stole away sheepish from their sight, with not a pause to say goodbye to the Hare he had helped (who in any case saw not his master leaving, the coupling with his love so enthralling), away from the pond he loped to shade of the tree, where the faithful Cow still stood, her eyes adoring that beheld him approach. He nuzzled her, planted a sloppy kiss on her wet nose, murmured nonsense in her dipping ear, from which he flicked a few fleas on her behalf, and then mounted her saddle, and rode away on her, out of the Connemara golf course back to the lanes that lead to her field, back home to her pining calf, her sole son, begat by a bony bull. And The Mad Monk lay with her that night, and felt a mild content.

So he did not stay to see the dread end met with by the loving hares.

I— C— C—, feeling tetchy, riled by Isolde Lovelace's background lament, took a furious swing at a golfball. The golfball flew, but not where he intended, not to the goal of the hole beyond the pond. It flew far from there where he was aiming, lopsided through crisp air it soared, and did not make it past the pond, where it fell down dropping on the head of a hare, and broke open a hole in her skull, and left a deadly dent.

I— C— C— did not see the damage he had done; heard only the low splash of a golfball, rolling from a skull with a plop to the pond where it sunk.

'Ah, fuck!' said I— C— C—.

'Language!' said Isolde Lovelace. 'What side of the bed did you get up from? Try again, we're not playing to win are we, and don't be so bloody babyish about it …'

So I— C— C— took up again his golfing stance, cursing, and swung his club and hit another ball, but his luck was no better; it did not pass the pond.

And that second misaimed golfball found a lodging stuck in the skull of the other Hare in the pond that was there, who had only just begun to comprehend the foul wrong Fate had done him, only just begun to admit that she was gone, scooping her by her shoulders to cradle her dead weight in his paws, admiring the cranium's crater the falling rock had dealt her, beholding streaming blood that bespoke not of the birthing of before, but rather of her dying now, gone away beyond his grasp never more the sun to see, lifeless and limp in his hands, her life leaked and her love lost for eternity to him now – all this he had scant time to take in, before he too was struck down blind in his turn by a bolt from the blue, felled and killed by a falling golfball that knocked him down dead.

'Bollocks!' shouted I— C— C— to see his second hit go awry.

'Not your day, is it, dear?' Isolde Lovelace purred. 'But you'd better go collect them, the keepers will complain, won't they, they'll charge us for any missing balls …'

'O let it all go to deuce anyway, let them charge!' I— C— C— barked, throwing down his clubs, and storming off in a huff away (this really wasn't his day).

Isolde Lovelace considered the wisdom of gingerly picking them out herself, eyeing the murk of the lukewarm pond into which she proposed to stick fingers, to grope amid grime to find balls, but quickly discarded this notion. For it would mean getting her fingers wet. A grisly chore beneath the dignity of a senior professor. And besides, she had heard all kinds of horror stories about silly golfers who came to bad ends in suchlike manners, like that fool with a cut on his finger, who stuck in his whole hand into such a filthy pond as this one, full of the piss of rats and sundry vile bile, the cut that got infected with some deadly disease, that thereafter killed him stone dead two weeks later. No, it was best to let the balls lie where they were. Let them be lost. And so with a sigh, and a roll of baleful eyes, Isolde Lovelace, academic, gathered up clubs, and sauntered away, following her angry buck back to the Lexus, their unhappy outing at an end.

So neither I— C— C— nor Isolde Lovelace went near the pond; so neither saw the two dead hares floating in the bloodied water, a couple as were they, floating lovers bonded by their swift extinction, entwined and entangled their fresh corpses that would shortly draw the flies, their ears flopping limply, both their heads bleeding freely from the craters in their skulls, broken by misfired falling balls, pockmarked instruments of death, that others of their kind may some day find, and worship as angry vengeful gods, a pair of hares floating dead in the warm waters where it was were they wed, and their batch of newly born babies bobbing on the pond in a little ring around their bodies, mewling quietly, four babes of four fathers, missing their mother.

CHAPTER EIGHT

Portrait of a Freshman After Five Weeks in Trinity:
An Abysmal Pseudo-Poetic Babbling Ramble by S.J.C.
(from *ICARUS*, vol. 58, no. 1, p. 30)

Hunched in Front Square he Sits and Stares and Mainly Glares.
His Gaze is Glassy, his Grin is Glazed,
Any Smirks or Smiles are Merely Sycophantic.
Youth has been Ravaged, Potential Ruined in its Prime,
All that Pleasing Promise has Gone a-Drowning in the Rhine.
His Face has Aged Five Decades in as Many Weeks,
His Hair Drifts from his Scalp in Dismal Dandruffy Clumps,
And his Hitherto So-Spotless Liver, Upon a Time Once
So Clean and Pristine, the Envy of the Nibelungen,
Has Since been Battered, Corrupted, Polluted and Soiled.
Oh Misery most Abject! Gloom most Complete!
However Shall our Weary Freshman Continue to Survive?
Though all but Poisoned by Hearty Helpings of the Demon Drink,
And with a Belly Starved and Empty on Account of Paltry Funds,
He Shall yet Struggle and Strive to Create 'Art' out of Life,
And out of 'Art' Try Make Sense of this Bitter Mystery, Life.

Shortly after his arrival in Trinity College Dublin, Simeon Jerome Collins, for the lark, and since the deadline was due, wrote the above emission in five minutes, and sent it off in an email to Boris Nigel Gillespie, that year's editor of the college's poetry periodical. Simeon expected nothing to come of it, predicting rejection, for he knew the poem to be rubbish, barely deserving the name, but reckoned it better to try, than never at all to try.

But he was mistaken in several particulars. For he had overestimated the general calibre of the pieces submitted and of those that were printed, and moreover, did not take into account the fact, unbeknownst to him, that Boris Nigel Gillespie was a fool. For such he was, one who no more knew a good poem than he did a wart on the phallus of an amply endowed rhinoceros, one who got the prime post on account of bribery, a position he craved solely for the little bit of power and swing it would lend him. He took one look at the piece in his inbox, and thought it quite fine, a 'hilariously accurate' account of what it was to be a student getting soused, beguiled by the profusion of capital letters, and further moved to admiration by the author's enigmatic signature, three telling initials (what did they stand for? Superstar Jesus Christ? Strawberry Jam Conserve?), the letters, separated by dots, arranged in a row, endowing the whole with an added layer of mystery and intrigue. And so thus was the dolt taken in by the cheap trickery, and promptly wrote back to the writer, requesting a brief biographical note, for to be included on the magazine's final page, to which request the cynical author (marvelling at the man's denseness, yet greedily willing to play along with the inane charade), obliged as follows:

> S.J.C. is Junior Freshman studying English/History of Art and Architecture. He is a 'lover of the moon' and strives to attain a 'shabby wasted grandeur'.

And Boris Nigel Gillespie was duly delighted with this succinct summation, whose sarcasm he failed to spy, and quickly replied with a smarmy invitation to the magazine launch, to take place in the GMB, at which there would be a reception, with lashings of free wine and cheese and booze, on a forthcoming Friday night at the autumnal tail end of darkest November. And the author wrote back that he would gladly attend.

Simeon could not credit his luck, nor the editor's imbecility, but it was not long before vulgar thoughts of glory, founded on next to nothing, began to enter his small head. And in the weeks leading up to the launch, almost without noticing, he began to act the part of writer, a part founded on the garb he wore, which he ensured would be shabby yet imbued with lacklustre grandeur, cultivating holes in the flapping soles of his shoes, always wearing the same ragged black coat, which, through constant daily weathering, exposed to the starching sun and the wetting of the rain, came to acquire a greenish tinge, its elbows and shoulders besmirched by seeming rust.

And he acted aloof, keeping far from the company of his contemporaries, nurturing the air of a detached observer, speaking seldom but looking at life a lot, squatting day by day at the foot of the pearl whitely gleaming Campanile, from which scenic spot he could survey the sweeping whole of the college's capacious Front Square, eyeing the pigeons that passed him, and ogling the gulls who flew overhead, giving false directions to any tourist fool enough to ask him where was where, his dark shape appearing in the background of their photos, sitting watching intently all the comings and goings of the folk who trodded there in the square, looking determinedly mysterious with his brooding scowl, clutching his black glass flask of steaming green tea, from which he always sipped, tea leaves especially imported all the way from China by a family friend, tea to feed the boyhood addiction formed when his family had lived there, an appetite for such leaves fostered in Beijing's Ritan Park Teahouse, back in the halcyon afternoons after the slog of school, when he and father Eugene spent hours sitting in the shady outdoors on the rickety chairs, under which the squirrels nimbly scurried, surrounded by the chirp of crickets in the trees, hearing the blather of the teahouse proprietor as she played cards with her cronies, their banter that would break out into bicker as they hotly disputed their winnings, and the faraway hum of old men singing snippets from the pentatonic operas, mimicking the Monkey King's moan, and the silver light that fell in dappling slivers through boughs of the pines, to lighten the liquid contained in the little clay cups, from which the foreign father and son drank and drank, as they read their books in silence, slowly lifted into an Elysium of mild lightheadedness by the enchanting tea, into the only true paradise the two ever knew, one that was lost as soon as they left – and one which Simeon thought he had in part regained, as he squatted at the Campanile's foot, a grubby black speck on its whiteness, slurping up the same stuff, keeping secure the past in his flask, sip by sip transported back to vanished childhood's lost idyll.

After several weeks of suchlike posturing, the Friday night in November of the launch of *ICARUS* came round at last. And before quitting his abode on Lombardy Road and heading out for the evening, Simeon took the time to don a long and voluminous black coat, one bequeathed him by his school-friend Ruarc Stokes, who was a bulky boy, an enveloping garment that was far too big for the weedy slim Simeon, that trailed at his heels threatening to trip him, and drowned his arms, the sagging sleeves of which he was obliged roll up. And he also clapped on his bullet head a black hat, a Fedora with a wide brim, which he fancied gave him a rakish look, though since it was likewise a bit too big for his small head, it only made him look the more ridiculous. And in thus such crass array he left his home, and marched out into the pale evening, rounding the corner to Arnott Street, where he jocosely accosted his former classmate Belinda O'Brien as she entered her house, one that had a red door that looked down Lombard Street West, the same Belinda who was the girl next door for whom in St Pat's he had formed a fancy, with whom he kidded himself into thinking he was in love, a hopeless romantic who always had to be in love, yet whose bitter and cynical cast of narrow mind forever daunted and soured the fleeting purity of his feelings, ultimately rendering them false. And Belinda, on whom he conferred the nickname 'Isolde Millicent Gilmartin', never knew a thing about his supposed affection, for he kept it quiet and never confessed it, a willing sucker for the allure of the eternal unrequited, and so nor now did she greet him with any great warmth or fondness as he abruptly accosted her, stealing up on her from behind and slapping her shoulder to startle her, and babbling a minute's worth of nonsense at her, the kind of high-flown pseudo-poetic gnomic baloney he now felt the primary duty of his fledging writer's role, crap about cabbages, kings and onion rings, before sallying off again on his manically cheery way, leaving her behind bewildered.

Simeon Collins came to his college when it was deeply dark, and sidled in with the start of a swagger, under the looming Front Arch, passing the templar facades of the chapel and the Exam Hall, and the sunken Buttery, and so then came to the GMB. And he mounted the steps, and was met at the entrance by a wheedling fellow, with a sly face of freckled zit, and a crop of slimy carrot hair, grinning goofish in a monkey's evening dress, dispensing mechanical handshakes, eyes agog as he took in the new arrival, whose apparel simply sung of 'writer-bloke', and, suppressing a choke, Boris Nigel Gillespie at once knew the newcomer to be S.J.C., though he had never before met him.

'S.J.C., I presume?'

'I am he.'

'You're very welcome. This is, eh, quite an honour …'

'Oh please. I know the poem was a pile of balls.'

'Oh no, no, I just thought, y'know, it was very, uh, funny, yeah, and eh, very well written, and eh – may I take your coat?'

'You may.'

And S.J.C. was divested of his bloated cloak of coat by Gillespie, who draped it over a servile arm, quacking a compliment at the hat, which he thought quite dashing, and S.J.C. blustered, and was bade enter the reception room, which he did, where he made haste to pick up a glass of wine, and a copy of the mag, through which he riffled to page 30, to feel a spur of pride to see himself in print, though he was miffed to see that the clause 'The Envy of the Nibelungen' had been cropped, and he brashly pointed out this inexplicable omission to the goggling Gillespie, who dithering cringed.

'Ah, I mean, I just thought it was just a bit pretentious, don't you think, I thought it was just a bit, er, gratuitous, do you know what I mean?'

S.J.C. shrugged, and sipped his wine in silence. And Boris Nigel Gillespie had other minor quibbles – he felt that, lest the author wish to bring out a new deluxe edition of the poem at a later date, it might be significantly improved, wait 'til you hear, by replacing the 'Life' of the penultimate line with 'Strife', like this:

> He Shall yet Struggle and Strive to Create 'Art' out of STRIFE,
> And out of 'Art' Try Make Sense of this Bitter Mystery, Life.

'Would that not be a lot better?' said Boris Nigel Gillespie.

S.J.C. shrugged and sipped wine.

The blurred evening passed him by. In a shoddy ceremony, a prize was awarded for what was deemed the publication's 'best pome' – that went to one Konrad Merkel, his poem a garbage love poem with an eclectic – or electric (it was all about light bulbs) – modern twist. The boy in the black hat shuffled around sipping, not knowing anyone, unwilling to play the tack of brown-nosing, hovering at the fringes of the milling crowd of hobnobbing jabberers, loathing the ponces in their suits, hating his own fraudulence. He sat down sleepily on a soft leather couch, where he was joined by a Norwegian lady of advancing years, Elisabett Jokullsdt by name, who blabbered earnestly about next week's impending publication of her novel, a frothy fiction about 'love, romance and hate, spiced up by a little bit of sex', so the blurb had it, which card she pressed on him, inviting him to attend, which he lied he would, and she rounded off by flattering his vanity, telling him he had a writer's face, whatever that was, with deep thoughtful eyes, and a strident chin, and an aquiline nose – and the hat, of course, the hat simply said it all – before speeding out the door into the night. And S.J.C. shrugged, and sipped wine.

The evening dragged to a close. The revellers were slowly leaving in their hordes, slipping away one by one, until soon there were none left, save for S.J.C. sitting disillusioned on the couch, a quartet of giggling girls afar in the corner, and the host Boris Nigel Gillespie, flitting about picking up the empty glasses and bottles, feeling alone again, moved in his loneliness to join the solitary straggler slouched on the couch, who he liked to think he had befriended, for he had few friends if any, this Gillespie – for he had a regrettable habit of fucking people over. And so he chatted with S.J.C. about capital letters and pseudonyms and possible literary influences, and S.J.C. responded sullenly, and quickly got up to don again his lofty greatcoat, to take his gloomy leave.

But it was only then that the quartet of girls, merry maidens, four babes of four fathers and mothers, got up from their corner nook, and swanned over in a flighty flock, to ambush the strange boy in the black coat and black hat, who was pleasantly surprised at the sudden advances he was receiving from these none-too-negligible specimens of the fair sex, for he had never before ever thought himself a worthy object of feminine attention, believing himself to be an ugly chap and scrawny sort, far too weedy, none too virile. But the gambit of the girls was this – skimming through the mag, they had chanced upon one writer who did not sign his name in full, a reluctant celebrity shunning the limelight, yet this gimmick of initials, paradoxically, served only to arouse the more the curiosity of the chicks. S.J.C. – who was he? – by a subtle process of elimination they had narrowed down the suspects to only he who it could be – and, well – was he S.J.C.?

'Aye. I am he,' said S.J.C., beginning slowly to smile.

'Yaay! I told you it was him! I knew it was him!' trilled the one who looked Asian, and she was the tallest one, and she was the prettiest one too, and she was the most forward too, who grabbed him, and linked arms with the mystery man in the black hat and visage wan, and shuttled out into the night with him, the others following, giggling.

And Boris Nigel Gillespie, left behind alone in the empty reception room, cleared up the popped corks, and sniffled not a little, and stifled a sob.

As they ambled over cobbles, four maidens and a man, heading east to the Pavilion, for a final slug of something before it shut, the differing identities and characteristics of the ladies began to impress themselves on the dulled mind of S.J.C. There was the little Agatha Honeypenny who also liked green tea, and there was the alabaster beauty Lucia Seward with her first-aid kit, and there was the pretty religious nut Kyrie Elysium, who had an impish smile and who was mad as a brush.

But over and above them all, the one for whom he was most in thrall, was she that held his arm, unknowing that her charm would later do him harm, she the one that steered him, the Asian one, Dublin born of Chinese parents, which heritage recalled him to mind of his own past out there in the East, her oriental descent reminding him of the heaven-sent Teahouse, an Abode of Fancy no more now, but held somehow still in her eyes, in those of she of the glossy silky hair smoothly black as a cat's, her face of grace an oval and sun to shine, the cheekbones fine, the mouth that always seemed to smile, the eyes pools of dark pearls, eyes that twinkled in the lamplight as she laughed at his corny jokes and tired tropes, pointing up his fakery, noting his insincerity, too soon already she saw he wore a mask, yet he was never better than then, playing up the part to perfection, to make them all laugh came freely unbidden easy, the quotes tripped off his tongue, and they lapped it up, and he revelled glowing, his ego ballooning, and she above them all he strove to impress, for she was so warm, so encouraging, fine and flirty she was, he was charmed, he was smitten, and whatever was her name, he thought at last to ask, Saruko, Saruko, a Chinese beauty with a Japanese name, and they came to the Pavilion, a poor replacement for Ritan Park, not a patch nor match, and they sat them down, in the outdoors on wooden tables stained by spilt drinks, and they partook of suchlike drinks for the company, Bulmers for the babes, and a Guinness for the guy, and he jested that its colour scheme, of ebony and ivory, was not far off from the dark garments that he wore, everything he did was colour coordinated, and o, she did chortle, mimicking his mixed accent, was it Yorkshire, or was it Bushmills, or was it Connemara, or was it indeed Dublin, but it was neither, a forgery, his own invention, and she reached across the table, and took off from his head his hat, and put it on her own, begorrah, but it suited her, fairly did, but anything would, and he cringed, and made to get it back, but she quelled his attack, it was hers now, all hers, and her girlfriends giggled, and all drunk up their drinks, and soon all were done but for him, his sipping was slow, and they got them all up, and he followed, still sipping, stealing a Pavilion glass, and he traipsed after them with his Guinness, and if by now they thought he was a nuisance, they were too polite to say, and the Nassau Street exit was on their way, and it was here, his pint of porter finished, that S.J.C., drunken not a little, apelike flung his empty glass hard at a wall, and o, it did smash, and he crowed, and the ladies did wonder, but Saruko was taken, she thought it exciting, and they went to Grafton Street's McDonald's for a burger, and he followed, in a stark violation of a lifetime's principle, and he stole her chips and chuckled, and she simpered, and into ketchup dipped her finger, and under his poem on page 30 scrawled her name, an unseemly mucky blotch he would cherish and later smell, and by now they were drifting off on their separate ways, Agatha was running off to catch her bus, and Kyrie her taxi, and Lucia her Luas, and Saruko too the same would do, and to the Stephen's Green stop he followed her, a stagger to his weaving step, and still his hat was on her head, she would not give it back, and it looked to be she who would take it home with her, his small bullet head left bare, all on show his greasy hair, and he told her to be wary, it was a good hat, his one and only favourite, he felt so naked without it, do look after it I pray you, dear child, for such she was, and she said o yes, she would, she surely will, and she would tidy it for him, give it a polish to spruce it all up of the dust it seemed to gather, and he blanched at this plan, and told her no, it was far too much trouble for her to go to the bother of tidying it for him, no, no, she mustn't, but she said –

'O no … it's not at all too much trouble … not if you love someone …'

That was all; it was in jest; but it was enough; and it did for him.

And she hugged him, once and warmly, first of many she would bestow, for hugs were her stock in trade, and he hugged her in return in joy, patting her back, far too hard, she told him he was rough, and then she withdrew, and hopped on her Luas, and through the window waved, and then her Luas left.

And later on that night, as he staggered home drunkenly without his hat, S.J.C. looked up at the starry sky, and blew a kiss at the moon, and felt, deep down in his heart, a mild, but not altogether inconsiderable, elation.

For Simeon Jerome Collins had fallen in love.

And the complications and hazards that would ensue as a consequence of this love, would hound the lad for days to come, and years on end ahead.

CHAPTER NINE

For it was not long before that love was thwarted. She whom he loved he saw only at intervals, in crowded places, in the canteen, the lecture hall, or the cinema, invariably in the company of others, for her friends numbered many, and she spread herself thinly among that babbling throng. So for Simeon and Saruko were never to be those precious seclusions, alone in a rarefied place, without which true love may never flower nor burgeon. And he noted, too, with dismay, that her public treatment of him had altered quite, from that first enraptured night, a dream that came to fade; for never again with him was she to be flirty nor coy. Instead, she was nice, but brisk: she had earmarked him as a friend. For circumstance had decreed, to quash in the nip his futile desire, that she, the sublime Saruko, did not for him share those selfsame amorous feelings he had for her – for these she dispensed instead on Edwin Galbraith, who was top of their class.

Upon him, yes, him it was who Saruko loved, he with whom, in the impoverished idiom of the age, it was she 'went out' with. This concept, of 'going out' with someone, was a foreign one to Simeon, who was schooled in the outdated traditions of a bygone age, who took as his chivalric model the nutty Knight of La Mancha. He thought love involved nothing more than loving, and impassioned protestations of that love to the beloved, who might initially quail and swoon to hear such potty pleasantry, but thereafter come round and consent. But little use proved to be the quixotic designs of the Don for his Dulcie, no, not here, not now. For silly Simeon, ignorant, unlettered, uninformed, the friend of old men and a decrepit youthful elder, a boy in a bubble in the shape of Beijing, denied the norms of his peers, mired in dull Dublin wherein flew by their childhood years, never knew just what exactly was entailed by the everyday of then, what with the facile formula of flirtation, with all the little looks and giggles, the first touch of hand, perhaps the first sloppy 'score', the medley of texts mired with 'xxx's, and then to follow the ritual so hollow, approaching the lady in the library maybe, requesting in a hush a moment of her time, and then to withdraw to some place more private, upon the steely Ussher staircase, say, and there to produce the staple flower, plucked with a tremble from an Arts Block bush, at which she would blush, and only then thereupon to recite the line, so shopworn, so stale, so alien to romance such as Simeon knew:

'D'you wanna go out with me?'

At which Saruko, breathlessly, had said Yes she would o Yes. And why not?

Simeon was painfully slow to discover all this. It was not until several months had passed that he finally found out the couple to be an 'item', to be boyfriend and girlfriend, to be 'going out' – ah, that explained why with him she was so aloof, and why whereas with Edwin she was so tender. It was one day, having sat in the library and browsed his books for some hours that he glanced up from Chaucer, and saw Galbraith seated at a distance, gaunt and intense and alone. But not for long. For then she entered.

Herself, the one and only, up stairs of Ussher she had come, along floors of marble swayed her stately leisurely way, Saruko who was never in a fuss nor rush, for life was simply too short to squander scurrying, meandering always a sauntering slow way of coming to places she had of hers, along the way open ever to impulse, to tangents of whimsy, that was her genius, to trapdoors leading dark down to an elsewhere to where new treasures and pleasures undreamt of unbidden never before thought might be found or sought, maybe an ice cream, or the chance to catch up prattling with a pal, or to slurping suck a smoothie, or to pick and pluck from the bush a flower for he and for she, though winter being then at that time what if any flowers there were to find were dying or dead, so none about there were to find, none, and she had wanted to have one for him, language of flowers that of her soul and mind, mind in the head of the body housed of the goddess as she came upstairs and entered through Ussher doors swaying at a lilt, in a flash of purple Saruko made her stately entry as yet unheeded, she was an artist was Saruko of the black hair glossy silky long tumbling past neck's nape and blade of shoulder flowing fell, shoulder blades where once angelic Saruko bore yeasty wings, gliding in her jacket purple clad, which went wonderful well with her inner garment of cornflower yellow golden as rays of Apollo's sun, no less a sun her face as she smiled as she saw, and her flowing dress of flaming fire hydrant scarlet red and tights of electric azure blue, calling to mind the sky of other days gone by, and logic would have these colours clash, and jar to repulse, but no, they did not, no, not the colours that Saruko chose, for those, they melted rather the one into each the other, melding meshing in a mellow perfect overall, for making a harmonious whole of dissonant component parts was her great gift, natural, innate, she was born with it, the sublime Saruko who had a passion for fashion, and it was the first floor she made for and entered now, and there he was, as she entered she saw him, keen-eyed Saruko saw with a smile that made of her face a sun to shine, that face that shone with the sheen of sun a face as soft as pillow to lie and rest and couch a harried head and heart upon, what a hero, what a saint, Saruko, Saruko, Saruko la belle, for she is so pretty truth to tell, so say it once and say it well, so it was she saw Edwin, over at a corner table he was sitting with head in hands, oh no why, a joke surely only, a hug will fix the fellow, and she approached him now slow coming sauntering padding on subtle feet she came, up behind the back of Edwin she came, her Edwin who had not then just yet seen her in her coming, his head in hands as it was, and she was upon him now, and she made to stretch out arms to hug, hugs her stock in trade and means and manner of barter and tokens of the affection for all the bodies her large heart bore, but then, ah wait, his inner ear quivering he heard a sound, the tread of a subtle coming foot on floor at his behind, a foot, whose, a sound coming swift a perfumed presence at his back, something divine, something sublime, soft and luxuriant to love, and yes, he felt love, for what he knew not yet, head in hands, though he had an inkling, a fair inkling, of what and who it was, and lifted head from hands slow wondering who, and then lo, he knew who, knew it was she who, and love he felt then at that second as he knew, and then she was upon him, ravished with embraces all over him she fell to hugging him

Edwin, in her large heart's love she drowned him in her all embracing arms, Saruko hugged Edwin, and Edwin was full to flowing brimming over with delight and love he was, heart and soul swooning giddy drunk on her oxygen, so high was Edwin who hugged back in turn in love, long and black of silk her hair falling on his face, and Edwin Galbraith knew a bliss in that place, in the prime of life and love and so and so Saruko and Edwin hugged, hugged, hugging, and kissing, too …

'You're so lovely,' said Edwin Galbraith to the sublime Saruko.

'I really like you …' said the sublime Saruko to Edwin Galbraith.

And Simeon, repulsed, averted his eyes and fled from the library.

Initially, numbly, he accepted it. God's will be done. God knows he had been disappointed before, he was surely used to it. And he did his best to hide his hurt, adopting, masochistically, the opposite tack: for this rival Edwin he befriended instead. He often tagged along with them, to be in her company if only barely, so pathetic were the depths to which the wretch was willing to sink, a sentimental sex slave starved of his tyrant mistress love, cracking her cruel whip unheeding with cackle, lashing the spare prick at the wedding, the comic relief hiding his grief, the funny old uncle who was harmless, treasuring what smiles she granted him, laddishly rubbing chummy shoulders with Galbraith, a best buddy and brother who was friendly and complimentary. And he went so far as to let the courting couple crash at his house, over and over repeatedly putting them up, feeding them food, dining and drinking, pretending all was well. And once, a besotted addict of hideous pathos, he did what he could to persuade Saruko to move in with him, to flee the familial, strife which she gave him to know to be gruelling, to be a tenant among tenants, one he might admire but never dare touch, his home become a sterile love nest. Yet this threadbare pleasure quickly galled and grew bitter.

And even when they were not there, he was always to be reminded of his life's lack – for under his nose, his inbred hairy housemates, horny Gallagher and filthy Freaney, with whom he shared his father's house, would enact their loveplay in his presence, babbling their banal babytalk in Tellytubby accents that set his teeth on edge, and by moonlight the knifing noises of their lively nightlife haunted and soured his sleep (he once had the ill-luck to discover in a drawer a giant dildo they had had delivered – was it perhaps because Neanderthal Freaney could not himself deliver?). And his thoughts, as he tearfully tossed and turned, would wander again, irresistibly, excruciatingly, back to the sublime Saruko, and her union with the wordsmith. He took especial issue with the manner of their match. How was it, over and over he dolefully wondered, as he wandered around his dark house alone in the evening, picking up objects and putting them down, after submitting them to a phlegm-laden sniff (like his wheezy mother, he had no sinuses), how was it, wondered the lovesick insomniac, that she could automatically love Edwin only after the fatal question was posed, turning on by choice a flood of feeling like a tap, feelings that, being so prompted, must surely be false, since being so manufactured (o he had a lot to learn of life!), and, worse yet, why, o why, did she even then proceed, but the day after their match was made, still to tell him, a witless oaf adrift, just before her Luas left, that tidying his hat was not at all any trouble, for she loved him? Ah yes, love. The one word that drove the silly world, foundation of all our folly. Why would she use that hallowed word so loosely, so thoughtlessly lightly, uncaring of the consequence, of the harrowing effect it might have upon a sensitive soul such as he was? How could she? How dare she? He cursed her at times, bitterly dubbed her a stupid bitch and fickle vixen. And only from true love could such ugly spells of intermittent hate be begotten. And such thoughts made him sad. And whenever she saw him to seem sad, the corners of his mouth turned despondently down, his face bestrewn with sad lines of grieving marble cut, Saruko would say: 'You look so sad!' And this she would say with a smile that riled him, and drove another nail into his aching heart. And the lovesick lad grew glummer.

And in his lonely desolation of isolation, he would cry and tear his thinning hair, and storm the city streets by night, cutting a sorry sight, a melancholic self-pitying figure meandering among the puddles and pools, haggardly hunched with hands in pockets, the hackneyed rain teeming down in clichéd sheets of sorrow, frequenting quiet pubs where he drank alone and solitary, mutely staring into the cream of his pint, the froth from which left in a ring a Ronnie round his maudlin mouth, and the glasses were splitting as does do amoebas, as one became two, and two became four, clouding his vision and befogging his brain, but from the jug no joy could come. And those who saw him sitting there sipping, all alone on his stool in a slump, moping and pining for love that might have been, must have thought him the youngest alcoholic they had ever seen.

But then, after a lengthy period prostrate in a sulk, he decided it would be best to make his pain productive, by turning for solace to the joy of creation. From the deeps of his hurt, he would forge an object wholly new. For his subject, he would plumb the depths of his disappointment, milking the great and aching sad lack of his life, his melancholy the fulcrum of a masterpiece. He started a short story that became a book that got bigger and bigger the more ambition and ego swelled, engulfing all from sebaceous primal soup to bloody nuptial's nuts. There would be room for infinity in the grandiose cathedral he dimly foresaw. Higher and higher the scribbled cluster of pages piled. Sometimes he was lyrical, sometimes rhapsodic, and sometimes he wrote monologues, sometimes dialogues, sometimes arias, sometimes he cartooned, sometimes he was sketchy. Texts from the past he took for templates, an ogling dwarf squatting on the shoulder of giants, angling piteously to see farther than even they, embellishing them with everyday experiences closer to home, all to make it a mite more his own.

For he resolved to put into his gargantuan behemoth of a book everything that he knew, cramming the rapidly fattening tome with facts and statistics and anecdotes all wholly true, like buying sandwiches at Subway, or snoozing in geography class, or admiring the manic tap dance of a seagull on the college green, or dropping one's best blue biro into the creamy oval of the avocado bowl of the loo, the prelude to entail damply awaking from a wet and soggy dream, a tasteless opening to be aptly balanced by a long and smelly crap by way of coda, the dog's own bollocks, copying out his lecture notes and painstakingly reproducing business cards, and menus, and receipts, and graffiti on the walls of toilets, and soporific haikus scratched by students on their desktops, and recalled conversations, and a plethora of other irrelevant errata, mining his memories and beating his brains, nothing changed nor invented nor omitted, an epic diary in which all of his monotonous life was set down precisely as it happened, in baroquely copious and cumbersomely serpentine detail, even at the expense of interest (which fast flagged).

He worked laboriously, with a wide-eyed lunatic's intent, by candlelight, frantically composing by night, typing up in a soapy lather the dreary doings of his day, furiously pounding computer keys to drown the noises of Gallagher and Freaney copulating in the nearby back room, their obscene groans and sighs punctuating the angry rhythm of his clattering typing. The bloating book became his rod and staff, and soon was making him mad. Everyone he knew was in it, their names unchanged, their foibles and faults held up for scorn and ridicule, their virtues venerated, their quirks revered, yes, all, all of them would be given their space to shine and their page to prance, he would pull their strings and make them talk and walk, like a demented crackpot deity.

In part it would be the Great Trinity Novel, a chronicle of monotonous classes and of rowdy parties, a college romance and a gossipy column stuffed with students and their paramours, paramount among them Saruko, and Edwin, and Boris Nigel Gillespie, and the Players, and the ghost of Matt the Jap, with his own selfish self at the centre, and peopled in the cluttered gutters by comic relief professors, like I— C— C—, or Isolde Lovelace, or Stan Gloat, or maybe even Eve Parker; and in part it would be a reverential memorial of his vanished schooldays, a pageant of praise to St Pat's, run by serious Mr Bevis of the dour monobrow, seconded by saintly Corbett, and the barmy Jim Bateman the starry-ceiling-gazing babbling man; and he would plough his own family's history, a golden Collins chronicle, retelling the lark of the marriage of his mammy and daddy, seeking other examples in the dusty annals of lives lacking love, digging out enchanting antique nuggets like the yarn of poor Peadar Lamb who fatally fell for his bull, or the frustrated homosexual Aloysius O'Muadaigh, who took a shine to him on their single memorable encounter a decade ago, hugging and kissing him (a grainy photo set on his shelf would testify to this, to be reproduced in an appendix), or his Granny Nutmeg; and for the supporting cast he would turn to his father's friends and bar-room cronies, the layabout lushes, the oddballs and the gems, the denizens of the crumbling Thursday Club, of whose trivial travails in his youth he was the satirical chronicler, lovingly documenting types like Chairman Arsene O'Colla, or the leonine Harry Carson, or the crooning tenor Mr Graves, or the corpulent alcoholic Albert Potter who always stole the show – yes, all bar none would be enlisted, stuffed in like sardines to populate his mosaic, ballooning to burst and sagging at the seams, the greatest show on Earth, and one among the dullest, too; and, for the irony, he would call it – IKAROS (what else?).

And then one day he got a phone call from his father, his father's voice that crackled and popped over the shaky line, across an awful abyss to come to the old isle. His father began the call calmly, telling a few amusing tales about Athens, and of the tenor Graves with whom they had stayed a space, and dryly dispensing the usual domestic duties, remember to start my car to keep it from breaking, remember to keep the larder full with food, remember to study to pass exams, remember to keep in touch through texts, for we are wont to worry, and, finally, do remember on Monday to meet the old man Arsene O'Colla on Nassau Street to give over the house key, that he might get in and out of our abode as he would, since he's coming to stay tomorrow.

Simeon heard all, and nodded gnomically, saying yes, yes, yes. And then there came a loaded pause, and he heard his father's breathing quicken.

'... D'you ... d'you remember uncle Ulick's brother?'

'Aloysius? The weird gay one? How could I ever forget him.'

'The same. He's ... he's been murdered ...'

'... ? ...'

'... only just got the call. We, we won't be able to, to make it to the funeral ... but if you could represent us, for their sake, it'd be good of you ...'

'How was he ... how did ... by whom was he ... m-murdered?'

'Some monkish chap, one they thought was trusty, apparently ... there's a manhunt on ... he was dying anyway it seems ... talk of mercy killing, they say, but unwarranted, uncalled for ... a White Dog bit him or something ... just remember Arsene ...'

And then the line went dead as his choking father dropped the phone.

CHAPTER TEN

The Mad Monk's Doggerel Epic History contd.
(Part Two of Three)

… So there I lay in my father's orchard,
Trapped once more in tracts where I was nurtured,
In our seaside fortress of discontent.
I wept. For I knew now I was not meant
For such a life as this, which seemed so dead
Beside what I dreamed. But by the deathbed
Of my father and mother now I knelt,
For while I slept, a storm struck, which had dealt
The killing blows to both, unlucky pair.
Falling rafters cleft them two, and a flare
Of lightning had cracked up my brother's brow,
And ripe with new knowledge did it endow
His brains, for now he knew the past, present,
And future of mankind too, heaven sent
Gifts that swelled his ego and my envy,
As we slouched mid wreckage, my heart heavy.
With quaking breaths our poor parents expired,
And we buried them in the marsh, fresh mired.
From mounds of rubble we went on our way,
And I pined for my dreamy yesterday,
While my brother remained full of good cheer –
He was the elder by about a year.
He swore to me we'd build a hilltop farm,
And cultivate ingredients to charm

Our souls and senses. As he spoke, I swooned
With joy, for waking life was like a wound
In my chest that longed for quaint FaerieLand.
Upon some slope we built our house of sand,
With pebbles and mortar made in the quiet
Of the countryside, far from the riot
And din of the dismal towns. And we dug
A hole for a pond, filled up from the jug,
By whose moist lank banks our mushrooms could grow,
With poppies too, and aniseed in tow,
In our garden of wonders might we live
In bumbling peace, not a fuck could we give
For any of the old world's bleeding woes,
Lulled by the languor in our heads, which shows
Just how callow and silly we were once,
With not one mere sodden shred of conscience.
Soon I was intoxicated again,
And returned to the heart of my heaven,
Where things were not as they were, for my wife
Had given birth to a child, a fresh life
I took in my hands, a baby female
Who was unique in her kind, whose shrill wail
Was the first the world heard. Her new feature?
She's a Faerie-human-hybrid-creature.
The mechanics of it bamboozle me,
But I shan't linger. I wrapped the baby
In swaddling clothes, and carried her away,
Freak that she was, waking the next new day
In our hilltop haven. This my daughter
Was like a memento, a souvenir
From Elysium, proof that I had been
And gone, and done all I did in heaven.
There snug she was sat in my trembling palm,
Scarce ever was seen a baby so calm,
And I looked and found myself in her eyes,
Though I could not withstand her rattling cries,
Leaving thus the burden of her rearing
To my queer bachelor brother, nearing
The wan period of his virile prime.
He was content to babysit time
And again while I was drunk atrocious,

And under his rule she proved precocious,
Learning her algebra lessons and sums,
Her alphabet whilst teeth sprung from her gums,
Walking and talking and toddling around,
Entranced by this world of colour and sound,
Her vision filled by her upright uncle,
And her father wretch sprawled on a dunghill.
Elijah's devotion was never faked—
He gave her love, and loaves of bread he baked,
Over which crumbs she nibbled and giggled
As she shat on his lap. I was niggled
To see my place supplanted, and oft would
Abandon my home for the heath and brood
Upon the mess I had made. Sorrow then
I felt as I prowled in cold of the glen
Alone, and resolved to flee. So I left
Them alone for years. A father more deft
Than I was he – she would not miss me much.
The whole great Earth did I wander as such,
Playing all parts, sometimes a pirate king,
More often leader of a gambling ring,
Pretending I possessed the prophetic
Skill of my brother, fooling lunatic
Beggars into thinking that I was God,
A shabby divinity, clad slipshod.
Yet despite pretence, to my great gladness
I hit upon my true Divine Madness,
The fruit of the gifts Oberon bestowed,
With which I was now so godly endowed,
Flying, vanishing and miracles make,
If not for good, then for mere magic's sake,
And mid the hordes of the mad I was feted,
A wacky Socrates undefeated,
Or a barmy Buddha with gleaming eyes,
Goofy Messiah groping women's thighs.
My beard grew longer, my skull grew sharper,
And at my approach brute beasts would scarper.
I had found my role, my immortal mask,
And so thus did perform my fervid task,
Conjuring tricks and casting spells on fools,
All in accordance with my made-up rules,

And in the desert I sought disciples,
Rejecting many hugging their bibles,
Finding only a scant few who were true,
And Watt and the Wizard comprised those two.
Archibald Theodore, the better man,
Was portly and stately, no larger than
A dwarfish elf, but his moral stature
Was sublime, and his salient feature
Was power of eloquence, his winging
Words that so oft did dazzle my spinning
Brain that breathlessly heard his rhetoric,
Confounded by his voice euphoric.
But ah, the Wizard was the wayward one,
Having been denied milk when he was young,
The runt of the pack, full of ungainly
Jealousy, feeling me, in his zany
And misguided affection, to be like
The father he never had – stupid tyke!
I saw these pupils intermittently,
And they both bonded with difficulty –
When first they met, atop a white mountain,
The Wizard, heart sick with savage disdain,
Attempted to murder Watt by dropping
Him off the cliff – he became a jobbing
Hangman later, and tried again to do
The same – these foul deeds he would some day rue.
Watt's great ambition, while under my spell,
Was to find an idyll in which to dwell,
Vague Arcadia, an Eden on Earth,
Returning once more to womb of his birth,
To effect with grand project he gathered
A merry band of drunks, tarred and feathered
Like the unruly mob of the barroom,
From whence it was they came to dispel gloom.
Upon certain bare patches of rough soil
They laid their foundations, and worked their toil
With sweaty brows for the day's sultry course.
I saw them too seldom, to my remorse,
For I was always elsewhere dallying,
Wasting my wares on frowsy whores sporting
Whiskers and scarves, those nimble Viennese

Foxes who gave me the pissing disease
Which nearly killed me while in France, where cheese
Was the sole relief that gave me to wheeze,
Whiles I rotted in kitchens shelling peas,
Flirting with the waitress who was a tease,
Then I worked in a vineyard, on whose breeze
I dimly scented my childhood – oak trees
Waved in my head as I plucked grapes, while fleas
Sucked my hot blood as I sunk to my knees,
In mind and soul disturbed and ill at ease,
Missing youth's awnings, the hillocks and lees,
For remembrance of things past did displease
My heart beset by maudlin memories.
What of my brother and daughter? My wife?
All the things I had neglected in life,
Wastrel that I was, an undeserving
Mandarin of the old school, surviving
So long because of brute vitality,
Not pious living or morality.
But moving on – the Wizard murdered me.
I offered myself to him shamelessly.
The deed was done at my express request,
To his delight, and Watt's touching behest.
We were shaggy fugitives on the run
From the law, he and I, clad in homespun
Rags and tatters, since he was thought to be
A terrorist, revolutionary
Intent on his part having roused the ire
Of the villain in charge of the empire,
Our unworthy rival, gay-Lord Acrille,
Who, like the Wizard, was hungry to kill,
Being something of a camp psychopath.
Hid in some rank bathhouse we shirked his wrath,
Nude and wallowing in frothy water,
When a chicken came in, and Watt caught her.
This first love of his, a Silkie bantam,
Had haunted his dreams and robbed his rest. Damn!
I forgot to tell you how I did say
To him once that he ought to find a wife,
Which he did – a plot twist like pivot knife.
Mark well that thread in the tale – it's juicy.

But as we lay disrobed, shaking loosely
The wetted locks that clustered on our heads,
We heard afar a siren from the Feds,
At which we depart with clumsy soaked haste,
And fled fast, and thought we could not be traced,
But then the hideous hangman Wizard
Came and saw me – well cooked was my gizzard.
He resembled some gross obscene lizard,
His teeth tombstones, and my mind a blizzard.
Like lamb for slaughter I knelt on my knee,
Looked him in the eye, and begged for mercy,
But none would he give, and none I needed,
Bearing my breast, Watt's protests unheeded,
As my gaunt executioner raised high
His flashing axe, and struck, and struck, and I
Erupted with a screech and howl, and blood
Pumped from my chest in pulpy clumps, like mud
Gushing and streaming through my finger's grille,
Wet palm to wound as I stumbled downhill,
And choking died, and from flesh life did pass.
And the hunter stood over my carcase,
And spat, grinned and gloated, then stalked away,
And that was how I did so die that day.
Queer feeling, being dead, lest feeling still
Remain among one's mound of bones that trill
While the wind creeps and sneaks, rattling the ribs
Of your witless corpse. Dribbling babes with bibs
Are divine, compared to the sullen dead.
It was Watt who wiped my corpse as I bled,
And hoisting dragged my cadaver downtown
To the undertaker, asking with frown
For the cosiest coffin he could get.
He bore my body in the box – forget
Not how small he was – passed down to the beach,
Where he found a leaking boat in a breach,
And in company of his foster son
Sherman, sailed out to sea – my will be done!
Through storms and typhoons those little men sailed,
Pummelled by the sky, their plot nearly failed,
Until at last with luck they reached the strand
Of some paradise, a desert island,

Tropical sandy luxury, peopled
By ghostly hens, whose feet the sand dimpled,
Chickens of that same Silkie bantam sort,
To Watt's joy. And for years in that resort
Did he and Sherman happily abide
And tend to my tomb, warding off the tide
Of looming progress across the ocean,
Daily doing great acts of devotion
On behalf of my shade. I was, of course,
Dead and gone for all this – so much the worse …

END OF PART TWO

CHAPTER ELEVEN

The morning after, at the very break of the new day, The Mad Monk awoke, beside the Cow and her calf, with tears in his eyes. He had been crying in his sleep.

For he had been subject to distressing dreams over the course of the dark night, where horrific portents of things to come commingled with sadder memories. He had seen a one-eyed cat with a bleeding tongue; seen a catatonic old man sitting in his bed as his mind cracked; seen a weedy youth shovelling sewage; seen a man spooning dollops of mustard into the gaping mouth of a kneeling female; seen his own death repeated on a loop, the Wizard plunging over and over that axe into his master's chest, and the screams that tore the air; or seen again that same Wizard, his corpse mangled and his busted head a pulpy mess, having been squashed by the wheel of an unheeding automobile, having lay down in the middle of the road to die; seen a young man's tight foreskin swell and bloat to strangulate the dying dickhead; seen a naked fat man dancing with a carving knife; seen two dead hares floating in a pond's bloodied water; seen another pond, the one where his own daughter plunged down her unhappy head to suffocate and drown; and lastly of all, all the sadder for seeming so happy, seen the gang of old stagers, sat around the dinner table in the Arcadian Nook it was once their privilege to call home, eating and drinking and making merry, as the sun in glory shone down from on high.

And as he sat up from the grass from sleep, and roughly wiped his wet eyes, feeling the dampness of the morning dew, in the grey light of dawn that matched his mood, he could not help but think again of that Arcadian dinner table, and of all those who had sat to sup there, his old friends, all of whom, bar himself, were dead. So many deaths he had seen in his time, he thought sadly, so many beloved lives he had seen dropping off and quitting from the race, never more to be seen or spoken to: there was his prophetic brother Elijah; his daughter Minnie, a peaky abnormality, a Faerie-human-hybrid child he had never done justice; and Cousin Peter the prim one, her protector and sometime lover, who could be relied on to be practical; and Uncle James and Uncle John, Jim and Jack the jovial ones, the avuncular good fellows, never failing to merrily crack a joke – wherefore were their dear jests to be no more? – and Colonel Buckshot, the ancient gargoyle, monumental in taciturnity, a block of wooden stone that yet did pine and wither; and young Sherman the wise fool, deadpan but always eloquent, smarter than his years; and Watt too, Watt above all of whom he thought, Archibald Theodore, the dwarf with the look of a titan, a giant among mortal men, his daughter's husband, his son-in-law, his devoted pupil, his best friend, he too long gone – and how he missed him.

And as he stood up, taking care not to rupture the slumber of the Cow and her child by his side, and began to pace about the field, touching the stones of the wall around them, he remembered with a pang their salad desert days, when first they met and bonded, as if by accident, in the wastes of the shifting sands; how he had appeared out of the drought as if a mirage to comfort the thirsting little man, so splendid in his conical cap and garden gnome's get-up; how swiftly he had befriended him, the both united by their effusive grandiloquence; Watt the younger who acquiesced to play at being disciple to the elder, lapping behind at the towering master's heels, picking up titbits of his supposed knowledge, his secrets, his gifts, his powers, his 'Divine Madness' – that was the name he had coined and the doctrine he preached, the term he used to describe what it was that made him who he was, that peculiar, ungraspable sort of enlightenment he possessed, that power he strove to pass on to a select few others, like Watt and the Wizard – but deep down he knew it was no more adequate a phrase than was 'Magick' or 'Lunacy' or 'Sorcery' or 'Gifted' or 'Bullshit'. For it eluded words, whatever it was that made him not as others were, that unsightly power, somehow preposterous, that came and went as he grew and diminished, though never obliterated – and at times how he did so ardently yearn to be a simple human man, such as Watt was, who had not this oppressive weight of empowering greatness forcibly thrust upon reluctant shoulders, that could not shake off their yoke – then this further burden of immortality to contend with, a novelty initially, though now more oft a drudge, conferred upon him when he was dead, and unable to give the go-ahead – for it was a mixed state, the pleasure of his own permanence soured by the dismal spectacle of all the other things and persons about who were not, as easily felled as were the trees – why try get close to anyone, only to see them slip away again like all the other passing shades, to be thus resigned to trudge on again utterly alone, to seek new fruitless intimacies? Alone, for he was always somehow alone, for all he may have known such intimate friends and family that had gone – Puck and Pooka there were still, yet to join him – but they were not family, not as dead daughter Minnie had been, nor like his Faerie wife, frumpy now and losing her looks – for even Faeries could not last forever, being subject not so much to dying, as to fading away to an extent so considerable, that they wound up as good as nothing. And nor for the Puck and Pooka could he ever muster the love he had borne for Watt, not with them enjoy the rapport he had had with that other smaller greater man.

He would never find another friend as Watt had been. And he acknowledged now how he had learnt far more from Watt than ever Watt had from him; for Watt was a Hero built on a tidy and diminutive scale, modest and approachable, human, wholly human, a state such as The Mad Monk always secretly envied; Watt who married his daughter, Watt who he devilishly encouraged to sleep unknowingly with her mother, spurred by the cuckold's cheap thrill, a low deed he now condemned, that yet did not ruin their friendship; for noble Watt remained unerringly faithful to his wayward teacher, and never swerved from his side even after he had died, and built for his corpse a coffin, and sailed aloft the perilous seas in search of a desert isle such as would be for the cadaver a sanctuary – and now Watt himself was dead, his master had overseen the wake and read the eulogy, and borne the body back out into the desert where they met, where Watt was entombed in that same coffin his resurrected elder vacated – and human Watt would never rise again – for he was too much of a man to admit of such a grotesque awakening.

The Mad Monk leaned on the stony wall, and watched the sun begin to arise, far away in the distance over the country's dipping hills, red rays beginning to lighten the cascade of far-off fields, illumining the woolly sides of sleeping tiny sheep, flocks huddled on the hillsides, rays alighting on pinprick haystacks, drying up the dew, casting light on his mood of melancholy. Such sad moods did not assail him as often as they might, considering all the sorrow he had seen, but when they did, they went down deep, the grave antidote to his customary jubilation. The Mad Monk's face at such times was the saddest in the world, his stooping figure as if cut of grieving marble, every line on the tired visage one that sang of woe, no light seen to shine in the large and downcast eyes, as they stared down the red and rising sun. He was alone in this place, this smaller world that had not the room for one as he was, a ravaged vestige of a bygone ghostly time, an age of Watts and Wizards, a time that knew not the contemptible poking of tongues into cheeks, unafraid to dream of greater things, that had the courage to strive enact their beautiful fantasies, for whom to be irrational was no shameful sin, who valued valour, who esteemed friendship and folklore, who made no mockery of magic and did not sneer at superstition, forever donning their ridiculous robes to roam the fields and pine for love as they tended to their flocks, an Arcadian age, golden and holy, that even if it did not exist outside of the world of dreams, then damn it, why not dream? To dream of happiness, dream with longing to be free, unshackled and untrammelled by the tyranny wrought by the unstoppable turning of time, time that sought to empower the careless, to keep them busy, to look at clocks, to rip up a pastoral carpet to drown in smothering concrete, to do one's duty, to scurry all over the bruised and sickened earth like the busybody ants, forgetting one's roots, getting overwhelmed by the trivialities, losing touch with what was human and animal, with all that was true and good in life.

In his mounting anger, The Mad Monk ground his teeth, and kicked the stone wall, sending it toppling asunder – but the falling stones made no sound. For an instant he bowed his head, overcome; then looked back up.

That red sun was a rising one, not a sinking one – so too might his own star rise again. And if this wretched world had no room for him – begod, he would make his own room to clear his niche, if it meant bringing it all down in a thunderous riot of rubble and ruin to shock the skies, and make the universe quake, and the stars shiver, but from the throes of such destruction might spring again a better place, a world in which his ilk would be welcome. And let him begin here, on this island of Ireland, as good a place to begin as any, a land thought for so many ages to be the end of everything, last bastion and outcrop of earth before the endless shaft of cold and cruel sea, yes, this place, once thought an end, let it be now, through his endeavours, the beginnings of the better. Yes!

He laughed aloud, awaking the Cow and her calf.

'You is okay, Sah?' she mooed in concern.

'Never better, Madam!' he chirped, whipping around to bend down to nuzzle her voluptuous belly, fingering the udder's teats he had suckled, 'But I must hasten to be gone, to redeem the world, to make it a happier one for cows as thyself, Madam, supplier of such milk so marvellous, like as unto the wine or honey of heaven, finer than any e'er I greedily drunk – but I must be away, yes, and look you not so sad, for there is a Day of Reckoning in the offing, where all will come together as one – easier said than done, hence my need to make speed. So fare thee well, and rest assured, I do love you, my heart you have won, how jealous would my wife be were she ever to discover the terms of intimacy we share – and bye, bye, my boy, your mother's all yours, my best wishes to you both – and now – pip-pip, tooraloom-tooraloom and zoom!'

And with that, he kissed her one final time, and ruffled the calf's forelock, and gave to both a wink, and then shot away over the wall he had knocked, and bound along on the legs of a dervish, over a dozen succeeding fields, tripping by their occupants, stepping on the toes of rabbits, rousing the rage of bulls, exciting the wrath of pigs, arousing the ire of donkeys, and the bewilderment of a few men in tractors, until he had soon quit all the cultivated lines of domestication, and was lost amid slopes of hills, a dot among the crags of mountains – and thereupon was gone from their sight.

And the Cow, bemused, gave a puzzled snort; whereupon her spoilt calf made noises in appealing for his morn's customary suckling bout; and so she lay back down, with her wobbly udder in the air, to let her son do as he wilt.

CHAPTER TWELVE

Mr Harry Carson awoke hung-over, sprawled on his couch, prone form still clad in the garb of the previous day, a dapper greatcoat and scarf flecked by diamonds of arabesque design – this elegance marred by the liberal spillage of cider all over his crotch – which dampness was the cause of his groggy awakening. He had been clasping a can in his palm while he slept, remaining through the miracle of innate reflex unspilled only until now.

So thus did he spill his cider all over his groin as he snored; so thus did he awake to feel wet; and so then did he groan and curse; and, feeling the throbbing in his temples, and the overall ache that beset his blinding brain, resolved thereupon to never drink again – a resolution he made upon the advent of every succeeding hungover morning of his rakish life, always broken come the alcoholic allure of the eventide's temptation.

Sitting up and moaning, a bulging vein stabbing his forehead, coated in peals of sweat, feeling the stiffness of his creaking knees and back, he flung the can across the flat to the unlit fireplace, and hastily unbuttoned and tugged off the dampened trousers, divesting himself also of the sweeping coat that was likewise stained, resolving to dress the better for work – though retaining the scarf, of which he was too fond to ever take off.

He lived in a tiny flat in a block with the moniker of 'The Bantam Cock', a room without a view, pleasingly central, pissing distance round the corner from Christ Church, near at hand to all in town that mattered to him most, location its paramount virtue – though not such a great venue to bring girls back to, such as he did on and off, to appease the waning fire in his sagging vitals, the place being too dim and dark, lacking in romance and space for shagging – the Russian Ivana, his last, and most lasting, flame, having once complained that there was not even enough space to sling a whip.

And Harry smiled to think of Ivana as he rooted under the couch for a new pair of pants, that busty Slavic peach with a sultry gaze and taste for flagellation, a ready ride, a great bundle of fun and barrel of laughs – though it was stability she ultimately wanted, for which reason in the end she did ditch him, in favour of a moneyed man she married, who could offer her that that Harry could not – though he comforted his wounded ego by fancying that he was better in bed than was this current chump, spilling over with cash, but all dry down at the root of manhood where it mattered, and perhaps she knew it too, the lusty fox. With relish he remembered, as he pulled on clean pants, their last autumnal encounter, having a valedictory fag together outside some dingy dive, when she did offer him, apropos of nothing, her shapely backside, bending down low to let him look, at the same time suggesting, with not a flicker of emotion in her cold voice, that he give her a groping about the cheeks of that ample place, for sentimental value's sake – to which saucy offer he readily acquiesced. But he would not fool himself into thinking any more would come of it than that – their affair now belonged to the annals only.

Moving about the flat, humming a Mozart aria, slowly getting dressed, memories of last night's debauch came slowly back to him, such as might explain the state of his home, which was not normally so cluttered with cans as this, so littered with the debris of gentleman's apparel, the effects of drunken visitors, left behind them as they staggered away when the party came to a close. He recalled how he had fallen in with a gang of obstreperous drunken lawyers outside of Grogan's, with whom he had been quick to bond, the bunch united by their refined accents and silvery vowels, Southern Prods as he was, with whom he went on the customary pub crawl, accosting bystanders with slurred requests for loans, in return for which kindness they would receive an eruption of Noel Coward songs, bawling fit to wake the dead, winding up in a sleazy wine bar on the north side, where ladies had lain in his lap, low trash and sluttish sorts, the kind of rubbish whores on whom these dreary nowadays he was resigned to spending his savings, having no better outlet, after which he brought a select some, of lawyers and ladies, back here to his humble home, where jollifications presumably ensued – he could not remember what followed – until the cracking dawn – hence the state of the place as he shuffled about in search of a bit of breakfast, hence his blistering head. And he gave a groan again, upon opening his leaking fridge, to see that it was empty.

This was no life for a gentleman, he thought again for the thousandth time, his path of thinking, clouded by the hungover haze, beginning to trace again that self-lacerating route to which, the more he aged, he was lately heading down the more often. For he came from a noble line, that of the Carsons, a worthy breed of good Protestant stock, in bygone days a distinguished distilling family, in whose esteemed circles he was viewed by many a disgrace to the name. For much had been expected of him, given his high standing and education, all the finest and most impeccable credentials, and he had singly failed to deliver. For years he had lived on his inheritance, which had amounted to a quarter of a million or something, word of which affluence quickly earned him, among the coven of the drunken, the reputation of a good chap to beg for a lend, to touch for a loan never to be returned (as Albert Potter had most recently done, cadging a sum to the tune of a grand or more, a transaction strategically conducted when Harry was in his cups, wheedling and yodelling, playing up their mutual Protestant roots, a tack the cunning knave knew would appeal to the sentimental in Harry, money which the man never saw again). Harry had by now drunk up the bulk of that weighty inheritance, making do with an undemanding job minding the stall in Mr Baker's Bookshop in Clare Street – a job he may very soon lose – he and Mr Baker did not get on. His only other hope of income, his shares having gone down the tubes, was one Granny Marge, elderly, Zimmer-frame bound, living in England, in whose will he was named, along with sister Anita, as inheritor of her (reputedly) astronomical fortune. He did the bare minimum of his duties as a nephew to curry favour, sending along annually a card with a printed message like 'Wishing You Well', which he had only to sign 'Love, Henry'. Painless, but it was sufficient to keep him in the will, or so he hoped (though rumour had it that she liked Anita rather more than she did him). The old bird, unfortunately, was taking a very long time to die. Touch of arsenic mightn't hurt. And otherwise, he was the perennial lush and layabout, a legendary rake and waster, his mane and fangs falling out, stumbling from bar to bar, the good fellow, life of every party, winning over a countless many with his wit and charm, the barfly, the ligger who always knew when the next reception would be held, at which the red wine would come down spilling as manna from on high, cultivating actorly mannerisms and tricks of the voice in the telling of his treasure-trove of tales, displaying a haughty air of ruined grandeur, striding about town with leonine head held up high, with a swagger, a guise of affronted dignity, earning him time after time the tiresome accolade 'a larger-than-life character', the last of his kind.

But it was only that – a part, one he grew tired of playing the more he approached the end of his tether, a mask that fitted him the less well with each ensuing listless year, one whose hollowness became impressed on him the more forcibly, which he had grown to hate. And, for all that he may know everyone in Dublin, he remained a lonely man. All the lonelier since his best friend, Eugene Collins, the only one who never patronized him, who would listen calmly to his woes and pass no judgment, had now gone away on a long haul to Grecian soil, with whom he still kept up a daily correspondence via text messages, which skill Eugene had imparted to him just before leaving, a little light on another dead day – how he missed the man.

Growling as he poured water from the tap into a glass, and gulped it down quickly to sate the dryness of his parched mouth, the lips of which were still dark with wine, Harry did what he could to fight back the wave of self-pity that every morning crept up in a welling tide. He bent his shaggy head to the sink, doused crumbling lion's locks under the whistling tap, shook his wet mop to wake himself, and then shambled to his toilet, to take a quick piss before he went on his way to work, already late.

What he saw upon prising open the tiny toilet door filled him with horror – a recumbent balding middle-aged man, unconscious but muttering in sleep, nearly nude, with a hairy flabby belly and fatty thighs spread, reclining in the narrow bathtub, full to the brim to overflowing with clouded water. Harry was so shocked that it took him another few seconds to register the rest of the place – the tiles of the wall and floor begrimed with vomit, the toilet bowl brimming with soupy shite, loo-roll paper, soggy and mottled and stained, lying all around in dampened clumps, and stagnant pools of the yellowest urine everywhere. Outraged Harry Carson cried out in disgust.

And then he looked again at the sleeper in the tub, only now recognizing him as one of last night's gang of drunken lawyers. And he nearly recollected his name – Peter or Thomas or somesuch. And only then did he remember why he had befriended this wretched chap outside Grogan's in the first place, who claimed to have been with him throughout their salad schooldays and during Harry's one year in Trinity, so he said, though Harry had completely forgotten, though did not doubt, an honest man who thought everyone else also honest; and only then did he remember, with qualm, the advances this individual had made on him, in the pitch black of night after he had brought some lawyers and ladies back here to this outraged flat; amorous advances, with a lot of rubbing of knees, and stroking of shoulders, and attempted groping of groins, hoarsely whispering sweet nothings in Harry's appalled ear; and how that man had told Harry how much he loved him, how he had always loved him, always from afar, never requited or confessed, ever since they were beardless schoolboys, even then he had nursed a crush and been smitten, and been harbouring a secret all these subsequent years, never ceased to love even when life drew them apart, doomed by circumstance to keep his desire tight in the closet under strict lock and key – until now, when they were here, together alone, in their cups, he could contain himself no longer, he must, he just must touch him, oh Harry you've utterly no idea – oh my god Harry how I do so love you.

Harry had told him to fuck off.

And at this rejection, like any lacerated lover, the man broke down and wept, pleading and beseeching him to have mercy, he was being torn apart by this torment – but Harry, though drunken and weak of will, remained firm, having all his life never looked upon another man with longing, and nor now would he waver from his straight course – and the lovesick lawyer howled again, and rose from the couch, and screamed blue murder, resolving to deal with this in the Latin Lover's manner, uninhibited by his customary Protestant's reserve, giddy with love's lunacy; and threatened to kill Harry, who lay uncaring in a stupor on the sofa, and when this threat failed to arouse the fear for which he was hoping, resolved instead to lay waste to his host's water closet, and thereupon stormed off in there, and slammed the door shut, after which Harry passed out clutching his cider can, and knew no more – until only now, standing in the bathroom doorway, when the melodrama of the inane scene all came back in a harrowing rush, as he gazed upon the dead weight in the tub, and saw that he had made good his threat.

Harry crept in gingerly, trying to avoid the puddles of puke and piss, and with an effort shook awake the hung-over comatose lawyer – who, after the usual groans and incoherent mumbles as he ran through the rigmarole of coming into consciousness, upon being questioned, professed not to know a thing about anything, declared he had never set eyes on Harry in all his life before, knew nothing about heartbreak or a lifetime of unrequited love kept closeted, but now let off the leash, and seemed affronted, expressing outrage that such a suggestion should ever be made, and wondered what the hell he was doing supine in a bathtub in a nearly nude state, accused Harry of being a filthy pervert who had doctored his drink, and lured him back to submit him to unspeakable degradations, and furthermore called his baffled host a scoundrel and a twisted blackguard, and thereupon, with much clumsy splashing, hoisted himself out of the tub, and blundered out of the bathroom, spluttering further curses, dripping copious puddles in his unsteady veering wake as he went, and having found, after much blind groping, the door of the flat, lifted the latch to let himself out, and so he departed, noisily.

And stricken Harry, left behind alone in the violated toilet, buried his face in his hands, and quickly cried for the dismal state of his jakes, the pain in his head, the dissolution of his fortunes and the listlessness of his life, then shook himself, and rose again, with a swing of his scarf, to head off to do his duty, contemplating the swelling progress of but another hectic day.

CHAPTER THIRTEEN

One day long ago, back in the beginning of everything, the giant Ben Bulben, old and tired and weary of life, lay down reclining on the land, and fell fast asleep, softly snoring, capacious legs akimbo, hairy cheek couched on a palm, peacefully recumbent in his great full length. But soon his snores fell silent, and the deeper grew his sleep the longer he lay, the land beginning to claim him, to make him a piece of its own. And so he came to be as stone, stone that swallowed his tender flesh to make it the harder, cracking his skin of soil that came to be of earth, from whence sprouted flowers, upon which grew grass and stubs of trees, and wherein whose hollows and upon whose crags there were birds built prickly nests, upon whose swelling cascade of limbs sheep and goats came to wander over the ages. And so it was, over the millennia, over the fall of the dying years, that the man became a mountain.

And it was in the shadow of this mountain that The Mad Monk came roaming one fine day, bathed in a golden eventide's dwindling glow, came walking down a country lane, lined by hedges of the heather he loved, scent of laburnum in the dusky evening air. He had spent a short while in nearby Sligo town, stealing buns from a café, robbing cabbages from the grocer's, and plucking apples from the mayor's garden, which goods he stuffed into the mucky sack he carried, over a shoulder swung, a swag bag he nabbed from the railway's tracks where it had been left discarded, emptied of the coal it had carried, accosting bystanders on his way down the central street, to ask for directions to the graveyard planted by the giant's toes, for his memory of the route, over the many years since last he had been by, had grown hazy. Most of the townsfolk he accosted proved of little help, put off by his size and shape that scared them (though he did try to seem cuddly), misunderstanding the antique cast in which he couched his query. And disgusted by their ignorance, he grew grouchy, and would spit at them, or shove them aside with the malign disdain he kept for little men, storming away with his bulky sack on his back, raiding a tourist office to rustle through the brochures, growling and cursing, terrifying the staid matron behind the counter, squinting at him through befogged lenses.

'Zounds!' he bellowed, throwing down the useless glossies stuffed with trivia in a scatter, temper quickening as he turned to face her, 'Is it so very hard, Madam, for a man to find a map of this wretched hole? Would it cost you too much, my dear good woman, to tell me where I might find the cemetery of Drumcliff, wherein is buried this country's most eminent versifier? Could you take but a moment to spit out at me that morsel?'

The cowering lady trembled, and murmured quietly that his hostile tone did not please her, and that if he kept this up, she was well within her rights to call the guards.

'Oh, fiddlesticks and petty bollocks!' he roared, beside himself, 'call them then, you whore, and let them come in their petty droves of minions, with their drooping cudgels, their puny sirens shrieking and their triple chins flapping! What the hell has gone wrong with this benighted isle? What has become of your fabled quality of welcoming? Mark my words, you slut, I shall be penning a venomous missive to your governor, your head honcho on your Bord Fáilte – I know enough of your lingo to know that's a misnomer! Was ever a poor foreigner as myself, a stranger in a strange land, made to feel the less welcome? You bitch! Let's whip up a storm!'

Overcome by his fury, he briskly laid waste to the place, ripping bulbs from their sockets, his talons scratching dents in the wallpaper, tearing up all the glossy paraphernalia, pulling down the posters and stamping on the billboards, reserving his especial malice for the rack of postcards, their insipid little squares stuffed with sunny scenes, so false they roused his greatest wrath, shredding them into fourscore figments, some of which he gorged upon, chewing and gnashing and swallowing to prove his point, during which such wanton destruction the poor old lady made good her threat, picking up the phone to call upon the cops. But she had barely done with dialling before The Mad Monk, his fury spent, had done with laying waste, and quit the place, bidding her a curt good day, blowing her a token kiss as he left, as he stormed away in huffy indignation.

But there was at least one good man in Sligo town, as he found.

Aloysius O'Muadaigh was an ageing bachelor who lived alone in his mother's house, a crumbling wreck of a place that stood on the main street, its dropping rafters and dusty panes and air of shabbiness an ungainly blotch on the streetscape, a blot to be obliterated, so it seemed to the town planners, who for years waged fruitless war with Aloysius in a struggle to get him to leave so they might bulldoze the ruin in the name of progress. But the old man would not budge, milking the system's benefits to get himself by, a hunched advertisement for the power of the squatter's rights. He was his own man, and would not bow to the dip and sway of the system's pendulum. Why should he leave? His mother would not have wanted him to. He had lived with her there, in his childhood home of bygone days, even as an adult, keeping her company in her twilight years for two decades, in the murk of their cobwebbed abode, amid the pile of Aloysius's broken old toys that recalled a lost boyhood, the pair of them slowly going mad together, ranting and arguing all the dreary day long, Aloysius often moved to threaten his mad mother with murder, the old baggage croaking back with similar rasping sentiments, as he ladled into her champing toothless mouth spoonfuls of bland and quickly cooling porridge, her dinner he pretended to doctor with poison, while she struck his ribs with her cane, and spoke of the knife she would so soon stick into his skin – but, for all their threats, neither mother nor son ever killed the other in the end, for their submerged mutual love would never admit such barbarity; instead, they were united in losing their minds. At the height of his hysteria, Aloysius ceased to turn on the lights, never lifted a finger to slay the rats who began to thrive in the shadows, and soon would not even leave the house to forage for food, preferring to subsist on rotting cereal carefully rationed, hearing queer voices, refusing to allow any visitors – not even his own brother Ulick, who came in vain repeatedly knocking on the mottled door, while on the second floor above, Aloysius peeped fearfully through chinks in the curtain's shroud, no longer recognizing the man with whom he grew up, who had sucked of the same sagging dugs he had: he later confessed that he thought at the time that his good brother was a British spy, or one of the Black and Tans resurrected from the grave to come by and kneecap him.

Then there came the day his mother died, and he was left behind alone in the gloomy place with her corpse, stiffly sat in the same musty armchair where she had whiled away her dying days, her corpse whose skeletal hand her bereft son fondly stroked, a tear welling in his eye as he watched the progress of a spindly legged spider crawling over the squishy couch of her lifeless gaping eyeball, from which the light was left, her cadaver attracting a brood of flies and ants he had not the will to bat away, reasoning to himself that they came to do her devotion as he did, she to whom he murmured lovingly, ardently missing her already, wishing that he too were dead, sticking by her side even after she had died, a faithful loving child.

Though her demise was also a partial liberation for Aloysius, who had lived so long in her stifling shadow – for only now could he cast off the yoke of her squabbling oppression, coming by degrees to live again the semblance of a normal life, reunited with his brother and surviving family, for whom he cooked dinners, and to whose garden on weekdays he tended, taking long walks on the beach with Ulick, jokily reminiscing about the painful past as they quaffed wine in the kitchen, and discovering finally, in the course of self-analysis, a truth about his divided nature, long kept quiet in the dark of the closet – he was homosexual. Now in his sixties, this belated discovery was the cause of much of his subsequent turmoil, for he could never reconcile his lust for men and boys with his equally ardent Catholicism – Jesus surely never had in Sligo town a disciple more devoted than was Aloysius O'Muadaigh, a soldier of Christ from the cradle.

He was in love with all the machinery of the Church and its mysterious doctrines, his rosary beads hanging close by his breast, hung on every one of his walls an imposing crucifix, spending days pawing over his moth-eaten Bible with grubby nicotine-stained fingers, in thrall to the feel of rice paper and swooning to scripture, whose stirring phrases and pious cadences could bring a tear to his eye, refusing to listen to any music that was secular, collecting by the dozen cantatas on vinyl, playing them at top volume, to the ire of his neighbours, never daring to cast his fanatical gaze on any painting that did not depict a religious scene – and, at the same time, revelling in the contradiction, sating his sodomy's lust by night, making up for lost time, struggling to pack into the years that were left to him all the cock and bum fun he had not had when young, cruising about the town's moonlit suburbs and ghettos, enlisting pimply tinker boys for his purposes, tearfully chiding them for tempting him, as he went about the act of darkness with them, waking afterwards feeling a blistering guilt, scalding his soul in the unforgiving light of a shameful dawn, guilt that could only be appeased by a stint in the local confessional, mumbling the story of his sins into the earlobe of a dozing clergyman on the grille's other side, relishing in the details of his debauchery he retold, secure that mother would never again lift a finger to stop him – though sometimes he felt a chill in his heart, as he imagined her staring down at him from the heights of heaven, sometimes thinking he heard the fall of her feet at his back, as he tiptoed around the dark house alone in the evening, once awaking in the middle of the night, vision clouded by tangled vestments of the erotic dream that had excited his slumber, only to see her ghost standing looming at the end of his cold bed, a wizened wraith that glared him down, wagging an arthritic and reproving finger at her son who had gravely sinned, haunted by her vindictive shade.

And the memory of that ghost was on his mind today as he sat in the crypt of his sitting room, the curtains drawn, letting in none of the gay light swathing the street outside, nursing a cup of tea, brewed from one of the teabags he was always recycling, sitting hunched in the dimness, nodding his head to the strains of but another Bach oratorio, whose swell blanketed the musty room, serving to shut out in part the memory of the ghost, consigned to slumber in another murky avenue of his brooding brain.

Aloysius O'Muadaigh had a small skull, whose bony edges stood out plainly beneath the thin pale veil of parched skin, black eyes set deep in their sockets, tall brow crowned by a sprinkling of sandy hair, greasy with his sweat, his hollow cheeks held down by his customary frown, but welling now wider as he gave a wolfish grin, expressive of the pleasure the music gave him, his teeth akin to a jagged row of tombstones, teeth stained black and brown from the incessant stream of fags it was his wont to smoke.

Grinning with lupine joy, he made now to roll another slender strip, with nimble fingers pouching the tobacco in the slim tube of Rizla, wrapping up with a lick of lizard's tongue to secure, and was on the point of lighting the whole, when suddenly a loud rapping on his front door took him aback. He yelped, starting up in his shock at the violence of the knock, dropping his roll-up, whose contents were spilled all over the floor, lost in the carpet of dust, never now to be found again. He cursed, hating whoever it was that was knocking, and resolved to sit tight and ignore the rapping, which did not desist.

Then The Mad Monk got sick of knocking, and thereupon kicked open the door, which broke open easily, flying off its defunct and rusty hinges with a bang. One hand holding his sack, the other hastily repairing the damaged door with a wave of enchanted fingers, he slid into the house, and barged through the tunnel of the hall into the sitting room, where Aloysius lurked by the fireplace with a poker clutched in his bony hand.

But the violence of The Mad Monk's entry stood in contrast to the kindliness of his conduct once within. He took one look at the forlorn figure by the fireplace, and saw a weak and lonely old man doing his pathetic best to seem upright and fearsome, small and emaciated in his drooping cardigan, eyes boggling at the intruder's imposing size, trembling grip on his poker weakening – and The Mad Monk smiled warmly at the cornered madman, sensing a kindred soul was there somewhere.

And Aloysius dropped his weapon at the sight of the smile that stung him, and held up his shaking hands to shield his eyes, to see no evil.

With cheerful grace, The Mad Monk came to a ragged armchair, and sat down slowly on the late mother O'Muadaigh's armchair (that held still, in its frozen contours, the imprint of her corpse that had sat there snugly so long), deposited his bag of gains by his feet, and leaned back in languor, beady eyes upon his quailing host, who peeped in fright through chinks in thin fingers, at the smiling guise of his singular guest.

'Pardon my rude intrusion, my dear friend,' the visitor said affably, 'I mean to do you no ill. I pray you, please sit down, and feel at ease, I beg you, do.'

Aloysius lowered his hands slowly from his face, and warily crept from the fireplace back to his chair, onto which he sank again.

'Much better. Now we may talk as men, civil talk such as which I am starved of. For when one is alone and friendless in a cheerless place as this town, rejected by its unfriendly inhabitants, lost and aimlessly adrift on a surly street, it gladdens the heart when, upon a sudden, one catches sight of a ruined house, from whence within can be discerned pouring the divine strains of Bach – well, one knows the inhabitant must be a man of some taste, one whose acquaintance must be made. Your name is …' (he narrows his eyes, fingers snapping the air, until it comes) '… Aloysius O'Muadaigh?'

'I am he,' Aloysius O'Muadaigh said with steel, 'are you on the planning committee? Come in here to run me off my land? I said I'm not shifting.'

'Oh no, no, no,' The Mad Monk chuckled, 'I'm from no committee, not I. I am on your side. We among the world's madmen know our number. And we'll all do each other a turn and a favour should occasion arise. For you see, I came by Sligo town, Mr O'Muadaigh, to forage for food' (with a gesture to his bulging bag) 'food to feed a pet of mine, a ravenous White Dog, big brute of a fellow, fiendish appetite. It has been years since he's been properly fed, and the belly of the beast must be growling. I last left him buried under a boulder, by the graveyard at the foot of the giant's toes.'

'Giant's toes?' Aloysius murmured.

'Ay. I think the locals call him Big Ben, or somesuch.'

'Ah, it's Ben Bulben you mean,' said Aloysius, pleased to be better in the know, 'the graveyard at the foot of which is where Yeats is buried, they call it Drumcliff.'

'The very same,' The Mad Monk beamed, 'you're better than any tour guide, good Aloysius. W.B. beneath the big Bulben, you say? How the names change. They linger about as long as doth the turning tide. It is the way of our time. Anyway, I came to you to seek directions to that graveyard, for the route I have forgotten. That is all I ask.'

'It's quite a walk,' said Aloysius, growing eager, stroking his thin chin, 'and no simple route to describe. But I can take you there on foot.'

'That would be an exceeding goodness of you.'

'Not at all,' said Aloysius, 'I'm always game for a walk.'

'Thank you,' said The Mad Monk, 'and hang on – permit me repay you in advance for this. Have …' (producing from air a Rizla roll-up, newly lit and set to smoke) '… a fresh fag for your pains, in exchange for the one lost to the floor, on my account.'

Aloysius reached across and took up the smoke, crossing and blessing himself as he did, mumbling gratitude, fingering the rosary beads by his breast, privy to a minor miracle. Then, having stuck the roll betwixt dry lips, and taken a deep suck to steady his jangling nerves, he stood again, and took from the corner his knobbly hawthorn stick, and made steps to the door, beckoning to the miracle worker to follow, and The Mad Monk did, rising up with a chuckle and swinging his sack over his shoulder.

And so the peculiar pair sallied forth into clear air, leaving the wreckage of the O'Muadaigh house for the street, down which they strolled together in silence, side by side, striding into the sun that was waning, soon to sink, until in time they had left the town behind them, and the sleeping giant emerged over the horizon, his lofty brow poking up the closer they came, straggling into focus as they mounted to higher ground, Aloysius taking up the lead, getting more animated, attaining elation from the rare weed his acquaintance had pouched into the spectral roll-up, like no tobacco on Earth he had ever enjoyed. And he grew more voluble the higher they got, and began to tell The Mad Monk some things about his past, a heady mix of madness and mothers, scripture and sodomy.

'Ah, sodomy …' The Mad Monk sighed, 'the name has a dated ring, and does not become the thing. Highest form of love, so some say, popular among those gay Greeks back in the day, that race on whom genius gushed forth the greater loot of her store. A noble love, but one that fell out of fashion, and made to seem shameful, though I hear it is supposedly making a comeback, in this age that prides itself on being permissive.'

'Bah!' said Aloysius, 'this bloody time is as straitlaced as they come!'

'I doubt thee not. But sodomy. There was an occasion when my friend Watt (God rest his soul) and I, on the run from the law, took refuge in the precarious safety of a bathhouse, a sleazy lair run by a gibbering loon, who ripped us off. But there we were anyway, Watt and I sat together in a steaming bath, all alone, talking rubbish about a Silkie bantam chicken it was once our mutual joy to know, the legs of whom are employed, way out east in the faraway orient, in the production of beauty products for women.'

'Silkie scent. I use it myself whenever I can get it. Some boys like it.'

'Really? The world shrinks. And we were naked the both of us, all our wares on show as we chatted of chickens. And Watt was shy initially, being a small man, the sort of dwarf I oft bade sit on me knee, but he proved to be amply endowed for his size, so far as I could see. For my vision was clouded by the fog of rising steam, and I was moved to sink lower to submerge myself beneath the hot water, as a dark sea lion I sank in the bath, to obtain a better view of my companion's nether parts, in the milky froth of bath. And I looked long upon them, the pride of Archibald Theodore, the genitals of genius. But that was all. I only looked, but went no further. Which is odd. It is not often that I hold back. For it has been my wish to be as complete a man as ever there was and as much as I can, cutting himself off from no part of life, all things being equal, and all worthy of a go.'

'I could help you,' Aloysius said, somewhat overeagerly.

The Mad Monk gave him a quizzical look, under which he coiled.

'I mean,' he stuttered, 'it's just, well, um, you are, eh, quite a handsome bloke, seen from certain lights, b-beautiful, one may say …'

'Thank you. My wife often said the same.'

'Oh!' croaked mortified Aloysius, 'o in that case, o dear me, em, just forget I said anything, I mean, eh, the sacred contract of marriage being beyond dispute, I would never dream of, eh, y'know, impinging on it, God's laws I shall never lay asunder, er, um …'

'Oh, cease your squirming, my goodly O'Muadaigh. Certainly I shan't be enlisting your services in that sphere, or at least, not today – nay, today I did not set aside for sodomy. But you talk of the laws of God – our marriage could hardly be said to accord with those. It was a different beast. I remember it to have been a convivial event that took place in the merry Court of the Faerie King, involving much speechifying and versifying and nectar-imbibing, our union blessed by lashings of booze, crowned by our being dunked in a giant barrel of beer, where first it was we conjoined and cuddled – so chaste we were before then, batting tricksy eyes across corridors like a pair of coy and giggly virgin schoolgirls – only until then, in a lather of liquor, when we met and mated.'

'O yes, yes, yes,' said Aloysius, liking the turn the tale was taking.

'Yes, we copulated. But even now, still can't quite fathom how we did it. For she was, like Watt (who later rode her, upon my wicked urging), so much tinier than was I – elfin, almost – the logistics of the act beggar belief – and none could credit it when she came with child. Ah, my wee wife! To talk of her makes me miss her the more. Small and dumpy little creature she was, frumpy and so matronly – hard to say what it was drew me to her, in retrospect. But I suppose it is the nature of true love to be inexplicable.'

'Ay. I second that. For my part, I never ceased to love my mad mother, for all we may have hated each other.'

'O, you Irishmen and your mothers! Lucky me, I shirked the tyranny of the nursery from an early age, a bright child who did not play with his toys like the other oafish boys, I who talked out of turn, who gave cheek at table, who swore and blasphemed, who dared to drink and fell under the spell of mushroom. But I was on the side of life. And it was not long before I got well away from the domineering bag who begat me. All I remember is her crone's whine. Can't even picture her face, the one my dog tore up. A mother's love was another love I never knew. Bit sad, I suppose. But then again, I've seen mothers enough … I made my own wife become one.'

'True. I myself have many nephews and nieces already. But I will never rear a child. No fruit of my loins. And while my Church may condemn me, my seed I will continue incessantly to spill on barren arid earth.'

'To make mandrakes grow, I'll have you know, lest you be dying as you spew. Insufferable squall of bawlers, I've born many, to my shame, in previous lives while I was hung, nameless infinities of bastards. But while we talk of dead earth, are we any nearer to the damned graveyard?'

'We are just arriving, Sir …'

Aloysius opened the creaking gate, and they entered the grounds of grave, passing nimbly between the stumps of tombstones poking impotently up from the earth. By the plots of sunken lives the pair passed, in the quiet of the eventide, golden light petering through the branches of brambly trees, gaunt yews and thin pines, long shadows cast by their spines. And The Mad Monk was pleased to see that the place had not changed in any noticeable particular since last he had been there. And one grave above all the others drew his gaze. He stopped to stoop to read aloud in reverence the writing:

Cast a cold eye
On life, on death;
Horseman, pass by!

'I met that man once,' he said in an undertone unheard by Aloysius, who was thrashing a bed of nearby nettles with his stick (riled by the reminder they afforded of the recent time he had rolled about in them writhing, punishment for having taken a tinker).

'He was a solemn chap, but when he laughed, there were none were louder. And a randy buck when it came to wooing,' The Mad Monk said.

'What's that?' Aloysius panted, setting down his stick.

'Your Yeats. Loved a dirty joke, he did.'

'Ah yes. Of course, some say he is not buried there at all.'

'I have heard that story. Seems to me to possess the underwhelming hallmark of truth.'

'Life is nowt but disappointment,' said Aloysius sagely, clicking rattling black teeth in a ghoul's grin, 'and on that subject ... we came to seek your pet, did we not?'

'We did. My hungry White Dog so famished.'

'I see, faith. And be he some manner of, er, magic mongrel, what?'

'To an extent. His powers are few beside those of his owner. He can alter his size, grow bigger or smaller. But that is the extent of his prowess. Naughty critter. Gave some silly poet a nasty fright long ago.'

'Now that you mention it,' said Aloysius, leaning lightly on the mossy rim of W.B.'s stubby tombstone, 'there has been talk of late. For my brother Ulick, you see, is a keen dog lover, his house is awash with the brutes, and his ears prick up always at the sound of a hound. And he tells me that he has been hearing howls emanating from this place, upon occasion. Coming by this graveyard in the course of a recent nocturnal lope, having just done a day's ramble up Big Ben, he heard that hungry howl, an underground growl welling up out of the darkness. Fairly terrified him, it did.'

'Indeed?' The Mad Monk said, setting down his sack, 'That rings true. Sooner I feed him the better, it seems, lest the naughty scoundrel run loose from his lair.'

Then The Mad Monk knelt by the poet's grave, to divest his sack of its contents, and as he emptied out all the edible items, a breeze that was chiller blew through the air swiftly on a sudden, a sharp gust that brought stinging tears to the eyes of Aloysius, as he leant on the tombstone, observing intently as The Mad Monk took out from the big bag food and more food: cabbages; cakes; scones; bananas; oranges; apples; oats; beans; grapes; biscuits; nuts; a jar of mustard; peas; pomegranates; olives; pop tarts; jelly babies; radishes; cloves of garlic; fruit pastilles; several varieties of veined cheese – and when all the bulging sack was emptied of its loot, and the plot of the poet was covered all by the goods he had gathered, The Mad Monk sat back with narrowed eyes to consider the collection, and knew then, with a snap of fingers, that something vital was missing:

'Meat! Meat! Meat! Body of me, what an oversight! My poor pet will be craving flesh! I'd best go get some – will you wait here, and keep watchful eye on these helpings, to ensure no scallawag steals 'em? I'll just hasten up the side of the mountain, shan't be long before I stumble upon the carcass of some sheep, killed by a headlong topple from one of Ben's great shanks, dropping to their death in a merciless ravine below. Failing that, I'll murder one of the buggers meself. Won't take a jiff. Do you mind waiting?'

Aloysius was agreeable to the scheme. And The Mad Monk rejoiced at the fanatic's amenability, and gave his friend a wave, who blew back at him a kiss, a queer send-off at which he grinned, and turned, and strode away through tombstones, his robe rustling the twigs, spangles of the setting sunlight filtered through branches alighting on his sharp head, over which a halo hung, so it seemed to Aloysius, who smiled at the fancy, left behind alone leaning on the grave of Yeats, humming in a content he had not known in a long while, eyes on the back of his friend who left him, as he made away through tombs and trees, size dwindling as he hopped over the graveyard wall, and soon vanished from view, as he began to climb from toes to thighs, from shanks to flanks, and with nimble hop, and many a bound, thus began to mount Ben Bulben.

But their separation was to prove misguided.

CHAPTER FOURTEEN

Atop Ben Bulben's brow, at rim of the sheer cliff, on the craggy plateau of the giant's head, stood a kingly Goat, surveying the land laid out below, as the sun sank. This Goat had had a good day – many meals had been his, and many ample she-goats had also been his joy to mount and buckle – and now he had ascended at day's end, to the utmost crown of his hilly home, on a vaguely romantic whim, to watch the setting of the scarlet sun.

And as he stood there proudly on his hooves, nibbling in content on what morsels of grass could be found that clung to the cliff, and saw the fiery orb before him sink from sight, he felt moved by a secret longing stirring in his breast, a something for which he pined and yearned to give utterance to, if he could but only find the sounds or words:

'Way-hay-hay,' the Goat plaintively neighed, as he quietly munched.

And with the sunset, and the daylight's dimming, and black night's oncoming heralded by the deepening dusk, the Goat saw mists begin to form in a blanket all over the land, as far as he could see. And these misty wreaths, that brought the cold in their chilly train, came to converge in particular profusion all around Ben Bulben's brow, settling on his peak of plateau. And soon in time, the Goat was surrounded by all the enveloping fog, a cloudy curtain that obscured the sight, visibility everywhere hindered, bar but a narrow radius of a few feet forward and back from where he stood. And the Goat grew afraid, and stood still, rooted to the spot, fearful of the cliff's nearby edge, over whose rim he might blindly blunder, and topple headlong through the swirling fog, fall to a rocky death at the mountain's foot, as so many of his kind had so often done, in suchlike manner of death as to which so many of his loved ones had been lost. And so the Goat stood his ground, his legs trembling from the coldness and dampness of the misty air, cowering there in his growing fear, unknowing, uncertain, frightened.

And then from the fog an apparition emerged.

For through the smoky veils of sheathing mist that swathed the sight, the Goat upon a sudden discerned a shape, coming forward from the swirls as it approached him. A form taller than was he, one that moved on two legs, so it seemed, though it rather floated than walked, though yet it had a hobble. Clad in the ragged vestments of the greyest grave, a pale and withered wraith, with a long and tangled beard that hung, a shadowy ghost with piercing glowing eyes, that froze the marrow of the terrified Goat who numbly beheld its approach. And the ghost came closer to the Goat, a grisly smile on its haunting face, and laid a spectral claw on the Goat's horned head, and patted him to calm, and took up a strand of his Goat's beard, and toyed with it, entwining and curling the bristly hair, softly stroking his head all the while, a faint murmuring issuing from its pallid lips, idle pleasantries and sounds to soothe. And then the ghost raised an arm from the heavy sleeve of its robe, from the hand uplifted a spindly forefinger to point upward at the hidden sky, and then the ghost spoke, imparting unto the quaking Goat its message, croaking forth in a reedy voice akin to onion skin:

'Mark you well this. A Day of Reckoning is in the offing, my bearded boy. Take heed, and do due reverence; and pass on the happy tidings to your kindred kind, so that to the good news I bring, none among you be blind …'

CHAPTER FIFTEEN

The Mad Monk meanwhile was climbing up the mountain in search of food for his hungry hound, so long kept cloistered. And the day's last red rays lit up his way as he ascended higher and higher, clinging to the cliff with powerful fingers, barking at the few sheep who made bold to 'baaa' at him as he passed them by, nervous flocks huddling precariously on the hill's steep side. He paused in his hasty ascent to slurp up a mouthful of crystalline water from the slim cascade of a slender mountain stream, its brook that tumbled bubbling by, and as he whetted his thirst, and splashed his parched face, he heard above the cries of ravens. And looking up he saw them circling low in the sky, their dipping and wheeling signalling the fresh mass of carrion they had surely espied. And The Mad Monk followed them, bounding higher by boulders on fleet feet, and found then, in the crook of a shallow ravine, the carcass of a felled lamb, a pool of blood spilling from its threadbare split side, the ribs poking through from the wool on view, its small body smothered by buzzing flies, its little head surmounted by the arrogant raven who had discovered it, boastfully croaking, pecking out the eyeballs with bloody beak. The Mad Monk shooed him away briskly with a wave, and spat at the flies who fled, and picked up the corpse, and held it tenderly in his arms, cradling lovingly the dead child, gazing pityingly into empty sockets, where once bright eyes had sat and peeped, with all the blooming curiosity of youth, mourning that it be so young, and doubting that it would provide meat enough to satisfy the appetite of his insatiable Dog.

But it would have to do. And so, mindful of the lonely O'Muadaigh below who might miss him, carrying with care the corpse, he turned around again to descend, when a queer noise from above halted him in his tracks, a sound that was not the croak of ravens, but sounded rather more like the neigh of a goat, coupled with an eerie babbling.

Curious, he darted up his yellow eyes – and only then saw the weird shaft of fog that draped Big Ben Bulben's blinded head – and in the midst of that mist, he saw a sight that stunned him, moving him to drop the dead lamb. For he saw above him the dim form of a floating Goat, enraptured in the thick of the fog, wide eyes transfixed by the figure who held him in the air afloat by his beard, that figure too that floated and glided – but the Goat was solid, whereas, it, or he, or it, was watery, or wispy, or wholly ghostly.

And upon seeing this vision, The Mad Monk, alarmed and unknowing, began to clamber panting up the steep and rocky side, keen to get the closer to the floating Goat held by the ghost – climbing higher into the clouds, until soon he was at one with the fog, and set foot on the mountain's utmost summit, coughing and spluttering as he swallowed icy gas swirling all around – treading closer to the floating forms that bewitched his curiosity – and soon he was close enough – close enough to touch the hoof of the floating Goat – close enough to behold in horror the profile of the ghost, dancing a foot above him in the midair – horror for he knew him to see – to see again that bald brow, that tangled ragged beard, liberally littered with knots, those shaggy brows cocked and raised in bushy crannies, to furrow the pallid forehead, to see those large and gleaming eyes that burned – and knew him to hear – to hear about him in the air dimly discerned a stream of pattering speech, issuing from chattering lips, intoning croakily to the floating Goat, in a voice from the past, one he knew well, had known from infancy – and all these attributes, together combined as one, equated to form a figure of old, one of his own, cast long ago of the same old mould, two sons begotten of the same sire, both once babes in arms, who suckled milk from the same drooping pap, his one and only flesh and blood brother—

'ELIJAH!' The Mad Monk bellowed.

The ghost started; and turned around above in the air to face him. And he beheld again, hanging amid mist, the countenance of his first and only sibling, the burning eyes of whom met his. And The Mad Monk quailed under their stare, and groaned, and tottered, and sank under weight of the sight, to be drowned in a net of the smothering fog, that wafted along, in a rushing mighty wind, to cover him wholly – and the last thing he saw, before he fell through fog, was a broad and toothy grin beginning to form on the grey face of the ghost, and the last he heard was a haunting chuckle petering forth in the swirling air – and then, as wind of whiteness merged to blanketing blackness – all was lost – and he was gone.

CHAPTER SIXTEEN

Aloysius O'Muadaigh leant on the tombstone in the deeper dusk, whistling hoarsely a few choice paragraphs from the *St Matthew Passion* to keep company with himself, flapping his arms, and hugging his chest, and fingering his walking stick to keep himself warm, as the dark brought cold to his stiff limbs, running his knuckles up and down the hawthorn's length, keeping time with the beat of his whistling, as if it were a flute upon which he were piping, missing the more the miracle worker as minute by lonely minute passed him by, as he stood in the shadows by the grave of the poet, all alone in the court of the dead.

A gust of wind, burped by the earth, billowed by, rustling crackling leaves along its breezy way, a gust he likened, in his morbid mind, to a pathetic plea, coming from one of the rotted occupants of the worm-riddled coffins, submerged in damp clay beneath his nervous feet, in a hopeless appeal for comfort, a futile spume erupting from the hereafter.

And his thoughts, fuelled by the sinister atmosphere of that gloomy place, began now torturously to follow a ghoulish bent. For he felt hemmed in and oppressed by all the dead lives around him, their suffocating souls surrounding him like flies, cramming all the chill air that was there, and he fancied that he faintly heard their wail and clamour as they arose, the banshee's nagging of his departed mother among them; and he wondered just how many of the dead were exactly numbered in this place, the soil below crammed full with festering bodies; and he wondered whether it was writhing in the infernal pits, or basking in the Elysian bliss, or lost in the listless wastes of limbo, wherever it was in the afterlife they found themselves, where it was they whiled away the incalculable infinity to which they were consigned, all those dead men, and dead women, and dead children too, or whether indeed they were no more than nowhere now, an idea he could not countenance; and he wondered whether they would be saved, when the trumpets sounded, and they arose from their little boxes, stumbling on creaking bones, from whence their flesh was long decayed or nibbled, the hobbling horde of Sligo's sarcophagi; and he wondered how long a time was yet to elapse before that Day came, how long was left to them to lie before the world was ended, on that Day when He would come again, clattering in a chariot in glory, to judge and save, or damn and doom; and he wondered too, with a pang of terror, whether he, Aloysius O'Muadaigh, was destined to be damned, to be tarred with the brush of the beast, on account of his contemptible sin, an unholy aberration in His Lordship's eyes, stained credit appeased by not one of his continual quailing confessions, with their false promise of threadbare absolving, an ignobly impoverished redemption as offered by a disinterested and drink-sodden cleric, muttering facsimile benedictions in soiled weeds, fluttering absolution with jittery fingers that shook – no, no, that would not and could never be enough, not for Him who cast a cold eye down in disapproval on the gay madman He set in His sights, a target to be shot, His dart to punish, that sinning specimen tormented by racking anguish, overeager practitioner of the sickly unnatural vice, delving and burrowing in forbidden tunnels and debauched zones, yes, for his black crime of sodomy would he be put in the pillory to join the mass of the condemned, to be utterly eternally wretchedly damned – and all these harrowing thoughts, buzzing unrelentingly in his troubled mind, found impoverished outward expression in the form of a choke and gulp, drowned by the rising wind, as he stood sobbing unseen softly, in the darkness of the graveyard, as he quietly wept.

Then a noise, emitted from near afar, ruptured the quiet, and upset the stream of his brooding. His ears pricked up; he raptly listened and heard. It came from nearby where he stood, wafted by the wind, welling up from under the ground upon which he was shaking, a noise he gleaned to be the sound of a hound, the low growling of a buried dog, a growl that was a call to summons, a command that could not bear disobeying, that bade him approach, to root and seek it out, to set it free from its prison in the clay. A ream of rheumy film fell over his eyes, that grew to be glazed and blank, as his hands fell slack to his sides, dropping his stick as he abruptly left his place by the tombstone, and sleepwalked stumbling through shadows, in a murky realm unknowing, in search of source of the sound, that grovelling growling he could not resist, passing sunken lives stepping on snapping twigs in the twilight, faint light of the sky's emerging stars glimmering through chinks in the trees, to patchily illumine his unwitting way, as he followed the path of the growling, until he found its ultimate subterranean source, in the cold graveyard's darkest corner, over which hung the pining arms of a willow tree, divided down all the middle of its length, jaggedly split by a flash of lightning from the past, the fragmented trunk, its pockmarked bark gnarled and knotty, haggardly bent in supplication, its bowing beaten shape echoing that of a keening crone in mourning, the weeping willow a wailing widow, beside of which was laid a big black boulder, about as tall as was he, from under which the low growling was issuing.

He could not afterwards with any precision explain just how he found the requisite strength to shift the enormous stone from where it sat, to disclose what it hid, but shift it he did, somehow, for all his arms were weedy and his age was weak. And the shifted boulder was revealed to have hidden a very deep and very narrow hole in the ground, over which he knelt and bent on tiring groaning knees, to gaze into that gaping pit of absolute blackness, greeted by the growling of the beast submerged in earth, whose growling grew in volume as he squinted into that looming recess, as deeply dark as the mouth of a wolf, or that of a giant dog. And he sensed excitement in the rising growling, erupting into raucous howling, and the patter of monstrous paws that dug into the pit's walls, as upwards the eager canine came clambering, with champing frothing jaws, overjoyed to have caught again the scent of nocturnal air wafting sweetly down. And he keenly heard the violent hunger inherent in that ravaged howl, as the starving beast came surging upwards, to greet and eat the man who set him free, to gorge on the lean meat set on his skeletal frame, to feed on the flesh of he who dopily froze, rooted to the spot by the hole where he knelt and gawked, numbly clapping his palms, mumbling inanely with the ghost of a grin:

'Good dog … nice doggy … lovely doggy … c'mon now me boyo, me beauty … time for walkies and munchies … time for dinner and dessert …'

CHAPTER SEVENTEEN

Ulick O'Muadaigh lay in languor, stubby quill in hand to scribble his scrawl on a curling piece of parchment, by the side of his wife Wilhelmina, her breast and belly rising gently up and down, as she breathed and snottily snored, uncaring of the unwieldy array of books, and pile of papers and pages, scattered all over their hectic bed of birth – for it was the eccentric custom of her husband to make of their bed a writing desk, to convert the site of their repose, and blue moon lovemaking, into a dour cubby den to do his writerly work. For he was a man both highly industrious and incurably lazy, who preferred to do his bookwork on his back, that it might feel the less like labour, and the more like leisure. Having taken early retirement, on account of high blood pressure, from his thankless job as a psychiatric nurse, he now bided away his housebound days in beavering away at his novel on De Valera, in which he would endeavour to prove (through means of copious, if slightly slanted, research, and by couching the fruits of his discoveries through the accessible medium of a daft and harebrained plot (about a gang of schoolchildren who stumble across illicit political secrets, tucked away on a high shelf in Trinity College's Old Library)) that the country's one-time leader was actually a British spy, who ordered the killing of Collins, the jealous wastrel who slew the martyred hero.

There he was, then, perched on his pillow, dimly lit by the lamp as he wrote, sucking on his puffing dudeen, whose plumes of smoke befogged their bedroom, occasionally pausing in his scribbling to pensively stroke his white moustachios, or pluck from his capacious nostril, into which he daily dug, yet another crusty currant of dry snot, and he was on the point of reaching an especially tricky passage (charting the revelation of a few choice and luridly sickening details, concerning the Long Fellow's curious sexual proclivities – not to mention his similarly long (and emaciated) physical endowments), when, of all a sudden, the phone by his bedside loudly rang.

Its shrill ring awoke his dog Pearse, who had been dozing beneath the bed, but who now rose and began to bark upon hearing the noise, at which his ears pricked, and his scruffy tail flapped and wagged, at the sharp sting of the ring as it rang out in the room, to the ire of the growling collie, who was bade with a hiss to desist by his owner, snatching a caring glance to his still sleeping spouse (for it would take a whirlwind to awaken the weighty Wilhelmina), as he reached out a flabby naked arm to pick up the receiver from its cradle, wondering as he did just who the hell on Earth would choose to call, at such an ungodly hour of the cold dark country night.

And upon putting the receiver to his waxy ear, he heard a voice that spoke across an abyss, from the crackly line's other end, the most beautiful he had heard in all his life.

'Is that Ulick O'Muadaigh?'

'Ay. That's me. Who are you? What kind of hour do you call this?'

'My ardent apologies. I am ringing from the mobile phone of your good brother – I picked it out of his pocket – you were his only contact.'

'What the hell? Aloysius? You a kidnapper or something? You holding him to ransom?' bellowed Ulick, suddenly beside himself (his lifelong passion for plots and conspiracy even now did not desert him).

'Nothing of the sort. Your poor brother is hurt, Mr O'Muadaigh, grossly injured and much wounded. I am afraid a dog has bitten him badly, and that dog was mine own.'

'What? Is he all right? Who the fuck are you? Where are ye?'

'Beside the grave of Yeats. He is alive – at least, he's still breathing, so far as I can see – but he will need much nursing. The comforts of home are what he most badly needs, to be back in the bosom of his family, of whom he spoke to me warmly, a few hours ago, when he was still fit to converse, on the right side of the land of the living.'

'Jesus fucking Christ ...' (with a gulp and quaver, his puffy face turning an ashen shade of grey) '... Yeats, you say? By Bulben, you mean. Drumcliff, yes. Right. Jesus. Em. This is a shock. I'll … I'll head on over in me car …'

'Good. I will stay by him until you arrive. Thank you for keeping your cool. I have been negligent. I am so very sorry about this.'

'Bit late for that …' (he sits up to get dressed) 'arragh, I'll be over …'

'See you. You shan't miss us. And o yes – as to who I am – think of me as an incompetent guardian angel – an angel who fatally slipped in his service – an angel who pleads your forgiveness – an angel whose wings … have been clipped.'

And then the line went dead as the caller hung up.

CHAPTER EIGHTEEN

The Mad Monk hung up on the call and wiped his aching eyes, and cast a sorrowful gaze on the forlorn form of his badly wounded friend. His face and throat were torn, a lump of one ear cut off, from a stump of one leg a sizeable chunk was bitten and gashed, his flesh riddled with nicks and cuts and bleeding welts, and all his frail body, and tattered garments, besmeared and splattered with his blood. He lay in a pitiful crumple at the foot of the wailing tree, beside the boulder he had somehow shifted, face down in the pool of his own blood, blood seeming blue and silver in the starlight, gossamer spools of the moon, that unheedingly shone merrily down. And discernible too, on the grave and earthy ground that had seen horrors, were the bloody footprints of the hound who did the damage, monstrous prints that left deep clefts in the soil, shining weirdly silver, as lit by lunar light, matched by the greater ebony of the unlit recesses of shadow all the way round, those darker places that threatened to swallow the path that petered out, of the trail that traced its bloody way to the gate of the graveyard, where they disappeared, as their victim's blood dried up. And where the brute had gone, there was no way now of knowing, and nor was now the time to go seek it – it was time to play nurse, to tend to the fallen.

The Mad Monk bent, and on his back rolled poor O'Muadaigh over, and put the phone back in his damp pocket, and lifted him up, and carried him back to the plot of the poet, and set him down, by the pile of food that had gone untouched, propping him up on the tombstone, and knelt before him, and from the soil, and the sleeves of his robe, procured obscure ointments, with which he gently bathed the rougher wounds, to ease in part the patient's suffering, which tender treatment provoked a response from the recipient, in the form of a low groan, a paltry sign of life, and a heart still beating.

And as he lathered on his lotions, to soothe the skin of the stricken, the mind of the nurse was not all there, for it kept wandering back to the mountain, and over and over again reliving the strange things he had seen there. He had awoken from his lapse to find the fog had long lifted, to unveil the iron sky of stars above, and standing, nearby where he lay, dim and dopey, the Goat, nonchalantly munching grass, as if nothing had happened. Jerking awake, he had set upon this Goat, to whom the spectre had spoken, pressing him with questions, fervidly demanding details, but all to scant avail, for the Goat was reticent and chary with his speech. All he would concede to say was that the ghost had sung of many marvels that were to come and still to be (one of them involving the love of an elder man of blubber for a tattooed younger), and of the Day of Reckoning – a portentous phrase that was The Mad Monk's own. And he would have further pestered the Goat with queries, had he not then heard, eerily echoing from the valley below, the bloodthirsty howl of the hound let loose to sate its appetite, coupled with the shrieks of its victim, the first morsel of meat it met on its way, at the sound of which The Mad Monk dismissed the Goat, and charged back down the mountain, passing by the dead lamb he neglected to retrieve, missing his steps in the dark, tripping and clumsily tumbling in his frantic blundering way, resorting to rolling to quicken his course, until finally he arrived again at breathless last only to discover the affair's dismal outcome, with his savage pet escaped and long gone beyond his reach, and unfortunate Aloysius left for dead. And only through a miracle, perhaps by a strategy of playing possum, had he avoided, by a hair's breadth, being killed by the creature. And all the business could only be accounted a cock-up, so The Mad Monk thought glumly, disillusioned.

And as he wiped O'Muadaigh's bleeding nose, and applied some spittle to the sockets of his eyes, to which he plastered dock leaves to quell the sting, he cursed himself for having allowed things to get so grossly out of hand, though certainly it was a bright idea to have rung up the other brother, as he had done. And it was natural that he should think of

O'Muadaigh's brother at that time, he who had, not so long since, seen his own brother's ghost. But though his brother had not deigned to speak to him, and had been so quick to disappear, his image lingered in his memory, and he was haunted even now, haunted by bright-eyed Elijah, dead but alive, tight-lipped but gnomically all-knowing; and he wondered, as he wiped away the blood, whether his brother had had a hand in what had happened here, which seemed to him askew, but perhaps was less so than it seemed; for it was ever Elijah's way to nudge things along in a little way or two, the better that they might get where they were going, and his prophecy the fuller fulfill, delicately hijacking events to suit himself the better, or rather the larger world; and perhaps, if this was true, then there was a reason for this outward randomness, and The Mad Monk's mistake something of a blessing in disguise, no more than another turn of the wheel. Such a thought was consoling, but troubling too. Where was one's will in all of this?

For even while Elijah had lived, and all the more now that he was dead, The Mad Monk had always been somewhat afraid of his brother, forever nursing, over all the long years of their acquaintance – they could never be close – a sneaking suspicion of his overabundant knowledge, envying his insight into the workings of heaven and Earth, baffled by that foresight, that filled him with such fear, often coming to quarrel with him whenever he refused to explain how it was he knew what he knew, resorting to bloodying his nose to squeeze a response from him – only in the physical sphere did Elijah ever seem the weaker – in the face of which abuse, the prophet might admit his abilities were linked to the flash of lightning that struck him in his youth, a pat response that to The Mad Monk smacked of fobbing off, akin to his own attribution, of his own gifts, to his childhood predilection for mushrooms – and yet it had to be allowed, for all it pained him, that he owed his brother much, and while he had lived, on him he had much relied; for when The Mad Monk took charge of his hybrid daughter, abducting her from Faerie-Land where she was born, and spiriting her away to the waters and the wild, to a house on a hill in the mortal world, where it was none but Elijah who was there to care; and it was her barmy uncle who brought her up, and fed her, and played with her, and schooled her in the world's ways, and protected her from the world's vagaries, while her mad father wandered far away waywardly elsewhere in that world, where he was killed; and in that house she grew up a spinster, after her dotty uncle so devoted, was deemed gaga, and carted off one day to be incarcerated in an asylum – the younger world, even then, was never ready to welcome the Divine Madness that ran in the family veins, with which both brothers were liberally blessed. But wily Elijah had escaped, and met with Watt, husband of his niece, to whom he prophesied his departed brother's second coming – and so it was Elijah who engineered the happy outcome of their travails, when all ended up in that Arcadian Nook, that Abode of Fancy, where all could live the life of their dreams – and how odd was it, further proof of his primary role in these motions, that once doddery Elijah's grip began to slip, his mind gone gaga again, that their hopes similarly began to break, and their citadel was smashed, and their Arcadia destroyed, to be drowned by repulsive blocks, and monotonous monoliths, to house the dour workaday drones, who filled in their life's allotted slots, and joylessly did their deadening duties; and so thus were they banished, refugees outcast from Paradise, to glum slums and cheerless city streets, where one by one they died as did flies, and Elijah was among them who died the lonely death of the dispossessed, catching cold from a downpour, ailing and failing, until, wasted, he stretched out on the pavement, and expired, his last words unintelligible gurgles – The Mad Monk had dumped his brother's body into the stinking river down by the town docks, for want of better resting place.

But he was back now, that was sure, to do more mischief – though it was dubious as to whether he was furthering or hindering the progress of his living brother. Suppose that what had happened here were for the better, and the White Dog let loose to perform some part – yet what good could come from the sacrifice of the blameless Aloysius, an event which reeked of evil, and so sickened The Mad Monk's heart? That was what so disturbed him ever always – the wicked and unseemly relish with which the old boy gleefully watched things shape themselves the way he said they would, the cold remorselessness, the inhumanity he could display upon occasions, tempered at times by such warmth and kindliness – it remained a puzzle to The Mad Monk the degree to which his brother was either wholly benign or wholly malign, for he was always a bit of both – and much the same could be said of himself. That was the way they were, the two of them, a pair of gods and devils, brothers bound by blood wherein swam good and evil humours both, the one who was bright when the other was black, and so on until infinity's end; and as he sat back, and sighed in the darkness, weary of ministering to wounded O'Muadaigh, The Mad Monk reflected on the nature of brotherhood, by turns in bafflement, in trepidation, in sorrow; he thought of his own brother, that enigma, one of life's enduring mysteries, like love, the labyrinthine mind of Elijah that encompassed the stars, posing a riddle he could not crack, a man he could never know, never known when he was alive, nor now that he was dead and walking – you could not grab a ghost.

And into the midst of his horrified contemplations, the honk of a horn, from over the hedges, shattered the stillness, announcing the arrival of another brother, come to collect his fallen other, the one who was Ulick, come to care for Aloysius, who was deeply in need, for whom he bore great love, love such as The Mad Monk and Elijah could never muster for each other, such was their muddled and uncertain state; Ulick who came from his car cursing, shining forth a torch to light up the night, the light of which fell upon the face of The Mad Monk, who rose to seek pardon for the wrong done, a guardian angel gone derelict, gesturing to the crumpled body of the other suffering brother, at the sight of which Ulick, in disgust and grief, ground his teeth; and then, master of his mood, produced, from the boot of his car, a rusty wheelbarrow, into which The Mad Monk, unbidden, laid in reverence the barely breathing body of his friend, resting him on the cushiony pile of the food for the dog that went uneaten; and so, after shaking hands in fellowship, together they wheeled him away, into the night.

CHAPTER NINETEEN

And so, to the house of his brother, through the dark was Aloysius wheeled in the creaky barrow, to be gently dumped in the boot of the car, the ageing engine coughing as they drove in the dark down leafy winding lanes, Ulick at the wheel clasping the clutch in despair, sitting, silently, to his left, the mysterious other passenger in the mucky habit, yellow eyes shining weirdly in the murk, so tall that his pointy skull's tip poked up out of the bonnet's open sunroof, fanned and kept cool by the rushing chill air of the night.

And headlights dimmed as they came to the hearth of Ulick's country cottage, its roof of reeds, its walls pebble-dashed, its chimney smoking, billowing forth a towering plume blocking the marmalade moon. And they took the maimed man from where groaning he was lying, hoisted by his brother with stagger to the door, opened by his yawning sister-in-law, summoned from sleep with reluctance, but who cried to see the state to which he was sunk, in no way placated by the bundle of stolen foodstuffs offered her gravely by the unknown other man, the unearthly visitor who followed shamefaced, stooping his height to fit in the frame, a dishevelled stranger, foreign to that place.

But they made him welcome, and bid him sit down at his ease by the fireplace, flickering light of the dying embers crinkling his face, as they lay the victim down on the couch, and divested him of his bloody garments, which in the morn they would burn in the garden, and Wilhelmina washed his wounds with wet rags, and draped over his ruined nakedness a heavy tartan shawl, though still he shivered, and his nose ran snottily red, while in the little kitchen caring Ulick brewed a pot of tea, and handed round the cups, the steaming beverage drunk by The Mad Monk gratefully down.

And then, when husband and wife were hunched and knelt before the fire, looking at him inquiringly, he spun the melancholy yarn more fully for them. And they accepted it all without demur, the will of whoever made the world be done – Wilhelmina was the pious one, though sceptic Ulick somewhat did scoff a little, but still did not complain. And that night, and for those that followed, there was to be for them scant sleep, for they were keen to keep vigil by the side of ailing Aloysius, to guard his mutilated flesh lest the prowling beast perchance come back to claim what he had left unfinished – and so they bided many a sleepless hour, twiddling thumbs, and pacing gloomily up and down.

For The Mad Monk, this deathbed sojourn made for a peaceful, if poignant, interlude to his travels. For he grew to love their compact cottage, with its sloping walls from which the flakes of caking plaster fell, and the numerous pictures that were hung from every cranny, paintings and photos of old friends and relatives, some of whom Ulick would identify for him, if asked when in the mood; and sometimes he would offer his editorial assistance for Mr O'Muadaigh's book, due to be a bestseller – a kindly offer brusquely declined with a grunt (Ulick's authorial pride would admit no editor). And come the dusk, one heard afar the chirp of crickets ringing in the darkness, and the growl of faraway foxes as they stalked cowering chickens, tightly clustered in their nervous coop; and when the morn was brightening, it was the lowing of the cows, and the bleating of the sheep, and the cries of the larches, that came spilling through their sunny windows. And once the invalid was installed in the spare bed kept for visitors, there was no room for The Mad Monk, who cheerily consented to sleep in the small shed adjacent to their dwelling, where he passed a number of nights slumbering soundly amid the straw, his snores rustling the hay their donkey nibbled, his humble lodging shared by the single pig they kept, whom he would hug by his breast for the while that he slept.

And, once he had won her trust, he would with Wilhelmina cook in the kitchen, ably assisting her in the making of their dinners, as once Aloysius had done before him, rooting among the pans and tureens and ladles that hung from the ceiling, peeling the potatoes that grew in the garden, dicing the juicy cutlets of piglet's flesh, skinning the onions and grinding the garlic, all such stuff that wound up in the bowl wherein was brewed and stirred their daily stew – and, whenever her back was turned, he would enrich and pepper the mix with some choice and tasty nameless powders, that had their origins in his robe's voluminous sleeves, to better the pot of their broth. And they would take turns in feeding the dying man, gingerly spooning the dripping soup into the wreckage of his mouth, that yawned almost always open, the fitter to drool and dribble, feeding him by mouth like his mad mother had done for him once, back in the days he was a babe, as he in turn had done for her when she was in her dotage; but he could only take in a single swallow, before painfully raising a trembling hand to shoo away the tentative spoon.

And the presence in the house, of many a panting dog (Pearse, Parnell, Wolfe Tone and The Liberator were their names), was a cause of fear and disturbance for Aloysius, his delirious foggy mind distracted, for the sinister pad and tread of their paws, the ominous rustle of their tails as they wagged, to say nothing of their growls as they caught sight of the three-legged cat (perversely dubbed by Ulick 'Eamonn the Divil'), served only to remind him of the like creature of their kind that had gored him – and so, at the sight of his distress, The Mad Monk thought fit to usher them out into the yard, where they would remain, until he was went away and gone.

For he had no will nor fire to live left in him, his eyelids fluttering, slipping open nearly ajar, half awake and half in a dream of the past, and he could but barely rally to the strain of speaking, his voice but a dim croak. And Ulick was especially saddened to be losing his brother so soon again, who had been locked up with their lunatic mother for years. But he would make the most of what time they had left, sitting by his side holding his withered little hand, masking his grief in a shower of cheerful words, as he spoke warmly of what had been, and of all they had seen in their time together on the Earth, while the dying Aloysius listened to his droning reminiscences in silent delight:

'... Arr, but we've had our bit of fun, haven't we, eh, me bold Alo? But to think you were one day only a coy little altar boy, clutching a quivering candle, drinking the holy wine when yer man the father wasn't looking? And school, ever the top of our class you were, especially at the fecking theology, while I lagged behind in me cups, drawing on me desk and playing with me marbles, the ones that you later lost. But we grew to be strapping lads, chasing ladies through the night, or I did at least, courting in the hedges, and romping in the meadow, earning my degree in bachelordom. Them days is long gone, Mina me love, so don't be scowling now, less of that puss on you. Ah, but d'ye remember at all, Alloy me boy, our days down and out in London when we were young, when times at home were tough, a little pack of grubby Paddies trying to make a go of it? That's where you got that cut-glass accent you have, for I'll be damned but it's not a Sligo voice you sport, ye mad mimic, ye pup. And we were in that poxy tip of a flat together, airless wee affair, couldn't invite any girls back it was so dire, not that you would anyway, closeted priestly celibate that you were. But the smell! Even bloody Eugene Collins turned up his nose at those dirty digs of ours, put off by the stink of our socks, and the mice that were many. It was near as bad as bloody Arsene's fecking mausoleum, down in the southeast. Remember him? Arsenic O'Colla that was, quare fellow, regrettable name, some chess player too, roundly trounced me when I tried. But yeah, baldy Eugene from Taylor's Hill was with us, one among me college chums. You two went to the arty French films together, the rest of us scared of subtitles. But French – ah, d'ye remember old Tadgh O'Mara too? Long streak of misery with a horse's face, a bit of a psycho too. Eugene told me how he once tried to murder his sister's fellah, clubbing the bugger down with a stone on a Salthill strand, took three men to pull him off when he saw the red mist in his eyes. Mad into all things French. Didn't want to be a Yank, and you wouldn't think it, to look at him now. Went over there a mere month, came back sporting this cod of a Gaul's voice, ye'd never know he'd been born in Louisiana. Forgetting all what English he had, bemoaning "zee lack of 'armonee in zee Irish beeldings". You two got on so well, spouting all me bum about Ludwig's Late Quartets and The Art of Fugue. Ah, that time you and me and Tadgh, we went to a Soho strip joint, got into a fair fight we did – wasn't it you insulted the bouncer, mocking his Cockney warble with your smooth syllables? Little shit stirrer, ye scut. Or perhaps you tried a move on him. Squeezing a sac here and there. We always did suspect. Any bloke who was too sensitive or refined was for sure a poof and pansy in our boy's book back in that bygone day. But Tadgh fairly was a crazy fucker, pretending to be a poet, yet remaining always something of a simple boy from the humid backwoods of the land of the faintly free, frightened of all them beastly blacks, a man of his time fleeing from the 'fear gorm', who brought him out in spots. A homophobe too. It was his hair you once tried to touch, planting down on his fluffy head a tender hand to stroke, and another horny palm clamped down on his bony thigh. Oh jaysus, Tadgh didn't like that! Ye had him bawling, he fairly fled into the night, didn't he just, we never seen him ever again after that ... O, the like of them lads you'll not be seeing again. And then you moved back in with our ma, when it was, I suppose, you went a bit bonkers. Cloistered in that house of death among the stricken shades. We did so miss ye then. Children we had, Mina and me, a brood of several sons and girls, some of whom are due to drop by to see you, by the by, but back then, as they grew, from babes, to toddlers, to talking teens, they always did be wondering about their mysterious absent uncle, the one who was shut up with their invisible grannyma. And I remember them sitting on me lap, and me spinning legends all about you, turning you into a myth for the craic, one they might pass on, and carry to their graves. You thought I was a West Brit in them days of darkness when we never saw you, and you wouldn't admit me, for donkey's years you seemed a stranger. But then she died, didn't she, our mammy, and we can ne'er forget that wet night we finally saw you again, when you came by banging on our door, howling and weeping, tears running all down your hollow cheeks, a skeleton you were, your own ghost, unfed and starving thin, to tell us she was dead, and would I care to carry her corpse to a coffin? And so I went with you in the rain, a belated bit of brotherly bonding, to that wretched dump of your haunted house, to detach the dead old goat from that foul and reeking armchair, to which she was stuck and rotting. Bizarre business. But it was good to have you back, if only for a wee while of a few short years. You had not changed all that much, I'm glad to say, once one found your offbeat wavelength. The kiddies were mad glad to have their loony Uncle Alo back among us. And trips we took, the old faces to find, like tubby little weatherman Arsene the gnome, and barmy Tadgh O'Mara, flapping arms like the daft goose he was and is, gone God knows where by now, and ay, down to Dublin didn't we go too, to meet Eugene and the son Simeon, to whom you took a shine I remember. He had a beaky beauty in your barmy eyes, if never in nobody else's. You made plaintive passes at him, ye did, to make up for time you lost, wrapping him in hugs and daring to kiss him, ye dirty old rogue, akin to those smooches you plastered on me own son Paddy's cheeks, but he spurned yer advances, like a good straight soldier, and so too did Collins Jr rebuff you, and in your pitiable rage to be rejected, you hit him, yes, and smacked him, and called him rude names. Ah jay. Don't get me wrong, me oul clown. For I will miss you, Alloy. And miss our seaside walks with the dogs. And our boozy talks and quarrels late at night. Suppose we'll sell your filthy house. You never did leave a will did you. I'll … I'll dedicate my book to you … only with your permission …'

Permission was granted through a slight squeeze of the hand.

CHAPTER TWENTY

Not long later there came a call from the children who had come by the railway, summoning their parents to Sligo town, where they were waiting by the train tracks having newly arrived. And so then did Ulick and Wilhelmina take their temporary leave, leaving their patient in care of the wayward guardian and administering angel, to clamber into their car to drive away as his final day was darkening, to be gone if only for a little while. So The Mad Monk sat by his dying friend's bedside, wallowing among blankets raggedly breathing, the wilting candlelight casting tall shadows on the walls, as the other man read aloud one of the more splendid stanzas from the Palinode to Chaucer's *Troilus*:

> *O yonge fresshe folks, he or she,*
> *In which that love that up groweth with your age,*
> *Repeyreth hom fro worldly vanyte,*
> *And of youre herte up casteth the visage*
> *To thilke rod that after his ymage*
> *Yow made, and thynketh all nys but a faire*
> *This world, that passeth soon as floures faire.*

'You read it very beautifully,' O'Muadaigh croaked in admiration. 'Do you have experience of doing voice-overs? Were you ever perchance a trained actor?'

'No. Though you would not be the first to say so. I have been a ham. But enough reading. Food for thought. 'Tis soon midnight. Been a good innings, I should say, ay?'

'Do you … do you think I shall be damned when I die?'

'Damned? O goodness gracious no, of course not. Why?'

'O god!' Aloysius cried, throwing off his blankets, 'I wish I had been born a monk, and could have spent my life alone in solace and bliss, by the side of a still lake!'

The Mad Monk considered this ejaculation for a space.

'Indeed?' he finally said, feebly.

'Yes!' said Aloysius with desperate hope, 'Has not this life of mine been such a waste? But might not the next be better, were I to be reborn? Might I not then become such a monk as I desire to be? You yourself, who do be a monk, must know!'

'Ah, but I am a monk in name alone, my boy. Certainly I did do a celibate stint in one of those joyless silent orders, to which I owe this handsome habit on me that I pinched, which I wore to the grave and back again, across the sea to land, by now a second skin. But the pleasures of the flesh I valued too greatly to enjoy an excess of inhuman abstinence, so nay, the monastic life was not for me, though I daresay it would be fitting for thee. And as to the next life? That's a matter of the lottery of souls. But Lordy knows, having brought thee to this sorry juncture, I owe thee a favour, so hence' (leaning over O'Muadaigh with burning eyes and hellish grin) 'I do now swear with a kiss' (planting a peck on the dying man's bloody brow) 'that I shall see to it that thou art thus transfigured, in just such a fashion as you would wish. This I do swear, so this I shall do.'

'Gadzooks!' Aloysius croaked in ecstasy, 'So do it now!'

The Mad Monk was on the point of considering just what he would do to live up to his bold-sounding ballyhoo, when then there rang out, through the stillness of the surrounding night enveloping them, a piercing scream, at the sound of which the blood of both ran quickly cold, upon hearing that chilling howl like that of a wailing woman, at which ungodly noise goggling Aloysius sat up in his frantic bed to bellow: 'The Banshee! She howls for me! My hour is come upon me! Do it now! Do it now! Do it now!'

And there she was, surely enough, her face leering at the little window above the bed where he lay, pressed to the pane, fogging the glass with her rattling shrieks, nails and talons clawing the frame and scratching as she screamed. And The Mad Monk staggered up from his stool where he sat, to behold in horror the Banshee, who had groped through the darkness, drawn like a moth by the flame of the candle that lit them, gawking in upon the two, her incessant sobbing that shrilly pressed him do the deed, the hideous old harridan moaning and groaning, clad in rags, clotted face clumped by wrinkles, and bleeding sores, and hairy warts, open pustules spilling forth globs of putrid green pus, her beaky nostrils flared, streaming sooty black snot, tiding down in weeping rivers, straggly hair greasily askew and wound up in knots, stringy tufts torn out by claws in her keening lament, gnashing what few fangs were left in her gaping mouth that spat spewing foam, her evil eyes ablaze with the roasting tears of a crocodile, falling down leather cheeks to scald the window's shivering glass, and wailing, wailing, all the while wailing without cease, a torrent of wordless woe a torment to hear, for all he did jam his hands to his ears to shut her out, as Aloysius, transported in the throes of looming death, rolled and thrashed and ghastly laughed alike, doing battle with his bloody blankets that rolled into knots that meshed him, sickly smiling as he screamed: 'Do it now! Do it now!'

The leering Banshee at the window wailed, as The Mad Monk, overwrought and spent, roared: 'FUCK OFF AND BEGONE, YOU HAG OF HELL!' then swung back a hand balling into an iron fist, and ran at the window, and smashed the glass, the shattering shards cascading all over like falling stars, and then, without waiting to see if she was hurt or gone, huffing and heaving he began to grin again, an avenging angel towering above the bed of death, rubbing his hands and flexing his fingers, the better for well-meant murder, as O'Muadaigh lay in the deep pool of his shadow, shining eyes bidding him do as he wilt, that he might to the better life come the quicker.

The Mad Monk bent over the bed, and sharply thrust two forks of stubby forefingers into O'Muadaigh's nostrils, which bled as they were jammed, and with his other hand clamped a heavy palm on O'Muadaigh's mouth, that he might not inhale nor exhale, the better to block his breath. And the man who was due to die complied peacefully, a slight smile playing on his thin lips. And so he was smothered and slowly annihilated. He twitched a bit initially, which was to be expected, but shortly then grew stiller, until soon he was unmoving, and thereafter moved no more, lost amid unending night.

And The Mad Monk threw back his head, and closed his streaming eyes, and with an immense effort of will contrived to rapturously imagine, and to bring into being by sheer dint of such effort, what it was they wanted, until soon it seemed to be so; and thus, in the hidden porches of his shut and darkened eyes, he saw the soul of Aloysius spring free from the lame cadaver of earthly carriage, clapping its hands and singing in joyous trill, borne on the tender gust of chimney smoke ascended, beyond the marmalade moon that was waxing, so steadily through space does our whirling world careen, buoyed ajar on an off-kilter spindle, like a butterfly giddily fluttering through the yawning firmament, cheerily skimming among the stars, skipping stones on a little pond, and the night sky was a sea, through which one swam, a deep sea diver, caught by the crashing waves of the wind that tossed you like a leaf, into the constellated ocean where stippled coral crags lay, the pebbles of planets, the rings of Saturn those of a sunken skiff, or rusting spokes of a bicycle spinning in a whirlpool, manned by its one-time skeletal peddler, the sunken hunter the drowned Orion, puny Pluto but a bubble on the brink of bursting, hurtling comets blazing jellyfish, the Milky Way the snail's trail of frothy sperm dripping from a virile whale, and the sea was shrinking the closer to the surface you swum, or either you were growing, goodly giant Alloy me boy, and soon you saw my sun was shining, his celestial rays puncturing the darkness of the deep, until then when you pierced the veil, and shot up on the other side like a darting dolphin, to spiral and cartwheel before falling again with a splash, shattering the stillness of the lake, and you floated, and paddled, and found your feet as you came to the shallows, and waded from the waters reborn a new man, hairy and bare of bottom, with a halo, as you came ashore again once more, and found a friend in the hermit Kevin, standing in silence on the sand with outspread palms, on which a bird had built a nest of twigs, and laid her blue eggs, hatching in a sweet eruption of twittering song, to which you hummed as you erected your own nest, by the lakeside built a beehive hut of clay and wattles, held in place by the paste of your spittle, a saint and sage's saliva, and lived forever thereon the life of peace for which you yearned, feeding on fish, and contemplating infinities, squatting by the lapping shore, to the dying echo of the singing spheres, resounding for eternity in a low hum, across the breadth of quiet waters – and then our kindly killer let fall O'Muadaigh's vacant head when he was dead, and back on the soft pillow his skull gently fell with a flop.

And The Mad Monk stood, and shivered, and heard the barking of the whining dogs as they banged on the door, for fear of the phantom, who had fled faraway; and so he let them in, and to the bed they bounded wagging in a brood, four pups of four bitches, and then he went out, and with a heavy heart he left that place, and wandered away into the deep black night. Exit the redeemer – whither would he wander then?

And when the O'Muadaighs came home with their children, they found Aloysius lying stiffly in his bed, empty eyes staring like a fish's, with the grin of a ghost, surrounded by the dogs who were whimpering, and while Wilhelmina froze, and Ulick gasped, young Paddy O'Muadaigh alone came forward from the family's huddled ranks, to lay a hand on his uncle's head, which was as cold as ice, and so then and there pronounced him dead.

And with many sobs and sighs, they all lamented his demise.

CHAPTER TWENTY-ONE

All was quiet in the residence of Mr Albert Potter, where not a sound was stirring, nor a breath of air leaked, no gust of wind to rustle up the leaves of pages of the many books laden with their dust, stacked in a jumble on tottering shelves sagging in strain. That place was an abode of books; they were everywhere, swarming and multiplying, seeming to copulate and fecundate, book begetting book with each and every fresh purchase, bought or stolen or grabbed from wherever. They took over, made the place their own, toppled down from their appointed niche on the shelves, tumbling to cram the couches, of which there were two, dropping low to litter the floor, to invade new territory, to mark their terrain, to vanquish and conquer. And they had all but won. One could tell just by looking at the place. It was a dark and dim subterranean flat, through whose cobwebbed windows little light was admitted, planted several feet under the earth, where the man lived as a mole, kept captive by his books. He had read them all, or at least tried to give that impression. The loot of the world's learning, all his, encapsulated and stored in these treasured tomes over which he daily pored and rooted and browsed, if only to grasp but a smidgen fraction of their wisdom, that would forever remain out of reach, for all he did try. Having read everything, it was said that all he now could do was merely reread, him for whom under the sun nothing was new, and nothing left in life for him to do, his copious reading leading him to barely but a brick wall, beyond which he would never get past, jammed in his crooked corner, stuck fast. And so he drank, drank heavily. And ample evidence for his drinking is also to be found in that place his flat, the colony of cans and barrage of bottles competing with the books for eminence, receptacles for the poison found lodged in his plant pots, or stored up in his sink. Drinking was his way of life – until, that is, he had a horrendous attack of diarrhoea one dark day, soiling filthy his dirty drawers as to the cubicle he frantically ran, bringing him to his knees there on the wet toilet floor, 'mid the mess and reeking stink. The body's revolt. And so the doctors deemed it meet to give him a death sentence, decreeing that drink was his destruction, thanks to which such over-imbibing he had only a scant eight months left of life to live.

'There can be no doubt,' said Albert from his bed where he lay, 'that Dr Johnson is quite right to say, that a man's mind is never more wondrously concentrated than when he knows he is to be hanged in the morning. It sharpens one's senses, gives one a new alertness, grants a clarity unforeseen, and makes each magic moment precious, especially when one knows, as I do, a rationalist, that this life is all we will get, and there is no happiness to be met in the hypothetical hereafter. O what a pleasing train of thought …'

He was muttering in his semi-sleep, his voice a dark and plummy rumble of velvet, muttering as he rolled over on his side, the rolls and flabs of his flesh akin to so many waves and rivulets on the simmering rippling sea, his skin that quivered as jellied water. His bed was an ocean, a mound of blankets and sheets and towels heaped atop its creaking mass to suffocate the sleeper, a soup into which he nightly sunk, to sleep deathly as a drunk, to toss and turn and grunt, his mind a muddle. He slept nude, as bare as he was born, and many were his tracts and folds of flesh, for of the naked Albert there was a lot to go around. One might call him a fat man – or a large man – or a chubby man – or a plump man – or an overweight man – or a morbidly obese man – or a strong man. For he was simply too big for the world that struggled to contain him, in which he was ever outcast, life fitting him like a glove or shoe a size too small, the perennial misfit – an ungraspable giant, whose barrel body and trunk and belly and thighs constitute a world of their own, the Planet Potter, one might say in forgivable flippancy.

The bulk of Albert in his bed, quietly muttering in his unsound slumber, his pork hidden by lank blankets that bestrew his body, damply sticky with sundry secretions, from pores of sweat, or a dripping penis, there in his bedroom, second principal room of his flat, the other chamber of the heart that was his house, linked to the living room by means of a connecting passage, a constrictive vein tightly lined with bony shelves, meeting the ghastly toilet along the ventricle's narrow way. The toilet was in particularly poor condition this season, for Albert had been having problems with his plumbing, and could no longer flush away his festering faeces with the previous ease to which he was better accustomed. For the tide of sewage had been blocked midway along the pipes, obstructed some way, somehow, and being thus blocked, could not go to where it should, but rather came up bubbling from the dismal drain to flood the flat, to poison his plants trembling in their pots, to make his home unwholesome, to give him anguish. If ever he received a visitor, which was seldom – he was a lifelong loner who did not encourage company – a pungent aroma would assail their nostrils as they descended the steps from the square outside to make timid entry through his grubby door, giving them pause to wonder at the cause, and then the sight of sewage, clotted and manky, seeping up from under the door, would be enough to turn them hastily on their heels away.

Albert had done what he could to contain the damage, scooping up shit with a spoon to fling it away over the wall, ruffling a few more feathers, but it was never enough. His friend Eugene Collins had also done his bit to help, being possessed of a pair of rods, long and cumbersome yokes that he would stick down the drain's gaping hole, to push and shove back and forth, sweat clouding his bald brow and steaming his spectacles (that readily ran the risk of getting speckled by shitty droplets), as he struggled in vain to get the flow going again, upon occasion rewarded with a faint gurgle as the foul matter made motion, such gurgling all too rare. And Albert would sit aside on the steps at the sidelines, squatting like a very Buddha, seeming to swell, his size morphing with every breath, with a lordly air looking on calmly at his friend's devoted labours on his behalf, making random remarks to temper the trial, dispensing worthless advice on how best to push or grip, or sometimes likening the tedious chore of shoving rods down holes to something else altogether – 'It's rather like fucking, isn't it, Eugene?'

And Eugene Collins would pause, and mop his brow, and say quietly, with a rictus of a smile, through gritted teeth:

'Yes, Bertie, it is, yes – but Bertie, this fucking sewer of yours is too disgusting for words, would you not think of getting a professional to look at it? All I'm doing is stirring it up.'

'Ah well now, Eugene, the expense you know, I'm a man of modest means, life is hard, and there's a recession on the way, so we've heard ...'

'Bollocks. We all know you're loaded. I've seen those deep pockets coming down with cash. And what me and all the other boys are wondering is, how do you get by? How do you manage to drink so much on so little?'

'By spending nothing on nothing else. My expenditure is carefully calculated, each transaction delicately weighed beforehand to test the pros and cons. You look unconvinced. I suppose it would be foolish to deny that I do not have my secret ways and means, doing the odd bit of double dealing on the side ... I have the dole, that's more than respectable, but then the repo business also brings in a few quid, though it's uncertain ...'

'And the loan from Harry, eh?'

'Hush! Less lip out of you on that score. That Carson creature bears a deep grudge. Still, when last we met, we got on amicably enough, I thought ... rather like Achilles and Priam in the tent, I felt, juh juh juh? ...'

'His own funds are lessening. Granny Marge is all he has left, and she's not dead yet. He'll be glad of that grand you owe him. Either that, or he'll stick a knife in you.'

'No, no, no, Harry is a Protestant gentleman, of excellent southern stock, and would never do a fellow as myself an ill turn, we're in the same boat. A knife, you say? How vulgar! We are not Italians!'

'You do have the look of a beardless Borgia, though, seen from down here at this angle – ah fuck! My glasses have fallen in!'

'Oh dear, you'd better fish them out, I suppose ...'

Then the dream dissolved: Albert was subject to a rude awakening.

Into the flat an intruder came blundering. The first sign of the intrusion effected was the sound of the front door creaking open, and the rustle of his soles as he rubbed them on the doormat, having plodded through poop to get there. At the noise, Albert, whose hearing was always acute, started up from sleep, sitting bolt upright in his hectic bed, like as unto a lunar landscape with its crags of cushions and sloping blankets, his ears pricked, his froggy eyes set deep in their pouchy sockets swivelling in a riot from side to side. Who the fuck? But he did not stay long to fall prey to panic, quick to make his move, ever brave. With a snarl, he freed himself of the sheets pinioning him to the moonscape, and rolled from bed in a sweaty fluster, feeling fury that his fortress be breached, and set down heavy feet on the floor, plotting his attack, eyes alighting on the machete by his bedside, a shining cleaver of which he was fond, which bending swiftly he grabbed, in the mood for murder, homicide justified for being provoked. And with weapon in hand, he tiptoed to the bedroom door, breathing heavily, and crouched in the darkness, listening intently to noises from the living room.

The intruder was the son of the landlord who owned the property, situated on the west side of Mount August Square, sole son of the trim family who lived above Albert, with whom they had some sketchy arrangement, none of it on paper, agreeing to let him live in their basement for a specified thirty-five years – as if he'd live that long! The family generally got on with their tenant, though they could not deny that they found him a queer fish who drank far too much in their abstemious eyes, and whose lurid existence they tried to keep a secret from their affluent neighbours. They also took issue with his unsightly behaviour of some years before, at the time he had his fling with his last lady friend, with whom he had a passionate affair, passion he flaunted, making fervid love to her in the garden, on shameless display to the eyes of all, to their consternation. No pleasant sight was the Potter posterior, no pretty thing to see the broad buttocks of Albert as they heaved and shoved and pumped and ground on the grass. Still, that was about the most outrageous of his escapades (that they knew of), and it was all in the past, thanks be to God, their subsequent squabbles having been over matters more minor, over little things like an excess of noise at night, or rent overdue, as was the case today.

The landlord's son, sent down by his father to bully the lodger and squeeze out of him the cash since last Friday owed, had found the door unlocked, and felt scant qualms about barging in without knocking (through the putrid swell of sewage did make his heart skip a beat, and his nosewings tighten). But once inside, in that nether realm, which knew little daylight, standing uncertain in the midst of the living room's rubble, amid books and bottles, unwashed plates and decaying kitchenette, wilting plants and couches host to tomes, he grew nervous, felt new fear, there amid the debris looking very out of place, a gauche youth of twenty summers, pimply and weedy, foreign to this alien abode of books and beer. He looked around the room, looking for a trace of the man he sought, who was not there yet whose brooding presence was eerily palpable, infecting all the mass of assembled objects with its implacably solid aura, every stamped item that bore his trace and mucky fingerprint, dusty objects that seemed to wince and coil at the shaft of unwelcome sunlight that fell through the open door, light admitted to the crypt, to the displeasure of its denizens. And made unwelcome by the hostile silence that hung over all, the landlord's son shivered, and resolved to fast get the business over, stepping over a discarded lampshade whose fabric was ripped, noting darkly that the smoke alarm had been torn out of the cracking ceiling, clearing his throat, and calling out weakly:

'Mr Potter, are you there?'

There came a terrible pause, in which he strained his ears to catch any sign of life, seeming to hear in the silence the soft tread of a bare and suspicious foot, lurking somewhere in the shadows, in the abode's darkest abyss of blackness, over in the area he knew to be that of the incumbent's bedroom. And stifling what fear he felt, doing his best to be bold, he had a mind to march on over there, to confront the idling ogre who would not show his face, to make his father proud, when suddenly there came a reply to his query that made his blood run cold, and froze him to the spot where he stood, as he heard a voice that spoke to him from the darkness, low and gravelly and laden with menace, the dark rumble of an expiring whale rolling over on the deepest ocean's nethermost floor:

'Mr Potter does not take kindly to uninvited visitors.'

Then the landlord's son was met with a vision, one conjured up from hell's blackest pits. Out of the shadows into a ray of the weak sunlight stepped the man he sought, but not in a guise that was appealing. For the landlord's son was privy to the sight of a naked man clutching a carving knife, a large fat mass of flesh that waddled forward to meet him, a devil brandishing a cleaver emerging from the darkness, in the mood to hack at a throat, taking swipes in the horrified air to imply the deed he would do, gnashing his teeth, leering lips contorting wetly in a bloodthirsty smile, his demonic eyes bulging with malice, naked, all too naked, all too much of him, too much flab and belly and nipple and navel and muscle and sheer mass, too much to swallow on a weekday morning not long past breakfast. And the landlord's son gave a gasp, and backed away, choking, struggling to quell the scream that welled within him, his mind gone blank, heart aflood with horror. And then the naked fat man came further forward, bounding archly in ballerina skips on his frog's feet, raising his knife, whose deadly blade caught a shard of falling sunlight and shone, casting a glinting radiance all over the room's murk, illumining the dim, casting hither and thither its heavenly rays, rays that lit up all the mass of bare body before the quailing youth backed up against a bookshelf, whose eyes were drawn irresistibly down, down, anything to avoid the burning eyes that glared him down, drawn down by the slanting lines of light that lit up all his nether regions, gaze descending to rest on the lower parts below the belly, the large legs squatly stood, and the fishing tackle between them, crowned by a small forest, the pendulous balls dangling and knocking, but the other thing, no, not that, the greatest horror of all – erect, solidly stood up a cruel poker of a porker, purple and squinting with one narrow eye, manhood's cyclopean sceptre, an engorged trident set afire, all too, simply too, just too, too … stiff.

And all this was coupled with the dark voice that growled again:

'Fuck off to hell or else I'll chop you in two.'

The landlord's son screamed and fled helter-skelter through the door of the hellish abode, up steps back to the square's safety, stepping in shit on his harrowing way, screams dwindling the further he fled, 'til soon he was gone again, and calm descended.

Albert, nude in his living room clutching his machete, was pleased with how he had handled that caper. He lowered the knife and sighed. Conscious of the faint chill in the air that blew through the door left open, which he felt all the more given his vulnerable nude state, he quickly shut the door, closing out the sunlight and the sight of shite leaking from his sewer, casting his abode into its accustomed darkness once more, and this done, he made room for himself on his couch, shoving aside an impertinent pile of books heaving in a mass of cluster, and thereafter sat down on his sofa.

Toying with his knife, recollecting the scene that had passed, embellishing its outlines with details the more grisly to make for a story more sordid, chips of wood to add to the fires and embers of his waning legend. He also felt the beginnings of trepidation, even guilt – after all, to indecently expose himself like that, to the son of the man in whose basement he resided, well, hardly the wisest of moves. But feck it all anyway, said another feckless voice from the other side of his skull, it will all blow over. And it would, more often than not, so he'd found over the scattered course of his ragbag life's dissolute lope. Doubts thus dismissed, he came to ponder on the new day that had dawned, on deeds that may be done and errands in all his mighty errantry he may run, if there were any, and indeed there were none – he always did his utmost to ensure he had nothing, or at least little, to do, leaving all the more time to read and think and drink, all those things today he would do, may begin with a bookish bout to complement and make way for the later boozing – was he cutting down on drink? – feck no, what could a quack tell him that he did not already know, let him lead his life his own way – oh hush, pray, scoop up a book to read, yes, he would read.

So he rummaged through the barrage of volumes sat beside his naked eminence on the sofa, taking pains to choose which to reread, which he had not yet reread to death. Dismissing *War and Peace*, dismissing *Tristram Shandy* (edited with an introduction and notes by I— C— C—), disparaging *The Idiot*, flirting with *Gulliver's Travels*, toying with *The Brothers Karamazov*, he elected in the end on *À la Recherche du Temps Perdu*, the one book he seemingly never exhausted, for all that he had read it umpteen times. And so he licked his blubber lips, and turned to the familiar title page, the paper crackling with its age and its curling edges fraying brown, a joyous glaze falling over his froggy eyes as he was transported, sedately sat on his sofa in all his naked flabby grandeur, a mountain of man, a swelling blob, a ballooning little planet alone in another better world, cocooned in his solitary pleasure, levitating in his quiet rapture as he read, beginning to smile once more again, perusing Proust for the thousandth time.

CHAPTER TWENTY-TWO

The Mad Monk's Doggerel Epic History, contd. (Part Three of Three)

... From my stagnant bones my green flesh decayed,
And in my guts the worms a banquet made;
Soon my sockets were empty of my eyes,
The jellied balls nibbled all by fruit flies;
Some shards of beard clung still to my skull's chin,
And my robes of mould stank my stale coffin.
Oberon then caught wind of my demise,
As told by one among his chicken spies,
And decided he would covet my corpse
(Prime jewel in his museum, of course),
To which end he despatched a grave robber,
Armed with his harp and a scumbag's honour,
Braving the ocean's frenzy of its sharks,
Scuttling into my tomb in black of darks,
His harp's twittering benumbing Sherman,
My coffin's guardian to shoo the vermin,
And as soon as the simple sentry slept,
Swiftly off with my bones the demon leapt,
Stealing away to some laboratory
Where the restorer stalled his oratory
In order to clean up my skeleton
He dismantled, dreaming of Babylon
As he greased my hips, for this restorer

Was my same good old friend, the Puck of yore,
Once my drinking companion in Babel,
Sporting now his surgeon's gloves and scalpel,
Lumping on new clods of caking baked muscle
And freshly fried organs onto my shell,
Upon my meagre frame he clad again
With skin and blood, and, when spruce, I was then
Transferred to Oberon's plush gallery,
A monument built for his family,
Stuffed like an animal behind his glass,
All orifices sown up (it was gas!),
Doomed to be a waxwork among waxworks,
A miserable fate that knew no perks.
Meanwhile Watt had dared to venture inland
Again, to confront the encroaching hand
Of Acrille's metropolis. Once onshore,
And reunited with his friends once more,
As they sat in a bar and dourly mulled
Over days they had seen with voices dulled,
Sipping their whiskies and choking their sighs,
There came unto them a chap with bright eyes,
Weathered and doddery, shabby-genteel,
With battered bowler he doffed with great zeal,
Twirling his bow-tie and salty whiskers,
As bold he claimed, mid scurrilous snickers,
That he was prophet of the coffee-room,
Come to foretell what fate for them did loom,
Predicting both tragedy and triumph,
And furthermore (at which Watt mumbled 'humph!'),
They had best get back to their island fast
To behold the wonder before it passed.
As to what said 'wonder' was, he was vague,
Couching all in poetic fog, the fake.
He spoke of new dawns, of rebirth's marvel,
Hinting life stirred within their isle's hovel.
That last caught Watt to the quick – swift they dashed
After that. The prophet's old head then crashed
Down upon the table, his duty done,
Free to drool and watch the arc of the sun,
Free from the madhouse wherein he was kept,
Into which the goons hauled him while he wept,

Reckoned unfit to look after his niece,
On whose padded walls he scrawled flocks of geese,
Raving of monsters all the while he daubed,
Crying her name to the harpy's applause,
My daughter's name, that same spinster alone
In our hilltop house where she made her moan,
An uncle and a father lost and found,
Her sad wintry life ended when she drowned
Herself in our pond by the lank willows,
But that came much later – me breath billows.
Meanwhile and earlier, while Elijah drooled,
Back in Faerie-Land where Oberon ruled,
A conspiracy was hatched, by the Puck
And his fellows, to pilfer, nip and tuck
As much of the King's Promethean fire
As they could afford to steal from the sire,
And to apply its flames to my dead limbs,
And restore my life – loveliest of whims!
Would that I could have composed such great hymns
In their honour – cunning Puck cuts and trims
My beard, sly Pooka pares my dirty nails,
And fairies catch my refuse in their pails.
Scrubbed and tidied like a revamped statue,
Liquid fire basted bones like snotty dew,
Until I awoke, lazily opened
An eye long closed, with gleam that betokened
I'd learnt lots since I slid from Mammy's womb.
Translated back to my desert isle's tomb,
Sitting on my coffin grinning smugly,
Breathing again the air with baby's glee,
Learning how to blink with a newborn's joy,
Flexing my fingers like an infant boy,
I lay quiet, awaiting Watt's return,
Fearing that his comrades might choose to spurn
Me, like the devil in an old friend's shape,
A macabre ogre born out of rape,
But this was not to be the case. For when
They saw me, every one of those good men
Was all exceeding joyous then and glad,
And though to say so makes me somewhat sad,
Only after death did I start at last

To truly live – my indolence was passed.
With nary a breath, I rose up and swore
That we would wreak revenge at our foe's door,
And wage war upon the loathsome Acrille,
Whose vile city we set alight with skill,
And watched its towers of greed blaze and burn,
Steeples asunder to make the worm turn,
Crawling our way through the wreckage to seek
The horrified overlord, the charred freak
Whose throat Watt slit; and we caught the Wizard
Whom I imprisoned, just as he deserved,
In a glass box, to make him learn manners.
Whooping our glory, we sailed with banners
To greet the fairies, our laurel's honour,
Where all was not well – Oberon's bower
Had become his harem, and I was shocked
To find my wife kept in a dungeon locked,
Whipped and beaten, the King's favourite sex slave.
Sick I was to see how grossly the knave
Had used her to satiate his rough lust,
And without ado, I squashed him to dust.
What a nerve he had to make me cuckold
While dead, while she was trapped in his stronghold!
I thrashed him to pulp, though I owed him all,
Feeling hero's hate as I watched him sprawl,
Bald defiler of my spouse, scalp uncrowned
As he whined defeated, prone on the ground.
My wife freed, the Puck and Pooka banished,
I pointed them to a place untarnished,
A homely hut on a tall desert dune,
Where they have abided many a moon.
It was Watt and I who brought them there,
And there, upon a whim's jovial snare,
Having heard her express admiration
For this gnomic dwarf of noble station,
That I persuaded Watt to woo and bed
My wife, midst shifting sands and moon's godhead,
An amiable cuckolding for sport.
Call me perverse, perhaps, a twisted sort,
Scant harm came of it, save gross dishonour,
Heightened when, afterwards, to our horror,

Having returned to our hilltop haven,
Our final refuge, we met my craven
Daughter, whom Watt proclaimed to be his wife –
There be that twist of tale, that flick of knife!
My own poor wife thus his mother-in-law –
Incestuous nest unforeseen we saw!
Ever after Watt thought far less of me –
I was a mere man, of stupidity
Surpassing that of most, no hero-god
Nor glorious redeemer of Earth's rod.
Otherwise all was for the best of peace –
Wrath cooled; Elijah returned to his niece
Who welcomed him home, and I embraced him,
Begging forgiveness – his eyes of cherubim
Showed up all my vain follies and ill faults,
But he, free at last of asylum's vaults,
Glad only to breathe, with ease forgave me,
Content instead to hear my history.
As it was, we passed many happy years
Secure in our commune of laughing tears,
Drinking and jiving and making babies –
My daughter bore Watt a girl, sweet ladies.
Yet as it must to all of us, death came
Knocking us down one by one, the old game.
Soon only Watt, his child, Sherman and I
Remained to hold up our family sty,
Whistling alone in our cavern of ghosts,
An idyll interrupted when, mid toasts
To the departed, a biographer
Showed up to be intrepid chronicler
Of a proposed Life of Watt, whose renown
Was widespread. Infirm now, in greasy gown,
The old man was all too willing to talk,
While his devotee doodled in fine chalk
Depictions of the yarns he spun, and told
The grand tales that I myself was so bold
As to embellish and embroider fine –
I was co-author – this was a goldmine!
The task was long and taxing; Watt grew pale,
His beard went white, his health no longer hale.
Excess of speech drove him nearer the grave,

So I took over – too late him to save.
I wrote the script that the younger man drew;
Day by day our tower of pages grew.
I beefed up my own role and stole the show,
For mine was the star part, I'll have you know,
And Watt well knew I plunder'd his thunder,
While his life was diced and laid asunder,
But such trite concerns were beyond him now,
And soon as mourners by his bed we bow,
Straining to catch his last words and wishes,
One of which was neither sick nor vicious,
And that was that his daughter Winifred
Should marry his biographer Alfred,
Which deed was done, and I was their witness,
To their delight, and his dying gladness,
And the old dog died then, too soon to see,
Complete with epilogue, his history
Bound, printed, published and browsed far and wide.
I took my leave of the lovers, who cried,
And carried his corpse back to the desert,
Where he would be safe from every hazard.
As for me, I did not overlong stay –
Having died once, I dared not waste a day.
For oft I did remember how Alfred
Suggested, nay, had eagerly offered
To write my own grandiose chronicle –
As subject, I was as much a marvel
As Watt was, whose book needed a sequel,
And I was matter made and equal
To the task of providing incident,
Stuff of a romantic or loony bent,
And so I made it my mission of late
To cross the seas before my strength abate,
And come to this isle, and fresh wonders work,
New friends find, new loves forge, and, with a jerk,
Pull the fatal plug on what vice I can,
Cultivate this land for tomorrow's clan,
And lastly, turn back time, and build again
A lighthouse of happier dreams, graven
In gold on vellum or papyrus scrolls,
With cast made up of all the finest roles.

Here now in our caravan we wake late—
Such a sweet whimsy that we met, good fate!
You alone shall be my wise muse, my love,
And strengthen me ever to onward shove.
Mark well what I say to thee, dear Maggie—
Welcome to my next ABODE OF FANCY!

CHAPTER TWENTY-THREE

Having breakfasted, on some stale ham he found in his fridge, and covered his nakedness, slipping, with strain, into tight black garments, that struggled to contain the loot of his lard, Albert Potter now felt the old thirst descend upon him, that could only be assuaged by a wetting stint in the local. And so he quit his abode, and mounted the steps to the air, and from Mount August's sunny square through the tunnel he strolled, emerging under the arch onto the avenue, crossing the road to the pub that he loved, The Mount August Inn, as owned by Mr Merriman, who was a meanly spendthrift sort.

And the portly publican, balding and glaring, greeted him customarily sourly, as he crossed over the threshold and came to the counter to quaff his daily share.

'You're starting early,' Merriman said with sneer.

'I'm keeping you in business!' Albert jocosely rejoined adroitly, as he hoisted his heaviness onto his corner stool with a struggle, and settled in his seat with a sigh, the crack of his pulpy buttocks poking out of his trousers.

A pint of Foster's, the cheapest the place provided, was duly poured, and set down before him, to be roundly slurped and swallowed, for he dealt in quick slugs and rapid gulps (any longer lapping would provoke an excess of introspection), and set back down empty, to be promptly replaced.

And so, at leisure in the lounge, with all that he needed, Mr Potter surveyed the scene in pleasure, for he loved the pub at this bright and early hour, when no lights needed be lit, since through the open door the sun was shining, the bejewelled motes skipping on the sunbeams, slanting columns of shimmering dust, radiant rays that shone rosily red through the coloured window, the golden light that fell in glimmering diamonds on the tables, on the stools, on the sleekly curving counter, on gleaming glasses, heavenly illuming all such surfaces, that afforded him such solace, and made him wonder why anyone would ever want more from the world than what there was to simply see; and, whenever the wind had a mind to blow, little leaves would enter meekly by the door, borne on the tender gust, inwardly wafted to litter the carpeted floor, over which so many sodden soles of drunken shoes had unsteadily trodden; and the lounge, which was distinct from the bar, as divided by a rigid partition, to quarantine the undesirables, a Victorian notion of Merriman's, of which Mr Potter quietly approved, the better to keep the peace, for he loved the lounge for its serenity, a placid place that knew no squabbles, or very seldom saw them, such as was conducive for his thoughts and ponderings, for he was always an advocate of a man's birthright to do no more than sit and think, and if the drink alone could help him think, so be it, so thought he, as he lifted to his lips his second, and duly drank it down, to whet and quench his thirst, with a smack of blubber lips, the lower loosely hanging, so shaped through years of wrapping round the rims of glasses to gulp, wet lips that so often did dribble, the dribble of saliva that did dry, as it trailed like a snail to his chins; and so he thought, and did not talk – his companion Merriman was no talker anyway – and for the while he thought of his chess, one of his gentlemanly accomplishments, in which he was among the country's champions, a shark, and briefly he mourned the dissolution of the Chess Club that used to cluster there on Tuesdays, whose company so oft he would join, to break the monotony of his solitude, for Eugene Collins was one among their number, for whom he bore a great affection, the son of whom, one Simon or something, was also a sometime regular of that August place; and so too was Harry Carson a chess-playing member, Harry to whom he owed much money, whose gaze these days he could not meet without a qualm of conscience; and among them also was little Jim Bateman, whose fragile mind was so prone to crack – whenever he started composing poetry, it was a sure sign his sanity was slipping (one among his better productions being: 'One Plus One Equals Two, except when you are in love, when One Plus One Equals One!') – who had lately cracked again, to be put in John of Gods, where Albert had visited him at Halloween, at which time all the inmates were clad in costume, which made for a troubling scene, what with ghouls and zombies and trolls eerily traipsing around, hugging the whitewashed walls, one tall man who held in a headlock a dribbling smaller, while one tried to converse with a gaping loon that was one's erstwhile drinking companion, one who barely no longer knew one; and then there was the elder man Arsene O'Colla, eccentric Wexford book dealer, with an addled mind no less prone to cracking, Arsene who was the only one among them who could match Albert's prowess at the noble game, only Arsene who was a similar topper of tournaments, Arsene the weatherman whom Albert had not seen in maybe fifteen years.

After some pensive hours had passed without incident, Matt the Electrician came in the door with a stumble, hailing Albert with a cordial mumble, as to the counter he came, hopping atop the stool by the bulk of Potter's side, to be granted by Merriman a bottle of Lucozade, for any other stimulant made his hand and heart shake and patter overmuch.

'What's the best news, Matt?' said affable Albert.

'She left me again.'

'Ah.'

And then they sat in silence for a goodly while, the two of them just, secure in a content of quiet neither bothered to break, loving the company of one another, neither having anything to prove to each other, the flabby Potter staring into space with a smile as he sipped, Matt the harried handyman (absentminded and saintly, of the county Limerick born, where by the Jesuits he was summarily beaten as a boy) perusing the paper, to come to the crossword, which it was his daily joy to do, which small victory served to swerve the train of his thought from his bereavement by his leggy broad, some of which crossword clues, the more obscure that bewildered his brain, he read aloud so the other man might answer, for Albert was the sage among the soaks, the bright spark often grilled by Merriman over impertinent matters of history, such as eluded their idler understandings, the resident intellectual whose thoughts were on a higher level, such as was belied by his corpulent carriage, his outward form and guise that of a grubby little alcoholic – yet what a piece of work was that man, and what a sight, his face! – for there was something apish there, Neanderthal nearly, from an earlier time and era, his face the face of our ancestors, a study to make Darwin drool, the way it was chiselled like the rocky face of cliff, something so hard and iron unflinching lay there, a bull unbending strong, and at the same time so jelly flabby, so fleshy with all its folds of fat, the loose hanging lower lip seeming wetly to betoken a soggy stupidity, and something then again of a ghost of Rembrandt's face was there too in Albert's face, and so tender a compassion and wise, such a kindness and gentleness there too that shone in the blue and liquid froggy eyes – and so to this man it was that Matt read out his clues:

'English author of picaresque novels who –'

'Fielding.'

'Internationally renowned chess player who –'

'Kasparov.'

'To which virtuoso violinist was Beethoven's Opus 47 dedicated?'

'Rudolphe Kreutzer.'

'Kreutzer will fit ... bejaysus, but you're fairly the clever fucker, Bert ye brainbox, what the feck are you doing in here drinking all day, eh?'

Albert only grunted, and sipped anew from his Foster's.

Matt's sentiment was shared by Donald the Barrister, who arrived inebriated, and, having given the ins and outs of the Four Courts case he was handling, for which Albert provided his usual expert analysis, no stranger to the legal system, with a lawyer's voice, the drunken barrister, as was his custom, began to chide Mr Potter for wasting his life:

'... Albert, please, do us all a favour and get up off your arse, for fuck's sake, I hate to see a man with a brain like yours pissing it all away against the wall, this fucking country needs you, for fuck's sake, honestly.'

To which Albert replied, very gravely and solemnly, with a sad smile:

'No. It is too late.'

The rounds kept coming, and when his dimes began to dwindle, at three o'clock, the tedium to temper, he took a cumbrous long lope to a Baggot Street ATM for cash to get, waddling by the canal en route, the scenic detour, the usual utmost extent of Mr Potter's daily perambulations. By the banks in bliss so then did Albert lumber, for so well he loved the water and the trees with their falling leaves, the ducks and swans and gulls that glided by, feeling joy to see ripples of sluggish water dappling flowing, to walk the paths by banks adorned with dead leaves of dying trees, pausing in his lumber to watch the water, stopping and bending to look into its dark depths. But the sight of his own fat face, reflected in that water, had been no happy spectacle to see. So he did not look for long, but rather went on to walk, and listen to the trickle and crash of the canal as it fell by the lock, the roaring torrent of waterfall. Beside the bronze Kavanagh he'd stopped again the scene to savour, standing by the crank at the bank, the green man and fool. And beside Paddy he'd sat down awhile, and knew for a time a peace. And the thought crossed his mind that this was a fit spot to set a play. And he wondered a short time why this had never been done. And he wondered if it was up to him to do it. And then a lone heron, keeping vigil on the bank beyond to watch the fish, had spread its wings with caw, and took off, and flew. And thus to his idea did it in parting a blessing seeming impart.

But nothing would come of it. The idea waned and died, as did the ailing fly who came to the counter to die, impotently buzzing, crawling pitiably around by the base of his beer, to be crushed by Mr Potter's fleshy palm, as it came smacking fatly down.

The hours dragged, and the minutes slipped by, and the sun climbed higher and fell, and customers came and went, and the day darkened, and behind the counter one saw the shifts of the rounds, as one who had his duty done passed on the baton to another one, as Mr Merriman retired to his nook on the floor above, leaving the business in charge of his minion Carter, who was the meaner barkeep, a sourpuss who seldom smiled, and the other one, Robbie, the kindly one, with voice of velvet, though his grip on a glass was jittery, and oft it was one's pint he would overfill and subsequently spill, but he was mannerly, and one's heart went out to him, being as he was an underdog, a husband henpecked, and likewise bullied by his peers, the hapless butt of Merriman's surly sneers, and his boss would berate and humiliate him for dropping glasses, cursing him in front of the crowd, once moved to cut his wages by half, for serving too slow and being too sloppy, a grief that Robbie bemoaned at length to understanding Albert in an undertone, to Potter who nodded in sympathy and sighed at his woes, for he well knew what it was to be down on one's uppers, gasping for breath like a dying fish stranded on a hostile shore, a world away from the rightful watery element in which one was at ease, and Albert sometimes thought he himself was something of a water creature, at home in the sea, and indeed he was fond of flaunting his flesh in the midst of the aqueous jelly, as he did down in Dún Laoghaire's forty foot, where once a week he bared all his belongings, and bathed in the nip, uncaring of who may see, oft bade desist by prudish old maids and cheeky little scuts, whose arms he would threaten to rip off, in the sinister bear's growl of which he was master, enamoured of his bountiful nakedness; and a similar story, of how he was accosted by the landlord's son this morning, he had already shared and regaled to his neighbour at the counter who was Matt, to cheer him up to help him forget his prodigal flame who did desert him, overegging the pudding to stress his self-proclaimed heroism, to the electrician's mild amusement, but still greater bemusement.

'I gave him a piece of my mind, I tell you, nude as I was, sent him packing like a frightened puppy, juh juh juh? I scared him so, the wretch!'

Maud the barmaid, who called Mr Potter 'petal' when she felt merry, but was very mean when she was not, then sundered his story by thrusting two empty glasses into his face, as harshly she hissed, with an axe to grind:

'See that? That's what you're supposed to be drinking – nothing! Nothing at all! What did doctor say, eh? Have we forgotten already?'

'Ah, but my dear, for me, my glass is always half full,' he replied charmingly, 'for you see, I was always an eternal optimist.'

Why, how many had he had? He had forgotten how many by now, but he knew that he had not yet drunk beyond his means, for all manner of small change yet filled his jangling pockets deep, enough to see him through to long last orders and belated closing time. It was his custom, and a small point of pride, to always be the last man in the Mount August as it shut. And even before that time came round, it was his habit too, as each and every dreary night wore on, to take to buying three pints at once, to get in as much as he could while he could, to increase and make a maximum of intake in the time allowing. And even then, when they shut out the lights at last, and catcalled and booed and shooed the sole sod not gone, egging him on to get up and go, even then was not yet the end for him. For then, upon a mumbled word, he would collect before going his typical 'take-out', a plastic bag of clattering cans passed over the bar to his flabby fist that proffered to pay what cash was left, a shifty transaction carried off shamefaced with stealth. And then, ushered, he would go and be gone, and steal away off into the night, with his plastic prize of bag of beer, to take away across the road and under the arch to home, where then to be guzzled, 'til he was full well tanked up, and on the couch conked full well out.

To each his own. All by now had gone home. Mr Potter drank alone.

But he was always alone, in one way or another. To be orphaned young had him for life left lonely. It was his mother who had died, his father who had fled. And it was this man who had left his foundling son abandoned to a second cousin, the harried stepfather, the only man that Albert ever loved, whose own subsequent death had shattered the resolve of his stepson. And this poor selfsame stepfather had been unhappily married to his mad stepmother, who used to kick her boy in the balls, as he lay bawling in the cradle as a child, the harridan who tore up the house, until her stepson, home from school in time to behold horrors, stepped in to give her a ritual dunking in the sink, only that that could quiet her. Misfortune begat a misfit. Even Albert Potter's very voice was an artifice, that accent so fruity rich as velvet posh, contrived and forged at a young age, when he'd remade himself, or so he said, to stand out from the drubbing Dublin drone of peers at school, when he'd become a new man, with a new voice to boot. It was around the time he was thirteen when he'd broken his arm, and had stayed home from school to heal, and once the arm was healed, had never again set foot in school. From then on an autodidact he became, the chip on shoulder ground, for he found that hours alone in the local library, browsing the loot of the world's best books, taught him more than any school or college could. And so he read, and thought, and drank, and stole bicycles, and became ringleader of a chain of gangs, and fought, and thought, and made money enough to cross the sea to travel a time, saw some of the world, went to England and Spain, and had some sex, and did some drugs and drank, and joined the British army, and did battle in the jungle, and killed some men, and read some more, and took up chess along the way, and became at that game a giant, storming the tournaments a colossus, racking up medals and prizes, a chess champion who went to Norway and Japan, and drank, and read the more, and took up kung-fu, and was a fighter, and broke men's bones, and went to Germany and Italy and France, and borrowed money, and grew in debt, and drank, and read the more and more, and so then in the end became all round a learned man. And what then, once he was become a learned man? What but talk trite talk to fill empty air, and drink until an early death? But what joy did the drink ever offer him, from the cup that did not cheer? These days he had not even the luxury of oblivion, of drowning in the dregs to forget himself, for the poison in his glass no longer even made him drunk – he was only, at the best of times, which were negligible, which were seldom to never, privy to a mild merriment and obscure elation. What then? What but waste for which he was doomed? And very soon he would be dead, and he would barely by any be remembered.

He took another gulp from his glass, swallowed and sighed.

And the warring pessimist in him now thought his glass half empty.

CHAPTER TWENTY-FOUR

So whither would ye wander then, o ravaged vestige, when you went and was lost to us for the space of a dark season midst the wintry wastes?

It was to the woodlands he went to seek some solace, trudging through prickly brambles, and stamping on the nests of nettles, that plagued his path and stung his crusty soles, as he bounded by a bit of bogland, and nearly got sank in the swamp. Alone he walked in the wood with heavy heart and leaden plod, feeling the chill of raving autumn sheathing through all the threadbare fabric of his robe, of which the sleeves and hems were tearing and fraying, browning like the leaves that fell from the balding branches as they shed, erstwhile tresses of the trees who lost their youthful looks, withering in the winter to ghostly bony stumps, chalk white in their decay.

He was lost, and he was being hunted, that he knew, hunted by the police, rampantly in hot pursuit of their lonely prey, whom they sought to punish for his criminal sins, those of thievery (that which was entailed in the robbery of the food that went uneaten), of verbal assault and battery (in the violated tourist office, to the scandal of the poor old maid), and finally, most malignly, of murder. It was the O'Muadaighs who raised the alarm, in grief and umbrage, for they had thought that they could trust him, this more than man who seemed a saint, and bitter their betrayal. Their enraged vision reddened, soon they were heaping all of the misfortune suffered by the deceased squarely on the shoulders of the swine who had posed as his saviour, going so far as even to assign the bite marks on the body as belonging, not to the White Dog, but to the weird old monkish man who came from nowhere and went by no name, yes, him it was who had bitten Alloy our boy and all but eaten him, their logic for this deduction resting on Wilhelmina's whimsical belief in werewolves. After all, he had had such peculiar yellow eyes, hadn't he? He was very hairy to boot. And the moon had been full that fateful night.

The guards on patrol, naturally, were sceptical about such a fanciful supernatural extrapolation from what scant facts were known (though they did acknowledge lycanthropy to be a viable possibility that history could readily support), but none doubted for an instant that foul play had occurred, and luckless O'Muadaigh had been murdered by a scheming blackguard who must needs be quickly captured. And so they lavishly launched their fervid manhunt, issuing descriptions of his person to all the television and radio stations, pasting posters bearing a scribbled facsimile of his face all over the walls of the towns, and on the swaying poles of the highways to which he may run, cordoning off all the surrounding environs to limit his frantic lope, and culling the grass in hope of his trace, and ransacking the corpse of Aloysius in the mortuary, rummaging and jumbling all over the pockets and pores of his deadness, that he might divulge further secrets concerning his slayer, who was vilified in the grubby tabloids, painted by the gutter press as a 'bloodthirsty psychopath' and 'cold-blooded merciless killer', and among the public, punters greedy for coarse sensation, vicious jokes were soon abounding about this 'Resurrected Rasputin', this 'Crackpot Capuchin', this 'Demented Dominican', this 'Cistercian Sociopath' (for they could never make up their minds from which order this alien hailed), as he became a figure of hate in the eyes of the islanders, made over into a man they loved to loathe, a national scapegoat who soon was even being blamed for the impending economic recession, which was looming large.

And so The Mad Monk was wanted for murder, and went on the run like a weasel. It was to the mossy woods he went to hide and hibernate, as the kindred creatures around him were snoring, the slumbering animals alone who bore him no ill, a lonely fugitive straddling the sloping hills, knee-deep in their clusters of forested bushes, seeking refuge among the crannies and nooks of jutting cliffs, from where he might espy from afar the officious male brutes below, combing the meadows in search of his prints, squeezed into their starchy uniforms like walking trout, meaningless medallions on their wheezing chicken's chests, boasting their puny cudgels and their newly patented newly fangled stinger guns, with which, if they saw him, they would shoot him on sight for to stun him, and thereafter descend upon him in a clucking swarm to net him, like the sailors and jocks on the liner so long ago likewise had done for him, in the faraway days when he was adrift on the ocean, rootless and free – and far happier in himself.

His mood in this season of setback was grim, though still he kept on stonily grinning, though his bright eyes grew dimmer and did not smile. His lofty aims on behalf of mankind he was obliged to put on hold, for aim of saving his own skin, keen to keep hidden until the storm died down, which would be a while in coming – he would be lucky if it were as soon as the spring. But how could he defend himself, how could he explain the frankly inexplicable, who would listen, who would understand him, a friendless outcast adrift in the dark, empty of sympathy and void? How could he explain that what looked like murder had been willed and requested by the slain transfigured, and who would believe that the soul of the lost was at blissful liberty now, squatting by a lake in another place at peace, a fate he might have wished for himself were he lazier, rather better than this tedious traipse through the wastes, a fox in flight from the oafish pack of dogs who lapped at his heels, the joyless plight of the scapegoat now his to endure?

'True greatness is never seen as such in its own lifetime,' he remarked to the nipping air over and over, to console and lift his despondent spirits. But then he would remember that his own span of years were now to be unending, and his lifetime of eternity, according to the glib logic inherent in his clichéd quip, was doomed to be forever clouded by antipathy always, and the malignant misunderstanding the masses bore him now would be constant and incessant. And thoughts as this made him feel the sadder, and all the more alone and lonely. Would that the Puck and Pooka were yet come to accompany him in this perilous place! But he was all on his own for now.

Then fortune took a turn for him. Mournfully wandering in the wilds in winter, with gloomy doleful tread, he came one day to an enchanted clearing in the woods, marked by the ghosts of mushroom patches, cooled by the whistling eddies of the wind. A glade once green and young, now deathly chalky as elderly bone of brittle skull. Snow was silently falling. The silver flakes descended from the grey sky to rest on his sagging shoulders, dusting his bristling beard like stars or dandruff. He shivered as he knelt, too old for fleeing, so weary of chase, knelt by the bank of what had been a babbling brook, a onetime waterway now frozen, covered all by cruel ice, the stream long halted in its cheery flow, blocked like the clogged artery of a hardening heart. He knelt by the bank of the frozen brook, and stretched out and lay on the icy ground, the falling snow enveloping him, his lowering blanket a coverlet. And he would have slept in the snow, uncaring of the cold, lying alone to dream of better days, had he not then heard a sound.

It was a cry, a stifled woman's wail, carried to his ear by breath of the wind, a plaintive call for company. And he seemed to hear in that oddly familiar keen a pining lament lovelorn, touching to the core his tender heart. He sat up sharply, and turned his head, seeking the source of the sound that moved and haunted him, and so it was he saw her. For there she was, surely enough, the same again he'd seen before, leering at the little mouth of a cave above him, on the edge of a conjured precipice that he wasted no time in proceeding to climb, all in thrall to her call. The Banshee, for it was she, was better looking by far than before, having hid her awful ugliness beneath a thickly laden layer of makeup, with tasteful lipstick liberally applied, gleaming dentures in place of her hitherto rotting gums, false pupils and false lashes fluttering to allure the one who climbed the crags to meet her, bewigged with a blonde and frizzy fright wig to cover her greasy hairball Medusa's knotty mass, a cracker welcome to all comers, having taken the trouble to tart herself up to thrill any wayward man who came by her way, like this handsome one here for instance, this shaggy hunk who dug his stubby claws into the niches of the cliff-face, as he clambered further upward, slithering sleekly like a snake up and up the slope, ever more eager, ever more hungry, ever more aroused. And his blazing eyes were flaring with quickly kindling desire, wick of the candle's flame of his throbbing loin's lust, as he smoothly scaled the sheer precipice, and made his mount, and stood before her, tall, dark and handsome, the dishy dude of her dreams.

Her keening wound up at once, and she fell silent, hotly breathing, belching bubbles of cloudy tufts of foggy breath in the swirling windy air, looking up with a crick in her leathery neck into the eyes of her towering admirer, who grinned, and gave her a dirty little wink (his signature stroke for seduction, it never failed him for wooing and winning). She blushed, lowering her bashful face to hide her shyly nervous smile, then mutely bade him be welcome, with a spindly gnarled arthritic forefinger beckoning him in, to enter her homely abode of a cave on a cliff. And The Mad Monk bowed lowly at her beckon, and, in beat with his bowing, briefly boldly wrapped his frostbitten lips all around her wrinkly prune of raisin's tapering finger, and sucked it tenderly, once, twice, thrice, from which chill of clinging lip she got a giggly thrill, and tittered, and then he stood and smiled, and she turned about and entered with a ballerina's pirouette, and he followed her stooping, ducking his looming height to fit in her frame.

Within her cave (whose dripping ceiling was low, obliging him to crouch and hunch and recumbently lie, which well suited their purpose) was a fire blazing in the glowing hearth, over which was dangling her soiled knickers on the washing line, and her puffing kettle, in which her yak butter tea was brewing, and all the gaudy wares of her colourful crockery, and all about the floor was draped a scarlet carpet of furry foxskins that she had collected and painstakingly knitted over many long and empty years, and on the rocky sloping walls her mementoes and memories humbly hung, sentimental monographs half hidden in the flickering murk (she was a spinster he assumed, until he saw the rotting ring on her finger, which would occasion comment in due course, post-impassioned coitus). And by way of a bed, she had a hammock hanging from the posts of two ancient tree stumps, felled by her own mottled axe, a swaying undulant riverbed with shawl of ferns, in warming mid-air serenely suspended, a bed of love into which the two were fast to fall, for they had no time to waste, certainly not at their age.

She led him there alluringly with her wagging curling finger, sighing moistly as she flung off her floral slip of rags, to unveil her shrivelled bodice that had known better days, 'twas fortunate that her figure be lit by the forgiving firelight, but he drank her up and loved her all the more, revelling in the drooping dugs of jelly he fondled, cupping her soft paps in his horny palms, as she dropped and slumped into the pouch of her hammock, and caressed and fingered herself, moaning wetly and stirring the juices of his vitals. And her godly lover grinned and gurgled, purring like a tomcat in scent of her heat, and likewise divested himself of his shawl, cascading a shower of wetting blobs from the melting snow as he tossed it away, and she gasped at the very size of him, the rippled miles and muscled miles of his hugeness, she couldn't believe her luck, she'd caught the biggest fish in the sea, hers, all hers, she was choking for that spermy whale who dithered, bending to pluck from a pocket a crystal vial he treasured, replete with the silvery slime of sea snail, the secret liquid of love, a known aphrodisiac that worked wonders on his own little wife, way back in moony days of lover's yore, and uncorked the container, whose glistening contents he poured all down her throat, into her mouth gaping to admit him, and she nearly gagged as she swallowed the stuff, and groaned, and thrashed in passion as it took hold of her, ballooning and gagging she clawed his hairy chest, and dragged him down abruptly on top of her, so heavy and huge he broke the flimsy hammock with his weight, and down on her doggy carpet in a riot of love the pair came toppling down, the impact of the crash driving him right up into her harshly, ah, o, so stiff, so sticky, so wet, flick, flick, flick, flick her woman's weedy beanie with yer dick, dick, dick, in, out, thrust and grind your purple prick, grunts and groans they emitted as they rolled, frothing she scratched his back and bled him, more, more, more, handling his harpoon in a fever, show and hide and seek the leak, their skins were spilling sebum as they sweated and writhed around, and he ploughed her mossy furrow cackling, his engorged trident set afire and bloating soon was spewing, a gushing geyser storming the volcano of her vulva, ah, ow, spew, gush, heady rush o blush, never, never known one to match him, not a lover, not one, and o, o, o, ooh … it was good.

(Phew!)

And so The Mad Monk and the Banshee met in a fever fit, and made hot love loudly and wildly. And they copulated together in such a fashion for some six or so days, trying out all the routines in the textbook, and varying the beat and tempo of the thrust, until soon they were all but exhausted, and the prodigious stock all but depleted, and the god in man all but unmanned, and so on the seventh day they rested, their work complete.

CHAPTER TWENTY-FIVE

'Christ!' The Mad Monk moaned in ecstasy, as he withdrew his dripping member from her mouth for a final time, 'Exhausted you have me, o most exuberant female! Insatiable nymphomaniac! How raw my old man doth feel! But by crikey's dicks – methinks these itchy bites on my bell end were administered by your own careless champers, no?'

'They were rather,' the Banshee grunted back (her voice was a croaking rasp, hoarse from a welter of wailing), as she wiped her lips on her soggy stays, replete with starch and stain that mingled with her minge's yeasty grain, 'It was just … too delicious.'

'Scrumptious!' The Mad Monk sighed, with a smack of his lips, as he fell back nudely on the semen-sodden furs of her carpet, clapping a palm to her pockmarked ass, her nutty buttocks dimpled by pimples and speckled by spots, dragging her back down to his belly to cuddle, 'This cave has fairly known fireworks. Never doubt the power of randy sea snail's humble slime. But my dear dove, come closer and kiss me, and chat to me, do, for Lordy knows we have spoken seldom if at all over this septet of sun-dawning days and sun-sinking evenings. To begin with, I must thank you fulsomely for your hospitality, and for lending me refuge when I was on the run.'

'It is nothing. I just liked the look of you when first I saw you.'

'By the deathbed, eh? I was rather rude to you upon that occasion, for which I am sincerely sorry. Heat of the moment overtook me, y'know. But wait, tell me now, if I may ask – do you have a name, m' dear?'

'In life when I was living, I was known as Megan Devlin – they nicknamed me Nutmeg since I was barmy. Mad Maggie of the duelling tribe of the bickering Devlins.'

'Really? "No shit", as my Stateside chums will sometimes say.'

'Ay. And now, might I in turn ask a question of you?'

'That you may, dearest Nutmeg.'

'Who made the world?'

The Mad Monk considered, stroking the grizzle of his bearded chin.

'Who made the world, Maggie? Me. I did. I see you when you're sleeping, and I know when you're awake. Yes. I, Madam – I am the man who made the world.'

'The man who made the world …' Banshee Megan Devlin dreamily purred, '… and what a lover too! I never knew a chap who could make me come like you do. Such a size!' (with a playful pat of his penis, coyly cupping and smacking his bloated sacs she tickled), 'Just look at the length of the lad!'

'Waay-haay-haay! Easy on now, petal! My ballooning balls are all gone burst! My todger is tender today. For you've drained it all out of me, you thirsty vixen, 'twill be some few moons before I am an upright man again. But enough already about me. What about you, Madam Maggie? Taking into account a remark you dropped earlier into my eager ear, it would appear that you were, eh, living and breathing once upon a time? That you have been, in fact, in life, a mortal woman? How does that come about?'

'Arragh, but don't you know, poppet, I was not always as you see me now. Being a Banshee is a tricksy knotty business, a post that wants its filling, a slot to occupy, a baton passed on, time after time, blooming from woman to souring woman, each becoming a witch and a bitch. We play the same part, you see, and wear the same mask, the lot of us resurrected divas and drama queens. And there have been as many of us Banshees throughout time as there's been crones who keen over the corpses of kiddies.'

'I see, faith. Not too negligible a notion, that of passing on the makeup kit, when one has had one's run at the role, said one's lines and done one's bit as best one could, with another budding understudy always waiting in the wings, to carry on the discarded torch. I could learn something from that. But how do you get cast? And by whom?'

'By whoever runs the show. I always assumed it was whoever made the world was our shadowy producer. So is it not you, then?'

'Never thought about it … if I am a puppet master toying with your strings, I assure you it is wholly unwittingly, a quirk of inadvertent fate.

Unless …' (his features darken and cloud, fear stealing into the hooded yellow eyes), '… unless old Elijah has a finger somewhere in this pie …'

'Who?'

'A sibling. An evil twin. The elder devil at my shoulder. My bad brother. Or is it me who is? Or am I he? There were many rooms in my father's house, through which we ran and played and battled as boys, and pulled one another's hair out. But never mind. We were meant to be discussing you, beauteous Banshee Maggie Nutmeg, one and only wintry queen of my heart, 'til the melting spring do us part, to render a running stream of our twinkling nuptial's icicles. But please – do tell me something of the life that you lived when you was a woman. Who were you and what did you do?'

'Ah well, only if you insist, dearest. I was born in a small wee place, they call it Athenry, a bit off the beaten track and plodded path, full of ferocious farmers who quarrel for their sport, with bitter tongues in their heads, and sharp knives in their deep pockets. My schooling was sketchy – it took place mainly in the local, unlicensed, after hours, where it was I learnt all my lessons in life when I worked as a waitress, spooning on the side whenever my pocket money was wanting. But O! such scenes of scandal I witnessed in my girlhood, as would scar a fainter heart than was mine, one that hardened. I remember one piece of work once telling another: 'You have a chest like a chicken', and getting a knife in his eye for taking pains to be cheeky. That was how me own father died, as it happens, the jousting Jasper, a wicked one, the like of whom will never be seen again. From him, my ever so naughty pimping papa, from whom it was I learnt all the ins and outs of whoring, taught to bare my pubescent budding bubs the sleazy counter crew would stroke and grope for a guinea, or whatever coinage it was we were using back in those misty centuries of long ago. How faraway now seem my wild young days of feckless freedom! My pride and joy, and the capstone of my temper that was so fast to flare, was my fiery head of glossy hair, russet red and luxuriant, my curls that were the delight of the drunks, and the envy of the other rival colleens, the spitting flirts.'

'Mmm. Oh, I'm certain sure you were no trifle, but a handful.'

'I was. And the rage of my wrathful race was instilled strong in my sparrow's chest, in my heaving breast that housed a storm. Often it was I would lash out at the local lads if they came too close, or boorishly overstepped the demarcated boundary lines of decency and prudery, which were rigid in them days – powerful were them priests in our grasping parish, and our people were pious, and so too was I a holy maiden in my way, for all that my virtue was mayhap, by bare necessity, somewhat besmirched and fatally tainted. But I sought saving, and many's the time I did my bit in the confessional's black box of night, spinning the story of my harlot's purple sins through the chinks in the wispy grille in a whisper, to the guilty pleasure of the dirty whiskey priest, taking sips on the sly from his compact grog, as he avidly attended to every sweaty detail of how I came to have my plundered maidenhead, fondling and sighing as he heard me bare it all, playing along with a touch of lilting spittle in me lisp to rouse the fool further, but I pitied him – for it was, after all, the only outlet those chaps had for their lust, snared in the crucible of their castrated profession that encourages impotence, only fit for geldings and eunuchs.

'But then there arose a time when I had to put a period to prostitution, and set aside all such assignations, in order to attain some scanty measure of propriety, and earn my living the decent way. And what did I become, would ye believe it, but only a schoolteacher, and a good one too – for I had a way of shedding light to which the children cottoned, turned on by the clarity I lit up on the fog of their little lives. So that was an end to my girlish giddy-gadding – gone were the days when I would flaunt my woman's wares, and haughtily toss the silky treasure of me locks – for now I cycled to school on a pennyfarthing bicycle instead, jingling me bell to accost the sweeping flock of yawning sheep who clogged the narrow lane, and waking the curious cattle who poked their sleepy heads over the stony walls to ogle me, as past their dull fields I glided by, red follicles done up in a spinster's bun and hid beneath a bonnet, the sight of my thighs shielded from view by a long and swaying skirt – that often got caught in the spokes of my slippery wheel, and made me come a cropper, as I dizzily wound in a weave spinning into the schoolyard, to the cheeky glee of my charges, their tousled heads peering out the chapped window of our musty classroom, grubby cheeks begrimed that beamed with joy as they chuckled at my clumsiness. But I was firm with them.

'And soon of course, there came that time of life when it was incumbent upon all us Devlin damsels to be betrothed, to snare some suitor to look after us, the done thing in them days. God knows we went to all the barnyard dances, did we ever, flighty colleens once more, where we stood in a giggly line angling to be asked by the stuttering hopeful, upon whose hopes we poured cold water with our icy rejections, about which we later laughed a lot, like a right catty pack of bitches, toying with the bleeding hearts of our victims. And it all went on for ages and ages in this fashion, as the shelf upon which we sisters sat came slowly to be cleared. And I was the last of us to be wed, the last of all of us to find a new bed, for I was picky, and prickly to boot, and it was a rare sort of man who'd put up with me moaning. It began to look like I'd never find my one and only, and my mammy worried, and wrung her teary palms she wetted as she fretted. But then –'

Banshee Megan Devlin hesitated, buried emotion's catch in her croak. And The Mad Monk, touched, watched her intently, noting the glance she gave to the weathering ring, a memento of marriage about which he had wondered, a faded gem set on the claw of her finger, her look of yearning that did linger, as the tears started in her red-rimmed eyes, wetly netted with bulging veins of searing scarlet ribbons. And he patted her shoulder kindly, to soothe her sorrow, while saying softly, to urge her on:

'Yes? What then? Do carry on. But then – ?'

CHAPTER TWENTY-SIX

Banshee Maggie the Seanchaí drew breath, and hastened on to say:

'But then I found him. Or he found me. St Francis Alphonsus Xavier that was, my solely only fearless Fran, my favourite Franny Joe, King of the clan of Collins, Donegal born and bred on yeasty barleycorn, hailing from the ebony valley of Dun Louis where the thieving badgers dwelt, where there lay a volcano way back in the long ago, didn't you know or not. A rocky land of lava swathed in the smothering grass that was so good to mow, and the honeyed hay of the harvest that always smelled so sweet, among which bales the bumblebees did hum as they built their hive, from whence it was from the piebald egg of his mum he came to me, my darling blue-eyed beau on a rickety bike, all the way from his originals come down to Galway town to make good.

'He was studious, and pious, and obliging, and kind, in training a doctor of medicine to be, a vocation about which he dithered until, whilst dossing after hours amongst Bunsen burners and a bevy of tumblers, he hit upon, amid the smoky maze of chemistry's web, the true joy and glory of his manhood, finding that he preferred the clink of an array of test tubes on a tray, and the heaving froth of their bubbly foam, to the more practical pleasure of heated fiddling with a cumbrous stethoscope, only to rootle out the deadbeat thudding of an offbeat human heart.

'But his own one was well warm, that I knew, that I deeply felt, though how I knew I ne'er could ever fully say, and where first of all it was I clapped my eyes on him also eludes – but no, wasn't it at the chuckling riverside's parish picnic where first it was we met, yes, he was in his reedy suit of dapper herringbone's tweeds, and his dipping cap of velvet felt, with his specs so shiny that made me blush from afar, flashing from the rippling light that fell upon their dimpled rims, as they eyed me up with intent at a slant, moved to approach me on pattering feet subtly weaving through the throng, and to idly chat about this and that, rubbishy nothings that sounded so nice, so soft and plush was his grainy voice of valley's breathy husk, to which I grew to long to listen and listen, all the days and nights of the weeks and years I could glow in tune to those tones, and perhaps I showed a little interest, after which he made his move, and maybe indeed a date was arranged, all alone and at peace by ourselves, somewhere secluded like the yawning yew by which, by day, both of us bicycled wheeling en route during our buzzing daylights, under a tree of sympathy where we practised our harlequinade of courtship, and won one another's fitful worship, carving our names in bliss on the bark, initials shelved within a little heart, vowing never from the other to part.

'And yes, I knew he was true, for I had known many men as you know, but never one for whom I felt such as now I did for this, one whose hand I would hold and hold and never ever dare unclasp, for he made me melt, and cracked the stern and brittle bitch's shell in which I came encased, and softened me, and mellowed me, and made me feel all mild and gooey inside. And, what's furthermore, my approving family found him to be a suitable suitor for me, for he was a marriageable man, bookishly in training to become a learned professor of his steaming chemist's art, a most eminently practical and respectable profession that knew no snags nor baleful hitches, from which fluting job he would in years to come a big bag of money for me make, o, he had simply everything and all about which we doting gurleens dreamt, security, and honesty, and looks, and wit, and ready cash in hand to hitch, too good to be true in so many far-flung ways.

'So he whisked me away, and made me his bride, done up to the hilt in the dress of a wren, with feathers in me hair and a rose in me blouse, and down the stony steps we skipped as a pair quite as cute as a button, linking our arms and joined by the hip at the waist, as before our cheering clans we joyously embraced. And now gone from the grasslands borne on a clattering carriage in a dreamy rush was I, hurtled down a highway into the raucous city of lights, into the metropolitan arena of mania so alien to a country hen like me, to giddy old Galway's teeming town through which the babbling Corrib flowed and skipped, wherein the smoking salmon hopped amid the churning hurdles of the stones of their wisdoms, there and then where we set up our house on a mount, in salubrious Lindisfarne set on Tailor's Hill, a miraculous mansion replete with rooms among which our hypothetical horde of kiddies could seek and hide in the rabbit's warren of their home, huge as a palace so it seemed to a bumbling bumpkin as myself, of a sudden strapped into an apron, and making for his lordship tea and toast.

'No, I flatter myself – for it was mainly he who served me – I was far too queenly and imperious ever to wait on one, no, not even he, unfailing Frankie mine, who always took my tantrums on the chin, and never stooped to bicker nor flag, unbending, never bowing, only he who fully knew just how to humour a harridan like me. For he loved me, truly did, and so too did I him, and he made me a mother come the harvest of the spring, siring urchins in a steamy pack, rearing up a sextet within my waiting womb that welled, and on the dot out of me they came popping in a trickle, four sons, all as bald of head as was he, and two daughters, both as bright and pretty as me, the names from the air we plucked like olives from the twig, truculent Trevor, and prickly Peter, and amiable Eugene, and shrewd Peggy Felicity, and Jacob Francis Hubert the sculptor and aesthete, and little Rosalind who was the last to arrive, a bit belated somewhat after her date was due, at a fallow time when all had thought my birthing days were dead and done. A barrage of births that robbed me of the fleeting bloom of my beauty, for so many childer in as many years coming in a crop that clung and stole my youth, such was my decade's worth of almost perpetual pregnancies, that my shifting moods of storm and gloom, up and down like a whistling tap through the tureen of a yoyo, meant that I was nearly daily depressed, such is woman's woe, the cross to bear of our fading postnatal nature, and after that the monotony of menopause settled down on me shoulder, and never again would I a babe within me belly brew, and only now did I begin to miss it too, the gore and blood and miracle of it, that fecund way a fertile filly has, with her furry black snatch's soft little lily pads of tissue, to soak up the dribbling bumbaclot.

'Perhaps I resented them a little bit, nay, a lot I mean, much malice within me festered and soured, such spite and ugly bile I fostered for me bawling brats at whom I never failed to bawl right back. For all I tried, I could never be a natural mother – I could teach them, yes, little bits of botany all about the twittering blobs of birds who sung on the branches, and the stalks of our garden's grass kowtowing to the godly wind, heritage of my vanished classroom days – but I could never bring meself to give any of 'em the bounteous suck of me bubs, the bite of their swelling canines I did so fear – so Frankie weaned them for me from a sterile bottle, with its plastic brown nipple around which they wetly wrapped their toddler's lips, full of the gloopy milk come from a furry cardboard carton, stolen from some cow somewhere. Their crying nettled me especially, and roused me to rattle their ribs with the wagging cane of a shrew, as they rolled recumbent in their cradles and cried, already so disgustingly spoiled and pampered, brought up in a bubble of affluence I never knew when I was a sooty nipper as now they were. I had not the instinct to nurture it seems, nor that fabled mammy's love, that eternal plume of worship that is never meant to die – it did in me, early on, by half too early, did it die.

'Perhaps elder Trevor got the worst of me, only since he was the first – on him like a guinea pig I applied all the studied tricks I filtered from the textbooks, those moronic manuals for mothers as written by stupid men who have never themselves been mothers, like Dr Spock, my one-time idol whose trashy tome I took for gospel, who recommends that one ought not to let the little ones sleep during the hours when they are most apt to idly do, but rather rouse them instead with a stick from their slumber, only to stuff unwanted food into their reluctant mouths, all in accordance with the specified hours he has allotted in his appendix, vacant numbers plucked at random from the air of his empty mind, no matter what the inclination of their appetites, no matter how oft the poor protesting darlings resist and bid one desist with the rattling chorus of their cries, those whines I so detested, as I clapped a palm to Trevor's gob in a huff, to shut him up as I brutally administered his antibiotics, pills that served no purpose and did him no good, me whom he came to hate, turning to his doe of a daddy Frankie for relief, my modest spouse who showed a far greater facility for fatherhood – he merely had to love them, and impose some limits, and thereafter leave them alone to learn of life – and they all adored him for it. I was the bad wolf in their beady rosary chain of hostile eyes, and he was the good archangel to whom they appealed with their plaintive cries.

'Yes, I confess I was jealous of the easy rapport with them he had, and though deep down and hidden within I never ceased in my soul to love him for all the years of our lives, from my mouth and from my hands he got nothing but abuse, forever being forked and speared on the diabolic tip of my tongue, forcibly made to weather a welter of unceasing sneers over the deadening span of the trying years, bobbing over complaints over nothing, treading water as he bore up under my non-stop nagging harangues, with occasional smacks and hurtling of pans. Such scenes of squabble my quailing brood was made to witness – I remember how, to soothe their distress, he would only roll eyes to the sky like the battered saint that he was, beaten and bruised by the punch I could pack, only to pass it all off as no more than a quirk of the full blue moon, the blinking orb of a Cyclops in the clouds, whose stare and frown makes all women and wolfmen mad.

'Alas! I weep now to think just what a trial of torment I made him serve, just how far I went in tempting him to hate me – but he never did, he never, never swerved in his devotion, for he continued still to worship the rosy wonder once I was, a happy memory of a nightingale belonging to once upon a time ago, one he kept carrying on to cherish in private, even when he later lost all his own marbles, about which gradual onset of doddery senility my children, by then fully grown and from our torrid familial nest flown away in a breeze of relief, blamed me at whom they pointed their fingers, me whom they blamed for their tortured daddy's pitiable loss of his mind. It was so sad to see him sink, lower and lower getting lost in his dementia's dark and knotty wood of sawdust, his brilliant brain befogged in the forest, a bygone bon viveur and life of every party, possessed of a quiet eloquence that could reel off every equation at a finger snap, reduced to a stuttering mute shell of himself, hobbling about our haunting house looking alone and ghostly, a stranger to his own turf, surrounded by mist, broken only by the odd petering shaft of light from his youth, imperfectly cleaving the curtain's net, expressed in the form of an incomplete equation he would shakily write on a napkin, in the eggshell scrawl of an elderly child, with a faltering and liver-spotted hand:

a as of 1 = … ? …

CHAPTER TWENTY-SEVEN

'O, but it crushed me to see my beauty fled – vain as ever, I did treasure still the memory of my golden bonny days of bounty, combing over and over with my decaying brush, as best I could with my useless shrivelled hands that could but barely bend, the locks of my glorious hair of bronze that somehow kept its colour, the better to mock the rotting rest of me, daily soured and disgusted anew by the obscene cripple I saw whenever I looked in the cloudy mirror of mildew in fear, loathing this cruel joke that met my horrified glance, squinting through my short sight as the snowflakes of dandruff peeled off my ruined scalp, to settle among my cardigan's threads, hating to death this sickening incontinent farting restless bitter housebound melancholic shrieking old sow and malicious hag and baggage I was become.

'O! A pox upon impotent old age and pestilence! What wouldn't I have given not to go on, but to take flight back again to the better! And there was I, all alone and lonelier, stuck in a rut in the frosty igloo of my home, a snowy palace of reeking ice that bit and nipped at me belly, with only my hubbie's body's empty urn to keep me company in my monotony, to whom never again was I to talk, as once we did when our hearts so sweetly beat in time, way back in another life that was more lovely, his gaping ear into which incessantly still I continued to spill the stew of me spite, for there was fuck all else for me to do but brutally hurtle the gravel bolts of me barbs, to flay him with bitter insults that cut to his core that quietly cried, sourly lacerating in a poisonous marinade of hate.

'And only once, and only then, and well about time too, did I finally push him at long last too far, far enough to rebel and escape, for one dark night in the harsh and cutting winter of a mellow year, didn't he only just stagger up from our bed and flee from me, packing his bags and stuffing his suitcase to the gills with his socks, transported by some subtle imp of spunk that we never did suspect him of having, and all the way away from me as fast as he could he ran, tottering to the train, onto which he hopped with a gasp, slipping as a sardine into a seat by the side of a commuting Chinaman, with whom, over the course of their journey into the tunnel of the night, he garbled sundry idiocies, a well-met set of mumbling men equal in eloquence, voyaging over the span of the tracks that wound all the long and rocky route to Dublin to seek refuge with his relatives, to kindle some solace from his sons he loved so well, at the door of one of whom, the baldy Eugene it was I think, he came banging in the howling wet of a storm, dripping adrift as a seal and hopelessly lost in limbo, yet somehow cheerful still, chuffed to have taken flight of strife, gently triumphant in his old-fashioned whimsical way.

'And they made him welcome, for all they were nonplussed, and bid him sit down and be dried, a wonder it was he did not die from the drenching he had borne, and there in state at the table's top day by day he sat looking smug, an amiable dustbin who ever would swallow the spares of their suppers, and polish off the plates they could not finish, delightedly lapping up the grease that turned his bunny's stomachs, this senile gourmand from whom, by degrees, they managed in time to get to divulge why it was he scarpered from my side, teasing out of him terse little smidges along the lines of 'o she's a torment and what have you', further fuel for the swelling bile they bore for me, petty little bitches.

'But at least he was happy in his absent way, St Francis Xavier of Alzheimer's Abbey, shuffling around knee deep amid the dead leaves of their gardens, with his pipping watering can and snaking hose that trailed at his heels, flourishing his silvery shears with which he trimmed their bushes, so splendid in his rubber gloves and boots, the sun that gave a halo's glow to the egg yolk of his gleaming hairless head, humming along to the burr of the bees, whose unchanging undying drone must surely have bethought him of his home, if only but dimly, if only but barely, to think again maybe of the bygone badger's valley of his birth, set low down in the volcano's undulant womb of voluptuous shadow, where once he played hopscotch or scatter, slurping the honeycombs his childhood sweetheart might have sucked upon, if only to allure him hither to kiss.

'And now today grandson Simeon, grown up to his shoulder, was there and near, and ready at hand to mind him and guide him, and mutter along with his monosyllables, the only one among his younger layer who really understood him in his decline, and only then the only time he knew him, making do with precious hints in the dark to gauge the upright gent he had been, holding his hand and doing the emerald rounds of their lawns in a litany, pointing to the poplars and fingering the flowers, rousing chuckles from the genial old oaf by pulling funny faces and making mirthful noises.

'And in the background, his hovering sons and daughter kids could not fail to wonder why on Earth he was here, for he was draining their funds for all that he was a talking point, an antique curio akin to an elephant's tusk, an ornery source of gentle genteel fun, the token senile sot every family needs, flashing the witless smile of the toothless cherub in the corner, with sagging belly and clipped and wizened wings fluttering vaguely, blustering and flustering as he struggled to stoke up a sentence from the blizzard in his brain that put a catch on his tongue, though all of what they said to him he seemed to understand, but never could gather the sense to reply.

'But as to me – it was the same third of my boys, rascal Eugene the baldy rogue who failed his finals through an excess of tomfoolery with a Teutonic tart who bore a fuzzy bust, him it was who gathered the balls of his courage to motor down to his childhood home, where still I was staying all alone going not a bit barmy, wheeling up the drive by speckled pebbles dashed, and parking his car by the groaning gate, ducking under the thickets of the overgrown hedge that had not been cut in years nor shorn, passing by, with a nervous nod, having seen, with a shiver, the ghost of himself when younger, the pockmarked apple tree under which as a feckless kid he had so often pined and skid, tossing the fruits of its branches at his brother, at elder anal Peter who once pushed him through the glass of our dining room's window smashing to bits as he fell and bled, all only for being overarch over some thorny point of theology.

'And now, through the teeming snow, to that same window, in the wintry night was he walking, peering through the pane to find his mother whom he could not see, for all the lights had long since burnt out, in my domain of darkness that dwindled to a muzzled dim, to sheathe the diva huddled hidden in the blackness unseen by her son, unheeding of the bell he wearily rang, calling out my name over and over, sounding so hollow in the rippling ocean of that night of echoes, as over an hour of listlessness he stood on the step sadly knocking on the futile door, until finally he could take no more, and kicked it down with the hoof of his foot.

'Passing through the broken frame that sprang so easily open, eager to admit him into the teeth of hell, he was met by dust, and shrivelled relics of his youth kept pickled in jars, as through that tomb in mounting alarm he jumpily walked on edge, starting at every faintest skip of sound, wondering where I was lurking in that mausoleum's gloomy murk, peopled by a pattering trickle of rats and mice who scuttled upon his footsteps, his scalp tickled by crafty spiders who spun their webs of gossamer in the rafters, to snare the stupid flies on whom they gorged and fattened, better fed than me whose leaking fridge was yawning empty, by which my son brushed by, lighting a stump of a candle to illume the mantelpiece that sagged, coughing from the catch in his throat as he perused the mottled pictures recording former teatimes, wryly smiling as he remembered just one among many crappy picnics I had spoiled, at which I sat in a sulk with me mug done up in a sour bun's pussy pout, and ruined everything for everyone all over again, and bending lower he found, deep in a drawer long discarded, the lanky greasy geek's journal in which he had jotted when young, groaning to find a memo of the day that their Jesuit master Father Grimly (with whom, after muddy sports of tackle and toss, his clammy chums had showered in the nip together, posturing jocks in the blinking baths of scandal) took them all to see *Ben-Hur* on the brand-new 70mm screen, which dross the young critic in pithy Eugene astutely dubbed, in a word, 'lousy'.

'And there I was too, o yes I was, the preying moth or looming mantis, letting him lie getting lost and distracted, as through the shadows I stalked on my webbed and cracking feet, building to the crackling summit of the peak, for a drama queen such as I knows in her bones anticipation is the secret of a scene, prowling up behind him beginning to growl like the wraith of a lost soul I was becoming, becomingly clad in my nightdress knitted from graveyard rags, a bangle about my spindly wrist made of bones that rattled, bearing aloft at an angle a lantern, within which a candelabra stood at a slant, melting dripping wax in a searing puddle on my onion's arm, the candlelight whose flare was hellish, and lit me like a horny study in scarlet of the devil, and finally he heard my moan and turned, and saw me only then as the demon to which in dismay I was reduced, and felt a wave of pity and torrential revulsion commingled for his poor old mammy, for whom he never before had felt such sympathy and terror as then alone he deeply did, his mammy Maggie who was become a Banshee.

'And I wasted no time in beginning to lambaste him, and riddle him with reproaches and prongs, dubbing him a fickle lazy idle useless waste of space, an insolent bastardeen who never said sorry nor please nor thanks, to whom I would not even pass across the table the rancid butter for to smear his worthless toast he always did be burning, all the wrath and hate I bore up stowing spilt out to scald the scarified face of my son, who stood in a sway and swallowed his pity, and hit me back with some slurs of his own, he had inherited my forking tongue if never nothing else, and so we stood there shouting in the hall for the space of an hour, the infernal flecks of our spittle lit up by our lamps, like the belching spurts of fire spat from the lizard lips of dragons who burp brimstone on a strictly daily basis, until soon the poor sod could take no more, and turned and ran out the door he had torn down, and I pursued him as quick as I could, to fling after him the bevy of his bags, fuelled by a power I knew not came from where, so deft was my aim that met its mark, knocking a block off his balding top, bringing him down to his knees on the twisting path to the rusty gate, there it was in the freezing snow where he fell, and there where I applied feeble crone's kicks to his stomach, to rub well into the welt of his bleeding wound just who was his mammy and who was his master, the witch who would hound him forever, and never ever once in her tidal wave of monsoon's abuse abate, until finally he staggered up hoarsely with a curse, clambering into his car to scoot off with a coarse spume from his exhaust, blackening me face with a shower of soot that sought the creases of me lines, as he left me in the lurch, alone again, and madder yet.

'In short, an eventful and spirited reunion was ours. But enough about me already. I am quite hoarse from all that talking. How are you doing, darling?'

But The Mad Monk made no answer; for he had fallen fast asleep, his shaggy head snugly couched in the pillow of Granny Nutmeg's lap, taking his rest, feeding on his ease, snoring softly while the snow still fell by her door, and Banshee Megan Devlin smiled as she gazed upon his repose, and gently stroked his tufts, a windswept orphan of the storm of the world, the world he said he had made.

CHAPTER TWENTY-EIGHT

But he awoke in the morning to find that the snow had stopped, though still the sun chose not to shine, since the clouded sky was white. Crawling naked on his knees from their furry bed to her door, he shivered and stood up unsteadily, grunting. Raggedly leant on the rock, he gazed out upon a land of blankness, whitely spread at foot of the craggy cliff. Not a whisper in the air was there. The trees below stood cowed, beneath their loaded shaft of flakes and drift, winter's ashen vesture in place of their leaves. All was still.

Solemnly, he took the place in, and bowed his head, yawning, weary, pounding brain still swimming with the tide of her talk that had haunted him. And looking again back up toward the sky, were his eyes not moister? Was there not all o'er his face a flicker of a kind of remorse, a tremor of a sort of sadness? And for what? Was it upon his mission he mulled, on the fatal delay that winter had wrought, on the enormity of all that yet awaited him? Or does he indeed still brood on what he heard from her, words that sent him deep to troubled sleep? And does he wonder what he may do for her, his bedfellow to whom he gave his ears in his sympathy, and his moisture for their pleasure? She sleeps; he stands; might he not move? But he cannot leave her, no, not now, not while naked at her door he stands uncertain and cold, wondering upon what boon he might owe her, what token of his love leave to bring her comfort, and grant her greater peace. And also, if he is honest, he may reflect anew on his failures so far, which outweigh any wins, if indeed there are any, and indeed there are none – for the hares that he wed were quickly killed by I— C— C— – not that he knows, though in his guts he surely senses – and his White Dog is lost

– and O'Muadaigh is dead, gored to the bone by the hound, but finally put to death and slain by his own bloody hands. All has failed.

Shattered at the thought, mildly beating his grizzly breast, he sinks anew to knees, back down to his bum on the cold rock, casting his thighs and calves and ankles jutting out over rim of the precipice, to let his legs hang dangling in the cold air, in quiet space. There he sits, disconsolate. What might he do now to redeem his checkered record? That he might ultimately erect a glowing Abode in the end, the house of happier dreams, built on brightness, an outside and an inside, lofty above the grabbling fray of filth, hoisted safely on its stilts, wobbly but steadily so, peopled by the select set due to be divinities, apostles to pass on his baton, who might fulfill the sketchy foundations he could lay, to fill in the gaps between his lines, and bring to final pristine fruition the greater glory of the grandiose cathedral he dimly foresaw, a vision in his clouded sights that ebbed and dipped as he sunk and tread the water, to which he must grasp and never dare unclasp, vowing for dear life to feed and sustain such fancy.

And what would his brother, he could not help but wonder, what would his brother have done, were he to be him? That reckless ghost who always seemed to prowl upon his snaking path, breathing over his shoulder, the pad and tread, pad and tread of whose shuffling footsteps forever haunted his journey of meanders, whose rattling exhalations upon his back even now he seemed in fear to feel, a musty gust of the graveyard that bade him glance behind – only to see nothing, only her homely cave, only the Banshee tucked up in her bed of snoozing furs, and a few last scarlet embers gasping and sparking amid the charcoals and briquettes of her dying fire – for it was only the wind, not butterfly breath of brother's ghost – but was his brother not indeed at one with the wind, carried along on its eddies and whorls, borne by the breeze that could not read but could see inside souls, and decipher the maps of minds, and the future foretell, and its clumsy course distort? And he cursed the ghost who spied upon him, and spat on his palm in disgust at his cowardice, though still he could not help but ponder, as before, whether they were not part of the same chapter of fate, pawns in the same plan, agents of good and ill bound to drag the other kicking down, wound to the same cause they would effect by different routes, and mayhap while the one's path was steady, the other's was made of meanders, and for the one his straight lines were deviant tangents, divergent to the other's parallels – and perhaps what seemed to be messes were neither wrong nor right, but both, or none – all being one, come what may of the world's abiding whirlwind.

He deplored this streak in himself, that of doubting, that of fretting, that of wasting precious seconds in idle introspection – he was not as bold as before – and cried aloud an oath to the air, whose coarse ring upon the silence was a spur, and brought him to his resolution. He stood up again, welcoming the cold morning, his pointy head sharply colliding with the low ceiling of her cave, a bump back to the earthy roof that gave him to bleed, his peeling halo that became a paling aureole of blood, one of life's petty irritants that fuelled his fury, and he snarled and growled as he stroked his tattered scalp that stung, moved to instant action by a nitty-gritty little thing.

And Maggie heard his growl in the deeps of her sleep, and woke, and from her pillow raised her tousled puzzled head, eyes yet blinking stuffed with sandman's dust, batting eyelids to shirk off slumber, and through the batting of her rotting lashes, she saw him, her lover, as she would a shadow, caressing his injured head as he bent down low, to pick up from her floor his shroud he had discarded, into which he slid afresh with many mutters, clothed, complete, nude no longer, in the mood for miracles. And she might have cried out to him, in a rasp from swooning where she lay, in a rasp to echo upon the rock of her home, to cry out what, why, what are you doing and where are you going, but not a sound she let slip – his very stance seemed to set an upright catch of silence on her throat. Thus made mute, she watched him, curiously, her mouth flapping dumbly like a trout, as he grabbed from a corner of the cave her mottled axe, and turning on a grimy heel he stormed out her door in a splendid wrath, out into the whiteness, hopping over brim of her cliff down which he skid and slid, tapering down her precipice with the skill of an adder, her axe slung over his shoulder, the blade caught in a crook of his arm, and in her fluster she rose from her bedding, and flurried over to her door to see what all his fuss was for, and gaping over the edge she knelt to admire the smoothness of his descent. What dexterity! What agility! Look at him go, sweet Nutmeg, those same fingers that cling to the crags once bore into your dugs! What a hunk! What a mensch! And now see, ha ha, you is smiling to see the old buck be climbing, stirring the vitals as he hits stony battered bottom, and came to the ground, feet set back on the earth's firmer floor, mid brambles and nettles, his old friends, nearby the frozen brook, the mocking stream of ice.

And now, to the halted river, from foot of her cliff, it was he strode, swinging the potent chopper of her axe in beat to the crunch and slap of his feet in the snow, and she beheld in awe as he bent by bank of the chilly brook, and raised aloft the shining iron, and swung it swiftly down, and o, the crack and snap of the ice that he sundered, and began to split, and the churning waters within, stifled so long, now began to peter and filter out from betwixt the splits he drew, between the zigs and zags he etched with quill of her axe, and he chopped and hacked some more and further, till soon the brook began to flow again, began afresh to gush and babble as before, the liberated liquid slithering out mid the jagged splits on the surface of the violated lid, the constipated torrent brimming forth in rapture to be rescued from its paralysis of hitherto, giddy to be set free from the prison of the ice, as chop, chop, the jobbing old man of the woods bore up and down the axe in the air, the hairy lumberjack of children's legends, the one who saved the lively waters from their deathly inertia, who cast off the suffocating shawl of Jack Frost, beaten back from the feisty young heifer who was a budding river, the stripling stream who was a deviant meander of its teeming mother river Corrib that was going to Galway, set free at last through crunch of the Banshee's axe, the very one The Mad Monk swung.

Hacking, panting, lulled by his labours and breathless, he stood aside and sighed, with fire in his head. Stealthily and steadily the brook petered out mid the chinks he made, glowing green and frothy, finding its feet, growing foaming, alive and flowing again. And the old woodsman sat down on a boulder and rested, setting her axe on his lap, and raising high his arms and hands to wave, and conduct the rushing course of the current he stirred to motion. And from afar, on the cliff above, Banshee Maggie looked down and on in love. Hastily draping herself, she made tracks to join him, clumsily descending her slope, slipping and tumbling and very near coming a cropper.

And as for him, he would reel in the spring, and bring back buds to withered stalks that were drooping, and clothe the bare branches with leaves of gold and amber, all this he thought in his valiant frenzy, shut eyes shining in his gay delight, knowing the joy of a wandering child from the hills, chasing a gypsy's caravan through verdant glades, his hands and fingers fluttering as he made music and hummed, weaving a tune from the trickle of the running waters that began to hiss and pound and crash, and he sang along with the stream in a trill, knitting and looping the golden baritone lines. And all around him in the sleeping woods of winter, wherein all the kindred creatures were snoring, in the bliss of their beds, feeding on their fat to keep away the cold, snoring in their fluff and down, cradled in their fragile nests of wispy feathers, they too, they too began to stir. For they felt in their sleep, somehow, felt something of the kindling he had brought, and the rhythm of the wakening river crept into their dreams, and bid them rise earlier than intended. So from their nests and burrows they rise and they rose, and from their dens and warrens they scurry, all of a flurry in a hurry, duly following the dictates of their dreams, inquisitive and puzzled, snuffling the soil and sneezing, all in a wonder as one, and vaguely too they also knew that their world was going young again, and not so dead as they had supposed. And in their mini-hearts the candle of joy was awoken again, and they rejoiced, the cute little ones, and cavorted and gambolled and frolicked, making merry while the wood was warming, and the frozen river's ice began to thaw and melt, making but more water, lifting up the shards of ice that began to float and bob. They were like the bass notes or the bristling discords in his symphony, The Mad Monk thought, the stinging C-sharp minors or something, humming along with the bubbling fire in the mind, buoyed on the allegro con brio that carried him through, bright-eyed vainglorious Vivaldi, orchestrating all that was good.

And Maggie was by his side by now, kneeling down by the rock he sat upon, moist eyes uplifted, and she opened her mouth as if to query, for she knew not in what way the world was turning – but he placed a palm of his to her lips, whilst saying:

'You've talked enough, Nutmeg. Behold! Dost thou remark upon this thaw before its brittle cue? I am composing a concerto for the spring, ducky my only, sweeter by far than any old Antonio could ever envision, much less enact, one well beyond the scope of that randy seducer of nuns. These cute little critters, who come from all sides in their humble droves, to do worship at your shrine and grotto, are to be the hustling chorus, and you, foxy doxy, you shall be my female lead, my soprano line, La Belle Dame Maggie the Diva. And I will marry thee covertly, here and now, and we will have us a wedding. Know that your shaggy saga of yesterday's evensong has moved me – so I will be Friday's Frankie for you. O yes. With my cap of satin felt and dew, like the silken hat your hubbie once wore, my rods of elm, my capering tubers, my ear trumpet and coppery bugle, together we shall be wed, and I will bring you fourscore happinesses, and anoint thee with precious fragrances, all the perfumes of the big smelly world, all to bring thy beauty back again. With ambrosia and lavender shall I daub ye all over, and honeysuckle, and peppermint, and ballerina fuchsia clad in flamingo pink, and comb the curls of your buttercup hair with nectarine and laburnum, all the smells of spring and summer to smooth over your scowls and paper your wrinkly cracks, and prod your navel to the gills with marmalade, and all that's sweet and light in life. So let us hop to it like the sun!'

And lo, the overjoyed bride-to-be slumped to the rock, and her lover, her suitor, her soon-to-be-groom, arose and uttered an incantation, at which, as quick as a cut, or a wink, or the snap of a shutter, her axe became a crozier. Maggie thought she felt a judder in the very earth beneath her, as her looming groom now donned the pinstriped garb of a lounge lizard, kitted to the nines in ducks and spats and dicky bow, a tulip poking from the pocket by his breast, busy hands warm in their spotty kid gloves, his beard oiled and combed and tamed, a top hat atop his scalp to hide his baldy's patch, a rose betwixt his shining teeth, snatching a pinch of snuff to pep him up and clear the cobwebs, with a quizzical monocle to sheathe his gleaming eye, eager at the altar, ready to be wedded. Only then did Maggie think to glance upon herself, to see with no small surprise the bridal ware she wore, white as the driven snow swiftly turning to liquid slush, robed in splendour such as she ne'er knew before, ripe and plump in the dress of betrothal.

And the tall man in the suit now tossed the shimmering crozier high up into the air, where it was caught by the beak of a hooting owl in the midst of his hunt, who came down upon them swooping, an able cleric with a fetching doggy collar about his fat neck – if neck really is the name – do owls have necks? – no matter too major. Descending to earth, he alighted upon a peaking rock the greedy welling river had not yet swallowed, and there and then, with a stern glare in his golden eyes that did not feel fun, and the dazzling crozier clasped in an ashen sooty wing, he cawed and croaked through the appropriate rigmarole, a bit-part actor well versed in his role. And the happy couple, the lady having been hoisted to her shaky feet by the dishy dude of her dreams, now stood as a pair in the slush, and gave their answers in the generous slots of pauses he provided, for no, no, they could think of no impediment that might mar their marriage, for she was an undead widow and he was the man who made the world after all, and an obliging badger stood up to become his best man, the ring was a little thing carved of cedar and pine, and a prodigal goose was her quacking bridesmaid, and yes, yes, they would truly live happily and lawfully and honourably and properly and so and so, and so thus did the reverend owl bind them together in a ghastly parody of matrimony, and having said all, he cast his staff into the heart of the river, and sailed away in a dream.

And O! what rejoicing then was there! The larks sang long, and fighting cockerels crowed, and horny donkeys neighed, as the happy couple embraced and kissed and cuddled, as if they never before had done as they did, and there was none in the world but themselves, and, high up in the sky, the moon and the sun briefly were one. The ceremony, such as it was, was followed by a riotous party, where both man and wife got deliciously tipsy, drunken as kites on the clotted dregs of a chunky goblet of altar wine, and a legion of overdressed foxes, scarlet charmers and shameless flirts, did a tap dance on the table, and sang many sentimental songs. With his Abe Lincoln stovepipe hat set awry, his mutton chops bitten off in clumps by his ravenous mate, the husband was blushing crimson as the badger-cum-best-man stood on a stool and made the customary cheeky speech, laden with anecdotes he fished from the top of his head, that had scant bearing in fact but were always outrageous, remembering the stint they did in the hedge school back in the day, tutored in pig Latin by a beautiful otter with a sleek lithe hide, who gave them both a ride as they dipped into choice pieces of Petronius ('I knew nothing, I wasn't there, I deny all charges, I swear …' The Mad Monk muttered to Maggie, who cared not a fig), blathering on and recounting the bawdy chronicle of their youth amid the reeds and shades, before finally he grew too drunk to carry on, and toppled off the stool instead, and could have cracked his skull upon a stone, had not the fluttering bridesmaid caught him in her arms (wings?), quacking pleasantries to comfort him (they would subsequently have a hurricane affair, as was only fitting, the dirty-minded badger and the quivering goose, his paws and fangs tearing her feathers to bloody pieces, in the clandestine hollow of a willow, stooping nearby bank of the brook – and some say they can still hear her last stifled squawks even to this day – for he ate her afterwards).

CHAPTER TWENTY-NINE

And so did o'er the long and jolly day and night the newlyweds carouse, 'til the tolling of midnight's bell did the groom arouse to make a move to erect a conveyance fit for their honeymoon's maiden voyage, a romantic cruise down the Corrib. And up he got from the depths of his cups, and to the riverbank he blearily weaved, where he gathered together a batch of logs and branches with which to build their bark. Sticky with love, Nutmeg looked on bemused, as he hammered and whistled in his work-aday overalls, with the help of a heron who dished up the nails and screws, to shimmy the sinews of the heaving mast and secure the captain's cabin, a tasteful lover's nest, as sticks became planks and a mass of lumber became a boat, as pretty a ship as ever a sailor sailed. No cowboy builder, to cap all off the artisan carpenter then dipped his brush into a pot of paint a cynical weasel provided, and to the side of their vessel he appended a solemn daub in scarlet, slowly tracing the letters he mumbled with tender care and love, dubbing the hull under none but Megan Devlin's very own name, which tribute made Granny Nutmeg swoon by the bank in tawny midnight's amber pool, bathing all in golden hue so yellow as an owl or eagle's eye.

And thus, the boat built, with the heron at the helm for want of better bosun, and an oily cormorant, ghost of a sailor drowned, enlisted as errant first mate, the romantic mariner set aside his monkey suit in favour of a naval officer's equipage, and beckoned to his bride to join him up on deck. She scurried thither puffing, tripping over the hem of her dress, scuttling up the ladder to sit at her champion's side by the prow, who patted her shoulder and lit a cigar, and nuzzled her cheek as he made a sign to his fellows to launch out into the current's raking drift, a doff of his skipper's hat that set them to steer, the lanky heron and his black cousin cormorant, hardy seamen both, a worthy crew. And as they departed from the land, the bank's well-wishers bid them good luck and bye, furry and scaled and feathered alike all cheered, and the seafaring pair blew kisses to their fans, as their chipper dreamboat glided down the gush and rounded a corner, hurtling round a loop in the seeping meander, making a foaming break back to its wily mammy river.

So thus by starlight they sailed serenely, murmuring low and puffing upon pipes, eyeing the sky and enumerating the twinkling constellations, some of which recalled the captain of friends he had in former lives, reclining in the shelter of a fluttering flag upon which their gnarled insignia was inscribed, their tugboat making cautious passage through the liquid corridor lined by the walls of willows, struggling free from their clutch into clearer country by verdant meadows dotted into grids by jumbled clutters of rocky walls, within which such wild gardens sheep and cattle drowsed and dreamt and nibbled grass, sometimes raising sleepy eyes to inspect the queer vessel of bizarre carriage that billowed by their bit of green ground.

Morning came along dawning in a parting of clouds, Aurora shook off her locks of dew upon the stalks and shoots, casting away her lunar mantle and twilight's gown, and Apollo's glaring eye arose afresh to find their ship pulsing down into the lap of the tumbling river, shining blue as the wrinkled mirror of the sky. Feeling hunger's pang, the heron and the cormorant took turns in hopping sleekly over side of the deck into the water's deeps, for to fetch fish from the dark lungs, catching some haddock and mackerel, salmon and cod to break their fast, seasoned by seaweed and whatever other nameless flavourings their captain could conjure, for him it was who lit the fire and stoked the flame of the stove, offering up the crunchy catch of the day with a helping of chips and spinach, laden with mustard and sesame garnished, their whistles wetted by wine, and all there on the deck who devoured his grub, beneath the azure canopy and swelter of the new sun, warmly lauded and applauded his prowess at the pan, toasting him goodly between their pleasured chews, which plaudits he spurred with bashful dancing hands, hiding blushes beneath his mushroom cloud chef's hat. And Maggie was of them all exceeding admiring, for she frankly admitted that a healthy part of the route to a lady's heart lay by way of her belly – and in this respect not even Frankie was his peer.

But Frankie – Frankie – only but to think of him again did move Maggie now to know that some miracles come too late. At which thought she sniffled, as she nibbled on fresh fish, sniffling that turned to tears in silence, quietly sobbing in the sun on the stern.

But he saw – don't think for a moment he never knew – and he stooped to whisper – what is wrong, what can I do – to which she made her request – to which he quickly acquiesced. For Galway town was along the route, one that wound down from the sticks to the suburbs, to branch into the priceless graveyard of ambition, western capital of the elder isle, into whose outspread arms they soared in their ship, by the cathedral's balding dome of lime, dodging the tricksy boulders that barred their ease of entry, brushing by the gravy college, within whose quadrangles her younger Collins kids had hammered in their brains amidst the books and shelves, sailing past canal banks and locks and russet walls of ivy glistening in the sunshine, beams illuming the queer quartet who crowded the little boat, the four being Banshee, grizzled seafarer, heron and cormorant, the latter pair whose ears (is that the word?) whose ears perked up to hear the piping calls and echoes of their fellows, of whom around the town there were many dozens, for the seashore was near and lapping, and Galway's bay was calling them home, home, home. To which end, the two seabirds took their leave and bade farewell to the adults, flapping their wings as they croaked an adieu, before diving off the deck into the gurgling surge, to fish and feed for all their days, to meet their mates and copulate in the churning foam, as any brainy fowl worth his peck of salt unerring would, and daily did and indeed does.

Left behind in the boat, the newlyweds wearily waved and sighed thereafter, made newly awkward. So the tall man took up an oar, for want of keeping busy, and rowed them in a frenzy hastily down the onrush of the churn, breaking to a halt by the sacred Salmon Weirs, nearby the Spanish Arch of times renowned, and hopped from their skiff into the shallows, since the tide at that time was low, hauling their hull into the safety of the rocks by the quay, dropping anchor and making moorings, to steady and still their ship. Splashing knee deep amid the flapping rivulets, anchor roped to an anvil and a discarded shopping trolley, mired in moss and weed and sucking molluscs, he glanced up with a savage flash of his eye, and held out a hand to bid her descend from her mount on the deck, and come down into the town about which she wished to make pilgrimage.

Haughtily descend she did, nose aloft in the air, following his impatient beckon up the steps that lead to Eyre Square, by way of Quay Street and Shop Street, passing by MacDonagh's (founded 1902), which window, fogged by the fervent breath of all within who fed and frequented, won from him a look of longing, a stare of pining hunger for mushy peas, and blobs of sweet ketchup, and the scent of cider vinegar, as was good for building blood, such riches and delights as he could not from his own impoverished pockets provide. To Charlie Byrne's bookstore she granted a nod, and so too did she the same for Kenny's bestow, an erstwhile art gallery – well did she remember the dimming days when she did share a natter with the wizened lady of that house, newly dead, fresher than she, two bags and crones who once enjoyed torrid gossips, over the course of a couple of cups. But wait – this was the wrong way – so back they turned the two, hand in hand like wraiths, ghostly revenants late for the revels, tripping along an inch above the cobbles, unseen by the ignorant, as they backtracked and crossed across the bridge, over beyond to near where lay Nun's Island's way, higher mounting until they found what had been her house, a sorry plot upon old Tailor's Hill.

But in the dour interim, she found their home had since been sold, following the squabbling of siblings, the bickering of the grasping brood she birthed, for it had been bought at an auction by some faceless capitalist with a mind to make money. The grand big house that she had known by the name of Lindisfarne had now been knocked, the cranes and wrecking balls wheeled in to sunder to smithereens her pride of the past, to reduce their familial home to rubble and ruin, the goodly walls rent and cracked, their flakes of chipped plaster dissolved and borne away by the racking breeze, the windows smashed, the grass mown to sooty nothing, the pockmarked apple tree chopped and hacked, to be pulped into paper upon which to print bills, and from the descending dust to erect anew a grisly complex, compact of granite and steel, concrete and glass, an edifice to loom and chill, a vision of progression embittering the former owner, the galvanized forlorn Banshee who shivered. And her haggard companion took her by her scrawny arm, and bid her move away in dismay from that haunted place.

Lastly, with faltering steps in gloom, higher progress further made they up the brow of the sloping hill, until then when they came at last upon the very graveyard where Professor Francis Alphonsus Xavier Collins was buried. Wind whistled through the trees as the arc of the sun declined, a snowy brush of slush lying dusted upon the tombstones, somewhere among which Frank lay dead in his cold box, hid beneath amid the wormy soil, with a few bouquets of sorry flowers laid by his grave, and upon his slab were writ these sickly words, composed and engraved by one of his nurses:

Frank was someone special,
Someone set apart,
He will live forever,
Engraved within our hearts.

And the widowed Banshee Megan Devlin fell down to her knees by the cross of her loss, and heaved great and lasting wails and sobs that were robbed by the passing wind, and wept and lamented piteously. And The Mad Monk stood discreetly aside to let her do her devotions, and leant against a yawning yew, and put tobacco in his pipe, and began to whistle sombrely, hoarsely whistling in the gathering darkness, in the quiet night.

CHAPTER THIRTY

In another quiet night, Tadgh O'Mara had fled to the mainland in search of his child, stowing away in the holds of the outgoing Bofin ferry, as in his youth he had hid in the bowels of a transatlantic liner like a beardy rat. The ferry hit the coast of Mayo, and the demented poet took flight before the ticket inspector could ogle his retreating gauntness.

From there, like the spit of a scraggly lunatic he wandered down deserted paths and camped in shivery fields, sometimes mistook for a scarecrow, as his bony frame was glimpsed afar, poking up from amid the pulsing sheaves of wheat. He fed himself on whatever berries and nuts might come his way in the threadbare hedges that he scoured with trembling hands. His bare feet were cut to shreds by thorns and stones that bestrewed the cruel roads down which he roamed lopsided. A wild man of the woods, he blended with the moss and bark. Sometimes he caught sight of herds of police, combing the meadows in search of a criminal's prints, and he hid from them in the Burren's rocky gullies. From drying creeks he drank his fill, squeezing melting clumps of snow until a few oozing drops of crystal liquid were imparted, to please his gasping thirst for water, a wandering prisoner lost in wetlands with not a fit drop to drink.

And he continued to compose as often as he was able in the course of his exile, jotting down stray ditties on crackling leaves he hoarded, as he crouched by cattle troughs to shelter from the storm. His poems during this period had a certain terseness, a raw power and honesty, that they had not hitherto possessed. Denied a dictionary, without a possession to his name save for stub of nib and the rags he wore, he was forced to use only the simplest words of which he could think, the most easy and potent that came quickest to mind, and such a style, of almost scrupulous meanness, paid off. And even when these poems were lost, rendered wetted when the rains came and he dropped the leaves that dissolved in petty clumps, he retained them in his mind, and planned to deliver them to his daughter. With his back to the wall, he was beginning at last to truly live. Sometimes he dreamt of the White Dog, and of the whimsical owner who had set him on the right track, and, upon tearfully awaking, he genuflected to the red and rising sun, and gave thanks to that shaggy deity to whom he was indebted.

One day when adrift in the midlands by dawn, he came upon a gypsy's caravan stationed in the centre of a tidy town, with a gaudy sign advertising the foretelling of fortunes and the divulging of fates. Intrigued, he chose to break his solitude briefly, if only to ask where in the world his child might be found. He knocked on the door. With a creak, it opened, and a silent figure appeared, tall and dark and brooding, bearded and hooded, with an eyepatch and an earring, poking out his shaggy head to dourly peer and glare upon the poet, whom he beckoned forthwith and ushered into the dim interior.

It was a smoky place wherein wafted fragrance of incense and faint tang of perfumed musk. Tadgh was roughly sat down with a shove upon a stool by the table round, where sat the psychic medium Minerva hunched, nodding snoring in tune to music celestial, stirring only upon a prod from her partner, which bid her raise aloft her ragged head of Medusa's curls with a wangling quiver. She gruffly asked for money.

'I have none,' Tadgh croaked in English, 'but I must know where my daughter is.'

She snorted and told him to get out. But then her partner, who had been eyeing the poet discreetly, seemed to tremble in a kind of recognition. He stooped, and mumbled something in his lady's ear. She heard, considered, shrugged, then said:

'My oracle says she's to be married in a Rathmines church.'

Gabbling Tadgh O'Mara thanked the wizened gypsy and her oracle, and left.

Some weeks later, having squatted on the roof of a bus he had hijacked, unbeknownst to the short-sighted driver, the poet arrived in Dublin, where he had not been in many years. With a bumpkin's awe he tripped about the streets, darkly noting the signs of change, the glittering towers and cranes that bespoke detested progress. Like a tramp he kipped in leaky alleys and dined in stinking gutters, avoiding the threat posed by surly youths in hoodies and trainers. He found Rathmines Cathedral, lured uphill by its lime and looming dome, but could find no trace of the marriage in the records – not that he could even remember his daughter's name, which was a setback indeed.

So he opted to squat on the cathedral steps until his daughter's wedding cortege arrived, however long that may take, banking on knowing her from familial resemblance. Bored in the meantime, he explored the town's nearby environs, getting reacquainted with Portobello and Ranelagh and the Grand Canal. No notice was taken of the lanky tramp stalking the pavements and hugging the trees by the banks, scratching poems on their barks, verses breathing lonely woe. Sometimes he forgot who he was. And sometimes he remembered all too clearly. And most of the time he could not care less either way.

CHAPTER THIRTY-ONE

Elsewhere today the ghost of Elijah roams abroad in the distant woods. Scurrying through thickets of ashen hedges, scarce discerned in his graveyard rags that merge among the shrubbery, gliding by clad in grey robes of rust that mingle with the falling leaves. A flitting sprite with tangled dripping beard, whose spindly fingers attempt to part the twining sticks to peer out midst the branches that bar the view. But his haggard claws have no feeling nor touch in them. Nothing will move at their bidding; all will stay still at his behest. What could be more dismal than the loneliness of his ghostliness? But Elijah never despairs nor complains, far beyond such all-too-human quibbling.

And after nights akin to eons, during which he yearned to work wonders, whilst his spirit was wont to walk and prowl, come the dawning of the yawning days, he would subside and merge into the shady hollows of desolate trees, kindred of the prickly spider whose webs were his duvets, for to slumber midst the veil of shadows, safe from the sting of the rising sun's red rays, the flames of which streaks might scald him, and burn him and melt him, such was his fear, mostly groundless, for he was airy and void of substance, at one with the wind and weightless, far beyond the domain of harm. He was nothing now but an insubstantial shred of a shape, and a hoarse last wisp of a voice, both remnants of life quite fine insofar as they went, but utterly impotent in the face of action. Glorious dreams he nursed in his quiet darkness, of great doings undone whiles he had lived, that might yet now see their fruit, would that he had but a body to do them.

So it became his latest mischief, asides from spooking the sheep and cattle with portentous words of doom, to take possession, every once in a while, of the bodies of unassuming animals, and to inhabit their petty frames apace. It lent him an insight he had hitherto been denied, having lived his life couched in the wizened shell of a man alone, but now delighting to see the big little world through their meek and shining creature's eyes, to scuttle down its paths on their cloven feet or furry paws, to sniff and piss and shit and mate as did they, which diversions he enjoyed, even during the day – for he felt securer within the shackles of their skins and skeletons, their bones wound round with the streaky muscles he so missed in his ghostliness.

One day he would be a little lambkin, the next he would be a brooding ass; come sunrise he might be a strutting cock heralding the morn, come the moon he might be a hooting owl swooping to murder the mice; on Monday he could be a virile bull, on Friday he could be a glossy otter; and not even the busy ant, nor the fluttering butterfly, nor even the sightless earthworm were safe from the taint of his unscrupulous piracy. Each of the failings and strengths of these respective species he tallied, enumerating their qualities in the looming tome of his deathless mind, which remained the mind of a man, no matter how godly endowed, a mind that soon again began to long for the glory of a man's body in which to be housed, such as was his onetime wont, after the fashion of his last life.

And so, fuelled by this desire to rule again the kingdom of a human body, flying free into the stars from the cage of the mammal and fowl, the ghost was whipped astride the tides of night, riding the lapping breeze like a stallion, subject of the wind's eddies and whorls that swept him along in his billowing shroud, through fog and cloud and mist and dew, until at last he alighted off the wheezy highway, and was landed in that part of the island where the bulk of its denizens did dwell, in the eastern coast's metropolis where a millions humans milled, amongst whose shoals the bold Elijah, his bright eyes raking the hordes from the heights of his eyrie, did then decree, almost arbitrarily, that only one greater man was worthy, to whom he would grant just one more last dull day of life to be himself, and to find himself, and to know himself, and then finally be bid flee into the ether forever. And who he was we soon shall see.

CHAPTER THIRTY-TWO

The old man Arsene O'Colla is arrived in Dublin. Off the Wexford bus he sets his foot and frowns, cocking a sceptical sneak at the Spike (in a city full of heroin addicts, putting up a giant needle is surely ill advised), and down O'Connell Street he dawdles then, to get a gander at Chapters, but this is short lived, owing to the fecking expense. Now he shuffles across the bridge, snail's gait at odds with the rapid scuttle of the milling throng, and in passing squinting eyes the swollen Liffey lolling by below, its golden rivulets, whorls and rococo eddies, sweetly dappled by the flirting sunlight that soon shall fade, sluggishly flowing in leisurely thread between the arches. At the lights, he sees the poet Pat Ingoldsby hunched by the bridge's balustrade, his swarm of signs screaming his status: *That Rarest of Species: A Dublin Poet. I'm Not Dead Yet, Sorry. Health Warning: These Poems Contain Imagination. Special Discount on Books Covered in Bird-Shit.* Feeling the nip, the poet blows on his cold hands, ruffling his white moutachios. Arsene grants him a nod, a nod curtly reciprocated. Their chilly acquaintance was a nodding one (Arsene had once tried to haggle with him over the price of a mediocre volume of verse, but the poet took righteous spitting umbrage at the stingy figure the Chairman named). A little green man alights within his sights, and Arsene the weatherman crosses the road, and continues up Westmoreland Street to his destination, at which he shall be by four. And so at four, in the second-floor café of Nassau Street's Kilkenny Design Centre he would be found were one to look for him, sitting solemnly waiting at a table alone, alone until the boy arrived.

He raised his hazy eyes as I ascended the stairs, seeming at first as though failing to see me – doubtless I was taller than he remembered

– and wet and scruffy I was too, on account of a drunken topple I had taken only yesterday – late from a lecture too, that didn't help, so belated was I, emitting burbling apologies for my tardiness as I sat down opposite the old man, and set on the floor my prop of bag, and dazedly scratched my dizzy head, and only then did I remember the point, and only then did I fall to rummaging mid jangling discs in my coat's top right pocket, the very place where I was so very sure I had put it.

'Hang on … I know it's here somewhere … Ahh, yes!'

With show, I withdrew the keys round which the transaction hinged. There were two, silver and gold, attached to a purple ring, keys I held out to Arsene, who accepted them with a nod and a mumble. He knew how to operate them? Of course. They were idiot-proof. I wondered was there anything to add as a heavy silence fell between us, in which a pin dropping might have seemed an event, a silence I briefly pondered how best to break, before deciding instead to let it lengthen, content instead to study my companion, to whom I must have seemed an unlikely foil: a small old man with a bulging balloon of a belly, a rat's nest atop his potato skull at an angle to slip, his dirty nails uncut and grimy, shoulders of his mouldy jacket sprinkled with freshly fallen snow of dandruff, greeting the world with mouth agape and vacant stare. I worried over what I saw, recalling his geriatric doctor who prescribed those deathly pills that made the gentleman so groggy yet so genteel a zombie. And I wondered too had he heard of O'Muadaigh's loss, a man he surely knew, and as I wondered further he took the initiative and spoke.

'Do you want a cup of tea?'

Did I want tea? The stream of my inconclusive thought resolved itself fittingly into a mild patter of vague murmurs and a noncommittal shrug.

'You do want a cup of tea, so,' said Arsene with no small firmness.

'Suppose I do, so,' I gravely conceded.

'Right. Great.'

He stood up from his seat to shuffle off. This relieved me – so he was going to pay! – something of a turn-up for the books, no? I marvelled at life's unending wonder as with squinted eyes I watched his slow shambling old man's progress toward the counter where he dipped a shaking hand into a cavernous trouser pocket, the deep pockets of the mean, and withdrew a wee plastic packet, of the kind once distributed by the banks, in which were stored some coppers and bronzes he counted out with care as he announced our order to the bored blonde who yawned at the till, refraining tactfully from trying out on her the execrably pronounced few words of Polish that were his to command, a man of many tongues in none of which he was proficient, I smugly smiled to think.

But my smile grew sadder when I remembered how he was and the days that we had seen. This was the man who once reduced us all to stitches some ten years ago in the Irish Film Centre, standing up and booming out: 'I'M GOING TO SCRATCH MY BALLS', and how we all fell about and laughed and roared at his immortal clowning as he dipped and scratched and sighed, his tongue panting with a Pantaloon's relief. All those wild capers, all those barbs and sallies were gone, gone, gone, for he was too much mellowed like a sour fruit going to rot, while arteries hardened and blood ran cold and stilled in its flowing. But I had never known the man in his heyday, never known the young Arsene whom my father first had met sometime in the seventies, that same young Arsene of whom only once I heard my father speak, in the shadows of a Galway bar as the saturnine singer Graves bitched about the Florentine lock the bastard had busted. Father had raised a hand to hush his harangue as the chimes at midnight tolled. No, the old man was not always as we see him now. A Lothario once, you know, an electric wit, a lady's man, life of every party. This was the man my father had befriended, the man to whom he kept his oath of friendship although that man was not there with us today. Where had he gone? Age had taken him away, leaving behind only a dopily blinking shell inclined to grumpy spells, a sullen curmudgeon, albeit not without his own brand of intermittent benignity. And into the midst of my reverie, I heard the clatter and rattle of the teapots and the teacups shaking on their flimsy tray, and the crash of the tray and the pots and the cups as they were set down on our table's glossy top.

'There we go now … there,' said Arsene.

'Thanks … you shouldn't,' I started.

'Ah, yer grand …' he said, raising a bared palm as he sat, 'sure, 'tis only …'

Rumbling gurgle from the region of his belly broke off his speech. He paused, drew shoot of breath, poofed and belched softly, excusing himself from another encore. And then Arsene, seated, at ease, at leisure, laid on the table his left elbow, raised next his left forearm, and upon his balled left hand, all balled save for the forefinger, he couched his left parchment cheek as the extended left forefinger began to tap his left temple, tapping in doleful, dolorous, slow-tapping beat and time, with all the drug-induced stillness and superb economy of motion of an Aboriginal sage, like Nandjiwarra Amagula OBE., at thought of whom I smiled as I watched the extended, temple-tapping left forefinger, in act of tapping, dislodge from the tapped temple a few fine white powdery dandruff flakes, scattering like falling stars. Then the temple-tapping forefinger of a sudden stilled and stopped. I turned my gaze from Arsene's finger to Arsene's eyes, which I found, with a start, were regarding my own. Abruptly, stuttering, I looked away and forced myself to speak.

'How was the bus ride down?'

Arsene considered his reply some small while, his replying delayed, rolling it about his tongue as if 'twere morsel of spongy meat ill cooked.

'Yeah … it was … nice … yeah … nice sunshine this morning … great weather … sunny southeast …'

'Ha ha, yeah …'

'… and of course, I have the free travel …'

'… Nice …'

Free travel. He had to mention that, of course.

'… Yeah … it's been warm for December … haven't even needed to turn on me heat at all yet this year so far! … y'know?'

Wonderstruck he looked, seeking verification of the wonder.

'Well, I'll be …' I supplied.

Warming up Arsene seemed to be, getting into the swing of it.

'Yeah … nice skies we get down in Wexford these times … And since I was in the Met Service, I'm able to identify all the cumuli, the n-nimbus …'

'Indeed.'

'How are the folks getting on in Athens?'

'Er, they're well, I think …' I said, scratching a nostril, '… they're well … Got a call from them yesterday … yeah, they're getting on fine.'

'That's good', said Arsene.

A portentous pause followed. And Arsene saw that it was good

'Fine …' I said again with something like desperation, gaze lowering and eyes alighting on Mealy's catalogue, its much ruffled, fingerthumbed head poking meekly out of Arsene's hairy suitcase. There was a topic.

'Are you, eh, going to Mealy's auction tomorrow?'

'Yes, tomorrow … I'm going, tomorrow, yeah …'

'Where's it on?'

'Out in Tara Towers at half ten. I'll take the bus out there, half nine the latest …'

'Right.'

'But yeah … Should be some interesting books there … a few valuable old Irish ones, in which I have a, eh … especial, er, interest, as you know …'

'Yeah, ha ha …'

Arsene riffled through the catalogue with an abstracted air. I sniffed and sought his scent – cobwebby, musty, like the odour of crumbling papyrus. Chapped dry lips parted now in preparation to form the Next Great Pronouncement.

'See … they know me down in Mealy's …'

'Uh-huh …'

'And … 'cause I'm a regular there, see …'

'Yeah …'

'… they know that I know books, like … my opinion matters … and when I arrive, eh, nothing happens until I'm there … and when I'm there, everyone's watching me … nobody starts to bid until I start to bid … y'know?'

'I can imagine …'

'Yeah … it's sorta like … I set the … I set the pace, like …'

'Hoom.'

I pondered upon this boast, about whose veracity I was dubious.Back down on the saucer I set my cup and on my jacket's shabby sleeve I briskly wiped my moistened mouth.

'How's the girlfriend?' the old man inquired, still smiling.

I scowled. He always asked this question, and my response was always the same.

'Non-existent,' I dourly replied.

'Ha ha. Ah not to worry, you'll have one soon.'

I grunted, and wrung my hands, struggling to exorcise the thought of Saruko …

'Yeah …' the old man mused, '… ah, that's very interesting …'

That was one of his catchphrases. He always said it so damply, so soggily and numbly dumb, so thus did Porter disinterestedly express his interest. Porter was his nickname, derived from his love of musical theatre – not his partiality to stout. And now Arsene 'Porter' O'Colla, gazing into the middle distance, spoke again to the air ambiguities.

'Yes … I was offered a place in Trinity once, y'know …'

'Oh?'

'Yeah … they offered me a place in … what was it, physics, yes … because I was so good at maths, y'know … I was so good at the maths I was, y'know … I tried all the questions at the paper, and I could do them all … even the calculus … that was really funny to do, yeah … and, oh, they were amazed I was so good … they were very, yeah …'

'I see.'

Pause.

'But you didn't take the place?'

'No …'

'Ah.'

Pause.

'And why didn't you?'

He considered.

'I just … the idea didn't appeal to me, y'know …'

He fell silent.

'Ah … I see …'

I too fell silent. And all the while we sat there the world outside the windows grew darker all that while. Then the old man Arsene with thinking eyes picked up again his cup. With morose delectation he sipped his milky tea, as did I. So in a bout of silence talk dipped as both of us alike together sipped in twain. His sip was the shorter, since he was in no hurry to finish. And on the shiny saucer his rattling cup with pale frail hand was set down half-drunk. Once, twice, thrice, he smacked his lips, and roundabout the scene he stared.

'Quiet at this hour,' he remarked.

It was, I agreed, my cup near drained.

'Probably about to close soon …'

That was very likely the case, I agreed, my cup all but empty.

'Yeah,' Arsene sighed, his gaze drooping floorward.

My tea was finally finished. On shiny saucer with deliberate hand I set down firm my empty cup, and there was closure in the clink that sounded, as I breathed in and out, hemming and hawing, nervily drumming busy anxious fingers on the glassy tabletop, wondering and wondering how best to wrap all up.

Arsene raised bleary eyes from the floor and took in my table-tapping.

'Do you need to go?'

By way of mannered answer, I cleared my throat, and made to rise.

'You're off?'

'Yes. Listen, er … should I wake you tomorrow morning?'

He mused a moment.

'No', he said finally. 'Yer grand. I'll get up meself.'

'Ah. Okay, so.'

Picking up my bag with faulty strap, I hovered, awkwardly looming and shifting on my feet.

'So …' I said as I lingered, 'what will you do now?'

Arsene thought this over deeply.

'I'll … visit a few shops … look for books … then I'll go have me dinner …'

'Right so … well, enjoy that …'

'I will, thanks …'

'And, eh, see you later …'

'All the best, Simeon …'

He raised his hand, his frail pale palm open and bare. And I took and shook his hand, a handshake brief but warm, and dropped his hand, and then I turned and strolled to the stair. And only as I was descending did I recall an act of humble charity (so callowly absorbed in itself is youth), and so did call back clear: 'Oh! And thanks for the tea!'

'No problem,' said the kind old man Arsene the weatherman.

I descended. And so we parted, amicably, for the last time.

And I do not like to think of him sitting there alone, forlorn and fatigued and left behind, a weary wasted figure sitting there slumped, grogged up by medication misapplied, zonked by ill-doctored drugs. I can imagine how, with a look of supreme haggard blankness, he might have contemplated the silver and golden keys I had left.

And if I say 'forlorn, fatigued, wasted, weary', please do not construe or assume, from the use of these sad adjectives, that there was anything dejected or defeated about Arsene O'Colla. For as he pockets my keys (yes, even now I can see it happen, him whom I shall see no more), you can be sure that his mind will be dwelling on nothing of a sad or sorrowful vein, but rather, he will be congratulating himself on how well he, the hero of his own narrative, has handled things, having once more again come out on top, making merry capital out of dreary happenstance. How he must have relished his independence and cherished his guile and cunning. Free lodgings tonight! He is very pleased with how he pulled this one off, so adroitly and adeptly, really, he amazes himself sometimes. Buying the tea the way he had, so off the cuff like, that was a fine touch, the grace note, and the unused Eason book tokens in his pockets, ah yes, they too could play their part, be employed to show gratitude. And now he thinks of the future, the immediate future, which appears bright. He will have a nice panini for his dinner, or a slobber bun … ah! The fun he and Ulick O'Muadaigh used to have with their slobbering competitions! Yes, he'd murder a slobber bun if they had one. But perhaps those Moroccan waitresses at La Boulangerie of Camden Street hadn't heard of the concept. No matter if so. And after, maybe even, he'd have a mild stimulant in some nearby licensed premises, to pep himself up a bit. Then to bed. And on the morrow, to rise and bid, in a book auction, one among his favourite milieus, in which he might revel. All was well. He very nearly smiled outright.

CHAPTER THIRTY-THREE

Mr Harry Carson was shutting up shop. First, upon the door he hung the sign: 'WE ARE CLOSED'. Next, he locked the till, and began to whistle as he did. Next, he switched off the lights. And then from the rack he took his things with verve and dash, slapping on his shaggy brown greatcoat, and with modest flourish clapping on his head his hat. A rakish black hat he had taken of late to wearing, to conceal his day-by-day greater baldness, to hide from the scorn of gougers his sorry rusty tufts, the vestigial remnants of a lion's mane once luxuriant. He had a certain vanity still. A pity, then, and an irony, that that tight hat may well have been upping the rate and beat of his balding.

Thus attired, whistling Harry, glad to be done, flexing his arms in the shadows, scooped up his keys, and turned around. And dropped his keys. For he saw then with a start a shadowy figure huddled in the doorway, a hairy suitcase clenched in its hand. Harry's whistling ceased.

'Yes?' he asked.

After a pause, the figure spoke.

'Howya, Harry ...'

The voice sent a tremor through haunted Harry. He was further disquieted by its familiarity with his name. But then again, he was a well-known man. He knew everyone in Dublin, and then some. Most likely another of those leeches trying to cadge some cash off him, for his comparative affluence was no secret among the coven of the drunken.

Brusque he began, 'To whom do I owe this pleasure –'

'You're looking well,' it cut him off.

Harry blanched. The flattering tack it was taking, to try soften him up mellow enough before making the crucial borrowing beg, a loan never to be returned. He'd heard that one before. With a hard heart, he tried again.

'Who is it this time?'

After another pause, the reply came.

'Yeah!'

(Arsene had misheard the question.)

Harry was getting heartily sick of this charade. At the belated end of a working day, he had no appetite for a bit of cloak and dagger. A couple of pints in the local was all he yearned for, and here now was a parasite with a taste for amateur theatricals.

'Oh, you're for it now,' he muttered coarsely, marching to the light switch he quickly flicked. But then, as the flickering light chased away the dim, the figure of Arsene was revealed to Harry, and that of Harry to Arsene. Taken aback, Harry beheld Arsene who beheld the form of Harry whose eyes widened in surprise at the sight of Arsene who cracked a sort of smile, to show off his good mood of the moment.

'Is it Arsene O'Colla?!' cried Harry, collecting himself.

'Yeah, heheheh,' Arsene kind of chuckled.

'Sorry about that, couldn't see you in the dark there, y'know …'

'Yeah, heh.'

'How you keeping?' said Harry as he strode forward, hand outstretched with meaty palm bared.

'Never better!' said Arsene, shaking Harry's hand.

Handshake with brio carried off, Harry withdrew his hand, and surveyed the creature before him stood, sort of smiling. The state of him. Needs a tidying, shouldn't wonder, shabby-genteel look he must be going for. But Harry had always gotten along with Arsene, Arsene whose vanity he was eternally ready to flatter and pride sycophantically wide-eyed boost, drawing the odd old man out of himself, spurring him on to greater giddier boastful heights. That was why Arsene always liked Harry, why he always admired and respected Harry, why he always had so much time for Harry, that man he oft called 'so handsome', 'so nice', 'so charming'.

And true to his reputation in Arsene's eyes, Harry, having got over his bout of surprise, now looked the old man in the eyes, and turned on the tap of his charm, in a steady gushing brook of banter and bluster.

'So ... long time no see, Arsene, how are you, are you well are you?'

'Never better, yeah ...'

'Is that so, ah, isn't that great,' said Harry smoothly as he bent to retrieve his keys, 'and what is it you're up to, are you just up for the day, is it, up from, where is it, Wexford, isn't it?'

'Yeah, up for the night, yeah, I'm up to see, uh, Mealy's auction ...'

'Really, is that so, isn't that great, so you're keeping well, eh? Feet up, enjoying retirement?'

'O yeah! Enjoying retirement, yeah, don't know myself since ...'

'What was it you were in, was it the weather, was it ...'

'Met Service. Yes, I was in the, uh, Met Service, eh ...'

'Really, yeah, yeah, exciting place that must be, say, did you ever get a gander at all at all at any of those nice lady presenters, did you?'

'Oho, y'know ...'

'Some fine ones, no? Fine bundles of cowflesh! Which of them were, eh, "easy", y'know what I mean, har har?'

'Ha ha ha, o well, yer wan, what's her name, Evelyn, Evelyn, er ...'

'McCarthy, is it?'

'Ay, yes, McCarthy, yes, she had a bit of a reputation for being ...'

'Arr, she's getting on though, isn't she, lately? ...'

'Oh, she is, yeah, getting on a bit, eh ...'

'Showing her age, she is, yeah, I saw her on the box, when was it, was it last night, was it, yeah, and jaysus, she had a lot of lines on her ...'

'Yeah, yeah, she's looking her age, lately, yeah ...'

'Happens to the best of us, doesn't it, ay, Arsie, eh?'

'O yeah, now, that's it, just it ...'

'Does it have its perks at all, does it?'

'Perks? O now, the free travel is nice, I have the free travel these days, since I was, eh, sixty-seven, and I don't know myself since ...'

'Isn't that great ... arr, I'm not quite at that stage yet, Arsie ...'

'You're not, no, are you not, yeah ...'

'I'm not, no, oh but god, I feel my age, y'know, oh now, Arsie, I tell you now, oh, after fifty, Arsie, let me tell you, we all, eh –'

Harry paused.

'We're stiff all over, aren't we, except in the place we want to be!'

This made no impact, for better or worse. Arsene's attention had drifted to the books. In his dull eyes the flame of hunger to pore over paper kindled and mildly burned.

'Well, you've a great selection, anyway, haven't you …'

'Suppose we have, ay,' (Harry was in equal measure relieved and disappointed that his quip had gone unheeded), 'though mind you, I was never one for the books much, meself, it's, ah, mainly the, eh, top shelf I have much time for at all, ahem, yes.' (It will be remembered that all the erotica, porn and general smutty fiction, so useful to Harry during the slow hours of business, was kept on the top shelf, out of sight to all save those patient and keen enough to look.)

'Oh, you say you're not a man for the reading much, do you?'

'No, no, ahem, no, no, I only did the one year in Trinity, you know, and the chap who marked my single essay, oh, he told the father it was purest drivel, baby stuff, a child could write better …'

'No!' said disbelieving Arsene with open mouth.

'Oh he did, yes, no, I'm no scholar, I was more of a lad for the partying and the courting, y'know, not a man of letters, me …'

'I must say Harry, I find that very surprising,' said Arsene with awful sincerity.

'You do, do you, you can't believe it, can you?'

'Yeah, yeah, I can't believe it, I mean, y'know, to look at you, anyone would swear you were a great man for the books, because you're so, eh …'

'So?' said Harry as he reached out again an arm for the light switch.

'So, er, er, uh …'

Harry's finger came down on the switch, casting them into a dim shroud of murk.

'… er, uh, so *elephant*.'

(Arsene had meant to say 'eloquent'.)

A pause followed, as they stood together in the shadows, Arsene's breathing heavy, Harry rather nonplussed.

'Thank you,' he managed after a gap to say.

Another pause. Perhaps the hint was not enough? He began to make subtle tracks for the doorway, his path ahead blocked by Arsene, who spoke.

'So, you've turned out the lights again …'

'I did indeed, Arsie, that's true, I did …'

'You're shutting up, are you, is that it?'

'I am, indeed, closing time, it is …'

'Ah, that's a shame, I had been hoping to browse in fact …'

'Were you, eh?'

'I was, yeah! Wanted to sample Mr Baker's selection …'

'Oh that Baker!'

'What?'

'The most awful gobshite, Arsie, bane of my life, utterly insufferable, that man …' Harry sighed as he deftly slipped out the door past the block and lump of Arsene.

'You say insufferable, is he?' said Arsene, turning his head to watch the other's progress, 'I find that hard to believe, now, I do, in fact … and so you're going now, are you?'

'I am yes, off on my merry way …'

'I see. That's very interesting.'

'It is. And now, you better scoot out of that, old fellow, before I lock you in for the night! And we wouldn't want that, would we, now?'

To further rub it in, with semblance of savagery he brandished his jangling chain of keys in the face of the other, and flashed and gnashed his teeth.

It worked. Arsene got the message, and as a bonus was rather amused.

'O no, that wouldn't do, no, ha ha ha, yeah,' he said, stepping out obligingly. Relieved, Harry bent and locked the door and pocketed the keys. Arsene looked on admiringly. So strapping and gallant a gent, that Harry. While Harry, shop shut, day's duty done, felt within his soul a bat-squeak breeze of elation. Freedom beckoned in the form of a few. And mayhap too a fag or two. He sighed, adjusted the angle of rakish hat's peak, smoothed out his coat, and looked to Arsene, who looked on at him admiring.

'Now then, Arsie …'

'Now, Harry.'

'What'll it be, Arsie?'

'Be, Harry?'

'Place down the road there, Arsie, I'm sure you know it …'

'No?'

'My local. My home from home. I hate the place but can't keep away from it.'

'Is that how it is?'

'Ay. Now, I know you're not a man for the poison generally, you're a scholarly sort, one of that breed of, er, bookworms who I sometimes have to try sweep out of the shop, prevent them from hatching their eggs ...'

'Ha ha ha.'

'But perhaps you would not say no to just one. Not seen you in a good while, after all, sure. Will you have one with me? A glass in the Grog?'

'Ah sure, might maybe have just a cup of tea ...'

'Bah, tea!' barked Harry brightly, with stealth moving a hand to the back of Arsene to gently nudge him forward and as they slowly westerly forwardly moved, Arsene mulled and hemmed and pondered seriously, and then conceded to have just a small glass of hot whiskey or port or somesuch stimulant. And Harry applauded heartily this sage resolution.

They passed into Grogan's, entering through the back door. At that hour, too early for most, its jam was all but empty, bar the typical pack of lushes secure at the counter, enthroned on their stools, muttering and supping and belching and farting. Garish artwork adorned the walls, below which many soft and slumberous seats were then free from the rumps of reprobates. Harry sat Arsene down at one of these and told him to be at ease, he'd do the honours (Arsene's heart leapt, he was overjoyed), and swaggered to the counter, promptly making his orders.

'Hot whiskey and Heineken, if you'd be so good ...'

The barman heard him and stirred into action and served, and while he served, Harry amused himself by making eyes at the barmaid Niamh. She was a severe but sexy thing, clad in black, probably good with a whip, with a tumbling Rapunzel stream of blonde hair much admired by Harry, who just now felt it good and right to comment on.

'Looking well, my love, your hair, I mean, and you too, of course,' he said sly, a rogue, a loveable rogue, onetime lady's man and errant gent.

She gave him a look of ice (but she loved it), then went out for a fag. Chuckling Harry, invigorated by the flirt, now next nodded to the counter crew, all of them who nodded back, all of them there who knew him, among them cartoonist Tom Mathews; the tramp-cum-poet in exile

Tadgh O'Mara (weeping into his wine); a jug-eared creature in a white anorak who was a part-time conspiracy theorist; and a certain Joe, glasses askew and raincoat much creased, an ostensible family man and supposedly a 'scholar', though what it was he was a scholar of was a matter of some dubiety. This Joe sidled over to Harry, leaning suavely on the counter with his hat at angle rakish, and mumbled in the porches of his ear words often heard. Trying to touch the affluent prod for a few notes, murmuring low in the drubbing Dublin drone so far removed from Harry's plummy proddiness. How's the granny, Harry, she keeping well is she, she popped the clogs yet has she, got yer inheritance yet, can you spare us a few at all for the love of god.

But Harry would have none of it. Hissing, with imperious scorn he dismissed the leech, bidding him wait 'til later, and to have a tad the more tact, could he not see Harry was in the company of a venerable old man of the world of letters. And so Joe saw Arsene, to whom at once he bowed, taught as he had been from the cradle to respect his elders (a bow that went alas unseen by Arsene, who was staring at one of the paintings and trying to think of what he would say when Harry came over).

Then the barman came up with the goods, placing before the eyes and nose of Harry the desired drinks. Harry thanked and paid and took change and left a sizeable tip ('buy yourself a good book, son, you Trinner chumps don't read enough these days'). And so Harry took his drinks and brought them over to the table where was sat Arsene, and set down his drinks on the table, and beside Arsene sat himself down with grunt and sigh, as Arsene looked on admiring.

'There we go now, Arsie …'

'There we go now, Harry.'

'Get that into you, Arsie.'

'I will, yeah, thanking you, Harry.'

Together, they lifted their glasses, toasted, brought rims to lips, drank and set down – Harry's slug was the longer. Together they sighed, smacking lips, thinking of topics. Harry it was who took the leap.

'That barman, Arsie, let me tell you, he's one of them breed of students, and they're a lazy low crowd of snoots as you know …'

'Is that so?'

'Ay. They were in my time, and I'm sure nothing's changed since. Wait – yeah … isn't … Eugene … you know Eugene, of course?'

'Yeah, I know Eugene, yeah …'

'His son, Eugene's son … that lad's in Trinity now too, isn't he?'

'Oh, he is, yeah, that's right, yeah …'

'What's his name, it's Simon, isn't it, what?'

'Yeah … I met him just now …'

'Who, Eugene?'

'The son. He gave me the key to the house just now.'

'Is that so, really. Yes, that lad Simon, Eugene used to bring him into the shop when I was there when he was small … quiet fellow, you'd never get a word out of him, but of course Euge thinks a lot of him, doesn't he?'

'What? Yeah, uh …'

'Fathers and sons … what a topic, eh, Arsie, what?'

'Yeah, uh …'

'My father, Arsie, he was clueless, you know, didn't know how to handle women, totally naive, you know, when he married first, had to ask a doctor what to do, he didn't know how to ride her! Hadn't been taught the facts of life, the poor silly bastard, hah!'

He laughed heartily. Arsene did not respond. Harry gave him an uncertain glance, his laughter checked, then carried on hasty over the hiccup.

'But Euge, yeah, he's a decent man, I'd consider him perhaps my best friend, see him now and again, y'know, sometimes I meet him on Tuesdays for the chess whenever he's at home, up there in the Mount August, you know it?'

'Yes, yes … he brought me there for chess once or twice, yeah …'

'Really? Ah, but Arsie, you were the champion in your time, weren't you, eh?'

'I was, yeah! I was a great chess player, yeah …'

'Weren't you, yeah, until the old, eh –'

The words 'mental breakdown' were on his lips already fully formed, but in the nick he checked himself from forming them aloud. He had a reputation around the town for tactlessness, but this ineptitude would just be too much. Instead, he said:

'The Mount August, yeah, nice spot, of course, my problem with the place is that that bloody Albert's always there, you know Albert?'

'Who was he again?'

'That lazy idle fat waster, Albert Potter, always at the fucking counter, always gulping away, nothing better to do with himself, and what gets me is, he cadged money off me a while ago, and won't pay me back in full, the mean old shite! Shameless, you know? Now, well, we, eh, made up after a fashion, of course, but oh, resentment lives on, Arsie, I'd never know what I might say to him if I had my colour up …'

'Potter … yeah, I think I must have played a game with him once …'

'He's a fine chess player, yeah, for all his faults …'

'Albert … yeah … I can't picture him at all …'

But Harry could picture the bloated Albert all too well. He was sorry to have brought up the subject, for it made his colour rise and face flush. So, he steered away with the following:

'But Euge, god yeah, I haven't seen him for a while, is he gone abroad again is he? I think in fact, no wait, yes, where was it they went, Euge was telling me this just the other day, I used to meet him most weekends, we would watch the matches together, and he told me, where was it –'

'Athens. They've gone to Athens.'

'Is that so? Yes, I went there once myself, few years back …'

'No, they've gone there, to stay with, er, Martin Graves, in his, uh, flat there …'

'Graves? He's the singer fellah, right?'

'Yes, he's a tenor. Martin Graves, he's a tenor.'

'I remember now, he sang at Eugene's fiftieth, didn't he, remember that, jay, yes, what a voice he had, he's a marvellous voice he has …'

'Yes. A fine voice. Martin has a fine voice, yeah.'

'Has he had any luck in the singing business at all?'

'Uh … bit … joined a chorus, I think … Lassus Scholars …'

'Oh yes, it's, what's her name, Franny Dunne in charge of that, isn't it, arr, she was a sexy thing in her day once, used to be mad about her, me, but of course, she'd be past all that by now, a staid oul wan she'd be by now, what??'

'Yeah … Martin … no, I tell you the thing about Graves …'

'What?'

'He has … he has the most wonderful … er … uh …'

(The word was on the tip of his tongue.)

'Wonderful … er … um … wonderful …'

(Breathless Harry hung, the word so near to trickling out.)

'… he has … Martin Graves has …'

('Repertoire', that was the word, go on, rep-rep-rep –)

'… he has the most wonderful *abattoir*!'

(That was not quite the word he wanted.)

Harry, nonplussed, looked on. He wasn't sure he'd heard.

'He has what?'

'yeah … wonderful … *rebbattoir* he has … great variety in it, yeah …'

Harry understood. He smiled indulgently, benignly chuckled, swearing silent to himself to remember that one, to write it down if he could. For a choice gem like that was no common thing, and cried out to be preserved in amber. That is the problem with people, they always forget, such leaky vessels are their memories, the best bits of life being always the ones that slide away the easiest, such elusive things, those the sublimities, the morsels that slip through our fingers as we attempt to grasp them, a myriad infinitesimal grains of sand scattering on the cosmic beach, forever lost forever. Such thoughts as these, on the frailty of memory, gave Harry's benign chuckling a more mellow flavour, until soon it ceased, and he fell to silence, mulling mellow over the matter. The matter of memory. The fault of forgetting. How much, he wondered, of his own life had he forgotten? How many moments, precious, transient, disgustingly ephemeral, how many such moments were lost? They might have lasted and lived as long as he, had he only remembered them, which he hadn't, and so because he hadn't, were gone now for good and all and eternal ever. Much of his childhood, his teenage years, his young manhood, all that was a great dimness to him now, and what scant shards were left to him seemed like relics of a fading fast dissolving dream, vestigial remnants no more than. In sepia he saw himself, a child in the grass, racing after a ball he could not catch, thrown by a man whose face he could not see. His father's face? In a dream he sat on a rug before a fire, warming his little hands, listening to a story read him by a woman whose face he could not see. His mother's face? Wisdom teeth had been pulled. Yet when and where? First kisses had been exchanged. But with whom and how? Where was first love found, if love it was, if love it could be called? Amid the haystacks, or in an alley behind the school? Stolen kisses hastily taken, before the call of a parent bid them part, racing to dinner in response to an anonymous summons from faceless fathers or mothers whose features he could not recall. For the faces of his parents, both of them a long while ago dead, those were murky, enveloped in gloom and fog, no more but a blur to him now. There were old photos about for him to consult, true, fading images of a stern man with a toothbrush tash, and a dowdy woman with her hair in a bun. They had reared him; they had stuck with him through his wails; one supposes they had loved him. Yet when he looked upon the faces in those photos, cold eyes staring into the lens with an air of hostility or fear, those faces appeared now as those of strangers he had never known. And perhaps, when all was done and said, he had never at all known them after all. A chill ran through his veins; he did not even want to consider that. What else was lost? He could not remember. Why had he forgotten? Perhaps because it was none of it worth remembering. None at all. Nothing was anything; everything was nothing. And that perhaps was the worst thought of all.

A stark and awful wave of sadness passed over Harry. Of a sudden, with a clarity he did not want or seek, he saw himself and Arsene sat there now in the murk of dim of Grogan's, spouting to each other inanities; the old man Arsene with his jowls, his parched papyrus skin, his glazed and vacant stare; and he himself, he, Harry, a rake defanged and going to waste and rot, putting on but a feeble pretence and show of banter to ward off emptiness, the old routines long lost their empty lustre; his one-time good looks so fast gone to seed, his hair falling out, his lion's mane gone to nothing, the rusty egg and pate of baldness atop his skull no hat could fully hide, his cheeks rough puffing out with flab of jowl, his ruddiness, his unhealthy flush, his beer belly ballooning as did that of Arsene, that all-over stiffness in his legs, his arms, his back, in all sundry parts save the very place he sole wanted stiffen; he was fifty-four; soon he was old; he would be old before his time; he would not even live as long as Arsene; and in what time he might have left, what could he hope for but more of the monotonous same, for there was for him no hope no more of change;

all fade, all pine, all grow old, and so too would he grow old, and he would be alone and old, and lonely old in his loneness; for Russian Ivana, his last and greatest hope, was history now, married to a rich swine who yet could offer her a banal security Harry never could; and there was none else left, for no other woman now could ever want him as once they might have seemed to have; and he saw further: how black and laden with tar must be his lungs after the forty-odd fags a day it was his wont to smoke; how bloated his sore abused liver after all these pints he downed even when he didn't want to but felt he had to; and how paper thin and fragile must be the sorry walls of his poor and weary suffering heart, a heart whose beat was an uneven uncertain beat, and may soon miss a beat, and after that one miss forever cease to beat and beat no more forever again.

Harry raised a hand, and roughly gave his leaking eyes a rough and furtive wipe and rub. He shook himself, feeling the familiar crave for the fag that alone could calm him. And then he felt the silence he had allowed to settle. Awkward, he ploughed back in.

'Heh, yes, yes, quite the abattoir I suppose your Martin Graves has, yes, a well stocked one, decidedly, yeah, with all the favourite tunes, what?'

'Yeah!' said Arsene by way of reply, cracking a sort of smile.

And Harry smiled back at the old man, as best he could in his condition.

'Just going out for a quick ciggie, Arsie, back in a minute ...'

'Right!'

CHAPTER THIRTY-FOUR

It began to rain. If one was outside one would be wet. It was thus meet for one who was outside at that wet hour to seek shelter within some nearby dry stronghold. So shelter was sought, and shelter was duly found. For in the drizzle and the damp and the mounting darkness of the dying day, a farther bar's open door promised a wealth of warmth within, glowing in the murk like a distant firefly. The old man approached the door, struggling to stem the mild chattering of teeth the downpour had spurred. Thus clenching his teeth, he passed through the door and entered the bar, in which doorway he stood and dripped and dried. The bar was largely empty at that hour. The electrician had long departed, called away on the score of faulty wattage. The copper was in the crapper and the barman was dozing. Only the fat man remained, secure at the counter's corner. Upon hearing the creak of the door, the fat man turned round to greet the newcomer. And then he started. For he seemed somehow to know this old man. And the old man, in his turn, seemed somehow to know the fat man, a fat man who had not always been fat. And so both men stared and marvelled in silence, the fat man who sat and the old man who stood, struggling both to recollect who it was they were, what friends were theirs to share, what passionate hobby once had bound them, what ravages the changes of time had wrought on both. The old man beheld aghast the layers of blubber that had drowned the onetime gallant, once so limber, once so lithe, the contours of whose face were enfolded now in rolls of fat, of which departed shade only his kind blue eyes remained alone unchanged. While the fat man coolly regarded the shell-shocked shape, the jowly mouth ajar agape; the many gaps between teeth; a hint of dry drool on the chapped lips; the shabby jacket lightly laden with freshly fallen snowflakes of dandruff; the glazed and vacant stare; the pot of belly bulging; the hairy suitcase in cold hand held; the potato skull topped by a bobble black hat, that gave him the look of a geriatric garden gnome; and the right shoulder a shade higher than the left, that sunk as if gasping under all the load of life. And from all this array of attributes assembled, he could but conclude only nothing. Who is the man? Who is anyone? What of those that on the street we see but do not see and brush by without a backward glance, spare souls going gone, all of them who like us live lives, lives upon lives of all who were born and grew and all who dream dreams, all who think and drink and wink and stink, and shit and wank and couple and beget, and thereafter sometime die, just as we are doing and will do, but none whom we know or can ever recall, those lost lives we passed over deeming unworthy of our time or attention, and we too for them thus dismissed, they who make on us no impression to last as they pass us by and by us are passed, and never again are ever to be seen, background players in our lives, and we too in theirs, window dressing, passing blurs forever forgotten lost and gone, like ghosts. And the fat man looked upon the ghost in the doorway, and thought then life so tragic, gratuitously so, too total, too terrible to take. And an overwhelming sadness for a second held him slave.

But he was never one to wallow – go on, go on.

'Hello there,' the fat man said.

'Hello,' the old man said.

'Started to pour again out there, I see ...'

'It has, yeah ...'

'Bloody miserable, this climate, eh?'

'It is, yeah ...'

'Come over here closer to the counter. It must be chilly near that door ...'

'It is, yes, it is, yeah,' the old man said, making shift to approach.

His hand that did not carry his hairy suitcase took off from his head his black bobble hat, his egg and pate unveiled. Slowly he shuffled over to the counter, his feet never far from the floor, heels dragging, the hold of gravity strong. The fat man beheld bemused his slow approach, and gestured then when the old man was nearer to the stool to his left that was spare. With a mumble, the old man took the hint, and with a grunt sat down on the stool. It was a small struggle, for his stature was short, and the stool was tall. Set down next the case near his feet. Set down his hat on his lap. Then he yawned.

The fat man waited for the word. But it did not come. Their eyes met. So he said it.

'… I believe we've met before?'

The old man eyed him. He was so huge and bloated, on the outside so rough. But his voice was gentle. So it was safe then to say that he thought they had.

'Good. But in what, er … what context was it that we met?'

'… Context?' the old man said, confused.

'Context. I mean, what, eh, were the circumstances? Of our meeting? I mean, you know,' he blustered, elaborating, 'this is one of the subtle charms and minor pleasures of this place, trying to figure out just who the hell is who, and where we met, and when. Faces from the past walk in a lot. And they're not always the ones one wants to see. Disquieting thing at times, I can tell you. But a pleasing pastime all the same.'

'Ha ha ha,' the old man said.

The fat man was pleased with his phrasing, and took another gulp from his glass by way of reward. Setting it down, he rolled about his eyes as if to think, then made to seem, through gesture, as if he had only just remembered. Make it more fun.

'Wait – I believe it was the chess world where we met, wasn't it?'

'Oh, yeah! Chess, yeah …'

'Some time back, eh?'

'Yeah!'

'Whereabouts would you say? In Kilkenny, I'd imagine …'

'It would have been Kilkenny, yeah …'

'Do you remember my name?' said the fat man boldly.

The elder man hesitated. Then conceded that he thought he did.

'I am flattered. For that matter, I believe I know yours.'

'Yeah?' the old man said, cracking a sort of smile.

'You are … is it Arsene?'

'Yeah!'

'Good. Sorry, I myself am Albert, Albert Potter. How d'you do?'

Belatedly he held out his hand to the weatherman to shake, who smiling did take, well pleased. Though he did suppress a wince to feel the moist fleshy flab of Potter's pulpy palm. And Albert in turn was disturbed by the cold of the old hand he held, not for long held, letting it quick to drop. So there they were, then, the two of them together then, Albert and Arsene.

'So … how are you, Arsene?'

'Oh, never better, yeah …'

'Good. And I suppose you knew all along who I was?'

'Ah yeah, I suppose I did, yeah, heheh …'

'Aha. Very good, Arsene, very sly. By that I see that you are a cunning and canny old rogue. You hold your cards tight and close to chest. Perhaps that's what made you so excellent a chess player in your time.'

'Yeah, maybe it did, yeah …'

'Ay, one needs to be as cool as a cucumber in that business, and as I remember, you were one of the coolest and cleverest I ever played.'

'Thanks!' Arsene said, 'you're, eh, very, uh … very *receptive*, Albert.'

(In fact, 'Perceptive' was the word he had wanted. Though to be fair, it did fit.)

'Oh, I take pride in my receptivity,' said Albert, not missing a beat, 'you pick up an acuteness like that in that game, you know, you come to read a person as you would read a board, like a grid held in head. You must have some stories of the game to tell, about where all the bodies are buried. Would that I could fish them from you, before you stagger off and die, your tales untold, juh, juh? Sorry, I am blunt. Anyway, long time no see. What are you up to these days? What have you been doing with yourself?'

'Oh, well, you know, I'm retired awhile, yeah …'

'Mmm, that must be nice. Regular work is such a chore. I myself could never get the hang of it. Never could stand it. Felt stifled. And I don't mind getting paid, not at all, that's the great thing, I feel the sting of thrift now that I'm unemployed, but still … it's the tyranny of the whole work thing that gets to me, this invasion of your life, you know, this authoritarian voice that speaks to you through a schedule, juh juh juh?, dictating that you must be here at this time, doing that and this! Madness! My entire energies these days are devoted to scraping by on the bare minimum without having to sink to do that, to work, I mean, to save myself from that hell, and keep my better self for my, er, better business ...'

But what better business, Albert?

A sound of flushing offstage. Jacky the Polis must have done his dump.

'Er, anyway ... what is it that brings you to these parts?'

'Well, I'm just up for the night, see, I'm just over at Eugene Collins's house ...'

'Small world! Sure I know him well, he used to play chess here before he went abroad. He's a decent fellow, a good sort, though not so much the man of action ...'

'Ha ha ha, no, not so much the man of action, yeah ...'

'Ah, but who is? Action is overrated, anyway. Those who do nothing do no harm. Though do no good either, I suppose. Ah, you can't win ...'

Arsene said nothing.

'But I'm much indebted to Eugene in my way ... you're staying at his house?'

'Yeah, 'cause him and the wife went, went to stay with Graves ...'

'Graves? Oh! Not the one who sang at Eugene's fiftieth?'

'That man, yeah, Martin, he's a great range, he's, he's practically a *charnel-house* of musical knowledge, he is yeah ...'

'Charnel-house? Storehouse, surely you mean?'

'What?'

'Never mind. But what did Mr Graves sing again? Some Schubert lieder, I fancy, and some sentimental something too, along the lines of *Some Enchanted Evening* ...'

'You were there were you?'

'I was well scuttered. Booze was plentiful then. But yes, somehow or other, I distinctly recollect being there ... I had to be there. It was the thing to attend that December, a night to remember. You too were there? How strange I did not see you. How funny again, the way paths cross, how we came so close yet missed the mark, back then, six years ago must have been, until now, at this place and point of time ...'

'Funny, yeah ... but, eh, anyway, I got the keys to the house off the son, see ...'

'Eugene's son? Yes, I know the son too, after a fashion – a civil if strange sort, I would say, but I suppose decent in the end, a son who takes after his father in that regard …'

Mind full with fathers and sons, he took a gulp from his thinning glass. Elder Arsene sat quiet, ruminating on what next to say. And then the younger, glass set down empty, smacked lips, and decided on another.

'Robbie!' he called, not too loudly, 'Robbie!'

Benign, bespectacled, smooth as oil, Robbie the Barman immaculate in dicky bow dress got up from his doze and glided back on over into sight to serve. The same again?

'Quite right. And oh, Arsene, what do you care for?'

'Eh … just a Lucozade, please, if you wouldn't mind, yeah, thanks …'

Robbie the Barman heard, and sidled off to pour. Jacky the Polis, looking red and shifty (the dump must have been a downer), came back furtively, slipping shyly onto his stool, avoiding the eyes of all. Then Albert Potter asked Arsene O'Colla another question.

'Say, by the by, must ask, there is doubt in my mind – your surname – which way do you prefer it? It seems to clash with your first name, which is so oddly continental. Gaelic meets Gallic in you, eh? But are you a Collis, a Collopy, an O'Colla or what are you?'

'Oh, any of them really, yeah …'

'Good. Though I suppose for the purposes of patriotism, such as I normally have no time for, I'd better employ the Irish form of O'Colla, eh?'

'Good man! One of our own!'

'Careful now, Sir. Nothing more mindless than getting too wrapped up in the tricolour. Romantic Ireland's dead and gone, as we know, so let it lie. For I'm usually such a cynical sod, deflating the debacle. I know my history inside out, and it's nothing but a catalogue of ineptitude. Pinch of salt with everything is best, I find.'

'*Erin go bragh*!' barked Arsene in a short burst of gusto.

He started to laugh. He had decided that he liked this fellow, for all he was a sad case. And Albert, though more demure, was also moved to smile.

'Ah yes, the old slogans … suppose they can still stir the blood, make it boil. I take it you are an old campaigner? A Sinn Feinner, even? Or dare I say a Fianna Failler? Please god, not that.'

'Yeah! And, eh, the old IRA, too, yeah.'

'Oh no!' cried Albert, smacking brow, 'I see there are no limits to lunacy …'

'And, and my, my father, he was a hunger striker in his time too …'

'I see. And a cradle Catholic too, I would suppose? Must warn you, by the way, I myself am a son of the, eh, other stock, if you like.'

'Ah … one of the others, are you, yeah …'

'I am, yes. One of that dying breed. But you won't hold that against me, I hope, if you are as good a Catholic as I'm sure you are, you will turn the forgiving blind eye to that, overlook that alien strain in my makeup …'

'Ah, less of that now, there's no ill feeling …'

'Thank you. But you're from Wexford, Wexford … isn't that the county that has the most paedophile priests at large? I recall a recent scandal there, perhaps the details will be fresher in your memory –'

If Arsene heard (for he looked as if he hadn't), he was at any rate spared from answering by the arrival of the drinks. Albert, with some reluctance, was the one who paid.

'But indeed,' he said as he sipped and licked his sores, 'it's a rich pedigree we have, literary wise at least, we Anglo-Irish prods … we have our Yeats, and our Swift and our –'

'Swift! I was just, eh, reading a great book of Swift I was …'

'The Dean of St Pat's, yes, one of my favourites. The clarity and poise of his prose, you wouldn't want a word changed, juh, juh, juh? Proper words in proper places.'

'Yeah, yeah, his, his *Tale of a Table*, that's a right book, yeah …'

'Table? Ah, yes. I see where you're coming from. But anyways, yes, literature is the richer for the input of its prods. Of course, well, they only go so far. Some figures you know, just stick out, excite a sense of awe with which you cannot quibble. Somebody like Joyce, say, boyish sort, just doesn't excite that fear you find in, say Homer. Shakespeare. Dante. Tolstoy. Proust, o he's the pinnacle. No novelist in English comes close. Tolstoy's the only one comparable. Did you read much of them in your time?'

'Oh yeah, yeah, loads, yeah, I love Tolsty and Prowst, yeah …'

(In fact, though he owned several editions of the major opuses of both, Arsene had never wholly gotten through them. Open up his volume of Proust, stowed on a Bannow Bay shelf, with rodent chorus. A bookmark shall be found on page 390, in the midst of *Swann in Love*, testifying to how far he got, and from whence he never proceeded.)

'Is that so. I'm impressed. You seem a well-read man, Arsene.'

'I am, yeah. I deal in books, see, I'm a book dealer ...'

'Oh really? An excellent hobby, by the mass. Is it profitable?'

'Ah now ... variable. Depends on the demand, you know ...'

'As it would. But do you specialize in some area or genre?'

'Irish books. Rare Irish books.'

'Ah. I should have known, of course, staunch patriot that you are. Yes, I can see that demand for those books would be apt to fluctuate ...'

'Yeah ... here, I'll give you my card ...'

He took out his wallet, and rummaged in its every cranny, coming up after a gap with a small rectangle of firm plain white, a simple unassuming card he passed across to the other, who took it up with interest and beheld.

ARSENE O'COLLA
Leabhair Gailige

Bannow Bay
Co. Wexford – Ireland
Tel: 053-473166

'I see,' said musing Albert, pocketing the card, 'very interesting. A made man, you are, then. You're enjoying a productive retirement, so.'

'Keeps me busy, you know? Good investments. And pays the bills ...'

'Ah, the bloody bills, they are the bane of mine. But yes, you're just up for the night, you said. And up to do or see exactly what?'

'Oh now, Mealy's auction is on, see, so I came up to see that ...'

'Ah, a book auction, good. I'm very happy to hear that a man would be willing to travel so far sole for the sake of his books. I'm a bookworm myself, as you may have gathered.'

'Yeah, I did think it, yeah ...'

'Between that and the chess, how much we have in common, eh?'

'Yeah!'

'Yeah. The two of us who do common worship to the printed page and written word, in thrall also to the graded board and all its army. You might be a brother I never knew. Must say, Arsene, I find myself thinking you a man after my very own heart.'

A pause full of feeling followed.

'Thanks, Albert,' Arsene managed.

He took up the Lucozade he had been lacking to lap, lifted to lips, and slurped a slug. Albert with Foster's followed suit to slurp. And Arsene set down his glass with grunt, then came a coughing wheeze of sneeze, a racking hacking cough that sneezing shook him. The younger gave the elder a look of concern, considering the wisdom of delivering a whack to back. But before he could, Arsene got up and stood down from his stool, and in a mumble excused himself and shuffled off to the toilet.

And Albert meanwhile sat at the counter alone again and staring into space thought deep and long, in wonder at what a piece of work was life. At times of hell he could not wait for it to end, as when at the height of his depths he had crapped incontinent and wept bitter tears as the trousers were fouled face down lying on the cold damp floor of bog crying out for a balm of death's relief to soothe; and still at other times he would wish for a bare second to span centuries, and nearly wept again to think that this time that was now could not be always, all but wept for precious time that was wasted and was lost. It was all too short. Like flowing water on the pebbled riverbed snaking through eroding stones, wearing on and on down to sand and grains that too would slip away gone from grasp, thinning like his glass was run and this day of theirs and ours that would too soon itself be done, and never again may we see the sun. We, he, you and me, to never see again the sun so long since sunk. And the day that was a life was wanting hours. All or most of them gone by already, and so much yet undone to do. How one yearns to fly free from all, tread time on tip of toe and nimbly play a never-ending game of go. But held always back and down by all those scabs and sores on soles of feet, and our warts and carbuncles and blisters, our pimples and pustules that swell to popping with their pus, our teeth decaying wanting brushing, our lips that are chapped, our rashes and bones so easy broke, our bile and spleen, our scales of skin that flaking fall, our fingernails full of grime so grimly fun to pick and eat, our nostrils full up stuffed with snot and phlegm that drips or crusty hardens to bolus balls, and our weary blinding eyes that darken dim and die, all the dross and dreck of these our damnable frames of filth that weary weave unsteady their all-too-mortal way through all the thickets of this time, and Why? Why? Why do people die? Why do babies cry? Why is the sky blue? Why does the Earth spin? Why does the sun set? Why do you never see any baby pigeons? For it is just so fucking random the way of it, this life, the point of it always eluding Mr Potter in his ponderings, as he screwed up his face in his perplexity's deeps, and clawed his cheeks, and tore out tufts of his ratty hair in his angst, full all of listless woe in his hapless pursuit of a reason why, but no, no, he would never cease to seek to try, for no more than try he could not do, and so would carry on trying do. Where do we go from here, for heaven's sake? What can be done that must be done? No man of action, he yet still feels there is something in the wings lying awaiting for its cue from him, the burden of its fruition resting on none but his own broad shoulders, bullish shoulders that sag under all their daunting weight of promise. There's the muddle mundane of life for you. A mad world, master mine, believe thee me, so do.

And into the midst of his wondering, he looked up and saw the benign eyes of Robbie the Barman watching his. The eyebrows raised as their mute gaze met. Same again? No –

'I don't suppose you wouldn't by any chance maybe happen to have a chess board and clock handy around the place would you, Bob?'

But Robbie the Barman did.

And when Arsene emerged at last back from bog, it was to find Albert setting up with care and glee a game of chess. And shy and sheepish he was when discovered, a slight bit bashful was Albert by Arsene found.

'Ah, Arsene, there you are ... er ... fancy a game or two? Normally it's Tuesday is chess night, but, eh, since you're here today, and Bob's come up with the wherewithal ... I thought maybe we might, er ... well, will we?'

Arsene hesitated. Lennox had told him to avoid excitement. He never disobeyed doctor's orders. But even so – the giddiness granted and lease of love of life beating anew in his breast bethought him otherwise. Why not? Give it a go, boyo.

'Yeah sure, a game or two, why not, yeah ...'

Albert was mighty happy this to hear. How many minutes do you care to have by the clock? Which side and shade will you take? For the elder and better must have the right of way to choose his terms. So Arsene chose to be black for this first game, and Albert would be white, and Arsene, in light of his age's malady, would have twenty minutes deciding time by the clock, while Albert would plump for a bare four or five, though a mere one or two was his norm, and this sum of time, big for him, on account of the respect for the prowess of his elder he bore. The conditions laid, they went and played.

And so they played a game, grimacing and fidgeting and scratching and humming and hawing they played, tortoise Arsene sedate, while eagle Albert was agile and darting deft, rapid reading the board as a book or music score, pursing his mouth and scowling sipping Foster's as he played to the quick coming end, he it was who won this game.

'Bravo,' at the end said bleary Arsene with pumping heart and staring eyes, 'you haven't lost it, fair fucks to you ...'

'Ah well, you had me in a tight corner a good long while,' modest Albert conceded with shrug, 'but then, that hole in your flanks started to widen, y'see, and once I see one of those, there's no stopping me – another?'

'Yeah, let's!'

Roles reversed: Arsene white, Albert black. Clock time the same.

And so they played again a second time, and this time Arsene won.

'Christ! You did for me that time!' the sweating younger panted, 'you struck me in my weak spot, you made right for my Achilles heel ...'

'Ha ha ha,' elated champion Arsene laughed.

'It's that bloody Italian opening you had to play to begin, nothing gets up my nose like it, I don't know what the hell it is about it, but it unnerves me like nothing else, I just crumble, I go to pieces whenever I meet it ...'

'Italian opening, yeah, that was always my specialty,' said boastful victor Arsene, 'I remember, yeah, when I was in, eh, was it Sweden, yeah, in the eighties sometime I was playing that, and I think Karpov or Kasparov came up behind me to watch, he'd just never seen anything like it, y'know?'

In wonder wide-eyed he looked, seeking verification of the wonder.

'Well I'll be damned,' said Albert with a pinch of subtle salt on his tongue in cheek, 'I can imagine that scene, two gods in awe of ye. Another?'

'Yeah! Yeah! One more!' said eager Arsene, in love again with life.

And so then they played again a third time, and this time together they drew a draw. And when they both of them this third time a draw drew it was pure and simple joy they both of them knew, Arsene and Albert knowing joy as they looked up to look at each other and smile in joy, sitting happy playing chess in the merry Mount of August.

CHAPTER THIRTY-FIVE

Alone again was Arsene who came to Lombardy Road in the quiet of the night, as the wind blew and the rain dribbled. At number nine he stopped, the black squeaky gate of which he opened, the red door of which he approached. Suitcase set down, in a deep pocket he made to rummage for the keys, noting the garden to his side, overrun with weeds, the wilting holly, the hawthorn that was less than hale. The keys golden and silver found, he applied them in their respective orders to the locks to which they did apply, and entered.

The first thing he noted upon immediate arrival was that he had left his bag outside, having forgotten to pick it back up having set it down.

In the hall with his bag, which he set again down on the floor, the better to ease himself, an old man weary, he took off from his head his hat, his egg and pate bare unveiled. The hall was dark, as was the whole of the house. To the right and east of Arsene there was on the wall, beside the alarm that was so seldom set, a light switch, to which pressure he applied pressing a finger, to illumine the dim, which did. And the light came on, and so he saw the hall before him:

the ragged red carpet at his feet, where were scattered odds and ends and ads and sundry bumf through the letterbox daily shoved; to his right a radiator; to the north ahead of him the stairs; to his left two doors; on east and west wall the large oblong mirrors facing each other in which he could see himself if he chose, which he didn't; the hall table at the left west, fine mahogany, under which were shoved some sets of shoes unused, and lain on the top were some unpaid bills for gas and internet, and set in the centre of that table serenely smiling with eyes closed and expression beatific was another souvenir from China, the huge head of a beaming Buddha, brown and broad.

Next, of the two doors on his left, it was the nearer that beckoned best. So he entered that room, the front room, and turned on the light, and saw:

the large windows by burglars broken once upon a time, their flowery curtains drawn; a bulb encased in a paper shade from the ceiling dangling; the computer on the table, an Apple Mac that rarely worked, with printer in tow, dusty from its disuse; snaking wires streaming the floor to trip up the careless; a grey swivel chair in which one sat at the keyboard to type; a bulky mattress laid on the floor, complete with sleeping bag and pillow, inviting a body to recline that never did, laid before the cold fireplace that was never lit; some statues bestrewing the floor, among them: a naked black lady, a woodcutter and a laughing oriental sage; a laptop and iPod belonging to the absent Gallagher and Freaney; on one wall a reproduction of a photo of the young James Joyce, hands in pockets in front of a greenhouse, wondering would the photographer lend him a shilling; a painting of Jackson Pollock done in the style of Pollock, painted by Eugene's brother the pun-loving Jake; shelves and shelves and shelves all round the four walls of the room, coming down with bric-a-brac and clutter: board games (Scrabble, Connect 4, Monopoly, some jigsaws), photos (Ralph Richardson in various guises and poses; William S. Burroughs mooching moody in a grotty bar), miscellaneous memorabilia, and most of all overwhelmingly books upon books, more books than could ever be read, books browsed, books discarded, books neglected, some among them being:

War and Peace   The Brothers Karmazov   The Gormeghast
Trilogy   Boy   Being an Actor   Rosebud: The Story of Orson Welles   The
Trial   The Virgin Film Guide   The Best of Hal Roach   Fantastic Mr Fox
Ulysses Stan and Ollie: The Roots of Comedy: The Double Life of Laurel
and Hardy   Life: A User's Manual   Notes from the Underground   Esio
Trot   Monkey
Ralph Richardson: An Actor's Life   Anna Karenina   Moby-Dick   Malone
Dies   Going Solo   The Real Life of Laurence Olivier   À la Recherche du
Temps Perdu (Volume One)   Inside Mr Enderby   Help!   Dubliners   Joe
Gould's Secret   Catch 22
Nothing Like the Sun   Charles Laughton: A Difficult Actor   Lucky Jim
Gulliver's Travels   David Lean: A Biography

A Tale of a Tub Don Quixote Egil's Saga The Essential Calvin and Hobbes The Life and Death of Peter Sellers Othello Pink Samurai A Portrait of the Artist as a Young Man Molloy Shooting the Actor The Narrow Road to the Deep North Damned to Fame Garfield Earthly Powers The Playboy of
the Western World King Lear The Mosquito Coast Paradise Lost Collected Poems of W.B. Yeats My Secret History
The Authoritative Calvin and Hobbes Journal to Stella Someone Like You Anthony Burgess Winnie the Pooh I am a Cat The Life and Opinions of Tristram Shandy Crime and Punishment My Name Escapes Me The Sea The Blackwater Lightship The Witches Mrs Dalloway
Frankenstein Treasure Island Le Morte D'Arthur Sir Gawain and the Green Knight The Canterbury Tales Hamlet Troilus and Cressida
A Christmas Carol The Picture of Dorian Gray The Guinness Book of Movie Facts and Feats The Koran The Mabinogion Great Expectations
The Narrow Road to the Deep North How Poetry Works Still Pumped from Using the Mouse: a Dilbert Book
The New York Trilogy Peanuts: A Golden Celebration To the Lighthouse
The ABC of Reading Donal McCann Remembered A Sentimental Journey Herzog on Herzog The Unnamable The Book of Illusions
Stanley Kubrick: Director A Critique of Pure Reason The Shining
Dracula Goosebumps Series 2000 Montaigne's Essays Mr Vertigo The Fearmakers Blessings in Disguise The Idiot The Rime of the Ancient Mariner Alice in Wonderland The Aeneid The Man without Qualities
Classics of the Horror Film The Hunting of the Snark Finnegans Wake
The Little Prince The Iliad Murphy Watt Moon Palace
Life of Pi A Heartbreaking Work of Staggering Genius The Van
The Odyssey The Butcher Boy Mephisto The Sorrows of Young Werther
The Portrait of a Lady Vanity Fair Selected Cantos of Ezra Pound The Lord of the Rings Extremely Loud and Incredibly Close The Hobbit
V is for Vampire The Far Side Gallery Mr Bean's Diary Mr Bean's Scrapbook The Hitchcock Murders Simpsons Comics Extravaganza
Paul Scofield: A Life George's Ghosts May you live in Interesting Times
A Mad World, My Masters Dead Man in Deptford Madame Bovary
Amerika The Master

And curious Arsene wandered round the room, admiring the paintings, inspecting the photographs, in thrall to the weight and quantity of all the junk and debris gathered. He was disgusted by the numerous collections of sordid porn bought to sate impotent appetites, and was amused by some of the funnier pictures.

But there was one photograph above all the others that aroused his interest. It was stored in an unobtrusive place, down on a shelf near the floor, easy to miss at a casual glance, a monochrome shot, nicely framed, a sizeable rectangle. And Arsene got down on his knees, to pick it up to bring it closer to his ailing eyes that he might see it better.

It was a black-and-white photograph of two men sat on a park bench beneath a tall and lofty tree. Both were bald. Both wore glasses. The one on the left, the younger of the two, had a moustache, his arms folded and a baleful look on the face, his smile a forced one, eyes looking furtively away (he did not trust the photographer). In contrast, the other older man on the right, was quite at ease. He sat with hands on his lap, legs apart, looking directly into the lens, a benign smile on his wrinkled face. The attitudes differed, but the familial resemblance could not be missed. For after a moment's mental cogitation, Arsene concluded that he was looking at a photograph of Eugene and his father Frank. That singular shot had been taken almost a decade ago, one day when the two were wandering abroad in the Phoenix Park, enjoying the sun and the deer, making small talk (most of it made by the son – the father's speech was failing), when they had been approached by a shady soul in a mackintosh, who begged for the privilege of picturing them. And though the son was dubious, his father was keen, and so the shot was briskly taken. And the picture wound up in the magazine *Magill*, and so the father and son achieved some faint fame among the circle that read the periodical and saw the shot.

And Arsene now remembered the old man Frank Collins, professor of chemistry back in the older day in Galway, Donegal born, hailing from the valley of the badgers at Dunlewey's foot, whom he had met way back, before he went gaga, and his marbles went wandering, remembering him to have been a saint, so sweet and good a man he was, ever gentle, unassuming and kind, never raising his voice, keeping forever in check his temper, ever the one to hold open a door to aid the passage through of the one behind who followed, husband to the crazy Megan Devlin, Granny Maggie Nutmeg, the both now long dead and gone, a mordant reflection that made him feel sad and cold.

(Though Maggie was since become a Banshee, not that Arsene knew.)

And from the front room old Arsene made motion back into the hall, and hither from there to the stairs. Slowly he mounted them, step by shuffling step, 'til he came to a landing, and lent upon a banister, ahead of him two doors beckoning. The one to his left was a toilet, the one in front was Simeon's room, the toilet door slanting open inviting entry (a humourous sign saying 'CACATORIUM' stuck upon it), but the latter door was firmly closed, a young man's monkish sanctum, which would admit no outsider. Faithful, the old man did not, his attention caught upon a sudden by a picture, another picture, one that was hung on the wall between the two doors, to which he came closer to inspect.

It was another photograph, larger than the first, the vertical frame rectangular, and the setting, so Arsene saw with a start, was none but his own home in sunny Bannow Bay, in the very same light dining room of brightness, where only this very morn he had sat and ate his aborted breakfast, and let in the one-eyed cat about whom he had quickly forgot. Everything to be seen was there in that photograph, yet younger, less fusty, less dusty, separated from today by the distance of a decade: to the right of the frame the mantelpiece sat, to the left in the corner the radiator squatted, and upon the floor the shaggy rug lay, draped in darkness save for spotted squares and shafts of sunlight peeking through the table's spindly legs, and higher up the picture's height one's enraptured gaze ascended further, to take in the chairs that clustered round the table's top, swathed in its stippled veil of starchy cloth, to drink up in delight the telltale stains and the brave little teapot, with its helmeted lid, glossy attire of ebony akin to the armour of an errant knight, and nearby stood also a carton of milk, long past its curdling due, and the little bit of melting butter, and a glowing jar of lustrous marmalade, and a stack of riffled newspapers, and then – the grace note – the couple of revenants sat at the table in a stupor, sole inhabitants of the dining room of then, on some faraway morning some many summers ago upon which it was taken, a precious second snatched from the dizzy and unstoppable turning of time, two living beings granted living death on a frame of film, frozen like flies in marmalade's amber, or withered figures in a frieze – Eugene must have been the one who took them, he had an eye, coming through the kitchen door brandishing his lens – the old man Arsene and Simeon Jerome, together alone again.

There they were, the pair of them, set against the sun beyond the heavenly bay of window's screen, seeming to shimmer on fire from the green of grass within whose reflected radiance they sat in their seats, and one could almost hear again the twittering of the cuckoos and the larches, for he had not yet then cut and mown down the lawn to limber, the young man's back to the glass and face to the lens, of whose prying gaze he was overtly aware, while the elder man sat in profile, seemingly oblivious to the photographer's scrutiny. They were themselves, but they were fresher than today, the callow lad but a fidgeting nipper of nine, who knew not yet the pain of love or grief, posturing and cringing, putting on a vulgar show for his father's camera, screwing his face up into his habitual scowl – a grimace that never left him, rendered into stone by every wind blown – and his elder senior uncle, an uncle in nickname alone, for it was not pulsing blood that bound them, but mutual sympathy's esteem that coursed in their veins, not to speak of the accident of lifelong association since birth, and the elder man was sitting gravely, seen from the side, shifty and itchy in the wig he wore, sat at a slant on the doming cone of his eggy scalp, a rat's nest darker than the scanty tufts remaining, younger seeming smarter, tidier, neater, a hand set upon the cheek of his teacup, on the brink of taking a sip, a slurp of tea too hot that would give him to gasp from the scalding on his burning tongue, fitting more snugly into the cleaner clothes he was wearing, belly not yet so grossly distended nor swollen, a pockmarked bulge of pale stomach potted from gluttony's excesses, or the gaseous evil of vapours and airs, sitting staring into the middle distance with an air of something inscrutable astir in his face, betokening perhaps the beginnings of a frown, roused to reflect, at a hint from the youthful shade that sat by his side, on the blooming glory days that were gone, and of all that had not been his.

And older Arsene who looked long upon the shot, following listlessly the rambling train of snaking paths of thought, those hazy byways down which his muddled thinking strolled, now found with some surprise mysterious tears starting in his eyes. For the weight of all that had not and never would, of destinies ignored and possibilities misplaced, of a life's rout of copping out and opting for the easier, of buses missed and books not bought, money lost or treasure stolen, of encompassing miserliness and meanness of spirit and purse, of bleeding noses, varicose veins, heartaches and heart attacks, paltry satisfactions and all too potent sorrows, all these lasting irritants crept up all over his hunching frame like tics or shivers, lurking over and behind his bending back like the shadow of his departing soul, or a wizened ghost with tangled ragged beard and blazing eyes, whose tapering fingers reached up to snuff out the lights he had turned on, now turning them off one by one, one by one the bulbs began all to nullify and die, as the shadows came stealing, until darkness lurked all over the black landing, which dimming he attributed to the failing and blinding of his own old eyes, mulled by rheum and the burgeoning inklings of cataracts, teary and crying eyes, so sad and so tired.

And he remembered youth, of childhood summers spent at play on Curracloe Beach, flying kites in the heights of the blue yonder, paddling up to the ankles in the lukewarm shallows, pottering with one's spades and buckets, building castles and fortresses from the powdered sand, sand scooped up to fling in clumps with giggles at one's brother – who killed himself subsequently, for some reason of his own, by wading into warm waters far out of his depths – while one's father looked on from the dunes in the distance – but he was always distant – nursing some secret grievance, nursing his lip he incessantly bit and chewed, wed to a woman for whom he could never muster love, their babes begat from some sterile sense of duty solely, rearing passionless offspring hurled into the brutish world to wallow and flounder – his breath halting, he raised a shaking arm to lean upon the wall, resting his brow upon the photo's frame to steady his sobs – and he remembered all the dullness and the tedium of his life of growing loneliness, and the hopes he had cherished that came to be quashed, and above all those he had held for her – why could he not summon the name – the one woman in all his life and in all the world with whom he fancied he had a chance, for she was troubled as was he, she seemed to understand him, and him her, unfed and starving thin by choice, a bony anorexic bulimic who binged and puked her guts whenever she did not fast, who seemed, for whatever why, to take a certain solace in his silences, whose hand he would hold and whose tears he would wipe, confiding in him over long and doleful hours, and sportingly submitting to his clumsy kisses, whom he charmed and wooed with the wit that was once his own, a ring for whom he bought, a proposal to whom he made, mid many stutters and bashful shuffles of shy feet upon the floor – but she gave him her word she would.

Her promise transformed him, and he walked awhile as one among the stars, roused to buy an oblong bungalow in Bannow Bay, the walls he painted glistening alabaster, the windows he scrubbed to shine and dazzle, splurging on the bric-a-brac he bought, all for her, a luxuriant lovers' nest fit for a family, cradles and cots he stooped to survey, a million miles away, pounding heart straddling the future far too soon, plush the golden ending he foresaw, no better close to the inconsequential chapter of his faltering days.

But his optimism had been premature – she thought it over once again – and decided she was overhasty – decided he seemed too childishly keen – and decided she did not like him all that much enough anyway – and so she called it all off with a cutting call on the phone, and went far away abroad.

He never set his eyes on her again. Broken, he cracked. For days and days on end, and maybe months, he would not rise to feed nor stir, slumped in his bed of sorrows staring at the ceiling, starving and freezing in the frosty cold of his icy burrow, hallucinating and intermittently raving, until his nearby fellows thought fit to break down his door, and summon forthwith the services of the sanitarium, as soon as they saw to what grim state he was sunk. He himself attributed his mania to the chaos of his heart that had missed a beat – and perhaps such a misdiagnosis was not all that astray – the paper of its flimsy walls was ripped and torn, a scabby wound that would not heal. So there it was, all too plain, chief among his many dismays, the one denial from whence all his sorrows start and troubles began, tucking it out of sight under the rug of an aura of optimism, which was at best itself no more than more denial, a lifelong lie he fed himself day by day and hour by hour, such impoverished comfort that could not sate his hunger for the love he lacked, starved of the seeds he never sowed, and the babes he never bore, doomed finally to grow old and be ever alone, the old man Arsene alone, old and lonely old alone. All these thoughts raced through his fogging head, wetting eyes squinting in the gathering dim, the blackness swirling around him as he peered upon a patch of the shot, as he stared upon the blurring shape of the nine-year-old child, of the younger Simeon Jerome.

And perhaps after all in the eyes of the old man Arsene he had always seemed something like the promise of a son that was never to be.

What happened next we cannot know. Know only that something stirred and scraped in the shadows behind him, a whisper, a croaking gust, the brush of a gown upon the carpet's fur, velvet draping of sleep that fell all over his brimming eyes, lids fluttering in relief as they were shutting down at last, to slowly sink and fall to the floor, folding to his knees, face first then to his belly, to flatly lie upon the landing's floor recumbent and supine, in the guise of a slumbering child, a dozing infant in a cradle rocked by the spectral prophet's soothing patter, prostrate and stonily still, as if dead. And the old man never knew what hit him, for there was no time for such a courtesy.

And that is something like the end of the story of Arsene the weatherman, after he lay down and did not wake up – and if he did, it was not as himself. He's nothing but an eggshell now, seeping yolk of soul gone soaring away, flown free from its cage, into which soon sometime some other quicksilver element might choose to petering enter, to take up residence and refurnish, and inhabit the petty frame apace. But we durst not presume. And that is why his whole long dreary day was followed through so thoroughly, as it was to be the last when he was as he was, in which every inconsequential second seemed of significance, and every shaky breath betokened volumes, after which every exhaustive snail's step we laboriously traipsed in his wake. And would we not all of us want to live every day as if it was to be our final day, such sweet days of our lives that are wanting hours, ticking ineluctably toward the ultimate stroke of midnight, if only indeed to live every day so surpassingly fully, such privilege accorded to poor old Arsene O'Colla at last, granted a final lease of life before his own was aborted and done with.

Where do we go from here, then? What of young Simeon?

CHAPTER THIRTY-SIX

Young Simeon returned home some hours later, and discovered the front door ajar.

Arsene had left it open the second time he entered, fetching his forgotten bag, which fact Simeon could not then know, as he stumbled dumbfounded around, calling out the old man's name over and over, crying Arsene, Arsene, Arsene, sounding so hollow in the rippling ocean of that night of echoes, the little name was as lonely as the moon whose light shone into the hallway.

Simeon ascended the stairs to the middle-storey landing, only to start upon the lump that lay in the dark by the door of his bedroom, the form of a body sprawled prostrate in the murk, in the glum dim gloom on the ground. Upon seeing this, the young man froze, and faltered in bleak foreboding, unsure of what to do, afraid of what move the recumbent form might make lest it was roused. Yet when he saw that the thing on the floor still made no move but continued to lie still, he summoned his courage to tiptoe closer, to flick on the switch of the landing's light and illumine the dimness by degrees, blinking as the flickering was revealing the prone old body to be that of none but Arsene, the old man Arsene, uncle Arsenic, Arsie, Porter, the Chairman Arsene O'Colla himself, lying face flat on the floor, splayed and still.

Uncertain awhile Simeon stood, barely able to register what it was it meant, what it was he saw; then he bent numbly to his knees, and crawled over closer to inspect. Dead? He can't be. Wait. Gingerly, he stretched out and lowered a tentative hand, to rest upon the elder stooping back, to find that still it was raising and lowering, as the dead weight was continually slowly inhaling and exhaling – so no, not dead – but sleeping?

With care, with struggle, for the flabby weight of the body was heavy and hard to shift, Simeon rolled old Arsene over onto his side, then over flat onto his back, that his face might face the ceiling and be lit by the light, a cold shell, a dishevelled husk discarded on the floor like a shoe, ditched by the soul. He looked long upon that face in silence, the face he knew so well, the face that told him nothing – the eyes lightly shut, imperceptibly seeming to be quivering, so imperceptibly it was more likely a flutter of one's own lashes obscuring the sight – the mouth agape an inch as he mechanically drew breath but did not snore, a streak of dry drool trailing to his sagging chins – the skin paler, pastier than earlier, ice-cold to the touch, as was found when one applied a palm to the wrinkly brow and puffy cheek – so no, not dead, yet neither quite asleep – if sleep it was, why choose to slumber on the bloody landing – a coma? Paralysis? Vegetative? A swoon, another heart attack? But surely the lips would then be blue, and the cheeks too.

The thought of calling a doctor did not even enter his mind – instead, he found himself strangely numb, hunched by the body dumbly, looking on with cold detachment upon the mute fish's face of the man he had known for all his life, with whom he shared a capacity for sullenness and terse quietude, for being gnomic and withdrawn, set at a frosty and elusive remove from the way that others were – and now the elder one was irrevocably withdrawn for good, and the younger left behind deprived.

But this much he had the presence of mind to decide – it might be a good, not to say sanitary, move to shift the old man from the floor into the toilet, that he might without any effort evacuate his bladder and bowels lest they be full. But the operation was not so easily executed, the mechanics being awkward – he must needs firstly sit the old man up from his stance of lying, and then shove his own arms under the other's fatty armpits, to hoist him back up to his feet – much exertion was required for this, the one-time athlete having fallen to fat, his gasping weight akin to several sacks of spuds – and Simeon, rather weedy, was never strong to start with, and it took many huffs and puffs to get the stringless puppet upright, and prop it clumsily forthwith, one bloody foot at a time, step by waddling step, kicking the heels to bid them forward, toward the toilet door, opened with a nudge of one's knee, to flick on the bathroom's clinical white light with a spare finger, and to catch from falling the tottering totem upon whom you had momentarily relinquished your hold, and thence to turn him around and settle him down on the throne, the lid of which was blessedly open and raised, and once sat down, one now was obliged to unbutton or unzip the rumpled trousers, to slide them down the legs to the pallid ankles, so frail, so dainty, their veins varicose, and next slip down the old man's underpants, stained and blue and smelly, spotted by starchy tokens of the blue moon nocturnal secretions to which he was prone upon occasion, letting loose a fetid aroma that made the boy blanch, and after all that, as one shuddered, wiping one's brow with a sullied hand one made quick to scour in the sink with soap, then to prevent Arsene's torso from drooping down and sinking back to the floor as it was wont, a listless mannequin denied his puppeteer, and so to seat him back grandly in state, settled and ready.

All this done, Simeon sunk in sweaty exhaustion onto the side of the nearby bathtub, and coolly regarded the old boy now sat on the pot, head aslant to the starry sky that the peeling ceiling shielded, seeming sleeping as he shat, mouth ajar to drool, one eye groaning open, its pupil glazed and blank, so vacuous it could not see, a picture of desolation, portent of our future fate. Simeon had heard tell of some scandal in some old nursing home, wherein the incontinent invalids were strapped to the bowl and tied to the toilet, while their minders ran amok with carousing and playing cards downtown – he had applied something of the same principle in this particular case, though rather more humanely, sans strings, without rope. But he had not the stomach nor heart to sit and wait for the sound of the foul matter making motion – when the first tentative trickle of the flowing swill lightly touched his ears, up got the boy from his slump by the tub, storming out of the bathroom in pity and disgust, to let him alone do what he may do.

From the landing, numb Simeon stumbled upstairs to the topmost floor, removing soggy shoes as he did so, their soles flapping from the holes he cultivated (crossing the road that morning, a motorist had called out: 'Hey mate! Yer shoes are talking!'), and once upstairs, he turned on a lamp to illume the long table, set over by the southern bay windows, at the top chair where he sat, beside his breakfast's remains, a bowl that bore the hardening remnants of his microwave-made porridge, and the vital white envelope containing the key originally intended for Arsene, seen too late, all too late. A bottle of red wine half depleted, survivor of revels bygone, stood by his teacup, which bottle he uncorked afresh and poured into the cup, noticing only now that the cup still contained a dribble of cold tea, stale tea with which the merlot mixed. But anything would do.

And so he sat there alone and silently, and drunk the queasy mixture in displeasure uneasily, craggy and grim in the tawny moonshine puddle of the dangling bulb above, as the wind blew and the teeming rain fell, casting mournful eyes all around the darkness of the large and vacant room, a blur in the blackness that enclosed him in his solitary spotlight, as he downed the ill wine right down to the lees, smacking dry lips as he poured out a finger further – the bottle belonged to Gallagher and Freaney, he now remembered vaguely, 'twas one they had been hoarding like beavers, and such a violation, on his part, of their paltry rights of ownership, would occasion a squabble in the morning, or whatever time tomorrow they returned, petty little bitches that they were, but he couldn't give a fig – and so he drunk their fill to smother wonder. But he could only shy away for so long from the overwhelming sadness of the evening's events, and soon an intolerable melancholy bit him to the bone, akin to the howling wind that petered through the cracks in the walls, peeking through the window chinks, swirling and curling in snaking gusts around all the corners of the cold and draughty house, all but empty and void of life, save for the defecating zombie in the toilet, and the maudlin youth supping lousy wine at the table's top, setting down the cup to rest his head in his hands.

Suddenly and briefly, he yearned for company of a kind, such as incapacitated Arsene no longer could provide, be it animal or vegetable, though preferably human and feminine, to whom he could talk and ask advice, who might lend a shoulder upon which he could bend his brow, to bury his face in her hair, glossy and sleek as a cat's, the hair of the same Saruko who ate up what heart he had – but just as soon as he felt the urgent inkling of buried desire, he set it aside in a frosty huff. Instead, he lifted up his cup to the light, and proclaimed, with a batting of his lips, a silent toast to the departed spirits of all the dead men and women he had ever known.

And as he toasted the spirits that swam in the ether of his sights, and gulped down deeply the vine's benediction, he wondered whether was old Arsene on his way soon to join their ferried ranks, and whether his present ghastly paralysis was only the portent of a final deathly perpetual stillness. But he knew no numbers he could call – for what family the fellow had were either distant or dead – nor could he even begin to articulate or explain, not even to himself, what was the full truth of what was going on – and thereupon decided that it would be best (though not bravest) to shield the shell from scrutiny, and set the enigma out of sight and safe, to keep the old man hidden away from prying eyes, in a spare bedroom or a shed, and carry on looking after him, in whatever way he could when he could – he owed him that at least.

Swallowing wine, setting down his cup, he rose and softly padded from the table through the dark back down the stairs to the landing, returning to the toilet to survey the patient's progress. He was sitting immoveable as before, though a new and fouler odour, heavily lingering in the leaden air, informed the nurse that the predicted motion had been made, and the poor old bowl now bore the crapulent deposit done. And now 'twas time for another cumbersome manoeuvre that turned Simeon's stomach, as he heaved the elder from the throne up to his feet, and leant him propping against the wall as he riffled some paper from the roll to wipe – the hide was mercifully clean for the most part, thanks be to Jesus, though still it was chastening to behold the wrinkled buttocks, dimpled by pimples brushed with downy greying fur that clogged the stippled anus – and then to vehemently dump the soiled sheets into the brimming bowl, to flush away the filth and slam down the lid, the air now newly alive with the whirling and gurgling of the waters wending their welling progress down the festering pipes, as they bore away their newfound treasure of turd with pride, down to the gutters and drains and all their loathsome remains.

And in the meantime, once more again the lowered trousers and drawers were rolled back up the calves and thighs, to hide his paltry pride and lend the wraith a smidge of his bygone dignity, and then the same wobbly tedious advance of exit to the landing, turning left as the young man gallantly sacrificed his own bedroom to the prescient basket case, for all it was the coldest room in the house, wheeling the bulk of his father's friend through the door of his sanctum, passing in the dim the shelves that held the crumpled relics of his youth, the scrappy comics (*The Beano, The Dandy, Batman and Robin*), the garish picture books (*The Cat in the Hat, Where the Wild Things Are, Fungus the Bogeyman*), the toys and action figures (those goddamn Mighty Morphing Power Rangers), ignoring all these tawdry tokens of moribund childhood misspent, pushing the old man forward one foot further, and stood back to let him fall with a flop onto his threadbare bedding, to slip off his shoes and socks and tuck him in as comfortably as he could, nestling the empty head on the pillow, covering him in a patchwork blanket leaking feathery pinches of its fluff, drawn right up to Arsene's chin.

So in monkish Simeon's cell would dopey Arsene thereafter thus lie, for all the sundry wintry days succeeding his body's arrival and his soul's departure, consigned to the boy's bed to slumber amid the cluttered debris of the room, one more bit of bric-a-brac among the clusters of junk, one among the books and the pictures and the reams of juvenilia, the budding author's immature and inept attempts at art, such as his crappy graphic novels peopled by his stock repertory company of cartoon characters, whose many starring parts and supports were indicated only according to the doffing and swapping of their different hats, the piles of pages throbbing atop his desk beside the bed.

And as he stood again and made to put out the light before he left, he took a final look at the potato face on the pillow – and froze to see both eyes bolted open, bloodshot and yellow. And he heard a voice, thin and reedy akin to onion's skin, like the growl of a bear, or the hoot of an owl, or a panther's purr, a voice that by some dark trick of ventriloquism appeared to issue from the old man's throat, though his lips did not move:

'*Mark you this. A Day of Reckoning is in the offing, my beardless boy. Take heed, and do due reverence; and pass on the happy tidings to your kindred kind, so that to the good news I bring, none among you be blind ...*'

Simeon Jerome Collins fled from the room screaming in horror, and bolted upstairs seeking the comfort of the couch, upon which he collapsed undone.

That night he slept but did not dare to dream.

CHAPTER THIRTY-SEVEN

At the same time, elsewhere. In Mount August Square. Where lies a tennis court round which looming lodgings stand stern, their brickwork choked by ivy, by vines that clog the fissures and strangle stone, and a glum dark park where, from the branches of the trees, dangle ropes tied into nooses. A fit site for suicides. In summertime, floating through air of square, one sees billowing by the blossoms of cherry trees, clogging the gutters, breezing into one's nose, stirred to dance by gusts of wind. But there are none now; the court is empty; the trees are bare. Dead leaves, hangovers from the party's close, lie around in a dull litter of sad damp clumps. Darkness reigns.

And into Mount August Square, a padding animal comes, with crooked back and burning eyes, coming through the soft night prowling mid the damp, with tentative scuttle. Hear the sound of the tread of its paws, to which some wet leaves stuck. Where are you going to, snowy my son? Where are you going to, my handsome young one? Many miles have you wandered, let loose from lair unwitting. You shiver as you stalk – for the spring your master hath wrought has not yet made it eastward. With the tang of meat in your mouth, the fangs and canines smeared by blood of man, mandibles you wetly scrubbed with all the floppy length of your tongue, licking quite clean your chops.

And towards one especially westerly residence something draws thee now, a mumble in your mind's ear, a murmured hint on the lapping breeze that nips. Meander over, puppy. Accordingly, by the foot of a foggy lamp casting light of pea soup, the creature paused at the dour blue door, its steps and eyes driven downward from the panelling that people admired, to ogle the rusty gate barring the steps to the basement beneath, the way down littered by potted plants, dying flowers and ferns, winding vines and sometimes thistles. Descending now, slab of stone by worn slab, in the quiet night wagging its ragged tail, pottering down the steeping walkway toward his sullen door.

Pausing there to scratch the boards, to poke a cautious paw, a curious snout, nosing and sniffing the letterbox's creaky flap, through which so few messages so seldom were passed, bar the bills, tedious bane of listless life. Scratching met with silence bare within – did he then slumber unknowing? Poor form, the hungry mongrel growled.

Looking down then, a pot of milk you saw on the doorstep, a rude and badly burnished bowl of chipped china, for it was the owner's way to leave an offering available for the sundry little kitties who flocked the square, wandering cats astray by starry night and cloudy day, rushing to lick and slurp up the moony pool in the creamy bowl he left them, some of which vagabond mogs he would admit enter into his grubby abode, and keep him company while he drank and dozed. He loved to watch their curling backs and vaunting tails, their glossy hides dappled by his flickering lamps, their shiny whiskers bristling as they warily eyed him from afar, stalking round beneath his tables and his shelves, vaguely afraid of the pack of tomes he hoarded in his silent keep, wary of the books that crammed his dismal den, dodging the bottles and cans that strewed his laden floor, all such things so blunt and heavy by which they lightly passed, weightless refugees from the terrain of his dreams. Moved, upon occasion he would rise from his slump, and all would scatter at his blobby approach, taking flight like geese or gulls, all whom would flee save for the friendlier, who suffered him to snatch them and catch them, and clasp them to his fatty bosom, to whom he would croon dimly remembered ditties from long-lost days best forgotten, scraps of old songs and childhood tunes. And sometimes, staring into tawny dubious eyes of liquid emerald as he sang, he would see himself mirrored, a fat and flabby drunken man singing badly to a sleek and pretty cat, whose cold and unforgiving glare would move him to drop them, away from his bulk from which they bounded, a man feeling sad and fat, forlorn and alone again.

He had been dreaming of the cats when the scratching of the dog at his door awoke him. He awoke, by degrees and blearily, to find himself ensconced on his couch, awash with a medley of tins and tang of staling booze, his mobile phone numbly clutched in his porky palm, the metal now wet with the sweat of his clasp, glistening from the slimy balm that fell from every oozing pore all over the skin of his body. For he had fallen asleep in the midst of a message he had been typing, with no small struggle (so fat were his fingers, so tiny the keys), intended for Arsene, which so far read:

> Good game or 2 tonight. When will you be up next? We must play again. Good chess in this town is hard to

To find or to come by? He opted to let it lie, for the sound of scratching forbade him ponder further. So the text remained unsent, as the phone was tossed aside, carelessly dropped into a cranny of the bloated couch, in which tight niche it would remain a week unfound. Up to his feet he heaved his heaviness with prosperous huff and gasp, and to his door he lumbered stately across the carpet. Such a sound of scratching augured a visitor of the animal kind, since a human body would be more apt to knock, though as likely as not they would not, as witness the case of the landlord's son of yesterday's morn – but was it really so far away as only yesterday? And such a noise of scratching, he figured more as he paused at the doormat, did not signal a guest of feline shape, not one of those purring ghosts who haunted his dreams, for they were wont to mewl or keen, rather than waste their precious claws in crude chore of scratching at the door. And so, all unassuming, he took his key from his pocket, stuck it in the lock, unlocked and opened.

Sniffing the air with an initial apprehension, looking down in the dark, from the stooping mound of his bulky height, the eyes of Mr Albert Potter met with those of a dog. A small dog. No more than a pup. A puppy lost and starving. Doleful and plaintive were those hungry burning puppy's eyes with which his measured scrutiny met. Snowy white of tarnished alabaster was the hair of that hound, whose lustrous furs glowed in the dimness of that quiet hour, some fine dark time to go before grey dawn was due.

The puppy looked up at him, and whined, pleading mercy. Beguiled, the fat man melted, stepping aside by way of invite. And the white hound took up the hint, and shuffled inside, sniffing the musty carpet, and nosing the kitchenette's cracking tiles, wagging his tail in weak and famished joy. And Albert Potter, sucking his jelly lip he bit to help him think, closed and locked his door again, observing mildly the erratic circling of the pale pup, scuttling about his cluttered floor. Of what breed? Bloodhound or basset? It was hard to say. Sometimes the ears were pert and pricked, sometimes they flopped and drooped. Bright eyes turned upon him appealing. To feed, yes.

He ambled over to a cupboard, wherein hid many cans of beer and beans, past which ranks he dug and delved as he bent, 'til he brought up some slices of queasy ham, and drippy bits of bacon past its best, the worried remains of a buried chicken, some curls of mince and pockmarked sausage, all the odds and dregs of such meat he could supply, dumped upon the tiles in a tidy pile, toward which bound the hound to scramble and gorge, for his empty gut to fill. A slobbering noise of munching and slopping, with long dropping pink of tongue, and spitting gnash of gleaming canines, gladdened brush of tail wagging up and down in the air, up and down slapping the dust from the rugs with every smack, feathery motes arising in a pillowed cloud with every thrash of the tail.

Mr Potter pulled up a stool upon which to sit, and looked upon the creature kindly as he chewed, with an inkling of growing warmth in the man-frog's bulbous eyes, happy to find company of a kind, such as here had come to him in the secret night. He had not kept a dog for some years, never since his stepfather's pet labrador had died, the handsome black the ailing elder bequeathed him, in a rasp from his deathbed passing on ownership of the friendly beast to Albert, that dog who was his constant companion for several seasons, who daily lead him on the leash round-about the square and city, such energetic perambulations as kept his frame chipper and trim, as gave him something other to do than drink. And though the crowded lodgings were not ideal for an animal, let alone a dog so large as was his labrador, the two of them had made do, and merrily so, the man and dog who were kindred in their creature comforts, loving the company of one another since neither had a thing to prove to each other, happy only to breathe and be. Then the labrador died of a pox, reduced to frothing quivers, writhing piteously until it croaked.

Thoughts of his dead dog of yesteryear swam back up before his brimming sights, from which welling threshold he was called back to earth by a lick – a lick on a dangling palm from a plump tongue, furry tongue of whom from him had sought and found such easy sanctuary. Mr Albert Potter gravely blessed the beast in pseudo-solemn benediction, and then patted the bright skull, tenderly scratching the ears and temples, stroking fondly the smooth body of the alabaster puppy he lifted to his lap and hugged.

'You're welcome to stay so long as you don't have rabies,' he mumbled dryly to the cheery dog in his arms, as he drowsily began to swoon and rock and dream again. And the White Dog, whose shape was shifting, barked but once and briefly, as if in tacit approval or agreement, and thereafter fell sweetly asleep, snugly nestled on the pillow of the giant's lap, the voluminous lap of corpulent Potter, whose blubber lips were leering as he smiled upon the dog's repose, and gently stroked his tufts, leering like the grimacing mask of a gargoyle, stony custodian of all the city's sorrows.

CHAPTER THIRTY-EIGHT

The morning after, a Tuesday I think, I woke up in a fevered haze, half convinced, half-heartedly hoping, that last night was all illusion. But such naive optimism promptly dissipated as soon as I went back downstairs to my room to check, to see whether indeed he was still there, and in the state I had left him – and he was. He had turned and thrashed the sheets amok over the course of the night, sign of the foreign spark now welling within him, to which I could name no name. And he looked upon me oddly as I entered, lemony eyes greeting me with a strange stare that was alien indeed, alien to his nature that I knew. The mouth dropped open, and I was told:

'*An elder man of blubber will fall in love with a tattooed younger.*'

Thanks for that, I peevishly thought, unable to think of any better expedient than to part the drawn curtains, to let in some light to the must of the stale cell I had bequeathed. He shrivelled and winced, raising a clawed hand to shield his eyes and face, as the shards and rays of glum sun fell upon him, for all that I felt it would be beneficial for a plant, or a vegetable, such as whatever he was, to be thus illumined – and watered. For yes, I thought also to set a glass of water by the bedside – plus the option of an apple and banana. And this was all the care I could afford him for now, that day, cold and selfish as the young often are, preferring instead to leave him alone. Dressed with bag in hand and shoes on feet, I parted from him, bidding the bugger an adieu with a muttered, 'I must be off now, Sir. Take care. See you later.'

To which he replied:

'*Ay, ay, and I— C— C— is coming again too.*'

Shuddering, I shut the door, and departed, setting a routine in motion.

For truly it is incredible just how quickly one falls back into a comforting routine. You may call me too young to be saying such things, if you must, but comfort I needed, and distractions I sought, and I found them plentiful. For thus lulled by all the ordinary of the outside world, life for me became again as dull as ever, notwithstanding the unnatural occurrence of which I was uncomprehending witness. (In retrospect, I suppose I was in denial – and perhaps I was going ever so mildly slightly mad too, mad in my own little way.) My days in college ran their typical course of tedious lectures at which I slept, chatty tutorials at which I kept mum and dumb, letting the loudmouth Yanks hold the floor, extended bouts of tea-drinking at the Campanile's foot, and even further extended bouts of bingeing in the bars. And come the dismal evenings, one staggered back home to find that all that had really changed, outwardly, was where one slept, namely the couch. This change of sleeping arrangements never roused any comment or question from my tenants, and nor did I ever bother to tell them. As for my secret guest, I had only to check on him upon my return, to see whether he had ate and drank the provisions I had left him, and more often than not he had, with the least of fuss or motion. After one unfortunate occasion when he wetly shat the bed, being unwilling or unable to shuffle to the toilet (assuming he knew where it was – it was impossible for me to determine just how much he still understood and was aware of), I installed a rude chamber pot of china in the room, a rundown relic from Lindisfarne we had hitherto stored in the shed, and this arrangement seemed to suit him well enough for the nonce.

As for Gallagher and Freaney, they never suspected nor remarked upon a thing, for they only had eyes for their trashy computer games and their sickly love games, ungainly kindred to the ant who sees only the grain of sand that is directly in front of it. Even when they heard weird noises issuing from my room, they cared not a fig, perhaps assuming the gurgling and chanting of Arsene was only my own lonely reciting.

Predictably however, they did make a tiresome fuss on the score of the bottle of their wine that I had drunk – I repaid them amply, like any fuddy-duddy uncle would, to no effect.

And I was, supposedly, all this lengthy while still desperately in love, futile love destined to be doomed, a life's lack of which, in my manuscript, I made a self-pitying meal. For what of she? Saruko, Saruko, Saruko la belle, a Chinese beauty with a Japanese name, who went out with Edwin. Can you picture them? So far they seem no more than ghosts, bloodless spectres granted nothing but names. In my stillborn book *IKAROS*, I submitted both to a sort of glorification, burying them in tawdry passages describing her habit of hugging him for a hundred pages.

It really was the most dreadful shite. I was a true sore loser, in the fullest sense, seeking paltry compensation through my wishy-washy words of wish fulfilment, willing that I was Edwin, being hugged and kissed by the woman he won. One could almost hear me drooling as I scribbled those soppy mawkish lines of drippy liquid length, the pulpy purple sentences dribbling out of me like spittle or mucous, making a smear on the page like fly's eggs. And I took pleasure in sharing such sections with Edwin, sending to him in emails gargantuan swathes of the stuff, and he was chuffed to see himself put in print.

But then there came to be a twist to this sorry business, occurring roundabout this time I recount, the hectic period of Arsene's interment and my mounting madness. On a certain day, having written and typed a typical purple passage, I mailed it off to Galbraith for his perusal, as was my wanton custom. And later on in the fine night of the same day, whilst I was tippling solo in the Pavilion, gloating in quiet over the words I had woven, stood alone on the veranda admiring the darkly empty cricket grounds, sipping Bavarian horse piss contained in a can, jostled and elbowed by the other wretches round me, in whose jovial mirth I took no part, who should I then happen to see afar, mounting the steps from darkness into lightness, but only her very same self, about whom I had only just writ.

There she was below me, and here she came toward me, the one and only. Today she wore her usual rainbow's riot of colour that spanned the spectrum, a scarlet jacket of fire hydrant red (or was it? or wait no, maybe it was her skirt I meant, but she had a purple coat that got nicked in a club ...), and a spotty yellow dress, tights of 'electric azure blue' that did justice to her amply curving calves, and somewhere else around her ensemble were spots of violet and green, on the scarf or on her bag I think, mere flecks, mere impressions was all I saw, she was like a pointillist painting in shimmering motion, for mine foggy eyes were misty as was customary, and I was rubbing them roughly as her own met mine, from down below from whence she was ascending, climbing waving as too did I in turn, catching my breath till soon full by my side she stood, the pair of us alone among the gabbling horde whose chatter we ignored.

I affected, as ever, a poor imitation of nonchalance, smiling gamely, accepting the token hug she offered, the same she bestowed on all she saw (since hers were so automatic, as the dreary years wore on, their onetime wonder wore off, as one grew to doubt their sincerity, sincerity such as she so often took myself to task for lacking). Released, I stood back an inch, and leant against the balcony's boards, to make the usual small talk, how are you, you're looking well, thank ye kindly and the same to thee too, the same timely inquiries as to the state of her health and mind, and all that jazz.

'The sun shines for you,' I might just then have said.

'You have such small eyes,' she would have said instead.

But after we had chatted for a minute, I noted that her eyes – those swarms of crescent moons, pebbly black pools wherein swam stars – that her eyes were moist. She had been crying, poor thing – witness the reddened rims, the lankness of the lashes. Her lower lip was trembling. Her glossy hair seemed askew. Some sadness had bit at her heart, and I did wonder why, but was too afraid to dare and ask, allowing instead a certain silence to fall, for her to fill and me inform, figuring she would, and indeed she duly did.

'I broke up with Edwin,' she said.

I thought I had misheard initially – for what she had said simply could not be, not according to the scenario I had scripted – for only that very day I had written cloying letters of their love, the same as I had sent him, such love that to mine own eyes seemed implacable and enduring – but now I learnt that their life in my book was not the life those lovers were leading. So blind I had been. A qualm of guilt flooded me. For now I saw, overwhelmingly, how people have an independence, an autonomy, always beyond what we say and write about them, so we ought never durst presume, as I had done so rashly – and if one cannot know oneself, how dare one assume one ever knows another?

It seems so painfully obvious in retrospect, but I was young, and somewhat less than wholly human, and the lesson struck me home and hard, as I stupidly stood and heard. For once more again she was weeping, her shining cheeks the gushing home of streams, and through tears and sniffs she hazily recounted the sad story of their split – her main motive appeared to be that he had not given her the attention she deserved, and felt to be her due. Cold and unloving she dubbed him. Calculating and dissembling she reckoned him. Dishonest and insincere she thought him. Overcome, she choked, and upon my flimsy shoulder bent and buried her lovely silky head, the showering strands of which I dumbly patted, fingering her hair as she rent the air with her piteous sobs.

And so, down Pavilion steps we descended and departed from the crowd, mine arm around her shaking shoulders, for to guide her pining stumbles, and past naked trees shivering in the chill breeze we went on our way, as glassy-eyed on she murmured shrilly more: 'I think, like, with relationships, people should like, fit together neatly, like your other half, like jigsaw puzzle pieces like, there should be no snags or anything like, I thought I'd found like my soul mate, but I guess we were just too different, and maybe he was just waiting for me to break up, wah wah, I hate men …'

On and on she prated thus, as we meandered past puddles through the dank and foggy city streets, and my heart sickened in the lamplight as she made her lament, on and on 'til soon again she was silenced by her sobs, and I stood glum, and knew not with what words I could comfort her. That night I took her home with me, for Gallagher and Freaney she numbered among her multitudinous bosom buddies, and with them I figured she could natter ad nauseam, whilst I might sit aside and ponder in quiet. 'You never give advice!' she had earlier chided me, in the tone of a helpless child, disgusted by a negligent parent that never gave good guidance. To which I replied, like the cocky shit I was then, 'I never advise since I do not pretend to be wise.'

And so in Lombardy, upon the front room's mattress, myself and my home's sullen cohabitants sat round her in a ring to listen, as she spilt the teary beans some more and further, for the worst she had still to divulge. You see, a goodly part of the reason for the abrupt timing of their break had much to do with her discovery, while nosily rooting through his bags, believing that all of what was his was hers, of one of his many journals, in which he had been confiding his innermost thoughts, the deepest passions of his mind.

This journal made distressing reading for naïve Saruko. For in it, he divulged details of his dreams, mainly wetly erotic, and of his various twinges of lust for busty girls quite other than she, of longings unrequited and desires unfulfilled, of his burning ardour to know a woman biblically, and fully possess a girl bodily (since for all the kisses they exchanged, he and she had never made love – virginal Saruko, old fashioned in her way, refused to have any sex before marriage, so protective of her treasure she was too afraid even to use a tampon), confessing in depth to the gnawing frustration and sometime boredom he felt for her, hating her obstinacy, her selfishness, her neediness, so clingy she would not let him be himself, so squeamish she would have liked to deny him the solitary manual pleasure he sought in recompense (to this I can attest – I once saw her cheekily quiz him as to when he had last masturbated – and when he replied, in all honesty, that he had not done so since Sunday ('Did you come?' she queried; 'Presumably!' he quipped), she haughtily took affront as if he had wronged her, and would not speak to him for the rest of the week), and so on and on she riffled through his private pages to show us instances of the dark heart her one-time darling had. At least one passage I found particularly revealing and hilarious, in which, in a vaunting stroke of vanity too far, he named his pet crickets after the canon's luminaries, among whom he himself numbered: Dante, Heany, Beckett, Joyce and Galbraith, kept in gourds to chirp. Here was a madness in which I sensed a kinship – and then I felt guilty, having sent him that day a gushing tawdry version of the romance that died, which gesture must have seemed unfeeling, resolving then to seek him out, and my apologetic sympathy to lend.

That night I left her to cry her eyes dry, in the arms of the ragamuffin Gallagher, and, having peeped in upon Arsene (who had been browsing my books for the day's duration, and who greeted me with the prophecy that '*A balding man shall incessantly spoon dollops of mustard into the mouth of a kneeling female*', which ambiguity I took on the chin with a shrug), I fell asleep naked in the chamber of my parents – a perverse impulse perhaps, but their bed had more comfort than the couch, whose small appeal was palling.

But I was awoken in the morning by her voice, murmuring lowly in her dulcet monotone, 'Am I a bad person? Am I pretty? Do you really think I made the right decision?' sundry such inanities that stirred me from my slumber, the drowsy veils lifted from my eyes, half in and half out of my dream, only to find her conjured up before me, stood at the foot of the bed like a gossamer fairy, padding on her gliding feet in a flurry of downy wool, shimmering into the room to slump onto the bed where I lay, laying her laptop down on the duvet – for she had an insipid essay due that day.

'I'm 5000 words over the limit. Can you, like, edit it for me?'

In a tone so plaintive and despondent, delivered with a look so prettily appealing, that I could not say no – it would be like slapping an injured puppy. So, reluctant and weary, with grumbles and yawns, I sat up from the pillow and attempted to oblige, by first cutting out all the adjectives with which the fatty piece was clogged, of which there were only a couple thousand, which made only a negligible difference; and while I tapped and deleted, and vainly struggled to make sense of her non-sequitur sentences, she sat there on the bed in splendour, scantily draped in a woollen shawl, and whined and whined, relentlessly harping upon her listless woes, both familial and heartaching.

And so utterly absorbed in herself was she, that she did not even notice my nudity, obscured in part as it was by the heap of blankets shrouding my length, and nor did she notice – thanks be to almighty god – the physical manifestation of my mounting desire, which was set in motion by virtue of the intimacy of her sheer proximity – forgive me for being boyish, but she had applied some sort of irresistible scent that morning, possessed of some mild aphrodisiac quality that acted on the instinct, some bewitching fragrance that lit up the animal's vitals, some delectable perfume that I found deeply arousing, whose feathery charms I could not resist, as the shy wafts of scent flitted along the sunbeams, to meet with my nose and enter my nostrils, tickling my hairs and setting all me senses tingling, the pulse pumping, the blood racing, rousing the dribbling spirits to focus in one especial spot, to lengthen, to elongate, to stiffen the hidden member beneath the sheets, beside of which lump she sat oblivious, staring at the ceiling, blathering on about how much she hated men, all of whom she thought cruel and crude, castigating all the male brutes who would never assist or do her any favours – whilst I continued to whittle down her unwieldy word count, at the same time struggling to stifle the mounting upsurge downstairs, a telling bulge of blanket that nearly brushed by her bum on the bed, but she had eyes and ears for her sorrows alone, of which torrent she would never quench nor weary, and by now I must confess, for all I was aroused to the utmost, and for all 'twas then I might have made my move, that I was growing more than a bit bored of her tiresome talk, and was no less irked to see my labours on her behalf go ignored and unacknowledged, and just as I was wondering how I might put an end to this sorry scene, I then felt a pressing flatulence in my guts, an eructation wanting escaping.

So without any hesitation, I slowly farted, silently, the quiet gas seeping free politely – and the noiseless killers are always the most noxious, the most pungent. Upward in the air my gaseous aroma arose, akin to foul vapours of rotted eggs or fish, windy result of too much roughage and porter, and soon the scent of my gassy perfume met her tender nostrils, assaulting her sense of smell that was more refined than mine, as she screwed up her nose, and winced, stabbing an accusing glare upon my innocence.

'Did you fart? You're so disgusting, Simeon.'

The strategy worked. For she could not bear to remain there a minute longer, such was the stink. Snatching up her laptop, she bolted from the room in revulsion, leaving me alone to cradle my secret erection in my quiet peace of loneliness.

From then perhaps may be traced and pinpointed the beginnings of my disenchantment. She whom for so long I had loved, the one woman above all whom I wanted, now that she was free and available to me, utterly attainable, given a little effort – now, shatteringly, I saw only her faults and failings, and could barely be bothered. For I saw now how stubborn, how irritable, how tetchy, how petulant, how childish, how difficult, how frankly impossible to please she could be – the very things of which poor Edwin had accused her in his grubby diary, poor Galbraith for whom I now felt fonder.

Yes, even now, years removed from the fact, clear as day I can see him in the mind of mine eye, a pallid bony figure muffled up in a long black coat and scarf, a melancholy aesthete seated gauntly alone in a Parisian café, glasses askew and greasy hair lankly awry, gimlet eyes red rimmed from the want of his rest, jotting down musings in his unkempt moleskin, the vellum on which his insights were laid by the minute.

We met for lunch later that day, he and I, in the spirit of being buddies, indulging in manly sympathy, tough luck, mate, life's a bitch, plenty of fish in the sea, all that bullshit. And I apologized for sending him the snippet of the book, that crappy rhapsody concerning her hugs, which on such a day must have seemed a gross affront, a crass reminder of the glory he had lost, the writing and sending of which, in my deluded mind, seemed almost tantamount to a curse, as if, in so writing about their love, I had subconsciously willed that love to be broken, and wrought a dismal curse. He dismissed these notions as fanciful, and kindly set my guilt at rest; and so, to heighten the merry camaraderie, I unwisely decided to quote to him his very own line:

'I was very amused by the names you gave your crickets! *Dante, Heaney, Beckett, Joyce* and *Galbraith*! Really, Edwin! And you've got your chronology all wrong, too.'

He blanched at this; he had not known that she had stolen his private journal, let alone that she had showed it to others, a breach of trust as was not easily forgiven. I had put my foot in it again, stirring up the shit. And so we gravely parted on this note.

He must have sought her out then, in a towering anger, and told her what I had said, that chance remark that betrayed my knowledge of what he rightly wanted hidden. And she herself in turn also took righteous affront, always sinned against but never sinning, figuring it was actually her confidence that had been breached, having sworn me to secrecy never to tell him that I had seen the journals she had stolen and shown me. In the evening she confronted me, by the darkening college gates, and took me to task for having said what I said. She reminded me that I had sworn to keep it secret – I remembered no such thing, and affected ignorance. I tried to make a joke of it, for the whole business was becoming so ludicrously overwrought, that the only sane thing to do was laugh. This did not impress her. She told me everything, she said, since she had trusted me, thinking me one of her closest friends. She accused me of being a two-faced liar, incapable of any honesty or sincerity, who never said what he meant, whose words were meaningless. She told me in a weeping tone that she could no longer trust me to be her confidante, nor even, for that matter, by extension, her friend.

'This isn't a book – this is life ...' she sniffed, by way of rounding off.

She turned away to hide her tears, and then went off to catch her bus, leaving me behind alone, aloof and standing; and then, for want of better, I looked down upon my shoes, whose flapping soles were talking to me.

CHAPTER THIRTY-NINE

'You were always the only woman I have ever really loved, insofar as I am able to love, insofar as I can be at all sincere and tell a truth at all, so it is only you who I love.'

The Pooka paused in his reading, his pince-nez slipping down the slope of his lengthy goatish face, and looked up from the paper across at his companion Puck, who pottered about Arsene's filthy kitchen, cursing the temperamental kettle he could not operate, and ransacking the fridge in search of a few eggs he deemed it fit to fry.

'What do you make of that bit, Robbie?' the Pooka called from the study. 'Bit of a *cri de cœur*?'

'Bloody bathos and bollocks!' the Puck barked, slamming down a saucer of water on the rusty hob.

They had travelled, and were weary. Their little ship had washed up in Wexford, on a Crosslakes coast from whence they had skipped, down lanes lined by blackberries and briars, toward the empty house of the absent weatherman, on whom the Pooka recalled having played a trick or two at some point in the past.

They had smashed through the window to obtain their entry, and as they clambered through the shards and jags they had startled the one-eyed cat as she murdered mice. And o, but her stomach had certainly swelled since last she was seen, bloated from the quantity of meat she had been eating, having overindulged her appetites in the banquet of blood and flesh over which she had presided, in the fattening course of the days since the old man admitted her, and unwittingly thereafter imprisoned her, bless her.

The Puck promptly set about preparing some more substantial fare while the flirty Pooka, purring to the portly cat honeyed words of old romances, had dumped a bundle of yak butter on the table, and, spotting the corpse of a mouse that she had only partially eaten, daintily prised the sticky mess from the side of the radiator upon which it was plastered, set it on a saucer laden with crumbs of bread and biscuit, seasoned the remains with a sprinkling of sugar and a dollop of marmalade, and rolled the bloody furry body round over and over on the surface of the saucer, to collect the crumbs by way of batter. And he nibbled gracefully on this small snack as he sat in state at the table's top amid the festering newspapers, kindly sharing the mousy guts with the mewling fat cat while disdainfully skimming through a relic of a vanished life that he had just unearthed, stashed under his chair – a long forgotten love letter of poor Arsene's.

'Bathos? Yes, bathos is the word for it,' the Pooka snorted, tossing it aside and cuddling the cat.

The water boiled, the eggs fried in an excess of oil, and with a tin of cold baked bachelor's beans to serve for starter, the matronly Puck returned, bearing a tray upon which all these goodly treats were placed, vaulting over to set the meal down upon the dusty littered dining table, and to take up his own seat opposite his horned and goateed companion, a friend and rival. And so they drank their sour fatty yak-buttery tea, and munched upon their pungent eggs (a few days too old), and popped the cold beans into their gobs like peanuts, and the cat sated herself upon whatever was leftover. Any mice that might scuttle by, between the spindly legs of the table, were promptly crushed and squelched by a sharp heel or hoof, and subjected to the same battering of sugar, marmalade and the crumbs of biscuit or bread, to ably serve as succulent dessert for the champions. A perfect picture of domesticity that queer trio made, the Puck, the Pooka and the one-eyed fat cat, sitting enjoying a tasteful breakfast or brunch, bathed in the morning's soft light that carved them out from the dwindling shadows in whose dark cloak hitherto the dusty study had been swathed. The Puck smoked a cigar, the Pooka a pipe, blowing forth curling blue puffs toward the ceiling, splendid in his dandy's dress, with spotted yellow suit, pinstriped dicky bow, waistcoat and cane carved from buffalo's tusk, whereas harlequin Puck made do with the floppy garb and cap-and-bells of a Pantaloon. And the Pooka fondly reminisced over the weatherman he once had fooled:

'... yes, queer creature he was. Lived for his hobbies, as you can see, what with all these stamps and books and antiques and chessboards that keep us company. These human men are so adorable in their trivial preoccupations that they think must matter. It was no hard matter to drive him batty, sheer solitude took care of most of it, that and the disappointed love of his life that came to nothing. No pictures of her are to be found, you'll note, so far as one can see, a telling omission in the collection of so compulsive a beaver. Bony thing, anorexic or bulimic or both – don't smirk – it took only a few whispers in her ear to put her off him. He was done for after. I scrawled engravings of diabolic visions for him too, to fly before his demented eyes to grant uneasy comfort.'

'You bastard. Why did you do it?'

'Why so serious, Robbie! Why do we do anything? Why spook out poor souls and terrify helpless puppy-dog mortals? Is it not in our nature, being exiled from our Elysium, to seek out sport elsewhere for to keep our talons warm? Like our crackpot collaboration over that farmer and his bull. Silly old bugger. Wonder where he is now ...'

The Puck sighed and passed a palm over his eyes.

'These pranks,' he muttered darkly, 'these futile jests and feeble capers of ours. To what do they amount? I get so sick of them sometimes.'

'Why how now, my dear good fellow, you are becoming impossibly sober in your dour old age! Were you not Don Oberon's waggish rascal of a court jester for so long?'

'Having been sacked, I do feel the need to let me conscience prick me. But I am well glad that our man in the mucky habit has seen fit to put us to some nobler use. I daresay he has a benevolent enterprise in mind, for which he has summoned us hither.'

Thus turning the topic over to their master, they speculated over why he had summoned them hither from their desert comforts, via that ambiguous missive the purple-eyed talking seagull had borne:

> Messrs Goodfellow and MacPhellimey! Hola there, my merry company! Long time no see! How's tricks? How's my wee wife doing! Am I missed? My

> long swim in the sea has brought me at last to the august isle of Hibernia. But I charge you, come follow me, and follow me fast! Hop into thy boat and set sail swiftly! Once ashore, make tracks for the capital, a Black Pool founded by Vikings with horns on their helmets, where we will meet among the bushes of the Park of the Flaming Phoenix! Cheers! –Your very own one and only: MM

This told them precisely nothing. They knew only that the 'Park of the Flaming Phoenix' may refer to a vast area of greenery to be found in the country's capital, where presumably they would find themselves after a spell. But they felt no undue need to hurry, so comfortable in this Crosslakes kip as then they were, content to talk of things and means. And they discussed their master frankly, wondering upon his obscure motives. The Pooka suspected he had found another woman here in Ireland, a notion the Puck pooh-poohed. Yet that would explain so much, the Pooka insisted, not least his compulsive tendency toward cuckoldry. One could not but marvel at his lax treatment of his missus and the incestuous fling with the late Watt that he had urged and she had enjoyed. Add to that her affair with the Puck that The Mad Monk had also so obscenely encouraged, all but indecently spying over sand dunes as they enacted their diminutive coupling. Robin Goodfellow lamented to be reminded:

'O! that good sweet Faerie woman! How could you even mention her! Those rosy nipples I suckled, those undulant bubs that served as pillow for my enchanted head! How I miss her. How we are fallen, two bachelor losers sitting here now in another man's home, with nowt but that flabby cat for company and poor sport.'

'Do not slur. I'm no loser!' the Pooka beamed. 'This here mog Molly – may I call you so, m' dear? – This little cat I have so charmed – I'm certain she would say something very otherwise, if she could speak.'

'Most creatures can, as we've found,' said the dreamy Puck, 'it is only shyness that holds them back, to say nothing of their quiet contempt for their noisier fellows, to whose idle babble they do not deign to respond. The Mad Monk was a great one for drawing them out of their shells of silence, to converse with gods and fairies. Talking polyglot tongues, the language of barks and clucks, of purrs and growls and squawks, of moos and neighs and hoots.'

'Would that I had that skill of sympathy that could transcend the divide betwixt the species,' the Pooka mused, 'would that she could chatter, this plump and pretty kitty on me horny lap, whose hide I fondle. Whatever would she say, I wonder?'

'My name is not Molly,' said the cat in a croaking mournful voice. 'My name is Moloch.'

The gallants rejoiced at this prodigious eloquence and resolved to reward her by granting her a new second eye in place of the one she had lost – a sad mishap that had occurred during a scratchy tryst with some lusty toms, so she deigned to add.

'Oh such sadness!' the Pooka cooed, stroking her drooping whiskers with a gentle talon. 'The evil that men may do is grievous, make no mistake. But you need fear no such violence from fellows of feeling such as myself and Goodfellow have the honour to be. For to the gentler sex we ever do show the utmost courtesy, chivalric without fail.'

'To be sure, to be sure!' cried the Puck, 'And furthermore Ma'am, I should love to do thee a favour – may I be so bold as to proffer you the very yolk of this egg that I eat?'

Moloch the one-eyed fat cat resignedly sighed.

'If it can do no good, it can do no harm neither,' she conceded.

'Give her here to me, Fergie!' the Puck barked, to which command his comrade complied, passing the cat across the clutter to the open arms of his mate, who hugged her, and bade her have faith. Then, producing a scalpel, he sliced away all the white of his little sloppy egg, and scooped up the yolk with a spoon, murmuring a quiet spell as he did. Moloch was on the point of protesting when then, quickly, deftly, he dropped the yolk into her empty gaping socket, where it snugly plopped and snuggled, and very soon settled. The cat blinked, perplexed, for she found it queerly fitted. Set upon the table, she padded archly, greatly puzzled anew by the fresh sensations, of depth of field and judgement of distance. And the triumphant Puck lit up a plump cigar, and leant back in his chair, and put satisfied feet upon the table.

'Would you be so good', Moloch mumbled, 'as to let me out into the garden?'

Obliging Pooka hoisted and passed her through the window's hole. Smoothly she landed down on all her sure fours, and leapt to the lawn.

There delightedly she cavorted and frolicked, rolling on her back amid the stalks of whistling grass, and spotted witless birds prying into the earth, waiting to prey upon what worms there were, birds she hastened to stalk and pursue, upon whom she pounced and caught in her claws, with whom she toyed and played as they chirruped for mercy, upon whom she fed and ate. Theirs was a stringier sort of meat than that of the mice, yet their wee bones were easily and harmlessly swallowed, milky rich in calcium, ideal for maintaining the glint and gloss of her fangs. So thus she darted and frisked, in thrall to the chase, feeling years younger, and through the glass her ministers looked on upon her antics, and warmly smiled in pleasure; and then, with a bottle of brandy Fergie had kept in the loot of his boot, they toasted, and declared her to be the solely only Feline Queen of their Hearts.

CHAPTER FORTY

Elsewhere, The Mad Monk smelt the air and said: 'Never ask, dear Nutmeg, for whom the world was made nor why – for 'twas made for thee by me.'

Daily this he would tell her thus, with an expansive wave of the hand towards the surrounds of the environs through which they would wander and dally, side by side and hand in hand, rustling leaves in their drowsy wake. Daily thus he would say this to assure her, and to set at rest and ease her doubts, to assuage her worries to which she was wont, and jittery oft, for well she knew his urge to fly, his mission to enact. And that she might be jilted, or that he might leave her in the lurch, this she feared, for she could never bear to be left alone bereaved again. No such thought was in his head, but nor would he stay still for a second – something in the very bare air bade him on. So he took her with him.

By the Galway graveside whiles she pined and keened, he took up an axe, and chopped some trees, and snapped some branches, and bore the felled plunder of lumber back to their boat, whose shape and build he tweaked and distilled, and with paste of his spittle wove together twigs with the knitting skill of a wren, latching on some spools and wheels he hauled in from the harbour, kitting out the caboodle with curtains and canopies, a roof and some ropes, a door to swing and within some bedding, piles of pillows and cushions riffled from bins, jangling beads and jingling rosaries, until soon their sometime ship had turned into a caravan, a vehicle worthy no longer for the rivers, but rather the roads. Aboard this wagon of wonders he hurled her, into the woody heart of their clattering carriage she was pushed without scruples, as he softly bade her lie easy, until he had found some fitting filly to haul them through, some proper beast of burden whose back he might beat and sting with his reins, to drag them along in his wheeling train, down dales and fens and dells, by hills and meadows, lakes and forests, and all the cluttered errata of the big little world of theirs.

Parked in their stationary caravan he left her to pout, by the ditch in the roadside encircled by many cascading fields, each by one he arduously combed, nose to the ground and ears in the air, until he came across at last an amiable ass, munching grass with meditative air. He approached, leaning o'er the stony wall to beckon hither the randy donkey, who cobbled closer following the curling of his eager finger, whose long grey face he stroked as he kindly murmured friendly words, his trust and assistance to gain. The donkey's name was Balthazar, and in a former life he was a movie star, or so he claimed. He was easily persuaded to join their retinue, for all he could be cheeky. So from his field's confines, the stones of its walls rendered toppling with a thump of his steward's fist, he was lead to the gaudy caravan, and introduced to his mistress Maggie, who reckoned him a handsome creature, into whose service he was sworn. Strapped to his dappled sides were bridles and ropes, all the heaving equipage with which their mobile lodging to tow, rusty wheels of which wagon soon began to scrape and grind into the ground, circles upon circles of sparks were struck as soon as the coachman sat in his seat, and took up his reins, and cracked and beat the back of Balthazar, who neighed and hurtled as he set out on his trot, and bore along their creaking lumbering caravan, moving easterly across their elder isle, from the setting to the rising sun.

For many moons and miles they travelled as nomads all over the midlands, resting under the stars by farmyards and country bars, snatching their provisions from village markets and jumble sales, dodging passing cars and beeping buses, evading the highways awash with gasping trucks, favouring marshy paths of mud less trodden, through which zone of winding lanes wheeled their queer carriage, the company of man and wife and donkey, idle wanderers upon crusty face of the sweet earth. By riverbanks and gushing streams they paused to bathe their bodies, to strip and swim and laugh like the young, to wash and scrub while humming to the buzz of the bees and the coos of the robins, and to make love behind teeming glissade of waterfall's curtain, frolicking wetly starkers among shiny rocks and glossy rivulets. And whenever his overlord's hold on his reins was slackened, Balthazar too would jaunt away to sate his amorous appetites, seeking comely womanly donkeys upon whom to mount astride and vigorously buckle, servant of the springtime and of his lengthy donkey's dick, so long that it would drag along upon the ground behind him as he trotted, his precious manhood's treasure scratched and pricked by the thorns, the nettles, the thistles, all the battery of the treacherous ground's armoury.

Crops that wanted tilling they stopped by twilight to dig, robbing spuds they stowed in their sack, potatoes to pop into the Banshee's bubbling pot for supper, in exchange for which theft The Mad Monk would leave behind a pile of conjured gold, the erroneous response to which gifts was invariably – 'Ah, them faeries are fierce good altogether'. And they dawdled in orchards to pluck golden apples from the branches, borrowing honey from the hives of bees, and suckling sap from ageing trees. Olives and fennel, nectar and pollen they collected to season their salads, and luscious grapes they snatched from vineyards, with which to squash and brew their tiny barrels of goodly wine. Wool that was shorn from sheep was used by thrifty Nutmeg in the knitting of rugs, to drape them when the nightly chill came, and of jumpers to clothe them, even of mittens to warm Balthazar's ears, to sheathe them from the rushing breeze's biting in the evening.

And sometimes, to keep chock-a-block their coffers, they would pose as wandering gypsies to whom the spirits had imparted all the secrets of the Earth, and unravelled all the mysteries of the heavens, kitting themselves out in shawls and scarves, kerchiefs and bandanas, and a medley of twinkling props to enrich their deceit. In tidy town squares their caravan would halt with screech, and out would alight the sign to lure the punters, promising the foretelling of fortunes and the divulging of fates, and loudly too their donkey would neigh, by which time a swarm of hopefuls would have gathered.

A creaking door would open then, and a silent figure would appear, tall and dark and brooding, bearded and hooded, with an eyepatch and an earring, who would poke out his shaggy head, and dourly peer and glare upon the curious crowd, and beckon forthwith the foremost, ushering them into the dim interior, a smoky place wherein wafted fragrance of incense and faint tang of perfumed musk, sitting them down with a shove upon a stool by the table round, where sat the psychic medium hunched, seeming asleep, nodding snoring in tune to music celestial, stirring only upon a prod from her partner, which bid her raise aloft her ragged head, lifting her Medusa's curls with a wangling quiver, to fix upon her customer a piercing glance all of ice and fire, such as might turn their bowels to water, and all their dauntless mettle to quaking jelly. She would style herself Minerva or Mirabella according to her mood or humour, entreating her client to cross her arthritic palm with a cluster of dropping coppers, upon which transaction effected, she would produce from folds of her robe an array of cards, an hourglass and an abacus (to reckon up their allotment of life), and lastly of all a crystal ball, within whose sloping glassy walls swam violet twining vapours, swirls like faces or skulls.

Their wrinkled palms afforded her some scrutiny, tracing and following the curve or incline of the creases of their lifelines and lovelines, all the while cooing impenetrable profundities with solemn intonation. Then would come the sharp and acid hiss of breath, the gasp that bespoke full certain doom, to stiffen one's tingling hairs upon the nape or scalp, upon which cue her henchman, 'til now stood immobile and mute in a solemn corner, would suddenly grunt, and lurch, and topple down to his knees, in paroxysms of ecstasy or agony, panting for breath and clawing the air, writhing and rolling all about the floor, clenching his chest and foaming at the mouth, gnashing and champing his jaws and chewing up the tip of his tongue, frothing spittle and bubbles of blood he dribbled and spat, garbling hoarse gobbledygook between his grunts, a wave of raving weird words that seemed wrenched up from his guts or hauled out of hell, a secret potty language of prophecy into which one could read whate'er one wished, which edgy spectacle was sufficient to stun the spectators, who were accordingly urged exit by Maggie, with some muttered assurance to quell their dubieties, such as – 'You had best be gone, for this here caravan is like to be set ablaze and burning, what with the sheer heat engendered by the psychic vibrations we have set off in the starry stratosphere – them gods must be angry.'

Whereupon, once they were gone, Megan Devlin would shut the door and turn to look down at her lover, having ceased to writhe in his burlesque of transcendence, looking up at her from the floor with a doggy grin, and then the two of them would chuckle, and warmly smile, for the hooligan had fooled but another fool again.

Though sometimes there was more to their act than mere horseplay. For it was an abiding peculiarity of The Mad Monk's, the way he could always with such artless ease become the soulful confidant of whomsoever he was in the company of, how he would worm his way into their deathless trust and at the flick of a finger reel off, without any apparent prior knowledge, the facts of their lives (a trick of brother Elijah's he was acquiring the more as he aged), for all that they were strangers to him, and he to them, and stranger yet how none of them seemed to find it strange that he should know what he knew, he who they seemed to treat as an old friend, for all that they had never in their lives clapped sight on him before, save perhaps in dreams long forgotten, but maybe now dimly remembered; and this disarming skill of deduction he brought now to bear on their money spinning scheme, sizing up the rabble and drawing his conclusions, then mumbling in Maggie's ear that this one fat man would win the lottery, that this lady there was pregnant, or that this here hairy chap was due to die of dysentery.

Or, as in the case of Tadgh O'Mara, who came wandering in one day looking ragged and asking where was his child, recognition kindled in the oracle The Mad Monk of the man his White Dog had bitten, pointing him easterly thus to Dublin's Rathmines.

Some customers were lavish with their tips, and others were more stingy (those were the ones whose tyres he slashed and whose engines he filled with sugar), but nevertheless they always made just enough to live off the land in the freewheeling way they were going, enough to buy the sometime snatch of moony hashish to season their sleep, pinches of poppies or any of the other numerous narcotics that were doing the rounds. And bystanders on the streets, well groomed in the zany world's ways, to whom their caravan soon became a familiar sight, began to nod and tap their noses knowingly upon sight and smell of the glassy-eyed occupants, numbly grinning and chanting dismal mantras, earning a reputation as anachronistic hippies making up for all the time that had gone by them. And no bad thing it was to be thought a silly pair of gypsy hippies, riding through town with a lazy donkey chewing their cud, preachers of insipid slogans that yet augured no harm nor hurt ('*LOVE HAS NO PRESIDENT*' became the tatty motto of their shrieking banner), since for a killer on the run, such as he was, there could be no more convincing cover, nor safer guise to beguile the gullible.

Sometimes he would dash into the shops to scour the tabloids on their racks, lest there be news of the forces who pursued him, and of what, if any, progress they were making – but never a word no more there was on that score, save alone for a forlorn obituary of Aloysius O'Muadaigh, late resident of Sligo town, murdered bachelor of sixty-three, which paltry tribute wrung a silent tear from the eye of the one who had helped him die, as he browsed the wrinkled paper with trembling hands, sadly marvelling at how little behind might be left of a life, no more than a few bland words of token summation, writ on sheets that would soon be shreds, destined to wrap up oily fish and greasy chips, to join ranks with rubbish and blow along the gutters, keeping company with the tide of detritus and all of humanity's dregs, lasting scarcely longer than ghostly memories left behind in the minds of those that knew you, who will in any case themselves be dead so soon.

But otherwise there was no mention made of the case, for the pressure was off and the storm had died – and the world had bigger fish to fry than he, and greater criminals to catch, as he soon saw. Turning pages idly, for minutes on end intrigued, without deigning to dip a hand in a pocket to purchase the paper (which earned him many a dirty look from sneering shop attendants, of whose contempt he stood oblivious as he pored), The Mad Monk read of wars abroad on account of oil, of bloodbaths and slaughters in the name of god and glory, of bombings and hijackings and vulgar battles, of self-appointed world's police and presumptuous bigger brothers, self-satisfied self-elected watchdogs of the Earth trampling over and toppling down some decrepit empires of olden days, young nations having childish tantrums, an army of morons with a baby monkey at the helm, mangling the language and all too trigger-happy, lavishing all on the crazed hunt for a turbaned bearded mastermind, a demented goat who had scripted some sabotage, taking lonely refuge in faraway caves, high among the hills of lands now steeped in wreckage and ruin, lost amid memories of vanished splendour, a cackling terrorist with a dream of a new world, which delusion he would erect by means of massacre, through pillars of blood that lead to blood, much more of which was spilt by his foes in dozens of gallons, those oafs who nursed a vision of their own, a cherished beacon of a shining city on a hill, crammed with supermarkets and malls and stores and fast-food joints and fatty chains, all bloated with the big green buck, puffed up with lies upon lies, which monstrosity of banality they would stamp upon the crippled Earth with all the mighty gunpowder that was in their copious store, to brand the land with their emblem of a beef-burger-bun, slaphappy land of the quailing free, with a prosperous few, who had cheated for their gain, lounging in motors heaving their exhausts, and an impoverished many sharpening their knives, injecting arms and vomiting pills, blowing out their brains and assaulting the elderly, raping women and children, murdering babies dumped into toilets and flushed away with the crap – it was all too much, this human folly that dizzied him.

Was this the same world he said he had made?

All this squabble and turmoil and misery – was this the chaos he callously presumed he could fix with, as it were, a mere swish of a wand? He regretted now having dared to read the everyday news at all, the routine catalogue of horrors to which the other common men around him were immune. But he was alone in this place, and had tarnished his ignorance that was also his innocence, his precious ty he somehow sustained – for though as old as the ages, his soul was a child's soul still, appalled by the blurb he read on the blaring page, and the warring cacophony he heard in his head.

His temples pounding, shaking, biting his lip and scratching his hairs that were full of fleas, he gazed upon a picture of what was called a terrorist, a grainy portrait of a grizzly ruffian no bigger than a postage stamp, with whom he felt some guilty kinship, for all he deplored them, and condemned their bloody ways – that was the problem with the world these days, things had simply gotten too big, and all dark deeds were done in bulk, mounting up to a lofty ghastly quota of rotting dead – but it seemed that perhaps, to his eyes unschooled, that every one of these conflicting buffoons nursed a vision of something better, but the forms they thought ideal were clashing against those schemes of others that were irreconcilably alien, such being the sorry incompatibility of human desires – but yet to him it seemed that still they dreamed themselves of something sort of like an Abode of Fancy, never mind what other daft name they would dub it, the fervid effort of enacting which, no matter what the wretched cost, was so disastrous for the rest of us – would that one could wipe out all these warmongers with one fell swoop and stamp of fist or foot – but no, he was no exterminator, not on such a scope – for all the grandeur of his aims, he was resolved to operate on a smaller scale – he could afford to effect his improvements slowly, having all the time in the world literally at his disposal (hee hee!) – and he would begin at home – but where was home, and what was home, what family could he claim, being always alone in the end? – but if he did not act, could he preach? – but preach what message? – of love and understanding? – the words repelled him even as he uttered them and tasted their rank vapidity – why can't everyone just be friends? – worse still – this sort of claptrap would not even hold up in a tavern sermon, surrounded by a sweaty coven of drunken geezers who knew bullshit when they heard it, nay, he would be laughed at and derided as an ignorant idiot, which in many ways he was – so why preach if one is not wise? – ah, go get thee gone – for the world's more full of weeping than you can understand, old man – poor child – silly fool.

And into the midst of his baffled contemplations, came a tap on his shoulder from a surly shop assistant scratching his numerous pimples, who bid him get out and get lost, an unfriendly request delivered in incoherent accents that wanted better elocution.

To which in reply The Mad Monk bellowed 'Fuck off, chump!' and dealt the boy a belt on the nose, which freely bled as he fell over tottering backwards, bringing down all the rack of newspapers with him. And The Mad Monk, disenchanted, tore to fluttering tatters the periodical he had browsed, then turned about, and fled from the shop, and ran off down the street, cackling as he ran, laughing to himself, mirthlessly, alone.

CHAPTER FORTY-ONE

It was one weekend, when the weather was warmer, and the old man Arsene seemed to rest in peace, lying mumbling impenetrably, blinking slowly his bewildered fish's eyes, though without stirring from the bed, that I took heart in hand and left him alone, whiles I boarded a bus to Sligo, to attend the funeral of Aloysius O'Muadaigh.

The event was long delayed, owing to the inquiries of the coroner and the lengthy vagaries of the post-mortem, which had been beset by hitches and snags, as they combed his corpse for clues pertaining to the obscure cause. Murder it seemed, or at best mercy killing; there was absurd talk of lycanthropy, of anguished howls in the darkness, of a White Dog (a phrase as reminded me of the monster that turned Tadgh O'Mara's shocked hair white), of a mysterious stranger who had lain in Uncle Ulick's barn for the days preceding the killing, a debauched monk who had fled from the scene, ineffectual pursuit of whom, through the woods and hills, the lakes and crags, had arrived at a dead end only. In hushed tones Auntie Wilhelmina told me of how he had helped her cook their dinners, sprinkling their broth with exquisite nameless powders of his own procuring, gushing with winsome eyes about that bizarre aura of sanctity he seemed to radiate, of the heavenly tenor of his voice, of the kindness and gentleness in his weird yellow eyes – an image of divinity most dismally dashed when they came home from the railway, only to behold Aloysius lying dead in the bed and bloody, cold as ice with the ghost of a grin.

The undertakers had done a good job of tidying up the poor bugger, as I was privy to witness before the lid was shut, his scars and wounds well hidden and masked, though they had somewhat overdone the quantity of lipstick and rouge with which his mouth and cheeks were plastered.

And I remembered the scratchy feel of O'Muadaigh's lips on my own reluctant cheeks, the same he struck when I coyly spurned his dismal advances, as he hotly cajoled me to come out of my shell of shyness, way back in Abbey Street's Wynn's Hotel, in its firelight lounge of stardust and sand – at which recollection I shivered.

He was buried in Drumcliff, not far from the rest of Yeats, not a pebble's toss from the site of his own attack, lowered down into the ground in the chilly light of noon, amid the whispering of the gusting pines that clustered round, and the whimpering of the sorrowful faithful who gathered close in queasy packs. I stood aside aloof, hands in pockets, restless feet pawing at the earth, an outsider, a token effigy of those who could not come. Arsene, it transpired, had also been invited, as I was informed, an invite that met with no response, which silence was interpreted as an unfeeling rudeness on his part – I smirked, and withheld, rocking on my uneasy heels.

And I did not stay for long after the burial, unwilling to watch the elder unknowns shuffle and mill as they rattled off their condolences, unwilling to listen to exclamations of surprise over how tall I had grown, stalling only to humour poor Ulick for a matter of minutes, as he laid a hand on my shoulder and affected an unconvincing cheer, thanking me so much for coming, filling me in on the progress of his *De Valera Code*, and expressing regret that I saw so little now of his son, a one-time friend of old:

'... you and that brat Paddy were so close once, no? Thick as thieves or liars. Has it been years since last ye spoke? Such a shame. What has happened to you? He's in the army now, a fool carrying arms. Ye must come up more often. At such a time as this ...'

I heard and nodded and smiled and grieved; and then I left.

Back on the bus, looking out the window listlessly, lamenting at interims uncontrollably, fluttering sunlight bathing my eyes, as by fields and streams our little bus rushed, a notion occurred, and an idea was born in my brain, whose provenance I could not place. For it seemed not to issue from me, but rather to have been whispered in my ear, from above or behind. Confused, I darted a glance at the passenger who sat in the seat at my rear – frumpy and bland, snoring and asleep, a girly glossy in her fat lap.

Turning back to regard the view, marred by the tint of maroon Plexiglas, and the intermittent smears of snot or squishy yogurt, as left by whomsoever brash occupant had filled this spot before me, I pondered over on the thought, and decided to follow it through. For it was no difficult matter to stagger lurching down the aisle, and breathlessly persuade the driver to stop his bus by the side of the River Suck, which was in any case one stop along our careening route, at which our engine screeched and halted to allow me exit, with nary a pause to collect my sacks or bags (for I always travelled light, carrying only the garb my body wore, my gasping pockets bulging), after which, the stuffy bus huffed and puffed, and sped away again, leaving behind a lone bystander by a bridge.

I breathed the air, and looked around. It was enjoyable to be back. This was the flat heart of the midlands, the scenery that paraded the dull show of my youth, so largely spent tumbling in Roscommon's verdant plains and wings, through which this same babbling Suck did wind and dip, trailing its dappling course by the squat and dumpy cortege of houses and bars and shops that comprised good little old Athleague, the birthplace of my mother, wherein so long her sires had resided, in a cottage in Carraroe, a bit off the beaten path I took, yet set in the same neck of these unshowy woods.

At ease, I dawdled by banks of the Suck that flowed by the graveyard (Granny Mary and taciturn Mick were buried here, their plots bestrewn by rosaries and tulips), hopping with a stumble over the turnstile, to venture into the beginnings of the same Suck's Valley Way, the dream of a rambler, bounding by the marshy boglands and schools of pools and muddy puddles, for it was the river's wont to overflow and flood during certain damper seasons of the year, its flanks that would spread wide and soak the surrounding countryside, wetting the frantic sheep who sheltered on stray logs, and cowered on higher mounds, beneath the twining arms of wrinkly trees, jagged and split by vanished flashes of lighting bolts, at foot of which the sullen mushrooms grew, in little circles that the locals nicknamed fairy rings, where by starlight the wee folk might gather to play their rites of football, or ritual bloodletting, or rosewater polo.

And it was by the bark of one such wizened tree as these, haggard stumps that bent their branches, tips of which dipped for their pleasure into the Suck's passing tide, by one of these where Peadar Lamb had been dumped by the horny goateed demon, that time he did a deal with a devil, and met with his dead Bull beyond the watery grave.

Dimly I remembered this folkloric nugget as I meandered by the riverside, the hoary old anecdote I heard from my father, to whom Peadar told his tale one drunken evening in the wake of a wedding, as they sat alone drinking firewater in the farmer's kitchen, an unlikely pair. The bulk of Father's recollection had centred on the person of Peadar himself, an Irishman of the old school, with a chestnut face and ears like jugs, a flat cap astride his eggy scalp that was never unveiled, an ancient figure who seemed hewn from oak or cedar, craggy and gnarled like a rocky cliff face much hacked by ocean's waves, totemic and immortal and stooped, with a slope to his shoulders and a crafty glint in his eyes, set deep in soggy pouches, cushioned snugly amid the crannied wrinkles of his face.

And he had huge hands, well used to digging and ploughing, with strong palms he kept clamping down upon my father's thighs, seasoning his speech with suchlike almighty slaps of his listener's lap, such claps of legs he employed to embellish his point, enlivening his discourse by utilizing his massive bulbous nose to rub it in further, which sacred proboscis he would stick the more into my father's ear the closer he leant, as his story neared its climax and his breath almost failed, snuffling and wheezing and groping his (literally) captive audience. And initially my father felt apprehensive, fearing that he might be grossly used, roped into some illicit act by this corseted pederast, afraid for his honour as a husband to my mother, taking into account how alone and confined in that kitchen they were (missus Lamb was nowhere to be seen), fearing that the excess of spirits had conspired to set free the latent beast of rape that slumbered within the upright farmer's frame, revealing by night a lustful man who loved men, contorted result of years of oppression and suppression, stifling fate of so many padded countrymen who live in a screaming quiet state of denial – but no – this Peadar Lamb was as straight as an arrow.

For he belonged rather to a fading race of Irishmen who fancied male proximity but not carnality between men, one of those who were shy around even their wives, blushing and stuttering in the presence of women, bar the nuns, yet most at home midst the unruly mob of the barroom, moved by muscle to heavily breathe in the ears of their fellows, coming all the closer to ensure that every precious irreverent word would be heard – so thus did my father recount to me the shape of Peadar, and evoke the contours of the ghostly tale he told, of how he was undone by love of his Bull, of how he lost his money to an oaf, and of how the natural laws got briefly bent.

All these things I remembered as I roamed by the riverbanks, and breathed deep the fragrant air that stank of silage and compost, half wondering whether old Peadar was still among the living's land, and how old he must be if that were so, struggling to recollect where it was along the journey his keep was erected, and whether he would know me from Adam were I perchance to pay him an unannounced visit, which I didn't.

Idling, toying with a stalk I had plucked from the bulrushes beneath the lank willow's drippy fingers, I passed the derelict factory that glared across from the other side of the Suck's crooked ribbon, returning to the bridge from whence I proceeded to the village's central street. The place had never been a prime contender for the annual national Tidy Town Contest, despite the best efforts of my mother's Auntie Nell to prettify its ungainliness with cascades of flowers and garlands, their florid petals vomiting forth from gaudy pots lodged on reluctant ledges, inclining rather to drabness and greyness, yet to me it held a shabby charm I found congenial. Deserted at that afternoon hour, in silence and seclusion I padded down the vacant town, by beloved bars of Hamrock's, King's and Waldron's (the latter a victim of the rising flood), by the decrepit church that stood at its nethermost outskirts, at which point the road gave way to lanes of trees and hedges, wiggling their track to Carraroe, and Granny Mary's house.

Some half an hour's stride it took me to arrive. Sat at a kind of cross-roads, overlooking the looping Tipperary Way, so beloved of childhood treks. A pebble-dashed house with popcorn walls of two storeys, with a trim garden and a lush orchard, a cavernous rusty shed behind, and beyond a maze of overgrown fields of nettles and briars, of thistles and daisies and buttercups, and yesteryear's fallow crops untold, with spuds and parsnips long untilled, with piles of bales of hay stacked from a forgotten harvest, tottering towers and steeples of straw that saw the feverish chases and taunts of youth, between whose niches and crannies amorous cousins toppled and fell, while doing their dares in the dark of kiss-an'-tell-an'-all's-well.

I came to the house, and leant upon the gate, crumbling now and wanting oiling with its rust, and surveyed the house's ruins, long neglected since Uncle Dick the Polis, sole son of me mammy's brood, white-headed boy among the gaggle of his sister geese, had become uncaring inheritor of the estate, letting it lie abandoned to rot and fester. Pasted on one of the windows was a tacky sign implying it might soon be sold and revamped, the same ugly fate of Lindisfarne on the other side of my lineage. A sorry sight indeed it was, I lamented as I looked, with its walls of one-time puffy cream now gone stale and sooty, like the tarnished wool of a vagrant lamb, streaks of mildew miring the looming door, one of the windows cracked and broken, and by the dead and decaying flowerbeds sat a wasted goalpost, an orphaned relic of some grandchild's game that went unfinished, with a punctured ball to boot, lying beside discarded like the deflated skin of a snake. And the orchard, home of the holly and the ivy, of the crabby apples that seasoned our Granny's sour crumble and cake, from boughs of whose trees swung tyres on straggly blue ropes, the swings of our makeshift playground – now impenetrable, congested by scratchy vines and branches that impeded any entry, debarred by thorns that might scar and pluck any erring intruder's eye.

Mourning, with a squeak of the gate I set foot on the estate, and walked up the garden path to the door, peering through the chipped windows, trying to discern scanty details from the midst of the reigning dimness within, which fog divulged only wreckage, with torn wallpaper and falling timber rafters, the steps to upstairs collapsed, desecrated wires from the ceiling hanging down in stagnant loops, and on the floor of the kitchen lay the violated sink, wrenched from the wall as if by a dervish, sadly lit by the gorgeous setting sun peering through gaps in the window's dust. Soft and rosy sinking light bathed the outside, quivering and soothing as I curled around to the backyard, where a broken car with defunct engine was parked, long dead and exhausted, backed against the hovel with leaky tin roof, by the hut where the mountainous pile of turf was kept, the same bricks of coal that my infant mother sometimes ate, chewing and nibbling with juvenile displeasure, vital briquettes that in later years warmed lonely holy Granny Mary, as she spun out the vigil of her umpteen widow's winters, alone midst the frost and ice and sleet that plastered the place, attending to the crackling broadcasts from the wireless and keeping pious silence for the Angelus, bowing low her kindly head of snow, silken locks so carefully combed, from which silvery flakes of her dandruff fell, mingling among her hearth's dying embers where they burnt, to crisps and ashes.

Knee deep in the grasses I plodded round the property, mildly startled by the curious intrusion of a pair of peacocks upon the premises, who came by me haughtily strutting as if in affront, pacing up and down with their glistening plumes wagging as if to warn me away, exotic guardians of this long-forgotten estate, casting forbidding eyes of almond upon my trespass, wreaths of flickering tails a dazzling miasma of flaming hues, vain captors of the glancing sun that lent lustre to their radiance, flares that bade me shield my blinded eyes, as stunned I froze, and beheld them pass me by.

Round a corner they wound as one, and then were gone, and I thought that I had only imagined them. I was lured to follow them then, tempted by their foreignness, inflamed by image of perfumed tails that wafted in the corner of my sights, stumbling blindly forward until I had turned the corner around which they had just disappeared.

And only then did I see what I had been sent to search for and find.

For the modest corner disclosed a pristine vista. There lay the breadth of Grandfather's fields before me, rolling down their undulant arms of green and gold cascading, pulsing sheaves of wheat and pampas waving to me softly, gently blowing in the mild blue wind that beckoned me hither yonder. And side by side through the wily meadow I watched the peacocks go, threading their way through a grassy labyrinth of tangles and eddies, toward the distant spectre of a yawning caravan, with its chimney smoking, betokening occupancy within, and with its sides gaudily emblazoned in violet and orange and lime, parked at an insolent angle on the slanting hill.

And as the peacocks approached, I saw, by one of the wagon's wheels, upon a wooden stool sat, that there was a tall old man, raggedly clad and haggardly bearded, puffing upon a pipe and frowning, jotting at intervals upon a piece of parchment with his quill (the feather plucked from one of his peacocks, I presumed, marvelling at the queer hippie types who were wont to insolently camp at deserted plots as these, and wondering whether it was my place to shoo him away, which course of action cowardice quickly persuaded me against). He took no notice of me, since we were at such a far distance removed from each other, and nor did his donkey give me heed, a fine grey ass who indolently lay in the grass by his master's heels, placidly munching his succulent cud.

And then the shape of a woman, draped all over in a floral cowl, her face seemingly hid by a gauzy veil, emerged from within the caravan, and came and sat down beside the man, who received her with cheery courtesy, setting down his sheet and producing a lyre from the air, at which she appeared to protest (I was too far away to hear a word they said, and the ensuing scene played out in an intriguing dumb show), and yet, with many bats of her companion's entreating palms, she was easily persuaded.

And then the tall old man (who seemed so oddly familiar) began to strum the strings of his lyre, strumming notes with slow fingers, in tender delicacy and dulcet grace, and started to sing, in a sonorous voice that faintly echoed and resounded across the meadow's breadth, with a pleasant enough mellow tone, so far as I could tell, lurking as I was in the shade of a hidden apple tree afar. His song appeared to have a profound effect upon his partner. She sat still, apparently enraptured; and then, solemnly, nodding vaguely in time with the music, she raised her wrinkled hands, and lifted her veil to reveal her face, staring heavenward and shining with grateful tears.

I squinted to discern her features – and then I started – for I knew her.

She was none but the figure of my father's mother Maggie, the ghost of my other Granny Nutmeg, half a decade dead, some five years buried and gone.

CHAPTER FORTY-TWO

In retrospect it seemed so obvious, crushingly so – so daily dogged was he by the horror of hindsight. It was when they had parked their homely trailer upon a certain slant of inclining ground, a rare slope to be found in flat Roscommon's grassy old heart.

A suburb of Athleague, by the same kind of Carraroe crossroads where once they were glimpsed, behind a house that held a sentimental significance for Maggie, having been before the domain of her sister-in-law, her opposite number in every sort of way, kindly where she was cruel, modest when she was coarse. Saddened she was to find the dwelling decaying, no less than ravaged Lindisfarne destroyed, relics of the dying generations, the older ways on the wane. But it pleased her nonetheless to be back, and to puff upon hookah pipes while the idle peacocks played amid wreaths of their smoke (Lordy knows where those birds had come from – likelier Mars than Munster).

There in that twilight garden the old ghost and her haggard aged lover now kept court in their caravan, discreetly relaxing after having plied their ruse in Roscommon's county town. The Mad Monk had kept his beady eyes peeled for the person of Peadar, whom he so dearly wished to meet, yearning to spot his nutty face amid the crowd, hoping to catch the elder goblin hobbling and limping along on the single leg he had left, clutching his crutch with leathery grip, wondering whither his demon Bull had wandered, but no, the old man did not appear, and The Mad Monk had pondered the wisdom of paying him a visit, if he could but only recall where was his home.

Solemnly, he watched his wife count the coppers they had earned, racking up their sagging coffers that daily swelled, as coin by coin she lifted close to her ailing eyes the better to scrutinise, licking her lips as she strummed and plied the discs of their abacus, before popping the pennies into their rubicund bronze boar, their precious piggy bank, crudely painted in screaming hues of which Balthazar disapproved ('it just looks so tacky, mate!' was his whinny to his master, which impertinence met with a slap).

Absorbed in her murmuring enumerations, Nutmeg paid no heed to the gaze by her side that drank her up. There was a fresh sort of sorrow, a baffled torment in his look, breathing puzzled despair. Ever since he had read what he had read in the tabloid, an incorrigible restlessness beset him, unrelieved by sleepless nights through which he turned and tossed, and groaned in bed while she snored, biting his nails and tearing his whiskers, softly thumping his pounding brow in an impotent attempt to quench the fire in his head, unappeased by any ceaseless stalking up and down the breadth of O'Connell's farmyard.

He would sit in the broken car and pretend he could drive. He would ransack the shed and chew upon clumps of coal that gave him indigestion. He would milk imaginary cows and suck their imaginary teats. He would brave the orchard's thorns by moonlight, forcing his way through the spiking briars scratching his skin that bled, collecting rotten apples that he ground into a pulpy mash, stamped into a paste that he spread all over his face, to soothe his sores and cool his prickly skin.

And he mounted rotting tyres on ropes that all the dead children had erected to serve for swing, but his weight was too great for the straggly string to bear, and oft indeed the very branch itself would snap, and so toppling he would plunge, landing in an ungainly tangle of limbs and broken boughs and splintered rubber, in a posture of dejection that afforded mirth for the curlews and starlings looking on.

He was at a loss.

So thus lost in his abject muddle of aimlessness, sometimes he would leave her alone to sleep by night, while he shuffled himself off to the village and its bars, in the corners where he sat ghostly alone disconsolate, nursing a quickly staling glass of stout whose frothy head was fast dissolved. A forlorn figure he must have cut, looking a touch the tramp or poorly queer in the eyes of the elders, glowering from their stools upon the stranger, whose awkward entry always initially gave rise to a surly silence, greeted by looks of suspicion that augured some threat, though soon subsided. For such pub visits, he wore a tatty suit of orange that Maggie had knitted him, composed of every kind of carpet or scrap of rug she could find, hurriedly stitched with all the rags and seams showing, a clumsy furry musty garment that gave off a rank and festering odour of donkey's piss (Balthazar, lifting his leg, had been earlier unkind, which awful whiff accounted in some part for the unfriendly looks with which the timid master was met).

His torn Panama hat tugged down low over his eyes, the lonely outsider would squat aloof and joylessly sip his bitter porter, half listening to the monotonous drone of gossip humming, disinterestedly surveying the crappy photos that formed the local Wall of Fame (among which cluster of portraits he might have discerned the younger Peadar Lamb, with hair of russet adorning his head and poking out of his ears, one grasping hand clamped tight on the thigh of a lass or lad).

He despised these tavern tours he made, but was powerless to do otherwise in the tempting face of this easily available outlet for his wayward energies. Once or twice he was verbally assaulted with a barrage of homophobic diatribe and xenophobic abuse, being labelled, among other unsavoury phrases, 'poo-pusher', 'nigger-tinker', 'pussy-queen', 'scruffy sodomite', 'rimmer in a Zimmer frame', and 'Greek cunt'. His response was to smash a chair on the skull of the sweaty creep who had been so bold.

'Fucking hippie faggot! Go back to Atlantis!' the bastard squealed as he lay in the pool of his blood, which last riposte rang in The Mad Monk's horrified ears as he hurriedly exited into the night. Reeling round to the back of the bar, he urinated copiously on the pebbles of the yard, admiring the silver splash the twinkling moon patchily lit, sad eyes alighting on a capacious barrel of beer whose flimsy lid he quickly broke, whose contents he slurped and gulped, burping and bearing the load on his back away from the hateful pub, until he found a field by the river in which he could lie and lap the liquor at his leisure, in which idle trance he passed the vaster part of that mellow eve.

As grey dawn embraced the day, shooting forth its primary streaks that petered through the turgid clouds, he kicked the emptied vat into the swollen water, and chuckled mirthlessly as the lolling current carried it bobbing away to sea by way of Suck. Staggering back up to his feet, ashen beard moist with the dew, threads of his ludicrous suit wet with the grass's damp, he drunkenly stumbled by the banks, vaguely returning to where their caravan was kept. Bleary yellow eyes squinted in the sunrise as he arrived, hopping over the rusty gate, ripping a trouser leg with a crick of the fence.

A squawk of the skulking peacocks gave him to grumble as he wound again through overgrown weeds, stalks of the breezy meadow that swayed and bowed as if to bid him obsequious pass, kernels crushed by his tipsy amble. The donkey was awake, chewing lazy cud with half an eye ajar, grunting greeting. But Maggie Nutmeg, ah, she was asleep, curled up under the blanket of their featherbed, reclined among the webs that were their duvets, as he saw with a smile while peering through the welcoming wagon's door.

Crawling back into the reigning dimness of the grey within, casting off his sticky garments with all the quiet that he could, while her drowsy snores ebbed and dipped, and her breathing breast fell and arose beneath the sheets. Naked and aroused, patting stiffening, he wondered would it be wise to waken her, that they might enact their wrinkled play of love again, drunken rabbits. But as he grew swollen, and made to lower a hand to tap her shoulder from slumber to stir her, he caught sight of a ball of her twining yarn, and her shining needles – she had been knitting while he was away.

What had she been knitting?

Aghast, drooping fast, he saw by the dissipated hearth the set of miniature clothes she had darned and patched as black night passed, wares for babies all infantile in style, blue socks for a boy, pink stockings for a girl, cuddly mittens and gloves, adorable skirts and jumpers, tiny scarves and small pants, all neatly laid in a little row by the fireside.

And as he gazed upon the garments that lay by the embers, a vision came to him, unbidden, of his lonely wife sitting knitting in her rocking chair unspeaking, humming abstractly perhaps at most, her crooked fingers, clawed by their arthritis, manipulating the needles with none of the dexterity of which in life she made her boast, crudely fashioning whatever came to mind, and was most easy for her fancy, Granny Nutmeg's motherhood remembered, similar socks she had stitched to clothe her bawling charges, nevermore whose whines by her would be heard, save alone in reveries and nightmares, imprinted wails submerged on the cushions of memory's walls, in the padded cell of her dreams, newly woken lately by a glimpse she'd had of a grandchild just the other day, cowering behind an apple tree to spy on them from the meadow's farther side (a wisp of a sprite who'd fled as soon as she saw him, before she'd had time to register the face of the scamp), which visitation recalled longing buried, pitiably rendered in these scrappy tokens, ill-sown echoes poorly patched, fabric quick to rip and crumble.

Rapt on his shaking knees, the naked giant fingered the children's clothes, admiring the miniscule socks that fitted on his very thumbs, wondering why she had found the time to knit these follies, doomed never ever to be worn nor owned, for never could a child of theirs be sired, not in her Banshee's lifeless womb, vacuous treasure of the wailing dead, a sterile patch of fallow ground he'd ploughed and tilled, with reeking moisture for pleasure that found no fruit. He mourned, and turned his head, and saw her face asleep upon her camel's pillow, cheeks still wet with tears she's shed in sowing ancient oats, husks of yeasty cheeks he tenderly touched, stroking her creases and gnarls, so gently as to be imperceptible to the sleeper, and he marvelled at his ignorance, and wondered what she dreamed or thought, seeing her reborn as if for the first, cursing the idle promises he had made to bring back beauty, to upend the clock and let her blooming springtime chime, with all the holly and the ivy and the vanity of stinking folly.

How little, he came to consider at last, how little at all, if any barely but, he really knew who she was and what she felt. Since that first wintertime in her cave, seeming now so darkly long ago, when she'd told him her tale, he could not recall a single word she had ever subsequently said to him, nor barely even he to her. She was a stranger, stranger still for all the innocuous innumerable hours they had together abided, yet all unknowing, afraid of one another, foreign to each other. With a jolt, he realized just how seldom they ever spoke to one another, and how pathetically little they had to say, or even dared to share, consumed by stifling mutual timidity that drowned a surface intimacy, playing feebly out this shabby parody of domesticity, an illusion of matrimony to shield the empty hollows of their spectral lives, that were themselves illusions only, to distil heart's chill.

Dismayed, he plucked the socks from his thumbs, and wiped his eyes that warmed to the scratch of their wool, adoring these tawdry mementos of a spirit drowning. Sober again, he could not sleep; naked he arose, and left her, crawling back out on hands and knees to the meadow's dawning brightness, on whose silken grass he lay morose, and thought what was to be done.

And of course, in retrospect it seemed so obvious, so utterly inevitable – he need merely take up the hint she'd given, and feed his need and hers, in subtle stages, of course. The notion was born in his breast by the time the noon had come (was it igniting birdsong that woke him up from his stupor?), and as the day warmed, so too did his eager fervour. From the reluctant peacocks he plucked some feathers to furnish his quills, whose ink he obtained by crushing a few rocks, and grinding coal and peat for charcoal, should he choose to add any accompanying engravings, to enliven the lines. In the process of so doing, he stumbled upon a potential vocation, and wondered why he'd taken so fucking long to come around to it, the bare-arsed bearded bard.

Initially he foresaw a suite of treats, for the moment modest in scope and rough in style, gradually broadening in scale to encompass the stars, and the vagaries of fairy's ways. Handling his implements did not come easily to him, he who had for so long been wont to wield a sword or spade as opposed to pen or a pencil, but in his mounting excitement he soon forgot the strain involved in inscribing, and all but lost himself, and dismissed his futile woes of late. Dimly he could foresee in the very faraway distance a solution of sorts, to be obtained only by dint of such laborious application, wherein no amount of blood need be shed, but rather umpteen gallons of ink be spilled.

Nimble words, he soon found, were ravishing, and versatile, and many in number, and could be spoken or sung, with accompaniment to enrich their import, if need be, perhaps, lest they be too weak to work on their own. For he would extend what she had done, and fulfil the job she had begun – through knitting her own particular set of socks and jumpers and mittens, she had created new objects never seen before in the world (as hyperbolic as that may sound for such humble things so trivial) – and so too would he in his way create new things, building objects less solid or tangible, fodder to charm the ear and feed the soul, not clothe the body and sheathe the bum – though papyrus and vellum, not to speak of paper, were surely recyclable, and could be employed, if occasion arose, to forge a tattered umbrella from crinkly starchy sheets of foolscap (likely though it was that it might be raped and dissolved in the rain), the written words on which paper the mind might retain, for all that they be lost evermore to the touch, scattered to the nine winds in gusting sheets.

Enraptured by the heady flow and gush of language that flooded his brain, he choked and gagged to set it down, couched in the coarse grid of a meter he would master through stint of a novice's blundering, squaring ten syllables and five stresses to the line, counting his cadences and testing his inflections, learning slowly the steady pulse, the stately throb of redoubtable iambics: if it was good enough for the Swan of Avon, well, he'd give it a go. And on the score of Shakespeare, it was also Will who granted the impetus and set him off his rocker – having poked about in the wreckage of the O'Connell household, he came upon a doggy edition of the Sonnets buried deep in the rubble of a closet, much marked upon and maimed by crayon, evincing the scrawls of schoolchildren from yesteryear's curriculum. Skimming the scrappy volume, he chanced upon a certain page, whereon one line leapt out, helpfully underlined by a dutiful pupil:

My mistress's eyes are nothing like the sun …

That was enough – after that, beginning was the only hurdle, and here was a ready template easily adopted. 'My mistress's eyes' became 'Banshee's eyes' … 'nothing like' became 'have naught to do with' … and 'the sun' became 'the moon' (for once). A poem in her praise evolved, framed instead in the simpler form of couplets (since a sonnet was too constraining for the minute), with run-on lines and lots of lame rhymes that swiftly proliferated. ('moon: June' … 'surfaces: places' … 'lady: gravy') Balthazar lent editorial assistance and even threw in a few words of his own. Couplets had been good enough for Swift, and so he would mine that field towards which his dead friend pointed from beyond his grave, far away in the quiet of the Cathedral's Close where he might pay pilgrimage.

When Banshee Megan Devlin at last awoke, the spectacle of his increasingly prodigious industry roused her curious wonder – there he was, straddling the donkey's back, buttocks bare and all belongings on show, with an absurd beret atop his pointed crown, furiously scribbling upon threadbare paper scudded by blotted clots and blotches of his ink, mumbling under his breath to see how it sounded when spoken, transported by the joy of creation, revelling in his artistic pregnancy. And Granny Nutmeg understood, and would not disturb him; she busied herself rather by threading strewn flowers together upon the bead of a stalk, bonny charade of knitting a weedy daisy chain.

He saw this, and grinned; and when his poem was done, he read it aloud with hammy gestures and musical intonation. She approved, though she did think it verged on the border of doggerel, albeit endearingly. Encouraged, he kept the newfound practice up, day by day to fill up the gap in their confines, littering his lines with half-hints of the later greater gift he would bestow, as was implicit in her knitted nudge. A searcher after truth, he wrote directly from the half-life they were leading, colouring in his pastels the surroundings around them as they endured their pastoral, finding the nerve to express in verse those things he could never dare to say to her.

He toyed with hackneyed conceits beloved of the forgotten, willing himself to believe that the dreamy look in her eyes begat in him an image of a hunter in a cave (the details drawn from all the caves he had known, like hers in the woods, or the seaside cocoon where awhile ago that silly Hare had come unto him, bringing portents and begging favours), relishing the rhymes, some of them stodgy and some of them fine, evoking homely pictures of supper and breakfast, the sounds of donkey's neighing or the piping of woodsman's horn, plotting on the side a larger work, a proposed doggerel-epic-history that would recount his own potted chronicle, that might do for his past life what her own protracted tirade had done for hers, that she might get to know him, in which he might pour all the condensed events of his story before he came to Ireland, a lavish yarn of the shaggy dog variety, one to be set aside for a later date and a future happy chapter.

In the meantime, he wrote smaller things. He would not kid himself into thinking them Great Art, all too aware of their rudimentary character and provisional quality, their trashier edges evidence of his poetic apprenticeship. But for now, thank god, they would serve their purpose, and as he strummed his lyre and sung them for her pleasure and delight, both he and she grew happier. And surely one could want no more than that.

Only two specimens of this first stage have survived. Though sometimes gauche and sickly, they possess, in their way, a queasy kind of charm: one prestigious commentator[1] has remarked that they seem to represent a happy fusion of Sterne and Yeats, two names one would not have suspected of ever being conducive to successful welding. Yet all good things must begin somewhere. With bated breath we will wait, be it forever, for this mini-Michelangelo to produce his true Pinocchio. For now, here are the pair of surviving poems from The Mad Monk's doggerel cycle in Banshee Megan Devlin's honour: let them speak and stutter for themselves.

I.) 'On Looking into the Eyes of my Mistress'

Banshee's eyes have naught to do with the moon,
They're bright and blue akin to skies of June.
Wreaths of rheum scud across their surfaces,
While her heart yearns for far-off misty places.
Look at her luscious lashes as she blinks,
Lids faster flutter the deeper she thinks,
Brow begins to crease as a dream is born,
Maybe a memory of hunter's horn,
Galloping by a cliff, some chalky haunt
Amid the wilds where he was wont to vaunt,
Seeking shoals of meandering bison
(His preferred food, as well as venison),
Whose quick sides might he spear, their blood to gush,
Knees to crumple, slitting throats in the crush,
Croaking hoarsely as wanly they slow die,
Kicking heels, down in dust, now gone well nigh.
Mourn those dumb beasts, poor food for an exile,
A banished king, doomed to roam many a mile,
A ravaged vestige of a bygone time
When folk still spoke in regular rhyme,
Now a lowly squatter in a grim cave,
Dicing and mincing his meat like a knave,

1 Konrad Lorenzo Matteo Merkel

Grilling and charring the flanks on his fire,
Forking and chewing the gristle to inspire
Forlorn verses for his long-dead lady,
Whose face flavours cutlets soaked in gravy.
And after, when his meal is done, he might
Sing his sad song, though his voice is quite shite,
But that matters not, for sentiment's there,
Alive in lines that enliven his lair,
Telling the tale of how they met and made
Sweet love by starlight in the verdant glade,
And knew the joy of some wandering child
Requesting of the moon, in accents mild,
To descend from her lofty throne above
And give up her light to honour their love.
But the moon is mute, and will not be drunk.
And the poor child, whose heart is now quite sunk,
Is coldly told by the frosty empress
That she is not so easy to impress,
Bidding them be gone, and tear out their hair,
Penance for impudence, awful despair
To be spurned. Tears are in the hunter's eyes
As he strums his lyre in his cave and sighs,
And brokenly croons of all that is gone.
And I see that look, one of abandon
And ecstatic grief, when'er I glance
Into Banshee Maggie's eyes, oft perchance
When'er she does not know that I can see
The unfurling clouds on the tapestry
Of her stricken face, wrinkled in her joy
And sorrow. For she longs to own that boy
Who chased the gypsy's caravan, and bid
The proud moon cast away many humid
Locks of her light. All this I'm sure I see,
Or think I do, or do I not? Ah, me.
Our love's a rotten bloody mystery.

II.) 'Our Grievous Breakfast Spat'

In the crisp morn's dawn our donkey doth neigh
For his brash rasp is herald to our day,
While within we stir from our soft slumber,

Ensconced amid furs whiles we lie under
The timber planking of our roof that creaks
And sways and jingles with the wind, and leaks
Most oft in the dread season of floods and rains.
But today's a dry day; warmth still remains
From sunny yesterday, when we went out
Into the town to work our wares and shout
Prophecies at some witless passer-by
Who looked aghast to be told they would die
Rather sooner than ever they would wish. I pat our donkey's ears; you cook your dish
Of porridge and haddock, eels and some ham
Sliced with our cleaver, not without a qualm
Of regret for the handsome sow whose throat
I slit, in whose blood on the ground I wrote
A piss-poor eulogy, extolling all
Her bounteous good nature. With your shawl
Around your shoulders, you ring the tin bell
For breakfast, the best repast. All is well
Amongst us as I sidle whistling in,
Grinning gormlessly, like a true gombeen.
We squat to eat, like them of Nippon do,
Whose pincers for biting we also have too,
Cedar chopsticks, whose tinkle I enjoy
As they play upon our plates. You are coy
This morning, it seems to me, with your head
Firmly down, never lifted from your bread,
Shirking my gaze like some virgin schoolgirl
Unlettered in life, not yet done a twirl
With hairy strutting top-notch local cocks,
Of whom I never was one – I hate jocks.
Our old ass Balthazar pokes in his face,
Braying for his pudding with scant good grace.
We ignore him. Thus ignored, he departs,
With his tail wagging huffily. False starts
To his day, such as this, are customary.
And still you are silent, dearest Maggie
My craziest Nutmeg – what dark thoughts prey
Upon thee, my sweet? I'll help if I may.
Is not the day a warm one, and our meal
The real deal? Admire how the sun on steel

Of our glinting knife doth refract about
In a dozen directions, so why pout?
They are assurances, such sights as these
From which we take heart. I try set at ease
Whate'er worries thee. Able Aurora,
Our stage manager, gives off such an aura
Of grace and calm, she's a model for you.
O come, why so down, dear, what can I do?
And now at last you look at me to say
There's naught that I can do for you today,
For your bitter mood is a lifelong one,
Unappeased by this our old young love, spun
So late in life, won in yer afterlife,
Already far too late. All the past strife
Nettles thee the much more, since unresolved.
You pine for the past, there from whence evolved
The happier part of thy sob story,
Of Frankie and family: their glory
Is all that moves thee now, and I today
Am but a sorry substitute, too grey
To oppose the brightly pigmented past.
And yes, I shrink to think just what a vast
Abyss lies twixt me and him who loved thee
First – how must I appear the worse? Ah, me!
Only a haggard ragged vagabond,
Poor pedlar in cheap shocks, an old fool fond.
You say you've seen your children since your death,
Grown and adult, and you've stilled your shocked breath
As they pass by your glum ghost unheeding,
As if some gauze prevents them from yielding
To the tentative touch of their mother
Reaching out from a world quite another,
Stretching hopeless fingers that long to pat
Your brood as in days of old – no more that.
Now you yearn for the chuckle of a child
Chasing a kite in the heights of the wild
Blue yonder. And while you tell me this wish,
You dissolve in sobs. And I look at fish
On my plate, numbly listening to tears,
And sit in silence, so it seems, for years.

CHAPTER FORTY-THREE

She was a nameless orphan abandoned in Edinburgh in a little basket. And it was a quare quirk, on the part of Mr and Mrs Temple who took her in, to dub their foundling with the ambiguous name of Jezebel. The priest had his qualms as he baptized her in the bowl, and his voice had shaken as he pronounced the name, one he had been taught to condemn and abhor. No less quick to take umbrage were the antiquated relatives of the sprawling Temple clan, among whom there was uproar, and the couple was quickly assailed with reproaches, subsequent to the ceremony, when then their adopted babe was branded.

And so, to mollify the controversy, little Jezebel's step-parents consented to address her, when in public in the pram, solely by the affectionate variant of Jezzie. And little Jezzie grew up amid an eclectic atmosphere, kept afloat on artistic oxygen in the realm of literature, or painting, or cinema, or music, put to bed by her foster papa with a nightly dose of Wordsworth, the wizard of the word he adored, whose phrases he rolled round with his tongue in cheerful treble, to his bright little stepdaughter's delight, she to whom he never gabbled baby talk, but invariably spoke sound sense and wisdom.

And it paid off. Little Jezzie was a prodigy. Her first words came early, and quick to come they were too, lines culled from dirty Limericks, salacious cadences that she would commit like lightning to her teeming memory, and loudly and obstreperously recite, always at the most inopportune of times. And she was quick to walk, and eager to learn, and soon was devouring the dictionary, and browsing lots of books, and came to conquer the canon, learning, by dint of diligent rote, reams upon reams of poetry, such as eluded even her elders, whose knowledge she soon surpassed in scope. And precocious Jezzie so gifted grew, and drew, and painted, and sculpted, and played the piano, and was top of her class, and wrote little rhymes. And she racked up a nest of faithful loving girly chums (among them a certain Saruko, and Kyrie Elysium, and Lucia Seward), among whom she was pre-eminent in accomplishments, and, indeed, dare we say, in beauty.

For our Jezzie grew to be pretty too, arousing excitement among all what men she knew, whose heads would turn to follow her with hungry eyes as she passed them by, as well endowed in body as in mind. For she was a sturdy girl, with a sensual appetite, who kept fit and fed, swimming and cycling and building up her biceps and her strength. And irresistible Jezzie, once she was of an age to understand the connotations implicit in her bizarre name, began to live up to it, with all the goodwill in the world. Figuratively, and literally, she took her many men in hand. From boy to boy she gadded around, for life was short, and she ought to try on as many men while she could when young, but none among the useless studs could satisfy, so she cultivated claws and pincers of her nails, with which, in frustration, she would scratch their skin as they scored.

Her latest conquest was a sap called Finbarr Froy, an incurable romantic and potential poet, with whom she was involved for a fortnight's whirlwind affair that began promisingly in kisses and embraces, and breathless expressions of undying affection, but ended in tears and jeers, such as she by now expected from love, that eternal unreliable.

The one thing insecure Jezzie did not have was a look that would last. Her hair, naturally blonde and tumbling to her waist in Rapunzel's loving locks, came to be cut. Her fringe was low, behind of which she hid, peeking fearfully out from behind the strands – whose colour, altered by chemicals, jumped from month to month from blonde to black to blue to brown – which hue could express the truth of her fragmented soul?

Jezebel Temple, by now well nigh nearly nineteen in Dublin, currently finds herself a pupil of Trinity College. By night, she cries herself to sleep. By day, in the lecture halls, her gaze is elsewhere, her thoughts are afar. She knows not what she wants.

And sometimes, while crossing Front Square to lunch, she would spare a glance for the boy in black who sat beneath the Campanile, sipping mysteriously from a little black flask, from whence spouting steam in a little plume spewed, exquisite vapours lost in the damp autumnal air, and she wondered who he was, and what he thought, and what it was he was drinking, and thereafter would continue to wonder intermittently on and off, over all the dull day. She suspected that he was something of a piss artist.

And then, one springtime day, she came to be walking down Lombardy Road. She looked bewitching, in a scarlet coat of bloody red, of a comely figure with fat in all the right places, her spiky hair of raven's black with a beguiling fringe hiding her shining eyes, grey or golden green, her beaming lips that set her pale face alight, haunting her ghostly pallor, with a beatific grin, seeming to nod to the beat of her feet that were small, with tights of fishnet that let slip slivers of her calves through their grids, faraway her dreamy pensive gaze, wagging slowly her hand in the cool air up and down, to the hum of a tune in the head, conducting an invisible orchestra, mirror of her mind, and then, upon a sudden, she stopped in her tracks by a certain house, having seen something.

What did she see?

His father's garden, overrun with weeds and reeds, throbbing in the pulsing breeze that blew, rustling the hedge of hawthorn choking his prickly gate, that squeaked as it opened. But a single flower plumed amid the debris, an opulent pearl that caught her own eye roving at random ever restless, white and frail and slender, one she longed to pick. And pick it she did, poking through the bars a lily hand, plucking the slim stem, the stalk that snapped in silence, her treasure took. She sniffed it, and smiled, and bore it by her breast, slipping her plunder in betwixt her soft and bobbing bubs. Swaying as she strode away, slowly taking her leave of the little lawn, whose house was this she wondered, half in jest or earnest, admiring the crimson door, a number nine emblazoned in brass beneath the dour godhead, the one that held the niche of a knocker.

And it was only then that her ascending gaze came to be gliding heavenwards, rising by the masonry's maze of bricks, the real Edwardian regal red, passing by piping fissures in his wall the careening eye of Jezebel went caroming, to rest on the windows above, at one of which she saw a face, pressed to the pane, misting the glass with his feverish breath, gaunt, taut, the scraggly hair greasily lank, the pallid cheeks hollow, the mouth held down in a narrow frown, such as lined a scowl near set in stone, the eyes that looked upon her, their gaze fervid and deranged, impassioned and afire, staring, staring, unabashed, unashamed, a crazy gaze her own wild eyes met.

What was a girl to do, in the light of such stricken admiration?

She winked at him, and walked away (it was the same, she knew).

CHAPTER FORTY-FOUR

There was a strange brightness in the air those days. One saw it in the beaming eyes of druid Arsene as he sat in my bed day by day in the grey room. One morning he went so far as to crawl out of the window and potter about the rooftop, preaching to the surrounding avenues of chimneypots. By the time I found him, he had pulled down his trousers (much to the consternation of the prying neighbours), and was dancing precariously near the rim (the drop was not much, barely six foot, but if he fell we were fucked), caressing the twining Russian vine, my father's pride that swallowed the windows and drowned the ledges, whose leaves he plucked from rope of the stem and dusted his scalp with their fragile crown the wind blew off. Uneasy, I grabbed his elbow, and ushered him back inside. Without protest he complied. Then, as I tucked him back under the covers, he asked me: '*For whom has love so undone you?*'

'SARUKO!' I snapped in annoyance, huffily departing.

But names change. In the fresh season, I made my dangerous friends.

Following the glimpse I'd got of Maggie's apparition (which I put down to lovesick effects of grief or the intricacies of mirage), I was in no fit state of mind to then be approached by Jezebel Temple, as shortly thereafter I was. Her hair had been dyed again, to a slightly askew hue of turquoise or silvery blonde, so I did not, at least initially, recognize her as thc one who had winked. Amid the bustle among the crowds of Front Square's stalls, her hand took mine, and mine own arm her arm linked and ensnared.

'I hear you're writing a book! What's it about?'

I was captive then. I knew her by name, of course – she was notorious – and it did not help that Saruko had been her school-chum. But it came as a surprise to suddenly have her marching us around the college grounds, jabbering to the nine winds, lots of all sorts of stuff about herself, keen to impress, always interrupting whenever I attempted to say something, but yet I put up with it – any attention from her sex was preferable to naught. And besides, her body, as we have heard, was beguiling, indeed bewitching – I was tempted, all in thrall and afire for flesh, the most bestial of motives for a young man hitherto so idealistic and clean-minded as I – such fervid lust was surely the natural by-product of such celestially futile and disappointed love as previously I thought I felt. Saintly virginal Saruko, god bless her, was too fresh and pure to ever dare defile, too much a child to ever contemplate copulation. But Jezzie – ah, Jezzie was a sturdy girl, a comely wench. Better yet, she gave every sign of seeming to like or fancy me, touching eagerly oft, dizzily brushing her fringe with a furtive snakelike gesture that seemed to augur a giddy unease, surely signalling that she was smitten. Furthermore, I seemed to discern something in her welter of blather that kindled recognition – her neuroses I thought akin to mine own, a psyche riddled with the same queasy uncertainties and insecurities, coupled with the same faltering efforts to erect creations, the same frustrated impulse to art – I liked to think she was the girl I could have been were I born female.

Thoughts of death and transience preoccupied her. She claimed to have written a requiem, or at least part of one, called off on account of nightmares she'd had of a figure in grey, beckoning her to the grave with gloved finger, cajoling her to finish this mass she was composing – in honour of her own imminent death! This did sound a shade disingenuous, not to say markedly unoriginal, but I was intrigued, and willing to leave leeway for her cock-and-bull – after all, I was something of a persistent liar myself, consistently striving to appear more interesting than I actually was.

Some days and nights of shy flirtation ensued, as I cautiously stalked her, donning again my charmer's fedora to win more rakish winks, continually contriving to bump into her all over the place, attending banal functions, much against my better judgement, solely on the grounds that she would be there, even accompanying her home on one memorable occasion, parading past canal banks by moonlight, discussing Larry Olivier's Othello and the way his greasepaint began to blackly drip like melting chocolate, admiring the snorting swans to whom we tossed our crumbs of popcorn, and adoring the whimsical heron who waded the shallows in search of his fish, all the way to her front door, beyond whose confines I was tentatively admitted, but no, nothing ensued – a cup of tea and banter was all I got for my pains. Still, I always liked to take my time. (Fool!)

Arose then the terrible occasion I sallied to a nightclub, lured by whiff of her perfume. For an amiable while she humoured me, leading me along through shoals of blabbing arseholes, her iron grip a clamp upon my limper wrist, leading me on the wily goose's chase upstairs and downstairs in vain search of her friends, whom now she could not place nor find, poor thing. Perhaps I should have bought her a drink. Perhaps, when she sat us down in a corner of the beery garden, at an intimate remove whose scenery could have been construed as romantic were one so minded, cuddling close to me and warmly, with low-cut blouse that did justice to her voluptuous bust, pretending to text to fill up the pauses in our prattle, batting painted lashes with an adder's flicker to turn me on – perhaps then I ought to have to leant in to kiss her lips, to rake my claim and yield to the wretched 'score' whose allure I did so abhor in days of yore, to find her unresisting and compliant – heaven knows she got around, apparently undiscerning, accumulating a catalogue of losers for lovers, scores of ungainly chumps who'd been there before me.

'I don't like girls!' she once tartly remarked, 'Most of my friends are only weirdo boys who want to get into my pants! Ha-ha-ha-ha-ha.'

This utterance always accompanied by that shrill trill, that screamingly false metallic laugh she cultivated to sheathe her sores, whose trembling quaver I grew soon to loathe. Her mouth alone smiled, not her eyes, which stayed sad, and did not partake of the mirthful noises implied by her monkey's jabber, that dire cackle of artifice.

No – I did not take the chance to kiss her when I could. Perhaps this disappointed her. Perhaps I failed the test. Up she got and fast was lost to my hapless sight, gone beyond the heaving shower of shoulders that bobbed in rhythm to the beatbox.

Forlorn for a period I followed and meandered about the clotted murk, seeking that silver streak that alerted her hair, tawny ragged and dyed, all contrived just like her painted lips and padded hips, like a lonely harlot or apprentice courtesan, with a heart that had been broken by good love gone bad, a bleeding organ thereafter consigned to snooze, a body resigned to seeking the momentary satisfaction of the Saturday night 'score'.

Then I found her again, o yes, dancing a curly jig and twirling reel, in the jaundiced light of the lurid disco-ball, in company of none but the figure of Boris Nigel Gillespie, my one-time admirer and unworthy promoter, on whom she had nursed a crush.

Yes, he was a better dancer than I was, let us give him that. He had perhaps more muscle too, result of his weekends spent rafting in Chapelizod, and his nights of lifting violet weights. I noted that he often paused to kiss his biceps of which he was proud. And like her, he was a frequent dyer of his hair – today it was alternately blue or pink or tampon purple – all depended on what deceptive hue was lit, what hint of tint the wriggling epileptic lights above picked out in strobes, flashing with a shutter flick.

And soon his jaws were champing froth, like hers upon his arm – a shark she was, administering such toothy vampiric bites as these to stake her claim, like bloody watermarks, a habit of hers as soon I learned, like pissing upon a post – champing upon her willing throat and soon upon her lips, locked on his in sloppy pulpy viscous union of mucus, slobbering bubbling saliva like foaming spittle from whence flies and maggots are born – there they were wrapped up the pair, daring to score on the dance floor.

Then her eye caught sight of me over his shoulder, sulking on the ring's sidelines. Her lips left his. Her hand shot out, and clawed me into the viper's thickets. Gillespie paid me no heed, but repeatedly bopped. She swung me about for a bit, as if we were a trio in a macabre tango, and pressed herself against my ear, to ask me huskily how I felt.

'JEALOUS!' I shot back.

(One always had to yell to be heard in these clubs. Romance's doom.)

'WHY ARE YOU JEALOUS?' she bellowed in return.

And I roared, 'BECAUSE I AM ENAMOURED!'

(In retrospect, the wording was inspired!)

Boris Nigel Gillespie by now had gathered, from our exchange, that the plot was thicker. Drunken, he swayed, looking blankly from one to the other of us, confused, deafened. And she was aghast, or feigning to be.

She had had no idea, she crowed. O, she was so sorry to have led me on, for she was a horrible person, she said, you must excuse her. But she loved the drama – I did too.

'NEVER MIND – I'M USED TO IT!' I hollered.

She winced at this – it was a bit much – and then, to make light, tried to instill a jocular mood by likening me to Falstaff. I thanked her, embraced her, and stormed off.

Back home, sleep denied, I told old Arsene what had happened, in broken phrasing decorated by displays of sniffles. I doubt he heard a word I said. When I concluded my maudlin recital, he smacked his chapped lips and quipped:

'*Rejoice! These shall be the best years of your lives!*'

I was miffed at the time, but in retrospect I suppose he was right.

CHAPTER FORTY-FIVE

In such an unstable state of mind as was mine those days, prone to seeing ghosts, giving up my bedroom to a goblin who had stolen the shape of an old friend, my equilibrium was as a consequence constantly jagged, easily upset. I became a tangled ball of nerves, fuzzy at the edges and icy at the core, keeping too many secrets and telling too many lies. My sleep was scant, owing to excess consumption of the greenest tea that was my sole relief – one kettle of the stuff per day quickly became four.

My father's jocular suspicions, as to the precise nature of the weird brew I kept in the flask, began to take on a more ominous import – maybe, as he had hypothesized, it was indeed an evil elixir I drunk, disguised as the most delicious of drugs, of which I was an addict. Though neither strong nor weak, never sick nor ill, I still was always ailing, nose compound of phlegm, stuffed with snot, waxy ears seldom siphoned, innate myopia unaided by lenses (ah, vanity!), growing increasingly suspicious and paranoid, sensitive to the most trivial of illusory slights, addled brain unhinged by dint of too much stewing in a bath of leaves – they sit before my eyes even now as I write, their petals finely veined, swelling from dried husks into splendid bobbing pads, undulant and waving, swollen with their weighty drink of water boiled, sucked up by their liquid stems and engorged in their ventricles, puffed with fluid soon to sink and descend, lost mid ballooning plumes of steam, vapours that fog our view of the murky green bottom of the cup, forming a dark forest in a pubic cluster where they lie imbedded, my salvation and my curse, the succulent fruit of Buddha's eyelids, peeled off expressly so that he may remain forever awake, petulantly flung away in a beatific huff, so as to sprout in soil.

Dates are a blur. I used to be so pedantically specific, watching the clock whose tick was my pulse, counting the seconds whose hum was my compass – but now only the change of the seasons made any impression on me. I found myself in a bar one night, still reeling from the sweetie Jezzie (to whom I sent a grovelling text ['fulsome apologies for my behaviour last night, I was drunk, and feeling a moment's passing bitterness vented my spleen on the person closest, you were caught in the crossfire, alas …'], to which, to her credit, she graciously replied in sweet and fulsome kind like the lovely girl she was).

I believe the bar in question to have been near Townsend Street, owned by Chaplin's, fitting name for a fallen idol, whose battered bowler and penguin's walk once upon a time I strove to mimic when bored in the schoolyard, aping the twirling of the toothbrush moustache I did not then possess, but which now was sprouting in a muzzy gristle of down, rather carroty orange, after the fashion of my father's straw. There was an open reading in Chaplin's, yes, as arranged by the Literary Society, to which I contributed, settling down atop an unstable table with a swaggering stagger, lending my Guinness glass to housemate Gallagher to hold (o, just to give the little bitch something to do with her beaver's hands!), while I waved a fan of my papers in the indoor air, drunkenly sussing up the contents of my encyclopaedia for idiots (that was cheeky – both Saruko and Edwin were present, safely sat in opposite corners of course, to avoid a catfight), before launching into a rendition of one favourite purple passage (something to do with old guys in a bar thinking of death – that lousy trope of mortality!).

My manner of reading was hammy and hurried, imbuing the words with a lilting up-and-down sort of singsong, to embroider dead lines with a false rhythm they did not themselves possess, chanting faster and faster so the fraudulence could pass unsuspected, winning accolades for the power of my Niagara speed and surge, the fakery rallying to a thunderous climax that rattled the bones and prompted a prolonged standing ovation.

Overcome, I blubbered sweaty thanks, slumped to my stool as an ocean of claps subsided, and shakily reached for my pint, which then I knocked over, like an ass, just as an Israeli got up next to read. It was not deliberate, merely a momentary loss of muscular coordination, but as glass smashed, and the foamy brown puddle streamed and pooled while uproar arose, with much oafish clamouring for tissue and toilet cloth to mop up my mess, suspicion was rife that I'd done it all on purpose only to upstage the doleful Israeli (who looked crestfallen, punched), hogging the limelight like a prima-donna prig.

Shamed, I took refuge behind my dear Galbraith who assured me as ever that I had done neither wrong nor villainy. So the evening passed, and soon the bookish crowds ebbed as the pub began to close, as shutters sunk and rusty counters were cleared.

But it was on my way towards the exit that one particular individual stepped forward from the rabble to accost me. And I shall have to watch and measure my words most warily while describing him, of all people.

Taller than I was, certainly, though oddly our heights seemed at times to fluctuate, for his shoulders were lower, on account of his head being bigger. Big black boots and torn blue jeans, their scars of rips carefully cultivated to cook up the diehard image of devil-may-care, clad in the striped vest of a sailor and the sooty leather jacket of a gigolo, with an earring in a purple lobe riddled by bullet holes from former pierces. Lurid tattoos could also faintly be discerned, on his neck and what could be seen of his tuba chest. His head was indeed very massive, sculpted brow bulging, crowned by a shock of dark locks among whose tangled curls some shards of early silver faintly petered, evidence of prolonged mental cognitions within that enormous skull – his process of thought was always visible, god bless him, every effect so artfully calculated – you could see the cogs and temples grinding when you put a point across to him, over whose implications he would mull and ruminating chew until he could contradict them to the full.

Yes, his face was long indeed, equine almost, with a square-ish chin recalling Adam West's, erstwhile Batman in saggy pyjamas from the sixties, with a Celtic snub of a nose with comely wen, a large mouth that almost always flapped (he never shut up), with a loud and resonant voice that carried far and cut across the laden air, light though softly deep, a bass-baritone with voluminous lung capacity, a songster to fill a cathedral.

His eyes were piercing, very large and blue, yet their steely intensity went usually unnoticed behind the lenses that framed their almond lozenges or orbs, those shining specs his mammy daily polished with her loving douche. The abiding impression was of an oversized kiddie, a boisterous child who'd knocked the scale out of whack – unmistakably adult, older than I, he yet still seemed a small and eloquent boy, a big and laughing baby. And as far as accurate introductions go, I can do no better than paraphrase Jean Cocteau's beautiful summation of the meteoric juvenile Orson Welles:

> … [Konrad Merkel] is a kind of giant with the look of a child, a tree filled with birds and shadow, a dog that has broken its chain and lies down in the flowerbeds, an active idler, a wise madman, an island surrounded by people, a pupil asleep in class, a strategist who pretends to be drunk when he wants to be left in peace.

He accosted me in the doorway, anyway, this specimen, laid a hand on my shoulder, shaking his head in a commendable simulacrum of speechless admiration. The words, when at last they came, seemed long looked for.

'Can I … Ah! … Can I buy you a pint?'

Ah! This seemed by far the most welcome form of flattery, so much better than any gush. After some burbling hesitation, I gave him leave and blessing to buy. He returned swiftly bearing a pair (a rolled-up fag behind his ear, rolled while pints were poured, during which process of rolling and pouring I later pettily surmised that he had rehearsed all he would subsequently say), and so on our barstools we sat astride our celestial pedestals as the barkeep's broom dusted the tiles beneath our elevation.

We sipped and spoke – usually his voice held court, while I only interjected before being trampled upon – he was excited, god love him, and could not contain his rhetorical flood, his verbal diarrhoea. (With displeasure I remembered chatterbox Jezzie's similar propensity for loquaciousness, a passing bitter recollection that soured my porter's creamy head.) Topics were touched on – the madness of Perac, the actor Burgess, the glory of Joyce, the blindness of Milton and Homer and Borges, the wisdom of drafting, the facility of Mozart, the speed of reading, the character of our respective magnum opuses/opi? (he would know – he was a classicist at that time), poetry vs prose, the spry way I had littered my piece with rhymes (had I?), whose ease he claimed exceeded his by far, those with which his own proposed 'verse novel' was cushioned. All in all, an amiable first meeting. (God bless our dangerous friends.)

Konrad Merkel. Konrad Merkel was the name he gave, one at first I found it hard to catch. It sounded foreign – indeed, his mother Esmerelda was of Maori stock – hence those tattoos he partially displayed, latent on the chest beneath fabric of his threadbare shirt. The full name was Konrad Lorenzo Matteo Merkel – had his original confirmation name of 'Andreas' made the cut, his initials may have amounted to an almighty crushing whopper KLAM! SHAZAM! CRACKING CLAM! K.L.A.M!

Initials! Yes, that was my foremost contribution to this our first discussion (insofar as any other word than his could be snuck in at all) – I spoke with winsome eyes upturned of the weird power I saw invested in them, revelling in my own of S.J.C., and dismissing those of others as less loaded. We rounded off by shouting those of James Augustine Aloysius Joyce at each other.

'JAAJ!'

'JAAJ!'

'JAAJ!'

'JAAJ!'

'JAAJ!'

'JAAJ!'

In this manner we continued until the publican told us to go, and so we parted. In retrospect it seemed inevitable that I should soon introduce Konrad to Albert.

CHAPTER FORTY-SIX

Mr Albert Potter and the White Dog were so far getting on well. For it was a bracing thing to arise from stupor, grimly expectant of another tedious day, only to be met with the panting greeting of an inspiring pooch, growling his affections and offering the paw for the fat man to take and shake. And so far the dog gave no sign of being mangy or laden with rabies – nor was he dirty, since being scrupulously clean, licking his furs to gleam with all the care of a cat, even evincing toilet training through his habit of scratching the door whenever he wished to make a deposit, servant of nature's call. As for Mr Potter's cats, those whiskered ghosts at first were wary, tartly spurning the new arrival's endeavours to befriend them, cruelly hissing as was fitting, scratching his moist nose that bled, shirking his dogged overtures, though still the kindly canine, undeterred, persisted to charm them, and in time had won them over.

Albert, enthroned on the swamp of his couch, revelled to find his burrow awash with the swish of tails both feline and canine, chuckling to watch their play of combat, their masquerade of ageless rivalry, as cats cowered while the wily dog advanced, hurtling through their tawny ranks like a moony bullet, barking and whooping while his bushy tail wagged, braving their fangs and the brandishing of their pincers, until soon all the peril of war had waned, and every creature in Potter's lair lay down to pout.

And Mr Albert Potter sipped his cider while the White Dog groomed the back of an alabaster cat, licking free her fur of all the fleas she kept. And Mr Albert Potter, like a darker Doolittle, became a man who talked to his animals as well as to his plants, watering the pots and stroking the vines whiles he bantered with the beasts. He felt like the ringmaster of a shabby subterranean circus, and briefly considered importing a few more species to enrich the grotty commune over which he absentmindedly presided.

A parrot in a cage, for instance, might be just the thing to attract the crowds, whose imitative eloquence could supply a pastiche of a human voice and pep up the chorus of mews and barks with some squawks and titters. But then again, such a move was very maybe misguided, given the predilection of the ravenous kitties for flesh of birds. He would have to think about it.

He finished his last can, and flung it carelessly into the cold fireplace. Outside was early evening; ample time to gorge beyond under the arch. And so, with struggle, he grunting slid into his shoes (bending these days was no easy thing, given the breadth of his belly that impeded his reach to the feet – so far away they scarce seemed his), donned a dark shirt (men of such girth, as Orson Welles would concur, are well advised to wear black, speckled by winking stars of dandruff, to make a gaping cosmos of their corpulence, inspiring awe as opposed to ridicule – and do make sure your garments are also stretchy), and lastly tossed a coat over the sweep of his shoulders. The dog's ears and eyes perked up – for the clever mutt, avid interpreter of every signal his master sent him, had learned to read an impending walk into these motions of dressing gear.

'Not now, Snowy,' the big man said, 'Merriman doesn't like having dogs on his premises. I'm not blind yet, anyway.'

The dog looked downcast, but nonetheless consented to stay.

And with a window ajar to keep them cool, through which chink the slim cats could escape were they so minded, Mr Potter departed from his abode, and staggered huffing up the steps to the dusky square, past whose sharp bars he strode to the purple arch, under which he went in lamplight wanly orange, soon come to the August Mount across the road (what an ascent, so crisp the fresher air there), into which he entered, passing through doors which had no handles (so cheap was the publican), in a sluggish manner akin to sinking back into the soup of primordial ooze, from whence as a reptile once upon a time he gasping crawled, from slime to sand.

It was disconcertingly quiet for a Friday – sign of the times. Word had it that Mr Merriman, his business ailing, might soon shut down his saloon (at which rumoured prospect Potter mourned – he would have to resort to the Lower Deck if so), since he had ample incomes elsewhere, and perhaps five houses dotted all over the plusher parts of Dublin. And neither of his daughters showed any interest in inheriting his doomed pub.

Nothing changes here. Still manned by the same decrepit barkeeps, the good cop and the bad, gentle Robbie with poor sight and jittery grip, and nasty Carter whose temper was waspish (he recently refused to accept a coin from Albert on the grounds that it was too sweaty – for which insolence the fat man threatened to tear off his testicles).

Not even Matt the Electrician was here to ask for crossword clues – perhaps he had gone to Australia in search of his prodigal squeeze. Only Jacky the Polis was present, afar in the corner of the counter, casting a surly face upon the new arrival as he settled on his stool, still grudging him that twenty quid loan he had tardily omitted to return.

What a sullen aspect the gruff copper displays, bitter eyes flashing behind those angry shades. The constipation must have been getting to him too, not to speak of the smarting crotch injury he had lately obtained, by dint of his inept topple down a Rathmines manhole, crushing his groin as he did the splits, for which misadventure he nursed the ambition of suing the city corporation, hoping to grasp a grand off them, in feeble exchange for the impotence with which their poor street planning had cursed him.

'How's the body?' said Robbie as he proffered Foster's.

'Fitter!' said the fat man as he conjured a fiver and lifted the glass, 'Nice thing to keep a dog to get you out and about, juh juh juh?'

'Ah I know yeah,' said Robbie, conjuring change from the squeaky till, 'I'm considering getting me daughter one for her Communion, y'know?'

'O really indeed? And is there, uh, an after-party in the works too?'

'Don't push it, ye chancer. Ha, ha, ha.'

Mr Albert Potter displayed his mirth by mildly leering, and emitting a kind of scoff. He had seldom of late little reason to ever laugh outright.

Innumerable seconds, of the same wanton nothingness, now took their dreary course in that den of squalid languor, lit by the smoky lamps whose day was their night, atop pedestals two huddled figures looming in the dimness, slumped at each hunched corner of the glossy counter the barman scrubbed, manfully sipping in the silence, broken by the television box chirruping on the shelf, whose flicker only dozing Robbie deigned observe, squinting through his foggy specs, barely hearing the breathing of the customers and their awful lapping, two bloated toads at the trough slurping their rations, relishing their mocking puny grandeur, while the ominous clock chimed when hung on the reddest of the bloody walls, and the painted horse's head glared at the swollen head of Mr Potter.

Around eight or nine, a young hand landed on Potter's shoulder, and bade him turn, blinking through the mug of grog, sad eyes blearily shutting, pressed and squashed mid the folds of fat that formed his face. Who?

'Albert!' the boy in black smiled.

'Simeon. Long time no see,' said Mr Potter gravely, offering a flabby palm to shake, at touch of whose pulp the younger suppressed a shudder.

'Quite right, been a while, ay,' the callow youth blustered, overeager to impress, with a gesture to his murky companion, 'I bring company with me today. I'm here with, ha, I guess you might call him a Bohemian Poet!'

'A Bohemian Poet? Quite a lofty title to live up to!'

'How do you do. I've heard a lot about you,' said Merkel seriously.

Albert Potter and Konrad Merkel shook hands and exchanged names.

'Can you see them now, old chap?' trilled the Puck to the Pooka, as through the pane of the August's amber windows they squatted outside and peered.

'Clear as day, shot by rosy hues of nightly glass!' the Pooka barked, the fat cat Moloch lumped in his capacious pocket idly purring, nibbling upon a crust of cheese.

And can we see them? Can we not marvel at this wayward trio here assembled on the stage of saloon? Don't we love the strange sense it makes?

The fat man of fifty years and the two lanky youths of twenty-odd sat on their stools in a tidy ring, exchanging energetic gestures. The boy in black twirls a lock of his hair whenever he does not speak, for the twirling helps him think. The drooping quiff slumps o'er the equine brow of the boy wearing glasses. The perspiration glistening on the piggy face of the eldest man. At first muted, their volume warms to a friendly hum.

Merkel, usually the most voluble, is initially silent, humbled to quietude by the spectacle of ruined erudition that Potter's paunch proclaims. He sits on the sidelines quaking timidly, as Collins banters blandly with the big man – Potter liked the boy, but thought his converse dreary, a shadow of his father at best.

But eventually Merkel is emboldened. When Mr Potter mentions Nabokov's *Pale Fire*, he is proud to admit that he has read it, a claim of which Simeon cannot boast. And Albert approves of this, and they clasp arms in fellowship, smiling at the similitude. Simeon, aloof an inch at the edge of it, displays a pained rictus of a smile. He had long had the feeling, begrudging tinged by both envy, pity and stricken love, when first he was introduced to Albert, that here was a mind that contained his own. And Merkel's mind, slippery as an eel, infinitely malleable and incorrigibly mercurial – this brain seemed comparable. So then thus was jealousy begat.

Having deftly rolled a fag, Konrad excused himself, and sauntered to the smoking area at the bar's back, servile Simeon trailing at his dashing heels that clip upon the linoleum. There, in the queer scarlet light by the groaning bins (in which the Puck and Pooka eavesdropped, while Moloch dug through rubbish seeking fish), the taller boy smoked and thought, and offered the younger a cursory drag, the fish that took the bait.

'Konrad'. It sounds so odd to call him 'Konrad'. For he was always 'Merkel' to most. That was the name he invariably gave upon introductions – 'Konrad' only came later, only when pressed to divulge, granted with reluctance. For he had glibly decided, long ago during days when he looked into the mirror, that to go solely by his surname would amplify his mythic status, and stoke the fires of his artful legend, largely self-wrought and finely forged. And he had also decided, if and whenever one of his proposed books was published (would that he had but the tedious patience and dogged persistence to stubbornly stick at a project long enough to finish the thing, before his restless mind grew bored and drove him to abandonment, when yesterday's brilliance grew stale and lost its waning dazzle – for all that phosphorescence was only tinsel), that only the letters of 'MERKEL' would adorn the jackets and sleeves – might lend an air of mystery, and bolster sales. But to be called 'Konrad' pained him, though this his pride would not admit, and the syllables grated on his ears with their pressing harshness – for when called 'Konrad', he could not help but be reminded of Esmerelda, his poor mad little wonderful Maori mummy he always strove to forget, she who loved him so much, more than anything else in the world, the deluded quacking wagon. As with so many borderline psychopathic only children, he found her overbearing, all-consuming love to be of the suffocating sort, his greatest setback, and sought instead to spurn her aggressive affections, hating her for her insistent barging into his bedroom at break of dawn when he would rather be wanking or writing, loathing her insistent prying into his privacy, drowning under the constant welter of fatuous advice she gave him, harrying and badgering the boy who longed only to fly free. One compelling reason for his studying classics in Trinity, asides from the obvious benefit his poetry might derive from a comprehensive knowledge of Greek and Latin was that it gave him a handy excuse to get out of bed in the mornings (getting a job was out of the question, his artistic temperament could never abide the tedium of working hours), and run away from his mammy to town. Though her voice continued to pursue him. Losing his mobile phone was one useful strategy in shirking her longing contact whenever he went outside to roam, though still she cooked up ways to keep in constant crazy nagging touch with him, resorting to phoning his friends instead, just as now she did by ringing Simeon, who answered the buzzing and listened baffled to the ranting on the other end.

'Just hang up,' said Merkel blithely as he smoked.

Simeon obligingly did, and their discussion reverted to the matter of the bright-eyed blubber of Mr Potter within, with whom Merkel was taken.

'What a man!' he gushed, his passion and purple colour rising, waving the fag whose blue plume twirled upward in the path of his waving, 'He's a discovery! He's rare! He really has read everything! I can't believe it! But Simeon, really, really, we have to save him from himself! It is our duty! We have to rescue this man before it is too late!'

'Hush, less of that now, Murky!' Simeon bade with a wave, artfully employing the derogatory nickname he had devised out of envy for his friend, fearing the big man might overhear these impertinent ejaculations should he pass them by on his way to piss.

Yet he understood all too well Merkel's excitement at the sight and state of Potter, a rare piece of devastated treasure. For Simeon had long loved the man in his way, ever since his father had secured him an introduction into the presence some two years prior, since when he had always longed to be in company with the great man he yearned from afar to befriend and follow, a longing compounded by the breakdown of old Arsene the weatherman. Yet he sensed always his inadequacy for this role of Potter's disciple, since he glimpsed there a mind he could never match nor meet in quality of thought, in precision of judgement, in awesome scope and breadth of knowledge.

Besides, he could scarce swagger into the August on his own, to casually take up his stool by the bulk of Potter's side – it just simply looked too *weird* for a youth of twenty to exchange intimacies with a fat old alcoholic of fifty (should not young men be in the clubs chasing girls if they have any life of their own worth the leading?) – or at least, even if he saw no strangeness in such a friendship, he was nonetheless made to feel awkward about it through dint of the barrage of suspicious looks that the other clientele bestowed upon the odd couple, whose offbeat association, in their narrow eyes, could only augur some ghastly hint of homosexuality or worse.

So Simeon had longed for an open-minded and clever friend with whom he could meet Mr Albert Potter on his own terms and turf. Just one other companion made all the difference – for three was a crowd, and would ward away the baleful eyes of others. By bringing Merkel and Potter together, he suspected he could effect a meeting of minds, and the ensuing result was indeed above and beyond all he had ever intended or hoped. If nothing else, never mind saving the fat man from himself, they could at least keep Mr Potter company – god knows it must have been a lonely life sat upon that stool staring blankly into space and listlessly sipping, denied fullest fraternity with his fellows in the pub, who could not care less about books and chess and all his other intellectual passions and pursuits – for perhaps, in some strange way, the hulk of flesh was young at heart, apt to blossom in the presence of intelligent and eloquent youth, such as the catalyst Merkel so triumphantly embodied. The association could only do him good, so Simeon figured, and all three would profit from their oddly apt conjunction – and anything at all, no matter how small, so the boy further figured in his naive desire to do good, anything to drag Mr Potter out of his rut could only be for the better.

For he would never forget the sorrow that consumed him when first he met and spoke with the man, whom from afar he had hitherto callously and ignorantly regarded as only another wasted barroom wit, guzzling and slurping like a gorilla peeling a banana, or a dinosaur hatching an egg. But within minutes of his father's introduction, he had discovered that the fat man shared both his knowledge and love of the actor Ralph Richardson, which mutual admiration, founded on the seeming obscure, had spurred him, in his irrepressible excitement, to clamp a desperate palm on Potter's shoulder as he burbled and spluttered through his tributes, to the fat man's doped delight, though outwardly he affected to disdain, spurning the young hand from his shoulder with a disgusted brush of dismissal. But there and then the bond was born. And when Simeon looked longer and harder at Albert Potter, and remembered what his father had said about how he had crapped his pants, and how the doctors told him he would die within months if he did not desist from his drinking, which habit he never relinquished, an overwhelming sadness beset the young lad, and made his young blood seem old. He knew then, more than ever, that everyone would die, as this man would die, worth unfulfilled.

And little did Albert know that later on that night long ago, after they had parted, he to his flat and they to their house, the young man Simeon had wept on the way, wept real and brimming drunken tears that stained his ruddy cheeks, wept on behalf of Albert, wept to see so good and wise a man sunk by choice so low, wept for a wasted life, wept for potential squandered, drowned in dregs, wept for Potter, wept for the world that begot such men, wept for he himself and for everybody everywhere. And Eugene Collins looked on appalled, and tried in vain to comfort the sentimental maudlin fool, his first and only son.

CHAPTER FORTY-SEVEN

And the memory, of those tears of two years ago, was in Simeon's eyes as he slavishly followed his friend back into the bar, to resume verbose intercourse with the great man. What bluster and vigour ensues. Time and again, Mr Potter will lift up his apish arms of brawn, knuckles clenched tight into boxer's fists, in the sure-fire posture of the seasoned street-fighter. Merkel's mouth flaps incessantly. He cannot shut up. He has a trait of listening only to part of a person's sentence, then extrapolating wildly from that threadbare basis, living in the blind fantasy of his head, playing court jester. Around him, conversation becomes a competition, and the rococo banter spirals in mania.

'You never let me speak!' Simeon will sometimes snarl unheard.

And Mr Potter, conceding that he is wont to betray a 'mildly sentimental' streak in his otherwise aggressively macho makeup, begins to feel something of a growing affinity with loudmouth Merkel, who seems his own self in embryo, full of the romantic fire that failed, before youthful resolve dwindled, and all childish illusions dissipated and were snuffed, leaving behind lonely mementos in their sadly smoking wicks.

'They look like Withnail and Marwood with Uncle Monty!' the purring fat cat Moloch remarks, peering through a hole in the Pooka's pocket.

'Seen it. Didn't like it,' the unseen Fergus dismisses.

The bar steadily dissolved around our heroes the longer they spoke; the licensed premises in Ranelagh became, variously, according to whatever motley stage the intoxication of their shaggy speech had led them, an Elizabethan whorehouse, an Oxford quadrangle, a Chinese opium den, a Grecian temple, a Roman sauna, or a Californian tennis court. Mr Potter professed more than once his undying conviction that he had been born at the wrong time, and was doomed to be a lifelong misfit.

'Had I lived in the eighteenth century,' he declared, pounding his saggy chest with barrel's thump, 'I would have been at home. Can you imagine it? Those racy diaries of Pepys, juh juh juh, with all the gritty ins and outs of the scullery maiden with whom he has been bonking, point forward to the tomes of dear Bozzie! His edited diaries patched up to become biographies! Fit for oats! No, sorry, oats for horses and Scotchmen! All those coffeehouses and those learned wits walking around on the cobbles! The Age of Enlightenment, my boy! Garrick poking his head through the curtains to display all the gamut of emotions a human face can convey. Truly anybody who tires of Johnson's London is tired of life. Augustan elegance, such as their letters unfailingly embodied, ah yes, the Augustan poise, proper words properly placed – that is a virtue distinctly lacking in this, eh, barbarous and, er, uh, degenerate age of ours we occupy ...'

'Ha ha! I get it. The two opposing poles sit at this counter, then,' mocking Merkel glibly quips, 'we seem, you and I, to represent the classical temperament versus the romantic. But I have to say, to be honest, Albert, that I really don't have much time for all those musty blowhards with their balanced prose. Prose. Prose. That's what gets me. Prose annoys me. I have absolutely no time for prose. Unless it be by, say, the likes of James Joyce or oh, I dunno ... Lytton Strachey. Otherwise, there's so much dry shite in those heaps of toilet pages. Poetry gets to the point. I mean, most of these so-called great novels are really just very dull and not very good at all. Novels are just too long. That's the thing about novels. They can never be perfect. When I was younger I fancied myself a novelist, but then I just grew out of that. That's all behind me now. I've moved on so much and travelled so far. It's like I've come to the end of all that prose can do. An Olympian ideal beckons me beyond. Poetry. My unicorn Parnassus.'

'Yes but –' Simeon began.

'Ssh, just listen to this for a sec. You love your eighteenth century, Albert (may I call you Albert?). But to my mind, it's contradictory to call it an Age of Enlightenment, when really what they were doing just amounts to stamping out the homely old beliefs like spoilsports, and stifling superstitions and questioning faith, their imaginations shrinking just as, paradoxically, their so-called knowledge was advancing, gleaning a more comprehensive understanding of how the world works and all that shit, and so on. I'm quite religious myself, and it repels me to think so rigidly, to countenance a world that never goes beyond the outside impressions and surfaces of things, that doesn't have the courage to risk believing in something more, something beyond, outside of us and all around us. Make room for magic and make-believe, I say!'

'Fair enough,' the cringing atheist in Potter conceded, 'I will admit that the only intellectually valid position to adopt on the score of God is that of the agnostic, who leaves room for doubt and questioning, and eh …'

''But just listen to this for a sec – there's got to be a reason why your eighteenth century didn't produce a figure comparable to Shakespeare, and I think it's all to do with the fashionable narrowing of imagination in that era. Footnotes to Homer, indeed.'

'Ah but Merkel, Merkel, hang on now, just hold it there, who said that in the first place? Be very careful of any such sweeping dismissals. Who are you only a naïf and waif? Come, come, you just cannot ignore the force of Johnson, juh juh juh?, rolling down a hill to quell his sorrow, the eh clarity, the, er um, what's the word, the sonority of his work, his articles, his letters, the one to Lord Chesterfield, they are all superb – he tamed the unwieldy English language, even if he erroneously defined a "sonata" as merely a "tune" – how Haydn would wince as he turned in his grave! But no. Sam Johnson, no less than Swift, gave cadence to English prose. The thing is undeniable.'

'Well, fair enough, I'll give you that, Albert, in fact, yeah actually, you're right, because I suppose there was always, in everything they did back then, a certain crispness, an elegance and cleanness of expression, of the like that we just don't have anymore, that love of compact eloquence, of rounded supple phrases – all gone out the window.'

'Bred of a knowledge of the classics. How to sculpt your words. The ancients are always on the make. Yes Merkel, I always had great time for a classicist. It's not a practical branch of study. No career will await you when you sally forth with your scroll on the day your degree is done. It can only be studied out of sheer love for the thing. Purest motive. Would that I too could so have done. There is nothing to beat an education. I warmed to you instantly when little Simeon here told me you were studying classics. For some reason, I feel that I have seen you somewhere before. Tell me, have you, ha, ha, read much of, ooh-err, Petronius lately? Ha, ha, ha …'

Mr Potter was unfailingly generous in buying drinks for the youths – though he did this with greater reluctance in the case of Collins, who he reckoned stank of an affluence that begat a meanness of spirit and purse – whereas Merkel he supposed to be a penniless poet of the suburbs, a destitute lord of language, a vagabond bard strapped for cash, who needed but one pint of the black stuff inside of him in order for his wings to sprout, and his converse to erupt like a rocket. And true enough, the stout had a restorative effect on his sometime taciturnity, and moved him to raise his voice as he levitated, manically gesticulating to enliven his ejaculations, to re-enact his careful assemblage of routine wacky anecdotes, to rabbit on ad infinitum. Simeon, more gnomic, progressively clammed up the more and more Merkel mouthed off, doomed to feel inadequate, tongue-tied and helpless before this gormless colossus of easy eloquence.

And as he stared fixedly at the black hole in the middle of the face of the boy who professed himself his friend, the yawning abyss of his always open mouth, from which the torrent of his incessant speech never paused to stream, coupled with the rising colour of the working purple cheeks and gloss of the champing teeth, their tips bared and somewhat fanged, the elasticity of his snakeskin, and the lightning frenzy of the angelic devil's eyes – he felt a mounting horror he kept in the quiet.

'Time gents, hurry up please it's time!' velvet Robbie intoned as the whirring clock ticked twelve and thirty.

'Last of the summer wine. Come on boys, let us sally out into the wasteland. For I confess I am reluctant for this rare exchange to cease,' said Mr Potter gravely as he guzzled off the final drops of Foster's.

Unsteadily down from their stools the ailing champions climb, shuffling across the carpet with a flurry of parting mutters to the huddled others, who winked coyly, and muttered obscenities to their trio of departing backs, speculating on who was the giver and who was the taker among the lanky Romeos that lecherous Potter had seized upon to be his boyfriends. (The Puck, overhearing this cheeky raillery, would subsequently slash the tyres of their wretched bikes to weeping ribbons of rubber.)

Outside, in the cool of night, they queasy wove the three, so firm were they in one, along the August cobbles until the moist shanks of the canal banks bid them hither over the curling bridge, pointing to the Portobello, a seedy establishment that stayed open until later dimmer hours. But here they could not be admitted, for both Simeon and Albert, in earlier months, had been both rudely barred from its doors (the former for attempting to break up a row between his father and a dumb scut over the insidious matter of American foreign policy, his pacifying instinct undermined by the filthy language he employed to sate the dispute, too salty for the mealy-mouthed staff to countenance – and the latter for having stamped on the toe of a bouncer in the reluctant course of his premature exit). At a loss, wondering where was near and not too dear, the three men stood tipsy at the crossroads on uneasy feet, scratching heads like stooges do.

'Tell you what, gentlemen,' said Simeon suavely, 'there's a few bottles of wine in mine, the finest four-euro vintage from Tesco. We'll go back there and talk things through. And maybe have a bite to eat too.'

This resolution was heartily applauded. It was an evening that none among them ever wanted to end – they would fry themselves for as long as humanly possible, and hurtle to their utmost limits of endurance, burnt and exalted by the shattered brilliance of their respective selves. So by canal and college, down Lennox lanes they strolled in the dark, corpulent Potter already wheezing at the distance entailed, marvelling at the maze of labyrinthine sidestreets down which they delved, passing Kingsland Park Avenue, a stubby excuse for a leafless street better called an alley, behind one of whose doors the crazy sexton lived, a nutty codger who wore woollen hats and spoke Latin to stool pigeons, idling his misty years in a leaky house whose shattered roof had long caved in.

And the three fond men crossed the South Circular's breadth, and came unto the Lombardy mansion, whose cold windows werc black – Gallagher and Freaney were in Limerick, thanks be to Jesus, and Arsene, when Simeon last saw him, was peacefully occupied in carving queer insignia on the youngster's shelves. He toyed with the idea of displaying the prodigy to his guests, whom he thought might be better equipped to interpret his coded ravings than he, but quickly dismissed this course – too soon.

Albert had never before been privy to visit the house of Eugene Collins, and he admired and envied the gasping spread of books that nearly papered the walls, a monstrous collection that dwarfed his own back home in the burrow or bunker. With glinting eyes he sized up the spread as slowly he ascended the twinkling stairs, huffing and puffing with the strain, spotting one bulky volume on a low shelf toward which he hastily lumbered, scooping up the bloated book with a grubby paw, whose crinkly leaves and dusty pages he fondly thumbed and fonder remembered.

'Ah, *The Anatomy of Melancholy*!' he sighed in bliss, 'glorious treasure trove. One of my favourites. Reading this is an antidote for any passing upset. The only book that could get Dr Sam out of bed on a bad day. Extraordinary section all about the melancholy begat by disappointed love. Surely we can all identify with that, juh, juh?'

'Aha! I would have imagined that to be just the kind of book you'd enjoy, Albert!' said grinning Merkel with a sneer, 'but ah, I don't like it at all much. It's just quote after quote after quote sewn together. Really badly stitched. Burton's a failed human. It just seems so long and dry and tedious and boring to me, written by a pedantic loser holed up in his study. Everything he knows is what he's read, not what he's seen or lived. I think it's kind of an anti-book. The arcane epitome of scholarly pedantry.'

'Hmph! But Murky, you strike me as something of a pedant yourself!' Simeon snapped, as he uncorked the wine, and poured out three indulgent measures into three calves of ruby glasses, shining carafes to quaff.

'What? What? Me, a pedant?' spluttered Merkel, abruptly indignant, 'exactly how am I a pedant? Tell me that! When have I been a pedant? Name just one single instance of me being pedantic. Bet you can't.'

'Ho, ho, ho!' Albert leered as he sank into a seat at the table's top beside the window, gulping wine and enjoying his patriarchal position, 'you have done well, Simeon. You have pressed the very button that will annoy the gallant most. Now we know where he is most vulnerable, o yes, ha, ha.'

'Hmph!' snorted Merkel, sitting down to drink and smoke, 'I reckon it's you and Albert here who are the biggest pair of pedants occupying the room right now, obsessing over every trivial detail. To be honest with you, Simeon, I've read your work after all, and I've noticed your exhaustive and tiresome preoccupation with all the minutiae of the mundane, building up a bible of banality, and always laboriously pointing out to me what is already so crushingly obvious and apparent to anyone who has a pair of eyes in their head, indulging in the kind of art that has no point, getting lost in marginalia and persistently missing the point in the process. It seems to me, Simeon, that you have sufficient neuroses to make a kind of art, but at the same time you fatally misdirect your energies. I really hate smug knowingness. You have too much for what you haven't got.'

Simeon, a perfect host, hid his hurt and affected to ignore this petty slight, as humming dementedly he turned on a CD of Mozart's *Requiem*, conducted by Karajan, fitting accompaniment for their long dark night of the soul, and then sashayed into the eastern kitchen, to cook up a meal for the miscreants. And Merkel and Potter further spoke with growing fervour, while Collins cooked his signature dish, of patented 'Salmon Rushdie' (assembled hasty and tasty enough to kill for, ha, ha!), greasing the oozing darnes with a succulent marinade of his own skittish device, mixing in whatever goodly things were near at hand, combining balsamic vinegar with soy sauce and droplets of oyster sauce, and bastings of feisty mustard, the lumpy curdle of viscous liquid yellowed, and tossing in sprigs of parsley to adorn the pink fish, and ample cloves of garlic roughly cut, flavoured and lathered until the cavern of oven opened its mouth to admit the ship of plate to heat, while meantime the spinach was steamed, and the rice was boiled on the fizzy hob, the snowy grains swelling up in the puffy bag, in a bubbling pot that overflowed and spluttered, and charred the burning grill to sticky little bits.

'I've always been something of a devil-may-care sort,' Merkel remarked having puffed his rollup, '… and an exquisite lover, too.'

'O really Merkel!' Albert leered, 'that's far too girly far too early!'

'Johnson. You mentioned Johnson earlier,' Simeon put in apropos of next to nothing, 'my sometime friend Paddy Bender, a tubby wee redhead leprechaun type from Donegal, once nursed a fantasy of directing me in a one-man show, *An Evening With Sam Johnson*. Designed by him expressly to exploit my talents. A doomed project from the word go, since he's a functional illiterate. But frankly, I just can't see myself as the good doctor. For one thing to start with, I lack the girth, being gaunt.'

'Indeed,' Albert boomed, 'an actor can never quite get over his physique. Makeup and padding will only work up to a point. All that greasepaint is but a sham. Not even the very greatest are immune to their bodily limitations. It's why James Agate slated your friend Richardson over his less-than-romantic frame, deploring him for his lack of conventional glamour, deeming that he could never be dashing, could never be a Romeo, a Hamlet or an Orlando. And Laughton too would often lament his grossness, his ugliness, his sheer lack of physical beauty …'

'He could play a good Albert Potter …' Simeon murmured unheard.

'… always flagellating himself, figuratively, over his lack of the aesthetically pleasing qualities that our young friend here so fulsomely embodies, har, har. O crikey! Can I marry him, Simeon? O but Merkel, why the blazing Dickens aren't you a girl?'

'I think it's being a poet does that for me,' Merkel mused seriously, 'Women just seem automatically to fall for you the faster if they hear that you write poetry. That's the other problem with prose – it's called *prose*. The very word just sounds so leaden, so dead, so bloody earthbound and plodding. I mean, as far as I can tell, from what I've heard of you, Albert, you seem to have some kind of aversion to surface prettiness of phrasing and ornamentation – you like ideas behind your words, intellectual meat and gristle. You would be dissatisfied with mere splendour of style. It leaves you cold. Why is that I wonder? I reckon it's because you read so many translations of your blasted Russian novelists, which translations are often, out of necessity, and a desire not to obscure the original thought through extraneous flourishes, very spare, very plain and bald, quite cut and dried. That's where we part company, you and I. Tolstoy bores the arse off me. So does that windbag Proust. I mean, are these big names really *that* good?'

Spinach and salmon and rice all done, the cook swung into the kitchen to procure some plates, white dashed by primary colours in Mondrian's manner, onto which he heaped the steaming goods in roughly equal piles, dumping the load before the quivering noses of his guests, who grunted thanks and began to fork globs into gobs mid quips.

'Mmm!' Merkel hummed, 'this is delicious, Simeon! Funny enough, I would never have put you down for a master chef.'

'Is it as good as the mammy's, eh?'

'Mammies – just listen to this for a sec. My mother really, really can't cook. I mean, people rave about their mothers and their wonderful meals, but mine would do discredit even to a fucking steak on Sunday. Like rubber she makes it. Crap chops. It slides around all over the plate, evading eating.'

Albert expressed his appreciation by gruffly holding out his plate in expectancy of a second helping, of which there would be none, to his brief chagrin – though there were two bottles of wine still to empty among them.

CHAPTER FORTY-EIGHT

'*Who is I— C— C—? Who is anyone?*' the old man Arsene murmured again and again, as he lay in the boy's bed of a morning on the verge of midday. In the corner of his great eyes that roved round in circles while his head remained still on the pillow, he could see where everyone was and what they were doing, and their distant activities afforded him the greatest diversion in the maze.

—Mr Albert Potter sat on his couch stroking the White Dog and thought about Proust's Madeleine tea and Merkel;

—Edwin Galbraith showed his best acrostic with pride to his Dartry Halls housemate David Lydon who was very impressed;

—Konrad Merkel rose from bed downstairs in nine Lombardy Road;

—The Puck and Pooka urinated on Ship Street South while Moloch toyed with wool by the Dublin Castle gates;

—Ulick O'Muadaigh smoked his pipe and polished a paragraph in their Sligo cottage bed while Wilhelmina snored beside him;

—Jonah Marzipan attended a convention of Goths in Chapelizod;

—Esmerelda Merkel and her husband Pipefitter Pat were arguing in their Phibsboro abode over the wisdom of phoning their son;

—Jacky the Polis entered Merriman's to stiffen his nerves for the morning patrol;

—Jezebel Temple updated her Facebook page at home in Terenure with a status all about the weird proposal of love some guy had made to her;

—Housemates Gallagher and Freaney were having sex with a dildo downstairs;

—Johnny Fritzl was masturbating in his toilet in his Swords household, while Marco Grimaldi and Lukas the Shag looked at porn on the internet;

—The sublime Saruko was entering the Lecky Library to study during her free period, then got distracted;

—Boris Nigel Gillespie proposed marriage to Hilda O'Mara in Rathmines;

—Jasper Kelly withdrew from the body and presence of Eve Parker;

—Simeon Jerome Collins prepared a bowl of porridge in his kitchen;

—Peadar Lamb's Bull roamed the Dublin hills munching the gorse;

—Isolde Lovelace and Paul Dennehy were having sex in an Arts Block office;

—Agatha Honeypenny browsed various green teas in the Asian Emporium, since she wanted to buy a bag for Simeon;

—Kyrie Elysium was guiltily masturbating in her Portobello bed;

—Lucia Seward agreed to be Harry Block's girlfriend on the Chapel steps;

—The Mad Monk and Banshee Megan Devlin came to Kildare in their caravan;

—Peadar Lamb hobbled along on a single leg through the wilds of Connemara;

—A dog took a piss on Aloysius O'Muadaigh's gravestone in Drumcliff;

—I— C— C— gave a rousing belly laugh as he read again the opening scene of *Shandy* and felt happier in himself;

—Tadgh O'Mara woke up on a bench in Walkinstown and felt afraid;

—And Harry Carson, taking a leak in Grogan's jacks, shook off last stray drops of piss from his penis (though this he knew to be fully futile, mindful as he was of the maxim writ on the wall in front of his face: 'No matter how hard you wiggle yer peg, the very last drop goes down yer leg').

Then the door opened as Arsene mused, and his nurse entered, bearing a bowl of gruel that would serve his patient for repast. Arsene's dead eyes lit up with a greater glow as the tray was laid on the bedside table, and the spoon was placed in his pale hand.

And the boy, who seemed the worse for wear, following so soon on the heels of the extended batter in which he and Merkel and Potter had been embroiled (which had ended after twenty-nine hours back in Merriman's with Albert, rather oddly, bidding farewell to his new friend Konrad in the continental manner, planting two brisk wet kisses on the boy's numb and unfeeling cheeks), stood and waited for further queries or demands. For it was becoming the habit of the old man to engage in a weird kind of ritualistic catechism with the boy every morning before or after feeding, from which strange game the batty elder seemed to derive undue enjoyment, even in the depths of his dementia, a formula whose probing questions rarely varied:

'*For whom has love so undone you?*'

'SARUKO!'

'*For whom has lust so undone you?*'

'JEZEBEL!'

'*For whom has envy so undone you?*'

'KONRAD!'

'*He rises, and he walks about thy father's house, picking books off the shelves. Tend to him and serve his needs, for mine are fine.*'

'Are you sure? Nothing more needed?'

'*No. Go tend to the tattooed youth for whom the blubbery elder fell. Shoo!*'

'If you say so,' the boy in black muttered, shambling out and shaking his disbelieving head as he closed the door on his boyhood.

'*Envy is a spur …*' Arsene the invalid said with a sort of smile as he began to eat, '*And you can't make an Abode of Fancy without cracking some eggs …*'

CHAPTER FORTY-NINE

'Just listen to this for a sec, Simeon,' said Konrad Merkel, waving around Kakuzo Okakura's classic *The Book of Tea*, 'it says here that the original Japanese name for tearoom, Sukiya, actually roughly translated as The Abode of Fancy, *inasmuch as it is an ephemeral structure built to house a poetic impulse*, he says.'

'Well spotted, Murky,' I said with a smile as I sat down by my window, 'I knew that already of course. Had to write a poxy essay on the subject. They also call it an Abode of Vacancy or an Abode of the Unsymmetrical.'

'Bah!' he grumbled, ambling from the shelf back to the table, onto which he plunked his booted feet as he skimmed the slim tome with bemused contempt, 'Unsymmetrical, indeed! Here's what he says: *Inasmuch as it is consecrated to the worship of Imperfect, purposely leaving something unfinished for the play of the imagination to complete*. I would have thought that exactly geared to appeal to a stodgy prose stylist like yourself! A wanton excuse for artistic laziness!'

'Sit down and have some more green tea, you fucker ...' I growled.

O reader dear! I find it hard to convey that sense of exhilaration I felt throughout the first few weeks of friendship with Konrad.

'You were the first man I ever felt jealous of!' I burbled.

'Well, *you* were the first man *I* was ever jealous of!' he grinned back.

Every pore of one's being was alive and every one of life's banal avenues seemed to breathe and exult in rapturous promise. In its way, it was very much like being in love again, albeit strictly platonically.

'I shall have to murder you soon, you know!' I jested.

'O give over and get over yourself. You always act as if I'm out to get you.

But really, I'm, I'm completely open. There are no sides to me.'

From that first encounter back in the bar, we persistently kept on bumping into each other at random and unplanned junctures. He had no mobile phone at the time, and our meetings were all dictated by chance. In some Players night of Shakespeare scenes, where I played Melancholy Jacques and hammed and slobbered through the grandiloquence of man's seven ages, he played Hamlet in a white mask for the nunnery scene, rather woodenly and stolidly I thought, though at least his diction was good.

'It may be the only chance I'll ever get to play the Dane!' he declared.

Then one day I met him on the Arts Block ramp as he smoked and thought, and we dithered around each other like sissy genii testing the wavelength and braving the waters, until I suggested that we skip our lectures and quench our thirst instead.

'Ah! That's the attitude!' he gushed, 'people in my classics class are so dry, you know what I mean, they're very unwilling always to go for a casual pint and chat. That was what endeared you to me from the start, you never refuse an opportunity for a drink.'

We went to Grogan's and talked for hours and then went on to my home where he stayed the night and ate my food and drank my booze and slept in my bed (somewhat to the chagrin of Gallagher and Freaney, whom he perturbed with his scaly affability, and kept awake with his torrential noisiness). The pattern of our friendship, conducted to the rhythms of my foolish generosity and of his studied leeching, was settling in firm plaster.

So from then on every chance meeting was always coupled with a merry midday venture to a nearby pub to talk turkey further happily. And in my first flush of delight, having long forgotten the basic joy of conversing man to man, I more than repaid him for that first round in Chaplin's he had bought me. He warmed to me for my propensity towards drunkenness, and I to him the same. And yes, charismatic he was, and magnetic indeed, and fun to be around; one felt more burningly alive when talking one on one with him, meeting the stare of those shining eyes behind the gleaming specs, entranced by the ready warble of the large and chanting mouth, the waves of the tapering finger's flick, the elasticity of his snakeskin, even on the neck that he could stretch to turkey's wattles, protean flesh that was as rubbery and slippery as his shape-shifting soul, and the loud laugh that would erupt when one outdid oneself in the absurd stakes of wit and wackiness, moved and entranced and lured by the seeming enthusiasm he displayed for every insipid suggestion one made, greeting every new nugget about oneself with a wondrously convincing similitude of fascination, avidly interested in all one said that was fuel to his continuing monologue, keen to dig in all the deeper, and burrow, and thaw, and hollow one through from the inside out for his own advantage.

For he had a strange gift of divination, of worming his way into one's deathless trust, of gaining confidences and knowledge, of appearing so charming and seemingly trustworthy, a toxic skill that quickly worked its lethal spell on me. Even though he almost never stopped talking, and was vocally dismissive of most other people who came into his orbit, since being an incurably bitter and nasty misanthrope underneath the veneer of kindness, every so often he met a person who made their mark on him, about whom he wanted to know more and more, in order to learn from them, to copy them awhile, to try them on to see how they suited him, and then take from them every little bit that he could. It was a great trick he had, and I the ready and gullible sucker, an overeager minnow gagging to be strung by his hook.

Hitherto so cagey, stuffed with secrets and lies, it seemed to me that he had appeared at the very right moment when I most needed to unburden myself – it was either that or go stark raving mad. Newly arrived on the stage of my life, he was all but a stranger and perfectly objective with a willing ear, whom I could easily interest and enchant – who better than he to hear me out? And so I began, fatally, to open up in his presence, and brandish all the jangling skeletons that were crowding my closets, divulging details I had never before dared to breathe or whisper unto another. Firstly he was moved to pry into the underlying purpose behind my literary forages.

'You've told me several times that your book was *born of a great and doomed and futile love*. Who was that I wonder?'

And so I was moved then to unload the baggage of stillborn love of Saruko, and the inky fray with Galbraith, that burdensome go-between's scapegoat weight for so long I had masochistically borne without telling a soul. Having this imparted (in Grogan's on a Friday as I remember), I felt queasy, and was quick to dismiss it all as trivial, knitting a mountain out of a molehill. But Konrad, dear and wide-eyed gaping Konrad, remained sympathetic to my whines, and pressed me egging on.

'Don't worry Simeon!' he cooed like a dove, 'when true love's involved, nothing is trivial. You and I seem to share that same strange mixture of remorseless cynicism and rhapsodic sentimentality, a curmudgeon one minute and a hopeless romantic the next.'

'Yes. I'm a Sentimental Cynic. I see my initials everywhere.'

'Ha! And in your converse, there's also a very persistent note of Self Contempt. Better yet, Self-Justified Contempt. But anyway, being a desperate and hopeless romantic seems close cousin to being shrewd and canny. Something similar happened to me onetime – but we'll save that for when we're better acquainted. For only when you have yourself fallen in love for the first time, will you finally understand the impulse behind every bad soppy crappy love poem that has ever been written. Never dismiss it.'

Emboldened, I went even further via email, the form of the age that was all too treacherously easy and handy. From the guts of my drafts, I dragged up the unsent lament to the sublime wench, and forwarded it to him. I was motoring down the confessional highway, and could not stop.

'You should have sent it!' he typed back in spluttering mode. 'Raging Dionysus had you by the scruff of the neck but then your sober Apollo stepped in to put a clamp on your lovelorn frenzy. Next time, follow up the dictates of the heart, no matter what scrapes you get into, you'll have better stories to tell …'

And I spoke of the demon Jezzie and my manic protestations of being enamoured, and he chuckled wryly as he rolled a fag, saying it was just more grist to the mill of my mounting myth – who else but I would have said such a thing and been so batty?

(Offstage, as it were, he was boring his other friends silly with details of the latest new 'find' he had made, shouting off his mouth about me, or about the version of 'me' he had made up in his mind, which contrivance the authentic edition soon began to fatally ape like an automaton, as he artfully built up a legend of a Chaplinesque laureate with a hammy actor's patrician voice of gravel, with talking shoes and flapping jacket, and guts made of green tea leaves, who never washed nor soaped, but always wrote ...)

And I told him all about the older men I had known, in whose company I never had to try to talk, happy to sit in silence with not a thing to prove, and dash off cutting caricatures, painting studies of Albert Potter, whom we met with so memorably on a long dark day, and of Arsene O'Colla who had gone to the quacking dogs in my bedroom, of Harry Carson, and Martin Graves who sang, and Aloysius O'Muadaigh, and Tadgh O'Mara, and maybe even of Peter Cherry (who?), and sometimes even of I— C— C—.

And he told me many things too, and he told his own tales better than ever I could tell my own, and he told his spoken stories better than ever he could write them down.

And since he seemed so interested in everything about me, under flame of which scrutiny I delighted, I introduced him to some of my more arcane and intense preoccupations. I showed him what Ralph Richardson films I had spent years collecting, *Long Day's Journey Into Night* being the foremost of these, and Ralphie's Tyrone a gem.

'I actually can't believe how good he is!' sycophantic Merkel spluttered, 'strange, though, that you would be so drawn to him, of all people. A guy who could have been the greatest but somehow missed the mark, or stopped just short of reaching the stars. You told me yourself how he always used to snivel about belonging to what he called the doomed second division. And the mad thing is, why was that? He's obviously very talented, but he didn't bother going the whole way. Something must have held him back. I mean, he was a good Falstaff, but he didn't seem to have it in him to reach the heights of a Lear. Strangely familiar, I think. Apposite to our case, perhaps? Ah, splendid fury!'

If you prod a tigress twice in her lair, you must not expect her to purr.

... And I fed him green tea leaves by the barrelful, which drink he found delicious, and proceeded to swallow and wallow with eerie fervour without remit, for he reckoned it was a key ingredient in my makeup, a goodie worth grabbing and testing. He had an obscene love of Vivaldi – so I pressed more Beethoven on him, forcing him to sit through the Late Quartets that stung our ears and wrenched tears from our retinas, and I gushed over the tormented dragon, that fatal Grosse Fugue that moved me so.

'Ah I dunno,' he snorted after the disc burnt out, 'if I was in heaven and had to pick a soundtrack for the backdrop, I'd much rather be listening to the Four Seasons than this shit, sublime as it may be.'

'No, Konrad!' I blurted with shining eyes, 'this Grosse Fuge is one of the most remarkable things we humans have. You'll never have a more profound fifteen minutes than that. It's the climax to Opus 130, which in fifty minutes covers more ground than Wagner did in fifty years, and those fools who separate it from that quartet to which it is the only right and proper finale, know not what they do. Remember the first subject? *Da-da, da-da, da-da, da-da, da-da-da-da-da-daaa-da-da*, and so on, it's a knockout, so fierce, so fiery, so full of a savagely unruly joy, and then that second subject that follows, so gentle, so lyrical, in every way its opposite, and then, that passage before the end, like the third movement of a single-movement symphony for string quartet, that moment when that same second subject returns after a lengthy pained absence that we've spent in an inferno of shrieking strings, like vulture talons trying to gouge out our eyes and spread our guts on the sand, when all at once that glorious second subject returns crashing back in, at full volume, tender and sad yet buoyed by such an exultant hope, singing loud and anguished against the blaring demons beneath, striving to shed over all its grace … that passage is, to my mind, the most moving half minute of music ever composed by any man.'

'Blah, blah, whatever!' he sneered, rolling his eyes.

CHAPTER FIFTY

So there we were, the two of us, like dreamy genies before mutual back-slapping turned to loathsome venom, exiled only children rapidly stewing in our lightning delusions of grandeur, sidling down cardboard alleys munching our chicken fillet rolls and shaking fists at the winds, settling down on opposing bollards that our addled fancies perceived as pedestals, suitable busts for our chisels, quacking absurdities to the bemusement of bystanders. By dark down Dublin streets we walked as one, and watched the silken canal glitter in the moonshine as the bulrushes writhed in the wind, the water dimpled by the paddling swans and wary ducks, and the herons who browsed the banks and culled the shoals, like idling poets stuck for refrains, or bony farmers with metal-detector beaks.

On our long nocturnal walks and talks, Konrad would fluctuate between his usual babble and an unnerving quietude. He was a lad who spent many long hours in his suburban bedroom alone, charging the batteries if you like, building up a head of steam, which vocal eruptions he reserved for the minutes he would venture to the city centre, forcibly stamping and branding himself unforgettably in the memories of others he would meet, cultivating contradictions in his character, filling his skewered outlines with blazing pastels, determined to be everything and nothing and many-minded, changing his slippery mind every minute, since changing a mind was proof of having one, and a mind was all he had, talking and opining and interrupting others with his winging words.

But sometimes, and creepily, at intervals in the long stretches of hours that we passed in the company of one another, he would fall silent, and gnomically clam up in a trancelike raptus, locked up in sullen solemn knotty avenues of thought, unspeaking and unreadable, responding to queries with surly grunts, behind the bars with deadpan face and faraway gaze, eyes clouded over with contemplation's mist, brooding on silence mutely, as side by side we wordlessly marched. And initially one would worry, since so accustomed to his blather being unceasing, and one wondered whether one had offended him, and why that was if so, and one fretted puzzled, keen to cajole and do anything one could to please mercurial Konrad, whose rich amusement was food for which one began to pine, desperately turning sweating court jester, if only to afford mirth for the sulking emperor who was down in the dumps. By degrees one eased him back to earth and learnt.

Great sorrows he nursed in his wounded bosom, or so he led or wished me to believe, memories of past tragedies playing back in cruel and merciless repeat, behind the screen of his appalled eyes that had known great trauma. In snippets he darkly hinted to me of the dread things he had seen. Always assiduously seeking drama, he more than often found it, and stirred up the pots of shit to make it splutter all the more. In the wake of his Leaving Cert (which he fooled me into thinking he had rammed, too cool for school and study in plush Belvedere), he had subsequently gone to a college of low repute in Wales, exiled in murky Bangor with the cokeheads and the dregs, which was a dark place indeed for this tattooed adventurer to find himself in, this bruised survivor of the holocaust in his head.

'Man! You must have seen some bad shit there, dude!' said I, lightly.

And in response, as he postured by a pine tree trunk, over-egging the pudding, and rolled another cigarette with liquid grace, and smoothed down the crumpled weed in the tube, and moistened the paper with a lick and dab of lizard's lips, and sucked upon the mottled stalk he lit with molten spark from his ruby wick, and puffed and deeply dragged, and scratched the ring in his punctured lobe, and flicked fluff from his torn sleeves, and blew a blue and smoky ring that wavered and dissolved in glimmered air, and then, then, he shot me a look out of the corner of a bloodshot eye, whose fire was hid behind the shield of specs, lest his basilisk stare burn me to crisps of embers, shot me a look from a blazing pupil that had sought and met the heart of worldly darkness, a galvanized eye that had known the Earth's sheerest terrors, and courageously confronted the starker evil that lurked in the hearts of all men, and his brooding eye met mine, and he sighed, and said, world weary, in a dark voice no more than a hoarsely gravelled whisper:

'Yeah, I seen some bad shit in my time.'

O good god! What awful torments the restless genius must have been through! He dropped hints of hellish revelry that spiralled into tragedy, of illicit substances, of needles and threads and sniffs of powder, weird visions, hallucinations and ghastly nightmares, of sleep paralysis and mass orgies, of feasts of flesh and blood, and blooming virgins deflowered and devoured, crowds of copulating naked bodies groaning in the sand and dust, of lascivious inhuman excess on the infernal beaches, and burying murdered bodies by milky dawn in the marshy boggy woods, painting lurid pictures for me through inspired suggestion, evoking scenes of unspeakable debauch and oppressive horror, overwhelming horror and darkness, a long dark way from the cosy confines of nuclear familial relations, which straitjacketed banality hitherto was all the bright-eyed youth had ever known in life. But abroad in the valleys, innocence was irrevocably lost forever.

'Yeah. I've seen pieces of hell.'

Yet there was a light in the darkness. For some great love had been his – 'the only girl I ever really loved' he said, with a histrionic pound of his chest that housed a bleeding heart – some pigtailed milkmaid with creamy breasts that sagged, bedding her down in the eiderdown of daisies, unstitching and ripping her bodice to expose her udder he groped and kissed, dreaming of those puffy bubs that were his pillows, whose knickers he tore when they climbed the hills and fell down in the flowerbeds, with whom he met and fucked, wetly brutally and bloodily sweating time without number.

'I don't like contraception. It's an impediment to my pleasure. Fucking condoms spoil the fun. She swore blind she was taking the pill anyway.'

But soon alas, the young mother came with child, young Konrad's child, a father in his teens with teeming loins. And they were married in secret in a seedy registry office, the papers signed by an unscrupulous clerk with a gap in his teeth, tapping his brown molars with stub of his leaking nib, as he eyed up the shivering juvenile parents and made some lewd crude jokes at their hapless expense. And she swelled and grew, and then her waters broke, and daddy junior raved and stormed off in a frothing huff, helpless and gloating in the face of the catastrophe he had cooked, while some drugged-up friends rolled her to the surgery in a rattling barrow. And perspiring doctors bloodily delved as she howled and pushed, but without avail, for the babe could not live, and their child died in a cold pan, a sterile cup for a miscarried corpse, cut off in its first breath, dwindling to nothing, choking and soon dead, pitiably dead. And chastened Konrad ditched his sorry wife, and left Wales with lowered guilty head, and swore off sex for an ensuing year of celibacy, in mannered atonement for last year's disaster.

In leaden tones he greyly told me his doleful tale, as we sat on a bench in sickly lamplight by side of the swirling canal, into whose dark waters his blank gaze stared, and I grieved and held his hand to comfort the poor devil, uncertain what to say, resorting to stuttering platitudes of feeblest consolation, for which he assured me there was no need.

'I'm fine. Though I do feel sad now, to be reminded of it, like that.'

O god! The horror! The horror! And the pain – such awful and delicious pain, such lasting scars that bruised the young gallant's ruptured temples, his pounding brain accursed by trauma, his requisite chip on shoulder dutifully sought and found. Only vaguely, in a detached undertone, did I hear him divulge the chary details of his dark mysterious tragic past, delivered with manly bluster, and dreamy gaze full of remorse and pain, rubbing his palms to warm their cooling bluing fingertips, in a recurring gesture that amounted to a mannerism, dry eyes unclouded and clear of sentiment's mist, regretting nothing, striving to be brave, to go on and live and err and conquer, and overcome the glum and dismal debris of his past, to forge an object of beauty from his agony, designed to evoke both pity and terror and delight, to resurrect a vanished joy from the ruins, to build a book in which to pile all the hard-won wisdom he had gleaned by drinking so deeply from the brimming cup of life, a great work to sit on the shelves, and plump its feathered pages smugly, a novel in verse with not a word out of place, lest the precious edifice collapse from a misplaced cadence that might dizzy the mortar, nor a careless stray hair be allowed intrude to jar and mar the succulent fruitcake, all his tools of metres mastered and the exquisite images arranged in divine and inevitable array, a perfect and changeless work of art to weather the storms, erected by an aching heart that had met the tragedy of humanity head-on with a hard-on, fearlessly facing down the Gorgon as the snaky hair hissed and spat, slaying the elder Minotaur and tearing down the obsolete labyrinth, spearing the Leviathan and the Kraken, grabbing life by the shoulders and shaking it loose of everything it could offer, running the gamut to fill the suite of treats with sorrow and pity – and ultimately subsuming all into an exultant roar of divine laughter, shaking his fist at the skies, playing heavenly notes with all the jaunt and verve, all the cracked and poignant grace of a childhood tune, rasped out on a sublime squeezebox, in the flossy carousel by the park's demented merry-go-round.

'I had found my mission. It had happened. I no longer had any choice in the matter. I had to create. It was either that or die. And by the way – if you ever meet a girl who really is smarter than you – please hold on to her.'

And I looked upon this courageous and heroic artist who sat by my gaunt and wavering side, and I trembled in my flapping shoes, for it seemed the very earth had rumbled with a seismic pulse and shudder, and I felt myself a newt, a stork sucking flies from a hippo's granite back, a mere child unworthy to squat by Merkel's marbled knee, not fit to share the volcanic warmth of his magma aura, nor breathe the bubbles of air he displaced, undeserving of basking in the pool of rhapsodized light exuding from his shattered radiance. I marvelled and I shivered as my future grave was trod and waltzed upon, and I suggested we set off homeward again, for the night of revelation was chill and sad, and we were firmly bound as one.

'You have a ridiculously high opinion of me, y'know,' he mumbled.

To look upon, in the light of fresh dewy morn, a girl might have called him handsome, or 'massive', or' gorgeous', perhaps even a beautiful man maybe, striding the earth lightly with the limpid grace of a gazelle, cast in the pearly Grecian mould, with fluted columns of shanks and arms, his rippled nubile torso echoing a relic of antique statuary, the blushing rose of his finely etched cheekbones and chin, the curls of his tangled swirls of hair, a crest of plumage atop the bust, wiry hair going grey from the stress and weight of a short life lived too fast, the blazing eyes glazed as he skimmed the pages of whimsical Okakura's tea book with bored contempt.

'Fuck this whimsical shit!' he snapped waspishly in the morning, 'seriously Simeon, we really have to drop this dreadful gentlemanliness that marks our encounters. Enough decorum. Let's be blunt and direct from now on, eh?'

O god! What would I not have given to go back there now, to live again the golden mornings we shared in my sitting room, as the new daylight flared through the shimmering windowpanes, flooding the deadened shelves of dusty spines, the slanting columns bathing all in plumaged glow, in light of which we basked, and I sneezed as my nostrils were tickled by the bejewelled motes that skipped upon the sunbeams, when I supped my greenest beverage from the cracked goblet, lightly clad in silken scarlet pyjamas, those I wore under my college clothes when days were nippy, a second skin of silk in lieu of long johns or whitey-tighties, slurping steaming tea as my friend sat aside smugly and brandished his jotters, totting off a few deft translations of Homeric epithets, for sake of the belated collegial assignment his wilting Greek professor had bid the erring devil do, sometimes abandoning his homework to peruse the pages of Proust for the sake of variety, snorting at the bedridden Frenchman's follies, remarking chuckling on how very fey we were getting, like the sugary pipe dream of an Oxford don, the walrus and the carpenter playing cards with the languid aesthete lounging in the cushioned boudoir, as I arose to manically wave my arms to conduct the glimmering noises of Mozart that shone from the wireless, looking out the window to wave at the young mothers who were wheeling their squeaky buggies by, my dressing gown billowing in the breeze that wafted away trails of his velvet smoke, turning to warmly greet housemate Gallagher, as she mounted stairs bearing a silver box of chocolates she had bought for her hairy boyfriend, coyly grinning with her lopsided beaver's teeth, chirruping in the lisping culchie twang that Konrad confessed he found deeply arousing, and we charmed her, and gently joked together like a family of elves, and soon she was persuaded to allow us consume the bulk of the winking chocs, popped into jabbering gobs that sang and warbled any old fruity bullshit, and then she would leave for a lecture, and we would sigh, sat together at my glowing table in rapturous contentment, and I would clap a palm to brow, and pray, to whatever god was hovering in the witching air, that this happy idyll might last forever.

'Sentimental balderdash!' Konrad Merkel would sneer, 'ah, but it was always soppy old codger Sterne for you, wasn't it? No time ever for the iron grit of Swift? He'd win in a fight, I'm sure. Hands down every time.'

Yes, Konrad. For a season you were the best friend I ever had, and the most extraordinary man I ever knew. And when then you would depart from my abode, when the shrill receiver rang, and the harridan mammy's voice squawked and bid you go home for your dinner, I would be left all alone in my echo chamber, with only Neanderthal Freaney slouched on the couch, twiddling the knobs of his asinine Gameboy. And how I would miss the chattering git who had gone, and devoutly long for his loudmouth return.

CHAPTER FIFTY-ONE

Konrad Merkel often went home through the green of the Phoenix Park. In the northwestern direction of suburban Phibsboro, he would meander through the trees and reeds, past stony obelisks and roundabouts, wandering homeward via the way of the zoo, where sorry tigers roared behind iron bars, and gorillas took their cheeky pisses. He could get lost here at his leisure, in Dublin's very own Eden, awash with springtime and deer, those idling speckled quizzical fauns and cheery does, whom oft he was moved to chase, scampering after the trembling fleet until their antlered horde was scattered.

Brooding the young poet would pine and sway, lounging deep down in the long grass, the stalks, which were wreathing the hidden cities of the soil, where many a time past he and his bohemian beaver buds had abided their skiving hours, lost orphans adrift in the sanctuary of wilderness. Always the same four of them, with whom he had made friends for reasons, an Evangelical barbershop quartet with his own cocky self always as their figurehead, dictating where on the lawn they would lie and stare at the sky, little lost boys dreaming their creamy dreams, stolen by the thieving breeze.

There was Marco Grimaldi the goofy cartoonist, who looked like a fasting Baudelaire, faintly Levantine or Semitic of aspect, and olive of sallow complexion, and promiscuous Lukas the Shag, who looked like a young Shaw, a virile bounder enviably laden with a lucky loot of the bindu, who kept a Nordic squeeze on whom he always cheated, and lastly the cuddly Johnny Fritzl who looked like a gentler Poe, who was compassionate and foolish and wise, in roughly equal measure. And Merkel himself, who looked like Egon Schiele, one of whose middle names was Matteo – Matthew, Mark, Luke and John, debauched apostles, makers of streetwise gospels, full of the ins and outs of leeching and binging, puking and stealing, forging and skigging, reptilian frequenters of the town's bars and clubs and house parties, fixtures in the smoking arenas, lost mid bluest plumes and stalks of roll-ups. These were his friends and this was his bandit gang.

And as the young man walked through the Phoenix Park, dreading the impending homecoming to which he was bound, anticipating the hectoring of nagging Esmerelda, wondering with hands on hips why he had not attended any classes, backed by silent Pat the Pipe who shrugged if he was drunk, or shared an omelette with his son if he was feeling mutely jovial – strolling Konrad pondered further on his new acquaintance Simeon, and the greater treasure yet of Mr Potter, and decided he would call a meeting soon, and mix worlds like drinks, and await whatever frenetic outcome might arise.

Thus lost in thought, contemplating the bubbling pot of tempers, the distracted poet ignored his surroundings, and heedlessly passed the base of the great cross that glimmered come the dusk, and shone winking silver by starlight, erected on the sullen hilltop mound, set up in the seventies to mark the visit of the Polish Pope, now lately deceased and since replaced by a leering Nazi who looked like Bela Lugosi.

Whistling thus as he passed, his loud whistle that carried so far, vague Merkel crossed himself with the rhythm of instinct's treble, a devout boy who once toyed with the notion of a priestly vocation back in his seminary Jesuit days – he always wore his mannered influences on his sleeve. Puffing then upon his scabbed fag, he passed on by the high cross unseeing, and so did not notice the stationary caravan parked over there by the hill's grassy foot, its misty chimney pluming in the golden haze of afternoon. And the shadows of trees were lengthening as the sun's arc descended from its blue peak, and within the wagon the somnolent occupants daydreamed under their florid eiderdown, the buttery bedspread knitted of feathery webs with all a gypsy's daring, beneath whose gauzy sheets the tall old man and his snoozing woman lay, newly arrived in Dublin town.

And nor did heedless Konrad Merkel, passing nearly out of sight in a farther leafy grove, heavy boots trudging on the pebbled path with crunch, nor did he notice the lazy donkey grazing by the sleeping caravan, munching the park grass with a flicker of distaste, loathing how these grasses must so oft be cut or mowed, missing the buzzing of the countryside's bumblebees, whose honeyed hums added a dish of rustic music to his frugal grassy repast, a virtue diminished in this man-made haven and human Arcadia, where all had been so groomed and coiffed, so artfully tapered to a curling topiary point.

And the old bones of Balthazar still ached with the strain of their lengthy journey, creaking through county towns where youths threw stones, braving the lurking evils of provincial idylls, the wheezing toils steeping the nearer to the metropolis they moved, risking the potted Curragh in Kildare, and the teeming highways adorning the capital's outskirts. The ravished master, eager always to amuse, had done his best to shorten the trek by chanting aloud his freshly written history, his doggerel epic that sagged at the seams and put Granny Nutmeg Megan Devlin straight to sleep.

'It's a bloody gardener you need to edit that behemoth, mate!' waggish Balthazar had offered, 'he might do you a favour and cut it to smithereens with his shears, haw-haw!' for which dismissal he was granted a cuff of his ears, with a doleful grumble from the underappreciated artist who hastily tore his trashy poem to pieces and shreds.[2]

But now at last they were finally disembarked in the largest park in all of Europe, fit for nothing but a bout of repose while they waited for the rest. And Balthazar was appointed to eye the horizons of their environs, lest their comrades-in-crime pass them by. And soon indeed, after several dull hours of inaction, marked only by the distant sighting of ogling tourists and melancholic park wardens, shortly after Konrad Merkel went by, the sly donkey caught sight of pinprick spectres, hovering afar over by the edges of the green ramparts, scuttling by the faraway trunks of trees and shadowy bushes where they lurked, shyly venturing into the sunny expanse.

---

2 The surviving found object, as quoted above in previous chapters, was subsequently pasted back together from what few tatters were seen to have survived, the missing remainder being painstakingly reconstructed from the partial memories of those who heard it, with a corresponding diminishment and/or enhancement of the work's impact.

Keenly smirking, the donkey regarded the motions of the further creatures as they threaded through the tall grass towards him, huddling down and peeking at intervals, like timid meerkats popping up in an exotic savannah. There were three of them coming, a dwarfish elf with pointed ears and Pantaloon's garb who consulted a compass, a tall suited chap with a stern goatish visage who was flapping a crumpled map, and lastly a hobbling cat whose bushy tail was often batted. And they came closer the three to the easygoing ass, who smiled and made no move but calmly watched them approach, brushing by the nettled stalks caressed by the purring wind as the trio wound, until soon they were stood before him, eagerly eyeing the caravan he guarded, remarking on the weather and the precision of the place, wondering whether where they were was right.

'Park of the flaming Phoenix,' the Pooka drawled as he scanned the map for clues, 'looks to be this, and none other than.'

'Fair enough,' said affable Puck, scratching a blister, 'but 'tis for sure a large one. He could be hidden bloody anywhere in this goddamn abyss!'

'Granted. Whether he is here yet begs another question. He could be sightseeing. I regret that we ourselves did not do enough of that en route.'

'Ah, we saw enough in what we did. I liked the brewery.'

'Yes. The black beery stuff is amiable.'

'Aye. And that fat man of two days ago – he was funny enough.'

'Mr Albert was his name. Certainly. And an acquaintance of my dear old victim, poor Arsene. Small world. But where do we go to now?'

'Well now,' said the Puck, glancing at the monument astride the hill, 'this here yonder cross seems a nice little landmark, no?'

'Deucedly so. And this here caravan, with accompaniment of gallant ass, is a nice and homely piece of work too. I'd live in it in a jiffy.'

'Damn straight. Me too. But when will he –'

'Arrive? Like I said, that was never stated. So little in this affair has been spelled out. He seems to expect that we shall meet through the charm of synchronicity, slaves to merry happenstance and disciples of clockwork.'

'Damn crooked. What now then? Pick our arses?'

'O, go and breathe the verdant air, Robbie. Take a roll down the hill for sport. May took a look inside said caravan, too.'

'Careful,' the fat cat Moloch abruptly growled, 'mind that donkey don't kick ye. I like not the look in his beady eye. Too clever by half.'

'No? I find him handsome,' the sporting Pooka said, passing a fine gloved hand over Balthazar's head, delicately scratching and patting the slope of his face and nose. The donkey, beguiled, grinned back at the goat.

'See?' said the Pooka warmly, 'see how he is smiling at me!'

The Puck meanwhile was warily inspecting the caravan's entrance, tentatively poking the jingling curtained door. Balthazar saw, and gave a sharp whinney to signal, startling both the stroking Pooka and the prying Puck. At which eruption abruptly, there came from within the caravan a medley of spluttered curses, noises of banging and slamming, whereupon the door flung open. And the newcomers then beheld the frame filled by the dim shape of a hulk, a bearded ogre clad in dressing gown and slippers and nightcap, stepping down onto the grass and squinting into the sunlight, gazing confusedly upon the fresh arrivals and intruders, brandishing his poker at the ready to beat their brains to brassy pulp and bits, lest their intent be malign.

But when the fiery prodigal steadied himself, and blinked, and focussed at the figures trembling before him, and saw who they were, he dropped his weapon and a radiant smile lit up his face. And they, who had not themselves seen him in umpteen years, having half forgotten what attributes constituted his beloved features, stared at the first dumbfounded upon an unknown tall old man, a bearded stranger with wild eyes, a wandering vagrant with savage leer in a trailer unkempt, camping out in a public park.

But then, as his smile widened, and they blinked, and closer looked and were charmed, they knew him then to be who they were looking for, and him who had called them hither, and then they smiled and then applauded.

'Mad Monk!' the Puck cried.

'Mad Monk!' the Pooka trilled.

'What kept ye?' he said brightly.

And every one of those three men was all exceeding joyous then.

And The Mad Monk came forward grandly on his thudding feet that flapped in their slippers, and picked up the little Puck and tossed him high up into the air, as was their capering jest of yore, and dropped him to the turf and chuckled, and grasped the hand of the Pooka who darted forward, and pumped up and down the hand, and squeezed it dry of blood, and waved the goat hopping up and down, then swung him up into the air by the hand, and let him crash against the hillside slope, and laughed at his dismay.

'You've not lost the old vigour at least,' said Fergus dryly, as he clambered painfully to his feet of booted hooves.

'My Indian summer, boys!' The Mad Monk roared.

'You're a model to us all as ever …' said bemused Puck, rubbing his rear. Laughing, The Mad Monk next picked up Moloch from the grass and stroked her.

'A new member of the cortege, eh? Who's the pretty kitty?'

'She hails from a Wexford household in which we passed a number of nights following the eve of our arrival,' the Pooka gravely explained, 'Moloch is her ugly name.'

'One-eyed at first,' chipped in Puck, 'until I conjured her a second.'

'That was gallant of you!' their master cackled, unceremoniously allowing the lady to drop as he turned to his donkey, 'You've met my ass?'

'Charming beast, of course,' said obsequious Pooka.

'His name is Balthazar, and in a former life he was a movie star, or so he says. High cheese, no? Equine royalty if you will. Wonder if I ought to pay him Equity rates. Good speaker, too! Albeit impertinent. And – ah yes …'

His grin darkened, and his hooded lids lowered till his eyes were slits.

'… one last introduction left. You've not yet met my little woman?'

The Puck and Pooka exchanged glances.

'We, uh … left your lady behind us …' said sheepish Fergus the goat.

'Sated after my last ravishing!' the satyr Goodfellow muttered lowly.

The Mad Monk, enjoying their ignorance, slyly smirked.

'Ah boys. But names and persons change, don't they? Like the weather, like our locale shifts, like the big little world turns. Hang on –'

He broke off, poked his shaggy head through the caravan door, and whistled and raucously bawled to the wizened dozer within.

'Beloved Nutmeg! Wake up ye hag! Rise and shine! We have company! Get up ye glorious baggage! Come meet my mates, what?'

And then, bashfully, forth from their bed of shadows she arose and coughed, coming hovering through from the perfumed within, past swirling dimness she came forth unto them to meet the new people, like a phantom quailing in the daylight, blinking in the sunshine that dazzled her greyness, clad in her floral rags and cushiony slip, emerging from the trailer's darkness, setting down a wrinkly foot upon the damp grass, taking the hand her husband offered, snowflakes of dandruff peeling from her dusted curls to crumb the gnarls of her cheeks, meekly smiling toothlessly through whorls of her papyrus skin, raising a frail arm to wave like a queen, waving in fluttering greeting to the Puck and the Pooka, who looked abashed, and swallowed aghast.

'This is my lady Nutmeg,' The Mad Monk said, 'the Banshee, Megan Devlin.'

'Hello there,' Banshee Maggie softly croaked.

'These are those friends I mentioned before. The shorter is Robin Goodfellow the Puck, a witty refugee from midsummer greenwoods and the court of Oberon, whom you might know from Master Shakespeare's comedy; and the latter is Fergus MacPhellimey the Pooka, an Irish devil not unlike yourself and your shrieking kind of hoary lore and yore, though more given to mischief than to dolorous keening.'

'Charmed, I'm sure,' said Banshee Maggie gently.

'At your service, Ma'am,' the gallants mumbled in blushing unison.

'Told you he'd found another woman!' the Pooka hissed to the Puck.

'But *what* a woman!' hissed back the Puck.

'How grand we are getting on this afternoon altogether!' The Mad Monk cried, 'but o god! My goodly boys and friends and dears, it has been far too long. It has been frankly years. So much to say and tell, so many gaps fill in. On both sides there is much missed history to recount, no doubt. But firstly, some sort of celebration of our reunion is clearly in order. I pray you all, let us pull our weight and we'll have us a feast, what?'

He clapped his hands, and all were swiftly united in the project. The Puck and the Pooka ran off to the woods, and returned with a length of log to serve for table off which to eat; Moloch the cat caught some sparrows to serve for flesh of fowl; Balthazar trawled the glades and collected sprigs of thyme and fennel to serve for seasoning; The Mad Monk chased a deer to provide their main meaty course (since venison, as well as bison, was his favourite food); and the Banshee handled her ladle and stirred her bubbling pot of broth that came to boil. And her lover woodsman chased the startled deer in his grubby gown, hectically tearing through the thickets and coarser undergrowth, until he ran the exhausted animal down to collapsing defeat, and crunched and broke its neck with his brute fingers, and sank his fangs into its throat to drain its blood, and sucked out its life until it was limp, and brought the body back to barracks so his helpmates could carve up its flesh, dicing into ringlets and cutlets to hang and spear on skewers to barbecue over flames of their furnace, the sizzling bubbled fat flung away to feed the greedy cat, the rest toasted and roasted and charred until tender, bulk of its breast served with spuds and apples culled from kneeling trees, doused and basted with juicy wine, oozing flanks stuck in the soup to be milked of fluid nutrient and tang, innards mashed and pulverized and ground into offal, fit for the circling crows and gulls who spied with envy upon their dinner, or the curious schoolchildren passing them by in nearby buses on the tarmac, to whom they waved as they sweated and forged their succulent banquet.

And soon in time, when all their chores were done, and the light was waning in the rosy sunlight of another Dublin sundown, all sat at their woody mossy table of log to drink and dine, man and wife, elf and goat, cat and donkey, hungry equals all, squatting on the grass. They toasted and talked and ate and forked, and gulped and slurped from their goblets of goodly homemade wine, handpicked grapes squashed in barrels by the Banshee's own chapped feet and toes. And when all were full and fed, they sat sedated in their languor, and shared their crumbs with the jackdaws who came wheeling ravenously by, whom glutton Moloch was bade ignore, for all that her trickling saliva did moisten her incisors and glinting whiskers. Dinner thus done, pipes and cigars and hookahs were lit and sparked, and men leant back to smoke, and the donkey lay down on the grass to absorb his fill, and the cat withdrew to nibble and gnaw a discarded bone, while the ghostly woman rocked and took out her knitting needles, and began to sow and thread again, darning the heel of but another damn sock. And The Mad Monk smiled upon his companions, and exhaled, warming up for their ritual after-dinner bout of declaiming.

CHAPTER FIFTY-TWO

The Mad Monk: Ah yes...it is for sure good to have you back, boys.

Puck: Pleasure unmitigated.

Pooka: Joy is all ours.

The Mad Monk: Quite. Seems like the old days again.

Puck: Ah! Them halcyon scenes! They is irrevocably gone and lost to the ether of pipe-dreaming.

The Mad Monk: Why, Goodfellow! You were never wont to be so gloomy! Leave that to old soaks like me, eh?

Pooka: He is getting more melancholy in his older age, for an exiled jester is quick to miss the former mirth of his past patron Oberon, such praises as he always enjoyed, on which he fed his snivelling ego.

Puck: Shut the fuck up Fergie, else I'll bite you.

The Mad Monk: Ho! Your comical bicker is touching, boys. And when the laughter stops, what indeed is left of the empty clown? His makeup running with his tears, his frizzy wig askew, and his drooping red nose awry. But really Robin, you must not sulk nor pout. A waste of breath to whine, a misuse of life to bitch. But tell me now, how long have you been here, lads? And what have ye done or seen, worthy of remark?

Puck: A week I reckon it's been, and little so far seen.

Pooka: Ah not so, Robbie. There are some tricky nuggets might interest you, m'lud. We stayed in the abandoned Wexford house of one Mr O'Colla, on whom I once played a fatal prank that cost him his sanity. Dunno where he's got to since.

The Mad Monk: *(butting in)* No more than I know where your pal Farmer Peadar is, whose demon Bull, so I hear, has been busy, siring orphaned calves and riding comely cows who are easily seduced by a skeletal male.

Puck: Funny thing, that!

Pooka: Coming back to Wexford, the place we stayed was empty save for good Moloch, of course. She was not hard to take on board. Procuring a map from one of the old man's cupboards, we made our way down dusty highways – this imp here refused to believe I was capable of reading the map, and persistently mocked my skills of navigation, for all that he made no effort himself to direct us in the right wind.

Puck: Ah shurrup and give over, that's an irrelevant aside!

Pooka: Anyway, pensioners on the way to their Sabbath gaped and goggled upon our crew. We hitchhiked for a time too, on the back of a city-bound bus, whose rudder we sat upon, unbeknownst to the driver, at least at first.

Puck: He was damn mad when he saw us waving in his windshield! Told us to fuck off, or something unsavoury of that sort.

Pooka: I took care to slash his tyres of course. Little shit. And from there, having been dumped in a place called Kildare, we shuffled the rest of the way. Been in Dublin now some days, kipping in the gutters and loitering in the alleys. Also some spying on arbitrary folk to kill the time too, most of whom are dull.

The Mad Monk: Dull? Yes, so too have I found among these islanders, which has so often moved me to seek solace in the company of the beasts. Human creatures here are so cloistered in themselves, in the monkish cell of their souls. And it takes little to upset them. They live to be offended, mistaking indignation for animation. Anything outlandish, or in any way not after the common rut, is bound to excite contempt. I myself have been bullied, not least in the bars where all I wanted was a quiet pint over which to think. Not that I am a victim. I know how to defend myself, as well you men should know by now, but the scorn still hurts, like a thorn in the side.

Pooka: Of course. But we saw some folk of interest though, most of all, a certain Mr Albert, a gentleman of no fixed occupation, frightfully clever and well read and versed, an animal lover like you, based on hints we heard him drop whiles we hid in the wings and eavesdropped, and all his baggage comes coupled with a rosy streak of self-destruction in his nature. He exults in his squalor, and revels in his decline.

The Mad Monk: Ah! Sounds much like the young man once I was, starry-eyed and foolish, quashing my promise in a bed of mushrooms, back in father's garden at the beginning of the halting world.

Pooka: Quite. And this Mr Albert lives atop an August Mount, and does nothing save drink and play chess and crawl the pubs with youths. He is quite simply tragically comical in a nutshell. You must see him, Sir.

The Mad Monk: Gladly shall. I thrive on new friendships. We know we're getting too old when we don't bother anymore to revel. Would that Watt could come back to partake of all this history! For when the fellows are fun, they are damnably so. A man I met myself in Sligo, dead and gone now, ruined by both my hand and the fangs of my pet – who is also on the run by the way – but this O'Muadaigh was a wondrous piece of nature, incorrigibly gay and religious, a devout crackpot who had a fondness for charms of tinker boys. Some other names have passed down to me too, like that of one, eh, I– C– C– or something. And – well – darling Nutmeg, of course. Queen of my heart, heh. Yes, Maggie's one of the more worthwhile of these islanders I've met … *(The Banshee looks up from her knitting and frowns.)* What, love? You do not care to be praised?

Banshee: *(hissing)* I am hardly what you might call an islander anymore!

The Mad Monk: Fair enough, dear. You're one of us I guess. But what are we? Are we indeed undead? Sometimes it sickens me so to think. I am growing fonder of my hobbies. Making things is the final proof of life I have left. Off which I thrive. Pinching myself to feel alive. Whittling buttered couplets, remembering our salad desert days I left behind.

Puck: And why was that, we've often wondered?

The Mad Monk: Lordy knows. But a golden time may yet be retained, be it only in the deluded mind, turning over on lunatic delight.

Pooka: Fancy will conquer all!

Puck: Strewth! Is there nothing left then but imaginings?

The Mad Monk: For a time this was true for me. Worsened yet by a glimpse I got of the big picture, chancing upon an inky bit of bum-fodder. I tell you, it's a mad and hellish place we're in. Enemies of olden days, like your Oberon and our Acrille, are lilies next to what we're up against here. But soon I found that my gloom, like yours, was fatuous. For there is a wisdom of a kind in the joy of a child, even, heh, even an enlightenment if you will, in mere unsullied cosmic jollity, of courageous exuberance in the face of disaster, blowing defiant raspberries at the monsters that men may come to be.

Pooka: *(carefully)* Sounds familiar …

Puck: Sounds like … Divine Madness?

The Mad Monk: Sounds more like I'm taking the piss again! And mixing metaphors like drinks. But the name is only a name. Fun is fun, eh?

Puck: Now see here, riddling maestro, we've been reunited some hours now. And, evasion aside, it might be about time to hear just why you left us, and why you summoned us hither to follow thee.

The Mad Monk: Ah, the dread of motive! I expressed all of this, or something of it, at copious length in a poem I wrote recently for my lady Maggie Nutmeg here, for which she cared little – indeed, my chronicle induced inertia in the wagon, and sent her straight to sleep.

Banshee: *(snorting, throwing aside her needles)* Hmph! Be that so, no more than you yourself went out like a light, when I spoke of meself!

The Mad Monk: Did I, dear? Why! So I did. Though I did get the gist. Ah, fair is fair in marriage I suppose. But I pray thee, woman, kindly hush – these our friends are but lately come – not yet accustomed to thy self-centred babbling – for I assure you lads, once she gets started on her favourite topic, of herself and her troubles, she will not stop for a second!

Banshee: *(seething, gnashing mandibles)* Well! If that is how you have always felt, I shan't trouble thee much longer. Why, I'll, I'll go down to the seashore, just as I did in me life, and throw meself in to drown – all that prevented me then was the consolation of a priest, into whom I bumped on the prom en-route to me death – no such obstacle I'll meet today, down on them Dublin docks and soulless quays!

The Mad Monk: A pretty tale, love, but I doubt drowning will really do so much to annihilate a teary Banshee such as thee, such an insubstantial spirit as thou art. You're here with me for the eternal innings, dear, like it or not, through thick and thin and worse and better by the skin of your fangs!

Banshee: *(rising, gathering her robes round her, storming off to the caravan)* We'll see about that! See what you say when me baton has been passed to me understudy!

The Mad Monk: Here, I'll check the time of the tides for you! *(The caravan door slams. He shrugs, blows an unseen kiss to the air.)* Ah love! The great jittery unreliable. Like women too, and war.

Pooka: *(dashing out ash from stub of his pipe)* Sir, turning aside from this passing display of pettiness, such as so often we have been forced to witness twixt you and your other kindred beloved, what is it exactly that you, eh, want … want to be done?

The Mad Monk: *(his face unreadable in the fading light)* Done?

Puck: Yes, done, what is our, our, our project?

The Mad Monk: Project?

Pooka: Yes! What fruit shall be born of your new ministry?

The Mad Monk: Ministry? Mine? So far, feck all, I fear. Inaction is all too alluring. Merely getting from place to place becomes more appealing when you attain a riper vintage such as I enjoy. I killed a man I also saved. I gave fresh sight to a gull. I lost my dog. I was matchmaker for a lovesick Hare. I met my woman, bedded her and wedded her, and made money with her by spinning yarns. And I, uh … wrote some poems too.

Puck: Right. So are we to turn poets, then?

The Mad Monk: What? No, but …

Pooka: Shepherds in furs? Arcadian refugees? Sentimental minstrels in search of sheep, lost in a city that is notably bare of sheep?

The Mad Monk: I didn't …

Puck: Really Sir! We know your tropes. If this be your game, it was hardly worth coming all the way just for this! What?

The Mad Monk: I feel bullied, boys. Your own pranks were hardly better …

Pooka: All right, then, surely, um, surely you have some deeds you want done, for which our assistance would be of benefit? Some tasks, some goals to be seen to, eh?'

The Mad Monk: Well, we won't be lighting any more fires, that's a given … and I should certainly like to find Mr Lamb's Bull for one thing … and the man himself, with luck …

Pooka: Easy done, his leg's cut off, he can't have hobbled far.

The Mad Monk: He wasn't in Athleague, when I looked while there … and I should like to find my Dog again too, he's on the loose, he's a danger … wonder where the poet got to too …

Puck: *(muttering)* Never liked that fucking mutt anyway...

The Mad Monk: … And above all else, I should like to unearth Elijah. Though dead, he lives. And we need him. He knows things, that elder devil twin of mine sneering over my shoulder, my better half, my best friend and worst enemy. And I should like to talk to him, to bid him desist from gumming up the works, if indeed that is his strategy, assuming he has set out to foil my good works, if good they be, if bad indeed he is. A saint dressed as a devil? He eluded me earlier, and now hovers in the air, flapping his wings. He knows more than I, we've always known this. Any gaps in my lines he may fill in, if we could but only find him, and shake him by the collarbone, and take off our socks and put them on our hands, and evoke the fonder memories of our kindred dead before we were estranged, if that remorse alone would melt him. And lastly take him in my arms and embrace him. As in days of old, when mother rocked us on her knee, before her face was slashed. Before the bolt struck him, and addled him, when our father's house was felled, and we was set adrift. O brother where art thou? I hate thee not. Where is the babe of grace that once you and I both were? Infantine angels twirling their curls and forelocks, the same tufts of hair we tore in our squabbles. O brother Elijah! Love me, mackerel!

The Mad Monk falls silent, and lets fall limply his uplifted arms. His shining eyes pool over with hopeful tears. His companions are quiet. The donkey is sleeping. The cat desists from gnawing at the bone, and begins to prowl through the vales of the nocturne, wagging her tail as she leaves them seated in the darkness. For the sun by now has long since set, sunken beyond the western hills in the while they have spoken, and the park in which they abide is all clad in nightly shade, blotched by silver pools and bruises of starlight that dust the dim. No other light shines, for their smokes are all extinguished, burnt out by their breaths, and gusts of the caressing breeze. But then The Mad Monk wipes his eyes, and relights his hookah, and his fine face shakes and crackles in the wavering light of the pealing fire's flame. He sucks, and puffs, and ponders in the gloom. And then another thought occurs to him, and he begins to smile once more, faintly if bright.

The Mad Monk: … Anyway. Tell me more about this Mr Albert of yours …

CHAPTER FIFTY-THREE

Mr Albert Potter had lately acquired a parrot in a cage, to add to the school of animals he kept. It was by default that he obtained possession of the bird, an elderly tenant of upstairs having died, and the landlord had reckoned it best that the basement's occupant be the one to inherit the florid warbler. The squawker's safety was a paramount concern, to which end he stowed it in his bedroom by the moonscape upon which he slept, out of sight of the swarm of hungry kitties that prowled his adjacent sitting room. The bird sang the fat man to sleep at night, lulled into guileless slumber by the lyrics its former owner had drilled into its brain by osmosis and chance. The parrot's finest set piece was its ability to recite the rosary and the Angelus, to the square root of ten thousand times, having heard its pious master of yore drone through the litany time after time over dinner. And the cringing atheist in Mr Potter bridled to hear his bird so tediously quote the stolid words whose import he abhorred, which drove him from his bedroom in the mornings to seek solace on the quiet of his couch afar, separated from the patter by a partition of walls and rows of shelves, sipping from spare cans while the vagrant cats padded by his heels, and his White Dog lay on his lap and snored.

And supping Mr Potter mulled over the unexpected events to which he had been recently privy, and the latest acquaintance and new friend he had found, the jabbering gallant Merkel. The youth aroused in him strange and unfamiliar feelings of kinship, not to speak of love, such sensations of love as had for so long in his shell of cynicism been buried. And a strange desire was born in his breast, as if he had found his past self embodied in a dashing younger shape, one which he longed to claim and grasp for his own again. And he began to grow greedy and covetous of the company of the youth, sending him texts with invites to play chess, such sessions at which the other duller Simeon was always unfortunately present. But Merkel in care of a chaperone was better than no Merkel at all. And fatherly Albert smiled to see the boy survey the graded board and grind his brainy cogs, pushing pawns through their paces over the grids, quickly mated yet never quite checked, a natural player with all the correct instincts on which the younger and more Napoleonic version of Potter had so prided himself.

And after the sessions of chess in the August, the boys would accompany him to the chipper on the corner, where all would gorge on grease and oil, stowing their purchases in grubby sacks, which they hauled back to Albert's abode, where the trio sat on stools amid the rubble and the grime, admiring the stains on the weeping walls, tasting the dregs of what spare cans there were, only to spit all out in disgust, decrying the vinegary taste the filth had acquired. He played them music on his gramophone and bought them dry pizza he badly burnt in his microwave. But notwithstanding all these allurements, the young men were quietly repulsed by the squalor of the dwelling, which disquiet Mr Potter discerned on their faces, moving him to make, of late, a greater effort to keep spruce his bachelor's pad, sweeping up the debris with a shovel, and cleaning away the festering muck that flowed from his leaking sewer. Furthermore, the floral tiling of his lurid kitchenette had yet to be completed, an improving project he had long nursed in what remained of his domestic pride, for which reason he set forth down the Rathmines Road one morning, in search of an eligible journeyman to do the job.

But while passing by the cathedral, he was witness to an incident. A wedding was taking place, at which all the gauche well-wishers clustered and cheered as the happy man and wife (Boris Nigel Gillespie and Hilda O'Mara) descended from the steps in their finery. Flowers were hurled and garlands thrown to bestrew the two, as the outsider Potter stood in the leafy shade and wondered how he himself would have coped in the midst of that fuss, if ever he had had occasion to be married.

But suddenly an altercation arose. From the dark side of the cathedral, having long lurked in the dimness waiting for his turn, a scraggly tramp emerged from the shrubbery, with a long and ragged beard and blazing eyes, staggering across the paving to accost the startled couple, who froze and glanced aghast as he brandished a wreath and quoted verses. He appeared to be gabbling a monologue of gibberish, so far as Mr Potter could see and hear, grabbing the hem of the bride's sweeping dress and ranting nonsense to the nine winds, waving his arms and tearing his hair. He fell on his knees before her and genuflected, while all the in-laws blanched and looked befuddled. And the piebald bride, affecting ignorance, stole away to the waiting limo in her hurry, pursued by a medley of biddies that blocked the vagrant's advance. And Boris Nigel Gillespie, spotting a chance to win acclaim, tore off his jacket and rolled up his sleeves, and dealt the vagabond a belt in the nose, crushing the derelict who whined and toppled, kicked in the ribs by the freckly zit, beaten to a pulp until he ceased to writhe and soon was still. And thus, the happy outing marred by this untimely intrusion, nipped in the bud by unwanted brutality that reeked of scandal, the wedding party hastily sped away in their automobile, and the stray pricks on the steps fast fled in their suit, leaving behind the beaten tramp, sprawled in front of the cathedral like a squashed blotch of a fly on a windowpane.

Compassion arose in the heart of the witness who stood and stared across the road. Mr Potter, his tiling project quite abandoned, crossed over the empty street and peered down at the sorry form of the beaten man, his swollen features black and blue, groaning faintly, words of apology and abasement, mingled with fragments of the flight of Mad Sweeney. And the paunchy Samaritan bent, and hoisted him up, and bore the gaunt body in his arms, bearing the bundle of rags and bones down the streets with waddling step, mumbling comforts all the while he strode.

And Albert carried the tramp round the corner to Merriman's, and set him down on the scarlet couch in the airy cool of the morning, and rapped the counter and called for ointments and sponges to anoint the wounds and sores, which the surly publican reluctantly provided, dourly muttering that he didn't want any trouble on his premises. Ignoring this, Mr Potter set to coating the cuts and welts with iodine and fennel, bathing the injuries with tangy soothing and sting, moving the patient to blearily sigh in his rapture. Alert to his recovery, Albert called out for two pints, which grumbling Merriman poured and brought. With a firm hand, Albert lifted the wounded man's head from the table, and parted his bloody lips, and let them rest on rim of the goblet, and tilted his neck to let the healing trickle pour down his throat with grateful gurgle.

When a judicious sample was administered and swallowed, the ragged man's condition improved. He sat up more brightly, opened his glowing eyes the wider, and seemed more cognisant of where and who he was. He thanked his redeemer fulsomely, in Irish initially until, upon learning that the fat southern Protestant to his side had not a word of his native gloss, he smoothly switched to English, for all that his command of that tongue was musty and arcane. He warmed to his surroundings, and was moved to unburden himself to a friendly stranger.

And so, through the forest of his serpentine clauses and outmoded expressions, Albert learnt by degrees of the man's crackpot mission, of his vegetarianism and intermittent teetotalism, of his love of women, of his lust for poetry, of his loathing of conventional matrimony, and of his aborted attempt to seek his child's forgiveness, as witnessed just now, most miserably conducted and halted. And Albert well knew what it was to have wronged a child for whose pardon one longed; he himself had reared a girl in Scotland, an unwanted birth he had callously ditched, of whose whereabouts he now knew nothing. And in the end, feeling sentimental, he invited the vagabond bard back to his lodgings, for a touch of supper and a cigar, a true vintage Cuban, long preserved for a special occasion. And hungry Tadgh O'Mara, seeing stars, eagerly agreed to feed.

So in the haze of afternoon Mr Albert Potter and the poet left the bar and crossed under the arch to the tangles of the square. As Mr Potter fumbled for his latchkey and began to descend the steps to his burrow, Tadgh O'Mara began to recount his ordeal at the paws of the beast, a tale that piqued the interest of his sceptical host. But once they were inside, in that subterranean lair that knew little daylight, in the squalid crypt awash with books and booze, the newcomer froze, his nostrils arched to sniff the fetid canine air, while heedless Albert dropped his keys and strolled to the fridge, to unearth some cans for dinner. Turning, he saw his visitor halted in the doorway.

'Come on in, I don't bite!' said jocular Potter.

Reluctant Tadgh, newly nervous and feeling fear, sidled into the badger's den, his unblinking eyes adjusting to the dimness, beginning to discern the swishing forms of silent cats that padded by their heels. And further on the couch asleep, snoozing recumbent among the empty bottles, was a larger whiter bestial form, whose identity he squinted to decipher, as Mr Potter popped open a can, and guzzled a mouthful, and thrust another drink into the shaking hands of his terrified guest.

'Come on into my study,' said Albert, 'I'll show you my parrot!'

But just then, as Tadgh stepped forward following the prompting of his host, on the couch the White Dog shifted, roused from sleep by the intrusion, having caught a scent, of a familiar hated whiff, that wafted along a tunnel of a sunbeam, borne by a cluster of bejewelled motes, a victim's smell that annoyed his nose and bid him grunt and wake. And the White Dog grunted and grew, and opened his yellow eyes that swivelled round the room, catching sight of the beanpole poet who quaked in the doorway, at sight of whom the creature growled then barked then howled, ignoring the bidding of his owner to be hushed, as the frenzied poet shivered and fell.

'Stop that, Snowy!' Mr Potter barked in his turn, catching the toppling tramp by his elbow, 'Must apologize for that. He's a stubborn brute. An orphan. Came to my door of a dark night. Sometimes just gets a taste of something off people that he doesn't like. Takes a set against them. Please do not be frightened. He's harmless really, afraid of my shadow. All bark and no bite, as the cliché-mongers say, juh, juh, juh?'

Fearful Tadgh shot out a snaking arm, and clutched his elbow that his host had grasped, clawing at the ancient wound with a shivering hand, as the hissing monster stared him down and barked and snarled, and rose, and hopped down from the bloated couch, and waded through the grime of the room, and circled round his enemy's legs as his owner opined, and opened foamy jaws to clamp on a calf, at sight of which frothing mandibles the lanky poet quickly made his excuses and left.

Disappointed, Albert stood at the door and watched him flee up the steps and disappear around a corner of the square. Another newfound friendship queerly terminated. Disgruntled, he shut the door, and looked down at his banal hound, an indolent corgi with a dripping tongue, innocuously panting and dumbly grinning, as he gaped up at his towering blob of master, and awaited commands which never came.

Then Albert's mobile phone abruptly rang, buzzing shrill and tinny from a cranny of his couch. Kicking aside his woofing dog, he lumbered over and fumbled amid the cushions, then found the rectangle of chanting metal that wobbled in his palm, announcing the call of an unfamiliar number, as he curiously pressed a green button, held the machine to his flabby ear, and heard enchanted the gentle voice of a girl:

'Hi, um, eh, Albert? Tee-hee. This is Jezzie, I'm, eh, Simeon's friend, we're, uh, having a party in his place, uh, would you, er, like to come?'

CHAPTER FIFTY-FOUR

She had heard about Albert from me, and had grown fascinated with the idea of him, lured by the lurid picture I painted of the badger boozer in his musty lair. For Jezebel Temple had rejoined our crew, having affected to have forgiven and forgotten my manic amorousness, such feelings as I forced myself to stifle, for all that they did rankle still. Tempted by the novelty, drawn by the handsome spectacle of the prodigy Merkel to whose elbow now I clung, the harpy came like a bosomy bumblebee to hum about our hive of rhetoric. Bewitching still, she came to us sailing in her kinky buggy with her girly chums, like the alabaster beauty Lucia Seward, and the kindly spinster Agatha Honeypenny, and the saintly Kyrie Elysium who had an impish smile and auburn pigtails.

Honeypenny, on and off, had seemed to nurse a crush on me, as evinced by her buying me bags of green tea, to feed my famous habit, these precious sacks of leaves that she delivered with flush and swish as under the Campanile I kept up my daily squat. And Kyrie Elysium was one for whom I too had fostered a fortnightly affection, escorting her from pub to club and house to shed in search of cans and craic. Oft in the course of our awkward fumbling converse would I exclaim 'Jaysus!' and 'for God's sake!', which impious ejaculations roused her, a soldier of Christ from the cradle, to shriek at me 'DON'T TAKE THE LORD'S NAME IN VAIN!'

The dear girl! She was mad as a brush in truth, and touched me with her tales of childhood loss and grief, rolling in a dumpster to drown her sorrows, which doleful stories moved me to weep and cry, to her affront and shock, bidding me hush with a hug and kiss, as I babbled hysterically on the score of great and aching sad lacks of love that pained the lives of most. I later heard that shortly after we tearfully parted, she decided to dive into the canal to take a dip with the rats, swimming nude and moonlit among the trolleys and bottles and swans, bade desist in this barmy sport by a sagacious tramp, whose wise advice she took in hand. She was struck down a week thereafter by hypothermia.

But these gossipy girls, whose tongues would always wag, these girls saw me on the streets, gallivanting with Merkel and his Evangelists, to whom I too had warmed, as one by one I met them in the smoky pits of nightlife, leaving the library to loiter and lounge on cobbles and kerbs, beating our chests and squeezing our bugles as we beeped our horns in the smoking arenas. They were Dubliners true and full, and a breath of fresh air after the arid swamp of tedium my home had become, courtesy of Gallagher and Freaney's sullenness, and mad Arsene's stagnancy in my bedroom. Johnny Fritzl was the cuddly Christ who loved his antique ballads, and Lukas the Shag was the pallid lady's man who loved to bed his chicks, and Marco Grimaldi was the toothy cartoonist who didn't love anything much at all. Sometime too Alan Marzipan, gangling brother of the dark horse Jonah, would also bumble by, with his large blue eyes he very seldom opened wide, their heavy lids being sleepy, a Bach and Mozart buff like me. Merkel's voice, of course, dominated the affairs of this his group in the main, spokesman for their childhood sores and shoulder's chips, supplying each with a ready-made intro he had made up in his mind.

'In many ways,' he would say seriously, with a gesture to the luscious Fritzl, 'Johnny is wiser than either you or I will ever be.'

There was some truth in this. For Fritzl was the sweetest of them, fluffy of head and beard, and warm of heart and soul, possessed, on first appearance, of a ferocious pride I initially abhorred and mistook for arrogance, since he was given impulsively to hate the primary impressions he obtained of a new person, a stranger to his ways, until, in time, after a sufficient period had passed in which he cocked his head, and studied one's moves with a panther's gaze, and figured one through like a botanist, he grew at last to like what he saw, and then to befriend and love – and truly no man could be worthy of so intense an affection as Johnny Fritzl bore for me.

'Ah Simeon!' he would fondly sigh with a bat of his lashes and a slap of my back, 'with you, it's like you're real but you're not believable!'

Then he would squeeze my testicles and smile a foolish smile, or pull back the silk of my scarlet pyjamas to inspect my buttocks and marvel.

'Here, man!' he would say in wonder, 'your arse is fucking mental!'

And he was perceptive too; one of the first utterances he ever made to me, in the dark of my kitchen, betrayed a piercing insight that saw through to the horrid truth: 'Thing you must know about Merkel is that, like the majority of only children, he is, fundamentally, truly, deeply selfish.' A remark he later denied, though it haunted me, and never left me alone. And like me, he was a romantic fool, forever pining for unobtainable girls who were already attached to unworthy boors far out of his bounds, like the plump optician Guinevere McCarthy, who was conjoined to the beanpole painter Cyril Kennedy. I met these two in a hole called Whelan's, and formed a liking for the lady, and a loathing for her lad. He was arrogant and ungallant and was mistreating the gem he had seduced, to the pain of lovesick Fritzl, who stood lovelorn on the sidelines and pined and wrung his heart. Such a pure love as he bore was sad to see go so fallow and ignored.

I had been in an unrequited plight myself before, as all too well we know, and so felt his anguish keenly, and soon endeavoured, in the depths of my drunkenness, to do something about this. What vainglorious course of action I then took I do not now remember, but it was reported that at some point in the later evening, I raised my head from the table upon which it was slumped, my lank ratty locks dropping down over my bullet cranium, and fixed weedy Kennedy with a bloodshot stare, in which hate and fury kindled and burned and set him ill at ease, and then I bared my fangs and hissed:

'Does I— C— C— get erections?'

Cyril Kennedy, befuddled and afraid, sensing a cryptic threat, glanced nervously to Fritzl, who giggled, and attempted to draw me away from the fray.

'I hate him!' I snarled to Fritzl, still glaring at Kennedy as I was hauled off roaring, 'I hate him! I hate him so much! I want to slit his throat!'

And Cyril Kennedy, in the face of an attack so seemingly unprovoked, let his lower lip tremble, and mumbled a bitter and inaudible reprisal. But such a surly feat endeared me to darling Johnny, and that was surely good.

Like Konrad, he also harboured a fancy for my housemate Gallagher, entranced by her cutie-pie beaver's teeth and chirpy lilt, that same awful warble I myself detested. Once, as I escorted Johnny tipsily home, we met her in the hallway on her way to bed, and he caught a strand of her curly mane, and minced and smiled, and slurred:

'Your hair, madam, is like *obsidian rainfall*!'

A charming phrase; the silly girl glowed, then felt ashamed of herself for glowing, and then pretended she had not glowed – I clearly had a lot to learn from this furry charmer. Yet his fancy was not guaranteed to endear him to the grunting troglodyte Freaney, who ground his computer games in the next room producing horrid noises, covetous of his little girlfriend, the only prize he possessed in life, one he had coveted all the way since school. Fritzl's repeated attempts to woo Gallagher thus became a bone of contention in the house; I was entreated to ban him from our doors when he went too far, which policy I simply could not enforce – I liked him far more than they, and with him had more in common, and something soon would give (namely, they at last would leave, and I would breathe a sigh of relief in their summer of aftermath).

In the meantime I had to tread on tenterhooks, and secretly motor in my unwelcome friends under the noses of my housemates who were worse than parents, saving our parties for the weekends when they went home and left me in peace, having my surreptitious fun on the sly. It was a dead and empty sort of life, though at least lively. My dwelling earned repute as a house of mirth whose doors were welcoming, and of this dear old Jezzie caught wind, and soon was elbowing into the throng, thus unwittingly kindling my desire, for all my outward show of companionable disinterest.

Her latest daft proposal, when next she saw me lapping on the ramp, was that we throw 'a mad tea party' at my place on Friday, to which 'the others' (so she incessantly called Merkel's merry men, to my chagrin, their raucous presence being a prerequisite for her own) must be invited, so they were. So in a bunch they tramped through my door the four apostles, the hairy goblin twins in boots, sallow Grimaldi with toothy grin and goofy laugh (like a minor actor auditioning for Ming the Merciless), and pallid Lukas the Shag, a torn soul who could never commit, who was sometimes cold and sometimes hot.

And then she came, my dark angel with her ghostly hair, came over with her cortege, little miss Honeypenny armed with a baking tray of butterfly buns, steward Lucia Seward with her first-aid kit, and militant Jezzie fleshy and powdered and all too comely, smelling of aphrodisiac perfume that made my loins arise, and took over my kitchen with a brush of her fringe and a slap of her apron, and downed her flagons of cheap white wine, and poured the contents of a tin into a pan that sizzled, and I looked on stricken as darling Jezebel Temple cooked us up a pot of lentil soup that we shared from the same spoon like steaming newlyweds.

I retreated to the toilet where I sat and shat on the limey bowl, drunkenly omitting to lock the door, raising dead eyes in the midst of my shit to watch Konrad strolling in to wash his hands and face and regale me with a bit of gossip, only then to sense my smell and cajole me to wipe well, my mental hide and downy butt that was too far for my codger's quivering hands to reach, to which end my errant friend hoisted me up and sportingly performed the jolly deed for me, with a wince and grin that tickled me.

'This is the kind of thing great friendships are made of!' he sneered as he flushed and zipped me up and propped me forward like dummy Arsene again.

And as he shoved me up the stairs once more, I told the old boy of my fresh designs on the wench's virtue, and he seemed sympathetic, like he always so artfully seemed, and he pretended he would lend a helping hand in that direction, errant matchmaker and tireless chaperone, willing to efface himself on my behalf, to be a shady cool friend whose coolness, in her starry eyes, imparted a similar aura unto me, a coy satellite to his blazing sun. He even, worst of the worst, offered to write a sequence of poems in her honour, which I could then pass off as my own, since ladies always did so love to be muses for poetry, no matter how poor the verses made, which imitation of Bergerac I stoutly rejected – I had a smidgen more pride than that.

'The funniest part of it all,' he mused too loudly, almost within her goggling earshot, 'is that you and Jezzie are actually *such* a good match! Both the heroes of your own trivial little dramas, making mountains out of molehills, always the star part in the spotlight and the centre of things. Thing is, I'm not sure that you're actually in love with her, you're just *obsessed* with her, and weirdly so. Masochistically, maybe. It probably puts her off. Anyway, you might stand a better chance of wooing her if you made it a little less obvious that you want to fuck the living dickens out of her. I mean, stop slobbering for the love of god, and stand up like a man! And for Christ's sake don't leave your fly undone with your dong waving around in front of our faces, you incontinent dope! And here's the ultimate clue to riding Jezzie – it wouldn't kill you to take a bath every now and again. I mean, to be perfectly honest, you stink of piss and shit and fart.'

In the meantime, as we came upstairs, as the three girls gossiped in the kitchen tittering, and he dumped me on the couch, he remained more preoccupied by the strange admiration that Albert had seemed to show for him, expressed so far in relatively safe and chaste continental smooches, always wetly administered upon greeting and parting.

'Fucking hell!' gauche Merkel exclaimed to Fritzl, 'I don't get it. He's been making far too many campy remarks lately. To listen to him, you'd think he was a Lothario in his day, always going on about all those women he's fucked – but now this … but he's not gay. I refuse to believe he's gay. He can't be gay. He fucking can't be. God, can you imagine it? Imagine if we didn't go to see him for a few weeks, and none of his texts were answered. Imagine if I stopped playing chess with him – wouldn't it be mad if the next we heard of him, he had gone and fucking hung himself?'

And at this proposed fate, dreaming of the death of one among my boyhood's heroes, a latent twist in a tale that stank of the tragic, the evil only child wickedly grinned in his relish, having hit upon a catastrophe's recipe.

'Albert!' Jezzie cried upon hearing the name at which her ears perked up, from whose lobes hung spangled earrings that jingled, poking out her bright head around the kitchen's corner, 'Always Albert! Tell me more about Albert! Where does Albert live? What does Albert look like? Can we invite Albert over? Can we? Can we? Can we?'

And once she had hold of a notion in her head, there was no point in stopping her, as I handed her my phone with his number displayed, which she promptly dialled and rang in her eagerness, speaking avidly to the dark man who gruffly answered on the other end, and heard enchanted her dulcet stuttering monotone.

And so he came to us with his bag of cans, big and sweaty and unwashed and gross, came wearily to our door ringing the bell at mention of the devil, full of excuses for his fatigue, telling Konrad and I, with a lie, that he had been playing chess all day, and was in no fit state to be witty or brilliant or charming, his mood muted, keen only to drink on the sidelines, and observe our childish antics with a superior's disdain.

And the girls, upon sighting the bear who mounted my stairs behind Konrad and I, were at first shocked, then amused, then struggled to stifle their sniggers like bitches, as he waded to a seat at the table's top, and sat down, and popped open some beer, and growled his hunger as he surveyed the youthful assemblage with dark and watery sunken eyes, blinking against their flab as he supped and licked his lips. (Timid Honeypenny, out of her depth in these sordid waters, now got collected by her parents at this point.)

Following his arrival, awkward silences were the norm of the gathering, until soon, when his liquid vigour was replenished by his sips, he grew livelier, moved to pepper the discourse with mock-sagacious put-downs, moved by remembrance, prompted by sight of the pair of fair maidens who remained, to recall the buried gallantry of his firebrand young manhood, begging dearest lady Jezzie, who had called him hither anyway and now was too shy to say a single word, to grant him the indulgence of her lily hand, which she held out teasingly, which he took in a fat hairy paw, and kissed and patted with all the grace of a bygone chivalry, as if he were in livery and hosiery, and she adorned in furs and wigs, a starlet empress paid homage by her paunchy courtier.

'Princess,' he called her sweetly. And when this would not serve, for his daughter was rightly haughty to be demoted, he called her 'Queen of my Heart' instead.

Konrad, an able master of the revels, found a judge's wig from one of my shelves whereon all my props were stowed, and placed the grey and dusty hairpiece upon our Potter's crown, and we marvelled at how well it suited, the sweep of curls cascading from his brow to his hilly shoulders, wondering at the absurd grandeur with which it endowed him, until the man himself, indignant, and sensing a smidgen mockery, tore off the wig and flung his laurels aside as he lapped his beer, and called us a pair of fruity pansies.

The drink flowed, and the affair grew rowdy. In a further corner Marco Grimaldi and Lukas the Shag polished off a bottle of Gallagher's unprotected vodka, and then Marco, upon the snide prompting of Lukas, withdrew to the toilet, to fill it full of his watery urine that looked and stank the same as the spirits imbibed (sometime in the aftermath the little girl Gallagher took a sip, and choked, and pronounced his piss to be water).

And over by the table Jezzie produced her pot of paints, and daubed the cute faces of Merkel and Fritzl with streaks of blue of whose sheen she approved, winking and flirting with the handsome tearaways, my unwitting rivals for her lusty fancy. And I frowned and itched to see myself supplanted in her favour, a jealousy compounded by the trademark champ of teeth upon flesh, her same bloody watermark whose amorous meaning I knew all too well, gagging to watch a toothy bite administered to Konrad's wrist, while one sly eye of hers watched my cringing reaction from its beady corner, as I turned aside affecting jittery nonchalance, and chatted to Albert about books.

But he was far more interested in whatever Merkel was doing, and was covetous of his attention and regard, his eyes roving the room to keep the lightning being in sight, grabbing him by the sleeve as the loud boy ran by, enforcing the lad to sit on his lap or lean against his belly, at which point the love-object, repelled by the whiff, suggested a compromise, and so knelt by Mr Potter's knee, gazing up into his piggy face on which a beatific dirty smile was leering, enraptured by devotion, as the boy pleaded with bright and earnest eyes for but one sip of the elder man's beer can, for he had none of his own worth the name, and was all but gagging with his thirst.

'So am I!' Albert huskily replied, 'And nothing for me in return? You're fresh, aren't you! Give us a kiss first, in exchange for a taster!'

Giggling flirty Merkel offered a rosy cheek, and then was grabbed in the horny bear's big hands, and forcibly clenched as he wriggled to be freed, and his face was plastered with a myriad filthy kisses, as I looked on appalled. And I turned away from the disgusting spectacle, only to see, in the flickering candlelit dim, Jezzie and Lukas the Shag sat aside on my mattress in a sultry corner, the latter stroking her hand, looking at her in expectation as she warmed to his advances, and turned to him and lay on the voluptuous pillow, and he dipped his head and kissed her face and caressed her breast, in sloppy pulpy viscous union of mucous like maggots, sucking that rang through my temples, as guffawing Marco Grimaldi did a jig in the foreground, capering and skirting with his weeping jester's cap-and-bells.

Merkel had squirmed free of Potter's clasp, and was darting around the shelves, so the fat man contented himself with catching the dashing Fritzl who was too drunken to protest, who he pronounced 'a beautiful boy', over whose noble profile he rhapsodized, hailing the slant of the marble nose, caressing his fluffy curls, comparing his sweet face, in its curvaceous delicacy and grace, to a choice Hopkins lyric.

'Albert Potter,' Johnny Fritzl solemnly proclaimed, amid his slurring with a drunkard's sincerity, 'Albert Potter has a beautiful face.'

And it was true; he did; as we all did; for we was as fizzling angels then.

And then Lukas and Jezzie stalled their scoring to smoke upon their fags, as thirsty Merkel blundered over, begging Jezzie for just a sip of her can, his trademark trick, but she smirked and refused, boldly telling him first to suck her toes to earn his share. Which debasement he did, no stranger in sinking to unspeakable debauch, bending down and wrapping his lips around her little array of nipple toes, even through the stinking fabric of their stockings that did not deter him, as with moist admiration he suckled their wiggling contours, like a calf on his knees before his mamma's undulant udder, before the fleshy jugs to sing of mammas everywhere, while she writhed and laughed and felt adored as virile Lukas slurped and bit upon her chubby cheek, as with her claws she scratched and tore his sallow tuba chest, and I howled and tore out clumps of my hair, and did a swirling loony's waltz in blinded frenzy, arm in arm with cackling Marco Grimaldi, sweeping around the ballroom to the cracked and demented notes of a danse macabre, as composed by all the chorus of the world's humming madmen.

Johnny Fritzl tore himself from Potter's hungry arms, and retreated to the bathroom, mourning for his captive Guinevere afar, and took his bulging staff in hand and squeezed, and masturbated furiously into my sink that caught every last one of his drops. And neglected Albert grunted – if this was what counted for a wild party, then standards surely had slipped; in his time, no fun was had until the cops were called.

Meanwhile Merkel desisted from his suckling of girly toes, and snatched away Jezzie's cider can, not that she noticed, being preoccupied with the hunky Shag, and the thieving magpie gulped its sweet and sickly contents down, and saw me reeling in the kitchen, a tearful host cracking open another bottle, and he floundered over, and waved his hands in my face, and hooted and hollered with his purple cheeks working, bellowing and shouting all the while he did, 'I AM THE ABSTRACT CONCEPT OF KONRAD MERKEL! I AM THE ABSTRACT CONCEPT OF KONRAD MERKEL! I AM THE ABSTRACT CONCEPT OF KONRAD MERKEL! I AM THE ABSTRACT CONCEPT OF KONRAD MERKEL!'

It was too much. I snapped and dropped the bottle that smashed into a horde of jangling shards at my bare feet, as I wound forward in my anger, and laid hands on his throat, and tightened my clench and drove him forward to the wall, as he gagged and choked and burbled mercy and remit in the prank, but no pity was in my frenzied eyes as I blamed him for everything, and brought him down to the floor to his final squeaky gasps, and strangled and glutted him as we rolled in our combat, his helpless hands batting me off and circling the air, his lips and cheeks deathly bluing to my savage delight, admiring the iron bones of my madman's fingers that made their clenches and dents in his blasted neck, pressing down upon the lump in his throat to squash out every last little drop of life that was in him, my best friend and worst enemy of all, the prospect of whose impending murder at my bloody hands filled me with a demon's joy, as I whooped and snarled and gleefully strangled the bastard Konrad.

But luckily our house escaped becoming a scene of homicide when one of his flailing arms caught me by chance with a welcome punch in the chin, as I released my grip on him and fell back against the wall off which I bashed my head, and fainted and blacked out and slumped, and bled upon the shards of glass that littered the treacherous linoleum of the deadly floor, as quailing Merkel choked, and fingered the bruises of his neck as he rose and scurried off and gave not a shit, as I lay in the pool of my blood expiring and prostrate and unconscious, deserving victim of my jealous folly.

Then the responsible adult in Albert saw my plight from around the corner, and called the alarm with blubbery cry, and lumbered to my side and knelt and shouted for help, and raised my tattered head and lay it on his lap, as the ready-made nurse in Lucia Seward popped up and produced her first-aid kit, and bent beside my body with her metal box, and mopped up all the blood that from my frazzled brow did flow in weeping pooling mid the winking glass, their drops and puddles congealed by the morning, and this blessed pair of unlikely guardians, the alabaster beauty and the corpulent beast, tenderly administered as angels to my damages, and bandaged and plastered my foolish head, as the rest of the party revelled in blithe ignorance of the nearby calamity.

And Albert lifted me up, and propped me against the wall, and sternly warned me not to have another sup to drink, and carried me downstairs to my father's bed, and laid me down to sleep, and shook his head and grumbled at our folly, and passed out the door and exited our house, with a parting kiss to trembling Konrad who ignored him, admiring in a mirror the black and blue marks left on his neck by my hands, as on a bed I sunk into my wounded slumber, ignorant of my injuries, unheeding of their help, remembering only my attempt to murder, over which I gloated, and sank to sleep as a latent psychopath.

And upstairs, the lovers Lukas and tomboy Jezzie fell to their repose and spooned with the steward Lucia on the mattress, while Johnny Fritzl tugged his rod, and Konrad Merkel and Marco Grimaldi dithered and smoked until the new dawn came, discussing lucid dreaming and the merits and demerits of Tennyson's *Lotos-Eaters*, and other stuff.

CHAPTER FIFTY-FIVE

But in the injured boy's grey bedroom the old man lies, his honorary uncle and godfather figure, his dead head lifted from the pillow, cocking ancient ears at the dwindling noises that leak through the door's chinks into the echo chamber, as the party fades, and the hangovers from its close begin to droop like crying twigs. And as the morning's rays alight through his window, on whose panes the snaking Russian vine taps with coils of its leaves, spilling light illuming the queer drawings he carved on the youngster's shelves with knives (cartoonish depictions of Watt and Sherman helplessly lost at sea, as well as impressions of his brother), so then does he rise, throwing back the blankets to stand and sway in the cool of dawn, on legs and ankles of seventy summers and winters, old Arsene the weatherman who is no longer himself.

Objectively, rationally, one might say he was only after having another crack-up again, suffering a mental affliction far beyond the understanding of his youthful host, and a spell in St Pat's sanatorium would do him the power and world of good. But this cannot explain the physical transformation his season spent in the bedroom has wrought. His face, hitherto bare as a baby's, has sprouted hairs all over, hairy as Esau, and from his nostrils spring twining white moustachios, and from his chin flows a long and tangled dripping beard. The effect of ceasing to shave? But it is in the old man's eyes that the greatest change may be seen; Arsene's eyes, so small of yore, have grown large and bright, gleaming with an inner vision that burns and glows. Standing in his vest and old man's undies, scratching under an arm and farting, and belching as he begins another day and life, this new Arsene seems the picture of a prophet. And the prophetic effect is further enhanced by the epic accoutrements with which he proceeds to bedeck himself.

Simeon's shelves provide a rich stash of theatrical props and costumes to choose from, over to which the old man, who seems to grow in size with every step, proceeds from the bed. Babbling Arsene, mumbling profundities beneath his breath, selects a long dark billowy gown into which he slips, and slaps on sandals onto his cracking feet, picks up a curving staff of wood with which to thrash the weeds, and lastly, to offset and jar, opts to sport a great stovepipe of a top hat to crown his bare bald patch. Dressed and ready for his trek, he gives the skull of room a final survey, waving his crozier and bidding adieu to the shelves and the posters, and the piles of paper and bundles of manuscript, and the toys and the books and the comics and the shoes and socks, and the tray upon which his last meal of bread and cheese had been served, and the steaming chamber pot beneath his bed, whose putrid contents he shall not miss. And he leaves his hairy suitcase behind him; belongings are a burden, and the dead travel light as well as fast. He glides to the creaking door that opens for him of its own accord, and so he exits.

First he visits the toilet to his left, tearing down the irreverent 'CACATORIUM' sign as he does (it always annoyed him). He leaves a floating deposit in the bowl, a nearly unsinkable Molly Brown compound of yeast and cheese, flushes and admires the gurgling that rings through the air, smiling to consider the plumbing problems that shall shortly find fruit in the festering back garden, when the sewer is blocked and wanting cleansing rodding, and everyone's shit will overflow the gutter to befoul the shrubbery. Serenely he trips upstairs, and surveys the tattered damages left by the party, threading through the sleeping bodies of children sprawled around upon the pillows at odd angles, Jezzie and Lukas and Lucia entwined and spooning, Grimaldi and Fritzl wrapped in each other's arms, as the old man in the gown glides dodging by the pools of broken glass and blood, and puddles of spilt beer and wine, pilfering a banana from the upturned fruit bowl, and pocketing an uneaten butterfly bun, to keep him going as he roams the roads.

And none of the expired revellers stirred as he wandered around the haunted ballroom picking up the crumbs, in the cold blue light that fell from the glimmering shafts high above the topmost shelves, for all were fast asleep and safely comatose, save for Konrad Merkel, who must always in any case be the very last to retire, leaning rakishly on the open rosy window ledge, watching the outside street awake at six, as he smokes a final cigarette, and composes an acrostic about Albert in his mind. His back is turned, and he does not see the re-arisen old ghost steal his fill of salvageable food, and turn again to descend the stairs and leave at last, haggard revenant from an older banquet.

But he stalls in the hallway at the foot of the stairs, hearing wheezy snoring from the master bedroom. He nudges open that door, a latent memory of his old self awoken by the noise he knew from his heart, and sees the bandaged sleeper Simeon supine on the bed of his parents, over whose unconscious body the old man stands and gazes, keeping vigil briefly like a watchful angel in an Abe Lincoln hat, admiring the frenetic batting of the young man's eyelids, tokens of the fiery dreams of murder he nursed behind his eyes, watching his attempted strangling over and over on a grainy loop that will not cease in its homicidal chore until the yakking boor is choked for good, and shuts up at last for once.

A flicker of recognition, and passing sadness, arises in Arsene's golden eagle's eyes, for neither himself nor even Elijah had ever themselves been fathers during their old lives, never knew what it was like to have a son or child, never felt that feeling, nor now never could nor would, making do with substitutes in foster daughters and nieces, and book tokens for nephews, unsent since one could not pay the price in full, and cursory birthday cards posted at the wrong date, which were in any case only consigned to the dusty pile uncared for, to be quicker ignored and soon forgot.

But any sorrow is quickly quenched and stifled by his new and greater joy. In a gesture of leave, the departing soothsayer lays a soft hand on the boy's head that has been bruised and bled, and gently strokes his brow, and ruffles his feathery hair that fast falls out through dint of constant curling, for the curling motion helps him to think, at thought of which the spectral guardian by the bedside tenderly smiles, and blows a ghostly kiss in gratitude for hospitality and secrecy. And then the old man floats away back into the hall, closing the door in silence behind him, waving his staff to bid the front door open itself to let him leave, under whose red arch he passes through into the scanty daylight, raising a sunny breeze as the door is shut and locked, last knocking thrice on the step with his crozier, to endow benediction for the blessed sanctuary he found within the redbrick site.

The squeaky black gate opens and shuts, as Arsene Elijah O'Colla sets forth with flowing robes to face the gale that hurtles down the street, quicksilver heart beating faster in anticipation of seeing through the doings of his newborn day, gliding by the brickwork and the dwellings, past whose glass his shimmering self is seen to pass a mere reflection in their haunting windows, floating soon out of sight around a Curzon corner, finally lost to Lombardy Road and Number Nine, from one of whose spyglasses Konrad Merkel squats and sees a queer apparition leave them behind in his haughty wake, a tall old man in a nightgown like an asylum inmate, with the battered top hat of a toff, and gnarled staff and ragged beard, a prodigal wandering fortune-teller who will find his brother in suburban seaside Eden once more again, and bring back childhood's lost idyll in a puffball dream, along with the powdered wash of the tea leaves, and burning scent of the lotus and gorse.

CHAPTER FIFTY-SIX

I was awoken in the morning by my doorbell's buzzing, at sting of whose tyrannical ring I rose staggering from the bedding and groaning to the hall, a hand to my bandage grimly remembering the ordeal undergone, and answered the door and its angry ringer.

This was our neighbour from number eight, a certain life-hating Mr Chesterfield, who jabbed a finger in my face and threatened to sue me for all the noise with which he had had to put up the night before, which distracted him from his unstable sleep, and made his tempestuous moods yoyo up and down, and prevented him from thinking or talking to the potted plants who crowded his arid garden, begonias whom he watered in the nip by nightfall. Foaming at the mouth, seeing red as he spat venom upon my fuzzy innocence as I blinked groggily in the harsh sun, I feared he was on the brink of violence, having been there so short awhile ago myself, and shut the door on him out of concern for my safety.

Shambling grumpily upstairs, stepping over the snoring corpses, I saw perky Konrad smugly sat at the table's top, smoking and looking lordly and drinking my green tea.

I decided again to blame him for everything, and so I gruffly saluted him, and called him an arrogant and insufferable prick and a fucking son of a bitch, by way of greeting.

'O come on, Simeon!' he snapped, 'give over and get over yourself would you ever. The way I see it, you are far, far more arrogant than I am. And by the way, if you can remember the moment last night when you attempted to kill me – could we perhaps, if you don't mind my suggesting, limit these psychotic outbursts to just once a month, say? Just for safety's sake, like. My neck can only take so much strangulation.'

I slumped into a chair beside him, sadly surveyed the devastation that the raped dwelling had sustained, buried my face in my hands and wept without tears. And sneering Merkel laughed, and patted my shoulder to buck me up.

'Merkel,' I croaked as I raised again my face, 'you're my best friend.'

'You're my best friend, Simeon,' he replied automatically, too swiftly and smoothly to be sincere. 'You know, I'm kind of glad that it's just the two of us again. If I might offer you some advice, you're likely wasting your time with that Jezzie. You deserve better than fucking Jezebel Temple. She seems to me to be a bit of an undiscriminating alley cat, the type who'll go with anything, all you have to do is simply kiss her. She has this unpleasant quality of seeking to acquire boys who count for no more than notches on her bedpost of scores. There's something greedy in it. I reckon she had her heart broken once, and now she's determined not to be hurt again.'

'She wants you!' I snarled with scrunched-up face and wringing fingers, beginning to unburden me brain's baggage, 'It is you, Konrad! Only yourself so sound to whom alone I have told all, poor you! Ah me, you have seen me at stool, and given me stern injunction to wipe my arse and wash my filthy body – just the stuff that the greatest friendships are made of, as you say! But Jezzie wants you. You have no idea, Merkel, how exotic you seem to her! For you were always the only one she has ever really loved.'

'O give over! You sound like Dumbledore talking to Harry Potter.'

'No, no, listen! I take it all back! I revoke my wrath. For I am from start to finish a drama queen who loves a silly scene, how rotten it was of me to make you feel guilty for being better with a babe than baby Simeon, o so childish! Hers is a post or tree that I have not, for all my chatter, ever pissed on. I have no right to her and no right to warn off others from having a go, she's a free body and she'll have what she wants. And it's your good self she wants, boyo, you are the novelty of the month for her, digging into your hand her toothsome giant jaws and fabulous fangs like a shark lusting for its prized prey to suck your blood she longs to lick and pincers into your shoulders to stab, and for all you may not love her, you ought to at least quickly give her a bout of what she wants,

I know enough about the feminine mind to know that she's making it extremely easy and obvious for you, after all, a gal with a fringe like that is fond of fingering, tee-hee, tee-hee, but perhaps I am out of date, perhaps already things are not as they were, and 'twas she who seduced thee, hee hee, while I bled comatose ...'

'You're talking complete shit. It's quite remarkable, really. Lukas, by the way, was very upset, since he didn't know you had designs on her ...'

'Heaven knows,' I continued frothily, 'that poor Kyrie Elysium is gagging for my company, hers is a faithful Catholic love, I ought to swallow my pride and learn to love that impish smile and uncluttered mind, and contemptuously ignore Jezebel's biceps, that lurid bleach-blonde fright wig, those fatty thighs, those sturdy shoulders, all shallow vapid surface effect. I had a remarkable dream last night, in which I was Shem the Penman holed up in his haunted house fiddling about with his worthless excreta, and you were Shaun the Post, the macho man who's good with the girls, a seedy Christ for the ladies, holding forth at length and them all hanging and drooling on his every last uproarious word. This then merged into a phantasmagoric rhapsody where we put on a Players production of Anthony Burgess's execrable musical 'Blooms of Dublin', where Simeon Collins played – superbly and movingly, I might add – the cuckolded Bloom, and Jezzie was the lusty Molly bored of her Poldy, with Merkel her blazing brute Boylan, and poor Kyrie Elysium was the poor Josie Breen, married to the madman and longing for Leo, who wed like a fool her friend. And –'

'You're high as shite. You've gone mad. It's all in your head, man. You'd make an intriguing case study for the psychobabbling crew.'

'For it was only lust in the first place that drew me to her, and for me it is quite certain she lusts not. For you see, I value true love as highly as any poet, and it's been many the night and many the month and many the year since ever I felt that feeling for she that was once so near and dear, sublimest Saruko. But perhaps after all, he, meaning me, cannot yet love a woman since he cannot love and does so loathe himself. And –'

'Aha. There's the crux of it. You know, I'm starting to think that I wouldn't swop places with you for a moment. Inside your head is not somewhere I'd ever want to be! Seems bloody nasty from what I hear!'

'As you must by now have more than gathered, I have a delusional streak in me, wherein my affectations take over, and truly my only love must be of the Dulcinea calibre. Didn't Jezzie herself say that she has grown to hate my laugh? For she can hear its hollowness that threadbare hides a petty despair that knows not its object. And you heard her cite her hatred of my habit of relentlessly talking of "the most depressing things", and didn't she compare your cordial converse so favourably to mediocre melancholy mine? For some people are just by nature incorrigibly flat-headed and flat-footed, and it is no coincidence that I have a small head and you have a big head, nor that my hair is lank and greasy while yours billows up into such a plume that all the girls find it so necessary to flirty comment on and teasing toy with, and that you are a poet who climbs to the stars while I play below in the sand castles with my prose toolkit. And –'

'Ah here now, you're making rather too much of the differences in our hair styles. I recommend less green tea and more sleep.'

'And I shall go further, since these days I've gotten so exhibitionistic, brandishing skeleteons with gusto. Do you remember I mentioned a biography I have read, about Larry Olivier, as written by Roger Lewis? It has the lurid revelation that the great man suffered from a condition called phimosis, wherein the foreskin has gotten too tight during puberty. The passage in question, over whose implications and details I have obsessively mused a thousand times, describes how the foreskin and the head of the penis were imperfectly separated, and when the poor lad tried to unsheathe his knob, he found that fibrous tissue had inflamed and deformed his bits.'

'Queasy ...' Konrad said slowly, making a face, 'I don't like where this is going. What did he do? Was he able to actually have sex? Or what?'

'He had to be circumcised. As I shall have to be. For I have the same thing as he did, as I found out the hard way, during a graduation day's painful tumble in the blood clots of hay, in the dunes when I became a demi-vierge, an act of aborted intercourse that was as nasty, brutish and short as anything Hobbes could conjure. Never having had a wank before, I was unaware of my condition until then. Or maybe I knew, and was always in denial. Unable to jerk it back to jerk off, for want of any elasticity in the vile skin I would happily shed in a second, were it not for the fact that I do so fear the pain and bleeding that the barbarous operation will incur.'

Stricken Merkel frowned and looked concerned. And I sat back and grinned, and nibbled upon a few stray tea leaves that turned my head.

'I am privileged with this information,' he declared at last, 'I shall hold it tightly to my breast in fullest secrecy. But really – are you sure you actually have that? I mean, maybe this is just another of your delusions. It's perfectly natural that the skin be a bit recaltriant at first, and not so conducive to tugging. I had to tear mine. Jesus wept. God. God, I can't believe you never had a wank before. Explains a lot.'

'Of course. This thing is the key to me. It contains my essence. Perfect, no? So silly and yet so sad, abominably moving in the very best tragicomic fashion. There is the man, all too plain and all too mad. All the more reason that pining Jezzie be rightfully thine, and I remain alone on the Earth.'

'O hush, no more of that shit. We'll sort this out. I'll be accompanying you to that college clinic if it's the last thing I do, we'll make you have a little chat with them and see where we stand. Christ. I feel ill.'

He sat in silence and nibbled his lower lip in distaste, as I chuckled at his disquiet. Then a thought, quite unrelated, struck him as of the blue nothing.

'O yeah, I saw some old man leaving the house earlier this morning.'

'What?'

'Yeah, just through the window as I was sitting on the ledge, I saw him strolling off and out the gate, clad in rags with long beard and top hat, exuding just the kind of shabby grandeur I expect you would enjoy, and I remember wishing that you had been beside me to have seen him. And I remember thinking that maybe I had only dreamt him, since I had no memory of such a person ever being at the party. Who could he be?'

But I had already risen in my anguish, and bolted from the table, and ran down the stairs to the room that was once my own, which I now found empty and bereft of its former tenant Arsene. He was gone without a trace, as I found upon checking every corner and niche in which he might hide beneath blankets or lurk behind curtains to pull on me a prank, vanished into air, all the evidence of his wintry season's occupancy left behind to remind me and sadden me, those bizarre pictures on the walls and shelves, the bits of paper torn into many pieces, the food unfinished on the unwashed plates, the staring tray, the discarded clothes, the books of mine he had thumbed and browsed, on whose leaves and spines he left his mucky fingerprints and the scratch of his grimy nails, the cobwebbed mirror in which he might have regarded the growth of his hair, whose flowing locks he might have combed with pincers of my brush to tame their shags, and the stinky contents of the chamber pot beneath the smelly bed.

And I sank upon my boyhood's bed and wondered numb at this dead room vacated by the ghost. A book token lay at the floor by my feet, which token I brushed aside with my toes in despair, brushing aside that which he had intended to give me as a gift, long ago when I gave him the key in the café and left him be, the very last time I had seen him as himself, the last time that we had spoken and been bonded over tea, before his soul was stolen and something took him away on the fading wind.

Konrad had followed me downstairs to that room of death, and warily poked in his large head, smart enough to know he should not speak, padding into the musty dwelling admiring the scattered feathers that had leaked from the duvet, scaring the spiders who fled to the corners at his heavy-booted approach, screwing up his nose at whiff of the excreta, as I mourned and pawed the stains on the tangled sheets, while my friend browsed, sensing an adventure, drawn toward an article into which I had not looked, none but the lump of the old man's hairy suitcase, rotting in a dusty corner. Konrad knelt by the bag, and blew off the layer of sooty dust that made me sneeze as he unlocked its hasp and unclasped its zip, and upturned the sack and dumped its contents on the floor, where they lay in an ungainly pile of dirty pearls for magpies, through which we sifted in search of treasure and enlightenment.

There were three books, by Beckett and Swift and Dostoyevsky, and a change of clothes, and a bobble hat, and a scarf and gloves, and a toothbrush and toothpaste, and a wristwatch and alarm clock, and a mobile phone that had long since died, and a straight razor, and a bottle of some shaving foam that had dried up to brittle paste. But most intriguing of all, as we found in our survey, was a set of notebooks, very ancient and weathered, tightly bound with crimson ribbon, upon which Konrad's eyes alighted and grew hungry, as he gave me a glance asking silent permission to delve within the volumes. For answer, I grabbed one of them myself, and excitedly undid the ruby string to release the exhaling pages, at which my friend chuckled and did ditto in his turn.

Spreadeagled on the floor and rocking on our reverent knees, we browsed the contents of these notebooks for hours, travelling in time through browning page after yellowing page of his cramped and scuttling script, inky as a spider let off the leash to blotch the sheet, a handwriting whose sense was difficult to interpret, looping and bending over many long years down the aisles of his memory, clarity fluctuating according to the state of his mind at whatever time it was he wrote those words, the margins riddled with charocal sketches of places and people he had seen, lukewarm illustrations to enliven his descriptions, to pass the time and keep him sane.

These were the manuscripts of his memoirs of which in the past I had heard him sometimes speak, with Volume One devoted to his chess exploits, and Volume Two to the arcane Irish books he bought and sold, Volume Three to hurling and the rising fortunes of his Wexford team, Volume Four to the prowess of the county's operas, and Volume Five to his love affairs, whether real or imagined, whether unrequited or unsatisfyingly fulfilled, all the matter discussed in a guarded prose that stifled passion. Much was unintelligible, dropping names and incidents, which meant little or nothing to ignorant Konrad and I, readers from decades later of a misty past he could but ill convey, though I warmed and cried to see frequent mention made of me and my father and the waspish tenor Martin Graves, his best and most enduring friends who never failed him, of the rosy trips to Curracloe Beach we made with him, those summer voyages to the dunes and sand that he always treasured in his rosy lights, for they brought back memories of youth, of how his father watched him fly the kites and paddle in the shallows, seeming reborn in me, unworthy successor to his festering legacy, so callous and uncaring, I who had barely known him, in whose high regard I unwittingly stood, guileless stand-in for dwindling hope and unaffected fatherly love. We read of his great romance, the woman he may have married had life been kinder and blander, for whom he bought and scrubbed the house, the anorexic bulimic whose name was always illegible, scratched out with furious swishes of his nib, who decided she did not love him and doomed him thus to solitude when she went on her way and left him stranded in her wake, going mad as a night watchman in the dark bowels of the weather station, affrighted by a man with a goat's head who taunted him with visions upon his playing cards that flashed upon the victim's retinas, and bid him crack, tearing open holes in his head and heart, pounding wounds that never healed in his sickness, expressed sometimes in nosebleeds that assailed him even while he wrote, dotting his page with drops of blood leaking from his sneezing nostrils.

Tears were in my eyes as I flung open my window for want of air, and crawled onto the little roof beyond the ledge, to drown in the vine as I hugged his pages, yearning and longing and missing him of such a sudden, such as never before I had felt the loss and chasm he left in the void, wondering whither he had gone and whether ever he would return, a lost brick in a gloomy city. Howling to the quiet winds, talking gobbledygook about constricted foreskins and elder men of blubber who fell in love with tattooed youths, drooling over the prospect of circumcision and weeping for Jezzie's curves, I grew elated in my grief on the sunny verandah, and beckoned to Konrad, raving of the urgent need to leave our domain and go and scour the streets, in search of lost Arsene O'Colla again, my bygone friend, of whom the singer had not heard in seven years.

So we left my father's house in its ruins, letting the sleepers lie and persist in their dreaming devices, locking them all in with a click of the key, a surefire fire hazard I had not the time nor sense to ponder, as we ran down the streets like squealing orphans, juggling his diaries and quoting our favourite passages, Konrad and I, witless losers on an invisible trail whose scent we could not catch. We traipsed by the Temple Bar bank, scraggly and ragged, eyes bloodshot and tails bushy, accosting a parade that had gone by, hailing the tatters of its banners and asking where on earth was our Arsene, dismissed as drunken thugs by the men who marched and passed us by, uncaring soldiers of Christ who had no time for our folly. Konrad raved about Albert's face and flab, as I brandished Arsene's papers and flung them to the breeze, juggling his memoirs as I wept and cursed the colourless sky that made me squint, leaning against the slippery marble of the Bank, and slipping and sliding repeatedly and incessantly, a Chaplinesque stunt at which Merkel roared in mirthless laughter that shook his sides and rattled my wobbling tears, clapping his hands and cajoling bystanders to throw us pennies to fund our forages, and perhaps maybe finance my circumcision, pricey as that would doubtless be, to drop some pennies into the Simeon Collins Cock fund, in exchange for which he'll clown for charity like a hobo on the run from the circus police, sporting floppy shoes and red radish nose.

We scurried and dived amid the shoals of traffic, for Konrad never looked at the lights, convinced that a poet could not be killed, and mounted Christ Church hill, catching no sight of our prodigal hero who might have been gone from the world forever, lost to a beauty that had been there before, and then I saw my school of olden younger days, St Patrick's Cathedral, 1432 founded, a running joke since then, beside of which Nash's pub did dourly squat, where I got drunk on graduation day when I found out my limits. And we ran on, till seven or eleven on doomsday's toll.

CHAPTER FIFTY-SEVEN

He knew that he was being hunted, Arsene-Elijah, and felt the footsteps of the boys on the breeze. He saw them staggering through the alleys and gutters some miles behind him, veering round the city in listless circles as they accosted the parades, avoiding urinals and pissing on the cafeteria's graffiti, quoting words from his maudlin journals, which meant nothing now to him. So in his guile and cunning, he inverted the proceedings, and hid in the quiet of the cathedral's close as they wound by Nash's and reversed their tracks, and then he followed them instead through the shadows, floating at their heels unseen in the white light, admiring the Russian vine that clogged the brickwork of the Deanery. Pursued by the prophet, Konrad and Simeon then swooped to George's Street via Ship Street and Dublin Castle's cobblestones, quacking and flapping their wings and scaring the tourists, as atop opposing bollards they slouched like busts of sages, striking contemplative poses that were almost constipated. Holding back, the gaunt fugitive stalked them around the corner, through the dark cavern of Arcade to Grogan's, where they sat outside on silver chairs, penniless and skinflint, and sipped glasses of water, served by sexy Niamh who had a blonde ponytail and was good with a whip. Arsene-Elijah tiptoed closer and stood across the street in a dingy doorway opposite the bar, smiling with his jagged choppers, watching their heedless faces, glazed as the undersides of empty fishes that had been boned, knowing he need not fear them now.

The poet Tadgh O'Mara, recast as a tramp, came stumbling by, and leant over the smoker's railing to ask the boys if they had a copper to spare for tea and a biscuit and maybe a whiskey within where it was warmer, for his bones were cold and he was getting older. But they had not a cent to spare between them, so they mumbled in shrugging apology, to the vagabond bard's chagrin. Tadgh was put out, but remained for a moment, pilfering a beer mat upon which he would later write a poem about the freckly man who had beaten him up, his unlikely son-in-law who stole his child who did not remember him, and the fat man who had later saved him, the ghastly hound's inheritor.

Recalling this incident, stalling for time, and liking the boys, one of whom he thought he knew somehow, he then quickly recounted the story of the dog who had bit him, which hoary tale had become, over the course of his travels in the city from barroom to eatery, something of a set piece, which he always recited in exchange for a ciggie, of which fags they had none neither. Disgusted, he stormed away barking like a dog, to the amusement of peeping Arsene-Elijah, and the bemusement of Konrad and Simeon.

Harry Carson, looking dashing in his swishy hat and feathered scarf, then came outside for a smoke. He accosted Niamh, in act of entering as he was exiting, and treated the barmaid to a suggestive jest, and she repaid him with a look of ice even though she loved the flirt. Chuckling, the errant rake sat down beside the huddled pair of boys, and sucked upon his Camel and puffed forth a blue ring in air. Konrad, roused by the scent of nicotine, harried the elder man for a smoke, his one-time charm quite muted by his torpor and fatigue. But Harry was affable, and proffered a stalk to the youth.

Simeon caught sight of his father's friend, whom he had not seen in months and soon was moved to catch his eye, begging recognition. And Harry took a second or two to remember his best friend's son, for he was always bad with faces if not with names, but once he knew him he was warmer. And Arsene-Elijah smiled to see them banter awkwardly as if nothing was out of joint, the gallant dying lion looking splendid beside the youths with celery limbs that flailed and slumped, recalling old acquaintances and stirring up some pots of gossip while sucking their fags in the dying day, as Harry asked how was father Eugene getting on in the surly abroad, and Simeon asked after the health of Tom Mathews and the counter crew team, and Konrad interpolated with some nuggets of

Petronius, mentioning the name of Albert, at which Simeon stamped on his foot to have him hush, for bad blood was between those two Southern Protestants Mr Potter and Mr Carson, on the score of exorbitant loans unreturned, a weighty debt unfit to boast of.

But smoking Harry, in any case, did not hear Mr Potter's name as dropped by Konrad, scratching his tufts of dwindling mane and shifting in his seat, for he was, by his own admission, a poor listener all his life, for whom what went in one ear was gone out the other in an instant, talking at people rather than to them, wagging his head and assuming all the details already, ending their answers with surmises of his own, knowing everyone yet knowing nobody, making noise to avoid his woes that welled up in the silence that fell between his beers, two of which he then bought for the boys, in a gesture of generous extravagance that he would regret by nightfall, when pestered by the crappy painters to buy their shabby canvases, at the height of his drunkenness when he was the most vulnerable to be gulled and fooled by a conman boasting beret and brushes.

And Arsene-Elijah strained his ears, and heard Harry telling Simeon repeatedly that his father was a good man, and that he was smart and had a head on his shoulders, such as he Harry professed over and over he did not have, beating himself up and bemoaning his age, lamenting his decline toward which he ceaselessly gravitated, awaking every morning cursing every choice he'd made the day before, always staying for one more in spite of the protest of his emptying pockets, and the warning of the coffers that soon would be airy, the stocks depleted and the liquid kitty robbed, loot of the piggy bank drunk up and the English Granny living on immortal, holding onto her fortune with cold and grasping fingers that would not relinquish their wealth to her wayward nephew of whom she disapproved, whose picture on her mantelpiece had been removed, supplanted in favour of his conservative sister Anita, with whom he always rowed.

And his words began to slur as the quiet hour flagged, and the boys shifted in increasing sadness, mingled with callous disinterest, as Konrad took off his glasses and sighed, and Simeon gazed pained at the large red face that had been more handsome once, addled and overloaded, growing repetitive in his remorse, pressing the boy to whom he longed to say a word of warning, struggling to summon wise advice for life that never came, for his mind was a drunken fog and his speech began to soon deny him.

Then Simeon's phone began to ring, for Jezzie and Lucia and the lads were woken finally, about whom the despairing adventurers had quite forgotten, trapped and restless in his father's house and gagging to be let loose. So Merkel and Collins rose from their creaking seats, and made their excuses to Mr Carson who was put out, and doffed his hat and bid goodnight and waved, as the young men left him behind alone on a silver chair outside of the tavern, forlorn in a lonely pool of scarlet light.

He shook and bowed his sorry head, slumped on his chest and contemplating folly, fancying another jar just in case his scholarly buddy Raymond (who had a Swiftian thesis always in the works, always on the cards yet never quite completed, due to be marked by I— C— C—, at least ostensibly) be free and willing to get wined. So Harry Carson did not hear the prophet's approach, gliding over from the niche across the street in which he had stood and spied, until he raised his face and saw then the shaggy apparition leaning over the railing before him. He saw nothing of familiar Arsene O'Colla in the face of Arsene-Elijah O'Colla, dwarfed by the beard and top hat, and the array of golden teeth he bared as he waved upon dumbfounded Harry who sat in silence, cowed by the glowing eyes, and heard the old man lay out the course of life.

Arsene-Elijah grinned and spoke in an italicized accent that bewitched his listener, numbed by a voice as fruity and rich as a ham's, mellifluous as Ralph Richardson's, yeasty as onion skin off which layers of pathos might be peeled, to disclose the laughing bulb of the clove that cared for nothing. He told Harry that he need not worry for too much longer. He told Harry that he was not as badly off as some. But he knew too that Harry would still despair awhile, and declare himself disgusted with Dublin's indolence, and in his lust for a remedy travel abroad to Hispanic lands, to foreign climes where he knew not the language, in the heat where he would not drink but also would not speak, on whose distant beaches he might roam and feel the more alone as the washing surf mocked him, writing letters to faraway Eugene that were his lifelines, forced to move back when his funds ran dry, to reconcile with Mr Baker and notch up the bookshop job again. And he would break down, lonely in his humbug, with not a happy prospect close in view, and proclaim himself depressed, obliged to pop pills to pep him up and improve his moods, doing workshops with others who climbed the ladder of twelve-step programmes, drowning in tedium, tired of his character's part, sick to death of life's dreary sameness.

But there was hope, Arsene-Elijah went on, hope waiting for Mr Carson in the wings even though he might not sense it. For all he may have thought his last Russian Ivana was the last of love for him, there were other Russian Ivanas with whom he could try his chance. His age bracket having arisen, he might try dining in the Sheraton Hotel, and bond with the wrinkly charlady there, another older Ivana who was kindly and sensible at saving, whom he might charm and woo, for love-making would win the day for all that she had no English and he had no Russian, for all that she was hardly in the league of the sexy bombs after whom he'd chased before, a wizened Russian doll in truth, but after an age one finds that, when fucking in the dark, most bodies are like most other bodies, and the more yards of flesh one has to fondle the better off one is, schooled in that international language of gropes and slurps that defy mere words, and so they might live and be content in the happy silence of easy companionship, a balm to ward off lonely angst, Harry Carson and Ivana Egorova, as cute a couple as ever you'd see on the street, the loudmouth Dublin rake and the pint-sized Soviet charlady, strolling along the sunny promenades teaching each other little words for oranges and condoms, though at her age that latter prospect hardly need be feared, an added blessing to a union that was so cosy and easy that a distant marriage may not seem too much out of place, no more fitting close to the sketchy chronicle of Mr Carson's hectic days.

'*Mark my words*' Arsene-Elijah concluded, '*Seek Ivana, Henry*!'

And the old ghost Arsene-Elijah O'Colla, his duty done, leant back from Grogan's railings, and lifted his top hat and turned aside from the puzzled smoker, and strolled away with his robes billowing and sandals slapping upon the pavement's grime, soon lost among the nightclub crowds, whose guffawing heads he whacked with his staff, disappearing into the darkness before they could protest.

Harry Carson rubbed his jaw and sniffled, wondering just what all that drivel had been about that had flown right over his head. And although the morning after he could not recollect a word he had been told, the deeper sense was distilled in his bones. Some time later, while dining in a certain hotel far beyond his means, he saw a plump hen in an apron wheeling her trolley by him, whose wrinkly arm he grabbed, feeling again the old hunger, turning on the oily charm as she blinked and spoke some Russian, as he flashed a grin, and told Ivana Egorova that he would very much like to lick her snatch.

To which she replied, in the only words of English that she knew:

'Joost think positiff!'

CHAPTER FIFTY-EIGHT

We could not find Arsene, who had vanished and become one with the city's masonry. Tiring and ailing, grieving over Mr Harry Carson's lament, Konrad and I gave up the chase, and so wound home upon the party's summons, to continue the mindless merriment. Bare-chested boys and giggly girls streamed out the windows of my father's house, sharing fags and exchanging gossips as they sat on the ledges, and waved upon our shambling approach below from on high, streaks of blue paint shining still upon our beatific faces. Upon Jezzie's suggestion, we decided to pay Albert another visit on his own grounds, over in the Mount of August, whose higher hallowed terrain we would dare ascend and defile with our waggishness, another adventure such as she loved.

Better yet, as one of his messages slyly informed us, today was his fifty-second birthday, and we could be his beloved guests, the only children who ever acknowledged the momentous import of the date, one that otherwise would have passed utterly unnoticed by an uncaring world in which he did not matter.

And detained by the maidens and their interminable ritual of makeup and its application, we were further sidetracked by a stop at Whelan's where Jezebel grew drunker from the foam of our stolen pints, oft collapsing upon the smoking area's wet stones, rolling under the tables in pools of her own green vomit, until gallant Konrad suavely hoisted her back to her feet, brushing her down and bestowing a warm and maternal kiss upon her pallid brow, at which smooch I seethed and gnashed my fangs.

It was not until closing time that we staggered to Merriman's, whose door was bolted shut by now, though light shone still within, as outside we stood despondent and rapped upon the glass while the rain began to teem. And ailing Jezzie slumped to the cobbles and writhed while we rang up Albert, who was predictably sat at the counter in his anniversary's languor. Defying regulations, he lumbered to the locked door and opened it of his own accord, taking over his local on his own terms, the birthday boy who would lift a finger to the surly Scrooge who presided over the premises, dour Merriman who eyed our drunken entry with intense disapproval. And a queer bunch we must have looked, the greasy youths of fluff and down and beard, armed with the comely reeling girl whose hair was ultramarine, almost as blue as were our cheeks, come to pay homage to the fat emperor, our glorious Fagan of blubber, ringleader of our bandit gang, who met the publican's glare with open palms, raised in a protest of false innocence.

'What? You didn't even stand me a drink!' Mr Potter protested, 'And on this day, of all bloody days too! Give me another round of vodka shots and salt.'

'This isn't on,' Merriman snarled, 'Who let those kids in? Didn't you see the door was locked? Do you run this place? If this happens again, you're barred, understand?'

'O give over, it's raining outside, and this is my birthday party. Now gentlemen, what'll you be having? A cider for the lady, I suppose?'

But our invasion remained a bone of contention, and the birthday round was spoiled by Merriman's insistent rowing with irascible Albert who held his ground and glared him down with paunchy fists at the ready, their knuckles clenched.

Then with a thud of her large head, Jezebel slumped unconscious upon the table, and we had no choice but to leave. Ushered out by the spoilsports, we crossed over the street and under the arch in tipsy array, the lump of Jezzie manned by Konrad with an arm around her waist, livening up enough to sing along to a rebellious ballad or two, such passions as they shared, shaking fists at the rain they would defy.

And down Mr Potter's wetted steps we schoolchildren descended, into our perverse mentor's seedy den, past the potted plants and ferns our chortling stumbles brushed, into the badger's lukewarm abode where he made us welcome, on whose dirty couches and breaking settees we settled ourselves. The fading lady, a sleeping beauty, was laid down on the dusty sofa in all her full and ravishing length, and it was Albert who attended to her with a most admirable adroitness, casting off his coat and spreading it all over her like a rich dark blanket to keep the woman warm, tucking her in with a consideration and expertise well schooled in comforts domestic, a wiser older man such as she always longed for, discontented with the callowness of her contemporaries on whom she was forced to simulate her crushes. And lastly, he took gentle hold of her dozing head for a fraction of a second, and in the interval slipped a silken cushion upon the sofa's arm, upon which then he laid down her snoring head to dream in peace – a gesture conducted so smoothly, with such seedy ruined elegance, such perfect liquid grace, that years of cultivation and generations of rehearsal could never have bettered it.

In the centre of the littered floor, by the cracked tiles of the decaying kitchenette, was a black plastic bag of goodies into which he bid us dip, guzzling the cans he kept in his hoard, some of which had been opened before and then ignored, and as a consequence tasted of acrid vinegar that made us wince at the sharpness, as our massive host strolled to his music box, and ground out tunes to swell the ruinous ambience. And though he had professed that music was his weak point, he yet proved as knowledgeable and Catholic in his taste as ever, tossing forth Rasumovsky Quartets into the haunting air at whose aching strings I cried, followed by grooves of Armstrong's jazz that moved Johnny to do the languid samba, wiggling hips and strutting like a ratty chicken, while Merkel and Grimaldi and Lukas the Shag drank their tins and smoked their stubs.

And Mr Potter produced his camera, given him for free by the Irish Chess Union to chronicle his games, and began to take shots like a tourist, keen to capture snapshots of such rare revelry, which pictures would afford him comfort on the darker nights alone that would inevitably follow, for his hours of loneliness greatly outnumbered those in which he kept company, even with mere wretches such as we, who were at least better than nothing. And I sat beside the snoozing Jezzie on whose back I laid a paranoid hand unseen, lightly stroking her thigh unperceived, which paltry contact of assumed intimacy photographer Albert observed from his throne, and snorted in disdain.

'Folly, Simeon! Folly!' he barked in glee, 'she does not fancy you, lad, so set aside those delusions. You may not remember at a certain point last night, just before you went to bleeding, but I saw you attempting to hold her hand, at which she recoiled and hissed – don't touch me, don't touch me! No, the body language is quite clear. You made the fatal mistake of becoming her friend first. Any other intentions she will disregard as out of hand. Take my word, speaking as an older man who has had sex in a cinema. And after all, there are others here on whom she has her eye, juh, juh, juh? …'

And I will never forget how he sat there on his chair, by his crowded desk on which all the rotting books were piled and littered, off whose support they fell and tumbled, sacrificed to the floor's filth and grime, and how the dim lamp's pool of amber light cast half of his enormous face in shadow, the lower lip distended and dribbling, the bovine jowls quivering, on whose prickly skin some unshaven hairs protruded, an early beard whose growth he did not notice nor deter, the watery eyes keen and sharp, sipping his can and sternly admonishing me with a fatherly glare. And when I had heeded his dampening lesson and taken it pained to heart, he directed his lens upon her sleeping cleavage, and drew down the black blouse to admit a peek of more creamy flesh for his focus, and took a dirty picture of her pert little tits. Then he cast a hungry glance about his room to land on his favourite jabbering Merkel telling a story, at sight of whom Potter's piggy face lit up with his lecher's intent, as he slurped and slurred and sighed.

'Yes …' he mumbled, '… it is him that she most wants to touch and hold to her … small wonder, too … such rouge on those cheekbones …'

We heard a barking, and all heads turned to greet the woofing dog that had popped up on his doorstep, the albino orphan bequeathed him by windy fate. So Mr Potter grandly introduced us to Snowy his pet, an alabaster brute whose tongue was long and dripping, lathering our calves with friendly licks, whose ample head I caressed, while listening confusedly to the farther droning of the Angelus that faintly petered through from another room in that circus tent, reciting the litany in a croaking accent that seemed inhuman, chiming oddly with the dog's bow-wows.

'That's only my parrot,' Albert said, noting my abstracted gaze, 'I call him Monty. Or perhaps Orson would be better. Or sometimes even Sam.'

Rowdy Merkel wanted a dare, blushing crimson under the hungry ray directed at him by Mr Potter's stare across the room. *Push the old man just a bit further, you'll have a better story to tell in the morning.* So, egging on his comrade Lukas, he stood and shouted, hailing himself 'a naked boy, a naked boy!' as he cast off his shirt and divested himself of his jeans, and did a jig in his boxers, stamping on the discarded cans and knocking over a set of plants in their pots, rousing Albert's anger, mingled with terrible desire.

'Yah! Yah! We're the naked boys! We're the naked boys!' bellowed the evil only child to stir temptation, grasping the naked arm of Lukas the Shag and cavorting about in a loony's nudie tango. Johnny Fritzl, a man of morals, frowned and looked on in disapproval and disgust, while Grimaldi cackled his laughter, and Snowy woofed, and I sulked, and Jezzie raised her head from sleep, blinking puzzled and brushing her fringe.

But Albert Potter, pushed too far, rose from his stoop with a dreadful leer, brandishing his camera whose lens and shutter were flashing, and waddled over to the pair of dancing boys who were nearly nude, prancing in their scanty cladding that barely sheathed their loins from our indignant view.

'Look at me, Albert!' Konrad roared, 'I'm a naked boy!'

'O no you're not!' savage Potter growled, raising a bear's arm to knock the loudmouth Merkel down, while timid Lukas retreated to the sofa where Jezzie lay. Beaten and struck by Potter's punch of shoulder, willing victim Merkel toppled laughing to the musty carpet where he rolled in a tangle of bare limbs, as his flabby attacker stood over him, and planted a firm foot on Merkel's throat to hold the wiggling creature down, and with one hand prepared to cock his lens, while the other reached out to Konrad's dark boxers, the rim of which he clasped while the writhing boy guffawed.

'You're not a naked boy, Merkel!' Albert Potter snarled in lusty rapture, 'You're still wearing your bloody underpants, after all! I tell you, if you are to be a writer, you must learn to be more precise in your language!'

His grubby paw tugged down the boxers, exposing Merkel's donkey dong.

'There! There! Now! Now we may well say that you are naked!'

And Albert Potter took a picture of the naked evidence shrivelling below him.

Lifting up his foot, admiring the filthy picture in the digital preview box, the fat man released his naked conquest, who trilled and scurried upright, and fled from the house as Potter protested, too large to pursue the flashing boy who bolted up the steps, and raced along the pavement to the leafy square in the drizzling darkness, ignoring the cuts lent his bare soles by the shards of broken glass, and did an unclad lap around the square dementedly jogging like a naked lunatic, before returning panting to the underground den of sin, by which time the orgiastic riot of disgust was on the wane.

Johnny Fritzl had nodded off in an armchair. Disturbed, Grimaldi had left to enjoy a midnight walk to clear his head. Subtly nudged off the narrow sofa to allow Lukas to lie supine beside Jezzie, I contented myself with lying beneath the coffee table, prostrate amid the ashes of fags, the rubble of violated plants whose earth was upturned, and sticky pools of spilt drinks. Albert Potter had switched off the lights, and was on the point of retiring to bed with Snowy when nude Konrad reappeared, flushed in the dim.

For some reason, perhaps to stir the waters deeper and make the shit splutter, he insisted on accompanying Albert to his bed and getting in beside him, under that mountain of blankets that swayed the moonscape in the dirty old man's bedroom, where Monty-Samuel-Orson-Johnson the parrot softly gurgled a final rosary. And in the dark, together in bed, they lay side by side quietly breathing in anticipation, the fatter older man and the naked youth, in a murky reminiscence of Greco-Roman times. Perhaps the deluded classicist in Konrad saw himself as Alcibiades to Albert's debauched Socrates. Perhaps he secretly craved to be raped by this version of his older self, longing for youth to be swallowed up by alcoholic middle age. For when one has within one's reach the one and only love requited of a life so monstrously prolonged, one is not assailed by those feelings of squeamishness permissible in the fainthearted, but which true love disdains. But the older man, filled with a guilty rush that illuminated his folly, got cold feet, and saw the lurid madness all too clearly. Instead, he gruffly rolled over on his side and put his face to the wall. He would not play along with the sick charade anymore.

'Well!' he snorted as he dozed off, 'we're hardly going to have sex, so let's just give it a rest for today … enough of that … fruity bullshit …'

And in the darkened living room, as seated Johnny snored, I lay on the mucky floor trembling, and heard Lukas on the nearby sofa whisper a saucy suggestion to horny Jezzie, who was only too eager for adoration. And on the dusty sofa-bed I heard them smooch and kiss, wrapped round each other entwined like gluey flies or mating snails, sliding out of their impeding garments to rub skin against skin, sucking and slobbering and screwing on the detested sofa in their arid passion. And naked Konrad, who had risen giggling from Albert's bed, bumbling by to the bathroom, flicked on the light, and wryly cast an eye upon their coupling, and loudly made a jocular comment on their black affair, hoping that they were enjoying their heterosexual relationship to the utmost.

They did not answer, but it was all too clear that they were, so far as I could hear, lying not even a foot away in the debris, listening to their dalliance for all the whole of the long dark night, as I fretted in anguish, and pretended to sleep amid the squalor.

The best years of our lives, Arsene had said.

O yes old man, the very best, indeed.

CHAPTER FIFTY-NINE

But the brother of Elijah was stirring ill at ease in the northern-facing caravan parked in quasi-Arcadia, tossing and turning under the heavy blankets while the Banshee slumbered. And some dim time before the new day broke, he awoke beside her with tears in his eyes, having been crying in his sleep. He had once again been beset by nightmares.

He sat up sharply, and roughly wiped his aching eyes to be rid of the gross visions that had harried him, and poked his head through the jingling curtains of their door as he cast off their duvet, admiring the blue moonlight swathing the wooded fields outside afar, sadly smiling to hear the snoring of the Puck and Pooka who slept by wheels of the wagon, in lumps not far from the hooves of dozing Balthazar.

And as he wrapped a robe about his shoulders to guard his bones from the twilight chill, and stepped down onto the wet grass, taking care not to rupture the repose of those who slept around him, and began to pace in sombre circles around their caravan, he wondered why he could have been distressed in sleep, when all that he had planned was seemingly in motion. For here they were together again, a merry band of knaves settled in an Arcadian nook – but for what? And this perhaps was what disturbed him most, this thought that he knew not what now to do, having assumed all along that inspiration would arrive the instant the moment came, dropped into his head on cue, which callous certainty had now been undermined, once their site was found in this foreign clime where all had gathered at his heeded bidding. Wise as he was, he did not know very much. All the more reason why he pined for his brother who might explain all, scent of whose ghost loomed all the stronger in these winds that blustered where now they lay, lurking somewhere in the city's brickwork, behind a hedge or beneath a tree, sprawled in an alley's gutter lying in devious wait out of sight.

He seemed sometimes scarce an inch away, so The Mad Monk thought, skulking upon the very air one breathed, so he mused as he padded in his brother's shadow through vales of the park's nocturne, and knelt by a pond to slurp some dribbles from the dark waters, whereon whose mirrored surface the insomniac herons still were on the prowl for fishes, scanning the pool with beady eyes in search of a telltale splash of fin, or ripple of a tail as they swam through the deeps, sucking through their scales and gills.

The Mad Monk watched them and envied them. He too had once been aimless as were they, living only to keep on living, and thriving on such drifting, until the encompassing notion of his improving project fired him and gave him purpose, however vague his aims. But day by grey day his weariness persisted, and worse yet, his health, so hitherto unfailing, had begun to falter. He was seen to grow hoarser in his speech, getting more stooped in his stance, crouching like an older man who hobbled the earth in pain, coughing up blood on Maggie's pillow, urinating in the bushes with mounting agony, displaying such signs of ageing as smacked suspiciously of mortality. The Puck and Pooka wondered at the evidence of his greater indolence that roused their unspoken disgust, uncomprehending of his desire for more repose that met his failing will, moved at times to ponder whether the liquid fire of the Faerie King, the same flame as they had administered to Lamb's Bull, whether that flame's charms and powers were temporary ones only. With their help, The Mad Monk had cheated bodily death; but he was not cut out for the ranks of the immortals, such as stones and rocks embodied, weathering the world's storms to be ground down to powdered sands by the waves. He would conquer no longer; he would submit. He would win no more wars and burn no more cities, but would rather put his feet up and puff upon his pipe, smiling at the stars, recalling languid days when he and Elijah had chomped upon their mushrooms free from cares.

Dimly, in the guts, no matter what was said or what lies he told, he sensed his fading day was done for good, and his fallow baton must be passed.

In the murk, he discerned a starlit clump of such fungi that had wooed him in his youthful days, sprouting from the lank banks of the pond's moist shanks where now he sat in gloom. For the sake of old times, he picked one such mushroom, and ate it, nibbling in distaste, for its bitterness repelled him, and made him fear for poison. And as he chewed and swallowed, he remembered one last notion that had moved him, which he had all but forgotten, a goal that was attainable, one that might put him at peace.

Writing poems for darling Megan Devlin had given him satisfaction such as nothing else in this place had done, and fulfilled him to a human extent he had not known. And he now recalled the impetus of the socks and scarves that set him going down that inky route, and the windy promises he had made in the tumbledown lyrics, with the talk of a child chasing kites in the sky, such a child as the former mother longed for. She might not give birth, but he could still create, and make such a child as would fill the void in their spectral lives, to carve the child of grace that all of them longed for, an inheritor he would sculpt himself, with his own two hands and homemade tools.

He smiled in the darkness. To build a son was a task not so too arduous, even with his fading strength, for still with his dwindling powers he could handle clay or chip at pliable marble, whatever choice material he chose. And The Mad Monk smiled again the wider to fancy himself in his new role of Geppetto-Michelangelo, crafting his firstborn man, an Adam or Pinocchio to enchant his childless mistress. He himself had never had a son; now was the time to rectify that lifelong omission for good.

Hacking, coughing, clutching his burning chest as he lurched up from the pond's banks, he sensed again how short a time remained to him to carry out this chore of hope, pressing again more insistently upon him the urgency of the task, a deed that wanted doing in the instant. He could stall no longer, and must act now or never, to ward off the beckon of night. Staggering back through clumps of leaves that scratched his face as he parted the branches, he saw their caravan parked by the cross, and on the horizon, where sounds of the waking city wafted, he saw the first rose of dawn. And crowded about the meadow he saw a herd of deer had gathered, their speckled backs dusted by the early lights, daubed silver by the sinking stars, and painted red by the emerging morning's sun.

Upon the snoozing fauns and stags he smiled as he approached them in hobbling, pondering upon what materials he might employ to make his child, whether it be of wood, or clay, or rock, whichever would be most enduring and versatile and simple to sculpt or carve for a dying man in his condition, not to speak of the tricky technical problem of how he was to endow the stillborn fabric with life, or at least imbue it with life of a kind – she might like a wind-up toy, fired by electrical clockwork that sparked as cogs ground and the creaky puppet wheeled, workings of which gadgetry he confessed he had not an iota, though maybe Fergie or Robbie could lend a claw in that direction.

But then, whiles stonily grinning and mumbling his plans, he caught sight of a thing moving among the herd ahead, a creature that was not of the deer, though moved as if it were, and they seemed to accept it as such. But whereas they were fulsome and furred, this thing was a skeleton, roving and jangling as it dipped to munch the grass, with not a peck of flesh clinging to its frame of bones, a cuckoo in the nest whose intruding horns sparred those of their stags. He watched the skeletal creature butt its fellows with prods, and he squinted in his wonderment at the bony orphan who mingled with the unquestioning deer, recalling a goose he had seen by the canal, a lonely goose who lived among the swans, and thought himself one of them.

And so The Mad Monk met at last with none but Peadar Lamb's Bull.

This long lost creature of legend and lore was a myriad yards removed from its pastoral origins of yore, doomed to a miserly life alone in its unearthly state of deathliness, seeking solace in the blue moon cows whom he rode, hiding elsewhere mid such herds as these, whose spotted backs afforded some downy camouflage for the bony beast who filled their russet ranks.

But The Mad Monk gave not a second to marvel as he hastened over, seeing only an opportunity – if he needed materials, here were some before his eyes, ready-made and fired, sparked already with elusive life he need but merely grab, and chisel down to the childish shape of grace he proposed.

'O me bull, me bony bull, ye shalt be a bull no more,' he wheedled as he prowled through the long grass on hands and knees toward the heedless beast, 'why, I need just take me hammer and hack off them horns, and rearrange them ribs, and whittle his hips to a human scale, and give him a thoroughbred brushing down, and tidy up his fiery eyes whose blaze allures, and fit him out with the equipage of a toy boy, o such joy shall be hers then, when she sees this bully boy recast as our own – c'mere, me son!'

All caution forgotten, the mad old man unwisely pounced on the Bull from behind, taking it short in the glum morn. It snorted and reared, scattering the surrounding deer glancing up from their startled grazing, all taking flight upon sight of the scuffle, as the Bull rattled its bones onto which the ragged man held on tight, howling to the brightening sky a crazed vindication of his designs.

'My son!' he squawked, 'My son! Dost thou not know thy maker?'

The noise of the clumsy squabble awoke the dozers who lay outside beside the caravan. Bolting to their feet, the Puck and Pooka rubbed their eyes and beheld the fray, keeping discreet distance, uncomprehending of his stifled yowls that enjoined them to assist his hopeless pursuit. Eyes heavy with their fatigue, they barely registered what they saw, uncomprehending that here was the treasure from their past prank, unearthed afresh at last for better ends, if it could but only be held down for a minute.

For then The Mad Monk lost hold of the Bull of bones, who snorted and heaved, and trampled all over his vainglorious captor, cracking his brittle ribs whose snap rang crisp in the dewing air, and kicked him in the face with a skeletal hoof, then turned and galloped off toward the east, facing down the red and rising sun. Distressed, Goodfellow and McPhellimey stumbled over to offer belated help to their defeated squire, who panted and gasped as he was hoisted upright onto unsteady feet whose soles were wobbly, ignorant of his streaming wounds that muddied his robes, eyes only for the retreating creature making for the hills in a final break of freedom.

'We've not lost him yet!' The Mad Monk babbled, 'Come quickly boys, let us make haste to give chase before he outruns us to the verge of the sea, at the very world's end beyond which there is no going!'

His minders had no idea what he was saying. Shirking their support, he tried then to run, but he was frail, and his own broken bones were ominously rattling in their deluded frame. Tottering forward a few steps, he then collapsed in an ungainly heap, bemoaning his injuries and growing infirmity. In sorrow and confusion the Pooka heaved him over his shoulder, as the Puck awoke Balthazar and bade him get ready for a last trot, while Moloch the fat cat stretched and yawned, and prepared to tag along one last time.

And onto the grumbling donkey's grey back the ailing hero was laid by the goat, pointing a feeble finger after the path taken by the Bull they must seek, whose bones would provide him with the means to make his woman a gift, the last and greatest he would ever give. He would leave something behind him, an heir to enact the Abode's building, to rally the troops of disciples to fulfill the sketchy foundations that were all that his weakening hands could lay, etched on sand to be drowned with a lap by the next surf.

'I think he's going senile again,' muttered the Puck to the Pooka, who gravely concurred as he whipped the donkey's hide to start him forth on this final journey.

'Fare thee well, Nutmeg me love!' The Mad Monk croaked, his bulk prostrate on Balthazar's back as they began their trek, raising a shaking arm to wave at the caravan from whence they departed, 'See you come sundown! I'm going to make a gift for you!'

But Maggie never received that gift – he never saw her again.

CHAPTER SIXTY

For upon awaking in the morning to find that her lover was gone from her side, taking all his retainers with him, she took his disappearance as her cue to depart at last herself, and see if she would be missed. Gathering all her shawl around her, knotting tight about her turkey's neck her scarf, she cast off the blankets and rose from the pillows, and quit their caravan for the dawning air. Threading through the grass laden with its baubles of dew, she made for a meadow of daisies where she tiptoed in her grace without a trace, spiriting herself away toward the sunrise in a cloud of haze, on soundless feet lightly brushing the moist earth upon which she padded, seeming without knowing where she was going, although deeper down she did. Her understudy, in any case, was nearby in the wings, brooding in a dank suburban house in Phibsboro where the baton might be left, not far from the leafy park gates. And it was to Phibsboro that Banshee Megan Devlin headed upon exiting the manmade Phoenix Eden, creeping along unseen in the downpour, over drab pavements toward the squat domain of the Merkel family.

They were lately shattered. The only son Konrad was abroad on adventures and never answered his phone. The Maori mother Esmerelda had thus been in a fouler mood than usual, which she took out on her husband, the meek Pipefitter Pat, whose brains were failing. And Maggie, stood outside and regarding the dark house, nodded recognition to spot the old woman crouched by a candle at a cracking window, hunched over her tarot cards and threads. And Granny Nutmeg smiled upon a dame to whom she felt akin.

For there she was, all alone and lonelier, stuck in a huff in the chilly wreckage of their home, a cold domain of stinking soot that snapped and entered their nostrils, with only her empty hubbie to keep company with her in their tedium, to whom never again was she to talk, as once she did when their hearts so sweetly beat in time, way back in another life that was more lovely, his ear into which without remit she continued to spit the gruel of her malice, for there was bugger all else for her to do but savagely fling the thrusts of her jeers, to scald and sear him with sour words that cut to his core that wept in silence, bitterly lacerating in a lethal marinade of hatred.

But only once, and only then, and well about time too, did she finally shove him at long last too far, far enough to rebel and flee, for one dark morning in the harsh and shivering weather of a mellow season, didn't he only just clamber up from their bed and escape from her, packing his sacks and cramming his suitcase to the gills with his shoes, transported by some impish spunk that they never did think he had, and all the way away from her as fast as he could he ran, shambling to the train, onto which he bound with a grunt, sliding as an eel into a seat by the side of a prodigal Belgian, with whom, over the course of their voyage into the funnel of the night, he babbled a myriad follies, a well met set of stammering men equal in eloquence, journeying over the arc of the tracks that spanned all the long and craggy path to his native Galway to seek refuge with his relatives, to kindle some solace from his sisters he loved so well.

And meanwhile his domineering Esmerelda was left pathetically alone, hunched by her window forlornly looking out, hoping against hope that her only son might deign return from his travels, biding her darkling hours in knitting him socks and shirts, with pinching needles that filled the silence. She saw no face of Megan's ghost pressed to the pane, keening and whining, cajoling her to drop her duties and join the lament, to become at last what was always latent. Then Maggie laid down her gown on the doorstep, and cast off all her clothes, and faded naked from the earth, and Esmerelda felt a jolt within.

For her son was returning, whistling, idling up the drive by dappled cobbles flecked, hopping over the groaning gate, ducking under the thickets of the overgrown hedge that had not been shorn in years nor cut, passing by, with a hasty nod, having seen, with a tremor, the ghost of himself when younger, a feckless kid again who pined and skid beneath the pockmarked apple tree, of whose illicit fruits he had eaten and flung at the dining-room window, on whose glass they slapped to a mash, to his mother's chagrin.

And now, through the teeming storm, to that same window, in the gloomy morning was he strolling, peeking through the pane to spot his mother whom he could not glimpse, for all the lights had long since died out, in her abode of dimness that faded to a muzzled black, to hide the diva huddled sheathed in the darkness unseen by her son, unheeding of the bell he blearily rung, calling out her name over and over, sounding so listless in the rippling sea of that evening of echoes, as over an hour of emptiness he stood on the step sadly knocking on the hopeless door, until finally he could take no more, and smashed it down with the heel of his boot.

Sidling through the busted frame that sprang so easily ajar, keen to admit him into the fangs of hell, he was met by mist, and puckered tokens of his youth kept pickled in glass, as through that grave in mounting fear he edgily walked and jumped, starting at every slightest hint of sound, wondering where she was squatting in that scriptorium's gloomy dust, peopled by a trickling patter of mice and rats who tailed upon his steps, his hair annoyed by cunning spiders who spun their webs of silk in the beams, to catch the oafish flies on whom they glutted and binged, better fed than him whose yawning fridge was all but empty, by which Konrad softly brushed, flicking on his snub of lighter to illumine the mantelpiece that rotted, sneezing from the dust in his nose as he browsed the mottled pictures depicting past dinnertimes, smugly smirking as he remembered just one among many wretched picnics she had ruined, at which she sat in a pout with her mug done up in a sauerkraut's sulky puss, and ruined everything for everyone all over again, and bending lower he found, down deep in a cabinet long ignored, the oily gangly geek's notebook in which he had written when young, in which he had recorded details of his nasty Granny's ghost who pushed his mammy down the stairs, cracking her hip and calling in an exorcist to dispel the malevolent presence, while Pipefitter Pat protested.

But there she was too, o yes she was, the grazing mammy or thirsty wasp, letting him lie getting lost and sidetracked, as through the shadows she prowled on her webbed and snapping feet, mounting to the crackling crest of the peak, for a Harlequin as she knows in her bones anticipation is the key to a scene, prowling up behind him beginning to snarl like the wraith of an old ghost she was becoming, becomingly clad in her night-gown knitted from graveyard dregs, a jewel about her spindly calf made of bones that rattled, bearing at an angle a lantern aloft, within which a candelabra stood at a slant, melting searing wax in a dripping puddle on her bunion's arm, the candlelight whose flare was awful, and lit her like a thorny study in scarlet of the Great Beast, and finally he heard her groan and turned, and saw her only then as the devil to which in despair she was reduced, and felt a wave of sorrow and torrential loathing commingled for his poor old mammy, for whom he never before had felt such pity and horror as then alone he deeply did, his Maori mammy who was become another Banshee.

And she spared no time in beginning to chastise him, and bedevil him with complaints and chides, hailing him a nasty foolish idle wretched waste of love, a spoilt bastard who never said sorry nor please nor thanks, to whom she would not even toss across the table the rancid jam for to daub his staling bread he always did be wasting, all the spite and wrath she bore up stowing spat out to scorch the haunted face of her son, who stood in a sway and swallowed his mercy, and hit her back with some burns of his own, he had inherited her spiking tongue if never nothing else, and so they stood there raving in the lounge for the space of an hour, the infernal flecks of their saliva lit up by their lamps, like the burping spurts of fire spat from the komodo lips of lizards who belch sulphur on a strictly hourly basis, until the sod Konrad could take no more, and turned and ran out the door he had kicked down, and she pursued as fast as she could, to fling after a bunch of his books, fuelled by a strength she never knew she had, so deft her aim that met its target, knocking a clump off his bushy top, bringing him down to his knees on the winding path to the creaky gate, there it was in the damp grass where he fell, and there where she applied weak sow's kicks to his belly, to rub well into the scab of his pooling sore just who was his mammy and who was his mistress, the witch who would pursue him always, and never once in her tidal wave of typhoon's abuse abate, until eventually he lurched up gasping with a sneer, hopping over the gate to scoot away to his friends again for safety, with a parting finger that mocked her scathing face with an insult that sought the creases of her heart, as he left her in the lurch, alone again, and madder yet.

In brief, an eventful and spirited reunion was had.

CHAPTER SIXTY-ONE

And what of those selfsame friends he would rejoin for safety on the southside?

Far off in Potter's house, of a morning after debauched riots, all was still and quiet. The uncaring door stood open, to admit the dallying sunlight fresh after the shower, whose dusty rays fell slowly down on sliding pillars of ballerina motes, through which door, one by one up the steps, past the desecrated plants, with lowered heads and wringing hands, guilty revellers had made their exit, fleeing far away from shame.

Lukas the Shag had awoken first, entwined in the spider-woman Jezebel's arms, stripped to her frilly black bra, huskily snoring, her pincers digging into the soft flesh of his neck, where she had scratched his skin as they scored. With all the quiet that he could, he disengaged his nakedness, and dressed himself in silence, a ritual of hasty escape with which his bounder's blood was well familiar, stealing away on creaky boots to the bus.

Johnny Fritzl next woke in his armchair, and felt again that similar fear that every morn beset his nerves, alleviated only by a brisk walk in air, invited by the vista of warmth that lay without, so much finer than this tepid dungeon where the random sinners lay, peopled by musty books and bottles, and prying cats whose piss was rank, and the strange White Dog recumbent in the corner, lifting up a shaggy head to bare his canines at the waking boy, scared of that dog whose unnerving glare bade Johnny Fritzl flee.

And in the ensuing silence then, as a holy Sunday dawned outside, and the cats padded around the ruins, Simeon's hand was seen to flail from beneath the coffee table whose edge the bony fingers grasped, hoisting his cadaverous self stiffly up again, sneezing from the ashes having a holiday in his nostrils, dishevelled in his greening jacket, his wispy hair awry. First he cast an eye on the dozing harlot so very nearby, wallowing plump and supine on the sofa, her blanket of coat tossed aside to display the cream of calves and ankles, her bust raising gently up and down as she breathes.

On hands and knees, unseen and alone, her ragged admirer crawls through the sea of papers and cans, to kneel by the couch where she lies unaware of his regard, and he eyes her sleeping face, her lips parted, her fringe muffed from the night-time thrash. And the shimmering lids of her eyes are gently batting as she dreams, sandman's crystals crumbing their lashes, grainy deposits powdering her lily cheeks, dots of rouge specking the dimples, beauty spots he briefly palms like diamonds to purloin.

And his gaze lowers further down in the direction of her rump, almost peeking out from beneath the rim of her flamingo skirt, two great undulant mounds of lard encased in her dotty knickers, on which her friend perversely lays a hand to rub and grope, sighing in his devotion as he strokes. Inspired to worship by Sunday morning's service, while none are around to snigger or pry, he dips his head and shuts his eyes, his lips screwed up to smooch, and on the melons of those cheeks he plants kiss after kiss, sucking the lard like a calf in the morning, kissing her milky buttocks through the scanty armour of her skirt, crying dryly as he kisses with tears unshed, for he knows it is the closest he'll ever get to make his claim, as the profane temple brightens again.

Mr Potter the dark priest was then arisen from his dreamless slumber, roused by the warbling of his parrot, threatening to launch into a tedious homily, which pious droning his burly master quickly discouraged, by lowering a curtain upon the cage to sheathe, so that the bird might think their day was his night, a parrot who made do with a daily carrot to keep him quiet. Having waded from the pillage of his bed, Mr Potter then entered the wreckage of the living room as one would a bathing pool of soup.

And upon hearing the superior's heavy approach from darkness into brightness, Simeon hastily aborted his solitary pleasure of kissing Jezebel's buttocks, and shot bolt upright blushing as he sprang from the sofa in his blustering flurry, scratching his head with whistle, pretending to admire a stain on the wallpaper. He need not have worried, for Mr Potter, emerging round the corner like a reborn yeti blinking in the sunlight, noticed only the disgraceful state of the room over which he sighed, and the absence of the other marauders, most notably the naked Merkel, about whose whereabouts he brusquely questioned the jittery Simeon, by way of greeting.

'Bah!' the fat man snorted, unenlightened by the monosyllabic reply, 'How very typical. He's always going off and having adventures all by himself. And the bastard didn't think to tidy up the mess he made of my plants either. Look at them, Simeon. They are ruined from his topple. How dreadful. We should at least be grateful that he did not go so far as to emulate Rimbaud by taking a shit in my fireplace ...'

'He's always like that,' Simeon grumbled. 'Utterly thoughtless and inconsiderate of others. He broke my father's fruit bowl too. Not to speak of the lock on our bathroom door. Though at least that time his motives were comparatively benign, since he thought that he was rescuing me from the drunken coma into which I could well have slumped.'

'Dormouse qualities, eh? Sounds familiar. You were perky enough last night, though. Your torpor must surely be seasonal. But yes, he's a destroyer, that boy. Something to do with the only child syndrome I would suspect, coming from a home where he has never had to clean up his own messes. He has it to an absurd degree.'

'I hate him!' Simeon spat. 'I'd have been happier if I never met him.'

'Why Simeon! He's really got under your skin. But you make the mistake of investing too much in friendship. Myself, I allow nobody to get too close. He merely amuses me like a child, but also disgusts me ...' (growing shifty with edgy eyes) '... but really though ... where the fuck is he now? This is tormenting me ...'

And Simeon watched his hero bluster as he changed the subject, espousing the loner's creed. And the boy sadly smiled at this instance of disassociation, this pathetic attempt to hide the submerged pederast the tempter had unearthed, now ashamed of yesterday's crimes he would endeavour with all his ingenuity to steadfastly deny, keen to pound again his chivalric chest and banish his darker version, and reassert his gentleman's straight credentials in the daylight of propriety, to deflect from the bender's queer lapse of the evening, brushed under the rug with all the rest of human weakness.

Jezzie stirred upon hearing noise, and slowly lifted her dreamy head, shyly snatching hold of the blanket to wrap around her broad and nude alabaster shoulders. Where were the others gone to, she wondered, those others who were so strange, so strange. Albert chuckled to see his daughter wake.

'Ah, the Queen of my Heart is back among the living again!' he cried, stooping to take her hand on which he planted a slobbery peck. 'And how did you sleep, my dearest, my petal? Did you have, har, har, a lively night?'

Rubbing his hands, flapping the invisible tails of his butler's coat as he circled his domain, the tubby host next put on the kettle, and rummaged in a drawer in search of some oddments to eat, of which there was precious little food to be found, save for some stale bread and a jar of Marmite. But Simeon found a stash of dust encrusted green tea leaves in Albert's cupboard, leaves the titan had hoarded since the Tokyo tournament where he disgraced himself by showing up drunk at chess.

And at Simeon's suggestion, to rid them of their hangover, the big man poured the boiled water into a pair of chipped cups into which the boy dropped some sprigs of leaves that swelled like flowers on the spread of a pond, bobbing like lily pads or lotuses, or steaming crocuses in the honeyed air. So in a triangle of stools, in the middle of the rubble, the three sat and sipped in silence, the large man upon whose knee the White Dog rested his muzzle to drool, and the gaunt boy cradling his precious cup, and the girl with purple hair sucking Marmite from her thumb. And into this oasis, the wandering prodigal Merkel returned from his travels, his shadow falling over them from head of the steps outside as he blundered down past the pots and entered the dim again.

'Christ!' he spluttered as he sank into a chair and wiped sweat from his flushing brow, 'But boy am I glad to see you guys again!'

'Ah there you are, you scoundrel!' Albert leered, chewing upon a greenest leaf, 'Where the devil have you been? We have missed you.'

'Clothed again? You look like you've seen a ghost!' Jezzie tittered.

'And your hair has gone greyer,' said Simeon dryly, offering him a taster of tea to calm down his frenzy to meet their serenity, and so be lulled.

'Greyer? Small wonder after what I've seen. Just listen to this for a sec – I went home briefly just to see if I could get some money off me ma, and begorrah, but me mother – o me mother – she's gone stark raving mad since the da escaped. Never seen the like of it. I had to bid her good riddance with me pockets still empty. Dunno if I'll be going home ever again at this rate, not with her in that condition. Inhuman. Absolutely inhuman.'

'I do so love the sound of your domestic setup, Merkel,' Albert mused, 'it all sounds so scripted, so dripping with cliché. And that wonderful evocative scene you painted of your taciturn old man the pipefitter –'

'The fucking spastic retard you mean!' Merkel spat bitterly.

'Now, now. Never dismiss your forbears. He made you what you are, at least in part. And I'm sure he loves you truly, what with that lovely vignette you mentioned, wherein the two of you would sit in silence at the kitchen table, musing on infinities, until he would break the spell by singing some old song, at which he would weep, for it made him remember some brother of his who had died by his own hand. Or the times when your father would be happier, and that homely way he would express it, by cooking up an omelette, which he would share with you if his mood was good, shoving the plate across the table and wordlessly inviting you to dine with him.'

'Won't be seeing that again …' said Merkel with a hint of regret.

'No, there is nothing like a father, my children,' said Mr Potter with shining eyes uplifted to the sagging ceiling from which the smoke alarm had been ripped in a fit of pique, 'and you only know for certain you shall die once you have seen your very own old man go that way of all flesh. Being an orphan, I found out somewhat earlier than most. But my stepfather, who was henpecked just like your Pipefitter Pat, him with whom in the rooms above I lived when I was young … he was the only man I ever really loved. Loved enough to call him my true father, father pure and simple.'

'When did he, uh … pass on?' said nervous Simeon.

'You mean, *when did he die*, Simeon, *when did he die*. I fucking hate those pussyfooting euphemisms that people employ to shroud life's starker facts, those harsher truths away from which they shy.

'It was some fifteen years ago perhaps. A miserable life he led, with a wife like that, a madwoman who was forever breaking up the fucking furniture, on which he squandered all his hard-earned wages in replacing, to no good end. She was the never the same after that gang of bloodhounds attacked her in the street. I had to take matters in hand myself when I came home one day from school and caught her at it. All of thirteen, I still was strong. You had to be in those days, to survive the boxing matches those Rathmines ruffians would embroil you in, juh, juh, juh? So I marched over as she snapped the leg from a chair, and took her by the neck, and shoved her down into the sink, and dunked her in the water and watched her gasp without a shred of pity, until at last she agreed to stop for good and all. Hands-on, that's my approach. The most practical form of therapy, juh juh? But when old father died, of cancer and a broken heart, he left me the dog. Then the dog died too. Until this here brute came to me in the secret night. How's it, Snowy?'

He kissed the snout of his dog, as perturbed Jezebel glided to the toilet, on whose stinking bowl she dared not sit, over which she rather lifted her skirts and hovered to expel whatever ailed. Their voices lowered, the men discussed her briefly in her absence, gossiping over her dalliance with the Shag, at mention of which Simeon glowered and Konrad smirked, as he laid out his speculative theory about her deeper orphan's pathology, longing for a father figure to supply her with the love her own old man had not bestowed, drawn to older men on whose laps she could sit and be warmly rubbed.

With a flush and a gurgle in the drain, Jezzie bounded back in with a notion of inspiration, bubbling with enthusiasm, keen that they should all make a trip to the beach right there and then, a belated pilgrimage to skinny dip, such an exciting outing as Simeon and Merkel had always enticingly promised, on which they invariably never delivered. But the boys were willing, and Albert also expressed a muted enthusiasm, for his weekly dip in the sea was surely soon due. So they all stood again the fair quartet, the happy family of oddball orphans in exile, and a leash was wrapped around the White Dog's neck, and so they left the sunken house and ascended above ground, and roamed through the arch to the sunny avenue for adventure.

But as they passed by Merriman's and saw his shutters being raised, Mr Potter abruptly felt thirsty again, dribbles of saliva appearing in trickles from the corners of his lips, bespeaking the dire need he must quench at once, to which end he diverted them from their course, with a suggestion that they make a noontime breakfast of the stout. None would argue – if this was how he ordered his unchanging days, who were they to dispute or judge? Gloomy Snowy was cursorily chained to a lamp-post and told to wait.

The first customers of the day entered the bright pub where the bejewelled light shone in rays and streamers through the window's rainbow glass. Merriman eyeballed Albert as he made orders for the kids, barking for drinks with a bland and unapologetic face that warred with the barman's scowl, still nursing antipathy after last night's fracas. He served them in a cold and unfeeling fashion, eyeing the boys with deepest suspicion, glancing at the girl with intense distrust, a look wherein burnt also a hint of faintest lust.

They fell quiet as they drank, softly lapping from their beakers, adoring the lounge's perfumed calm all round that descended, the first of the day that would always be the best, in the cool of a morning before the porter's rot set in. And Jezzie returning from the bathroom, her beauty hailed by addled Robbie who was sweeping the toilet's tiles, scraping and bowing with his dripping brush and mop as the chortling empress passed him by and winked as was her sexy wont. Back among the men with whom she felt at home the most, around their table's circle on which their glasses drooled, they discussed art and music, painting and drama, and touched upon the best techniques of seduction prevailing in their era, which had greatly changed since Mr Potter's heyday, when all he relied on was a forthright manner that verged on the vulgar, and a bottle of cider slipped under the belt of a babe.

'Ah, but women like honesty, don't they, Jezzie?' said wise guy Konrad, waving his hands, 'Always be yourself, so we're told. My ass. Just listen to this for a sec – and with all due respect and no offence – but if the likes of Simeon were always himself, sure we'd be screwed. I had to laugh when I heard that story about him giving manly advice to some Edwin guy. According to S.J.C.'s manifesto of charisma, all you have to do to get a gal is to affect a dark and mysterious limp. Bizarre. But god, I'd really hate to be a woman though. It'd be kind of shit. They're good for hugging, at least.'

With a playful pat of her shoulder, coupled with a telling grope of hips, under which parody of homage she glowed, alarmed by his misogyny that she struggled to despise, which only drew her all the more, loving what she ought to have hated, allured by that atom of self destruction in his genes, the same nucleus of immolation in which she saw a spirit like herself. And when Simeon sallied off to the lavatory to weep in private unseen, chuckling Merkel lowered his voice to whisper to Jezebel that their smelly mutual friend had a chip on his shoulder, or rather in his pants, which could only be solved by circumcision, a bloody secret she found immensely interesting.

Albert interrupted their courtship to recount an arousing story.

'This reminds me of a trip I once took to a hidden French beach where it was the local custom to swim in the nude, of which bare practice I knew nothing upon my arrival, with trunks and buckets and all. But then this pair of buxom fillies descended upon me as I clambered over the gate to meet the dunes. And they were naked, the pair of them, and they cut a fine figure with their curves. You will pardon me, Jezebel petal, but the sight of their beauty made me, har, har, erect myself just that little bit more sternly, juh, juh, juh? But then, worst of all, they were asking me to take off my trunks, to do in Rome what the Romans did. So, blushing from the heat, I was obliged to lower my loincloth to display the poker I had grown. But they did not seem to mind. Perhaps they were used to it.'

'Ah, a naked boy!' Merkel smiled, 'We have an understanding.'

'Which only brings me to my other greatest nude escapade that took place locally some years ago. I found myself in Kennedy's, with a bunch of obstreperous and drunken lawyers, a seedy set of human types in a veritable legal eagle's peanut gallery of posturing smugness, to say the very least. But whatever happened, they must have slipped something into my drink or whatever, but I passed out thoroughly, juh, juh, and I was so ruined that I was moved to take off all my clothes as I sunk, as if I were on the point of going to sleep at home in bed. So, thus divested of my garments, I lay down on the smoking area's floor – don't know where the lawyers had got to by then, unless they were loitering on the sidelines laughing at my prodigious display – and fell fast asleep. To this day I remain in the dark as to why the management did not kick me out. Perhaps they thought I was a religious activist launching a protest, making some sort of statement about, er, uh, the grosser indulgences of the boom that then we knew, juh, juh. Though at least I had the decency to slip a sock onto my cock to preserve my modesty, for to keep the pecker warm in the cold of that night I spent on the stones.

'But a downpour in the morning woke me up, wetting my naked hide and giving me to shiver, like the naked Noah discovered by his Ham or something. And there I was, bare of bum and chest, alone in the midst of that deserted bar on a hostile weekday morning, the doors locked and the floors swept, the stools upturned upon the counters, last night's glasses scrubbed and stored in the dryer. And as I groped about the cobbles, spitting out the ashen butts that had been dropped in my mouth, as if I were a naked human ashtray for their fodder, with a splitting headache on me too like a fat frog, I could not find a single one of the clothes that were mine, for those bastard lawmen must have robbed me blind while I lay supine, juh, juh? Though at least they were kind enough to let me keep the stocking that hid my puckered member. I had to vault over one of the walls to get out, no easy feat when you are naked and heavy, cutting my feet on the glass in the dingy alley where I fell and all but slipped a disc. And then there were only more barbed walls and gates lined with shards and prickled wires over which I was forced to climb before I could at last escape, much cut by the thorny army. It is just as well the city was as quiet as it was as I made my way home, accosted only by some ungainly youths who mocked my unclothed condition – and, to be fair to the fucking buggers, I was, admittedly, something of what you might call, har, har, an easy target for their scorn. You see a different aspect of Dublin in those early hours that preface the dawn, especially if you are Adam-naked as then I was, and the walk to leafy Ranelagh suddenly seems all the longer. And when naked, you become more conscious of the filth that bestrews our dirty streets, and more wary of the hazards that lie in wait for the vulnerable foot, those booby traps of dog turds and broken bottles, that usually we ignore and take for granted when wc are safe in the straitjackets of our coats and padding. Brings one back in touch with the unclad animal in us. Anyway, I got home finally, having avoided some stones that a bunch of wretches hurled at my nudity, and got to my front door, shivering and bleeding and all but dying of hypothermia and exposure, only to find that, of course, my door was locked and I had no key, since having no trousers or pockets, robbed and ruined. It took the best and last of my strength to kick the door down, and collapse on my couch, which I occupied for the space of an invalid week thereafter. Some night out. But in a way, it was, in retrospect, the most glorious day of my later youth.'

Thirsty from the exertion of the telling, he gasped for a slug, and downed his glass to soothe.

Sandy tears shed in the sink, Simeon returned with invigorated jauntiness, twirling his imagined bamboo cane with the strut of a penguin, breathlessly extolling the virtues of the Sentimental Cynicism that he endorsed and indeed to a degree embodied.

'O Simeon!' Jezebel cried, clapping a hand to her mouth to muffle her earnest mirth, 'You don't have a single cynical bone in your body!'

'I overheard your talk of nudity just now,' Simeon babbled, 'which reminded me of a story of my childhood, wherein, at the age of about two or three, I interrupted a party that my parents were giving by barnstorming in to accost some old biddy whom I hailed as a witch. And I was sporting a little erection too (o yes Jezzie, I am coarse and shameless!), as I looked her in the eyes with a blazing glare, and declared, having learnt off by heart the quote from Larry Olivier's *Hamlet* film (which was the only video we had that I watched every day in the monotony of my toddlerhood), and declaimed, with my baby's poker sticking up rudely – *Frailty, thy name is woman*!'

'That's rather disturbing ...' said Albert Potter gravely.

'O Simeon!' Jezebel guffawed, 'You've been alone for far too long!'

'How tight was the foreskin then?' Merkel smirked under his breath.

'And a good story too,' Simeon ranted on, 'is the strange case of my uncle Arsene the weatherman, who's gone quite mad. Do you know him, Albert?'

'Not very well ...' Albert considered, '... he came in here once in the winter, and we played several chess games. He's a remarkable player. Very cagey, but by far the finest competition I've had in years. Has he really gone mad again? That is sad.'

'If it was madness ...' mad Simeon murmured, '... I probably ought to have told someone earlier, but I am only an irresponsible adolescent after all. Then he went on the run, and we lost him. Sad and strange and sad, sad, sad ... God! I wiped him ... but wait –'

Waving a finger in the air to prepare them for his trick, the scruffy conjuror dipped into a lapel of his festering coat, and rummaged about a loaded pocket, unearthing the first volume of the old man's memoirs ('from the horse's mouth, the unedited truth!' he added as a blurb's disclaimer), which he passed across to Mr Potter, who browsed with interest as Simeon told Jezebel the history of Arsene before he vanished from the scene, while Konrad filled in the gaps. Snorting, Albert flung down the notebook.

'Disappointing,' he concluded as he sipped, 'very hard to read and not really worth the effort. I remember he told me that he knew all the secrets of the chess world, which is a bitchy one, I assure you, peopled by ruthless cutthroats. And he swore blind that he had all the dirt and the insider's gossip, assuring me that only he knew where all the bodies were buried, and what skeletons crammed the closets of the champions. It really whetted my expectation and fired my curiosity. For I have made many enemies over the course of my playing, juh, juh, whose scandals it would be nice to know, if only for the sake of blackmail, rowing with cheats whom I flung bodily at the bathroom's walls, villains who crossed me once and were never allowed to forget it. One of my rivals once had the nerve to swim in the forty-foot at the same time as I was taking my dip, for which insolence I swam behind him, and grabbed his testicles, and threatened him that I would tear them off. But no. Mr O'Colla's recollections are a disappointment. Very guarded prose that shies away from any real red meat. Unless he expects us to read between his lines or decipher his metaphors. Which perhaps implies a streak of complexity I do not think they possess. Don't send them to the publisher anytime soon. Still. Pity to hear about that fate he met … how very strange and sad …'

His mournful eyes, contemplating dust in space, sank to rest on the grubby book, and he lightly tapped a finger on the ring-bound spine of Arsene's mediocre testament with longing, wishing and wishing with all his heart that it had been better, this last gasp that was too hard to hear, the last words of a man he never really knew.

'Yes …' he said to himself softly. 'How very sad to hear he has gone mad …'

Nobody spoke of Arsene again.

CHAPTER SIXTY-TWO

Arsene-Elijah O'Colla, who would never sleep again, walked around the city for the length of a great night through downpour in a jaunty humour, doffing his top hat to the unfortunate and scruffy who peopled the alleys and cul-de-sacs, to whom he prophesied on cue, cajoling them to seek the silver in the cloud and vice versa. Most responded with obscene graffiti writ on their outdoor dungeon's walls.

But Elijah's star was rising while his brother's was setting.

And on the following morning, while Potter and his children were drinking afar, Arsene-Elijah came to the DART station by the college's eastern back, on the redbrick of Westland Row beside the church. And on the church steps, Arsene-Elijah saw the poet Tadgh O'Mara lying ruined again, snoozing with his limbs all splayed. But Arsene-Elijah prodded the tramp in the ribs with his staff, and when he was awoken, blinking confusedly at the starry apparition who towered over his stiff and bony length, Tadgh O'Mara heard that great voice bid him arise from his slump.

'*Come with me!*' said batty Arsene-Elijah, '*I am going to Portmarnock Beach, where I shall show you fodder for the Great Gaelic Epic you always said you'd write!*'

Half asleep and more than half-mad, this sounded promising to Tadgh O'Mara, who allowed his arm to be grabbed as he was lurched up from the steps, and his body then forced forward by the pushy hairy prodigy, with a voice he rather seemed to hear with his mind and not his ear. Arsene-Elijah bought a one-way ticket for two, and they shuffled onto the train, ignoring the looks of disbelief and threat with which their duo was met. Zipping by above the maze of roofs that flitted past their window,

Arsene-Elijah exulted while Tadgh O'Mara rubbed grains of sleep from his eyes and picked snotty crumbs from his nose. And his companion, casting a critical eye over his down-at-heel apparel, tacitly removed some fleas from his bearded sleeve.

And to his numb new friend, Arsene-Elijah explained further. He knew that Tadgh had failed in his reunion with his child, but this could be rectified, if he would but wait awhile. For daughter Hilda would surely approve of being the dedicatee of a new Tain, such as her father surely had it in him to compose, the last and greatest gift he would ever give. A new Tain with a new sort of Bull set at its cadaverous centre, quite fitting for their unhealthy age, red in tooth and claw, like rats or falcons.

'*Such a Bull as my brother is giving chase to,*' Arsene-Elijah went on, '*and we ought to arrive just in time for the scrappy climax! You need but only cast an eye upon their debacle in order for thy slumbering Muse to stir, and golden words of most Gaelic harmony come unbidden to thy quill.*'

And even if he did not have a quill, he could recite aloud his poem to the blind air, or scratch with a bulrush reed the shapes of words in the shallows of the sea, surely a most enchanted Celtic notion, that art that thrives on exfoliation, like peacock tails or wreaths, or the spirals on the shell of a snail, or ripples on the surface of the water, those concentric circles that go on and on, bobbing like the universe expands.

From the Portmarnock station Arsene-Elijah and Tadgh O'Mara walked almost a mile to reach the beach, passing by the pubs where the golfers drank, and the swathes of green where the flocks of ducks were marching as armies to fight the seagulls for the discarded crusts of Brennans loaves. And the two old men ascended from the tarmac to the sandy dunes, the beanpole poet and the coffee-room prophet, splendid in their rags and filthy beards, swaying past the pampas grass until the sheerest blue was in their sight. On some distant headland, a grassy tower that overlooked the whole breadth of the shore, they stationed themselves to lie in wait for what they were to witness.

In the distance, trotting unworried at a canter around their Sunday's noon, Peadar Lamb's Bull emerged first, all its frame of bones jangling as it ambled down the beach, snorting and snuffling as it chased its skeletal tail, pausing by the lapping waves to slurp its repast and cool its heat in the midday sun. Tadgh O'Mara squinted and shivered like a hare facing down a hunter's silver barrel. Arsene-Elijah chuckled like a meerkat in grass.

'*Dost thou not love the brute? Does your heart not lift?*' he cackled amiably, '*and look you now, here come the hounds of rescue*!'

And there they were, the dozing cavalry who barely cared, appearing from over the hilly dunes in scampering dots, the little Puck skipping forth at the front, bearing the fat cat in his arms, followed by the grave Pooka who led the donkey by the bridle, on whose dull back, at full length wobbling, the ailing conqueror lay, the jabbering senile hero, in whose nostrils came in a breeze the scent of sea again, such memories of salty brine and weed that recalled his seaside childhood, rousing him for his day's final tackle.

With a last spurt of strength, The Mad Monk raised himself with shining eyes, and tumbled off the back of Balthazar, and rolled in the sand until he stood upright, and madly laughed as he saw Peadar Lamb's Bull drinking from the nearby waves.

'Nowhere left to run!' he roared to the wind, 'catch him, boys!'

'Anything for a quiet life!' the Pooka grunted to the grumpy Puck, who snorted.

And the ancient creature sensed his pursuers nearby, and turned and saw them charge into the waves, the Pooka and the Puck and the fat cat and the warrior donkey, egged on by the demented skipper who hopped and giggled, waving a baton of a reed he had plucked.

The combat was brisk and unequal. Balthazar was gored in the side by a horn. Moloch got trampled on by a hoof. But the cunning Puck and Pooka kept to the side while their animals provided distraction for the beast, and got injured for their gallant efforts, while meanwhile their crafty owners conjured up a fishnet from the garbage weeds that were washed in by the current. And then they caught him well and truly, and netted and bound him in their clasp as he looked the other way, and he roared and thrashed as he was hauled in like the merest catch of the day to be fried. They gasped and wiped their brows, these foolhardy champions, and dragged their treasure over to their frail old master, who was gathering logs and bark to build a fire.

They roasted him on their afternoon bonfire as he snorted undying, bones quivering as their glue began to melt and he fell apart to little pieces on the pan. And the warriors rested on their thrones of log, their bleeding ankles set in sand that stung them, and mopped their sweat and wondered as they watched Peadar Lamb's Bull be burnt down to almost ashes and cinders, the melting marrow stinking like the most pungent compost. Yet this dust still kept hold of life, Promethean fire of Oberon long ago stolen for their riper plans enduring, and the grains of onetime bone shivered and trembled like shells of pollen, such powder as need only be gathered up in clumps like turf, to be wetted with bathe of the first surf, to make a kind of lively clay with which the dying god could sculpt for his wife a mobile minotaur child.

And The Mad Monk squinted, and poked the burning debris with a stick, bubbling and spitting in a sticky mess on the ashen pan, and smiled to think it ready for his fruits. And he raised eyes to the sun, and prayed he might have strength for his last task, and fulfill it in whatever scant time remained to him before he died again. He thanked his helpers, who were unenthused (the Puck and Pooka were still in the dark, while the surly animals bemoaned the wounds they had incurred in the course of obscure capture).

'Well now, me pirate hearties!' The Mad Monk beamed, 'You can rest now and kick up your heels. Take a dip in the water if it suits ye. As for me, I'm a-goin' to make me lady a chiseller boy to keep us company in our oldest old age!'

'Such a strange little group of men …' uninspired Tadgh O'Mara mumbled from the headland, having heard not a word from the distance. And Arsene-Elijah grinned, and raised a finger to his lips, for the best was yet to come.

CHAPTER SIXTY-THREE

Meanwhile, the golden quartet of friends had quit Merriman's come the sunniest early afternoon, when their master Potter's pockets were empty.

And when Albert left the bank and came forth into the sun again, he saw Jezebel and Simeon sitting side by side on a window ledge watching Konrad badger a tourist for a fag as usual. And the grotesque young old man in the shabby jacket, and the sweet girl with melon's hair in her juniper skirt, the two of them formed so pretty a picture, with the White Dog cuddling beside them, whose mane they stroked as they laughed, seated side by side like a pair of chaste doves freed from the rafters of a deanery's ceiling, so pretty a picture that Mr Potter produced his camera and snapped the memento he would treasure like a light in the dark, plucked from life's bush like a rose that would wilt just like a leaf falls and a photograph also fades, to ghostly sepia's autumn hues.

Albert Potter and Konrad Merkel and Simeon Collins and Jezebel Temple herself – it was at times like these that Jezzie decided that the four of them were at the centre of the world. And then they went next to Slattery's across the road, dodging the trucks uncaring. And Jezzie hid her disappointment that the prospect of the enchanted beach trip was dwindling alas, forgotten somewhere around the third or fourth round, the liquid diet on which vampiric Albert exulted in his tragic addiction. And Simeon, whose round it was, played a clumsy game of peeping tom's peek-a-boo with the haggard barman, who looked the myopic spit of an older John Lennon if only he had lived, or maybe even sterner De Valera, ducking up and down from under his counter like a hare.

But new plans were formed over the next exorbitant round, with a new scheme painted of perhaps a picnic by the canal's radiant side, munching sandwiches and cherry sausages at the foot of the Kavanagh statue, at which prospect of cocktails Jezebel's heart leapt and her face lit up, as they discussed where best to head to buy the provisions for their lyric idyll, their pastoral interlude on urban grasses by the lapping bank where the swans swum – doubtless Tesco (for it's always better value, swear to god, and the four euro red can't be beat, especially in a recession like ours).

And Mr Potter, their flabby Bacchus who stank of the stale cologne he had earlier applied, horns drooping as were the tufts of his hair, then expounded the gist of the play he claimed he would write, one that would be set by that statue's foot (a papier mâché green man could be contrived on the cheap, or even polystyrene), a divine tragicomedy on whose stage all the human dregs would pass by in the barge when the world was flooded for their sins, a concept that sounded awesome in scope and infinitely preferable to some of those worthless Players pieces that were always being put on, some of which scripts Simeon had shown him earlier, trite things that the elder critic hastily skimmed and rubbished – they would not last, they would not last.

But his play, which *would* last we can be sure, if only it were ever written, this play he would entitle *ENCOUNTERS*, and he would tailor parts for all of them – Merkel would be the leading rascal sporting tattoos, and Jezzie would be the timid maiden who sold flowery butterscotch in her bicycle's wicker basket, while Simeon could be the gay policeman who spoils all their fun (typecast again, the boy bridled).

And Merkel applauded the brilliance of this notion's kernel, and slipped out to the street for a smoke and to keep company with lonely Snowy tied to a bollard. And disciple Simeon followed his friend like a lackey, pausing to admire his own face in the mirror of the snug's window that disclosed a reversed picture of the street corner scene, reflecting shelved beer bottles in the shady foreground, cars beetling by on the radiant road like bees, the balding limey dome of the cathedral afar, the smoking knight at his shoulder, and then his own crazed face sat splat in the middle.

What a face! A ham sandwich whose arching nostrils were winged, drawn and set tautly in their grooves, sporting the beginnings of a scarlet beard that hid the sensual overbite of his dental palette wanting brushing, a vinegary ginger man who took pride in his skin's aching lines, well engrained from lacerating strains of self denial and want of sleep, a nutty moon prince with bleary eyes whose bloodshot vessels pulsed, squinting rims reddish purpling as patchy lashes fell out, wispy hair beginning to billow in his mousey mania of sebum's grease, like the plume of a bantam atop a sunburned demon's sneer.

For truly it is wonderful the way, as people age, that they begin to look so much more like themselves, whether or not what's inside be ugly or pretty or a marvelous mix of both, the mess within beginning to taint and enrich the without, prevailing with those painful secrets writ large on faces that spend their tidy lives keeping mum on the civil rack, gnomes clamming shut and too afraid to talk the truth, undone by love that cracks the resin of the flapping sole, for we Irish are a shallow people, albeit perversely fair perhaps, as cruel to others as to ourselves, treasuring the unconsummated and the failed, making shallow friendships founded on fatuous fun that runs so cold in the bitter end, backbiting and bitching and kicking our enemies when they are down, snide wise guys who refuse to acknowledge the depths, emotional retards embarrassed by awkward topics away from which we shy, making nothing but a mess of our feelings, those horrid truths we would prefer to edit than be undone, to find the latent fun embedded in the torment, and make lukewarm comedies from the hash of our life's little disasters.

Similar sentiments to these were roused in Simeon's blood as he examined his new mask in the mirror, but instead of grief he felt only queasy triumph. Jubilant, stroking the creases of his face that had aged so very much in far less than a year, he was giddy at the discovery of his new physiognomy, to which he alerted Konrad with gusto.

'Look at my face! Just, just look at it, Konrad!'

'This body! This face! This mind! O heaven! My shining stars and body! Wait, I'll go get Albert and Jezzie to come out and take a look too!'

The fat man and the girl, assuming a house was on fire, came out eagerly, wondered what the fuss was for, and then went quickly back in, disgusted by the paucity of the discovery that surprised them not a jot, for they were not so easily impressed.

And once back within Albert and Jezzie discussed the latter's homelife, while outside Konrad and Simeon discussed the condition of the latter's penis (again).

'O but I am so afraid of circumcision, Konrad, I must have you know! I don't want that veil punctured, that mask destroyed, this cache that made my life's baguette! I do not like pain. I shirk it, a sucker for my creature comforts.'

'Jesus. You are *obsessed* with your penis. I mean, the number of times your cock has been the topic of our conversations – I gave up count a while ago. The details are becoming distressingly familiar to me. Me and Johnny must try give you a tutorial in masturbation next time we're alone.'

'Case of penile fixation, some Freuds might say, ay? Case of the chicken or wolf-man, who got it bit by a rooster in the midst of an eclipse? All the hairs on me head that I cut are kept in a bag, lest the cloning geneticists ever want to have a go on me! I kissed her ass this morning! And she didn't feel a thing since she was asleep!'

'O Simeon!' cried sentimental Merkel with reborn warmth, 'C'mere to me, ye big mad smelly old crazy fool and give me a hug again you stupid cretin, you bloody madman, in the name of all that's true and good in life!'

And they joyously embraced, and sang a duet then, a telling paraphrase of a medieval ballad, Simeon's favourite song in the world, the only one whose verses he knew by heart, where he took the part of the mother and Konrad that of the son:

– Where are you going to, Lord Merkel, my son?
Where are you going to, my handsome young one?

– I have been to the greenwood; mother, make my bed soon,
For I'm weary with hunting, and I fain would lie down …

Deserting Slattery's for the adjacent Tesco, when bellies growled for the picnic's treats, Mr Albert Potter took a trolley and wheeled it down the squeaking aisles, with his trio of children walking the dog beside him, like a family of elves without a mother witch to bind them, an unruly guardian paying court to foundlings dropped on his doorstep, steeped in fumes of his drink. Rows of shelves offered goodies they chose without discretion, happy to splurge and reap the most bounteous harvest. Jars of jam were dropped in the buggy, loaves freshly baked with stinking cheese to adorn their fluffy slices, and crumbed and salted ham, vines of grapes in lightly furred globes both purple and green, more jars of Marmite to keep Jezebel happy, a packet of tobacco for the virile roller Merkel, and bottles of wines both white and ruby, and the inevitable further beers.

– And what did ye meet there, Lord Merkel, my son?
And what did ye meet there, my handsome young one?

– I met with me true love; mother, make me bed soon,
For I'm weary with hunting, and I fain would lie down …

Standing queuing at the till, as the goods were reckoned and slid down the snaking treadmill to be added to the mounting bill, one might have seen again that familiar passing sorrow make flight across the fat man's face, as he stared into space in silence while the boys flirted with the girl, displeased by the cost incurred, costly both in financial and spiritual terms alike, such was the poignant novelty of the scene, such a parody of a family outing as he never before fully knew. In silence, while the boys sang, the scoutmaster dourly led them back to his house around the corner, at which the heart of Jezebel Temple sank again a little – it seemed the canal grass was also too far to go.

– And what did she give ye, Lord Merkel, my son?
And what did she give ye, my handsome young one?

– Eels fried in a pan; mother, make my bed soon,
For I'm weary with hunting, and I fain would lie down …

'Spare us that clapped out bullshit,' Mr Potter grunted as they descended and entered his domain again, where the sunlight grew a darker golden, falling through his door down his steps that from the downpour of before had long since dried. The gurgle of the gutter went draining by for countercurrent. The leaves rustled on the breeze that wafted down to breathe on their indoor dinner in the lustrous dark of their hidden idyll. Dandelion seeds, flowing down on sunshine's corridors, drifted through to stir them. And faintly the rattling parrot was heard attempting an aria in its cage (for Lord Randal's familiar rhythms had clicked in his brain – he remembered it had been part of his past repertoire).

> *– O, I fear you are poisoned, Lord Merkel, my son!*
> *I fear you are poisoned, my handsome young one!*
>
> *– O yes I am poisoned; mother, make my bed soon,*
> *For I'm sick at the heart, and I fain would lie down …*

Dancing motes toyed about Jezebel's hairs on columns, spots of almond halos for her rainbow crown. O for those halcyon days that pass us by in such a haze. She sat on the couch curled up like a cat, and licked some Marmite and smeared it on the biscuits they had bought. Torn sleeve jackets and pamphlets bestrewed her seat, some of which she perused with brown fingers. Humming the old song still, Simeon sipped wine and nibbled hammy slices, while Merkel glutted on cheesy watermelon, the fruit of paradise whose luscious juices dribbled all down his squaring chin, like the drying streams of saliva that creamed the stubble of Mr Potter's darkening jowls. And the large man himself sat at a remove to their circle's side, brooding in his armchair drinking wine, having made do with the scarcest bite of bread, very grave and hunched and sad, while children hummed.

> *– And what do you leave to yer true love, Lord Merkel, my son?*
> *What do you leave to yer true love, my handsome young one?*
>
> *– I leave her hell and fire; mother, make my bed soon,*
> *For I'm sick at the heart, and I fain would lie down …*

But Albert Potter rose up from his hush to turn on some music of his own.

'Raindrop Prelude,' he mumbled darkly as the disc wound in its dusty groove, 'raindrops to start us off with … twinkling keys, discords that jar … on so sunny an early summer's day. Some languid jazz to bridge the gap. And then … the, the, er, Satie piece I told you about. There is one number whose name I do not even dare pronounce … I … I can only listen to it once a month … it was the father's favourite too as I remember …'

That hour they heard it, while the sunshine faded as somewhere else a pianist soared, a dead man's notes petering down from another further room. A tower of sound melting in the air, noise that washed and swayed from the confines of a muffled record, filling the basement with jangling thuds and half submerged shrieks, shaking bones free from cracks of their dust. Their faces lifted, the listeners four, sunken in chairs while hearts were shook, into the air they stared as if there had been stars or clouds on that mucky ceiling above their heads. As if there had been a voice in the sunset bidding them heed and giving leave. A vessel onto which the gondoliers might board to sail away with the dead king's coffin that wanted interring among craters of the moon. Bereft in that other world that always looked back with longing to the home abandoned and in ruins.

The fat man perspired beside the luminous girl, a slip to his looming dome, a pair of angel's faces the snake Mantegna might have caught in butterfly's net of pigments. And the rosy sinner smoked and watched his blue perfume ascend. And the ginger gargoyle, whose scorched heart was fading golden like the setting sun, looked down from the ceiling to watch the rest as they listened, loving again the pear of her face uplifted, some sort of false love to which, like Lord Randal, he might wish hell and fire before wisdom became forgiving. His friend and enemy then, his evil hero who turned them all inside out for his amusement. And he gazed at the fat man last and longest, studying the hinted tears in the room's oldest eyes that still stayed blue, unchanged since birth, remaining the milky same while beauty sank into the pit of the gross, mottled and scarred something like a pockmarked Rembrandt's face, beneath whose keen unblinking eyes the telltale pouches sunk in bags, scowling from his easel and accusing the mirror that looked back without mercy. If you need a cheap model, try and get to know thyself the first.

And when Satie's tune was ended, stark silence was let fall. None of the children dared to speak, but waited for their dark father to break the gap in speech that lingered like a bell as yet not tolled, pregnant in the air of dust. A lacuna of time where all looked inward darkly, to see such a chasm in themselves, all of them lonely only children, foster orphans bound now to weird brotherhood, three of whom in their different ways loved the devil Merkel one and all, while himself alone loved no one. And then Mr Albert Potter heaved a sigh, and raised a palm to scratch an eye, and shook his flab and mumbled again. Growing confessional, he flatly described himself as a functional alcoholic, which label moved the children to protest, but how could they deny it? He spoke again of his father's plight, and the ordeals his baby self underwent at the hands of a crone who kicked her boy in the balls, as he rolled in the cradle bawling as a helpless child. A child's sad scream that papered memory's walls, in the sad padded cell of his dreams and nightmares that kept him from his unsound slumber. Of army days and horrors seen, fighting perhaps in the Congo or Cameroon, some place whose name always changed.

The beginning of his end was on his mind again as he sipped the last of his can. Jezebel's eyelids fluttered as the princess grew drowsy. And Merkel, whose glass was also dry, got down on his knees before Albert and begged him for just a slurp of his can. No chaste kiss this time was offered in exchange. Disappointed Mr Potter refused, and sadly chided him and poked him in the chin. And conceding defeat, seeing no beer was coming his way from the man who kept his cans close, jocular Merkel made a joke – 'Ah well, fair enough, I suppose your need for alcohol is greater than mine!'

An ill quip that made the big man shudder and sadder. With watery eyes, smiling through sheen of tears, he stared across an abyss of haze at the kneeling boy he loved, and stroked his chin, begging forgiveness in his silence, apologizing for the imperfections that on his head were heaped, for being wretched and pitiable and human, all too human.

'Merkel ...' he sighed, 'Merkel ... Merkel ... Merkel ... oh Merkel ... '

Being human was their greatest crime. In the wane of day, as evening's nip passed through his door and chilled them, Albert owned up to the dabbling in paints he once had indulged in, as prompted by a former flame who was a minor artist of the Sunday school. Eager to see some samples of his stuff, what little remained he had not destroyed, the children begged for a glimpse he eventually provided. Through the dimness he led them in single file to his bedroom's study, where under the gown encaged the parrot gurgled:

When that I was and a little tiny boy
With hey, ho, the wind and the rain,
A foolish thing was but a toy,
For the rain it raineth every day ...

But Mr Albert Potter lit a waxen candle, for the bulb above had blown out. In the flickering light his listening visitors stood close in chiaroscuro. And he raised the flame and pointed to the wall above his desk on which the books and jottings stagnated. On the mottled wallpaper where his favourite stain was found, the one patch at which he always stared at night when lost in melancholy contemplations, there hung a sizeable easel in a frame. Intrigued they peered forward, Merkel and Simeon and Jezebel, squinting in the sallow candlelight. Suppressing gasps of admiration when they saw Albert's great self-portrait of some twenty years earlier, intended as a gift for a girlfriend and never received.

But when I came to man's estate
With hey, ho, the wind and the rain,
'Gainst knaves and thieves men shut their gate
For the rain it raineth every day …

There he was, the younger Potter, dashing in his vibrant oils, sat by a window through which wintry sunlight fell in thick crepuscular strokes, brushing the side of his squarish face with pollen's illuming, sharp eyebrows uplifted and cocked as if to listen to birdsong from afar, the same brows that child Merkel shared and inherited, warily eyeing the light he did not trust, with such a fire and intelligence in the brooding eyes that had cause to be suspicious. Such an attractive catch as Jezebel Temple today might well have fallen for, a bloke about whom she might have dreamt and longed.

But when I came alas to wive
With hey, ho, the wind and the rain,
By swaggering could I never thrive,
For the rain it raineth every day …

Younger Albert Potter had been handsome once beyond a doubt, trimly muscular and dishy even, clad only in his shirtsleeves as if just after shaving, the hairy hamstrings clenched, the foamy bowl in a corner where the danger of razor was stored, the stubble about the erring chin, the beginnings of a beard like Gaugin's, devilishly romantic with a hint of a sailor's earring. The piece was very accomplished, the paints slapped on fearlessly, angry strokes that were livid and breathed passion, stabbing the canvas with a brush like a knife, as good as Van Gogh on a less inspired day.

And when I came unto my beds
With hey, ho, the wind and the rain,
When tosspots still had drunken heads
For the rain it raineth every day ...

But perhaps it was this professed want of original inspiration he so bemoaned, this lack of genius that so drove the frustrated artist in Albert to despair, hugely skilled and talented but not remarkable enough, a man for whom nothing less than the greatest could ever be enough, and if one were anything less than the best, one may as well pack it all in and wallow instead in squalor at the opposite depths, doing nothing at all rather than filling the world with just more mediocrity. They encouraged him to continue, but he would not listen, dismissing his efforts as mere Sunday painting, a lifeless forlorn dead end. And since, he added, he would in any case be dead quite soon, it was far too late, and simply not worth the bother any longer.

Long long ago when the world began
With hey, ho, the wind and the rain,
But that's all one, for our play is done,
And we'll strive to please you every day ...

Not worth the bother any longer. The picnic was eaten, and the flagons were empty, and they were sleepy, and staying any longer was not worth the bother any longer. They began to make excuses to prepare for their departure, the timid kids, yet they felt something like guilt to leave him be, alone in his quiet darkness underground. And he was saddened to see them go, and bid them prolong their visit by saying their goodbyes slowly, protracted by some final group photographs and the ritual continental kisses. Smiling through the wind and the rain, Albert Potter gravely shook Simeon's hand, and wetly pecked Jezebel Temple's cheek, and lastly embraced Konrad Merkel fully, and hoisted him off his feet in a bear hug that squeezed out all his breath. Then he dropped his love to the floor, and let them all depart, ascending his steps waving and calling their last quiet farewells to which he mumbled accord as he closed his door. Then he turned to survey his dim abode, alone in the dark again. And he lay down on his couch, and looked at the wall, and lastly blew out his candle, and so lay alone in the darkness.

CHAPTER SIXTY-FOUR

On the Portmarnock Beach he made his child, with all the care he could, while his companions drowsed and healed and lay in disconsolate piles. Scooping up the ashen dust into which the Bull's bones had dissolved, he carried the clumps to nearer the waves, and laid them down on the seashells, and wetted his fingers in the surf, and sprinkled his clay with the drops. And he sculpted the dampened grains and clumped them together moistly, and moulded and welded them with his nails as he found the shape of his child, until the vague form of a torso could be discerned in the sandy pile, with neck and arms and legs attached, weird bones fitted together oddly again. And the sun shone and baked what he built, and hardened the parchment sediments until they fused. In need of organs with which to fill the body's hollow, so his son could breathe and respire and excrete, he cast about his yellow eyes, which landed on the fat cat Moloch snoozing by the dunes.

'She will be glad to donate, at least in her afterlife!' he cackled.

And the madman reached out a quivering arm, and grabbed the cat by the bushy tail, moving her to screech as the Puck and Pooka awoke and blanched. But The Mad Monk was firm as he held her writhing down on his hands and knees, throttling her throat as he picked up a rock and bashed in her skull, the blood splattering his nose and lips as he struck again and again until her mews were silenced, and bits of her brains dashed out in the sand. The Puck and Pooka, who had loved her dearly, made feeble efforts to protest as their cat was murdered, to no avail, for he would not listen anymore.

'It was either her or the donkey!' he screamed as he hacked the cat to death, 'And I have gotten to know Balthazar rather better than she, let me tell ye!'

Balthazar, who was lapping salty water from the shallows, looked up and frowned to hear his name, and expressed disgust with his master by defecating.

Giggling and chuckling as his fellows mumbled disapproval and shook their heads, he next picked up a seashell and sliced open her belly and dug past the streaming pulpy gore and lardy fat, and roughly dissected the dead cat's cadaver, and hauled out her heart and lungs and liver and silken intestines, and laid the bundle of extracted organs in a pile on the sand. With his bloody hands he stuffed them all in a jumble inside the body of his son, without order or sense, relying on the abiding fire to gel the whole. Some of Moloch's stray bones he chopped in two, and siphoned forth the orange marrow and also stuffed that into the package, to fill the gaps. Then he turned to the sculpture's head, within which was nothing but airy noise, and within the cavity he dropped little crumpled pieces of the feline brain, which was better than nothing.

And he crafted the face of the clay child with all the more care, giving him a pointed snout like his own, and bags and pocks and scars to decorate the banal skin, rubbing the sandy flesh with his palm, making hollows for the eyes with his thumbs, and scooping a deep cleft for the mouth, in which he stuffed the legs of crabs for teeth and fangs. Pebbles and shells were stuck all over in pores of the creature's skin, to decorate his gingerbread man and lend him colour. For virility's sake, and to distinguish the sex of the beast, he next told his men to avert their eyes, and then, with much groping and gasping beneath his sodden robes, he donated some sperm of his own with which he washed the skin all over, trusting sacs would sprout between the legs, and from there then a planted member grow. And as the day drew on, and the sun began to sink, he delighted to see the parts were slowly fusing, and jerky tremours of animation began to flicker all down the length, as a finger twitched and a toe shifted. Grabbing dirty lumps that Balthazar had shat, he ground them into a composted heap, and basted the body in the grime, turning it over in the shit as with a rolling pin. Urging the Puck and Pooka to rebuild the dissolved fire, he passed his child's body through and through the flame to bake the body better in the spurting crackles, then laid it down again as he groaned and clutched his own heart, for his burning chest was full of spasms. Gepetto-Michelangelo had not long to go. In a profane ceremony of baptism, he bared his arm while his helpers danced, and cut a vein in his wrist, and howled at the sting as he allowed the pooling blood be sprinkled all over the puppet's body, blood that landed in the creature's mouth, at which it began to champ its forming jaws, and lick its emerging serpent's lips.

'It's alive! It's alive!' in ecstasy the creator cried, as he fell backward and gazed.

The moon rose as did the sister stars. He shore off some of his own hair, and dusted the sallow skin with sticky fur. And then it sat up, this thing he called his son and heir, and began to grope and feel and claw the sandy ground that surrounded, a being still blind and mute and eyeless, though it knew it liked the taste of blood. Appalled, the Puck and Pooka looked on in horror at its first motions, as its maker laughed hysterically. As his ailing heart beat faster and he coughed up blood, he ransacked his mind for a name with which to dub the brute he had unleashed, and hit upon the first that came the easiest.

'My son! My boy!' he chuckled, 'I call thee – CLUNGE MONKEY!'

'Thou hast unleashed a monster unto the world, Sir!' the Pooka wailed.

'He will destroy us all!' exclaimed the Puck.

'Nonsense!' The Mad Monk roared, 'this is the future! And what are we, my men, if we are not all of us monsters already? Here's to the new race of amorous apes!'

His disbelieving comrades cried hell spawn and apocalypse, as The Clunge Monkey raised its ugly head, and bared its gleaming fangs and spat. And between his spindly Rumpelstiltskin's legs, freshly seeded by his father's juice, a phallus was growing now, initially shrivelled and puny, gradually mounting to a dimpled walnut's size, with pendulous testicles with which he began to toy with his filthy baby's claws. But The Clunge Monkey, no matter what his critics said, was neither bad nor good nor evil nor even wise – he was pure life force, pure libidinous instinct, and was born only to spew on arid land and thighs, and never mind begetting as he entered chambers he would defile, attempting to copulate with whatever he met or smelt. Something of a precocious child who found his vocation early, the first likely thing he smelt on Earth, as he wallowed in the moonlight and enjoyed the emergence of his tackle, even before his eyes were formed, were the hooves of Balthazar scraping up the sand nearby. Emitting a gurgle of cackle that would become trademark, The Clunge Monkey blindly crawled over following the arousing scent, and mounted and shagged the donkey's hooves, to Balthazar's intense revulsion, and The Mad Monk's deluded nighttime pride.

'That's my boy!' he bellowed, 'Go, go forth, my precious! For life is short! O Nutmeg Maggie, thou art vindicated! I have made you a child! Now may I die in peace!'

'*And by thy brother's hand*!' came a voice from behind them.

All stopped and everyone froze within the fire's ring. Even The Clunge Monkey briefly ceased to shag, raising his sightless head to sniff the breeze. The Puck and the Pooka trembled and turned around, as did The Mad Monk, collapsed on the sand by the burning logs. A dark figure was coming forth from the shadows, in flowing rags and sandals, with a top hat and staff on which he leaned, followed by a hobbling tramp whose approach was shyer. The Pooka squinted as the hairy old man stepped into the firelight, and he recognized something of Mr Arsene O'Colla on whom long ago he had played such tricks. And The Mad Monk ceased to grin to meet a ghost unglimpsed since Ben Bulben so long ago, as the glowing eyes met his, unseen since the glory days, and the towering coffee-room prophet stepped into the firelit circle and stood over him again, another refugee twin from their father's seaside house long since felled.

'Elijah?'

Arsene-Elijah made no answer, but gave merely a sign to Tadgh O'Mara to pay heed and mark well what he would do, for this was part of the poet's lesson in life, or life of a kind, to a degree. And Arsene-Elijah threw down his staff, and flexed his fingers.

And The Mad Monk croaked: '*Must it be?*'

And Arsene-Elijah replied: '*It must!*'

And Arsene-Elijah bent over his brother, and sharply thrust two forks of stubby forefingers into his nostrils, which bled as they were jammed, and with his other hand clamped a heavy palm on The Mad Monk's mouth. And The Mad Monk complied peacefully, a smile playing on his lips. He twitched a bit initially, but then grew stiller, until soon he was unmoving, and thereafter moved no more, lost amid unending night.

And Arsene-Elijah threw back his head, and closed his eyes, and in the hidden porches of his darkened eyes, he saw the soul of The Mad Monk spring free from his earthly carriage, clapping his hands and singing as he ascended on the gust of bonfire smoke beyond the marmalade moon that was waxing while the world careened, buoyed ajar on an off-kilter spindle like a giddy butterfly fluttering through the firmament, cheerily skimming among skipping stars on the sea of the night sky, through which he swam and was caught by the crashing waves of the wind that tossed him like a leaf, into the constellated ocean among the crags of coral, where planets were pebbles, and Saturn's rings those of a sunken skiff, manned by the skipper Orion through blazing shoals of jellyfish comets, the frothy Milky Way the snail's trail of sperm dripping from a virile whale. And the sea shrank the closer to the surface he swam, and soon he saw a sun was shining, and pierced the veil, and shot up on the other side like a dolphin, to spiral before falling again with a splash, shattering the stillness of the canal, and he floated, and paddled, and found his feet as he came to the shallows, and waded from the waters reborn a new man, as he came ashore again once more, and found a friend in the hermit mister Albert who sat on a bench contemplating infinities, squatting by the lapping bank where the swans swum and the barge went by, to the dying echo of the singing spheres, resounding for eternity in a low hum, across the breadth of quiet waters – and then Arsene-Elijah let fall his brother's dead head, that back on the sand fell with a flop.

And Arsene-Elijah stood, and shivered, while the dumbstruck Puck and Pooka cowered on the sidelines, and Balthazar gave a whinny softly. And Tadgh O'Mara coolly surveyed the wreckage as he made notes for his Epic, the hero's body sprawled dead on the sand by the fireside, bloody in his robes, while his ghastly son, The Clunge Monkey, who was as eyeless as Cyclops, crawled gurgling amid his father's ashes he stirred as he blindly shat. And Arsene-Elijah chuckled, and gathered his cloak around him, and doffed his hat to the goggling mourners, and suggested that they might pass the night in doing homage, and perform acts of devotion on the shade's behalf, like funeral games.

And so, with further sobs and sighs, all again lamented his demise.

CHAPTER SIXTY-FIVE

Lying on his couch, he could not sleep, tossing and turning in the restless dark. So to keep himself busy in the lonely night, Mr Potter sat back up with sigh, and reached for his camera to review the pictures he had taken in the rare course of his birthday weekend.

He saw them all, and remembered fondly each occasion in its turn; there was the August into which the children crowded in surprise to keep him company; the salted vodkas and the potted plants the brash wretch had knocked; the reeling Jezebel who slumped on his settee, whose plunging cleavage he snapped, fingering now the soft flesh of the bubs his lens had captured; and then the naked Merkel who rolled about the ashen carpet in his bare and tattooed flesh, the waggling todger slightly blurred and out of focus; and the golden morning after amid the debris, with sweet Jezzie looking fresh as a daisy after plucking; and the sight of her and Simeon snugly sat as a pair on the ledge of the bank, rocking feet like cherubs do; and Slattery's where she bowed her head as he prodded her nape; and the picnic in the afternoon, recorded in a few tasteful still-life details, of smoke and cheese, of shining bread knives and glowing ruby of the wine; and a final few group shots, taken by whomsoever was not in the photo, of the boys and the girl, of the portly courtier and the queen of his heart, and lastly of the man and his boys.

And Albert looked last and longest upon a shot of himself and Merkel alone, the gallant lad trim and suave with his fag, enveloped in a yeti's embrace by the larger man, flattened by the flash like a cardboard cutout, the flare picking out every last drop of grease and drool and evidence of slur shining on the distended lower lip, looming sickly white like a grisly pancake with his sagging stubbly chins, looking so unlike the handsome self-portrait he had shown them, a monument to excess and liquid gluttony, testament to the poisonous course upon which he was embarked, of the most delicious slowest suicide. And older Albert who looked long upon the shot, following listlessly the vague associations stirred as he watched the photo flicker, now found with some surprise mysterious tears starting in his eyes. For what would he do tomorrow only more of the same after a weekend out of the ordinary, which may have seemed a new beginning but in deadly fact was sterile only, stillborn for him whose need was greater than theirs for his life was ordered round the bottle and not around other people, waking only to cross the road and drink and drink and never question himself as he counted his remaining pennies, pawing his phone and texting his children who brought pathetic breaths of air to him in the solitary dungeon he had erected for himself, pining for comely princess Jezebel who made him wish he had not let his girl-child go, while he grew childishly dependant on Merkel's visits, which were his lifelines, obsessively longing for the younger man whose loner's mind alone met his, as if they were travelling along the same track of thought while cocking their identical eyebrows, such a heartfelt kinship and soulful union born there as he never before truly knew, sickly love of a kind met only now in his twilight saga's forlorn close, all this sorrow roused as he gazed upon the shot that Simeon had taken, of himself and Konrad Merkel, together alone in the frame again.

And perhaps after all in the eyes of Mr Albert Potter he had always seemed something like the promise of a son that was never to be.

What happened next is hard to say. He laid down his camera, and shut his streaming eyes, and leant back on the couch, while elsewhere a breath of wind or brush of gown upon the carpet's fur might have sounded in the quiet night. And he might have been left there forever in the dark, slumped on his couch alone while dreaming of better days, of the weight of all that had not and never would be, or destinies misplaced and books not bought, had he not then heard a sound, at which he sat up sharply and squinted.

It was a cry, a stifled woman's wail carried to his ear through a chink in his door. And he looked about his room in search of that sound that moved and haunted him, and so it was he saw her. For there she was, surely enough, leering at the little window above the couch where he lay, pressed to the pane, twisting his plants as she squatted on his steps, scratching the frame as she keened. And Albert staggered up from his sofa to behold the Banshee Esmerelda, who had groped through the darkness drawn by his heat, clad in rags, clotted face clumped by wrinkles and sores and warts, open pustules spilling globs of pus, her nostrils flared, streaming snot, greasy hair wound up in knots, hid by a fright wig. For she had made an attempt to hide her ugliness beneath a layer of makeup, with lipstick and dentures, false pupils and lashes fluttering to allure the large man who stumbled to his door to admit her. And he twisted the key and opened his door, and stood before her on his doorstep, tall, dark and handsome, the dishy dude of her dreams.

Merkel's mother wound up her keening at once, and fell silent, hotly breathing, looking up with a crick in her leathery neck into the eyes of her blobby admirer, who grinned, and gave her a dirty little wink as he cast out a wide arm to welcome her in. She blushed, and bowed lowly at his beckon, and then she crawled in after him as he shut the door on her, bidding her arise once she was inside his house.

And he led her to bed with his wagging flabby finger she followed, sighing wetly as she flung off her ragged slip, to unveil her bodice that had known better days, but her godly lover drank her up and loved her all the more, as he likewise undressed and cast off his shirt and trousers and stretchy boxers, and she gasped at the very size of him, the rippled muscled miles of his fatty hugeness, as he grabbed her and tugged her down on the bed, remembering his moony days of lover's lore of before, and she groaned, and thrashed in passion, and clawed his hairy chest, and they writhed in a riot of love, and he drove harshly right up into her, ah, o, so stiff, so sticky, so wet, flick, flick her woman's weedy beanie with yer dick, dick, dick, in, out, thrust and grind your purple prick, grunts and groans they emitted as they rolled on Potter's bed, frothing she scratched his back and bled him, more, more, more, handling his fat harpoon in a fever, their skins were spilling sebum as they sweated around, and he ploughed her mossy furrow and crushed her, his engorged trident set afire and bloating soon began to spew inside her like a gushing geyser, ah, ow, spew, gush, heady rush o blush, and o, o, o, ooh … it was good.

(Phew!)

And so it was Mr Albert Potter and the Banshee Esmerelda Merkel met in a fever fit, and made hot love loudly and wildly. And they copulated together in such a fashion for about six hours, trying out all the textbook routines, and varying the beat and tempo of the thrust, until soon they were quite exhausted, and the godlike man was quite unmanned, and so at the night's seventh hour they rested, their work complete for now.

CHAPTER SIXTY-SIX

Back in Lombardy Road, the children returned and retired, all save Simeon, who had too much to think of, who sat upstairs nursing green tea during darker hours at the dining table. Konrad initially lay down on a mattress in the front room, but was put off by the stench of a dead rat whose whiff leaked up from under the floorboards. Chased away by the putridity, he sought refuge in the backmost bedroom where Jezebel had just tucked herself up, giggling as she slid down the cover to invite him into the warmth she wished to share, her gallant prince. And side by side in the dark the boy and the girl chatted lightly in the bed of love, on the plight of Albert, and of Simeon's fictitious circumcision; and then Jezzie made her first hungry advances, for she loved him so, leaning in to peck his cheek, overtures, which, being human and lusty, he could hardly ignore, and so with sport Konrad Merkel repaid her in sultry kissing kind.

And as they kissed downstairs, one pans upward to watch the insomniac paranoiac who paced the boards upstairs. And he dimly heard their courtship from afar below, the noises of romance rising through the ceiling to lend sloppy echo to his footfalls. And he mourned, and lay on the floor, and wished for sleep, and the ignorance begat by blissful repose, but no peace would come, only the scent of leaves that bade him drink further and madder from his chipped china cup. He imagined their coupling, with every stroke and tug, and tore out dregs from the roots of his greasy wig, and rolled around on the floorboards with palms to ears to shut out the sound of their laughter and smooches. And he took refuge in delusions, talking to himself about I— C— C— and the whereabouts of vanished Arsene, slurping his tea and wrapping up his legs in the lotus posture, and on the stumps of his knees he walked with locked legs, until his kneecaps cramped, and he fell over flat on his face like an amputee monkey. Finally, at his wit's end, with none around to witness, he decided to try (again) to masturbate. Gravely, he mournfully contemplated his bits, then halfheartedly tugged at the skin that would not submit, and never once had in all his life – so far.

But then, upon an awful awesome sudden it did, and lo and behold but the veil slid back for the first time in well nigh over twenty years, and slid and looped unstoppably about the cap, but then, once back, it stuck, and set like plaster, and would not go back, the bald head bare, and the retracted skin began to form a ring that swelled, one that might burst and bleed from all the discharge incurred. Like a fool dumbstruck he surveyed the precious damage done, afraid to touch or pull, wary of the pain he always shirked, and lay on a couch and draped a shawl over the evidence, and for the rest of that night he wept, believing he was ruined now for the rest of his life too, victim of his own mutilations. Thus had the phallic mask been whipped off at last, to unveil the mottled ruin beneath, a globular purple planet smeared with clotted streaks of smegma, a sight that excited only repulsion and loathing in Simeon's sad and horrified eyes.

And the sun rose to find him hobbling about his house like a limping elder (for o! the scrape of searing denim against the unclad head did so sting), rooting about in his drawers to find his silken scarlet pyjama bottoms (for the silk, though ticklish, hurt just a little less than the scratch of cotton underpants against the bared godhead, which was so sensitive), which then he wore under his jeans, the ruby bottoms poking out, slivers of scarlet that would excite scurrilous comment as to the queer secret life he lead about which none knew (ow! The fleshy ring, the ring!). Now he was forced to sit or kneel to urinate, hunched like a lady over the creamy oval bowl, for the warped lump of deformed flesh he carried, now shaped likc a mushroom cloud, hanging forlornly between his legs, could not piss in a straight arc without splattering yellow drops aimlessly everywhere.

Jezebel awoke, and scurried away to school, batting not an eye upon his crippled condition, which was just as well. He tartly noted the disarray of her hair and blouse as she exited, which appearance of breathlessness he attributed to the lust of lively Merkel, who now ascended the stairs for a breakfast of leaves, whistling and rubbing his palms.

'Konrad,' Simeon croaked, 'I am … grossly injured … things have, er, come to, uh – the pun is unfortunate – a *head* on the score of the Collins cock …'

Konrad roared with laughter, and roared still more as the victim attempted to explain his self-inflicted condition, which had the virtue of being rare. Attempting distancing from his agony, he evoked flowery metaphors to describe his weird state, dropping words like 'vice' and 'clamp' and 'veil' and 'an Elizabethan fat man choking his flabby neck in a wormy ruff' – this last image moved Merkel to simulate vomiting.

'You're a complete fucking cretin!' he sneered, 'You absolute piece of shit! Get down to that clinic right now and get it sorted, I'm sick of hearing about it. Anyway, you don't even fucking know you have this bull-shit phimosis thing, you're not a doctor, it's all self-diagnosed and totally fluffy, you just want a brotherly link to Larry! You ham! You fake! I look at you now, massaging your maimed groin, and I laugh! And I think – Uncle Toby! Uncle Toby! Uncle Toby's come back to haunt me! You sentimental fool! Ah, but it was *always* soppy old codger Sterne for you, never Swift's remorseless grit …'

'I am laid bare for your inspection, Gov'nor! I am … what I am … I have made circumcision the only viable … option left now … Ow! At least … at least when I – ah! – when I engineer my own catastrophes … at least I take the – ah! – trouble to – ow! – to ensure that – eek! – only I – ow! – only I ever get … get hurt … ouch …'

'That is an unutterably stupid remark. No more.'

Delirious Simeon lay horizontal for most of the day, watching the dancing play of sunshine on his walls, and the passage of clouds overhead, their scudded wools glimpsed swimming past in the blue disclosed by the skylights. And Merkel snorted and mocked him, and sometimes went out to buy fags, and sometimes lay around riffling through his ailing host's many books, and sometimes rang up his comrades to excitedly inform them of the latest 'mad story', an object of pity and hilarity commingled. Jocular Merkel cheered him by speculating that it would most likely turn purple and then fall off entirely, so squeezed and constricted was the blood flow by now. Erections were therefore a thing of the past – as the unharmed base of the trunk stiffened and filled with blood, the topmost prepuce only felt intense pain as the fleshy vice-ring was further strained and stretched to bloody breaking point, resulting in a chastened retreat of arousal – thus, in so pulling back the skin, he had submitted himself to a kind of bloodless emasculation, doomed to loveless celibacy like a monk, steeped in denials of life's essentials, castrated without a knife, left only with a dangling tuber flower that had a bloated head. And he and Merkel blandly discussed theories like botanists confronted with a uniquely abnormal case that defied all the categories, a mutation of the species in a manner of speaking, an affront to the norms.

Sometimes, in his mounting madness, he fancied he might hit the record books, as he madly resigned himself to this absurd condition, so much did he fear the surgeon's knife that might snip or shave away this strangling layer of flesh that clamped him – what if a vein were burst or he bled to death? Thus he wondered when left alone in his haunted house when Konrad left to go to class. This last possibility awoke in him a gorgeously tragicomic fantasy in which he envisioned his own premature demise, dragged bleeding and dying from the operating table, carried arm in arm by Merkel and Fritzl, who chatted nonchalantly through their smiling tears like professional undertakers, as they hauled his dying lump out to the college's cricket pitch, leaking a trail of blood from his punctured groin all the miserable way, the whole sorry funereal procession conducted to the poignant strains of Albinoni's ever-popular Adagio in G, early on some bright and misty morning as the rising sun still melted away the foggy dew, to lay him down on the moist grass where he might expire in peace while the ravens wheeled, and his friends doffed caps and chortled, and Jezzie threw garlands as part of the funeral games while Edwin Galbraith read the eulogy, and mopped up the path of blood that dripped from his wound and bled into the trickling gutter of the Liffey, like the Nile turned red by staff of Moses.

A whole day long he recuperated, sometimes wishing it were all a nightmare, hoping that he might awake in the morning to find the skin had miraculously retreated of its own accord and gone back to how it was – only upon waking did he see in dismay that it had only swelled the more, poised on the grisly verge of popping, to burst like bubblegum in an explosion of milky blood. Foolhardy or heroic or stubborn or insane, he forced himself to keep it secret – not as if the slippery bastard Merkel wouldn't go tell everyone anyway – and staggered all the way into college to attend his wretched classes as normal, limping at every painful step, lurching and staggering at a geriatric snail's pace, the vulnerable head feeling so exposed, rubbing and brushing against the scratchy denim through the many torn gaps in the ripped fabric of the silken undergarments, at every scratch of which he would gasp and wince and clutch a post to catch his breath and whine and moan and curse his self-wrought fate of auto-impotence.

And if anyone asked him what was wrong, or wondered aloud why it was he walked so strangely, he assured them that he had only his own ineptitude to blame, and that it was only on account of his having done the splits as part of a drunken dare last night – a silly story that convinced nobody, but raised eyebrows aplenty, suspicious gazes drawn downwards to the telling bulge he displayed at the busted crotch.

Between classes he met with Merkel on the college benches, and masochistically bore up to his friend's mocking lashes and slurs, pretending to laugh at the offensive barrage of raillery, determined to see only the funny side of his penile predicament. Once he summoned the courage to stagger to the clinic, only to arrive too late to make an appointment, not even in time for the hour allotted for emergency cases, as his surely was, resigned to limp off huffily complaining of the system's inefficiency to anyone who would listen to his crotchety gripes. He learnt to live with his affliction, daily bathing his deformed manhood in steaming waters that soothed the sting awhile.

And the strain of secrecy was sometimes too much to bear, and he decided to confide in a choice few others, besides the bastard Konrad, who would spread the word elsewhere in any case. On the Wednesday of that week of woe, the sublime Saruko sweetly and curiously inquired, by lamplight, as to the cause of his gait, which was hardly the result of doing the splits, when she caught sight of him limping along cobbles (such a limp as Byron or O'Mara might once have borne to incite the interest of a lass!).

So he was moved to unwisely divulge his plight to his one-time love beneath the bell tower, grasping her hand, and crying, and laughing, as he nosed her fragrant hair, and caressed her back, and copped a final desperate feel, as he inarticulately raved about ruptured veils, and of onion rings, and of circumcision, and of the inverted penis gourds that some African tribes employed, and of Olivier's cock, and of his fellow phimosis sufferer Josef Fritzl. And the naïve child understood his complaints only in part, for it was very much a man's problem, and she had enough of her own already, and she knew not whether to laugh or weep or console him, and often winced in her disgust, and shortly after made her squeamish excuses, and left him alone to limp home in the cold.

'I miss hanging out with you!' she called in parting, as he cried inside morosely.

And meanwhile Merkel was lodging in Lombardy, so fearful was he of his mad mammy back home. Sometimes he would ring the Banshee nag, only to meet with no response. And nor did Albert Potter respond to his calls, which lead Konrad to assume he had hung himself as predicted, a gross speculation that crippled Simeon pooh-poohed, as he clutched his mutilated flesh and whimpered. And sometimes, to lacerate and sting himself the more, he resorted to tediously quizzing Konrad about the tryst with Jezebel.

'Did you fuck her, yeah? Did you fuck her real good and hard, yeah? Did she scratch you did she? Did she ask you to hurt her real bad yeah? Was it a good fuck?'

In response, grumpy Konrad told the pervert to fuck off and leave him alone.

The smelly masochist chuckled mirthlessly, and picked up his flashing phone. He had received a text from Galbraith, who had witnessed his hobbling, and now wondered what was wrong. And tears filled Simeon's eyes as he typed a terse reply dictating a time for a belated meeting. And it was only right that he tell Edwin Galbraith too, this man who, once the inadvertent partial cause of his self-pity and sorrow, since spat out by the infantine Saruko, teeth of which dragon he had escaped and subsequently thrived when freed of captivity, this man who was now, in so many varied ways, perhaps the most admirable man he knew. A truer and a better friend who always wished him well, in whom he could confide and trust, who had stood by him steadfastly and unflinchingly, even when overshadowed on the sidelines, no matter how much the prima-donna Merkel hogged the limelight and stole the show. Edwin Galbraith was since become a Scholar, earned solely by unstinting diligence and the sweat of his brainy brows, and had comfortably settled in palatial lodgings in Front Square with a certain David Lydon, and was chasing scores of girls with whom he was a hit and catch, all of whom adored him for his wit and ingenuity, his good nature and mad cheer. An earring in his ear and a baguette under his arm, swishing through town with a satchel full of tomes, draped in a long black coat and beret, he was the picture of a studious thinker who did not stint at imbibing the divine grape, gaunt and intense and wacky too, living life to the full with fingers in all pies, wooing and boxing and fencing and writing and excelling. He resembled an acidic pipedream of Beckett pretending to be Dennis Hopper on speed.

DAVID LYDON AND EDWIN GALBRAITH OF HOUSE 7, FRONT SQUARE

This was the motto emblazoned in brass on Edwin's door, which plaque Simeon eyed unceasing after crawling up the stairs, and ringing the bell for his friend within. And for some reason he found the twin names, coupled with their locale, so inexpressibly hilarious, and once he found something funny, he milked it dry, no sophisticate when it came to comedy, repeating the motto over and over again, as if in a tranquilizing mantra:

'David Lydon and Edwin Galbraith of House Seven, Front Square. David Lydon and Edwin Galbraith of House Seven, Front Square. David Lydon and Edwin Galbraith of House Seven, Front Square. David Lydon and Edwin Galbraith of House Seven, Front Square. David Lydon and Edwin Galbraith of House Seven, Front Square. David Lydon and Edwin Galbraith of House Seven, Front Square. David Lydon and Edwin Galbraith of House Seven, Front Square. David Lydon and Edwin Galbraith of House Seven, Front Square. David Lydon and Edwin Galbraith of House Seven, Front Square …'

Edwin had been busy slicing off some spatters of menstrual blood that had flecked the pages of his Rushdie book. With a bread knife, he quite butchered *Midnight's Children*. He opened the door with a towel around his naked waist, fresh from the sauna, and wondered why his visitor did so gibber. Simeon fell through the door without ceremony, clutching the walls for support as he stumbled down the corridor, and veered haphazardly to a couch laden with copybooks, on which he collapsed and clutched his crotch, and whined. And his perplexed host offered him biscuits and tea, and listened to his complaint with an uneasy attitude. And having heard the baffling details, he stroked his thin chin, fingered his jittery earring, and looped a drooping forelock as he worried.

'In short, I am bollocksed, you might say!' Simeon beamed in conclusion.

And then Edwin licked a finger with which he cleft the air to announce his idea.

'Let us go then, you and I, to Chapelizod by and by. I have always wanted to walk there myself, and this evening seems the perfect occasion for so doing, don't you think?'

And Simeon blinked in his confusion; and then he smiled.

So off they went on the most meaningless of treks, having chomped upon cookies as prelude to their pilgrimage without purpose, a lengthy stretch of legs that was greatly unwise. They made haste from the college and headed for the riverside where cars were beeping, down by the bridges where they westerly roamed. And every inch of the merciless way Simeon limped and winced – the whole journey must have taken all of four or seven hours. He clung to Edwin's shoulder for support as the sun set, whimpering.

But Edwin absolved him of his suffering like a cleric, and airily assured him it was all no matter, pointing up to the uncaring stars that shone down on their stagger as they traipsed the gutters by the bridges, and drank up the swollen river's velvet drapes.

'You complain of circumcision that you purport to fear,' Galbraith said gravely to Collins. 'But once it is done, you'll feel so much better. And really, it's been done many a time to many a man. It's practically the norm in America anyway. And a Jewish man learns to live with his bishop bared. And anyway, from what I've heard, a cropped top both feels and smells better, according to the evidence of both parties in the case …'

They wobbled along the two, so firm were they in one, and stopped by Collins Barracks come the winking hours, where an unostentatious public house called The Millennium Bar opened its red doors wide to admit the thirsty strays. The barkeep, having enjoyed a pinch or two too many of snuff in his back room, gave them several rounds for free, for which they were exceeding glad. And they grew maudlin in their drunkenness, the young marauders, and babbling Simeon clasped Galbraith's shoulder, and confessed to having loved his former squeeze Saruko before, even ages ago when she could not be obtained and was out of his bounds, even then he had always loved her from afar, spying from his vantage on the side-lines, left on the shelf in the dark, which loony fancy Edwin had always somehow suspected on his part, since it had been so obvious all along, but never could ever bring himself to fully say, with a tact bred of politeness, being a gentleman true and full.

And drunker Galbraith lovingly spoke of debauch, and of women he had known, and of anuses, and of pudenda, of solitary pleasures, of breasts, of the worship of beauty, of the tinkling urination of maidens into chamber pots, of furry honeycombs he had tapped in his time, and of the aesthetic manifesto of the libertine he espoused, of excess and indulgence, all of which were so surely on the side of life. And the loser Collins bemoaned having wasted the greatest days of his youth, despising himself for always holding back, loathing himself for having let every chance of love slip through his fingers and disappear like sand, mourning the losses of Saruko, of Jezzie, of Kyrie Elysium, even of bloody Honeypenny, even of the Russian. And now the flaccid puppet was deformed forever, maimed and distorted by his own hand, twisted all out of shape at the very root of manhood where it mattered most – so what was left to him now, when he had put paid to all his chances, and bodily ruined all his hopes for a normal life, unhappiness ensured?

'Ah, but is it really though?' jocular Galbraith slurred, slapping him on the back to dispel his fatuous gloom, enjoining him to partake of the delight begat by wisdom.

They exited into the cool of night after the fourth or fifth serving of fuel, swaying and toppling under the purple sky speckled by toothpaste flecks. Past the gates of the Park they staggered inert, and soon limping Simeon was supporting the reeling Galbraith, ostensibly the healthier with all his private parts in place, but who was now the more drunken of the two, stewed in the barleycorn that fuelled his corny blarney. What a picture they made, the gaunt aesthete who could barely stand, leaning on the hobbling fool, his legs apart with inverted prepuce that grew the more swollen with every heavy weighty step, whose pain he noted the less, numbed by the alcoholic anaesthetic of which he partook. Into the night past the Phoenix walls they went, roaming in orange light by the stones, shaking fists at bushes above, passing the rowing club where discarded boats were moored and bobbing on the liquid rush. A chill wind carried away Edwin's bleary words on its breeze, as his slender belly grumbled and prepared to expel the vile poison imbibed. Some three more hours awaited them as they walked down that lonely midnight road, until soon about the spookiest witching hour they rounded a corner and entered the grounds of Chapelizod village, where an abandoned house stood by the churchyard, and the chapel's windows were of the finest stained glass. Through long grass they tripped to the river to watch the waters glide, bearing swans on their sweeping tide.

And the boys stood by the reedy banks and admired the rising mist on the river, through whose swathes the soupy moonshine basked, glowing sallow through the bulrush veil. And in the moist grasses sickly Edwin fell to his knees, and vomited copiously. He retched and smeared the grasses with his puke, into which his glasses fell as they slid off his nose, while Simeon, lurking nearby in the shadows of the trees, so his mangled bugle would remain unseen, pulled down his trousers and squatted to urinate in a mushroom glade, like any washerwoman would. And he moaned as he pissed, for the scalding trickle stung his swollen ring of flesh, as blinded Edwin wallowed damply on the ground, unseeing fingers groping about the pile of vomit in vain search of his lenses. Pitying Simeon crawled over to assist, and dipped careless fingers into the stinking puke to snatch out the tainted glasses, much smeared with clotted food, and he wiped the filthy specs on the damp grass to divest them of their muck, and slid them back on their owner's nose, who now saw only a haze of fog, clawing the air with giddy paws.

They stumbled a few feet further into the village's heart, but there was nothing doing at that godless hour of the desolate night, and they hailed the next taxi they saw. Edwin puked again on the way, necessitating a hasty abandonment of their transport midway home, hurled from the cab by a raving driver who took no pity on their plight. In the end, Simeon all but carried Edwin for the final mile to his college gates, sweating with the strain as the zipper of his jeans incessantly scratched the fleshy tip of his cock.

The morning after, he finally obtained an appointment with the college clinic. The lady who pulled down his trousers took one look at the damage, and exclaimed, pained:

'O you poor thing!'

And she sent him to St James's, for which she paid the taxi fare ('look after yourself!' she smirked in parting), and in the hospital his case was classed as 'urgent'. He was lain down on a stretcher, and told to keep calm, and then a chap called Adrian curled his lip as he surveyed the ruins of his loins, and applied numbing gel to his swollen bits.

'Am I going to be circumcised? Do I have phimosis?' delirious Simeon jabbered.

'You don't have phimosis!' Adrian laughed.

'But the veil … the onion skin … the masks … ow!'

'Be honest. Did you actually try to get it back once you'd pulled it down?'

'I … I …'

And then kindly Adrian tugged back Simeon's foreskin for him, and wiped away the flood of discharge, and set the boy back on his feet, and prescribed some anti-inflammatory pills to ease the process of the swelling in reverse. And as he passed the scribbled paper across the desk, he gave his patient a disbelieving look, both pitying and amused, as if struggling to stifle his laughter. And Simeon, reborn a new man, went forth into the world, scratching his head, confused. He was at least glad he could walk again.

CHAPTER SIXTY-SEVEN

Mr Albert Potter and the Banshee Esmerelda Merkel were so far getting on well. For it was a bracing thing to arise from his stupor, grimly expectant of but another tedious day, only to be met with the wholesome sight of a naked lady recumbent beside him in the bed, in which they passed their nights in boning and spewing on his bursting pillows.

She was wrinkled and decrepit no doubt, far from being a spring chicken such as once he lusted for, but after a certain age he had nonetheless found that, when fucking in the dark, most bodies were much like most other bodies, and she was at least full-bodied in her way. And they indulged in a charming parody of domesticity, like a weeklong honeymoon just before life's curtains closed, wherein he would slouch on his couch and hum, while she cooked up a succulent breakfast for her champion, and brewed divine tea in his pots she polished with her flannel. Cut off from the world and content, they would dine and sup in the underground dimness of his mole's hole, flinching at the sun's rays she braved whenever she ventured to his doorstep to water his plants with her hose. She knitted and darned his socks while he placidly observed, and grew the hornier in his idyll as he scratched his dog's belly, whose fur the haunted woman had washed and combed.

Albert and Esmerelda spoke little to each other, and most often it was she who held the floor, and whenever she spoke, it was about herself and her woes she liked most to speak. She would pine for her past among the Maoris, and lengthily recount the rosy history of her former love, her solely only Pipefitter Pat to whom she was wed when she crossed the seas. Albert listened disinterested to the bulk of her sentimental recollections, warming to her spiel only when she made mention of her only son Konrad, who was a trial so it seemed, and had been ever since birth, when the doctors dragged him forth drenched in blood, and she squinted on the bed in her blindness, unable to discern the sex of her child, to which end Dr Grimm dangled the lad closer in front of her specs, only for the brat to spurt forth a dribbling jet of urine from his little peg, dousing his mother all over the gnarls of her cheeks, at which skittish anecdote Albert much delighted.

Sometimes he wondered whether he himself was already dead, and whether this dreamy wraith of a wife had come on cue to keep him company in his ghostly afterlife.

As he sat on his sofa and watched her sow and thread, he heard a vague beeping emitted from under him. And after burrowing in the crannies of his couch, he found he had received a message on his mobile, a long-delayed reply to one of his own texts, one which, strange to say, he had never himself sent, since it stayed on the shelf with the drafts. And he scratched his head and dumbly wondered, as over and over he read:

```
Yeah, they was some good games all right. I'm
still in town, on Portmarnock beach as it happens. Come
join me, and we'll play a few more – your friend, Arsene
```

CHAPTER SIXTY-EIGHT

But Jezebel got her wish – there was a trip to the beach in the end.

It was in the course of my hours of recovery, a sadder and a wiser, but not a better man, a spiritual cripple in whom all the natural instincts, so innate and easy to the others, were so sorely quashed in me by artifice and mannerism. I brooded in my home, shying away from the summer sun outside, and examined my swollen bits that daily grew the less inflamed as they deflated, until I could urinate again without pain. I sent messages to dearest Edwin, thanking him for our night of triumph, and cast a cold eye on lounging Merkel who filled the foreground, his boots on my desk and his smoke filling my air.

'I'm not convinced about this whole penile affair of yours,' he sneered. 'It seems less to have been fixed than to have been just indefinitely shelved. Seriously, you need to get it sorted once and for all. That kind of experience could result in some long lasting psychological trauma, one of your own making, better still. I wouldn't be surprised if you did some time inside later in life. Hah! Wouldn't it be mad if you got locked up!'

'You shall visit me of course,' I sighed as I chewed a leaf, 'and keep me posted on the gossipy affairs, denied me as I sit in my cell and scrawl on the walls. Just as Arsene must once have done, come to think of it. For ours, Konrad, is an undying bond in spite of all your villainy. You shall be with me always, dearest of Maoris. I absolve you.'

'O fuck off! Get off your pedestal and join the human race for once. But you mention gossip, so listen to this for a sec – Johnny claims he got with that barmy Kyrie Elysium one you used to like. But she wouldn't let him enter her, since she's an eternal virgin and crackpot to boot, and was content to have him simply lie on her, erect and naked as he was, with his hairy arms spread like an airplane, a magic carpet parody of intercourse. Then she produced a shining knife and tried to shave off all his fur. Fucking ridiculous. There goes one mighty Yeti who shan't be shorn by that loony Bo-Peep!'

'How lovely that tale rings!' I cried in lazy rapture, 'I am glad for him. After all:'

Johnny Fritz could do no wrong,
And nor could Murky Con,
But Colloseum Simeon, ah Colloseum Simeon,
That tight old shite could do no right
Since he never did nowt but wrong – bum-bum!

'How sweet. Your first, and last, and greatest poem. Anyway, I just got this syrupy message from Jezzie, apparently she's with that Chinese one, they're just around the corner, and they want to drop in for a visit. Our fan club is knocking, darling!'

'My doors are always open for the flower girls. I hope they bring some incense.'

They did not bring incense, but instead brought butter and eggs and some ham. Jezzie produced a serving of whiskey from the pocket of her tweedy tramp's coat, and she passed the bottle around to her fey male foils, who sipped the spirits and opined. And ravishing Saruko smiled and looked adorable as she invaded our idyll, mincing and batting her silken gloss as she took over the kitchen, and fried us up some Jacob's crackers laden with all the yolk of the hen. She made an ungodly mess, but at least the result was tasty, served on palms with sticky thumbs, the remainders sucked from under the painted nails that had ground the lumps of cheese. Konrad explained the significance of his tattoos to his smitten conquest of last week, the girl with orange hair who giggled at the tiger on his thigh and the dragon on his back. And she loved the sound of his colourful mother from whom he had fled, and, for a dare and one of love's little ruses, snatched his phone and dialled his mammy's mobile, tittering all the while. And on the line's other end, faintly, as if buried underground in hell, we heard a dismal chanting, in a hoarse and ghastly voice, muffled like a scratched record, its torn vinyl grinding on:

'... *the snoring baggage in me always brooding was now the mask I was made forever to wear, emblazoned in lime on me branded cheeks that leaked their tears* ...'

'Enough!' cried perturbed Konrad, grabbing the phone and hanging up.

And Jezzie was also keen to discuss the matter of Albert further, our honorary father for whom we bore such love, mingled with fear that warred with our sorrow, missing the fat man whose absence galled us, about whom curious sheltered Saruko nursed a fascination. We had varying memories of the encounters with our Fagan, all of which was seen through intoxicant's delirium, and the sorry truth was hard to filter from our blurred recollections. Both Jezzie and I agreed that Merkel played up to his lust too much, which flirty charge he flatly denied, claiming he was the victim in the case, a lumbering innocent who ran the risk of rape in spite of himself, cursed by his charm – truly, his only genius was that of constant self-justification and acquittal of his crimes, I decided smugly as I shared my tea with Saruko. Sniggering, she whispered in my ear that she had heard my affliction was cured, and she rejoiced and was glad for me, so she claimed. I frowned and kicked myself for having told her – surely all the grapevine of gossips knew now where I had erred.

'You're an amazing person!' she gushed fondly as I gazed back across a cynical abyss, 'And a new life deserves to have a new look, no?'

I sadly smiled back, and marvelled at the death of love. But she was still a sweet girl, albeit as impossible to please as an abandoned child denied her candy, with a heart as golden as the light that fell through the glass. And she looked up and down the stinking wardrobe I wore, on which surface the diamond motes were skipping from their homes, turning up her nose in disapproval while eyeing my festering green jacket that had once been black, the laughing clown's shoes I never removed, and the jeans that were ripped at the crotch, through which hole my testes sometimes poked for air. And she snapped her fingers, a wizard of fashion for which she had a passion, and declared the time was ripe for my closet's makeover, in which fatuous pursuit Konrad and Jezzie gleefully joined.

And so, like a geriatric pursued by the nursery cops, sirens ringing from their buggies, I ran around my house and yelped as they chased me upstairs and downstairs squealing like kittens, until guffawing Konrad grabbed my waist and tugged me back down, and carried me captive writhing in his arms to within where the girls were giggling again.

And they wrestled me down to the mattress as I thrashed in hapless protest, and stripped me of my coat and shirt and jacket, reeking garments they tossed in a bundle out of the window, landing on the street where they sprouted legs and hooves, and ran off like gazelles or unicorns, for this was the mating season, prime time for bulls as well as bees and birds. And I rolled about wrinkled and naked as Jezebel sprinkled holy water on my innocence, showering dollops of the finest vintage from Knock contained in a clay pot shaped like a pepper dispenser, and Saruko took up her scissors and snipped my fuzzy beard she trimmed to a rakish taper, and clipped my lank fringe neatly, and brushed my hair and gave it a perm of a wave until it was springy. And the matronly ladies sponged and hosed and towelled me down, wiping dry and clean my every stinking aperture, sprucing my navel and anus and bellybutton too, and the glorious bitch-goddess Saruko coyly eyed the bulge at my underpants, and clapped a hand to her mouth as she purred: 'Ooo! It's big!' And in the corner, the stylist Merkel riffled through my father's drawers, and selected for me some fresh armoury as yet unworn, a shirt of navy blue, and a swish jacket striped by tweedy lines of green and brown like Sherwood. Into this new costume I was hoisted, and I blinked and flexed myself, bemused by the novel sensations, and eyed myself in a mirror, and learnt how to walk and breathe again, faltering on my ageing baby's pins as the mandarin princess guided me by the hand. Lastly, I plucked a bowler from the Buddha's head in the hall, and crowned myself like Charlie would. And all agreed it was a huge improvement, and Jezzie warmly suggested that we take the outfit on an outing to inaugurate the cladding, and all of us joyously plumped for the beach.

And so we set forth into the Saturday sunshine, skipping down Lombardy Road on invisible ropes, two men and two maidens, the tattooed wastrel and the reborn jester, the messy empress and the genteel harlot, plucking scarlet flowers from the bushes of neighbours to bestrew our laurel scalps, painting hearts on our faces with Jezzie's crayons and Saruko's lipstick, rings in our ears and bubbles in our heads, filling our baskets with fruit and wine and honey, and other juicy provisions for the picnic at Portmarnock to which we were cheerily bound. Dublin town was never prettier than then.

In delight we strolled through her dirty streets, past the dying generations of youths in arms and ducks on the ponds, the romantic etchings on barks of the trees, under whose boughs sailed the babes in the prams and the elders in wheelchairs, the scattering pigeons fed crumbs by the tramps, scabbing fags off the tippling clerks in the pubs, nearby the smoking barge honking as it drowsed on the canal, by whose banks the bony herons roamed and chomped on trout, startled by the hum of thumping swan's wings galloping in the sky above, disdainfully surveying the smoking wreckage of traffic winking by the stuffy green where harried shoppers cursed and cars were crashed, and in the shrill air sang the trill of school bells ringing as the Leaving Cert was crammed and rammed, and from St Paddy's doors the pupils swam in a cascade to freedom, released from the murk of the chamber wherein they wrote exams in dust.

In music stores Marco Grimaldi and Lukas the Shag were lurking by the racks, browsing porn without passion, next door to the teashop whose shelves of crinkly bags were scoured by kindly spinster Agatha Honeypenny, her laden bag bursting with flour for the buttery cakes she would later bake, ignoring the windows where Ulick O'Muadaigh's bestseller *The De Valera Code* was now being advertised among festoons of crepe, coupled with signings by the crusty author who puffed his pipe and scowled at any smarmy charges of implausibility the punters might offer, who glimpsed our quartet as we dipped past the Eason's entry in our hurry, avoiding the loitering Mr Denis Merriman, en route to a skirmish with his mistress, with whom he would run away once he retired.

And we travelled through the college grounds hand in hand as we sallied and chuckled on the blinking cobbles, spotting shady Edwin Galbraith lurking at his window, leering face pressed to the sweaty pane, a palm to brow, struggling to remember our Chapelizod pilgrimage while a monotonous mantra blared inside his head: *David Lydon and Edwin Galbraith of House Seven, Front Square...*

And we delightedly noted none but the furry bear Johnny Fritzl sitting on impish Kyrie Elysium, lost to love on the lush carpet of the rose garden's grass, scratching her bony rump amid the fallen petals that browned at the slightest touch, thumbs pricked by the spiking hedge of thorns, and I doffed my hat to him and told him to keep up the good work, while on the pitch the seagulls danced to conjure the buried worms, observed by the happy couple on the benches, seated gallant Harry Carson who was attempting to explain the rules of the game to beloved Ivana Egorova, the amiable Soviet charlady who could not comprehend the cricketing sport at which her ripe and rakish boyfriend had once excelled, before he dropped out to mop up drink with his shredded degree, sunburned kindred to the sundowner revellers sprawling on the Pavilion's idle steps.

And at the college's rear we boarded a train, juggling pennies we dropped as we jumped over the barrier for free, and jaunted down the tracks to the coast, and Saruko thrashed me with a baton loaf, sprinkling fluffy breadcrumbs that mixed with my moustache, as Jezebel hooted and Merkel looked out the window to the rosy afternoon.

In Portmarnock station we disembarked and ambled on the sandy path, scattering the woollen dandelions blown apart by our breezy passage, detained by the dizzy ladies who were always applying some more eyeliner, or forgetting where they had put their stupid purses, and we smelled the rush of coastal air that greeted us on the wild wind, harping in the swirls of our blustering hair as we passed the golf course, where I— C— C— and Isolde Lovelace swung their clubs and talked in the shroud of code about Toby and Tristram (she wanted to adopt a child, but he wanted to only imagine one), the hilly grounds littered by randy thieving hares who stole lost golfing balls, and bore them underground to earthen altars, where they were worshipped in the dark warrens as pockmarked gods.

We came to a great plain where flocks of ducks were squawking, chased by the girls who envied their feathers and bright beaks, geese eyed with longing by the restless Maori bard who tore off his shoes and socks in passion. Ducklings were hatching in the warm puddles, four babes of four fathers that eschewed their shells and waddled along in military file, as did we upon coming to the moors where the girls ripped their wetted nylons as they tripped on the earth's many dips, dodging the marshy bogs where clumsy Saruko nearly sank and screamed, as I eyed her comely calves to which I doffed my bowler, and Jezzie grasped her dainty wrist, and savage Konrad rolled up his trousers like a hunter-gatherer, and carried our picnic's cargo on his shoulder as if a weighty urn were set upon his deadpan head, as we regressed like cavemen in care of the tigresses and their pronged caresses, in search of fire and a site for our repast, nearing the humming dunes on the horizon ahead, the reeds that waved in greeting to our adoring troops.

We ascended the headland, and exulted in the spread of the beach below, waving our arms and skipping in the blanket of pampas. We sunk to feed the four of us in the long grass, guzzling our cucumber sandwiches and slurping the last of our summer's wine, clinking bejewelled carafes in the radiance. Saruko plucked a weedy blade and tickled Konrad's chin while jealous Jezebel knitted a daisy chain, mourned the distant sea and the faraway schooners she would never board, as she threaded the buttercups with her restless fingers, under whose nails congealed still the blood of all the male brutes she had conquered. A pair of six-spotted burnets were copulating in thickets of the heather nearby, rubbing together their inky sexes, whose progress I drank up with my magnifying glass, a dedicated naturalist. A flightless ladybird got stuck in our butter, rescued by Konrad who dangled a rope of reed to which the ruby beetle clung. Inspired, as if having seen his face in the sun, Jezzie then turned to me, and asked, very softly and tenderly:

'Do you think Albert would agree to pose for a portrait? God knows you're always saying he's an oil painting. I'd like to capture him with my brush before he …'

Before he died, alone in the cellar with a broken heart whose walls were papery, with all his arteries clogged and blocked, squatting in a final evacuation of his own filth as he expired from a stroke, dropping his last can as the pulse's beating stopped, his passing unheard, ignored by the world until the landlord's son came to collect the rent from the dead tenant in the basement, stench of his corpse caught by the dogs, a demise that would pass for weeks unreported, unknown even to the counter crew and the decrepit barkeeps across the street, until they chanced to glance at the inky obituaries and saw the name of their most loyal customer set baldly down, whose departure we ourselves would learn of too late, too late to attend his dismal funeral at which we would have been the only mourners, crying out our eyes and dropping bouquets of wilting roses, as

Potter's decaying paunch was lowered into its little plot, in the wind and the rain, in the cold.

I hailed this as the most excellent idea she had ever had, a worthy memento for such a folk hero as ours, and together we warmed to the scheme of artistry, as she excitedly decided she would work from photos, since he would hardly be the most amiable of models, gruffly shifting and itching and crowing for her cleavage as she attempted to scrawl his sculptural features on her easel, struggling to depict a tragic Rembrandt's face hauled from the butcher shop still bleeding in acrylic gouts and slashes, such a father as might have been hers, orphaned young as was he, ditched in the glens.

Then the wind stole my hat and carried it tumbling down the hill to the beach's sand. And I spluttered as my comrades roared, and rolled downhill myself to collapse in sand and chase my flighty bowler I barely captured. And Merkel and the girls descended, and knelt to play in the sandy nursery. Rival sandcastles we would build, one for the boys and one for the ladies, dug from the sand with our bare hands, denied our spades and buckets as we rebuilt Babylon from the seashore's clay. The girls built little before regressing to chasing, tossing clusters of sand at each other, stuffing grains down their busts, littering their bras with dusty crystals. And meanwhile Konrad and I, sworn artificers both, dug and dug together in allegiance, and erected a noble edifice out of the ground, a house of happier dreams where the brighter phantoms of passing fancies could abide, scooping up a castle out from the earth like Atlantis, like a godfather's house in which there were many ballrooms, with seashells and cockles for windows, a garland of flowers for a flag to adorn the mighty fortress of content we sculpted in sand, a seaside citadel where we might live in bumbling peace, lapped by the foam and elbowing the nearby brine, toying with the gurgling mollusks I could claim for mine, and hang around my neck in a lace, which Saruko thought was gay, pinching my face as she surveyed our house of sand in envy, stamping on the outer walls and tunnels with a giddy kiddy's foot.

'Your sandcastle is absolutely massive!' she trilled foolishly, lisping to distract me from my tunnelling labours. '... I think it's just to make up for something. Tee-hee!'

I could have killed her then and there.

Jezebel was eyeing the serene horizon, a lily hand to brow to shield her eyes from the blinding sun that spat down its rays. She spotted something farther away, and called out to us to look. And we all looked up from the sand, our gazes carrying over to the edge of the shore where she pointed, to a huddled group of figures and the remains of a bonfire or a memorial pyre, solemnly arrayed beside the gentle waves lapping at the beach's cusp. Our castle's building halted, our chains of daisies dropped. One by one we rose from our edifice, to stare unknowing in wonder, our voices hushed until soon in a row we boys and girls watched, in unspeaking reverence and awe, the distant ritual unfold.

And we stood in silence on the sand, and beheld from afar a hero's funeral.

CHAPTER SIXTY-NINE

Tadgh O'Mara, besotted bard of our Erin, sat on a rock and observed all while the waves lapped, and the tide went in and went out, sashaying over the shore with blooms of surf. And Tadgh made a note of everything that was enacted before him, scratching gnomic memos on pebbles with a shell, squinting with his ailing eyes that were blinding, so long denied their spectacles. And as he watched, he polished harmonies in his head relating to the proceedings, beauteous lines it were meet for some scrivener to copy as he chanted, lest all this brightness be lost, sucked up by the swarming flies who nibbled upon The Mad Monk's dead body, shooed off by a swish of Balthazar's tail.

It was not easy for Arsene-Elijah to convince the Puck and Pooka of the honesty of his designs, reeling from a stranger who had emerged in the dark to murder their master, refusing to believe that they had come all this way only to watch him die, and thereafter transport the body away again to whence they had come. They were sullen and hostile towards the wizened killer for much of the first night of their vigil on the shore, until he provided proof of his identity and professed credentials, in the form of recounting, from memory, the entire history of their fantastic group's exploits, which took a whole night to recite, while the firelight ebbed and the cadaver rotted. But so intimate a knowledge of their chronicles did the prophet provide, right down to the most precise details of Watt's conical cap, even to the smallest touches on the final panel of page 492 of the comic book, that at last they could quibble no longer, and swallowed their doubts, and accepted him for whom he was as the new week's sunrise came up, and believed him in his good intentions. And they stepped back from their indignation, and acknowledged his preeminence in wisdom, and appointed him master of ceremonies to whom they bowed, whose commands they would obey with unquestioning faith.

The Clunge Monkey, a servant of his nature, made numerous outrageous efforts to copulate with his father's corpse while the others were busy arguing, a balding sightless hobgoblin mounting the thigh of a felled colossus. But his grotesque attempts at defiling his maker, once detected, were nipped in the bud by the disgusted mourners, who grabbed and slapped him, a punishment the sadist creature rather enjoyed. Arsene-Elijah fashioned a cage for the brute, into which he was thrust by the Puck and Pooka, on whose hands he spewed seed as he was locked in behind the wire mesh of netting, thrashing about in his confines, resolving to have his way with himself thereafter, for want of any other object. And Arsene-Elijah's henchmen wiped their soiled hands on their sleeves, and beheld in repulsion The Clunge Monkey's further convulsions, a thing to which they could never warm, their former overlord's final bestowal to the world, which rather smacked of an upraised middle finger saying fuck-you-all-I'm-boarding-the-gravy-train-to-eternity, an insult, as opposed to a gift of beauty that had not yet come into the earth.

Then they turned their attention to the carcase, which they cleaned, and the Puck shuddered to find himself a restorer once more, embalming with lotions and wiping the body dry of the congealing blood, sprucing the cheeks and washing the filthy tangles of the beard, brushing and polishing the jagged teeth that were now set forever in an undying grin – perhaps he knew he had had the last laugh. One such looser tooth the Pooka discreetly detached from its gums and pocketed in secret, thinking it might fetch a good price as an arcane bauble to fool the elves, when he vended his stall at the forthcoming leprechaun's fair at the rainbow's end – Fergus was always an opportunist.

But Arsene-Elijah alone had the nerve to lay a hand over his brother's face to close his eyes, that their unblinking stare might be withdrawn, that haunted gaze that chilled the onlookers. Balthazar stoked the funeral pyre's flame with his hooves, a poker betwixt his jaws, humming to the crackle as The Clunge Monkey cackled in his cage. Lest he starve, the

Puck sadly passed through the bars the mess of the dead cat Moloch, on whose tattered flesh the monster gorged. And when The Mad Monk's body was presentable, Arsene-Elijah trawled the shore for some vessel in which to place it, and came upon a discarded canoe he dragged along the sand, into which they gravely laid the dead man. And they showered the body with an array of daffodils, and buttercups, and daisies, and bluebells, and violets, and roses, and funereal lilies, and a sprinkle of all such flowers that they plucked from the waving dunes, and heaped in a blanket of petals to drape in fragrance the remains of their lost and greatest saint. Tadgh O'Mara, who now understood that he was attending the funeral rites of the one-time owner of the dog who gored him, swallowed his past resentment, and threw in a few laudatory woofs himself.

And sometimes they wept and sometimes they laughed as they mourned and made their tributes. And they sat around on the sand in a circle around the coffined hull where he lay, and they fondly remembered his glory days, his biting wit and bravery and charm, and recounted how each in turn had met him, whether it be in Babylon or FaerieLand where wine was imbibed and fortunes told while lifelong friendships were forged. And Arsene-Elijah rose to read a kind of eulogy on the sundown of the second day succeeding his passing, remembering their salad days of childhood in their family's seaside citadel, such a distant keep as might have been erected on any fair shore as was Portmarnock's, in memory of a hero who was both divine and profane, who dared to be imperfect, a warrior who was once a toddler by whose side his wiser brother had grown up, tearing out one another's hairs as they browsed their cellar's beers, spying on the lovemaking of their torrid sires, and racing through the ballroom swinging from the chandeliers, mounting stairs to the topmost observatory tower, to spy at the stars for the first time, as seen through the lens of their astronomer father's telescope, wondering upon the other worlds in the night sky where they might pry, and alien domains infringe for richer adventure.

And Arsene-Elijah raised his top hat in reverence, and dropped ashes from the bowl of his pipe all over the body he dusted in farewell, and bowed and prayed and cried. And then they played their funeral games, performing charades in which episodes of the dead man's life were reenacted, sparking off fireworks and diving through hoops, swallowing the shingle and the brine they wore as laurels. And Arsene-Elijah leaned over Tadgh O'Mara's shoulder to inquire as to the progress of the Great Epic whose shape was forming in his brain. And Tadgh O'Mara assured him it was good – though he made request for a dedicated scribe to whom to dictate – and the subject made him queasy at times – for he questioned the dubious morality inherent in lauding the transformation of a skeletal Bull into a gross Clunge Monkey, which metamorphosis was not one he felt comfortable in celebrating. Surely a new Tain ought to be more ... gee I dunno ... elevated or something, no? But Arsene-Elijah made no answer, only tittered at his greatest prank.

Sometime later, just in time, after they had done reverence for a week, two more mourners joined them. Coming over the headlands two by two, descending toward the shore they came, the fat man of blubber and the ghostly woman, armed with a basket full of provisions for a picnic, tripping along down the hilly dunes hand in hand. Mr Albert Potter had never looked better. His parrot was on his shoulder, and his panting White Dog was safe on his leash, and his new beard was lushly growing all over his thinning chins, luxuriant shags she had often fingered in her fondness. Ever faithful, they came upon the summons of an ambiguous text, one that Arsene-Elijah had filtered along the airwaves through the motions of his mind. He saw them approaching from afar, and grinned and waved and beckoned. Tadgh O'Mara flinched at the sight of the dog, and skulked behind the Pooka's shoulder. The Puck made flirty eyes at the Banshee Esmerelda Merkel, who coldly ignored him, and scratched her tattoos. And Mr Albert Potter came closer with shyness to the shore's damp verge, wary of the wild bunch of elfin folk that clustered round the canoe wherein a smiling corpse was gravely lain, whose noble face, grinning bearded with a hooked nose, reminded him of something.

And Mr Albert Potter halted before the figure of Arsene-Elijah, and cautiously surveyed his unfamiliar hairy features, with mad grin and luminous eyes of lemonade hue, seeking a flicker of the version he had known, as the fiery orbs beamed upon him.

'Is it ... Arsene again?' he said slowly.

'*You have come for chess*!' Arsene-Elijah trilled, '*Pray, be seated, I shall be with you in a second. Fergie and Robbie, your time is come! Launch forth*!'

He clapped his hands, and the undertakers nodded, and genuflected in a brisk adieu. And the Puck and the Pooka produced a great sail caught by the windy gust, a makeshift crest that bore his motto, billowing and pluming as they latched their sheet to the mast, and stepped aboard the little canoe that rocked with their weight, spurting flowers blown from the body by the breeze. And Balthazar, unprompted, bent his great grey head, and nudged their boat forward to meet the encroaching tide, and Tadgh O'Mara took the hint, and pushed the rudder's breast in turn through the splashing eddies, until they were afloat on the shallows and floating, borne by the current along which they were swept. And they steered and veered and shook as the waves began to carry them away from the shore, toward the faraway desert somewhere over the farther horizon, where lay the tomb atop the tallest sand dune in the world to which they were bound, if ever they would see that mystic place again, where he might be interred beside his most devoted disciple, and his temple tended by his long-neglected wife. And the sailors at the helm who manned the flimsy oars and rowed, turned and blew back kisses to their stranded fans as they sailed away bearing The Mad Monk's corpse, waving to the coffee-room prophet, the blinding poet, the amiable ass and the puzzled new arrivals on the shore, all who stood and bid them bye, casting off caps they tossed into the sky, whooping and clapping their palms, as the passing skiff sank out of their sight, and the funeral barge was lost to their view and drowned among sea mist. And a chorus of seagulls sang and wheeled as he departed, in a last flurry of wings and caws and hoots. And lastly, a gull with purple eyes was seen to descend and land by the donkey's hooves.

Arsene-Elijah sighed and snapped from his reverie, and brought forth a chessboard from his robe's folds.

'*Right Mr Albert!*' he chortled, '*Goodly brother mine so long unseen. You're looking well, I say. It seems we were separated at birth, you and I, doomed to wander singly before we were twinned. Let us catch up again, over this long belated tournament.*'

Brother Potter scratched his whiskers and mumbled in wonderment as Banshee Esmerelda squeezed his hand in encouragement. Tadgh O'Mara, overwhelmed, nuzzled and caressed the mane of Balthazar as he shredded his beard. The seagull with purple eyes, nosing too near the lethal cage as it performed its final tap dance, was grabbed by The Clunge Monkey's paw, whisked through the bars to be torn to pieces as it was bloodily shagged. As for the purple eyes, they were popped from the sockets like grapes, and appropriated by The Clunge Monkey for his own, plopped and settled into the hollow grooves to fill his own empty pouches, that he might see all through veil of violet hue.

And Arsene-Elijah was on the point of laying down the chessboard on a sandy mound and lining up the pieces so he and his brother might play, when then he sensed the others onlooking, and turned toward the distant pampas dunes, at the foot of which the children were gathered and standing in a curious row, with the lump of their sandcastle behind them, the building halted as they witnessed the departing skiff sail and sink.

'*Hola*!' Arsene-Elijah called to them, brandishing his staff, '*Don't be shy! Do but come approach! Look, sirrah! Your fan club has come for the inauguration too*!'

Brother Potter leered as his ears perked up, hunched by the chessboard as he turned, and greeted his boys and girls who tentatively neared, lead by Simeon who lowered his Chaplin's bowler, followed by quizzical princess Saruko licking jam from her teeth, and the diamond empress Jezebel, twirling her skirts and smiling at her father.

'The queen of my heart!' he said, 'I didn't like it when you went away. So glad you came back. I might have a going off myself one of these days. One of these days ...'

Konrad Merkel caught sight of his barmy Maori mother in her rags, and blanched, anticipating scolding, but she merely chuckled at her rascal son of old, and linked the elbow of her newest god in man, a great ape squatting by the seaside, whose thigh she patted while his parrot squawked on his shoulder. And the White Dog, let off his leash, bounded over to greet the kids with licks and bounds in which they delighted.

And Arsene-Elijah grinned and spread his arms, and welcomed the newcomers. Their revels were only just beginning, he joyously declared, and a fine high time awaited their band. For the former weatherman was become a coffee-room prophet, and the grubby alcoholic was now become a mad potter in the mud, sculpting beauties in his clay, a lover woodsman to the Maori Banshee, lately mother of the boy he loved, the great erector in Albert who might build their brighter abode from logs he would fell and whittle with his chisel, and embellish the grounds the boys had laid in their paltry sandcastle the Chinese princess had petulantly stamped on with a kiddy's heel, humming as he raised a tower of salt, while his daughter flicked her brush to capture his attempts on canvas, distilling in oils every loving detail of his blubbery face on which the spread of fresher beard was so becoming, draped in his toga of raincoat that swelled in the drizzle, to a monkish habit's breadth, a cape and cloak to cover his foster charges, whom he would hug warmly by his breast for the while they bore the whirlwind's perils, windswept orphans of the storm of the world, fleeing to the better place they would craft together.

But first the reunited brothers would play some chess.

And they rallied their troops on the board by the seashore, and pushed pawns both creamy and ebony over the swathe of grids, checking and mating and castling and storming, as the breathing tide came in and out, bearing rearing stallions of frothy surf who neighed and crashed upon the rocks. And their games were cheered by their captive audience, of children and animals and witches and bards, of Konrad Merkel, Simeon Collins, Jezebel Temple, princess Saruko, Banshee Esmerelda, Tadgh O'Mara, Balthazar the Donkey, and The Clunge Monkey in his cage, peering through the bars with violet eyes, all did hail and admire the tournament, which ended in a draw. And having drawn and knowing joy, Arsene-Elijah O'Colla and Brother Albert The Mad Potter raised their eyes and smiled in joy, sitting happy playing chess on that merry strand of August pleasantness.

EPILOGUE

It took the singer Martin Graves the better part of the night to sift through all the evidence, from which assembled mass of dizzy cribbage he could draw but only imperfect conclusions, unsatisfied by half, and sleepier by far. Dazed and wilting come tomorrow's dawning, squinting as the fresh sunshine shone through the tall windows and bathed all the assemblage of objects in her plumaged glow, scattered across the Lombardy dining table from which the dust of angel's wings was arising in curtained haze of yeast.

And Mr Graves laid down the thousand pages constituting the comic book, whose yellowing leaves he had skimmed while sobbing, and rubbed his eyes and yawned, and rose and padded to bed. With no sign as yet of his invisible host, he presumed he would sleep in the room on the middle landing, in that same grey crypt where his old friend Arsene had passed his winter of madness, insensate in Simeon's chambers, catatonic in the young boy's bed. And into the cobwebs the fearful tenor Graves entered, a chink of sunlight peeping through the ripped shroud of the blind, casting down his baggage and taking off his trousers, lying down on the duvet and wincing at the stains as he drew the blanket over his body, to stare at the ceiling whose paper was peeling, and shut his lids and struggle to sleep, not daring to dream in fear of nightmares, lulled at last to rest by memories of the cricket's song, chirruping in his mother's chimney long ago.

Sometime later, he heard a noise, and bolted upright in the bed alarmed. To see the doorway filled by the timid shape of a princess, shocked and huddled in the entry, startled by the sleeper whose repose she had disturbed, having come to collect her effects.

'Mark?' said the sublime Saruko.

'I'm not Mark,' said the shadowy Graves.

'Sam?' said princess Saruko.

'I'm not Sam,' said the murky singer Graves.

'Oh!' said the mortified little girl.

And so logic thus dictated to the child that this man who was neither Mark nor Sam must therefore be some quite other different man. And after delaying to pick up her bags and bouquets, she fled in fear from the darker quarters where the crooner scratched his head and started from the bed, lurching in his briefs past the dead shelves, to hunch by the doorway. And he stood puzzled and watched her glide downstairs in her flurry and worry, as she skipped panting down the bannister, and sally out of the house to where the carriage was waiting, grinding its steam and puffing from the wheels.

And curious Graves saw the vehicle's shape through the chink in the open door as she ran outside to meet the noonday brigade, and he stroked his chin, and knitted his wrinkly brows, and decided to follow. Dazzled in the glory of the brightness he peered out the door, and saw the carriage parked on the paving by the lamp-post, in which they were all assembled again, ready to trek and tour, and rack up coppers to stock the dwelling they would build. Baffled in the radiance, Mr Martin Graves stood on the doorstep and admired as Saruko was hoisted into the carriage, grasping the celery hand that Simeon offered to haul her into their cart with a shudder, inside of which Konrad and Jezebel also sat, and kept a wary eye on The Clunge Monkey's cage (the beast was admiring the calves and ankles of the ladies through his drooling bars). Balthazar was pulling them along, bridled in his finery and nibbling the hedges of ballerina fuchsia whose sweetest nectar wetted his dry and lolling donkey's tongue. The Mad Potter was acting in his capacity as coachman, looking magnificent in his cloak of foresting ware, with a plume to his peaked cap and a tassel of his scarf, and his adoring Banshee sat by his side on the saddle, bonny Esmerelda, lamented Mrs Merkel, grand astride the lover's wagon. And Arsene-Elijah and Tadgh O'Mara were the topmost seated, sat highest in air on the open canopy of the carriage's roof, tossing blooms to bystanders who saw their caravan pass, spokes of its grinding wheels sparking as they plashed over alley's puddles.

And The Mad Potter, who soon might swap his hunter's fashion for a monkish habit he would defile, spotted the quizzical singer who observed them from the gate of number nine, and he alerted his brother Arsene-Elijah, whose guidelines for wisdom he often adhered to. And the fortune-teller twirled his moustachios and cawed to the singer. He stood and tossed his stovepipe hat, and gaily bowed and beckoned to the miracle's witness, and Mr Graves did likewise as he humbly approached to stand in the pool of their caravan's shadow, feeling ridiculous in his unclad state so nearly naked save for his loincloth, shivering in the sun as he felt his grave being trodden upon by a tramp in the future. Familiar Simeon peered out the caravan's window and waved to his guest, and said sorry for his absence, as did Saruko quietly request pardon for her foolish intrusion. But all joined in urging him to come aboard and join their crew, and accompany them as they journeyed round the city's streets, miming on the thoroughfares and performing silly slapstick routines to amuse onlookers, tossing pennies they turned to liquid wines to fund their endless revels, divulging fates whiles rubbing crystal balls, twining yarns and embroidering quilts with depictions of their knitted legend, sold as rugs and pawned as carpets in the city's markets, to fumes of opium and unending scent of Le Fanu's greenest tea. And dithering Graves stammered and mulled, and then was pulled aboard by effusive Simeon who begged him for a rendition of Feste's song, and then good old Lord Randal again. And the demon coachman grinned through his mane of beard like a fatty imp or rubicund lion, and cracked his whip, and so away they rode into the wonder of sundown.

And they ran through their routines for weeks and months and years on end ever after, and camped amid the squalor of litter, and lurked in the parks where they shared breadcrumbs with the ducks, and drank in the bars where they enlisted recruits, and tore up the stools and filtered fags from the stray bowls, and enjoyed themselves and felt beloved as they squashed their gobbled crisps and fishy chips. And they always returned to their beach to add further joyous touches to their sandcastle, that palace of grains that was daily swamped and drowned by the rushing waves, foaming slaves to the rhythms of the lapping cycle, servants of the moon and its motions that made the women mad. So their lair of bliss, ever destroyed by the encroach of waters, was eternally rebuilt over and over and raised again from dusty nothing by the erector Potter, lifting marble weights he hacked like a stonemason, sweating in his forge and chipping his axes, firing weapons in the kiln and stoking the coals that Collins collected from the sodden turf, heaped up in the oven where Jezebel baked her gingerbread men in the infernal cavern of the smoking pits, an army of clay warriors who peopled the flowerpots that Saruko sculpted, while her sister crafted pawns and rooks of clay to fill the grids of Arsene-Elijah's chessboard.

And Tadgh O'Mara finally completed his Gaelic Epic on the backs of bills and receipts they hoarded and kept, his words transcribed by the younger budding bards who copied down his recitations as his sight left his eyes and he grew blind as he died, choking and composing to the very utmost last before expiring on the bridge, thereafter dropped from Potter's brawny arms into the watery grave that awaited him in the river as the shabbiest laureate floated out to sea. And the copious sheets on which his words were writ were sown together by the flower girls to form a seamless tapestry of endless melody, whose lyrics were drilled into the head of the pallid singer Graves by the stern conductor Arsene-Elijah, who rapped his baton and hummed to the poetry's music, a stream of unceasing song that transported the pale songster as he sang forever on the sidewalks, his cap bared to contain what coppers were tossed by the besotted listeners.

Simeon and Merkel's torrid friendship remained a fraught affair, and they often duelled by dawn on the score of the woman for whom they once competed, the lovely Jezebel who preferred Konrad anyway. They later married. Arsene-Elijah was their jubilant priest who showered their bond in juniper berries, and a leafy bus shelter was their chapel, the same in the rain where Simeon proposed to Saruko in drizzly jest, enjoying the rebuff she bestowed, turning on her heel to rejoin her parents, who upped stumps and moved back to China.

And Collins, whose shoes were talking about I— C— C—, shrugged and twirled his bamboo cane, and sauntered away down an avenue of gingko trees breathing indifference, to cry unseen in the orange grove under the bowers of lilac streamers, lost beside the grassy maze for juveniles.

And Arsene-Elijah and The Mad Potter daily played numerous games of chess in which their younger jesters were schooled, massacring shivery pawns as Jezebel sat aside and snapped pictures of her fatherly ogre as he loomed over the board and scratched his itching temples while slugging liquor through a straw. And his loving daughter papered the wagon's walls with her photos from which she made her first tentative sketches, before at last catching up her easel and canvas amid the dunes, and painted Potter's portrait in the starriest nightfall, massaging her pigments that stuck under her nails, painting and smearing her father's face with all the blobby crepuscular passion of a later Goya's slaughtered pigs, strung to allow the streaming tides of blood drip and puddle in gushing gouts. The resulting portrait was hailed as a minor masterpiece by her sneering husband Konrad who was always unfaithful, hung on their godfather's wall beside the dashing earlier version, beside of which Monty the parrot gurgled and began to recite O'Mara's Gaelic Epic about Peadar Lamb's Bull, tutored in its verses by the untiring crooner, the priestly deity Mr Martin Graves who beat his tapping metronome.

And Arsene-Elijah covetously guarded The Clunge Monkey lest he should escape and destroy the world, snarling and ejaculating in his wicker cage, in whose netting he tore holes with his talons in which to stick his dick. But one day in the latest beginning, as he drowsed in a gutter and patted the cage, the haggard chuckling keeper was then approached by an ancient old man of some one hundred and twenty years of age, whose shadow fell over the squatting prophet who lifted his eyes and nodded in recognition of the prodigal vagrant who abandoned his farmhouse and all his lands of centuries earlier.

Peadar Lamb was limping along on the single withered leg that he had left to him, with a stump of a wattle peg to fill in the absent limb he had himself sawn off in the madness of despair, so old and tired, wearily peering at the world that had betrayed him, doomed to wander forlornly in the abysses of lonely roads, in quest of the fairies he could no longer find, to beg their favours anew, and catch back the pot of gold they stole, and embrace his vanished Bull who never loved him even when a skeleton.

And gracious Arsene-Elijah stood and bowed as the farmer approached him, and Peadar halted and eyed the cage at which he squinted, from which an awful growling was erupting in masturbatory treble, and the prophet looked the ancient farmer up and down, a grizzly antique with a gnarled face puckered as a wrinkled lemon that had been left on the sill to rot, crafty and doped the glint in his sunken eyes that wallowed in their pouched sockets, leaning against the brick of a wall to steady his tremble, sensing nearby bones of a Bull he had loved – but god, how sickeningly altered and twisted out of all proportion.

Arsene-Elijah bent and lifted the latch on the cage, and The Clunge Monkey crawled out displaying an erection, with liver spots on his hideous scalp, his violet eyes gleaming as he slobbered and spewed. He wrapped his claws around the farmer's woody peg leg, in whose nodules and chinks and crevices the lusty monster stuck his own wood, and bore and ground into the hole more peacefully. And the false leg came unstuck, and the horrified farmer fell, cracking his skull on the harsh paving, and his brains then spilt from the dent in his eggshell. And so he died, redundant and disconsolate on the street.

The Clunge Monkey escaped, bounding on all fours like a hare. And Arsene-Elijah saw that it was good. The new lusty age was begun, inaugurated in a murdering splurge. And the smiling prophet strolled idly away from the farmer's corpse, and his ears perked up to hear his tenor friend singing around the corner in one among the homestead's meadows, as all about him in a little ring the happiest faithful camped and lit their incense. And the singer's words sang of what was, and what had been, before this final seaside banquet, as the monkfish were fried and the surrounding cast remembered the parts they had played in Tadgh O'Mara's Epic.

For it really was the simplest of stories. Of how The Mad Monk came back home to Ireland to die; of how the body of Arsene the weatherman was stolen by the ghost of Elijah; of how S.J.C. was undone by love and lust and jealousy; of how Banshees pass on their batons and why silly women are wiser; and of how Konrad, Simeon and Jezebel found a more human hero closer to home, in the shape of that divine debauchee Mr Albert Potter, lord of the drunks, the latest and greatest of the world's maddest monks.

THE END